NO COUNTRY FOR OLD MEN

BY WARREN EYSTER

Far from the Customary Skies

NO
COUNTRY
FOR OLD MEN

BY WARREN EYSTER

 RANDOM HOUSE · *New York*

*A portion of this novel was written with the assistance of a fellowship of the
Centro Mexicano de Escritores.*

19,453

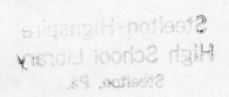

To my grandfather, Samuel J. Orndorff

CONTENTS

PART ONE: 1889 - 1894

I

THE MEETING was held in the village hall. The fire-wagons had been pulled out into the street and there was room for everyone to sit. The shortage of chairs was being taken care of by two men who seemed to have no foresight, but this was really a part of the courtesy and welcome, each family waiting until their own chairs were brought to them. Women would have held babies and small children on their laps, except that it was a political meeting, and the more space occupied by a family, the more importance as a delegation it could assume.

In the hall was the noise of people crowded together and bumping each other as they took off their wraps. Mr. Lang, holding his arms forward and high, was having one after another turn their backs to him. Tad Stevens was thin enough that his coat fell off in a quick sliding movement, but Selvinius had to broaden his shoulders and shove them about to free himself.

"Without scarf on a day like this, Monroe?" said Mr. Lang.

"So I am, so I am," said Selvinius, craning to get a view of his chest, brushing at the lapels of his coat, uncertain whether the scarf might not still be about his person. Big, broad men seem particularly victimized by wind and cold, and Selvinius was a little nervous about his health. "Well, I didn't miss it, so I suppose no harm's done."

Miss Addie Harnet was addicted to feathers and gloves. She had so many things to talk about that Mr. Lang gently removed her wraps without involving her participation. She was eager and pleased to see him and had a multitude of things to tell his wife, which, encountering him first, were offered. Addie had reached the gentle age at which she did not notice that men had interests differing from her own. Mr. Lang thought that splendid.

Henry Pierce quickly slipped out of his coat, folded it across his

3

arm. His father waited to be assisted. Jonathan Pierce would enter as he was, rather than remove his coat. It was a mannerism which extended through his entire nature. Yet he and Mr. Lang were particular friends; before investments and family pressure had forced him to move to Harrisburg, the two men would sit together evenings, talking, smoking, sharing satisfaction from being in each other's presence. They had the rare quality of not exerting pressure on each other.

Mr. Lang took him by the hand with a cordiality less demonstrative than the others had received. A warm greeting was given to the son, a hearty welcome to manhood, at which Henry seemed to have arrived during the time since they had last met. For Henry there was the discomfort of feeling friendship offered from another generation, but he was a very cool and mature young man, particularly attentive, extremely courteous.

James Dressinger was feeling about among the coats for a place to hang his own. He had a thick, dust-colored mustache and was little known in the village. He was interested in land along the river, an interest which he claimed stemmed from an investment his grandfather had made in the Pennsylvania Canal, which now had its greatest traffic in fishermen and skaters—a quick way of getting to Harrisburg in wintertime. Dressinger was the only one of the group who could be described as wearing a waistcoat. With a touch of the gallantry a younger man might have shown when visiting his aunts, he made himself acquainted with Mrs. Rowiger, Mrs. Lang, Mrs. Pierce and Miss Addie Harnet.

Tad Stevens paced back and forth, shaking the cold out of himself. He described himself as a wolf who would keep tearing and fighting his enemies, then one day crawl onto a flat rock and die alone in the hot sun. It was not much of an exaggeration. He was a cross, furious man who might at any moment grab his coat and, without explanation, practically without reason, throw open the door and go out, not even bothering to use his coat until he had gone enough distance to feel the bitterness of the wind.

Tad was political boss of the county, a long lean shank of bone with the country hardness which a man who has not used his inherited strength retains longer than those who have farmed all their lives. Shrewd, always a bit angry, a man who had approached politics from the outside and cautiously worked himself into the center, he had grown more fierce in recent years.

Farmers came to him and shook hands and pointed out where their families were seated. Tad was one of their own kind, a friend

4

by instinct, and they could talk and haggle with him. He would not pay the least attention to their opinions unless he agreed with them. He made it a point to get one thing done every term his party was voted into power, one thing for the farmers, no matter whose feet got pinched. Everything else he did was of his own making, for his own purposes. He was corrupt in the worst sense of Pennsylvania politics, where it was difficult to surpass previous corruption. The votes he lost among the farmers were because he was lax in his religious practices.

Tad had a reputation for getting what he wanted. He had used a smallpox quarantine to delay vote on a proposed turnpike-tariff increase, and had solved the need of a new courthouse with a timely bit of arson. He denied responsibility, but was willing to admit he had made the statement, "Providence is not always divine." Every ounce of his lean, bony figure was proud of his reputation, the good and the corrupt, and many people were proud of him. He raked his tithe, doubled it in good years, did not deny it, and in turn could be trusted to do what really needed to be done.

Tad's son was a heavy, powerful young man, better than his father and worse—more honest, more likely to fail in a crucial time. He was a penny-raker, but a good enough replica of his father; and in spite of being townish, too modest and having a cringing manner of making a statement, he was certain to carry the majority of his father's supporters, at least for the first two offices which should be chosen for him. Then he would have to begin to do some proving of his own.

Mark Stevens knew what he was about. He knew it was better to be a bit of a sheep, a kind of loyal body servant to his father, than to make a vigorous effort on his own. It was better to stand prepared to take over when the old dynasty was ready to go, and not put pressure too soon. Mark was cultivating strength among the young and the mill workers.

It was a unified group, of stronger stuff socially than their individual manners would indicate. Mr. Lang, who ordinarily would have thought poorly of himself not to have made everyone comfortable by this time, realized there was involved privilege of delay and of indirection. The form and tradition of a town-hall meeting were maintained on only slightly different lines from those which had existed in the first part of the century; but the meeting had come to loosen itself and give more expression in the fringes, in greetings and partings. It was natural that on an evening of importance there should be a certain amount of reluctance and procrastination.

Mrs. Rowiger made her appearance, breaking through the doorway with ponderous forward thrust. She had a way of making the biggest space seem no more than a parlor and as easy to manage. In a few moments she had already decided that she would keep her coat and had sent two young men on a hurried errand. Gathering the women, she marched them into the central portion of the hall. Mrs. Rowiger was the only woman present who could be considered politically important, and she believed women must be represented through the influence and pressure of their personalities. The duty of most wives was to strengthen their husbands, but from others, such as Mrs. Lang and Mrs. Pierce, a more general effect was needed.

The women selected chairs which did not place them in a row, yet had centrality. With a minimum of shifting they could bring themselves to face each other. There was a tendency toward grouping, toward being where they could lean and speak in lowered voices. Mrs. Rowiger violated this by choosing a broad and definitely masculine chair, which she promptly dropped into and took command of by gripping the arms of the chair as she would have a rocker.

Jonathan Pierce had to be satisfied with a straight kitchen-style chair, and he showed his disapproval by standing behind it, arms folded across his chest. His son was not so far into manhood as to renounce the advantages of being at his father's side.

Selvinius, notably, through the attentions of Mr. Lang and the more compelling gesture of Mrs. Rowiger, who reached forth and patted her hand on the seat, gained a more comfortable place than he would have chosen for himself. He was nervous about his health, but without consideration for his physical comfort. It was a big enterprise in which he was involved, and, as a father with small children must worry about the possibility of death, so he, already deep into the range of the probability of death, wanted to see his enterprise through its infancy, to see it rooted and lasting. He sat down and drew his head erect. White hair, which was combed flowing on each side, hung a little over the edge of his collar, in the frontier style which he had preferred ever since his hair had begun to be grayish.

Tad Stevens chose a bone-style stool and sat with his back near the wall.

Mark Stevens stood, since there was beginning to be a shortage, and it would have been necessary to carry a chair overhead to get through. He kept turning the keys and coins in his pocket. He was the only one in the hall who carried money in that loose manner.

Mr. Lang was too provident a man to choose a chair which would make others feel uncomfortable by being unsatisfactory to himself.

6

He was at ease most of the time; he had a calmness and gentle dignity which people had come to rely upon more than he did himself. The Langs, his forefathers, had proven they could be trusted. Mr. Lang continued that policy. It was natural to him.

The men had reason to rely upon certain qualities in each other, and to have nearly accurate foreknowledge of each other's views. They knew where they stood on matters. It was only when something such as the Selvinius proposal was put to them that they found it difficult to have a fixed point of view. For this reason the opinions of men who were firm would be of more importance, since they would carry with them loyal supporters, people who trusted them more than a proposal.

The men tended to use the spaciousness of the room. They were men of sound voices and of unwillingness to group at a political meeting. They retained the right to be free from the prejudice which comes from sitting near one's friends. Tad Stevens could make himself heard across the river when there was a light western wind.

Only Mr. Lang was soft-spoken. Yet his voice was never difficult to hear; it had a quiet firmness which had won respect for him on more than one occasion. Mr. Jonathan Pierce was somewhat the same, except that in recent years his voice had taken on a precise enunciation which made it seem too curt. By moving to Harrisburg, he had lost more prestige than he could ever have imagined. His son saw it, and saw hostility in the eyes of some of the farmers.

The hall was an hour in filling, depending on where people were from, outlying farms providing both the earliest and latest arrivals. There were encounters among families which had not seen each other since harvest, families which would never have come for a social gathering, and families which Mrs. Rowiger had rooted out. There were equally forceful handshakes among people who saw each other nearly every day.

There was another group, all men, predominantly Hungarian and Serbian, who worked in the mill and lived in shanties along the river. Some came in and claimed places to sit. Others remained by the door and along the wall. They were a different breed from the farmers and villagers, and were making that visible to the people in the hall. Mr. Lang and Mr. Snyder had done their best to show courtesy and respect to these men whose eyes remained suspicious and insolent. Mr. Snyder was one of the few people born in the village who worked in the mill.

The men were a hard-cut bunch, mostly dressed in clean work clothes and leather jackets, and some wore boots. Three men stand-

7

ing together, talking in undertones, had their hair savagely chopped. Some were ex-railroad laborers. There was a group of bricklayers and other craftsmen, several of whom were building homes, but as yet had made no attempt to become acquainted. Outside, gathered around the door and making entrance difficult by position and not by discourtesy, was another group, young, loud, with a smell of whiskey about them.

This group dispersed when the foremen arrived. They came in a mass and with the marching tread of having prearranged coming in that fashion. Almost without exception they were big, heavy, tough-looking and unsuccessfully well-dressed. They were neither intelligent nor educated, but there was a stability about them, an air of confidence. A couple of benches were all that could be found. They all managed to get seated, though for some time they kept leaning and shifting, glancing at one another. The man at the end of the largest bench used his hand to clamp himself fast.

It was Tad Stevens who rose.

"Let's get down to it," he said. "I didn't come for the jawing. I came to find out where we're going to stand." He put his hands together and gripped them. "Selvinius, it's your doings, so put it out here," he said, motioning to the space at the back of the hall, "and we'll get to it."

Selvinius looked around the hall to see if this opinion was general.

"Tad," said Mr. Lang gently, "I thought you held November comes soon enough."

"I do," said Tad, "and this *is* November. I also hold that if there's something smells, you got to decide whether to keep it perfumed or else get it aired out. So which're we going to do?"

"I suppose Selvinius better talk," said Mr. Lang.

Selvinius mounted to the speakers' rostrum, which was really a portion of the rotted-out boardwalk, slightly repaired. He looked first to see if all the people he considered important were present. The barn lanterns hung from ropes made the hall seem large.

"I've come to ask you people to give up one way of life and try another. It's a hard thing to ask. Fifteen years ago I began setting up a factory to make iron and steel. Twenty-five years ago I had a vision. I came here with it, and I told you then you need have no fear, I would keep trust, I would abide by your laws and decisions. I believe I have.

"My vision was this. I dreamed of producing steel in a steady and practical stream, a steady market for it, and a steady source of supply.

8

Well, I have. Beside the river, water power. Beside the canal, transportation. Now the iron canal, a transcontinental railroad. Limestone comes from exactly five miles away. Coal comes from thirty miles. Iron ore less than forty.

"But the end of one vision is always the keyhole through which to see another. The new vision is not as good as the first. I would reject it, except I cannot. I can only restrain it. For it's no longer my vision, but the vision of the whole state, perhaps that of the world. I don't speak of the future. I speak of now, what's begun and can't be stopped—but if it's handled properly there's no reason why it shouldn't be utilized.

"Pennsylvania's too complicated to be disposed of in a speech. It's a nation possessing a self-sufficiency enjoyed by few nations in the world, indeed the keystone to the East and the West. Commanding in agriculture—corn, wheat, buckwheat, oats, potatoes, apples, peaches, cherries. The Civil War gave us the strongest railroads in the nation. The most powerful state and the most industrial. The largest producer of oil. Only a man in my line of business can see the value of oil. I do not know yet where it may lead.

"When I started, other men were starting. Now they are no longer starting. They're going and going. I've not believed in that. I don't, won't and couldn't. After visiting central England I found myself hoping the frontier would keep using all the steam and let people like ourselves move in our slow, steady, better way.

"But it's not happening. We've got Carnegie instead. And a tough one in Frick. We must realize that the steel industry in this state threatens to extend beyond anything we've imagined, beyond the nation, into the heart of world finance. I'm already under pressure. To sell out. Ordinarily I would simply refuse. But the railroads are expanding tremendously. They want contracts, guarantees, bids —so much in so little time. I cite the quality of our steel. I get the reply, 'Fine, but we want miles of rail and switches and wheels and rods, not handfuls of the steels of Toledo or the blades of Damascus.' Bethel is beginning to cut off my major markets simply because I can't produce enough. Lesser consumers are not steady enough in need to keep us working full time. Without full time, my workers are going to head for the coal regions. In short, I'm faced with the necessity of expansion or selling out.

"You know me. I won't sell.

"I believe the plant can be expanded in a manner satisfactory to all of us. But it calls for a new way of life. For me it means another

9

blast furnace, an open hearth, converters, a frog shop, expanded coke ovens, and a minimum of two thousand workers. I would then be strong enough to hold at least two major consumers. But it means changing to a corporation in which I just barely retain control. I'll retain control, I promise that. For if big business gets hold here, this village as it now exists will be destroyed. We don't want a Lykens, a Wiconisco, Shamokin, Bethlehem, Pottsville or Scranton. We want Coverly.

"I spoke of a new way of life. In one sense I'm trying to prevent a new way of life. With your assistance, we can retain the best features of this village, keep it in the condition we have all come to believe is right and good. It will have to expand. But there is no reason why that expansion should be harmful.

"It must be made clear how far-reaching a change this will be. Many of you, I can see, are thinking that this has nothing to do with you. You have your families, farms and fences. That's not enough. Not nearly enough. For two thousand workers will outnumber you, and if I don't get co-operation—if I fail—that number will become twenty thousand or two hundred thousand.

"Businessmen here know and understand. I've talked with most of them. It's really a golden opportunity—if we handle it right. It's an opportunity for the village to expand peacefully and vigorously—a chance for many of you to sell produce near at hand. With care, a strong community of industry and agriculture. Without care?

"Without care I shall have to provide places for my men to live, food for them to eat, clothing. I or my successor. I don't want company stores, I don't want row houses, I don't want to buy up land and push and push you people inch by inch across the mountain. But to prevent this I need better village organization, an assurance there will be homes available, homes for rent. I want some decent people to run decent boardinghouses until the workers get settled. I want to make sure that this village is not overrun by Harrisburg and its commerce destroyed simply because of lack of available goods.

"The big thing I need is—accept me and my workmen. Realize they are men hunting a future, life, liberty, a little happiness. I don't want to see what I see tonight. I don't want to see workers distrustful and you people resentful. It's these conditions that lead to the Maguires. Twenty hanged. Scranton's not far. Nothing is far. We've got to get that into our heads. Time and distance are crawling into our hands, into the very palms of our hands.

"Now, more specific. I want my workers to live here and be as steady a people as you are. I want them to form the habit of loyalty and of pride. I can give them fair wages and enough work. I could give them houses and stores. I prefer not. I know enough about men to be sure that they feel—even in the best managed situation where the employer provides everything—like a stick which is being wound with string, tighter and tighter bound. I want them to have independence in their personal lives.

"These things I propose. To donate funds for the building of a larger school. To donate to all churches which show need and to donate materials and labor to any congregation or sect which does not have a church. To share one third of all the costs of paving the streets with brick. To make available all company fire equipment, in addition to what I have already supplied. To found a small library. To offer a plan for the community which will assure uncrowded residence. To offer a water-purification system, including a filter plant. A police station. An actual town hall.

"In return I ask this. A fair tax rate to be assessed on all property, and a guarantee that the tax rate will not be altered once formed. The right to call on town police to protect my property the same as any other property. Sale to me of all property on both sides of the canal which belongs to the town, at a fair price. Purchase of land extending further south along the river, along the mountain, and between here and Harrisburg. Petition for a new charter of incorporation. And the guarantee of a sewage system, as well as my continued right to use the river for that purpose.

"It is give and take. But unless I am given these securities and others, I will no longer be in a position to give guarantees. I will maintain the same loyalty as before. I am, simply, an old man who would like to leave his company well founded, and the town in good health and prosperity. It must be clear to you that the village cannot continue to exist separately. It must expand or be expanded, the latter possibly becoming a bitterness among us all."

There followed hours of debate. Mr. Pierce spoke for the company, having recently invested and gradually pulled together eight per cent of the holdings. His son spoke to the young people and urged co-operation, pointing out that present expansion was only the beginning, and that without some foresight into the needs of industrial life there would be cause for sorrow later.

Tad Stevens spoke simply. No. He urged the farmers to go ahead with their lives and Mr. Selvinius to go ahead with his own. "I expect," he said, "this village will grow as the people move into it. As we don't have no laws against buying and selling, none against going to church, none against a man building a roof overtop himself, I fail to see why we should tax ourselves just to buy land and call it part of our village. It sounds to me like the cart before the horse. And I confess I for one am not too interested in seeing the glad hand shown to everyone who comes and takes a look. I say no. Donate what you please, if you please and when you please."

Mr. Lang spoke as a man who was trying to sight through underbrush.

"Selvinius is right in so far as he states the need to expand. I've needed to expand my tobacco factory longer than I care to mention. Where Selvinius and I part company is that he's going to do it, I'm not. And I confess I'd stick to steels of Toledo the same as I do to paying more for tobacco that's been picked leaf by leaf as it's ripe. Because . . . There is no explanation for our preferences. I believe I shall be able to continue to provide a living for myself and my workers, while Selvinius believes not. He is probably correct. And I express here and now that although I disagree with Selvinius, although I feel he has in this instance reacted more to a point of pride than a necessity, I believe he will expand as carefully as he began, and will keep our interests in mind. I think it only fair that we should offer him co-operation. First, a fair tax rate. Second, the right to call upon our police to protect his property, except in the case of a labor dispute. As to purchasing land to the south and along the mountain and between here and Harrisburg, I confess it might be wise to do so. Principally because we are believers in local government and we should assure our children of land on which they can build homes within the same local law as ourselves. But that must be agreed upon by vote and not made as a guarantee. We have no right to commit the future. As to the sewage system, I have too much interest in it myself, at my factory, to offer any opinion.

"I must say that I'm opposed to anything being given to this village except through outright endowment. Our school must remain without bondage of any sort. I feel certain Selvinius means well with his offers. I hope indeed he will carry them through. I should like myself to subscribe toward a water-sanitation system, a library and a larger school. I should like to see many of you do the same. But these points must not be bargaining means. Their acceptance on that basis would cause trouble."

There was a hurried conference among the businessmen. It had been expected that Mr. Lang would lend strong support to the proposal. Mr. Tafenton hurriedly stood up, and his nervousness was that of being unprepared. He stooped several times to confer with his friends.

"I—I think we should accept Selvinius' offer. I really do. I feel that as a businessman and a citizen we could not do wiser than to accept this offer. We need to have the streets paved and we need a dependable fire company. . . ."

"What you mean," Tad Stevens thundered, "is you're afraid of a company store. You might have to change your God-awful prices!"

Mr. Dressinger rose. "I think I can settle one issue," he said. "This matter of land. Most of it is already in my possession. It is not for sale."

Mr. Lang said, "I wish that when we vote, we will vote according to our feelings, and not by what we stand to gain or lose."

"You've no right to take this attitude," said Mr. Jonathan Pierce in a low voice.

"I too have stock," said Mr. Lang quietly. "But there are other things to consider."

"Let's vote," said Tad Stevens. "Right now."

Selvinius shrugged, sensing defeat. Mrs. Rowiger was talking heatedly with Mrs. Lang.

Henry Pierce rose. "I think the workers are entitled to vote," he said. "They have an interest in this matter."

For a moment that seemed to throw a new light into the subject. But Tad shouted, "Let them come forward and show their registration cards, and we'll let them vote."

The meeting ended with an overwhelming rejection of the Selvinius proposal.

Mr. Lang then proposed that the intention of the village to cooperate be shown by applying for a charter of incorporation and purchasing such boundary lands as were available, up to the amount that subscription without taxation could provide, and this to be continued annually for a period of ten years.

Due to Tad Stevens, this proposal was also defeated.

There was more bitterness than usual when the meeting ended. Some of the men put on their coats and hats and left without shaking hands with anyone. One farmer nearly came to blows with two young workers who said something to his daughter as they were climbing in the wagon and lighting the sideboard lamps. Tad Stevens was standing beside the door, shaking hands with his friends and slapping them on the back. "Say, thanks for that pumpkin pie," he said to one of them. "I'll be out your way one day right soon."

Selvinius and Mr. Lang shook hands. "Sorry you had to see it that way."

Mr. Lang nodded, and said, "I am too, Monroe. But I promise we'll do as much as we can to make things go along smoothly. And don't you sell out."

Selvinius smiled. "If you hadn't known I wouldn't, I guess you might have come on my side."

Wagons began to move along the street, and out toward the countryside.

Winter came trumpeting in. Thanksgiving there was a great snow which bundled all the houses and made their quaint tallness purposeful. Wind mulched the snow against the western sides of the houses and made white stripes on one side of the trees. Fences appeared about a foot tall. For quite a while it would not matter what color roofs were.

On the fifth of December, 1889, a bitter cold came sweeping eastward and south, howling among the seven mountains and the rolling hills, heralding a new snow. Even Philadelphia was alarmed. Instead of swinging on eastward, or down the valley to Virginia, the wind whirled round and round in a two-hundred-mile circle, then sat down on the snow and stayed. It waited for people to step out of their houses. It made horses hard to drive out of their barns. It made trees sound as if they were suffering from rheumatism.

Snow remained on the ground until late January and was clean enough to be acceptable in the best Christmas tradition. Smoke from the chimneys must have blown onto the mountain, for there was no evidence of it on the fields. Snow stayed on the roofs because there was good insulation overhead as well as on the four sides—never more than four. The houses had big chimneys which were in use five months of the year and little chimneys that smoked all year round.

Germans lived in these houses. They tilled their fields from fence to fence, and conquered the land. They built stout barns and silos and houses that would last, and reaped good grain and raised good stock, planted early and fought frost, and went out again when frost beat them. The men were a hard-bitten, stout lot who would work in the coldest weather but demanded that the house be hot when they came in. They were not the sort of men who would be satisfied merely to go to stoves to warm themselves. The women made hurried trips to the barn and the well and relied on shawls which they

14

wound about their heads and shoulders in one swift swing of the arm.

Only in window-making were these Pennsylvanians careless: twelve to thirty windows, all draft and rattle and paper-stuffed, and the houses still too dark. Fixing a trace, mending a shoe, straightening a plow blade, repairing a fence, making a wall—these were second nature to them. Firewood made an extra padding along one side of the house, and more was cut whenever boys could be caught in mischief, for even punishment was productive. There were few houses with less than five children.

Yet Coverly might have been any of a number of villages ranging from the Lykens Valley to as far south as Lancaster. Except for one detail. In 1867 the first practical production of Bessemer steel was done there. The plant, although small and spread along the Susquehanna River, was a major producer of rail steel and pig iron.

On the fifteenth of December, three more inches of fresh and very light snow dropped windlessly out of an almost clear sky. It was so fleecy that the former snow by comparison seemed broken and crumbled plaster. With the light, jiggling flakes came an enchantment which was to last through Christmas. Silence seemed to drift in from the hills in the evenings and move along the streets, replacing windy afternoons. It brought people to their windows, leaning their heads close to see better and in a moment frosting out their vision. It was a curious feeling of something happening outside, something which could not be defined, a premature yearning for spring, at which their hearts scoffed, weather conditions being such. They felt it more as a desire to put lighted candles before the windows and to visit and be visited; they felt it as an inarticulate desire to break with solitude, without knowing how, without having the means. Stars in the crisp cold of night burned with quivering quick glints, making the night faintly blue, and the sky at one place seemed to have been rubbed with chalk.

Church bells, which seldom had song or pace in their ringing, had a clear, vibrating tone which traveled so far through the lower skies that even villages across the river could hear. The river was narrowed and decorated with white, and the current channels were pure blue. It was an ideal river for farm land, seldom violent, giving constant drainage. It acted as an enormous resonance for bells, allowing villages to remind each other of their presence, and trains to hoot warnings ahead of their arrival in Harrisburg.

The sky had no sediment. Sound carried with fidelity of tone even when distance had diminished it—so clear, so real, that a man walking along the street looked upward, searching with his eyes. To hear was so ordinary that one never became aware that he had paused, feeling a brief instant of possession, of bell sound stretched through the air after it had already touched against his ears; feeling the spiritual intention of a bell which merely summoned congregations and marked the hour for men to leave the fields.

Christmas approached through tones and intonations, silences and pauses, moments when hearths filled with brightness, when a candle lighted, when wind raked through the snow, when roof joists creaked. It was in the smell of candied apples and kitchens steaming warm. It was in the smell of pine needles when snow cascaded, leaving branches swinging green amid tinseled air. Baskets of cookies had it. Cows cudding and pulling mouthfuls of dry grain on the barn floor had it.

Christmas was coming. It was heralded by things less noticeable than a bright star rushing across the sky. It was a season, a span of time. It was coming to the farm land, to thrifty people who were provided for it, who had been provided since harvest and canning. It came toward them and they waited. No one was going to need a tree. No one was going to walk far to get a nice one. No more required than the quick stroke of an axe, an exaggeration of the way umbrellas are shaken as the tree was brought into the house. Then tying of candles, stringing corn and candies and taffies and ribbons.

The rush of spirit was a hearty one, without nervousness, with emphasis on cooking and baking. The best turkey had been used Thanksgiving, but there was fruit cake which had only been sampled in November, and had since been wrapped in damp cloths which had been soaked in wine. There would be puddings and tarts and dropcakes and sandtarts glazed and honey cakes and candied apples and dates.

They were people accustomed to raising their arms and hailing each other across a respectable space. When they did meet, it was usually over a fence or beside a tree or in front of the church, meeting with a curious shyness of face, almost bending into each other in the fulsomeness of shaking hands. There was freedom of spirit and good will that came from the freshness of the air and the renewal of friendships. It would have been hard to find people who had more in common, their religions varying from Amish and Mennonite pacifism, to strict Lutherans who sang nearly every Sunday "Onward, Christian Soldiers" and "A Mighty Fortress Is Our God." The same principle, the same hard emphasis on law and order and family strength and freedom, could be seen in all of them. Conquer and maintain. The roofs were steep, set against the hardest wind, dry in the heaviest rain. The furniture in their houses was indestructible, rafters a basic lesson in carpentry, pottery remarkable for heavy simplicity and the ventilation for the barns skillfully and artistically designed.

They had so much in common and were forthright, frank, strong-voiced, and yet it was hard for them to find reason to visit one another. If it had not been for marriage, which made kinships between the neighboring farms, and which gave them a form and a means of communicating, they would have been a lonely people. It took death in the family or fire in the barn or a sale of livestock to bring them together. Christmas inclined them toward visiting, made them more than willing. Yet it seldom came about.

And would not have if it had not been for another element in the village, a few people who were more wealthy and educated, the Langs, the Pierces, the Rowigers. Out of the productivity of their ancestors, these families had arrived at a position touching upon aristocracy, which, because they lived north of the valley of Virginia, because they were democratic in the Franklin as well as the Jeffersonian sense, was used only toward building and directing social enterprise in the village, and toward more extended luxury and leisure. They were the only ones in a position to make the holidays take on the same festive air in the houses and the streets as the snow had given to the trees and the roofs and the barns.

So the Rowigers visited the Langs, and the Pierces visited the Langs, and Selvinius came too, and there were announcements and invitations sent out. There would be a cantata in the church and a festival in the schoolhouse and a party at the Langs' and a party at the Pierces'. There would be apple-dunking and mistletoe. With this beginning, so it was through the entire village, like a spreading fire in straw fields, until there threatened to be more activities than so few people could provide for.

Mrs. Lang baked fourteen cakes in three days. She never baked a cake unless she made three. Women in the neighborhood were accustomed to hearing "oo-hoo," which meant Mrs. Lang was at the gate, her arms full with a pudding, a pie, a roast, in a clean white apron which was forever her excuse for not being able to stay. She was a provider for church banquets, organizer of social and educational activities, peacemaker of difficulties which village women are so apt at scheming or imagining among themselves. Men not merely tipped but raised their hats, standing still and to one side as she passed, as they would have for a very old woman who had been known and respected by their fathers. In their homes she was always made welcome through courtesy, and then, after their hands were washed and their shirts changed, they would come again into the room where she was seated with their wives, and with shyness and yet pride they would offer her short, earnest talk.

Mrs. Rowiger baked fewer cakes, but visited up and down the narrow valley. She was a widow with one son and feared by all men and not by bachelors. She traveled on foot with the fury of a woman who despised walking, with the additional annoyance of having had to sell her carriage and horses because her husband had managed to lose most of their money before he died. It had not really been necessary to part with the carriage and horses, only to retrench a little, but she had in bitterness put this indignity on herself and before the eyes of everyone. Her mission was to make sure everyone attended, to find out why various families had not answered invitations.

So Christmas came and was brought to Coverly. Old festivities with the comfortable history of having been established by earlier generations assured everyone of success and gaiety, so that even the strict sects found it difficult to find fault. There was joy and cheer and heartiness. The young and the older children and a few small children went caroling through a village so small that no one needed to be slighted, not even deaf Mrs. Seiders, who had to sit by her window all evening, watching for bobbing and swinging lanterns, so as to be sure not to miss it. Little Raymond Rowiger came to her window so she could see his face and tell what song they were singing, and Henry Pierce, the best baritone, walked around the group holding his lantern high so that she would be able to see how they were dressed and how cheerful they were. Raymond was sent away from the window to the door and then to the carolers with a bag of apples and nuts, and when he went home, three hours later and very sleepy, there were in his pocket two niggertoes which were warm from his efforts to break them.

Middle-aged people, bundled around their legs and in big coats, with their faces covered to the nose in scarfs, were sleigh riding, jingling their bells at each other. In the morning the streets would be slashed with rust marks. Even Jake and Jess Dreher, with their high-hubbed wagon, a barn lantern before and behind, went bumping along, sitting high and straight, gliding forward in spirit, while the horse pulled with the same pull that had brought out many a stump.

There was skating on the canal and many went hobbling about on Christmas. Some gave creditable performances. Mr. Lang drew a round of applause for his figure eights and back-skating on a pair of wooden skates which had been his grandfather's. Tad Stevens did well for his sixty-fifth year. Mark chased everyone from the ice in a demonstration of speed. More than a hundred people gathered round the bonfire, and thousands of fire sparks blew from the canal bank out over the river, and the snow fried, and tales of long ago were recounted.

It was the old people who were surprising. Children looked at their fathers and mothers with new respect. For these were people of enormous vigor, who had a good time when they set out to have one, who were so innocent about fun and frolic that they behaved outrageously and ridiculously, which only made them snuffle and chortle. There had never been any Puritan strain in them and never would be. They showed what it was like when serious, hard-working people get to thinking about youth and happiness.

Christmas was a quiet day. After dinner the old people sat around the fireplace, and then went to bed early, confident of having fulfilled the obligations of their heritage.

2

In a Pennsylvania Dutch house each brick has had individual attention and bears exactly its share of the total burden, for it has been constructed by men who know that time will strengthen and improve walls made firm in the beginning. The Lang house was not pretentious. It was the oldest house in the village and gave promise of becoming historical, representative of a former period and way of life. Despite monotonous structural composition, the walls had a graceful autumnal tone. Bricks, having lost their strong red surface color and false radiance, were more convincing because they had depth and blemishes.

More important, the house was snug and comfortable, easy to warm in winter, trellised with honeysuckle and ivy against summer. Four generations of winter had thrust the amount and force of wind, rain and snow that a large two-story house deserved. Now the winters were beginning to subside into mildness, cadenced with light snows, bright, bitter-cold winter days, thaws that burned brown spots on the hills; the walls and the large chimneys from which smoke could boil out were remnants of an earlier period which the house had outlasted, unneeded reminders of a time of great snows, roaring winds and violent temperatures. The mortar was still firm. Degeneration was measured by new window bindings, door sills, furnace, roof and the almost imperceptible lathing that hands had accomplished on doorknobs. The house was rising in value.

Brick steps led to two small and sturdy porches on which there was little room for sitting, so that in summertime the lawn with its maples, white chairs and little benches was popular. The maples were small, a multitude of big leaves assuring that it would have to rain long and smartly before the grass beneath became sodden. They were afforded a dignity of posture, which small trees seldom have, by the slender straightness of their trunks and a shapeliness which was not merely the result of pruning. By July their leaves were large and as heavy and firm as metal, so that not all breezes were recorded. By August there were flecks of ripe yellow, and autumn came easily.

From a distance the trees resembled green bushes, dwarfed by the spaciousness of the lawn, which was bordered on three sides by tall hedge. The sizable flower garden seemed a rectangle of red, yellow, white and pale blues, painted on the ground, slightly engraved. It appeared as if cultivation and selective seeding had bleached the flowers of their poignant colors into something more pleasing and less disturbing.

Two cherry trees wore white in April, prim delicate whiteness more clean than a remembrance of snow, especially when a breeze set the color into a slight shifting. The pink cores of the blossoms gave softness and drift, promising bright red berries and rows of jars on the second shelf of the cellar storage. Birds came to these trees more often than to the maples, birds with wild, shrill calls sometimes heard in the mountains, and left behind clusters of black seeds still clinging to stems. The wastage of greed gave the air along the lawn and the southern walls of the house an aroma of faint passion.

An old arbor which had once given vines a place to cling was now wired into broken firmness by the constriction of the fruit it had mothered. Blues sometimes got plump enough to burst and attract wasps, while the pale green sweet grapes were less dependable. Perhaps out of respect for its age, perhaps out of fear to meddle with the ways the vines had chosen to wind and bind, the arbor looked a little neglected and drowsy.

The apple tree was unresponsive to the fertility of the soil. Hardy enough and sprawlingly rooted, its very appearance was a crotchety cantankerousness, and it bore apples with disdain in isolated clusters. Malice was suggested in the deformity, the knobby unroundedness of the apples. Small, pinched leaves more gray than green, brittle in appearance, without tenderness, were rather unheeding of the seasons. The leaves came early, struggled with frost, showed not the least gratitude for rain or interest in the sun, and hung vertical in shriveled brown until a winter storm caught them and sent them whipping across the lawn and made the sides of the hedge look like an insucking ventilator.

The lawn was ample enough to prevent the apple tree from infecting the quiet, formal atmosphere. Never satisfied in this soil abounding with limestone, grass had choked the weeds and embroidered the brick footpath, and had actually crept through and beyond the hedge, making the Lang property appear even more extensive than it was. Where the grass ended, or had halted for this particular year, stood a tall old poplar which shielded the house from the noise of the street.

Three or four carriages and a few wagons were the traffic—an increase over former years, the result of village growth and of its becoming unfashionable for gentlemen to ride saddle. Sometimes dust would appear above the hedge, and if Mrs. Lang was not careful, that was her only chance of being warned. For it was a house visited many times by many people. In winter the cracking of ice glaze would penetrate the brick walls which kept out so many other sounds, and a few moments later the front door would be thrown open. In summer the gate stood open; the chairs and benches were dusted every morning.

Mr. Geoffrey Lang owned this house and a cigar factory. He also had two of the finest horses in Coverly, one of them sired by an award winner at the Gratz Fair for three consecutive years. The groom, the lone servant, was certain of employment; and his duties, aside from the two horses and the carriage, were keeping the grass level and tidy, shearing the hedge, and delivering occasional messages.

Mrs. Lang was a good wife and a good housewife. Her cooking and her garden were famous.

Into this security Irene Lang was born.

Irene eagerly began to explore, pulling the broken skin of her knee apart to look inside. The red portions of her fingers she pushed her mouth down over, tasting sweet, faint furriness, rubbing around and through her fingers with her tongue until they were clean, except that her fingernails had red rims. The taste did not satisfy her mouth's expectation. She reddened her fingers again on her knee and made lines on her face and went to the mirror. What she saw in the glass made her laugh.

The broken skin was pinching at her knee without hurting, except little hurts which were something to be curious about. One place there was a little blood going down along her leg as rain drops sometimes ran down the windows, and then it went inside her little white sock and made a pink place. It tickled.

She watched herself bleed for a long time. Then she put her hand over the cut and for quite a while believed she was holding the blood in. She began to be afraid all the blood would run out, afraid for her leg and not for herself, and she drew up her knee to her head, and her mouth leeched itself over the cut. The taste was different in direct contact, warm and almost thirsty, but soon nauseating—she swallowed only in the hope it would go back into her leg.

Irene ran and showed her knee to her mother, crying, "Stop it, Mommy, it hurts me."

Mrs. Lang became excited and did not know what to do. Irene had blood on her hands and legs and face and even on her dress. Against her pale complexion it made her appear completely white.

"But how did it happen?" Mrs. Lang cried, wrapping the knee with a dish towel. The sight of the towel turning red scared Irene more than anything previous had, and Mrs. Lang was a little rough in her haste to tighten the cloth. "How'd you manage to do it?" Mrs. Lang said brusquely. "It's letting up a little, but hold still! How can I do anything if you . . . ? Now hold still, Irene, I'm doing the best I can."

Mr. Lang came out of his office-study and used a piece of ice, his thumb and breath from his mouth. He was patient and persistent.

"I believe her coagulation is poor," he said.

Irene did not understand that, but knew who had stopped the bleeding. . . .

The man with the black bag who sometimes came to see Mother came. Irene saw him because Mother said she had to. It was usual to meet people in the parlor, so she was a little cautious entering the office-study where the man was opening the black bag, taking bottles out and shaking them and looking at them. One he looked at and compared with another bottle, then took the cap off and sniffed.

"No label," he said, holding it out for her to smell. "Label's always falling off. You can put your nose closer. Laudanum. Not much help . . . Useless."

The man patted his hand on the chair beside him.

"Hop up," he said.

Irene was convinced then he had really come to see her—not like all those people who pretended. When she found out he wanted to see her leg she was even more pleased. Since he found her knee as interesting as she thought it was, she found herself telling him about her new dress and new shoes. Irene was concerned about her knee too; it was very odd about that knee. But the man would not let her look as often as he did, so she became interested in his face and the top of his head. She kept blowing softly into his hair to see white places until he reached up and rubbed his head exactly where her breath had been going. She laughed because he did not know.

Mother came and told her to be brave and not cry, and Irene could not help but cry a little, although she did not want to. After that she could like the man only so much and no more, and would not even look at her mother. The scratch was cool and there was no redness and the man swung her leg for her. Having her leg swung put her in better humor. Irene wanted to see what her knee felt like now, wanted to peek under the white cloth, but Mother would not let her. For a while she had to put both hands on top of her head to remember to obey.

Father and the man lit pipes and talked back and forth too fast, nodding their heads, and Irene nodded her head several times, then slipped off the chair, sliding-board style, and went to the black bag that had made her nose tickle soon after it was opened. There was a big gold buckle on top and the bag was so strong she could not push it more than an inch or two. She put her face inside the bag and breathed big and could not locate the smell as much there as she could in the room. Yet after a while she had to put her finger in her nose to catch something which was crawling up into her head where it was not nice—like the time an ant had gone into her ear.

When the man was gone, Irene was lifted onto her mother's lap and hugged and shaken and cried over. She had to take hold of mother's dress at two places to hold herself erect, trying to get the two sides of her rump to share equally. She held her face upward so Mother could see her disapproval.

"I want down," said Irene. "Don't shake me. I want down."

"I knew all along," Mrs. Lang was saying. "I knew in my heart something was wrong. But the doctor had to know better and you had to believe him. No one would pay the least attention to me. My poor darling," she said, hugging Irene. "Never you mind, Mother will look out for you, she will take care of her own dear little girl, she will see to it no harm comes."

Irene, quite bewildered, kept looking from Father to Mother for explanation. Her knee was completely forgotten in this new excitement. She even forgot at moments to want down.

"Now, now," said Mr. Lang, "there's no reason to take on so. It won't make things a bit better, and you'll frighten the child over nothing."

"Over nothing! Well, if that's all you think of it!"

"You know what I mean, Ilsa."

"If the doctor had known his business . . . But no, he had to ignore my warnings. And now you make light of it. I shan't. I'll not have it said I neglected my child."

"Nor I," said Mr. Lang quietly, watching his daughter, trying to see what effect the conversation was having. "You know very well what I meant."

"Down, Mommy," said Irene, in a patient, hopeless voice.

"I'm not giving anybody the blame, except the doctor." Mrs. Lang pulled Irene tight against her. "I'm beginning to think he was wrong about me. I've thought that all along."

"I expect there's very little he could have done," said Mr. Lang. "Try not to let this upset you. We'll follow the diet he suggested and see if she doesn't improve. We'll work it out together, the three of us. We'll manage. Am I right, Irene? I'm sure you're not going to let it bother you."

Mr. Lang took his daughter from room to room and pointed out things she was not supposed to touch. Irene felt quite important. She trotted around after her father, staying near in case her knee should hurt again.

Mrs. Lang followed them and mentioned things forgotten or missed, and she raised a number of small items to the shelf above the fireplace, which was nearly out of reach for herself.

"I'm sorry I spoke so sharply," she said. "I just can't forgive myself for leaving the sewing basket where she could get into it."

Mr. Lang nodded, and in looking at his wife, his eyes were kindly and loving. He was the sort of man who could remember all that a woman has been and therefore keep a level view of her and appreciate her shortcomings. He could also remember his own faults and through them make stronger the good and honest qualities in his wife.

When he had completed the tour, he said, with a smile, "Now, Irene, if you can remember all that, you have a better head than mine, and if you obey everything I've said, I ought to turn you over my knee. So just be a little careful, and I suppose that will be enough to ask of you. Perhaps too much."

"There you go making light of the matter."

"Well, Ilsa, what would you have me do?"

Mr. Lang took a pipe from his pocket and placed it on the mantel and took down a larger pipe and packed it with tobacco. His thumb carefully prodded the strands. He looked around the room, hunting the chair he would enjoy smoking in most, one which had broadness and depth. Choosing an armchair he gradually adjusted the pipe to fit his mouth. Irene came over and stood beside the chair and looked up at him and patted his knee three times. Mr. Lang lifted her and then waited, holding his arms out of the way, until she had found a position where she could be still. Mr. Lang knew that getting seated comfortably was an important part of how long she would be content to sit on his lap.

Irene put her hand beside her mouth, but she would not speak until Mr. Lang stooped his head.

"I think it's going to bleed," she said softly, nodding her head seriously and emphatically.

"What makes you think that?" said Mr. Lang, amused.

"It hurts."

"Why, now, let's find out if it hurts. It wants to be rubbed, doesn't it? And it sort of feels as if you ought to look at it, just for a moment? Is it something like that?"

Irene nodded.

"Well, then, rub it a little. Not hard. And take a look. That's it, not hard. You see, it only hurts not to rub it."

Irene rubbed, now that she had permission. She gave her daddy a big smile.

"Now then," said Mr. Lang. "Whenever it hurts, you rub it a little. But not hard. And in about ten days you're going to have a new knee, the skin's going to be all new, and you won't even be able to see where it bled. But to have that new skin, we must cover it with this bandage, just as you have to be covered at night in your bed so you don't wake up cold."

Mr. Lang struck a match and let Irene look at the flame so long that another match had to light the pipe. Irene blew and missed and the flame came nearer, and she blew and the flame wiggled and made a noise. She felt a little air on her forehead and then the flame vanished.

"I blowed it," she said. "Let's blow another."

"Let's smoke a while," said Mr. Lang, putting a little white circle near enough so that she could smell.

Irene smiled, willing to wait. Waiting sounded nice the way Father said it. He seemed bigger than he had been earlier in the evening.

Mrs. Lang was getting dinner. It was the latest she had ever been, and from the kitchen came a fury of sounds.

3

Selvinius foresaw a new era, one which would replace the flow of men and ambition toward the West, and would take the sting out of the chagrin with which men finally realized America was not after all boundless. He foresaw internal growth, a new nation rising out of one which men had only skinned the pelt from.

Selvinius believed in industry and believed that men were in their hearts more willing to create, more willing to shape and design, than to destroy. Born and raised among Germans, he was convinced a man would rather be a shoemaker than a soldier. He saw no reason why a craftsman in steel could not be as proud and satisfied in his work and his life as a farmer in his.

He had read and studied in England, with attention to the problems of industrial depressions and industrial-political panics. His con-

26

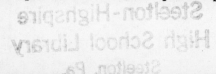

clusion was that they could not be avoided, but that if an industry was willing to reserve a margin of its profit, it could pass through such times without endangering itself or its employees. He guaranteed every man who worked for him assistance whenever no employment was available.

He initiated a stock plan which allowed his workers to purchase shares through small weekly payments. This plan he intended to retain, even if it threatened his margin of control.

He established individual and unit bonuses, based on quantity of production, minimum defective or rejected materials, and years of service. In addition, there was a general bonus, divided equally among employees, twenty per cent of all profits of the preceding year.

He established pensions for men who served twenty years, full pension for thirty-five years of service. The amount of this pension depended on the times and the condition of the company, but full pension was never less than half of the existing wage. Men totally disabled received pensions regardless of time of service. The partially disabled were provided with light work.

There was a small hospital and nurses to visit the sick among the families of workers. The public school was given funds to provide evening classes in English and American History. A library was established in the front parlor of Mrs. Kublenski's boardinghouse, and tools and equipment were provided for an industrial-training course, which the school board reluctantly voted to include in the curriculum.

A group of stockholders, led by Mr. Jonathan Pierce, were fighting Selvinius every inch of the way. The stock profits were so low that they were threatening to sell their holdings. But Selvinius did not budge. Mr. Lang supported him and so did Miss Addie Harnet. The production of steel was increasing, and there was an atmosphere of health in the workers' attitudes. Money was being sent to Europe to bring the wives of men across the Atlantic, and women were coming across the ocean on the promise of marriage and a wonderful new land. The bank was beginning to have a major business in currency exchange and in workers' savings.

Selvinius was keeping faith with the village.

Yet he turned a stone face against unions. As he stated his position, "I'm willing to talk to any worker or group of workers who believe they have a grievance, one which their immediate superior has failed to adjust, or which is beyond his authority to adjust. But I shall never speak with a man who represents another. I shall immediately dismiss the man who comes to me with a threat. On this I stand. I am one man, and the advantage of my position allows me to be just or unjust, and that I retain as my right. I no more believe in this proposed honeymoon of the worker and the owner than I believe in slavery. I shall not stand by and see the dignity of man and the aspiration of man made into a mathematics of power and number."

4

The parlor was warm and softly lighted and silent, except for expansion noises which made Irene peer down through the square holes into the darkness along the bottom of the register. Heat pulled at the corners of her mouth and gave her eyelashes more weight and length. Hot air blew out of the register making her dress balloon, enticing her to hold her arms in bird fashion. Flapping with gracefulness, swaying the two portions of her arms and also her hands in different but similar lightness so that her shoulders rose and fell—a feeling of rising, of soaring.

In summertime the register was the coldest area in the house, a different cold than she could feel reaching into the icebox. She was suspicious of cold air. A great blast of heat had once made her scream, but had not frightened her, only made her worry and examine her skin, puzzled that the skin had hurt so for a moment and yet was perfectly all right. But chill and the damp, early-summer odors from the register seemed to creep inside her flesh and linger and do harm. Shivering, continued beyond the initial excitement which was as funny as laughing, warned her of a vague, uneasy anxiety within her, something inexplicable, like the morning there had been frost on the window and steam coming out of her mouth and no covers on her and she had had a feeling of not being able to move, an awareness of the skeleton around which she was formed, and an almost sickening sensation of feeling the contours of all the principal bones in her arms and legs. There was something about cold air which she could not understand, a squeezing, pinching pressure which she did not like to feel around her knees. She did not like the sounds that came from the cellar on very cold nights or the noises from the windows.

Most of the things Irene was forbidden to touch, glass and metal, were cold.

She peered into the darkness of the register, trying to see the blue button, the penny and other things she could not remember, which it had taken from her. The blue button in particular she wanted. It had dropped in the middle of the rug, and she had chased it, and, as her hand reached, the register had sucked it down.

The parlor was softly dark and therefore the windows were bright, and Irene spent much time looking at light and glaze on the rectangular panes, holding her head in various askance positions to see different shapes at the exact same place on the glass. She did not have the least idea there was world outside. It would not have interested her if she had been told. She would have preferred to watch flecks and spasms of bright yellow on the pane of glass.

She seemed to sense, even so young, that the full light of the sun was not meant for her and was to be avoided.

If kindlings of light confined themselves to a pale yellow glow that stretched shafted between window and rug, holding the straightness and obedience of a searchlight, then Irene was brave, swinging her arms through to see if some of the yellow would rub off on her skin, cupping her hands to discover the weight of light, polishing her fingernails on her dress so they would sparkle, fingers which felt strange because Mother kept the nails trimmed short. But all these were done with Irene standing in the mild darkness with her arms reaching out to the sunshine.

She had learned, from trying to rub out the bright temporary stains on the rug with her shoes, the existence of shadows. She had learned how to make her own hand a great dark mark along the wall. But she could not understand why dust particles twisted and floated in the light, when in the darker areas of the room the air was clean and still. She was in the habit of holding a hand over her nose whenever she had to walk through, and even her eyes would feel dirty and she would have to rub them.

With the shades drawn the room was floated with air that had a soft scent of wood and of leather, and all the nervousness would settle into a cool quietness. Irene preferred the room that way. Her eyes would become much more alert and bold, and against the insides of her ears she would detect the softest pelting of minute sounds, more like a weightless sediment stirring in air than like sound. She had developed a confidence in solitude that made her more timid when in the presence of anything which moved quickly or made big sounds. Her awareness of and interest in the ordinary world, all that which went on so rapidly and brusquely far above the level of her eyes, was reduced into something meaningless. In the baffled, crazed wanderings of an ant which had somehow stumbled onto the carpet, where it whirled around in frantic circles, hunting its own scent and the way to return, Irene was likely to find more enjoyment by trying to make a path with her finger, a path toward safety or further danger, depending on her mood. For as she developed confidence in her perceptions, as her sensations became more intricate and acute, the great bustle of the world in which Mother and Father existed, the parlor invaded with people and noise, aroused in her a sensitivity and nervousness which made her want to peep in and watch carefully before exposing herself. Mother was always forcing her to enter, pushing her inside before she was ready. She was aware of something different about herself, something which made her distinct; there were so many things she was not allowed to touch which other children could. Everyone had been told about her blood, and now when people fixed their eyes on her she could see their eyes change.

Solitude was easier. Some of her happiest moments were when all was silent, without perceptible motion or sound, when odor was so even and placid that her nose could smell nothing. Irene, in these moments of tranquillity, was able to absorb the excitements and discoveries which the previous hours had brought and prepare herself for new ones. Childhood was for her a scientific and artistic and microscopic examination of the world of one room, the world of another room. Her approach was timid curiosity, a rare kind of stubbornness, grave quietness; and the result of her discoveries was delight or disappointment. Her eyes and ears were not selective enough to slip past the hundreds and thousands of minor miracles, from which her mind gained no wisdom and small learning, but which sensitized her eyes to quick correct movement, alerted her fingers until they could make minute decisions, and blew into her the unusual combination of a great hunger for life and a delicate appetite.

The parlor was her favorite room.

The kitchen was the biggest room Irene had ever seen, and it had three distinct odors, the inky, irritant smell of stove polish, the sharp scent of soap, and the more bodied, fulsome odor of new warm bread. The wallpaper was white except in one corner where smoke from the stove had made a shadow. Woodwork had the soft, shineless cleanliness that comes from being washed often, with even the lines between the panels kept clean by dipping a cloth in soap and water and then wrapping it around a match stick. Six blue and squarish chairs surrounded a table that could be made big and different by putting boards in the middle. Whenever the table was long Irene knew there would be visitors.

The floor was cold and hard, clothed with a few scatter rugs, and when the boards were stained dark gave off an odor so pungent that Irene would not enter. The table and the kitchen cabinet sat on tiny wheels, but it took Father and Mother together to push them about. Irene did not push since she might hurt herself and because her push did not help. She learned by accident how to pull on the leg of the ironing board and make it fall.

The stove was hot even to its legs. Pieces of coal were always falling inside and sounding heavier than they were. Irene sometimes looked underneath to see if fire had fallen on the floor, but never once thought about the house burning. When there was wood fire something was sure to be in the oven, and there was a gusty swirling and a sound like someone coughing into a handkerchief. Woodfire made even the draught holes red, and the wall behind the stove had bubbles in the paint.

The sound Irene enjoyed was the crinkle and hiss that came from the big black skillet when sausage was put in, but she was afraid to go close. It spit. When the skillet was rubbed on top of the stove, shaken back and forth, it would get furious, and even Mother would have to put the lid on in a hurry. Father had held her on his shoulder so she could watch eels squirm, but she had been afraid and lost confidence in what he told her. The eels crawled and splashed grease all over the stove.

Irene liked it more when Mother let dish water go down the drain and there were funny noises and laughter and squeals, and long after there was no more water, when everything was quiet, the drain would give a big burp.

She liked to sprinkle a little water on the stove lids and watch the drops act silly and bounce around, but Mother scolded, saying it was bad for the stove, the lids would crack. These were things Irene did not believe were so. And besides, to see little balls of water giggle and then vanish was far more mysterious than to watch steam from the kettle, which Mother seemed to think should be so interesting.

On warm winter days when the stove was used merely for cooking, Irene liked to rub her hand along the edge of the draught-slide and feel the coldness that came from inside and pushed against her palm. Touching metal gave her a sensation of both respect and distrust. The stove was interesting in almost endless ways, how it made food smell and change color and shape, how it pushed warmth out through the kitchen without moving or disturbing the air. But its real attraction to her was that it taught her so many curious things about her own flesh, about tenderness, and new confidence and new apprehensions.

Irene was also comparing herself with her mother, who could lift pan lids that released great gushes of steam, who thought nothing of thrusting her hands down into the fire to put wood in, who would taste soups that were simmering and test boiling sugar-water icings in the palm of her hand. Irene admired, but there was also distrust which kept her at a distance from her mother.

In the Dutch pantry was an iron kettle so large that when Irene sat inside she could not see over the top. It was difficult and dangerous to get into the kettle, and once inside she was forced to remain until Father came and lifted her out. She allowed him to do that for her, and when he had put her down, she would curtsy to him.

Irene would sit inside the kettle and frown and look straight ahead with her dark eyes. The imperfect, fragmented darkness which did not hinder vision, which was more nearly a light strained of all brightness and glint and color, would settle around her. The iron surrounded her with a coldness that made her know where the warmest and most tender parts of her were, seemed to pull heat from her body at a thrilling rate, and even to raise in her a slight fear of her flesh sticking fast. The curvature of the kettle made it difficult for arms and legs to understand what movements would keep her balanced, making her feel the same giddy, new-seeing awe as when she stooped her head and peered backward through the arch of her legs. The smallness of the kettle and the shortness of her dress made it impossible for her to twist the cloth enough to protect her legs from the iron, and the two tiny parts of her rump quarreled and disagreed over where she should sit.

But it was another chilliness, that of the air which surrounded her and seemed to keep descending, air tanged with the pinched scent of iron and with a different pressure which Irene could feel creep into her and inform her about parts of her body which were not ordinarily sensitive. The faint sound of iron seemed to blend into this chilliness, the sound a bell always carries in its hollow, the sound of water receding from sand beach, the sound which came when she held her hands over her ears, and with it the earliest recognition that silence too, silence which she loved, had a fearful quality of being vibratory and nervous. Her eyes would seem to contain particles alien to sight but infinitely delicate to temperature. If she touched herself on the forehead or on the throat the impression of that touch would linger, would even heighten, until she could not resist rubbing it away.

There were other moments when she would giggle and wonder many things, such as what it was like to be cooked. She liked to pronounce certain words in the kettle because they sounded so funny and her voice so unlike what she knew it was. It was a good place to practice the little rhyme Father had offered, "Biddy Beider baked a bitter batch of butter batter while Peter Piper picked a peck of pickled peppers. . . ." But never was she there to hide. She was secretive, she hid toys. There were times when she would have hidden from visitors, but there was such shame and disgust in being found, in being forced to come out, surrender without excuse or explanation, while her mother's eyes stared at her with indignation and cold fixity. And Irene would never have hidden in the kettle, because that would have spoiled it, the way the parlor was spoiled by visitors sitting around in chairs.

The eyes of people were beginning to bother Irene. She was beginning to feel the emotions that make people want to hide their bodies. She was becoming aware of how naked eyes can be, probing about with vulgar curiosity, squinting in a manner that was nasty and humiliating. Irene felt this in particular about Mrs. Rowiger, whose eyes were large and bulging and seemed to throw merciless glances, to gaze with a fixity that was worse to endure than having sunlight shoot straight through her, the way it sometimes seemed to do. Irene got so that she did not look at people's eyes, but that was hard too, and was an indignity which made her hands clench. She was getting so she could scarcely endure it when people touched her.

It was a house of many doors. Two Irene could not manage, one that stuck, another, which led to the attic, because the knob was beyond reach even on tiptoe. It was a door mounted on a high step, so that it seemed more like an enormous cabinet, and Father was the only person she had ever seen go through it, and then she had been able to hear the ceiling, and after a while he had come down with

33

something of dark metal which he kept blowing on and brushing lightly with his fingers. All the other doors had outlasted their purpose, were always open, held open by all sorts of items, a miniature of Grandfather sealed in a glass rectangle, a seashell which was colorless and not very roary. One of the upstairs doors, which did not need anything to hold it open, was nevertheless blocked by the pellet-filled base of a kerosene lamp.

Irene was the first person in three generations of Langs to form the habit of closing doors. There was continuous conflict between Irene and her mother on this matter. Part of it was simply the miracle of hinges. But it went deeper. Irene always slipped out of bed and made tight the door of her bedroom, with only the slightest sense of wrongdoing, and with an almost immediate feeling of tranquil isolation in which happiness and then sleep came to her. She did not like the door even a tiny bit ajar. Of course in the morning, the early morning, she was quite anxious to re-establish contact with her parents, and she chattered quite a lot and was affectionate and gay. But she knew the real purpose of a door.

The kitchen door had a keyhole big as her eye and an amazingly big key, longer than her hand. Her eye cooled and got clean almost as soon as she put it against the keyhole, and although she could not see nearly as much as through the kitchen windows, what she saw looked more interesting; her eye could see far without the uneasiness and bewilderment that distance usually brought to her, and color was more vivid, a splashing brilliance of sensation in itself, and therefore a reason for continuing to look. Through the keyhole came the first clear insight into the complexity of grass and trees, and through it she learned the advantages of watching one select area for a longer time.

For a whole week she went around with a piece of dark paper which she constantly rolled into a tube whenever she wanted to see or study anything. For a time she trusted more what she saw through the tube than what she saw with both eyes. She had a problem too. Her left eye was contrary and would not stay open unless she held the other eye covered; even then it did not really want to look at anything, saw because it had to, because she made it. Such disobedience caused in her a sort of petulance.

The kitchen door, biggest and thickest, was easy to push shut and only a little difficult to open. It was used by people with baskets, people who stood and talked and gestured without entering. Women who came to see Mother often simply walked in, but men who came to see Father or Mother stood a little away from the door, with their hats between their hands. Irene could have fun when Mother was not in the kitchen, for when someone knocked she would knock too, and then there would be another knock from outside. Irene would hide and watch the peculiar look that Mother would be given when she opened the door.

People Irene had never seen, people who sat in the parlor or on the lawn, came in through the front door. The front door often jingled when it was knocked on. Irene could not make it jingle from the inside no matter how hard she hit. Irene did not like that door, and anyone whom she had never seen would have to be very friendly with her to make the suspicion and alertness go out of her eyes and to make her forget to keep at a distance. Father used that door when in a hurry, but he was not often in a hurry.

The back door was used for just everything.

If Irene pinched the sandbag at the base of the door the grains inside would grind together and say something she could not quite understand, no matter where her ear was. That sandbag was the heaviest thing in the world, but she could drag it along the floor and even pick up one end. She called it, "My pussycat."

5

Toward evening the bustle and activity in the Lang house would diminish into a time of mellowness, a tranquillity which prepared the family for the long night of deeper repose, which stilled their hearts, attuned their hearts to the unmoving silence of the village. In winter the silence was something nervous and alien, with only the fireplace to indicate that there was activity outside, stirrings in the darkness. Coldness would sit in the corners; the family would sit in chairs drawn toward the center of the room, before that curious radiant heat of pine logs and hot brick which made them expose one side and then the other, and made Mrs. Lang sometimes stoop and rub her legs. If there was snow on the ground, they knew it only through a sense of isolation, a knowledge that the steps of the porch would still be a smooth white until morning, when it would be gotten after with a broom. Or by those tiniest of glints and tip edges of sound as sleety flakes met and stuck fast a moment or bounced away from the windows.

Summer had a different stillness, the blowsy odor that drifted in from the lawn, of cool wet grass and grape sweetness, and the sharp cries of insects which were clinging fast to the edges of the blades. Evenings picked up the scent which daytime heat matted, and brought it sifted through the screens, where moths would sit, white, frantic-eyed, wings fluttering in endless urge toward light. Even though the Langs would be sitting without much light. For it was the time which they devoted to communing with each other, letting the tensions and frictions of the day ease from magnitude to a more affectionate stage in which there was humor, tolerance and love. It was the time Irene had come to regard as her own, a time when Father and Mother were patient and understanding, when they would listen to her questions and do things to amuse her, and give her a great amount of affection of the right sort.

Irene was sitting on her father's lap, smoking her bubble pipe exactly the way he was smoking his pipe, and they were both laughing. He always had time to amuse her, a few minutes at the dinner table, a short while in the afternoon, laying aside a book or putting down his pen; but these were pleasures foredampened by their brevity, and it was the evening which he gave to her and which she gave to him. There was a lamp burning, most of its light held close, so that eyes were drawn toward it. Mr. Lang and his daughter used it more for silhouette as they compared smoke rings with bubbles. From time to time, Mr. Lang had to reach out with the pipe and tap it in a basin of soapy water, and once Irene inhaled the liquid into her mouth and needed a handkerchief to wipe her tongue, but that was the most discomfort they encountered.

The office-study had larger and heavier pieces of furniture and a stolid comfort that was not weakened by cushions or fabric upholstery. It was furnished in Mr. Lang's own tastes, in his belief that wood and leather properly assembled were more restful to and natural for the human body. One of the chairs, his favorite, had been his grandfather's, and it was in this chair that he was usually to be found. The chair was actually a little large for him, particularly in width, and yet something in his bearing, not the regal attitude which makes a king fitting to his throne, but a respectability heightened by appreciation for repose, made him seem suited for it.

Mrs. Lang was sewing. She was therefore closer to the lamp, but with her back toward it, so that she was sitting with one shoulder lowered, and from time to time she raised the material high. It was a very dainty piece of cloth and the little skirt would be amply pleated, and she was using slender thread and the tiniest stitches to keep the miniature proportions true in every respect. In the basket on the floor beside her was a piece of lace which had been intended for the blouse, received through the mail from Philadelphia; but it was a disappointment, not so attractive as she had been led to believe, and she was going to turn it to some other use. The movements of her hands showed that she was quite aware of the sensitive qualities of pleats. With clothing of this sort, care had to be taken with the child's petticoats or the whole effect would be spoiled, and so she had made that first. She preferred dresses in which the tone of the color was to some extent dependent on the petticoats, yet without the underclothing being visible except through the blouse, and then only if lace was used.

Her eyes missed the daylight a little more than theirs. Yet, despite this, it was perhaps more relaxing for her to be seated beneath the lamplight, with dinner and all the worries of the day past, with nothing further to be done except to put Irene to bed, and from time to time watch her husband and the child playing, than if she had tried to be a part in their amusement. It was no bother to sew, and she could always let it rest in her lap until she felt like taking it up again, sometimes with the faint surprise of finding that she had accomplished more than she had realized. The cool air from the window which drifted toward the fireplace passed by her, making her cross her legs one way and then the other.

After his wife had finished sewing, Mr. Lang went to the lamp and sent the room into darkness. It was, for an instant, an act of violence. Then it became apparent that he had done what the room and the atmosphere needed to complete their mood, and had indeed offered their eyes something fine to see, rather than shutting the eyes out. For the darkness lost its vivid pigmentation, the room stilled and regained dimensional security. Everywhere was an absence of radiance and the very softest shades of light. Through the windows could be seen the soft brightness of the horizon, stars and moon hidden by their height, visible only to Mr. Lang, who went to the window for a moment. He gazed out and then upward in the crops-to-sky movement which a man never loses once he has learned it. The stars and the moon were making the sky blue, faintly blue, and smoothing the sills with faint edges of light. He returned to the chair

37

and sat in it, finding more warmth than he had left. His eyes were still aching. He did not bother to close them, and after a while his eyelids lost their nervousness and functioned with a sort of indolence, as if confident no harm could come to his eyes from such delicate gradations of light.

On the floor moved in slow pantomime shadows so little less than darkness, so void of light as to seem ultimate culminations of the perceptive power of Irene. It was only she who watched these nebulous shapes. In daytime she would have known them as the shadows of branches of the tree, but in that different shadow of the moon, lineless, they were and had to be taken as a plaything of the faintest lights, as a picture for the imagination.

The crickets were louder and more shrill, wailing, and further in the distance there was music, or at least a co-operation of sound which sometimes touched upon one tone, one tone only, that was definitely violin. Mr. Lang nodded his head, as if measuring it against a remembered sound in his ear, yet was entirely unaware of the kinship in himself to a far-off sound. Irene only felt as if the windows had been thrown open wider, as if more and more came in through them.

Mrs. Lang had almost protested when her husband went to the lamp. It had come to her all in that one moment, many little items which could have been taken care of, out-of-the-way things which ought to be done now that she had the opportunity. She had thrust the needle into the sand cushion in the sewing basket, and the skirt was still on her lap, and she did not know whether she had really quit sewing or had only paused. But after the light went out and after her eyes had hunted out the shadow of her husband and had seen his posture as he stood by the window, gazing out into the night, she had folded the skirt and put it too in the basket. Her body remained stiff in protest of this giving in long after her husband and daughter were again comfortably arranged on the chair. The darkness made the chilliness around her legs more uncomfortable and gave her a feeling of being at a greater distance from her husband and child.

After minutes in which she heard no sound except herself and the meaningless chatter of insects out over the fields—a sound clearer now that she had nothing to do except sit in the dark, now that the moths had ceased thumping against the screens—she said, "Irene."

There was a long silence.

"She's not asleep," said Mr. Lang.

Mrs. Lang felt herself stiffen again, this time in spite of herself, and she sat, waiting for her body to do what she could not make it do. She had a momentary feeling that she would remain sitting this way, stiff and unvaried and alert, through the rest of the evening. And then in a moment she found her way clear to make a compromise and a surrender, to relax into the darkness and close her eyes over her nervous need to see and to share. Her head drowsed even while her arms and legs were still tense, the leather upholstery became a substantial odor, the chair seemed to fold away and out of mind, and when the darkness began to skip about, she was really asleep.

Mr. Lang could hear breathing and knew by its placid, long evenness that his wife was napping. She commanded his attention for a while, drew his thoughts to her and to their life together, in the comfortable pleasure of reviewing in a loose and uncritical fashion what his mind chose to remember. He was disturbed that she should find life so much more difficult at a time when they were most settled. He knew that she was too active, and not finding in activity that which formerly had been so good for her and for the entire village. But he saw that it was a change which she must make for herself, and in which it would not do for him to interfere.

He knew by the posture and weight of the little girl on his lap that she was alert. His eyes were not completely rested, making his face feel more wrinkled than it was, and his cheekbones seem thick. But he was tranquil inside now, the darkness having brought him more than he had supposed it would, and he had fortitude toward minor discomforts; they were something in which he found amusement, and even a certain sweet joy for the diversity of life. After forty, when a man began to feel younger simply because he could manage himself and his affairs more easily, the spirit of life seemed to dwell upon such small matters. He had learned that he did not like business any too well and that he preferred to spend his time with his family, with his books and his musings over life. There were kinds of indolence which he definitely enjoyed, leisure in which the mind could select as the keys were selected on a piano, moving lightly and quickly, then dwelling on one theme, holding it as long as the mind found pleasure and sometimes beyond.

Irene was sniffing in the dark, hunting for the grape odor which had been so strong, and now was gone. The odor of grapes she thought of as something she might be able to lift and hold against her chest. It made her eyes wider and made her feel the slight balance problem of sitting on top of a person, a feeling that she seldom had when with her father.

"I like dark," she said.

39

"Sometimes," said Mr. Lang, "I do too."

"I like it always."

"Yes, I know," said Mr. Lang. "And I'm glad."

"It's exciting," said Irene.

The pipe was warmer against his fingers in the darkness. The smoke had a more acrid reality in his mouth. As he puffed, his eyes could watch the intense swirling core of fire in the bowl of the pipe, noting the violence with which tobacco burned. When his mouth released the pipe, the light would instantly dim, not with the quickness of fireflies, but receding behind the crust of ash. He was more calm and satisfied than at any time this evening.

"Ah-h, so I supposed. Exciting and mysterious and alive," he said. "And to me it's more like dreaming without the bother of closing my eyes."

"What's dreaming?"

"Oh, it's seeing pictures when you're asleep, doing things you've never done and never will do, doing again and again things you should have done, things you're sorry you did. It's a chance to be young again, a chance to be old, and sometimes be just as you are, only walking in the purest air through the finest land—that's dreaming."

Irene could see a rosiness in the air and in its center her father's hand, and she could hear the pipe stem tapping against his teeth. She could not smell the smoke.

"What's dreaming?" she said.

There was a long silence.

"Why, it's seeing pictures when you are asleep," said Mr. Lang softly.

The moon had risen higher into the sky, and the shadows on the floor had quietly gathered at the base of the window where they were piecing together a rectangle of light. Mr. Lang and his daughter could feel the warmth which they gave to each other, and the chair had come to be the most intimate part of the room, allowing them to share each other without discomfort. The basin of soapy water was forgotten, and the sewing basket was hidden, and neither of them could have pointed very accurately at the lamp. Irene leaned her head against her father, and was touching the buttons on his coat with her fingers, merely to feel the tiny band of thread in their centers and to assure herself of their roundness.

A little later the doorbell rang.

Mr. Lang sat motionless, undecided.

Mrs. Lang was heard bumping into something, and then the room was brilliant with light.

Mr. Lang had a little difficulty putting Irene off his lap, and then another difficulty rising. He went into the hall.

Mrs. Lang gathered up her sewing basket and the basin of soapy water and went to the kitchen.

Irene sat with her hands over her eyes, keeping out the brilliance of the light, turning her head toward where she could find the most darkness.

Mr. Lang opened the door and saw at least three men, bunched together. He tried to look between them and see if there were more.

"Selvinius is dead," said one man.

"Selvinius is dead."

"We were counting so much on his living."

"We were counting too much on him."

Irene went to her father and patted his knee three times. She held her arms straight out so it would be easier to lift her.

"Not now," said Mr. Lang.

"What we have to know is who gets control."

"I think I can tell you," said Mr. Lang. "For ten years it will remain exactly as it is, and then the stock will be thrown on the market. His niece will receive the interest and half of the final proceeds. My daughter will get five per cent and Mr. Pierce's son the same. So that for the next ten years things won't change, and then—then we'll have to see."

Irene patted his knee. "Now?"

"What about this expansion program?"

Irene looked at her father but could not gain his attention. Her eyes began to search for some place she could go. She could feel herself standing between four men. Mrs. Lang was still in the doorway, listening to the conversation. When Irene came to her, she stooped until her face was almost touching Irene, and her mouth spoke through the loose hair curls, "You get your little chair with the pillow and then you can sit here and listen. It would please Mother if you did it."

But Irene went into the office-study and crawled up on the chair. It was still faintly warm from where Father had been sitting. For a while she smoked the bubble pipe, waiting for the visitors to leave; then she went to the desk and took a piece of paper and a pen. It took experimentation to remember how she had seen him write, and, holding the pen in the center of her fist, the way a broom is gripped, she tried to make marks. The point kept sticking and pulling the paper about.

"You better," said Mr. Lang, and his wife went for Irene and whispered again. Then she and Irene came to the edge of the parlor and waited a moment for a lull in the conversation.

"My daughter has something she wants to say to you all."

"Good night," said Irene.

"Good night," said one of the men, and the conversation resumed.

Upstairs, Mrs. Lang waited until Irene was in bed. Since she did not have time to wait until the child was fully asleep, she tiptoed through the hall and down the stairway, then walked faster than usual to the parlor.

A little later Mr. Lang was summoned by noises which brought him out of his chair, where, standing, with head turned upward, he tried to hear. It sounded as if Irene were having a bad night. Mrs. Lang was the first to arrive, but was unable to do anything until her husband came and quieted the child. There was blood on the sheets. It was not noticed until Irene was almost calmed, crying now rather softly, and Mr. Lang had to lift her out of bed before he found the cause, a tiny but deep gash just above the knee. After it was washed and bandaged, after Irene was convinced that she was not in much pain and would be all right, Mr. Lang inquired.

"I woke up and I was bleeding," Irene said promptly.

"You didn't fall out of bed?"

"No. I woke up and I was bleeding."

"Then we better have a look," said Mr. Lang.

He threw back the bedcovers and searched. Mrs. Lang ran her hands along the corners of the bed.

"I don't see anything here. Are you sure you didn't fall and then crawl back into bed?"

"She hasn't been in bed fifteen minutes," said Mrs. Lang. "She was perfectly all right when I left her."

There was silence for a time.

"I suppose we'll have to wait for daylight," said Mr. Lang, still holding the kerosene lamp near various portions of the bed.

"We can move her into our room."

Mr. Lang studied over that. He did not like the idea of having Irene become afraid of sleeping alone. He did not want her to be afraid of anything.

"Are they gone?" asked Irene.

"Oh!" said Mrs. Lang.

She hurried into the hall.

"Tell them I'll be down in a minute," said Mr. Lang.

Irene waited until the footsteps were almost to the bottom of the stairs. "Aren't they gone?" she whispered, watching her father to see what effect this would have on him.

Mr. Lang continued to walk about the room. He seemed preoccupied about something. The lamp made the light change places in the room and the shadows swing and stretch, discovering and losing in the same moment. Then, kneeling, with the lamp held away so he could see without its brightness directly in his eyes, he sprawled his hand across the carpet, with the slight inaccuracy that vision has even when eyes see well.

"My pen," he said.

Mr. Lang stood up and brought his eyes and the pen and the lamp into closer proximity, closer than need be. He took hold of the steel point and pulled it from the stem of the pen, jerked it loose from the binding dried ink, and put the point in his coat pocket. The pen he tossed on the bed, beside his daughter.

"I'm all right now," said Irene. "I can go to sleep."

Mr. Lang nodded. When it seemed he was not going to say anything, he said, "Good night."

Irene knew she was being watched. She could tell he was not looking at her as kindly as he usually did. She drew the bedcovers over her eyes, bound them tight against her forehead, and waited until she heard the door of the room close. Then she peeped to see if the lamp was burning, but her eyes encountered all darkness.

Much later in the night she heard the door open and knew someone was looking in. She could not tell who. She pretended to be asleep, made her breathing audible. The darkness was not very nice after doing that.

When Mrs. Lang dressed Irene she almost had to force the arms through.

She would hardly eat unless a spoon was pushed into her mouth.

She was always acting as if dirt were going to hurt her. She had to be taken out of training pants before Mrs. Lang thought she was ready, and now she would not use her little pot if there was anything in it. Irene was old enough to use the outside toilet. Only try to get her outside!

Neither Mrs. Lang nor her husband had ever been able to coax

43

her out, and Mr. Lang held that to force her would be the worst thing to do. He said that seeing the sky up so high and far, the world so suddenly big and wind blowing, that could frighten the child too.

Mrs. Lang could see what most women were thinking, and it made her angry. They were thinking she was ashamed of her own flesh and blood and that she did not have so much to be proud of after all, even though Irene was pretty. Some brought their children simply to flaunt before her, and they seemed to think red cheeks and a lot of loudness were the only things that counted. Mrs. Lang would not trade places with anyone, in spite of all the worry the child had given her. She had even come to be sort of taken with Irene's paleness and to believe firmly in the rightness of the child's delicacy. No one was going to catch her worrying her child about being different or threatening her with what might become of her if she did not get over some of her ways.

The trouble was not being able to get Irene to forget. It was more than a year since she had been bumped by the front door, and she still could not be gotten near it, though she would play by the hour beneath the back door, where there was more danger.

It had started the afternoon Joseph upset the smoking stand. Irene had cried terribly, not hurt, just scared. Joseph made it worse with shouting apologies and saying how he knew he should never have accepted parlor privilege. He loved Irene as much as anyone. But from that time on Irene was difficult.

Now she was afraid of almost everything. The only things she continued to enjoy were when Mrs. Lang drew the shades and made the room dark—or if she were left alone in a room with sunshine, after a while she could be seen playing some form of game with her shadow.

Irene never had liked Joseph. She was always being corrected for holding her nose. It was so embarrassing to Joseph, especially since he was clean, as far as men go.

Mr. Lang was concerned too.

He took Irene into the parlor one afternoon when he had a little time.

"We may have trouble getting her to watch this," he said.

He got down on his hands and knees in his good clothes and made his wife push the smoking stand so it would fall on him. He was a man who should never have had to get down on the floor. He was so accustomed to chairs that he scarcely knew how to.

Irene watched everything they did. She did not take her eyes off her father even for a moment.

44

Mr. Lang tried to coax Irene to push the stand.

Irene was stubborn. She simply would not.

Mrs. Lang was all for making her push it.

Her husband said no. Instead, he had his wife push it on him again and when it hit he let out a whoop and a laugh. It was the kind of laugh he used when he wanted to see Irene laugh.

Irene was solemn.

Mrs. Lang noticed before her husband did that it was no use. She never had had much of a way with her daughter, but now she saw her husband did not either, not as much as she had supposed.

She pushed the stand a little hard. Mr. Lang stood up straight and said, "Damn, Ilsa, you don't have to throw it on me."

That was the end of that. Mrs. Lang did not believe he was hurt, simply discouraged and using her as a way out.

Irene would not come in when the minister visited.

Mrs. Lang had to lie directly to the Reverend Harper's face about why they did not bring her to church. She could see he did not believe.

So, as he was preparing to leave, with the slow hesitancy of a man whose work is precarious and who must therefore preserve a tone and demeanor rather than strike a finality, Mrs. Lang went into the living room and took the child up in her arms, bound and determined for once to have her way. She told the minister what was wrong with her child, using a parable, so Irene would be safe from embarrassment.

Reverend Harper smiled and said she would come to the church in her own time and that they must take joy and consolation from a love so great as to admit of no other.

Mrs. Lang felt better hearing that.

But there were things the minister did not know. Irene did not love her mother. She might her father.

6

Mrs. Lang went into the living room. She was sure that was where Irene had run as soon as the front door had been opened.

Mrs. Lang looked around, then stood still and let her eyes hunt. She had a misgiving. She was looking as hard as she could and yet could not seem to see, as sometimes when she mislaid something and between searching for it and thinking about it could not seem to do either. She caught her eyes staring at the picture of her mother, hung there above the fireplace.

The child had heard her say that she was going to bring her in. Mrs. Lang told herself that probably Irene had run upstairs or into the kitchen. She would not be out of the house.

The reason Mrs. Lang was having such a time getting herself to look for Irene was that she wanted to walk into the parlor and say that Irene was playing and she was not going to disturb her. Mrs. Lang was tired of making the child do what she didn't want to do. Now she simply wanted to find Irene. She wanted to see if she was all right.

It was more than the shades being drawn which gave the room an unusually still atmosphere. There was something defective in the light, something which made the furniture and walls seem to be all straight vertical lines. Then Mrs. Lang saw.

Irene was not hiding, at least in an ordinary sense. Mrs. Lang must have looked right past her several times. Irene was standing straight and rigid and still.

Mrs. Lang thought she herself was going to cry out and was not sure she did not. If Irene had been standing in the corner with her face against the wall and her hands over her eyes, Mrs. Lang would have understood. But Irene was facing her. The child's eyes were looking right at her and must have been watching her all the time.

Mrs. Lang got closer. She prepared herself for those eyes.

The eyes were not seeing her. They were motionless and black, with false shine and meaningless fixity, like the eyes in the owl at the head of the stairs. Mrs. Lang remembered having a notion of waving her finger back and forth. Of course she didn't. But there was a sensation of the room being extremely bare, swept of everything, and she felt as if she were being held gripped.

The eyes did not move. Mrs. Lang was almost too scared to touch her. It came to her how she was always running into the parlor and seeing Irene on the floor in a still puddle of white, how it had always given her a scare.

Mrs. Lang did not have much of an idea what she did then. She did not think she touched the child at first. She thought she knelt. She thought she told Irene she did not have to see anybody, not ever. She thought she promised Irene everything a mother could promise.

When Mrs. Lang took the child into her arms, it was like holding stone. She tried with all her eyes could do and say to get Irene to look at her, to get one glimpse of recognition. She squeezed with her hands until she was sure the child would have to scream or at least move. Irene did not. Mrs. Lang grabbed hard then and shook, and it must have been a full minute that Irene remained as she was, and then began to be shaken loose and her head bobbed and in a moment she was at Mrs. Lang's feet, kicking and screaming.

Mrs. Lang was so relieved to hear those screams that for a while she knelt there, looking down. She gathered Irene up and took her to bed.

Mrs. Lang took Irene to her room and undressed her and put her to bed. She stayed there until Irene was quieted and she herself was quieted and could be sure everything was going to be all right. It must have been hours, for her husband was home. When she heard him coming up the stairs, she ran into the hall, intending to tell him about it, and instead found herself telling him to go downstairs and get his own supper this once.

Mrs. Lang went back to the bed and knelt beside and against it and stayed with her child until her husband came up a second time. Mrs. Lang noticed it was dark in the room. She went to the door and said softly that he could sleep in one of the guest rooms this night, but Mr. Lang was so worried he would not leave. When she saw that, she told him everything would be all right and explained what had happened without going into detail. Mr. Lang was a good bit surprised that she insisted on remaining with Irene, but finally he went, and Mrs. Lang hurried back by the bed and knelt. After a while she took the combs from her hair and laid her head on the bed and took one of Irene's arms and slipped it in among her hair and that comforted her. She supposed she slept.

She threw up her head of a sudden, for no reason she could think of, unless she had been dreaming. She saw light in the hall. It was such a dim lamp and so far away that she did not in the beginning need to move from where she was.

But there was the odd sensation of feeling more disturbed by the light when her eyes were closed and her head against the soft hardness of the bed than when she had looked at it. She went toward the light, intending to blow it out, but instead closed the door and leaned against it. Then, she would never be able to explain why, she turned the key. She could hear and feel it, for she had to press against the door to make the key turn all to one side. She felt such relief when it

47

was done. She was kind of upset at the same time, scared of herself, listening to her own breathing and her movements with a peculiar attention. Then she took off all her clothes, every bit of clothing, and got into the bed and took Irene against her. She could not remember when she had been in bed without a nightdress.

She never saw darkness as she saw it that night. She never lay so long without thinking, with her eyes open, not worrying about getting to sleep, not thinking about tomorrow. Sometimes she even forgot Irene was there against her, except as a kind of warmth. She could only think of it as having periods of time in which the world seemed absolutely still, not in the way of silence, but in that of motion. It was as if everything had for a while fallen away, leaving a stillness which was almost certainly physical. And it was during one of those periods that she felt the mouth begin to hunt on her. She was startled for an instant and put her hand in the way, but then she knew that Irene was still asleep and that if the child had been awake she wouldn't have. And she felt as if the wet mouth touching her were acquainting her with something which could not be described. So she took her hand away and kept her eyes open, looking at the odd blue darkness on the window. And then she closed her eyes and was not long in going to sleep.

7

One afternoon several ladies came to see Mrs. Lang. There were the usual exclamations of surprise which are scarcely surprise, and then an introduction; for Mrs. Lang had never met Mrs. Alfreda Haas, though of course they were positive of having seen each other. Mrs. Clarissa Rowiger refused to wait for the introduction to be completed, and, leaving this task to Mrs. Wagenbacher, sailed straight into the parlor and shoved herself into the rocking chair; she was such a big, stout woman that although she carried her weight magnificently when walking, when she sat, had she been a bit younger, her appearance would have been little less than obscene. No one dared laugh at her. Having pushed herself into the rocker, she began to slap her hands on the arms of the chair, as if this would help her to catch her breath. Her breathing was always audible, for she was troubled with asthma, and now she added to this with a constant, "Pss-chew-w-w, landy me."

Her son attended her to the chair and then stood dutifully and solicitously by her. Raymond did not resemble his mother. He was tall, thin and quietly nervous. Mrs. Rowiger looked about, then pointed at the coffee table. Her son walked to the table, took up the fan, went back to his mother and began to swing the fan gently over her. Mrs. Rowiger sank into perfect contentment.

The three ladies were detained in the hall. It was whether Mrs. Lang might not be related to certain E. V. Langs who lived in Ephrata, which was the birthplace of Mrs. Haas. When Mrs. Lang said that to the best of her knowledge she did not believe her husband had relatives there, Mrs. Haas would not let her escape the possibility that they might be distant relatives, and she bolstered this by saying what nice people she remembered them to be. Then there was a discussion concerning Mrs. Haas's hat, whether she should surrender it, or whether the ladies could stay only a minute.

Mrs. Rowiger turned her head a bit to get full benefit of the fanned air on her throat, that being where heat bothered her most. Her son glanced occasionally toward the hall, but devoted the main stream of his attention to his mother. He was fanning her in a manner that did not divert any of the air to himself.

"Do take off her hat and bring her in here," said Mrs. Rowiger with some exasperation. "All that bustle only makes me the hotter."

This seemed to bring the ladies to a decision. After Mrs. Haas had removed her hat and made proper apology for the state of her hair, and after a disclaimer of the need of apology for such lovely hair was offered sincerely by Mrs. Lang, the three ladies streamed into the parlor and arranged themselves in deference to the position Mrs. Rowiger had taken. Mrs. Lang had to move one of the heavier chairs so that Mrs. Wagenbacher would not be sitting behind the stout woman, who had by this time recovered enough to rock herself a little.

Mrs. Rowiger wiggled her finger, and her son obediently took the fan to the coffee table and put it exactly where and as he had found it. He remained standing stiffly erect until all the ladies were settled before seating himself. He was not cowed. He was simply unusually courteous. His eyes were quick and watchful, yet quite gentle when looked into, and seemed to get milder and more pleasant the longer one observed them.

"Forgive me for charging in and sitting down ahead of time," said

Mrs. Rowiger, in a voice that did not ask forgiveness. "But the hill did me in so I expected my legs couldn't last another minute. There's nothing to beat having to walk that hill, nothing to beat it. . . . You see, we were expecting a carriage." She shot a killing glance at Mrs. Haas, then continued. "And the Lord knows there's nothing worse than expecting a carriage, counting on it, depending on it, one might say, and then having to walk—especially on a day like this."

"I'm terribly to blame," said Mrs. Haas, quickly. "It has all been my fault. You see, at the very last moment my husband found it necessary to go to Harrisburg. I could have cried when he told me. But what was there to do?"

Mrs. Wagenbacher wagged her head in sympathy, for she could understand so easily how it had been. Mrs. Wagenbacher had been married.

Mrs. Haas gave a detailed account of how it had come about that she was not able to get the carriage and followed this with an effusive apology, amidst some embarrassment, but she was not allowed to finish.

"Well, my dear," said Mrs. Rowiger, "there's no sense talking about it. The milk's spilt, the harm's done, and I'm sure I shall recover. . . . I really didn't mean for you to upset yourself so. Those things will happen."

She tapped the arm of her chair.

"Yes, to the best of us," agreed Mrs. Wagenbacher.

"It's because you feel a little new among us, and you'll soon get over that," said Mrs. Lang, with real kindness in her voice. "We don't really know how fussy we are with one another, we're so used to it. But I think we will find it cool enough here in a little while. I've had the shades drawn the better part of the day."

"It's perfectly beautiful!" said Mrs. Wagenbacher, who was too cool and airy to be envied. She was so much too youthful for her true age and her spinsterish life that the youth in her was a mockery, having served no end, except to prolong her withering on the vine. Young men still glanced at her when she walked the streets of the village in her sprightly manner, then turned their heads in embarrassment at having done so. But she appeared to be quite happy with her situation, and to find a great amount of pleasure in life.

"I'm sorry all the same," said Mrs. Haas, giving the stout woman a resentful glance. "I wouldn't have had it happen for the world. I feel I've been treated badly for what wasn't my fault."

Mrs. Haas was the youngest woman ever to have been appointed

50

to the entertainment committee of the Ladies' Missionary Society of Saint John's Lutheran Church. This was her first committee participation. She wanted so for it to come off. Then to be unable to provide the carriage she had promised! To be taken to task for it! And, above all, to have Mrs. Rowiger, presiding head of the society, refuse to introduce her to Mrs. Lang.

To make matters worse, she was not sure her husband had needed the carriage. He might have taken it out of spite. He had not hidden the fact that he thought it ridiculous for her to be trying to maneuver into a society of women so much older than herself. When she had fixed her hair in a modest, old-fashioned bun and worn an early-fall dress to make herself seem older and more tranquil, he had laughed and given her a slap on the bottom.

"Pss-chew-ww, landsy me, when I get perspiring I stay perspiring," said Mrs. Rowiger. "Well, I'm here, here I am, though I confess I'd never have made it if I hadn't had my cane." She looked sweetly and with pride at her son, then wiggled her finger at him, not in request this time, but simply as a token of affection.

She began to arrange the sleeves of her dress and arrange her limbs in a manner which indicated there had once been an elegance and delicacy of feeling in her, but that now she had reached an age at which she could take on or reject her breeding at will. Her ascendancy in village society having been attained by the withdrawal of Mrs. Lang, she could now allow herself a certain freedom with the confidence that it would merely affirm and consolidate her position.

"I rather enjoyed walking. I like to get out and bounce around," said Mrs. Wagenbacher. "I need a little youthfulness."

Mrs. Haas gave her a glance of gratitude.

"If I had only known, I would have sent Joseph," said Mrs. Lang. "I'm so glad you came over."

By which the ladies understood that they need not walk home.

"The fact is," said Mrs. Rowiger, "we came about the church supper. But I'm still too hot to talk." Drawing a handkerchief larger than a woman usually finds convenient from where it was folded over the belt of her dark violet flower-print dress, she patted her face a few times, then placed it against her neck so that it made her look as if she had a sore throat. "Ray-mee, I do believe you should have fanned me a few minutes longer, I'm not as recovered as I thought. No, no, dear, not now. I only meant that you should give us a little more of your attention."

Mrs. Rowiger glanced significantly toward the living room.

"You needn't worry, Mother," said Raymond, quietly.

"Don't scold him," said Mrs. Wagenbacher. "I only wish I had a boy as good."

Mrs. Wagenbacher smiled at Raymond, pleasantly, wistfully.

"Have you ever seen a prettier boy? Isn't he simply beautiful?"

"Never," admitted Mrs. Haas, and then she looked.

Raymond and his mother exchanged glances of repressed amusement. Both knew he was anything but pretty. The glance was also to assure Mrs. Rowiger of her son's loyalty, and to assure Raymond that his mother did not enjoy needing to correct him.

Mrs. Lang found an opportunity to go to the kitchen and prepare iced-tea and set little plates with brownies. She tried to be quiet so that the noise of fixing the tea and setting the plates would not carry into the parlor, though the necessity for this was doubtful, since the ladies knew what she was about. It was simply one of the refinements which had crept into Mrs. Lang's vigorous, usually forthright manner, a need not to be ostentatious in hospitality. Then she went out on the lawn to arrange the chairs in the event the ladies would rather partake there, for she was not sure it was cool enough in the house, even though the shades had been drawn since sunrise.

Mrs. Haas and Mrs. Wagenbacher were having a discussion about flowers. Mrs. Haas had planted iris which had not developed. Mrs. Wagenbacher could not say for sure why they had failed, no, not even when it was explained to her how they had been set and the almost exact date and a general survey of the weather since—but Mrs. Wagenbacher could tell her what to do next spring. She could tell her how she did it.

"Iris," said Mrs. Rowiger, "can be thrown out the window and they'll grow."

Raymond was looking into the living room. He was smiling.

"I could have felt more at fault," admitted Mrs. Haas, "if they had failed to bloom. But I never even had an opportunity to tend them. They never came out of the ground."

"Probably poor bulbs," said Mrs. Wagenbacher. "I have failures with my flowers too, but I tell myself there's next year. I treat my garden simply as a little hobby. To be honest, I simply use it as an excuse to get out and plunge my hands into the ground and work it between my fingers. I so need an excuse to get outdoors, and especially after a rain. That simply wonderful mud!"

She held her smooth, plump, strengthless hands forth as evidence of her desire. Her eyes had taken on a passionate cast that was a betrayal of her helpless white face. It could be seen that she was becoming a bit anxious about her life. There was in her during these recent months a tendency to make startling discoveries about herself.

"You're still not minding me, Ray-mee."

Mrs. Rowiger warned her son with her eyes, then swung them upon the other two ladies, and said in an amused, light tone, "Mrs. Wagenbacher gets more sprightly each passing year, while the rest of us simply become older and older."

"Well, and why shouldn't I?" Mrs. Wagenbacher replied gaily, quite pleased.

"No reason. None whatever," said Mrs. Rowiger. "I wouldn't be half so fond of you if it weren't for your sweet nonsensical ways."

Mrs. Wagenbacher blushed.

Mrs. Haas suddenly felt the tightness of the bun into which her hair was drawn. She felt keenly the age of the women and the hopelessness of ever becoming really one of them, accepted by them. Yet this made her desire to do so even stronger. She wished Mrs. Lang would return.

Irene had been standing in the relative darkness of the living room ever since the ladies had arrived. Raymond had been the first to take notice of her. Mrs. Rowiger had seen her son peering into the other room, and by leaning a little in her chair had been able to make out the cause. She was quite furious that her son should continue to disobey, and she really felt quite oppressed with the heat, and then to have to cope with this social upstart, Mrs. Haas; all in all she was quite put out.

"Yes," she said, "Maude and I have known each other ever since when, and I declare I grow more fond of her daily. Indeed, I have known everyone here for so many years, almost forever, I might say, that I confess feeling quite strange toward you." Mrs. Rowiger smiled. "So that I'm not surprised you should have felt, what was it —wronged?"

"Yes, I did a bit," said Mrs. Haas, biting her lip.

"Well, I suppose there's no reason I should take offense at that. I suppose, as Mrs. Lang put it, we'll improve with further acquaintance. I confess I shall have to learn a great deal more about you first."

Mrs. Haas flushed.

Raymond, certain the girl remained in the living room because of shyness, was careful not to observe her too steadily. In the presence of adult dominion and domination, children have a way of seeking each other out, even while not seeming to pay attention to each other.

53

Raymond had other reasons for his interest. He knew quite a bit about Irene from his mother and his own observations. He pitied her.

He did not want to be defiant. But with his mother attempting to force him into obedience, he was released from the responsibility of being submissive. His eyes spent all the time that could be spared from the conversational activities in the parlor in watching Irene, urged by a realization that she was not in the least interested in him, in fact seemed to be unaware of his presence. This in itself was not enough to command his interest, nor lead him to take the unfair advantage which her inattention to him offered. He knew well enough what it would be like for her, if she was as shy and sensitive as he was beginning to suspect, when she discovered eyes watching her. It was a gathering conviction that something of importance was going on inside Irene that held his interest.

Raymond had never seen a child so beautiful, had never seen a child stand so long in silence, had never seen such grave, mature eyes, terribly black when they fixed on him, as they had at that moment. The reaction which he had expected did not take place, and this disquieted him until he realized that he had not really been seen, that the dark eyes had been too filled with concern to notice what they were seeing.

Her lips were moving, and sometimes her eyes would close, squeezed shut, but he could not hear any sound. Then her arms began to make little gestures, and he began to believe that she was carrying on a conversation with herself. He felt embarrassed to watch, until he noticed that Irene was now looking toward Mrs. Haas, Mrs. Wagenbacher, and, more furtively, his mother. He noted also the extreme seriousness with which Irene was regarding everything around her.

Mrs. Haas inquired about the condition of education in the village. She confessed ignorance.

"Of course I teach," said Mrs. Wagenbacher, "but I should say good—very good."

"Glory, glory, glory," said Mrs. Rowiger. "All we offer is six grades and call it twelve."

She continued to recover from fatigue which had been prolonged beyond simple discomfort from the heat, which was the least, in fact, of her present distresses. The handkerchief which had given her the appearance of a rather careless old nun fell on the floor without being noticed by anyone except her son. She did not seem surprised when he discreetly handed it to her. She smiled up at him, then

54

crooked her finger. He leaned politely to catch a whisper. His expression became perplexed, so she caught the lobe of his ear between her fingers and drew his head until it almost touched her mouth. Raymond nodded gravely, and said, softly, "No, Mother."

"Are you sure you don't have to?" she said more significantly.

"I said no," replied Raymond sharply.

"But you were squirming so."

Then, resigning herself to having been mistaken, she patted her face with the handkerchief, and, holding her dress out loose with one hand, wiped between her breasts and blew cool air into the hollow. "Twice as long for half the result," she said. "That's our school system. It makes me want to send Raymond to a private school."

Raymond was staring straight at the wall.

Shortly after this Irene made her entrance into the parlor. Her shoes made no noise on the carpet. She was not trying to walk quietly.

The manner in which she walked made Raymond aware of soft upward push against the soles of his own shoes. In a little while he found that by watching he lost part of his own self-consciousness and felt more detached from his mother.

Mrs. Rowiger saw Irene, acknowledged her with a nod of the head, and resumed the attention she had been giving her son. Raymond would not look at her, and she could see there was more anger than embarrassment in his expression. His cheekbones were prominent in the way her husband's used to be when he was brooding over something.

Mrs. Wagenbacher had been giving information about teaching school when Irene entered and waited politely for the ladies to finish their conversation. Irene did not retreat, so as to make herself obscure, nor did she walk around to where the ladies could not possibly have avoided seeing her. Mrs. Haas declared she did not understand how teachers could remain patient day in, day out. Mrs. Wagenbacher said it was all in the attitude; for herself, she loved children, and that was why she had remained as a teacher even when she no longer needed the income.

It was at this point that Mrs. Haas saw the girl, and for a moment she drew her hands to her throat.

"Goodness!" she said.

"Did I fright you?" said Irene.

Raymond leaned forward and watched. He had a feeling of it being important to his own happiness that she should carry off successfully this self-introduction. The girl was so small and frail that he perhaps thought of it as being more difficult than it was. He felt his mother's watching on his left cheekbone, but it fixed rather than deterred his attention.

"I'm Irene," she said. "Who are you?"

So far she had carried it off. Mrs. Hass seemed startled by the too-perfect imitation of adult gestures and civilities.

Raymond understood suddenly what she had been doing in the living room, those gestures and silent lip movements. He watched more closely her separate, precise movements, for he was beginning to sense the preparation which Irene had made. He was beginning to admire.

Mrs. Haas looked at her companions for advice.

"Don't you have a name?" said Irene, puzzled. Then she understood and smiled. "My daddy gave me a dog that didn't have a name. Daddy said, 'Think a name.' Spots. He has spots. Big one here," said Irene, patting the back of her neck.

Irene waited for a reply. When Mrs. Haas simply stared at her, the girl began to look from one woman to another.

Raymond noticed that she was without the stomach protuberance, the peculiar knee and elbow, and the large head of a child. She was in general symmetry an almost perfect miniature of a woman. Her dress was fresh and clean, the collar, sleeves, and very narrow belt in better proportion to her size than was usual. Her slenderness made her hair seem long.

"Her dog," said Raymond. "Her dog."

"Oh, you have a doggy," said Mrs. Haas. "Well, now isn't that nice."

The little girl frowned, held her head askance.

"But I call him Spotsy," said Irene, no longer quite sure of herself. The tone of her voice was intended to indicate that she considered it very important to have changed her dog's name. "Can I tell you something about Spotsy? Can I?"

"It's Mrs. Lang's daughter," said Mrs. Rowiger.

"Her *daughter?*"

Mrs. Rowiger understood the woman's astonishment.

"A little late," she said shrugging, wrinkling her nose.

"But my goodness," said Mrs. Haas, leaning so that she could see toward the kitchen, lowering her voice. "How old *is* she? I would have supposed . . ."

"Not as bad as all that," said Mrs. Rowiger, good-humoredly, more companionably.

56

Neither woman was as yet aware that they had laid the foundation for a way of solving the animosity which they felt for each other.

"Well, I only hope I won't have anything like that in my life," said Mrs. Haas, who had already, for all her youth, become embarrassed and indignant about her husband's habit of patting her on the bottom.

Mrs. Rowiger laughed. Then, seeing her son, she put her two hands to her ears.

"I was only telling Raymond not to listen," she explained. "He never likes to hear me talk about anyone."

"She wants to tell you something about her dog," said Raymond, staring at his mother.

But when Mrs. Rowiger did not choose to see or to hear, she was expert at it. She waved her hand at the unimportance of all things, shifted a little in the chair.

"She's very shy usually," Mrs. Rowiger said, looking at the little girl very directly. "I spent nearly a month getting her to say a word to me. And now, for some reason, she has decided to talk. Hasn't she?" said Mrs. Rowiger, raising her eyebrows in that special expression of condescension which she used with children, pets and poor people. "Go on, talk to her, since she seems to have taken a liking to you. But you will have to be careful, Mrs. Haas. She's, well, let us say very nervous." Mrs. Rowiger glanced significantly at her son.

"Oh, I see," said Mrs. Haas. "How old is she? How old are you, little girl?"

"Don't you want to hear about Spotsy?" asked Irene.

"Why of course! Of course we all want to hear. But first tell me how old you are. Do you know you're a very sweet little child? Yes you are."

"Sweet, sweet, sweet," said Mrs. Wagenbacher, who had been motioning to Irene with her hands. To see a child go near another woman always reminded her of her own maternal instincts. "Do let her come to me. I adore children." Mrs. Wagenbacher gave Raymond a smile which indicated that she included him. It might have been intended to signify to the boy that he was her favorite.

"Spotsy ate my glove!" said Irene importantly.

"How terrible!" said Mrs. Haas.

"He *ate* it," said Irene.

She made her mouth move the way she remembered the dog had used its mouth.

"Her father bought a dog, hoping that might make her less shy," explained Mrs. Rowiger. "They've tried everything possible. I'm really quite surprised. You have no idea what she's like most of the time. I confess I think the dog must be doing her some good after all." Mrs. Rowiger nodded at the little girl. "Irene, what on earth has made you such a chatterbox all of a sudden? Have you decided you like us after all?"

"Oh-h-h," said Mrs. Haas, "that's a shame, I mean a child being shy. It's so bad for them later. You mustn't be afraid of *me*, Irene. You're not going to be afraid of me, I hope."

"Have you ever *eaten* a glove?" said Raymond. "Her dog *did*."

"Ray-mee . . . Careful . . . Mind now," said Mrs. Rowiger, and then she abruptly took charge of the conversation, directing it toward the church supper, sounding the ladies on what they felt inclined to contribute. Mrs. Rowiger could grasp conversation as if it were a basket and take it where she willed, leading it through the narrowest of spaces or swinging it safely across the widest fields of generalities. "What we need for this supper," she said, "is nothing different to eat, like we've been trying of late, but simply to get out and sell tickets."

"Mother, please . . ." said Raymond.

"Sell tickets," said Mrs. Rowiger, "and it doesn't matter whether they come or not."

Irene was beginning to suspect that something was wrong. Her eyes, terribly black, lanced the air and swung with a swiftness which revealed both nervousness and determination. Then, after hunting, her eyes returned to Mrs. Haas and remained there with a keen and alert fixity, a patience which must have been difficult for them, a concentration of gaze such as eyes assume when peering into the limited circles of binoculars.

Raymond felt helpless and defeated. He sensed what was about to happen, what was already happening, and knew it could not be prevented. His hands were limp and he could not even find strength by wrapping the fingers together and pressing them. He looked at Irene and then could not look at her, fearing that she would find out from his face what she would find out only too soon. He knew his own tendency to feel too strongly, to magnify small things, and it seemed to him possible that it would not be seen by the child as it was seen by himself, that the suffering was to be all his own. But that only seemed to make more important the need of justifying the situation.

For now they had her. Or his mother had her. They would talk above her head and control her and make fun of her or ignore her, do anything they wished. They could even be kind to her. He began to realize that the tiny wisp of a girl, whether she knew it or not, was fighting for the privilege of remaining in the parlor; oh she could come in, she could walk around, even play, and no gate would bar her. But her actual right to be there, that was being stolen from her, was being denied to her. He began to suspect that one way or another she would recognize it.

"Mrs. Lang will of course provide the flowers," said Mrs. Rowiger. "You haven't seen her garden? It's famous. Really. She's the person to ask about iris."

"I most certainly will," said Mrs. Haas enthusiastically. She had a feeling she was going to be accepted by these women after all. She saw that she must simply not thrust herself so much, must let acquaintance be more gradual and natural. To be on good terms with Mrs. Rowiger was the important thing; without that there would be little chance of success. She suspected that Mrs. Rowiger could be very nice when once she liked a person.

"I suppose the chicken and noodles will fall my lot again," said Mrs. Wagenbacher. "I really would like to try something more exciting."

She simpered and pouted a little.

"But you're so good on chicken," protested Mrs. Rowiger. "I swear I believe half the men wouldn't attend if they knew it wasn't going to be *your* chicken."

Mrs. Wagenbacher blushed. "Oh I don't suppose that's quite true," she said, still wishing to try her hand at pies. "I have a new recipe for pie. Squashed blueberry."

"Nonsense," said Mrs. Rowiger. "Total nonsense."

Mrs. Wagenbacher lowered her head. She was consoled by the thought of men eating her food. And chicken was her strong point, that could not be denied.

"My dog is out there," said Irene, pointing toward the window. "He lives out there. It's his house."

Raymond saw that the girl was fighting what he had always avoided, what he had pretended did not exist by clothing himself with courtesy and good manners. He saw that really, in only a slightly differing sense, it was the same treatment which he had always received and which he was most certainly receiving now. It angered him to realize that he had never seriously resented it, that he had even considered it, recently, with amusement. He felt a sense of guilt for what was happening. The indignity implied by his mother in her question as to his need to go to the bathroom struck him as fresh insult, as something more malignant than his embarrassment had allowed him to suppose. For some reason which he could not completely define, he knew that his mother should not be forgiven for that. It was more than being twelve. His clothes felt tight and miserable on him. There came to his mind a horrid image of children everywhere being suffocated by crude and callous people like these.

"Is he?" said Mrs. Haas patting Irene on the head. "Yes, of course." Finding curls, her hand stayed and began to dawdle among them, while her attention had of necessity to remain with Mrs. Rowiger and the other woman. She was trying to share her eyes with everyone, but in a manner which would let Mrs. Rowiger know of the changed attitude which she had decided upon. Mrs. Haas knew when to be sensible.

"I think it only fair," said Mrs. Rowiger, "to let Mrs. Haas choose what she would like to provide, since this is her first time."

"I'm afraid I'm not the world's best cook," said Mrs. Haas, her hand resting in air in the manner of a careless benediction, in which position Irene, drawing away, had left it. Then the hand dropped absently, falling to her lap in a curve, touching and feeling the material of her dress, as if still finding curls. "I'll just do my best with whatever you assign me."

"Nonsense! How are you on potato salad?"

Raymond stared at the women. He was affronted by their conversation. He sensed how it must be for the girl to wait out this conversation, how each minute must blow out into an endlessness for her. He recalled how she had practiced in secret, how she had tapped in the palm of her hand and recited to herself, perhaps for a longer period of time than he was aware of, and how she had waited until her mother was not present. He felt a strong need for her mother to be here and do what he could not. He felt almost as if it were himself who needed Mrs. Lang. He found himself thinking of her and trying to decide whether or not she was capable of bringing about the change in atmosphere which would at least protect Irene. But he realized that he did not know anything about her, or about these women, not even his own mother. He knew only that he had misjudged his mother and could not forgive her for having been the one who had put Irene in this position. It made him try to seek out his mother's eyes and command their attention.

The conversation was jumping back and forth too rapidly for

Irene to follow, although her eyes moved as if she were watching some game in which a ball was being thrown from chair to chair. She knew now that she was being ignored. But she was only perplexed as yet, and stood watching everything intently, hunting for some interest in herself, hunting for words she could understand.

"We are glad to have you here," Irene said. "We must like visitors," she said a little experimentally, but could not remember more.

Her voice was lost in the midst of great, loud, raucous woman talk. Raymond had to lean forward to hear that pale and soft voice, and it gave him a sudden urge to run to the kitchen and tell Mrs. Lang that she was needed. But what could he say? Mrs. Lang, come quick, they're hurting your daughter? That? Hardly that. How could this be explained, where did it permit itself to be exposed? For it was the very common, ordinary appearance, the crimeless talk of women planning a church supper—that was what made it so nauseating. It was as if the room were being tilted and no one but himself noticing it. He began to feel that he had suffered all his life, that there had always been a cloth across his face bound tightly, with one tiny hole through which he by infinite struggle had been able to draw enough air to live without ever really breathing. He felt he must breathe. And looking at Irene, he could not believe she was innocent of it all. She was still even conscious of her posture.

Mrs. Haas was satisfied with potato salad. The details were being brought under attention. Mrs. Haas was trying to remember if she had seen napkins in the church kitchen or whether, as Mrs. Rowiger hinted, they had been given to Mrs. Zinnerman to wash and not returned. The light from the window, a thin, bright band beside the shade, was now at such an angle that when Mrs. Rowiger rocked, it struck in her face; but for some reason she did not call upon her son to remedy it, and shifted the chair a little instead.

Irene too had retreated to a new position, or rather approached a little further into their midst. She was standing very erect and with her eyes fixed upon the wall, revealing their preference for things which did not move. It was intended to be made clear to each of the ladies that she, Irene, was being courteous, and that they in turn must accept that and no more. If they would be kind enough to acknowledge that she must now return to the living room, that she had been with them already much longer than she had planned, she would detain them no longer. She was only waiting for enough silence to be able to excuse herself, curtsy, and then withdraw. She even sighed with the troublesomeness of waiting.

Opportunity came, but not as opportunity, for Mrs. Haas noticed the child was still standing near her. Now that her part of the dinner was settled, she could be a little more at leisure. Mrs. Haas smiled, moved her leg a little and patted a place on her chair. That she was a young woman made that smile and gesture more humiliating to Raymond.

"So you're Mrs. Lang's daughter. And that's a pretty dress you have on—and you didn't tell me how old you were when I asked. Don't you know? Can't you tell me?" she said, holding up fingers and then tapping them with the forefinger of her other hand. "I'm sure you can."

"I'm Irene. I told twice."

"Well, but that's not what I asked. I asked your age."

Irene was drawn against the woman's knee and held there. She did not resist. Mrs. Haas began to turn the child about so as to see the dress from a number of positions. "It's rather cute, isn't it?" she said. "I never saw so many pleats in anything so small."

"Don't!" said Irene, as the woman began to loosen her belt, and then suddenly she tried to squirm loose and there was a furiousness about her efforts.

"You better let her alone," said Mrs. Rowiger. "She'll be screaming next thing."

"Why, she's only a little shy," said Mrs. Haas, holding the child firmly. "She really likes me, don't you, Irene? We're going to be friends, aren't we? I'm not going to hurt you, I only want to take a peek at your belt, your pretty, pretty belt." She turned her head toward the other women. "I believe the whole dress is hand-stitched."

"Maybe she'd rather come to me," said Mrs. Wagenbacher hopefully, stretching her arms forth. "Would you like to come and visit me a while and sit on *my* lap?"

The resistance went out of Irene. She stood perfectly still, pulled her dress down where the woman in carelessness had exposed her underwear. She closed her eyes. Her eyes were pinched tight shut so that the lids were wrinkled and old-looking.

That was when Raymond leaped from his chair. He did not realize that he was standing until he had a sudden need of the balance to stand. His mind seemed an instant ahead or behind of whatever he did.

"You better turn her loose," he shouted. "You better take your hands off of her," and he advanced, not even knowing that he was

62

threatening the woman with his upraised arm. His body heaved, shaking off some bondage of its own, real as rope about him. "She's not yours, she's Mrs. Lang's daughter," he shouted furiously.

"Ray-mee . . . Sit down and behave yourself. You're making yourself look ridiculous."

"And damn you too, Mother," he shouted, whirling. "You did this and I won't let you do it any more."

But no sooner had his eyes encountered hers than he caught hold of himself.

"But—but can't you be *decent?*" he said. "Can't you listen to *her* for a minute and—and at least try—instead of . . . You know what I'm talking about."

Mrs. Haas did not actually release Irene. She was simply so startled that the girl was able to pull loose and run. Irene did not run far, only to where the boy stood and then tugged at his trousers, as high up as she could reach.

"Hey, you."

Irene was thrust aside. Raymond was giving the women furious, quick glances.

"Just give her a chance. All she wants to do is be nice and tell you—oh, damn, you just tramp all over people, you just don't care about anything at all, you just can't . . ."

"Ray-mee! Go sit down. And after you've thought over what you've said in this this room, you apologize to Mrs. Haas. Because you're going to regret this."

There was a certain grandeur in Mrs. Rowiger which had not been present earlier, and there was also the honest earnestness of a mother who realized that she had reached a crucial moment in her relationship with her son. It had not shocked her, what her son had said, for she had sensed long ago that such a moment was inevitable and had wished to postpone it only until her son was old enough to understand more. But now, although it was an embarrassment before these other women, she was almost relieved.

"You know what I mean," she said, "and you better listen to me."

Irene came back and tugged at the boy's trousers again.

"Hey, you."

"But what did I do?" Mrs. Haas was asking Mrs. Wagenbacher. "What in the world is going on?"

Mrs. Wagenbacher knew no more than she did. Not able to use **one** of her understanding smiles of sympathy on the boy, she merely withdrew and pretended to notice nothing. Her eyes blamed Irene for having brought the boy to defiance of his mother, which always made her own position so distressing and helpless.

Raymond looked down into the uplifted face, controlling his anger, and tried to see what the face wanted. He knew. It was something the child could not explain, but which the child expected him to understand. And that was the only reason he did understand, with a sort of faith. So he sat down on the chair again.

Irene went quite close to Mrs. Rowiger. She was not afraid. She made the most correct curtsy of the afternoon, straightened, and said, looking straight up into the face of the person who had always seemed so enormous to her, "I hate you." With dignity, with her head high and proud, Irene marched into the living room and out of sight.

The room was silent for a long time.

"Of all things," said Mrs. Haas softly. Then regaining herself, "We shall have to tell her mother!"

"We'll do no such thing," said Mrs. Rowiger. "My son is the young man to blame for this. He knows it. And he will apologize to you. He will apologize to me, now, here."

Raymond did go to Mrs. Haas and apologize, and he appeared to be sincere.

"And if you can use him in any way, to run errands, or help clean house—he's good in the garden, better than most boys—" said Mrs. Rowiger, "you simply call on me. He'll be glad to do that for you. Won't you, Raymond?"

"Yes, Mother, I'll do it," said Raymond calmly.

"He's helped me innumerable times, innumerable," said Mrs. Wagenbacher, pleased that peace was being restored and everything was turning out so well.

"And now you will apologize to me," said Mrs. Rowiger.

"I wish I could, Mother," said Raymond, looking intently into her face, shivering.

"You can—if you put your mind to it."

"No, I'm sorry, no."

Raymond looked up quickly, and then he smiled. He looked at the two women and his mother and at the walls of the room.

"Why, yes," he said, smiling. "I suppose I can. I apologize, Mother."

"I accept your apology," said Mrs. Rowiger, but her eyes were still hard.

Mrs. Haas and Mrs. Wagenbacher were relieved. The conversation soon became sprightly, and when Mrs. Lang joined them no one felt the need to mention the incident, and the plans for the church supper were completed. Mrs. Haas learned as much as she wanted to know about irises, and in fact took home with her a few plants and a promise that Joseph would bring her a little lime and bone meal. Mrs. Lang was somewhat surprised at the friendliness between the women and at a slight hostility which they seemed to have toward herself. Mrs. Rowiger was more quiet and thoughtful during the late afternoon. She knew she had lost her son.

PART TWO: 1896 - 1910

8

IN THE SUMMER of 1896 a track crew repaired a section of rail unsafe after flood. A mild spring wash had softened the western banks of the Susquehanna. This valley of earth was so soft and rich that the river had spread and fattened, thereby losing strength and swiftness, losing treacherous rapids which had prevented deer from swimming to the islands; now the river was too shallow for any large boat except flat-bottomed paddle-wheelers. The railroad and the canal had taken from it the little burden of commerce.

The rough, burly crew of men tore out old ties, graveled and reinforced weak places in the rail bed, and put in new studs, splice plates, and ties stinking with creosote. They washed their faces and the palms of their hands in the river, tied dirty clothes to stakes and let the river wash all night. The colorless urine of beer was emptied on rocks along its edge, this too in night-time in total darkness, or by the helpless yellow light of lantern, when the urine which shoots from a man's loins is clean and hot and joyous. The shanty was judiciously used in the daytime.

These were foreigners who came to America for gold and found sledgehammers. They were sour and disillusioned, and the vengeance of muscle succeeded in putting them out of work sooner than was necessary. In the middle of July the rail section was completed, and the men, with the exception of a few regulars, scattered over the countryside in search of harvesting and fruit picking.

Times were bad. The promised land gave little evidence of promise.

One man remained, living in the shack the gang bosses had used as headquarters. He had been west, would not go west, had been south and given part of his life to the Mississippi. Now he was near where his travels had begun. But Mijack was not a man fleeing homeward, not defeated, for the coincidence of four different railroad jobs had brought about his return. He regarded this as a continuation of the search.

Mijack had splendid eyes and good vision. His eyes and his teeth were young, set into strong, blunt features and fastened by flesh smoked and chilled inflexible with years of outdoor life, flesh hardened still more by the stolidity of his nature. His body did not smell fresh, nor did it have the soft, clean, flowing movement which could be seen in younger railroaders, but there was an alertness in the way he knelt that made it seem he had been young until recently. Licking his lips he felt age, but a hard day of work could force him to admit nothing. He was clinging to youthfulness beyond its natural time, not in foolishness or fear, but because the work he was doing demanded that a man remain flexible and quick.

Mijack had not mingled with the railroaders. He had worked and worked, holding discontent in his eyes and his stiff posture, not on his tongue. He had viewed the men about him with mild, disinterested contempt while his large white teeth bit into loaves of hunkie bread with the consistency of habit, not hunger, though he ate three loaves each day and drank little water, even in the heart of summer. Never except at lunch did his eyes note anything of a personal nature about these men, for he put work above all things.

It was working beside the river that had made of his discontent something seething and bitter. One day when the handle of the pick was wet and had softened the glove of coarse dead skin on his hands, when his eyes were pricked sore by the afternoon glinting on steel track, he had looked out across the blue river, so calm it did not sparkle. The water flowed with such sloth and indolence that it gave the impression of being pulled along against its will. It seemed incredible water so shallow could be blue, or could have the same unnaturally rich quality as rinsing water.

There was deception in this, for he had bathed in the river, and the water was clean and cool, good even to drink, and there was a fierce undertow. There were fish in abundance, bass, suckers, eels, catfish, pike, which were known as Susquehanna salmon, whitefish, perch, chubs and great carp. But since the river had lost its original purity, that purity of fast-moving water which exceeds cleanliness, and since coal mines to the north were choking creeks with black stain, the trout had fled, leaving behind a less delicate kin with green, soft skin and red, inflamed eyes.

Mijack had no interest in rivers or any waters, for it was land which fascinated his eyes, land set upon high places, land which could be owned, fenced, developed. He would never wade into the river for pleasure, only to wash. Rivers told promises that were lies, big rivers were danger and hunger and flood and typhoid, and the Mississippi led nowhere except to the sea. This was one lesson from his youth.

Rain was different. Rain splotched across the sky was more attractive than any sunset. Rain drops darkening the soil had the effect upon Mijack of summoning through his more than forty-five years a tenderness which had found little occasion to be used in life; but the most incomprehensible and useless sight of nature was the fall of rain upon a river.

It was land which caused Mijack to remain behind when the other men saw no reason to do so. On the opposite shore, several miles to the south of Harrisburg, was a dense concentration of smoke. Smoke meant work, smoke meant money. Through and above this was a mountain, easily the most prominent in an area of rolling green foothills, crested with a massive rock pile which remained dark, no angle of sunlight changing its appearance, for the bulk of the rock hung forward and created its own lines of darkness. It was the stability which caught Mijack's attention, something steadfast in a valley and hill world that shifted before every whim of light.

Even at such a distance he sensed in himself some feeling, some vague need, one almost obscured by the years of wandering. He wanted to take his eyes closer to it. Instead, he spent an entire day sitting on the edge of the river, flicking pebbles at the water, where minnows were trying to swallow them, and eyeing the high-set rock girdled with a green plumpness which made it an eastern mountain; idle, a man who despised idleness, who gave the Sabbath to the Lord only because it was the Lord's, who found it a long day and one of deep unrest. He sat waiting for his head to do for him what it should do, old enough to be patient with his thoughts. He had will power. This trait his eyes showed, eyes which looked upon the mountain with a quickness unrelated to movement, with a piercing steadiness never shallowed by monotony.

It was near sundown when Mijack made his decision. He looked at his hands, at dark blue stains which had been there ever since they had picked slate in the shadow of the colliery, at the finger which he had twisted in that first year on the Mississippi, at marks which had no definite effect upon his memory.

"So be it," Mijack swore to himself. "I build my house."

Mijack did. Two years later the house was.

Mijack set out toward the coal country of his youth, with the river as guide. He walked steadily and with the determination of a man who has not seen his birthplace in many years. His pocket contained all his money, and slung over his shoulder was a small sack of bread, cheese and dried beef. He knew the purpose of his journey and brooded over it as he went. There were few creeks to cross and not often did a fence run right to the river's edge, and the land was level, so that he made the horizon change three times the first day. There was time for remembrance, but so far from childhood it meant so little that he had to reconstruct the early years in a pleasureless, painless, historical fashion.

In the earliest part of morning he woke, damp and cold, and went to the river and wet himself all over to keep from being chilled. He scrubbed his blood into motion. While squatting, he saw his face in the water, and peered at the surprising accuracy of the reflection, then put his hands behind his back so that drops would not distort the image.

"It's coming," he admitted. "Age. I'll see it before I feel it."

And, crouched there, with his shoes gradually deepening in the earth, he vowed not to let age harm him as it had others, and knew there was no fear in him, but knew too that a man is allotted only so much time and no more. He clutched at the river with his hands and drank from the middle of his own reflection, and went away fortified and freshened.

By afternoon the Susquehanna had narrowed, but was still wide, for most of its water came from far to the north, along the New York border. It was the loss of the Juniata, river of laughter, which made the western side calm as a small lake.

In early evening of the second day, while moving across a farm which barred his progress, Mijack was attacked by two lean, snarling dogs. He had put a few good throwing stones in his pocket to be prepared for this, but did not use them, for he was the trespasser. If followed beyond the fence, where duty and training should halt farm dogs, he would not hesitate. Meanwhile, he was in for trouble. The dogs were of good size and did not bark, came in low with fearless caution, crowding, working as a team, seeking the best means of attack. For a moment Mijack thought they were going to allow him to escape, merely to force him from the property, but then they came at him.

He was warding the dogs off with his sack and with clods of earth when a young woman came running across the field and called out.

Mijack watched the dogs until he was sure they had decided to obey. Then, pointing at his footprints in silent demonstration that he had not trod upon the young corn shoots, but with no indication of gratitude, he went as near to the woman as the dogs would permit. He stood still and gave her time to look, time to judge his appearance.

The young woman did not move either. She had the quiet, firm stance often apparent among people who live on and by the soil. The dogs had taken nearly identical positions on each side of her, their eyes still hostile, but now looking more often at their mistress than at the man.

"Damn fine of you," said Mijack.

The young woman nodded.

"A body could get hurt from a pair like yours," he said.

The young woman acknowledged this with a more vigorous nod; it was almost equal to speech, this momentary enthusiasm, but then she lapsed into firm, unyielding alertness; it was a slight tenseness around her mouth which convinced Mijack of her youth, for in general appearance she might have been in the middle of life.

That which was hostile and alien between them was more than strangeness; it was their mutual sense that a man does not encounter a woman. It had been the duty of Mijack to pass on. Yet it was apparent that the time for this was past and it was therefore forced upon the woman to await, to be obedient to a courtesy which was not polite.

"Is there water nearby?" said Mijack, making as if to point at the dogs.

The woman kept silence, taking what she thought was her advantage; but it was not. The man was at peace, had stated his need and his desire, and could afford to stand still and, if necessary, long. So she nodded.

As they walked, Mijack looked at the land to see how well it was tended, how much had been planted, and where the boundaries ran. At the same time he studied the woman who was walking a little before him. She was short, sturdy, thick-boned, with broad hips and strong feet. She was young, without childishness. She walked heavily without lifting her legs, yet with forcefulness, and she never touched the dogs. He liked the plainness of her, liked the thickness of her waist, and how she kept her chin high and looked straight ahead. It did not matter that her lips were thin and long or that her hair was sand-colored without curl.

73

"I'm not often thirsty," said Mijack. "When I am—it's a bad feeling."

The dogs, at the sound of his voice, looked backward at him.

"With hunger it's otherwise. I'm almost always hungry. But I don't have to eat. I can go well enough without food."

The orchard swung his head here and there in another kind of admiration, for though he knew something of trees, he knew nothing about fruit. The apples were small and bright green, some so small they were not shaped yet. The trees appeared to be a little old, past their best seasons, but the woman told him the next five to eight years would be the most productive ones. Mijack looked at the trees again, with more respect for them. He felt a fitness in himself to be walking among them.

As they emerged from the shadows and the faint overhead rustling, he caught sight of the barn, clean and beautiful, with a weather vane pointing in the right direction, and a pattern of latticed windows for airing. Two piles of manure hid part of the side. The windmill had shining blades and a high tower. It did not matter that the house was low, rambling, in need of repair, especially along the porch. He did not have to look further to know he was among his own kind. He did not need to speak to show that he approved.

The woman stepped on the platform, took hold of the handle and began to swing it up and down. The pump sounded of metallic retching, and then as the water began to rise was more quiet.

"Am I welcome to water?" said Mijack. "Otherwise I could not drink."

"You are welcome."

Mijack took down the dipper.

The dogs had run to the end of the trough. He threw the first dipperful in their direction. He liked dogs, without liking them to drink before he had.

The woman watched the pump working.

"I have been drinking from the river," he said, to explain why he was waiting for the pump to chill.

Her face moved toward him to indicate attention; she was not going to commit herself to any point of view in what was his own affair.

Biting into the long-handled dipper, leaning beside the pump so that the excess of water fed into his mouth would spill into the warped, faintly lichened trough, Mijack drank. Then he paused.

"You have hands," he said. "I been noticing them."

The tone of voice was harsh. The young woman saw that the man's eyes were more steadfast than her own, both commanding and challenging. The surface coldness of his features had a pleasantness about it.

"God's will," she murmured.

Mijack tasted iron tang in the water because the dipper was tin and the white strainer cloth-bulb that hung from the spout was red-brown.

"Yes," he said. "His will and your willingness."

Being plain of appearance, the woman was acquainted with flattery. With outright suspicion she looked him over, her eyes bold in defense, almost sassy. The dog touching her skirt was warmth.

"How old?" asked Mijack.

The woman made no answer.

"Has this been your life always?" he said, waving an arm toward the fields.

"If you've got all the water you want," she said, "you'd soon be moving on."

"That depends," Mijack said. "Maybe I'm going nowhere further than here." He drank the best part of a second dipper, then hung it on the pump. "If you don't dance, card-play, idle over books, or look at men other than you did at me."

The woman tossed her head angrily, threw off suspicion, and seemed to settle into a sullen resentment of her situation and his presence.

Mijack went close to her. "I'm not speaking idly," he said. "I'm taken with you. Are you married or in prospect?"

The woman did not answer at once. Then she said, "You'd best come to the house."

"Yes," said Mijack. "Take me. I wish words with your father."

"Walk with me," Mijack said to her.

Now they were in the orchard.

"Abide with me," he said. "Be my companion."

He pulled a leaf until the branch tugged loose and swung upward, jiggling with freedom. He opened one of her hands, and put the leaf on her palm, and studied her fingers in this new relationship.

"Take me as easily as you do this. Judge me now," said Mijack, "without further proof."

"But I will not," said the young woman, her color rising.

75

"A man can't stay from his work."

She nodded, acknowledging, yet resenting.

"I've asked all my questions," said Mijack, slowly. "I let for you to decide."

"Stay on here three, four days," said the young woman, angrily. "I don't know nothing about you yet."

"In your heart you do not need more time to decide," said Mijack. "We aren't children, you and I. Haste? In a man approaching fifty? I have chosen you, Susie. If you can't choose, then I'm not for you."

He made as if to take the leaf from her, but her hand closed upon it.

9

When the house no longer contained sufficient mystery and delight, Irene was drawn to the windows, sometimes sitting content, sometimes slipping from room to room in an impossible attempt to decide which window pleased. Life was so—so umphettee dummphettee! Sometimes glass took duplicates from her fingers which were exactly the size of the pale ovals on her finger tips, and other times she could not make a mark no matter how hard she pressed. Glass breathed coolness at her when her face was near, and her nose was different in shape even though it was not touching. There were spots along the pane where she could see colors and glass within glass. The poplar tree had two trunks if her eye could find the right place to look.

In winter it sometimes rained white. Lines would curl down out of the sky, and the ground would whiten and puff with big hills during the night, and the trees would make sounds like the gate. If it happened in daytime the sky would lose all brightness and come close, and she would get a vague impression of the house sinking. She would blow with her mouth huffs and puffs and make water come out of the window and form a big circle with thousands of pimples through which she could barely see anything; and wiping with her hand made the window so glassy and made the trees and the hedge seem smeared and crooked; and while doing this she noticed that the air in her mouth was much hotter than that in her nose.

Irene never struck her hand against the window, for she certainly did not want to cut herself. If something broke, which was very seldom, she would stand perfectly still until Mother picked up all the pieces. Her eyes were alert to anything shining.

Spotsy ran off. Irene refused to have another dog, and she explained that very seriously to her father, pointing out that she simply did not believe she could bring herself to like another dog. After a while she did not even want Spotsy to come back.

Encouraged to discover the spring and summer of the lawn, Irene chose to remain inside and watch from a distance. It was easier to understand and appreciate the blue slow motion of the horizon through the limitations of windows. It was better to be able to hear the wind rubbing along the house and see flowers bending all to one side and trees showing the white sides of their leaves than to go out onto the lawn and be alone in that big place, where even Father and Mother were not of a very secure size. She did not like the activity which was always going on outside, nor to have to keep sticking her little parasol at the sun to protect her white flesh.

Winds of springtime made her feel many parts of herself simultaneously with new sensation, and made her familiar with the bone structure of her face and the penny size of her black eyes. But it also made her feel tired and hurt. Wind burned! It made her change her opinion about some of her prettiest dresses. Grass was not the soft fur green and tan it had seemed when seen through glass and distance, not a big green rug like the one in the parlor—grass was fierce and cruel.

Irene was a little afraid of the discoveries she made. She was hurt by things which do not really hurt. She did not know what to make of the enormous world in which even her eyes, the most confident things she possessed, were helpless.

Irene asked that her red jacket be put on. She went outside alone, marching with a definite and determined purpose. "There," she said, "I touched snow." Her hands gathered some and tried to hold in a manner which would keep the whiteness soft and light. Mother opened the door and gave her a jar. Irene made Mother wash the jar before she would put the snow in it.

Later the jar had water in it. She shook the jar, blaming it.

Father explained. He told her what happened to snow and other strange things about freezing. Irene listened. But she still blamed the jar.

She filled the jar with water and put the lid on tight as she could and then got Father's strong hand to tighten it more. She put the jar outside in the cold and then did not feel as bad about what had happened to her snow.

Mr. Lang was never too busy to have a chat with his daughter. A look of quiet joy would creep into his face when he was called upon to explain marvels and perplexities that Irene was encountering each day, as if he sensed that he was about to regain something time had lost for him. Never did he explain in language that could indicate he did not believe she was able to understand. Nor was there laughter at her questions, although he might smile and shake his head after he had answered, amused at himself. He was a well-educated man and fine in his thinking; he was aware of the rather perplexing circularity and contradictions which any real explanation involved and which Irene would not permit to pass unnoticed and uncriticized. He felt that knowledge was a kind of sorcery, a kind of adult fantasy, which no one could enjoy until he had developed a taste for the confusion and the undiscoverable portions of life.

Mr. Lang had a narrow face and large, dark eyes that did not often change intensity. When he turned his head, a person who did not know him would have thought he had a stiff neck. He wore dark wool suits and white shirts and did not remove his coat or vest in summer. He had innumerable shoes, all very much alike. He would not have been appalled if he had been unable to put on a fresh shirt each morning, a clean collar then and before dinner. But this had never happened to him.

If the arrival of guests in any way surprised or disturbed him, or if he was about to attend a function for which he was not prepared, he simply spent a few moments longer upstairs changing his collar and looking at himself in the mirror. This simple action prepared him to meet almost any situation.

Mr. Lang was quiet and could be depended upon to be preoccupied with business or a pipe. He did not permit tobacco to lose its pleasure and had developed an extensive ritual of preparation, spending a long time loading, screwing tobacco into the bowl, with many short twists and prods of his thumb, selecting the more moist and tawny strands from the pouch. He did his most important thinking

78

in those few moments. His voice was soft, too soft, but his mouth formed words distinctly, and he spoke with directness and vigor and originality when his hands were occupied with one thing or another. He could not be considered a nervous man.

Irene liked to close her eyes and listen to him. His words made pictures and songs. The rather bare office-study and the all-wood chairs and the hearth brick which could no longer be made to seem clean became a place where she was comfortable. Although past the age in which the intricacy of smoke whorls could hold her in lengthy fascination, she still liked to see him smoke and sometimes asked for his pouch to smell and sniff the tobacco and apple odor. She adored the faint stiffness and formality with which he treated his wife, herself, pipe and pocket watch; for some reason it melted her own reserve, allowed her to be more open with him and allowed her to make confessions of which she was afraid, as if she could trust her father never to become too intimate.

The poplar tree was aging. Root hills made the brief front lawn difficult to walk on and had broken into the cellar and were threatening the sewer. A branch tip which had trapped itself in the rain spout was beginning to imitate vines. Lower limbs were bare and stood too firm in the wind, without swaying. The moving shadows on the parlor carpet which Irene had watched and chased were stable now. There was darkening of the foliage and the tree was in silhouette earlier in the evening.

It caught snow in its crotches almost as deep as snow on the ground and went shining black with rain and softened until the bark was spongy and sticky as black ink. Its autumn was to shed itself in one big, sudden heap of brown and yellow. It shouldered to meet winter, coating itself with scale and dry crustings even as the ashes and skeletons of its leaves scudded and tumbled downhill and gave false fillings to the wagon ruts. Irene knew that much from the window.

But now she was running in a ring around the tree until so dizzy that the world ran faster than herself. She had to lean against the tree or else fall. Even as she clung to the bark furrows, the tree felt as if it were swinging. It was too big for her arms to encircle and it made her dress full of black spots, but when giddiness made everything into slippery brightness of new color, like, though larger and more violent than looking through wet windows, it did not matter about her dress.

She listened to the leaves pretend to rain, green of many shades shaking, flapping, whirling in obstinate directions, revealing colors no leaf really has. She saw one leaf using to the utmost its small freedom. She watched until her eyes lost perfect focus, until she seemed to see with the whole surface of her eyes. She sniffed until her nostrils were minty and narrowed and slightly different in size and structure. She was overcome by a quietness and content that made her whole body elongate and let the muscles splay into softness, so that her faintly chilled flesh held the muscles in a hammocked manner. "Coo-coo-cool," she said to herself, feeling the faint electricity that is transmitted from trees to all things nearby. Her toes pointed in gentle ballet imitation, then drooped, hung like bits of white putty from her foot. Even her eyes felt green.

It did not occur to her that she might climb the poplar or swing its branches or use it as a target for stones. It did not occur to her to want to hurt or to test its strength. It was a discovery of affection and certainly of fondness. She did what she could to protect the poplar from abuse. Whenever the ragman's horse chewed on the bark, she would stamp her foot and say, "Shoo . . . Shoo . . . Shoo, you," and then run around to the front of the horse so she could be certain it was disobeying, not merely unable to see. The heavy harness had cut blue scars on which flies liked to sit, and on the occasions when the horse obeyed she would chase the flies, once.

The baker had a big white mare to pull his little wagon. All the mare wanted from the tree was shade, and from the girl, sugar. Its eyeballs fascinated Irene. She stood before that horse with confidence and sometimes ran between its legs to get to the other side. But she was the tiniest bit fearful of its teeth. "Horsey," she would say, "take the sugar but don't lick." The mare would elongate her neck in the graceful movement which centuries of reaching up had taught her breed and blow a little hot breath into the curl of the girl's hand.

And then one afternoon, not sure how long trees live, not even sure they die, yet filled with the knowledge that the poplar was getting old and shabby-looking, Irene chose the greenest of the autumn leaves and planted the tips of their stems in the ground. Her hands did not mind getting dirty for the tree.

Smallness of hands no longer compelled Irene to be cautious with her knife and fork. She was nine. No longer did sitting before the table in a new dress make her knees and lap tense or cause her to sit with her chest tight against the edge of the table. So graceful were her motions that she gave the appearance of flirting with food, of enjoying the gestures of eating more than food itself. But this was only when she was at the table alone. For she was able to control the imitative gestures which she had learned from guests and her father, and to eat gracefully without attracting attention to herself. She had learned to enjoy food more when the best silverware and plates and the tall, thin glasses were spread in definite settings across the white lace.

Mrs. Lang was rather commanding, allowing her arms to rest on each side of her plate, eating with briskness and purpose. She was always a little late in getting her apron off and hanging it on the back of her chair, yet demanded that no one wait for her, even after all the years that her husband had waited without showing the least sign of impatience. She had a habit of watching people serve themselves and would bring it to their attention if anything had been slighted. She never could quite understand appetites being varied and uncertain.

Mr. Lang ate slowly, in quietude, and was always the last to finish. When he took his napkin to his lips he was finished, except on the rare occasions when, to make a guest feel more comfortable about accepting a second helping, he would put a little something on his own plate. He would talk across the table, but only on the lightest matters, and with more inattentiveness than was usual with him.

Mrs. Lang was somewhat self-approving of her cooking. She had recipes handed down from her great-grandmother's time, written in old script German. She liked to cook things which took a long while to prepare, even days, and it naturally peeved her to spend so much time over the stove and in all the minor preparations and anticipations and then have her husband eat nothing but potatoes, or nothing but meat. She could never understand that he seldom took more than a spoonful of what he enjoyed most. And she had to solace herself by making constant reference to her daughter's small appetite, which she did often while looking at her husband.

"How are the sweet potatoes, Irene? Candied too much?"

"No, Mother, they're fine."

"Why don't you eat some, then? The dish hasn't been touched."

"I had some, Mother—honest."

"But you didn't taste the corn. I'm sure of it. I think there's the right amount of butter in it, for a change."

"I have some. See!"

"Puf! That little bit, two or three grains. Here now, let me."

"No, Mother, please, I'm full. Really really full."

"No wonder you're so peaked. People must think I don't feed you."

81

"*Please*, mother, I don't want any more. I—don't—want . . ."

"Hush now, leave her alone," said Mr. Lang. "The girl knows her own stomach."

"She won't *have* a stomach if this keeps up," said Mrs. Lang, pursing her lips. "It'll shrink to nothing."

Mr. Lang cut a slice of meat. A second carving, this time on his own plate, resulted in a small deposit in front of Irene. She stared at it, then turned the meat over and began to scrape the gravy off, putting it at the very edge of her plate.

"There!" said Mr. Lang. "That bit I'm sure you can eat for your mother's sake."

He looked at the piece of meat and demonstrated with touches of his fork its miniature proportions. His fork had gravy on it.

Irene sighed. She cut very tiny specks and ate a few. She knew Mother considered food left on a plate a worse offense than eating too little.

Irene was not graceful in appearance when in distress. Her mouth and throat had to make motions she abhorred.

There was gravy. She could taste it even after she had scraped it off.

Irene attended the village school, but her education was actually in the hands of her father, who tutored her. Dante, Aristotle, Plato, Francis Bacon, Thomas Hobbes, John Locke, Immanuel Kant and many others were names that were freely exchanged and discussed at dinner when certain guests were present. Irene did not understand the subjects discussed, but she would listen, looking from one person to another, sensing and respecting the seriousness of the conversation.

Mr. Lang had educated her in a curious manner, beginning with his own family history, which had had its earliest firm roots in Germantown. He had shown his daughter portraits which had to be brought from the attic and dusted before they revealed much of anything. He also had his wife hunt out clothing which had been worn by earlier generations of Langs and even dressed himself in a few garments which were puzzling to the girl, stressing the wide variety of occasions for which they had been used, and pointing out the quality and skill which was still evident in the handwork. Her grandfather had served at Antietam, and Irene could point in the direction of Gettysburg almost as accurately as she could point toward her father's factory and toward the steel mill.

Mrs. Lang did not approve of the directness with which her husband exposed some of the less noble portions of family and national history. She found reasons to contradict certain information which she herself had given him about her own family. But on the whole she kept away from them when Irene was being given lessons, and she approved that her husband should tutor the child, since the village school was particularly poor in educating girls.

Mr. Lang himself did not think that. He thought it was only poor in educating a girl such as his daughter. He favored academies and each year made a small but substantial donation to the one in Harrisburg. The public school was, he felt, a secondary and less favorable method of education, good enough in its intentions, except for the problem of state and local authority which would have to be solved before anything serious in the matter of education would ever be done.

He heartily enjoyed teaching his daughter. It was not merely the revival of feelings which he had lost and forgotten, nor the pleasure of dealing with a fresh and surprisingly intricate mind, nor even the constant attention which he found himself giving to his daughter, an attention which increased when he saw that a strong-willed and lovely girl was emerging from what had been a prolonged and fearful infancy. It was somehow a fulfillment of the relationship which he sensed his daughter wished with him, a filling to the brim of the cup which Irene drank so greedily that she did not always digest it, and a continuation of the confidence which they now had in each other, and which Irene had always had in him.

When they were talking together, often in a manner which made it difficult to determine who was the teacher, and still more difficult to determine what subject was being discussed, the hearth would burn to such a low line of red ashes that flames would appear from time to time like bursts of light, and Mr. Lang would lift the book which had been folded across his knee only to find that it would have to be brought nearer to his eyes.

Irene was ten when she discovered Grimm and Andersen. She read the two books over and over, never tiring of them, her head whirling with excitement, her body and legs calm and nearly forgotten. Words came to her as vivid images, splendid with color, enlarged, exciting versions of reality slightly weakened by mist along the outer edges. She was able to feel, after having read the adventure of a princess, how delicate and white and unsubstantial her own flesh was. At such moments she regarded herself with breathless awe, viewing her person as distinctly separate from herself; at such moments her dress was stiff and weighted and strange, the way blankets were the first minute in bed.

Irene found poetry. She found it and was charmed by it even before she realized that it was poetry. There were images which flooded her with almost incredible delight, and she was fascinated by rhyme, intricate rhyme, as earlier she had been by self-invented sing-song. Her first really acute insight was in noticing its cleanness and neatness, which made words seem to have been stitched across the page and to fit each to each the way the innumerable colors in the sky at sunset were joined. Poetry had beauty, pleasure, delight, even sadness, but she was still incapable of seeing the human being behind the lines, the pain and anguish of the poet. She was looking into a new kind of mirror, finding herself, and sometimes someone who was not quite herself, and often encountering what she could see only so dimly that she had to put it aside, with bewildered, timid impatience.

While reading Blake she discovered how sensitive the two reddened nipples dawning on her chest were, not by touching them, but through an internal quiver that was strong enough to make her fold her arms across her chest and press, to remove the lingering itchiness. Reading could make her eyes wild and her nose too sensitive for breathing, her ears have internal parts they did not normally possess; she would have to put the book aside and rise and walk about. She would find herself nervous over the least things. The cries and calls among birds would make her hold her hands over her ears, and the fuzzy appearance of dew was often like a faint dizziness, and the smell of greenery and hedge was much more pleasant than walking along the flower borders.

Yet the sensuous and passionate outpourings of Keats and Shelley did not arouse this bewildered eagerness in her nearly to the extent Blake's lambs and Wordsworth's daffodils and lakes and rivers and soft fogs did. It was enchantment she sought, enchantment in a new sense of the old theme of sleeping princesses. She wanted to hear a bugle from beyond the horizon sound a pale, slender note which would be hers to remember forever. She wanted to hear a brook as she had heard it in a book, see a star as she had seen one sleeping in dreams. But she believed the most precious feeling in the entire world was to be given a Wish, to have a Wish. It was to possess the Wish, to be entitled to it, to keep and perhaps never use, or to cast it away suddenly upon some bit of nonsense, such as, "I wish my toenails were moons," or, "I wish my heart were a daffodil."

Splendid possibilities, made real to her through the two books of fairy tales, had really always existed for her in the general temper of her mind and emotions. They revived the awe and mysteriousness which she had felt sitting alone in the nighttime, a tiny lighted candle in her hand, the burning of tallow the only sound audible, in the suspended instant when her mouth was already hooped to blow the flame sideways and then darkness and darkness and darkness. They revived dreams of old dreams and wrapped them in new circumstance of such sweet sadness that she sometimes was impatient with herself in getting to bed, only to find herself lying there, impatient for morning to open the window with light that she might have that first look down across the lawn and garden.

For it was in this period of fantasy that she began to see the magnificence of the world and most particularly of the sky, the deepening sky of sunset which could hold two stars and a transparent moon and a violet horizon, the tawny orient moon of summer making the steel mill seem Halloween black and the river smeared with orange gloss, the blue flintiness in stars that was the only coolness her flesh could feel on hot nights. Heat lightning breaking across a clear overhead sky in pale glimmerings seemed to her so much more pure than sunlight and made the lamps in the house seem dim and without purpose. The air of evenings, even in perfect stillness, had a freshness which made her alert while her eyes watched intently through the twilight, seeing new things arise.

She began to taste pleasure and sweetness between her lips and on the very tips of her teeth. To feel beauty and happiness made her face too responsive, as if her face were an actress giving too dramatic a performance that sometimes left her hands and heart chilled and lonely. For the first time in her life, Irene was a little shaken and worried about the responsibility which her body put upon her. She had a vague notion that her person wished some attention given to it which could not be satisfied by bathing, nor by selection from among her prettiest dresses. To look into a mirror made her faint mute agony even more poignant, and even though she could see deeper into it than ever before, though she could see straight into her own eyes, or could stand and see herself as through a doorway in a slightly darkened hall, the image seemed to follow her rather than to be herself. In the glassiness of the mirror, and the deepened colors, she could begin to feel a certain importance in the curve and the gathering fullness of her hips, in the supple leanness of her waist, and above all along the curve of her throat. She simply had to throw her head back upon her shoulders, even if it did make her look ridiculous to Father and Mother. There were moments when she could not bear to wear anything except the very lightest dresses and very soft slippers. There were moments when she felt so much self-pity that she would run upstairs and throw herself upon the bed and cry.

These new emotions made her nervous, and they aroused feelings of not wanting to be near her parents. She was having feelings for which she was not quite sure she wanted explanations. She was a bit ashamed of not being as quiet and placid as her father, of having so many fears and strange, incomprehensible impulses—like spending an entire afternoon lying in bed, pinching water on her eyes and along her cheeks and even on her belly with an eyedropper. Such things were frightening when she thought about them later, and then she would feel a need to be near her father, to reassure herself of his mildness and stability. For he was the voice of truth. She was beginning to feel humility in his presence. She was coming to rely upon him in ways that she had not thought protection was needed.

And yet she had this feeling of physical estrangement from everyone and almost everything. She suffered at times a form of loneliness which was so acute that she would lie sleepless through most of the night, the pillows pushed off her bed, rubbing her forehead against the wooden post nearest the window. She would find herself imagining that she could feel the earth turning, ever so slowly and not steadily; opening her eyes did not fully restore her, and it would give her a feeling of the enormous space within her own room, of the house setting high above everything. It seemed that in the enormous space there was so little real air that her mouth had to keep opening wide to catch enough to satisfy her own need. Breathing went in and out of her without catching upon the places where it was most needed, without leaving any satisfaction of being restored.

Mrs. Lang's hip was giving her trouble. Irene became mistress of the garden, which consisted of common flowers, with emphasis on spring, yellow and white and lavender iris, and red-white tulips in abundance. In the middle and late summer the roses came on in all their boldness, while the bluebells and lady-slippers hung pale and shrunken. The maples would golden and compete with the garden for attention, while near them a parsimonious, crotchety old tree still bore enough apples to maintain its identity.

There was a regular season of butterflies, when the whole garden was twinkly and the air seemed to jump in little fragments. Irene was not fond of butterflies and was never willing to watch for long the erratic flight of their bright wings. She often shooed them off flowers or took hold of their wings and carried them as far as the hedge and blew them toward the village, stooping to wipe the powder from her finger tips. Butterflies were tainted with the same masculine ugliness that could be seen in the feet of geese.

The only time a butterfly was pretty was when sunlight struck it just right, one instant of glow. The one truly fascinating and beautiful trait was the way it knew whether a flower stem was strong enough to bear its weight, and knew before it landed, wings fluttering at extra speed to hold the flower straight. Yet butterflies were rather clumsy and were often unable to solve the problem of balance. The least bit of wind was their undoing.

Bees had terrible black heads and she blew breath against one if it came too near, while the palms of her hands pressed tight against her legs, the palms more afraid of being stung than her body was. If the bee circled about her head, she stood stiffly erect, and if it pestered her, there was nothing she could do except close her eyes. At such moments her little breasts seemed to enlarge and the nipples felt like tiny, hard buttons.

Her terror of wasps and hornets was so great that it allowed her to run for the house with all the speed her legs would give her.

Irene had a better opinion of birds. Sometimes she would take a crust or a slice of hard bread which she feared Mother might use for toast and throw crumbs on the lawn and watch birds wrangle. Their greediness amused her. And then, in the midst of fighting and wrangling, one bird might suddenly be as polite as can be, offering its crumb to another. There was one robin who had a habit of hopping quite near to the young girl and scolding whenever he failed to get a crumb, and so she would save one piece, coaxing him almost to her shoe.

Songbirds apparently found that the steel mill offered too much vocal competition; at any rate they preferred to voice their melodies across the distant fields. Meadowlarks and bobolinks were common, and the eerie whistles of the upland plover were sometimes heard breaking across the twilight of dawn.

What Irene liked most about birds was that they were unwilling to have her walk too near, that birds maintained a certain dignity and independence for all their silly ways. Except sparrows. She chased bold sparrows from the lawn with flapping motions of her arms. Sparrows were so bad mannered that other birds seemed to be ashamed of them and would fly away from food rather than be in their presence.

87

Yet there was little reason for Irene to be outside except to get a breath of fresh air, a fleeting touch of sunlight, and to tend the garden and cut flowers for the table.

Her bouquets were tiny, select, focused about the beauty and freshness of buds. This annoyed her mother, who believed in abundance, who always cut the flowers nearest death first, and then padded the bunch with a few pretty ones.

But Irene did not care what her mother thought. *She* was mistress of the garden now.

Raymond Rowiger was her only friend during these years. The difference in their ages did not seem to bother either of them. He would sit down and join her tea parties, and sometimes play the role of two guests by speaking in a high voice and then in a low series of grunts which made him hold his chin against his neck. Irene could sit across from him and laugh and make replies which kept him going.

Or she could give him a pretty interesting game of chess.

But Raymond was going to college in the fall. They did not talk about it more than was necessary. It gave Irene the mixed feeling of being left behind, of falling backward through time, and yet it also warned her that before too long her little world would burst. Neither of these was very comforting to her.

10

Marriage was performed with the light of the sun around them, in a little church without stained-glass windows. The atmosphere was clean whitewash and privacy. Near the altar the floor was broken. For this reason the ceremony took place near the choir box, which made the organ's silence conspicuous. The bride's sisters and one brother-in-law were present. Mijack met them briefly in the rear of the church. The ceremony was held early to enable man and wife to begin walking toward their home immediately after the wedding dinner. Mijack carried the ring himself, as he insisted it should be, but in other respects he conformed.

The bride took with her more than her wedding dress, and Mijack's sack was full of good things to eat. There were warm buns that would harden before sunset, and so they ate them as a sort of final contact with the activity of the morning, although the farm was two hours behind.

The wedding night was spent in a field. Although it was agreed between them not to enter the sanctities of marriage at any time or place except within their own home, a chill and mist blew off the river and took out warmth which the earth had been hugging, and man and wife were forced to bundle.

In the morning, Mijack said, "You did not sleep."

His wife made no reply.

"Listen," said Mijack. "I understand. I'm not insensible of your feelings. You hesitate, even now. But there are times when a man must say yes or no, say it firmly and without hesitation. This may be said for a woman too. So don't worry at what lies before us. But do your duty, consult me when you doubt, confide in me, remember that we are sworn one to the other, I to you, as you to me, and we shall live to make the Lord God proud of His creation."

Susie seeded, hoed and harvested the garden, erected a chicken coop and wired the chicken yard, sewed dresses for herself and made curtains for the narrow windows; in a longer and more leisurely span of time patched together two quilts and a comforter. She slept on a double-thick rag-knit rug beside his high, narrow bed which he had made with axe and knife, without nails or glue, and sprung with a net of leather thongs. The other rooms upstairs were not furnished and doors were closed in winter to save fuel, but they were kept bare and clean and in readiness.

With a certain remote, bitter, combative eagerness she approached her new life, with suspicious, haggling haste for things which they could not do without, but behind this was the careful planning of a woman who saw that the remainder of her life would be spent here. Though the house was strange to her, so different from the rambling cosiness of a farmhouse, she was silent and did not complain. That the house was stone made it easier for her to settle in it. Her husband had built the house and for that it must be respected.

It was ugly, crude, roughhewn, the work of a man who had no real sense of beauty or form, but who had an abiding knowledge of basic structure and simple masonry, of strength and of time's effect upon material things. There was one room for each window. The sills of the windows were of flat purple stone, the windows unquartered slits of glass set too deep within the walls to gather much light. Light would have to force entrance.

There was a single doorway leading to the outside and facing south. Susie learned to use steel fiber and no water on the unpainted pine flooring. The cellar was paved with small white and tan pebbles which had been gathered from the banks and bed of a stream which rushed down the mountain so swiftly that it made an almost straight bounding line to the river: the pebbles were quite pretty, pale egg color tinted with faint pink, and there was a worn cobblestone effect which Mijack himself admired. Fire would leave a complete skeleton on which a new house could be strung.

The roof was slate and bought.

Three years Susie was obedient, for in pleasing her husband was the promise of her own happiness. The small Lutheran church of wooden pews and uncarpeted floors received her and made her welcome; a voice soft and unremarkable was added to the choir, and her husband was elected to the council. This was all the social life they had. It seemed enough to them, those first years.

There was little home life. Susie was alone in the house six days of the week, and in winter had little to occupy her except to feed the chickens, sew, knit and make mental preparations for spring. Even in the evenings husband and wife had little time together. Mijack went to bed early, rose at four, without a clock in the house. He never talked about the mill. He never talked much about anything.

Susie did not suffer. She developed a habit of talking to herself during the day. Although she did not regard it as such, feeding the chickens was the most solitary and vaguely unsatisfactory part of her life. Bringing peeps and young runners into the house on cold nights was a further extension of this. Her mind seemed to become more fixed and stubborn, and a little of the freshness and bloom went out of her, but without making her less healthy. Her religious faith, which she had always practiced obediently and punctually, grew into a kind of sharp, embittered morality.

Mijack, since his return to the church, had rediscovered the Bible, and had become an enthusiast. He did not seem to remember his past reasons for uncertainty. She, on the other hand, was silent about her beliefs, accepted his opinions on right and justice and man's final intention here on earth; but there were moments when her straight, thin lips almost whitened, when her face was old, tough-looking and suspicious. She had never been passionate in regard to life and appeared to have settled herself into life firmly and enduringly. Yet there was slipping into her speech a tart, stingy accent, a clipped, prying bitterness.

Both were silent people who avoided displays of affection. Mijack had arrived at this more naturally, more by his own choice, and found more value in it. She had learned merely to endure it, at the cost of a certain amount of crossness, at the cost of the little pliability her nature had contained.

In the summertime fierce thunderstorms came down from the mountain and threw trees to the earth and acted like a pruning knife upon nature. Whether it was that the rock at the crest of the mountain contained ore or that this was the highest point in that part of Pennsylvania, all the more energetic and ominous clouds raced to the mountain, congregated above its peak. They sent down white flashes of light, sometimes in continuous minute-long discharge, searing, splitting into rock. A booming noise rolled down the mountain side and across the flatness of the river; small sounds came back from across the river, weak, imitative acknowledgments, no more like thunder.

On one of these occasions, in twilight made night by storm, Mijack was standing with his face pressed against the small kitchen window, watching the white streaks leap and fork, watching pale impact dust rise from among the rocks. It was more strange and impressive because he was unaccustomed to looking through windows. The bending of trees was disturbing because he could not feel wind. The extreme whiteness of the lightning made it appear to have more direful intent than an ordinary storm, and he saw the mountain not as a whole, but in sections revealed at random, so briefly and in such violent light that his sense of familiarity was shaken. Altitude was restored to the mountain. The slopes were ragged with trees, mostly second growth, but with a few originals, not huge or ponderous, instead firm and hardened and more widely rooted, with the grasp of an octopus upon the earth.

Mijack called his wife to him, and when she did not respond, called again, and though she approached hesitantly, as if still doubting she had been summoned, wondering what use she could be to him here, Mijack paid no heed, and for the first time in their marriage put his arm about her waist and held her against his thigh.

"Faugh!" he said. "You missed . . . Ah-h-h, but you missed something splendid—splendid, I tell you!"

There was nothing to be seen except darkening twilight and

nearby trees and occasional bright sparks as rain drops shattered themselves on the window ledge.

"Up there," he said, pointing into the darkness, "the rock is broken. It is broken deeper than I was able to see or dig. I have been there when lightning fell. I have been there when I had to cover my eyes."

His arm tightened, holding his wife pressed against him, and his voice was excited, yet unusually gentle.

Susie was there because she was held. Her eyes looked dutifully through the window, without attention or interest.

"I have seen lightning *crawl* into the earth. I have seen it run over rock, hunting an opening. Yes, and *splash off*. And I have seen it *smite through*. I've seen stone *flame*."

He put his hand against the window and wiped at something which must have been on the outside. It was now light from the stove which made the pane visible.

"This house, my house, is built of that same rock, marked and burnt and broken by lightning. Isn't it good to feel that—that you have something . . . ? Oh hell, I don't know—I get so contrary with words . . ."

Mijack put his hand on his wife's hair and drew her head against him, but did not look down. He was still watching every movement on the mountain.

"Do you know," he said softly, "I never use a chisel until I cannot find a stone that will fit. A chisel is not right for stone."

He wiped again, more vigorously, at the same fault on the window.

"I undertrenched. That's how I got the stone out." He made a swooping movement with his hand. "I went down under and let the stones fall loose. Like I used to take out coal. Do you see?"

Susie looked at the stove. He had put her in a position where it was difficult to keep an eye on the things which were cooking.

"Do you know," he said, extremely gently, "I could go outside and point at every stone in this house and tell where I found it and what day?" His eyes swung for a moment and scanned the wall. "But I can't tell from the inside." He frowned, as if puzzled by this, then clutched his wife hard. "Look, did you see the lightning? Did you see it claw? Did you see how it—how it *kinks* right when it meets the mountain? Doesn't it make you feel strange down here?" he said, releasing her, and pressing his hands to his abdomen. "Doesn't it—

92

how are the words?—make you feel big, make you feel marked? As if there was something fierce, something—ach, women!" he said, seeing she did not understand. "Women can feel nothing!"

He turned from the window and went to the table and put his head between his hands and squeezed it.

"Put on supper," he said, wearily.

Susie's eyes made a quick hunt over the small windowpane. She went to the stove.

She felt better when she saw that he was going to eat. It was a comforting pleasure to have a husband who ate quantities worthwhile preparing. Though his eating habits were not polite, though he was least courteous in this respect, he nevertheless had a hard-bitten, clean dignity at the table, the authoritative air of a man who believes in food and in eating. She was proud.

"The bread is all, wife."

She flew to the pantry. It was a serious mishap.

"Yes," he said, "I found that good stone is worth the trouble of careful digging. I learned respect for it. How sometimes good building rock is out in the open, and how a rock that won't come loose, one that makes you sweat and figure your damn head off, that's the kind to get." He thrust his fork into the mashed potatoes. "It's really a feeling to get so you can look and tell how much is hidden and where it's hidden. To be able to feel at the first touch whether prying will bring it loose. And I had a hunch I was coming upon something—something big in my life."

Mijack pushed aside the plate, the bread which he had called for.

"Go to bed. Get your work done and go to bed," he said quietly, pulling the lamp to him, turning the wick, and peering into the enlarging flame. "I want to be alone."

There was little kerosene in the bowl, so that the greedy sucking of the yellow flame was nearly visible, and the loosely curled wick was blotting at the fluid.

When he heard no sound of movement, his head swung, and he looked darkly at her.

"Damn you, stand there looking at me. Stand there looking and see what happens!"

Later, he went upstairs. She was in his bed, waiting. He flung his clothes on the floor.

"I suppose you prayed," he said. "I suppose you think that made everything just fine and dandy."

Mijack was not often unkind. He bought glasses for her eyes which had never been strong. He had noticed how close to a book her head read, how she could not thread easily, and although she protested, saying she did not need them, he would not hear of it. When she consented, it was to buy at a local store which had many kinds lying on a counter, no pair costing above a dollar and many as reasonable as twenty-five cents. Mijack said no. He forced her to go to Harrisburg to a real eye doctor.

In such things they retained respect for each other.

Nor did Mijack begrudge clothes to keep her warm and keep her decent. If there was any shortage, as he suspected, it was of her own making. He urged her to purchase things which would make her appear more attractive, insisting there was a difference between a woman who kept herself attractive and one who made herself enticing. He saw therefore no reason why his wife, who was so exceedingly plain, should not wear, at least on occasion, clothes which had a bit of color. Susie did not agree and, except for fitting her hair with a bun and two gray combs, did not alter herself.

Mijack was fair in almost all things, but when privileges were abused was quick to put his foot down. She wanted a coal stove and he bought it. A few months later she began to talk about a stove with an oven. She complained it was so difficult baking on top of the stove.

"Then don't bake, boil," said Mijack. "Damned if I see the difference."

She urged him to make a bed, she practically nagged him, but he was firm on this point, and warned that he did not want to see any of his wood missing.

He would be silent for weeks at a time, the dark, brooding silence of a man not given to patience in emotional matters, but with strong command over his tongue. His discontent was worse than before he had built the house. They talked over having children, because they ought to have had children by now. Mijack pretended more concern than he felt, because in his perplexity as to why they, and particularly he, could not find happiness or contentment, he seized upon this, which she could understand and feel.

The silence would be broken by some bidding for Susie to eat more or get out into the sunlight or spend less time reading, but then a period of days might follow in which he was kind to her and told her not to worry and that they must be patient and bear this adversity. Once so deep was his concern that he patted her hand, clumsily, in the manner of one who does not know how to comfort or console.

"Let it be," he said. "We'll get on well enough."

He brought home a box and placed it on the middle of the table and went to do chores. The box was wrapped in tan store paper and quartered with ordinary string. Susie, thinking it his, carried the box into the other room because she was preparing supper. She did weigh it with her hands. She did handle it carefully.

When Mijack finished chores there was a tub of hot water on the coal stove. He pulled off his shirt and unbuttoned the long underwear and let it hang down over the back of his trousers. With waddling steps, he carried the tub outside. Susie held the door open for him, because the tub was a close fit, and he had once pinched his hand. It had been her first experience with his anger.

"Well," he said. "Did I do right?"

"Do right what?"

"Nothing," he said. "Nothing at all."

Mijack washed, kneeling over the tub, using a large yellow bar of soap made from meat fat and grease. When he had scratched and kneaded his flesh into a yellowing color, he pounded on the door.

It was wintertime. He pounded hard. "Faugh, faugh, faugh, faugh," he said, slapping and wiping at his wet face, and peered impatiently at the faint light of the kerosene lamp, none of which reached as far as he was, yet filtered into the darkness in mist radiation sufficient to encourage Mijack in looking to see how clean he had gotten himself, without being able to tell.

"Damn woman, hurry a little, can't you?"

His wife came. She lifted the tub and emptied it over him and dried his face and hair with a huge towel which they shared, each having a tendency to use a different side. Mijack had his eyes pinched tight shut. Frog-squatted, he offered his head, swaying it a little, and the towel was used by Susie with a hard scrubbing and jerking which made him grasp her shoes with his hands. It was her way of showing him she had hurried, leaving things on the stove as they ought not to be.

"God in hell, get done with it."

He grimaced as she prodded his ears, both at the same time, with the towel like a bandage across his forehead. His face was red afterward.

"All right," he said, pulling the towel from her and feeling his

95

face for wetness she might have missed. "Get on in before you catch cold."

His body Mijack dried himself, with great care. He did not like wetness inside his underwear. It was the act of putting on soap and rubbing it into his skin which made him feel clean. Brisk contact with the soft, stringent cloth made him feel a revival of the remnants of his youth, part memory, part real, forcing from him furious, inarticulate, guttural sounds of anger and good humor.

He felt this exuberance even more because he had done something youthful, something bordering on foolishness. For the box he had brought was a gift. He cursed the absurdity of feeling so alive, so intensely masculine. The effect of water was more startling in winter darkness, leaving his flesh naked and vigorously unsatisfied, except for his hands, which were roughened beyond any possible return to sensitivity.

It was cold outside, but he waited a few moments, tramping back and forth along the house. The stars had their one opportunity of catching his attention. He hooted his breath into the chill air and watched it, then shouted, looking out across the sky, listening to the vast freedom of sound. The chickens were roused as he thumped the tin roofing. He was innocent and eager as a child, foolish and rash exactly as he had been in his youth, doomed to the eternal and unanswerable curiosities of sky and earth, beating on the ground with his heavy work shoes, snorting and snuffling, browsing about.

He was staying out too to give his wife opportunity to see her gift. He was worried about her response to it, worried about his own mixed response to having bought something which had cost too much and might reveal his ignorance of luxuries and femininity. He was annoyed with himself for having denied his own decision not to interfere with his wife's personal life. His pride made him yearn to be uninterested in her.

Yet he saw in himself a number of faults which he could not seem to be rid of, plain bad humor, which came inexplicably, without cause, and lasted sometimes for days. Each day seemed to depend upon those first hours of the morning, and a bad morning meant he would be out of sorts until bedtime, even if he got to feeling better. He knew that often he brought home from the mill an ill temper which she met with placid obedience and sometimes indifference.

So that he was staying out, doing what he thought at this moment and in this mood was cunning, staying out because he wanted to provoke his wife, who was all the while making sounds at the stove which meant supper was ready, to provoke her for no reason, or perhaps for every reason, simply to be and to live, to have a response, to feel hated if not loved, to at least have something in his life which would end the routine which marriage had become.

But Susie did not call him to supper.

Finally, buttoning his underwear, mounting his suspenders, shaking his shoulders until his skin had reaffirmed its contours against the stiffened cotton, he entered the kitchen and sat shirtless at the table, alien for a time to this room which he most possessed. The freshness of the upper part of his body soon made his legs feel tired, made the work trousers have an almost cured odor. His enthusiasm was gone. The soft whiteness of his shoulders was a great contrast to the dark of his arms, arms and hands fire-tanned, and made his face old and deeply lined. It was the bone structure alone which was keeping in his face a grim, unrelenting dignity.

Mijack took the rest a man is entitled to after a day of work. Arms folded on the table, head sidewise on top of them, he made no resistance against fatigue. It did not last long, two, three minutes, and then he was Mijack again.

"Well, old woman, are you expecting someone for supper?" he said. "Or will you grace the table with your presence?"

His wife hurried from the stove and sat too, head bowed to within an inch of her plate; she pulled nervously at her dress, smoothed her hair, composed her features, and again bowed her head. Mijack prayed, his face turned up toward where God was, the flesh of his face still bearing traces of redness.

"Lord, we thank Thee for Thy many kind blessings, and know Thou wilt continue to provide for us, Thy humble servants. We thank Thee for the bread and the corn and the meat which we have gathered and set before us. Amen."

"Bless us, amen," said his wife, softly, in unmistakably separate prayer.

Then she hurried to the stove, and after stirring into the pots with a large wooden spoon, tasting of each, shifting pots to where there was more or less heat, she served his dishes and placed all the food before him. She began to set a place for herself.

"Your dander's showing," Mijack said.

"Let it," she replied.

"I may," he said. "And I may not."

The manner in which they ate was as if fortifying themselves, biding time, waiting.

97

"Where, might I ask," said Mijack, "is what I brought home?"

"Where it should have been put in the first place."

"Ah-h-h-h," said Mijack.

After supper he put the kerosene lamp near his elbow and turned the wick flame high and broad and horned, so that the throat of the chimney glass charred and there was much black smoke rising. He broke open the Bible which Susie had brought with her and took it up in both hands and read aloud, while she washed the dishes as quietly as possible. He read in a voice monotonous and liturgical, but when he came upon a passage which his eyes viewed with favor, or one which he felt his wife was in need of, he used loudness to indicate to her that she should listen.

Susie was listening. She was waiting.

"What do you think of that?" he said, smacking his lips. "Eh? The Lord God formed man of the dust of the ground, and breathed into his nostrils the breath of life, and man became a living soul. Mark it says here a living *soul*. A *living* soul. Now what do you think of that?"

The chair creaked as he made an almost imperceptible imitation of rocking.

"Ah-h-h come now, give me your opinion. This one time. It has been so very long since you have been so kindly as to—give an opinion. Come, my dear, walk with me, abide with me, yes, in high things, in higher things. . . . We've had our meat and potatoes. Give me a *magnificent* explanation, one that will comfort me, one that will comfort us all."

He leaned backward in the chair, closed his eyes, and waited.

"Oh, surely, did I hear something? Would you repeat it?" he said, eyes open wide, smiling. "No? It wasn't you? Only a dish being dri-i-i-ed. Ah but one, one, one pearl of wisdom, one stroke of tenderness, something that I may sleep with and dream of, then rise and go eagerly to the mill. Yes—but that I go eagerly enough anyhow, don't I?"

She shook her head, negatively, in warning.

"No? Must I coax? Well, then, what about a little, tiny, ordinary, *common* opinion? That shouldn't strain you—if, *if*, mind you, you —have—a—o—pin—yun. Have you an opinion? Let me guess, have you? But wait, wait, hold on here. . . . Do you, that is, do you know what an opinion *is*? Do you *know*? Can we count on that much? Can we assume, depend—or shall I spell for you? Would that help!"

"Be careful," said Susie. "You've said enough."

Mijack shoved the Bible away from him, knocking a marker of gilt versed with Matthew on the floor.

"Be careful," he shouted. "With you? Faugh! You, who've never spoken one damn word which interested me since the day we married. Yes, it's true. Not one damn word. Well, I'll tell you what *I* think. I think it's a stinking shame a man has to have a living soul and a wife like you at the same time. I think it's a Goddamn stinking shame. There now! Have I made it clear? Have I set things straight between us?"

And he went back to his reading, sliding the fingers of his hands over his ears, still reading aloud, in a voice that gathered calm and pause, then weariness, and finally something of the air of the defeated.

Susie picked the marker from the floor and went into the other room and put it among her books. She did not return immediately.

Mijack continued to read aloud, using a finger to follow the lines. The stone walls gave his speech a long, clear sound, not so much hollow as not touching, not absorbing that edge which is attached to all human sound. The table was a bare, clean piece of wood, with only the marks of his own eating upon it. In the other room the fireplace seemed to be whining. . . .

When the dishes were clean, stacked beside the cupboard, his wife went outside and threw the dish water away. The light swayed and yellowed. Mijack had to put his eyes nearer to the book, and after that read in silence, and found passages that spoke as his own mouth had often wanted to speak and was now learning to. He was finding himself at the very time when he felt lost.

Late in life to begin, to have the beginning pain, to be wroth with his own ignorance, to sense that his native intelligence had been nearly destroyed by the very years in which he had been so hopeful, the years of searching. Late in life to feel the hunger of the starved. Above all, late to discover that he had never begun, that he must begin, and that his wife would be of no assistance to him.

And in his anguish he turned to her, saying what he could not have said yesterday, nor probably tomorrow. "Forgive me this once." He thought that was all there was to say, and fell silent. But into that silence came her silence, then the silence of the room, of the stones of the walls, darkened and dried and aged with the smoke of four winters of hearth heating, and three of cooking with coal. He did not have pride in those walls any more. He seemed scarcely to have remembrance of that time, except by the inverse feeling of being alien.

99

For he was staring now into the great and empty silence in which he had always lived.

"You're a good woman and I have no complaint," he said in a tired voice. "You bear your adversities, and—I don't. No, don't turn away. Forgive me. Perhaps . . . I don't know. . . . I suppose we need to have children. I suppose that would help. We simply don't have enough to keep going like this, day after day—at least I don't."

"You ought to finish your supper," his wife said quietly. "You didn't eat much."

Mijack looked toward the stove and saw she had kept things warm. Even though all the dishes were put away.

"No, I couldn't eat," he said. "Not now."

Later, his wife hurried upstairs and said prayers. Since her marriage she had taken to wearing more underclothing. She undressed herself and got into his bed and waited for him. Here the wind could be heard pushing against one corner of the house, and she could see her breath make vague clouds. But there were no drafts in this house of stone, and it was the very quietness of the air which was chilling.

Mijack undressed in the kitchen, where there was warmth, and carried his clothes upstairs. He was now in his fiftieth year and she in her twenty-fourth. It was his recent law that they should never undress before or within sight of each other, and that their bed should be without light. When he came to her, Susie was careful to give no enticement to her posture, her voice, or her eyes. Her hands remained idle among the bedcovers.

"The box was for you," he said. "You might at least have opened it."

Afterward, Susie rose from his bed and dressed, leaving off several petticoats, and finished her work in the kitchen, cleaned the table which she had not touched while he was reading, bolted the door, sewed a little at his work clothes where they were in need, and fixed the fires for the night. She gathered up his shirt, in scarecrow position on a chair back, and the work gloves he had left behind, put the Bible in its proper place among her own things, and then, just before she went upstairs and covered herself with the rug, opened the box.

She unfolded the white dress with dark trimming and held it against herself, and then went close to the fireplace, which had been banked of its light.

She was silent, and the night on the mountain side was silent, and wind moving along a slope in such continuation and with such slight variations came to be silence too, and the hearth hugged its heat to stay alive. Down in the village the stores were still lighted, and over in the mill the curfew whistle blew for children to heed quarter to nine.

She rose in the morning before him, renewed the fires with squirts of air from the bellows, and made breakfast. In the heart of winter, or when cold spells caught them by surprise, she brought the rug downstairs and slept near the fireplace. Mijack would not have the narrow bed brought down. He disapproved of her sleeping below.

In the morning Susie took the dress, box and string to the store where it had been bought. She refused to exchange. When she came away with more money than she had ever considered spending on a dress, her mouth was flattened into a straight, bitter line.

Mijack never brought her another package.

II

The mass production of steel was being born out of the black holes of shops in which there was a struggle as primitive and unsystematic as any the world has ever seen. Any man who spent an hour in the open hearth, blast furnace or coke ovens should have seen that men were forcing into their own hands instruments of destruction. The miserable working conditions of the coal mines were being reapplied, combined with an almost medieval sense of mass. An art was being changed into a scramble for power as men hunted for a new slavery to which they could chain themselves.

Yet, as in the coal regions, steel was breeding a tenacious and fantastically healthy tribe of men, at least among those who survived. Blacksmiths worked in temperatures ranging from twenty-five degrees around their feet to a hundred and fifty pushing into their faces and through their hair. Hookers would have frostbite one winter and the following summer have fingers nipped off so neatly that not until they took off their gloves did they realize it was more than numbness.

The gloves they wore were of stiff leather which made them keep clenching their hands so they could trust to grab hold. The leather made their hands cold the moment they stopped working. The fingers would fall into two halves because acid ate the thread. It was the men themselves who slit the gloves, making them wristless, open on one side, where they flapped loosely. Only a habit of keeping their hands clenched or holding them as if they had been washed and were waiting for a towel kept the gloves from falling off. They accepted small cuts and burns, so that when they felt the tug, they could jerk their hands out. Or at least have a better chance.

They kept smelling life where there was death. They kept being clever in small, individual ways, playing their wits against a whole philosophy.

There were the darkest of working conditions, black, moist earth underfoot, darkened brick walls and closed roofs. From a row of smoked windows there fed downward a gray mist of light which seemed to hang in puffy, humid forms. The light fed downward but made no man's shadow, and seemed to the men to remain overhead, above reach of their outstretched arms. It was like fog spread across the cleaner darkness of night, in which at least a man knows what he cannot see.

The coke ovens were like scattered fires on a wasteland, fires red, showing the torsos of men, showing the division between their legs, the variety of stances men have. The fires snarled and hissed with heat and intense inner glow, making only a thin radiance instead of true light. From each of the fires poured smoke, oil, and watered-coal steam, wrapping the darkness tighter as the chimneys of the furnaces and forges and pot-burners emptied their draft and carbon into the higher portions of the building. Even flames seemed to have black edges.

Finally the shop doors would open, four or five men pushing at each side, and a yard engine would come puffing in and drag new freight cars in and old ones out, leaving behind more soot and gas than the doors had opportunity to remove. Men swarmed over, beneath and around—their trousers flapping in the exhale from among its wheels, cursing and shouting as if it were a monster which they were trying to attack, while the engineer stared at the ground, calm, measuring, one arm thrust forward to the throttle. Through the open doors came sweeping across the black ground at ankle depth a cold air, biting into socks and making the cuffs of trousers stiff. Everywhere the sound of walking was greasy and gritty and uneven. It did not seem possible that it could become so bitterly cold in a building with so many fires.

At the far end, near the doors, hung three lights. From a distance only the coils of their filaments could be seen burning white and sometimes yellowish. But below the lamps there was enough light for men to write by and enough to make the earth gleam of grease. Here orders, calculations, and paperwork were being done; men in clean and soft clothing, but men who suffered more than the rest because of their nearness to the doors, and because they were not physically active. They put cotton waste on the wooden seats of their chairs and folded the legs of their trousers bicycle-style and tucked them into their stockings. When the doors were thrown open, they would clutch the lapels of their coats against their throats, writing with the curious stiffness of one arm, using their raised shoulders against the wind which fluttered papers and forced hurried elbows to be used as paper weights. When they rose to walk, they resembled puppets, hobbling about, stamping. One man kept cotton in his ears.

Throughout the building were departments—or areas referred to as such, since there were only those separations which men made from each other. A week of walking about in the building would not have given anyone a clear picture of what was going on. At least six languages were being spoken, and men moved here and there, doing now one thing, now another. Wooden horses were strewn about, piles and buckets of coal, waste rag, sawdust, piles of scrap steel, chains, hooks and eyes. There were miles of rope, and yet men could never seem to find a piece long enough to do a job; they were always waiting for someone to make a splice or a tie. There were cranes cranked in the manner that a well bucket is raised. There were jimmies, pry bars, knuckles, clamps and little cranes which had to be weighted on the opposite side to keep them from tilting. Some men did nothing except put their weight on or against one thing or another, at one place or another, as if they were engaged in a varied game of see-saw. There were things which had been trod into the ground, lost forever. There were things which men stumbled over, discovered, examined, threw away again, or stuck in their pockets for some vague future intention which seldom arrived.

Men had hiding places for their lunch pails, ranging from having them simply locked in tool chests to suspending them from a block and tackle and hoisting them twenty feet above the ground. There were old crumpled hats almost unbelievably dirty which men wore on their heads as carefully as any of their better hats. The bands were used to stick screws and nails and shims into, men using their hats as fishermen do. Men looked stout and clumsy from the troublesome weights in their pockets, hammers, short bars, punches, bits; most of them never knew what was in their pockets and had to pull everything out to find out. Men were always hollering for someone else to come and give a hand. They were constantly dragging heavy things near the fire so they could see what they were doing.

It was the chaotic struggle of individual men, of a man and his helper, of a boss and his gang, all engaged in activities with which they were familiar, but which were seldom identical. No two blacksmiths made the same tool alike. Every rigger had his own way of balancing a load. There was respect and lack of respect. There were men with tremendous ingenuity and men who were mule-headed and men who had to be told in what direction to push.

It was an atmosphere of the enormous, gasping effort of men who did not deal with force in terms of pounds but tons, and who still thought of their bodies and arms and the heaviness of their muscles as the principal means of achievement. They got together in great gangs, men who knew how to heave simultaneously as trained rowers know how, men who could move anything, because they knew how to lift, where to lift, when to lift, how to make every single one of a hundred hands count. They could lift because they had no consideration for themselves. They could lift because they had physical arrogance.

Among them were a group of specialists, men who dealt not only in strength, but who used all the cunning which could be applied to strength, wrist movements which gave their arms perfect leverage, careful stance and balance of their legs and flexible knees to prevent loin and back strain, swivel movements which brought a weight forward and upward along an invisible but real inclined plane. They knew when to jerk and when to swing evenly, when to use motion to advantage, when to have their hands underneath or on the sides. These men had a knowledge of their own body structure and its natural rhythms, a sense of anatomy and of the relationships between their joints and their muscles. They would not have understood a diagram. Yet they had an intelligence of the flesh which permitted them to live on a higher physical plane than the men about them. They were the survivors of a race of men whose ancestors had formed myths.

There was another atmosphere, men driving toward promotions and foremanships, of bullying and bluster and curses in every language of Europe. There were small, mean, underhanded tricks by which some men tried to rise above others. There was favoritism, bossism, and the quarrels of nationalities and bloods. Czechs and Slavs and Croatians and Ukranians were getting a stranglehold on the shops. Italians were falling into two groups, the proud and the excessively humble. Germans were taking over most of the technical and specialized work. Negroes were being bound into a second slavery, not so much by the workingmen, but through the employment office and high officials, who made work available to them only in the open hearth and blast furnace, where they did brick lining in heat so intense that their heritage was of little use to them.

It was only sound which seemed to give unity to the work and the men. Voices could be heard like those of two choirs, one base and guttural, clinging and joining with the sounds of the machinery, the other overhead, shifting along the high ceiling and the steel rafters. The multitude of voices were a chant in which nothing except the sound of voice could be distinguished. There was the ringing of steel, the unendurably long sound of thin plate set into vibration, like the chattering of a million teeth, the small staccato of hammers, the snapping sound of steel being cut, the sharp, high sound of one piece of steel being thrown on top of another. There was the hiss of gas and coal being burned under streams of air, the fierce and then weary whine of flame being forced to its utmost heat, the unmistakable sound of chain in those moments of its looseness, and the different sound of chain taking grip. There were the screeches of rope thinning, and the tiny sounds which men could make with their arms, the equally tiny sounds men could make with tools, men so accustomed to noise that their eyes never flinched.

The men had learned to talk to each other fantastically loud, had learned to set their mouths in line with the nearest ear; two men working together often looked as if they were kissing each other on the neck. They knew how to keep their mouths ready to use every instant of silence. They were so adept at lip reading that they did not even know when they were not hearing. Their hands and arms talked for them, sending signals more primitive than semaphore, signals which could often be understood and acted upon more rapidly than any formal transmitting method.

The noise was so loud it could not have any of the qualities of music, for music requires tempo and pause and mutations and percussions of clear value. The noise was a hazard to those who tried to hear. It was deafening to an outsider. But behind the noise was another sound, the sound produced by many sounds canceling each other, the wooshing roar of continuous impact, of actual motion in the air. It was a feeling in the ears like being underwater. It was only when this became a kind of platform of silence that a few extraordinary sounds could be distinguished, sounds as delicate in their own way as tunes played upon varying thicknesses and lengths of glass. It was as if through the roar of thunder one could hear the whispering of candles.

The men did not think of it, would have scoffed; yet it was this cancellation of sound, and this thin tune, which kept them sane.

The darkness was not darkness to their eyes. They had learned to breathe smoke and fumes. Grease and acid were part of the very fabric of their clothes. They would have washed themselves roughly at any time, even if their pores had not been permanently dotted black.

They were full of high individuality, men of all nations, men who drank, some on the job, men who would never touch drink, men with wives in Europe, men with European wives, men without women, men exported and imported. They were the hive, the swarm, the mass, and they made the steel that would ravage their own nations. Nothing less than work and money could have brought them together. Under that same principle they were, bit by bit, grudgingly, being made alien to themselves. They were being made into men with neither past nor future.

The steel mill nestled along the river, slowly growing, slowly sending out its tentacles, rail mill, coke ovens, switch shop, blast furnace, bridge shop, frog shop, open hearth. Rail tracks were the only clues to the relationships of the buildings. There were rows and rows of cars loaded with ingots of pig iron. Trains came in one after the other from the coal fields. Fire belched in the night, silhouetting black what was already black.

Selvinius was dead. The machines were working. The wisdom of man had turned a wrong corner and was pursing a straight line. The winds could not spread the soot further than the nearby land, but the real soot was spreading to the corners of the world.

12

Snow began to fall, the classroom was whispery, children were looking out of the windows. A vanguard of big flakes fell straight on the earth and lay there like white coins; one veered and pasted itself in the middle of a window where it made the pane seem lead-tinted and the classroom darker. The teacher, Mrs. Snyder, took a minute to go to the cloakroom and see if Susan Pore had returned her galoshes. Two carriages appeared outside and stood there gathering white trimming, the horses nervously pounding their forelegs and making dark ovals on the street.

Irene could not see Joseph, and she was a little anxious.

The four teachers of the four classrooms stood in the hall, stiffly erect, and four columns of children, marching in pairs, tramped down the hall toward the exit, across white-brown wood that would be stained and wet after the children returned in the afternoon. Near the exit the marchers broke into a run, and at the door there was squealing and shouting as young bodies threw themselves into the snow and cold, arms whirling. Three teachers were clapping their hands in a futile attempt to keep administration, one shouting, "No snowballing! No snowballing!"

Mrs. Snyder was still sniffing about the cloakroom.

Irene remained in the classroom until the school was quiet, watching, through a window now large instead of distant, for her carriage. She looked haughtily upon the children below. She felt mature and confident when the room was empty and she could talk with the teacher on a more equal basis. She could understand the weariness of Mrs. Snyder having to teach such children as these. But since she could not offer her teacher a ride in the carriage, Irene remained by the window.

At last, with a sigh, she gave up this vigil, and slipped into her coat, and by the time she was outside, the snow was deep enough to make her shoes feel unfamiliar. Children were making a slide. Big boys slid farther and faster than little boys, but the little boys were more excited; the little boys would be the ones to miss lunch. Two girls were brave enough to take turns in the line. Other girls tried once, and then, when coaxed to do it again, declared they had four or five times. Six times! Some of the little boys were so eager they would run back from the end of the slide and try to slip in ahead of turn. One boy was trying to open a new long, narrow slick of ice, but he would not get much co-operation until this one became worn.

Irene did not watch long. Last month Albert Nosowski had forced her to slide, dragging her behind him as he ran, and even after Irene had fallen he kept pulling. Irene had been surprised to find it could be fun even if she did hurt herself. It was the first time she had ever laughed at pain, and she had thanked the boy for helping her to rise.

Now Irene resented the idea of being forced, and felt worse because she had always considered Albert a polite boy, better mannered and more intelligent than the others, and here he was, pushing and shoving, showing off in front of these children. His name was always appearing on the blackboard above or below some girl's name, her own once, and she was sorry she had been friendly with him for a while, and glad he had not paid any attention to her since, and there he was sliding now, casually, with his hands on his hips, and she hoped Albert Nosowski fell! If there was some part of the memory that made her hesitate, wish to join the other children, she thrust it aside.

Irene edged along, and the mincing steps the snow forced upon her put the house on the hill at an unbearable distance.

Irene noticed the snowflakes suddenly were no longer touching her and looked upward in time to catch a glimpse of black very near her eyes and to feel her elbow taken and her own pace altered by the light, awkward gait of narrow trouser legs scissoring back and forth beneath an overcoat. The man had the collar of his coat pulled too high and his face hunched too deeply to be simply protecting himself from the snow.

"Once I knew a lovely girl who believed angels paint snowflakes, but refused to accept Chinamen painting butterflies. Do you know her?"

"Raymond!" said Irene, laughing and blushing.

"I thank my umbrella for the courage to approach," said Raymond. "For with the snow falling and my eyes such as they are, I kept expecting you to turn toward me and break the recognition in my eyes, and then I should have had to bring the umbrella in front of my face and hurry on." He smiled and turned his collar down, patting it into position. "I confess I had already decided that if it wasn't you, I wanted to meet that young lady all the same." He thrust his hand beyond the umbrella and grabbed at a snowflake which was falling more slowly than the others. He watched the flake melt into a nothingness which he could feel for a few moments after it had ceased to exist.

"You're making fun of me." But her eyes were alive. "You didn't used to tell such big fibs."

"No, because I didn't used to feel afraid of you," said Raymond. "I used to be only afraid you'd be afraid of me."

"Now you *are* making fun of me."

"Cross my heart never to do that," said Raymond, and the grip on her elbow was more firm. "I am only trying to say that it has been more than a year—you change too much in a year, you become so very new. And so I have to act as if I've changed a little too." He gave her a very earnest look. "Remember that I said one day the wand would wave over your head? Did it?"

Irene nodded, blushing.

"Strange," he said softly, "that what a young man would give his very soul to be able to do . . . But do we need this?" he said, shaking the umbrella. "Why shelter the sky?" He brought the umbrella to where it served more as a shield for his chest and looked upward. "Now is the time to be high on a hill. Now is the time to listen. If there is anything to be heard, anything really to be heard, it would come at a time like this. Listen, it is not a whisper, not a whimper. . . . It is not music—but could it be less—could anything be more quiet and yet heard?"

The umbrella collapsed when Irene had given consent, giggling, for she had not been protected nearly as well as he believed. His arms were careless when he was excited, yet he was completely unaware of having shaken snow on her. His physical innocence made Irene feel closer to him.

"I got in the habit of carrying one about. . . . Mother still always at me—rubbers, scarf, overcoat . . . Oh yes," he said, reaching in his coat pocket, "gloves. Feel as if I'm going to sink to my knees in this snow from sheer weight. While this," he said, pointing the umbrella straight before them as if sighting on the horizon, "is the most wonderfully useless thing that has ever been put into my hand. It makes me feel as if I'm walking around holding a pocket watch in my hand, counting the time it takes me to go from corner to corner."

"Your mother's right," said Irene, holding her head a little high and making her face imitate the authority of a mother. "You need looking after." She put a forefinger to her mouth and studied. "Now why, young man, do you have your gloves in your pocket, when you know they should be on your hands? You know very well that's the place for them."

Raymond looked at her in mock surprise. "That wand really waved," he said, laughing. "Well, let me see, I believe I took them off to make a snowball. I don't have the least idea what I wanted to make a snowball for, but I believe that was it."

"Quite likely," said Irene. "And you had better look in your pocket and see if you still don't have that snowball."

Raymond Rowiger really laughed then. "Well," he said, taking the gloves from his pocket and giving them to Irene, "there's only one way to make sure I have them on."

But Irene did not manage putting on his gloves as easily as she would have wanted to. She was somewhat embarrassed. She was sure that he only pretended not to notice.

"And you, Irene," he said softly, "I have often worried for you. Is the world still an awful place? Is it still below your expectations? Seeing you now, I can hardly believe you still . . ."

"Oh no! I love it," she said, brushing her hair and shaking it free from heaviness. Flakes imitated confetti, sticking to her coat and in her hair, alkalized her upturned eyes, tapped her nose and bade her sneeze, which she declined to do, and one went in her mouth, so small a flake she did not get a chance to taste. "But still I'm afraid sometimes. I'm afraid everything is so pretty and so wonderful right now that it won't last. I think, tomorrow I may wake up and find it gone."

Raymond smiled at her. "It won't happen, Irene. Not to you. Some day you may discover that you no longer feel it all, that some of the loveliness has gone, and that will be painful—but you will always remember that you have seen it." His umbrella waved through the air in great, careless arcs, indicating all that lay around them, houses with new roofs, straws stuck at aimless angles into white fields. Snowflakes bobbled to avoid the swing of the umbrella. "That will make it more beautiful than it ever really was. I promise that much. No, Irene, you will not be given your finest hour too soon. The wand has still many times to wave."

His face was flushed with tenderness and a smile which was all his own and every time a little different. Irene looked down at the snow. She knew she was important to him.

Raymond had detached his hold upon her elbow and she saw

him remove one glove and put it in his pocket and then felt her hand taken and his fingers weave among hers. She let her hand loose, feeling the length of his fingers and the slight incompatibility of their hands to join naturally. But her hand did not feel as small as she had for an instant feared it to be.

"There now," he said, "I don't have to feel I'm leading an old lady across the street. I can walk along like a man should with a young lady."

Irene looked up. Her eyes examined his appearance in a new way, one that almost startled her.

"I was so happy when I saw you," he said. "All day I've been walking around punching holes in the snow with this," he continued, tapping the umbrella against his kneecap, "so I could find my way to return home. I was so sure it was you."

"Then I haven't changed so much," said Irene, turning her face a little defiantly toward him, letting him see if he wanted the new prettiness which she knew was there. "I'm still a little girl." But she kept her voice teasing, as a precaution against her own feelings.

"Listen, Irene," he said, "a while ago I was beginning to think I should have punched holes in the snow all the way from college. I mean I was thinking of not going back. Maybe not so bad as that," he said. "But I'm not the sort of person colleges thrive on. They keep wanting me to cut down a whole tree, when I find it more interesting to take a leaf from here, a leaf from there, and then sit down and see why leaves have so much variety, why the oak and the elm so disagree."

Irene felt her hand gripped tight. But she knew that he did not know.

"Do you remember planting the stems of the poplars? Did they ever grow?"

"No," she said, looking at him quickly and seriously, almost frightened at his memory, since she had not recalled that herself for many years.

"No, of course not," said Raymond. "Now we know it's seed. And yet I can't help thinking I should prefer to see leaves grow. That's the sort of thing I'm up against. Do you understand?"

"Maybe," said Irene, pretending to be thinking over what he had said. It was one of the times she was being completely dishonest with him.

"But now, right now, I see it all differently," said Raymond, jabbing the umbrella straight down through the snow until it struck something solid. "I've really won a sort of victory, simply by admitting to myself what I am. . . . Irene, I am free now. I am free of Mother. These don't mean anything," he said, tapping his rubbers. He gave her the clear look which only a person who considered everything good in life as more beneficial to others than to himself could have. "And I am happy, too, happy as I never thought I would be. . . . I've decided what I'm going to do." He nodded his head at her, eyes serious. "I've gotten hold of myself, found something worthwhile—something I'm suited for."

Irene turned her eyes full upon him and let be seen the warmth and admiration which she felt for him, but which he had been hurting. She hoped that something splendid would be revealed to her.

"And today I nearly threw it away," he said. "I almost shut my eyes to it."

Irene did not know that he too had come from the school, that he had been talking with the principal.

She found herself hoping it was something to which she too could dedicate herself. Her mind leaped for a moment beyond her years into the vital blankness of her own future, and she felt the need of a glimpse of herself. The enthusiasm of his voice spoke for her, and she turned, facing so directly that he could not continue to walk. She felt revived between them the wonderful intimacy, the sense of identity which had made her trust him when she was little, and which she had not been able to feel since his umbrella had swooshed in over her head. "He feels *everything* I feel," she thought, peeking at him through the points of her lashes. Only then was it apparent to her how much she had missed his companionship.

Irene was standing with her hands against his chest, looking up at him, and when his eyes fixed on her face, radiant with their own thoughts, she could see them slowly come to focus on her and then hold fixed, as if a little surprised. "Tell me," she said, "I so want to know. I've always believed you would choose something—something beautiful." His eyes studied her a moment. Then they became confused, and Irene could see them look on past her without seeing.

"No," he said, "I can't tell you now. I mean if I told you, it would be a disappointment, it would not be something you could think of as—oh, beautiful or worthwhile." Raymond drew his eyes on her, to see whether this explanation would satisfy her. He began to feel that his intention was not as good or meaningful as he had believed it to be; and yet even more convinced that it was, after all, one of the few things for which he was suited. "Remember the snail? Remember how we had to look at it and look at it before we decided—its soft, shineless chalk shell and the strange head that made us decide it was a sea horse in a clam shell and belonged at the bottom of the sea, sitting on pink sediment? Remember? Remember that we could never decide if it was beautiful or ugly?"

Irene nodded, biting her lip.

"What I'm going to do is of that sort. . . . At least I hope it'll be . . . Ah, well, next year at this time you will be able to see for yourself, and I only hope that you'll have the same look on your face you had a while ago."

He smiled. He looked suddenly older and a little tired.

"But why must you be so secretive?" Irene said, half-angrily, for he was smiling at her in a way she felt was not right. "I'm never that way with you."

"Ho!" said Raymond. "That's one fib for your side."

Irene flushed.

"I suppose you don't remember the house and the ugly hill and the dirty creek, how we were going to use nothing except what was on the hill itself, do nothing except pull weeds and carry stones down to the creek and let them tumble in? How we were going to see the land become beautiful by itself, have the beauty it wanted and no more . . ."

"And live by the poems we wrote," said Raymond tartly.

"You never said that."

Raymond winced. "No."

"All right, don't tell me," said Irene.

"Don't be angry," Raymond said softly. They were walking again. He had kept her hand, but it was not until they had walked a distance that he really felt her permission to keep it. He was surprised to discover that he minded when she was angry with him. He was even more surprised that she had forced him to think of himself so seriously, had made him hesitate and see himself from a viewpoint which was scarcely admirable. And yet, what he was going to do was a little like that house on the hill, only it would be so difficult to see in that light.

"Through the snow. There is something fine about walking forward through the snow." Raymond looked at the overhead sky. "I always think of snow as springtime falling right down through winter. I remember when I was very little I once put snow on a plate, and it looked so pretty, and I was so sure it would taste wonderful. What a disappointment!" He laughed.

Irene did not reply. She only nodded her head. The snowflakes gave her something to look at.

"Through the snow!" he said. "Snow on a plate. Going forward to know what was the best that was behind us. Making footprints to get a better idea of ourselves. Carrying an umbrella to feel more reckless. Talking . . ." He laughed. "No, not that."

"I put some in a jar once." She averted her eyes, as if to keep them from making an appeal to him. "When *I* was very little." Ever since he had kept her hand when she first tried to withdraw it, she had felt as if he was hurting her with everything he said.

Raymond gallantly, a little too gallantly, handed her down from a curbing.

"Nonsense! Why now look, you come clear up to here," he said, his hand marking a position on his shoulder a little higher than she actually reached. "And besides," he said more softly, "you're exactly the height I admire in young ladies."

"Next year I'll be taller," said Irene tartly.

"I expect I'll admire you then," said Raymond, leaning toward her, noticing the radiance was gone from her face.

"Oh don't!" said Irene.

For a time they walked in silence.

"I suppose you're on your way home."

His voice was one of apology. He had a habit of bending toward her whenever he wanted to be kindest.

"Yes," she said. "Home from school!"

In her bitterness she began to swing her arm, knowing how foolish it would make him feel to have to swing his in childish arcs.

"I'm awfully silly," she said, in crabbed, abrupt aloofness, to herself. "You have to forget things I say."

Raymond gave her a very fond glance. She let her eyes be bold, as if to say, "Now why are you looking at me like that?" She let her eyes even not recognize him.

"You always have to take into account that girls are silly. They may act grown up one moment, but the next . . ."

And with that conclusion, Irene pretended to have nothing further to discuss with him.

Church bells were remembering noon, and the flake-filtered music, disarmed of its clangorous and shivering iron tones, came to them sweet and light as birdcalls, then hurried on to further parts of the village. All sound was a little breathless from its rush. The snow was

114

from time to time falling sidewise. Irene allowed a little defiant song to bubble out of her throat, a wordless little tune of mock gaiety. She did not care whether her voice sounded well. She even carried it a little to the very edges of its limits.

Home from school. They were both home from school. They would both be returning.

Two minutes later the whistles of the steel mill shrieked their version of noon.

"I hate them!" she said passionately. "Every day and every day."

Fluttering her lashes to defend her eyes, Irene peered upward at the dark flakes, her face pretending a sophistication it could not hold. Raymond made no reply, but picked a snowflake from her cheek and looked at his empty fingers where it must for an instant have been. It forced her to look too, simply to know what he had found on her cheek, why he had touched her.

Suddenly they both laughed, and, gripping their hands together more firmly, marched along the street in identical manner, in a sort of parade step, Irene still holding her head high, but now to see which part of her flakes would choose to strike and if she would agree. She began to feel the wetness of the flakes more than their coldness. Her hair was weighted and pulled at her throat with such a slight force that she only found it pleasant to keep looking skyward. It was amazing how many flakes missed her, swinging past at dizzy pace, blurred so that she was not able to see their patterns, some behaving like fast-moving insects with definite intentions which they went about accomplishing rather crazily.

She forgave the wind for hiding the new little song which had risen in her throat, for hiding a rich sweetness of tone that had never been there before. She felt a bit courageous to be able to hide from Raymond Rowiger something which would make an impression on him. She felt suddenly glad that she had a coat on, that she was wrapped about in thick, straight wool, and that all he had been able to notice about her was that she was taller and that her face had become more intense and deepened in tone.

"I've become a horrid, vain person since you knew me," she said. "I don't get along with anyone at school. And poor Joseph, our groom, must think I'm simply the worst in the world. I treat him as if he were dirt." She peeped out of the corners of her eyes. "Yes, I'm afraid I shall wind up a very wicked girl. I've gotten so I just have to have my way in everything. I don't help Mother half as much as I should. Father is spoiling me more every day. I read Byron and Browning and Shelley and I don't study any of the things I should. I'm—I'm godless, I suppose."

She was lingering. The gate was just ahead. If he went with her beyond the gate and into the house it would be different. The atmosphere of the house would change her more than it would him, and she was afraid there would be an embarrassment, partly because he had not visited for so long, partly for something which she could not define. Yet she wanted him to come along with her and only wanted to prolong the walk a little before they went through the gate.

"I wish I weren't so vain," she said. "I don't have many friends—real ones. I practically don't have any." She sighed. "I wish I would be going to college next year. No, now. I just have nothing to talk about with the people here. Except Father, and he's busy so much of the time, and I get embarrassed going to him all the time, with every little thing, just because I don't have anyone else to talk to."

Raymond nodded. He seemed to be preoccupied with the landscape.

"Well," he said. "I suppose I won't see you until summer. I deeply regret it. I've so often thought I would like—but I'm not worried for you now, I see that you are going to become . . . That you will have everything you want out of life."

"But aren't you coming in?" said Irene. "I'm not going to school this afternoon."

She wanted his eyes to look. They did not.

"I have so many things I want to show you and talk with you about." She knocked snow from around the gate to make it open more easily. "I was so sure that we, I mean that you were going to come in and have lunch. I—I thought this was only the beginning."

"I'm afraid not," he said. "Not this time. Because . . ."

"Listen," said Irene, taking his hand in both of hers and holding to it, "can I write you? I mean would you mind if I sat down sometimes and wrote—oh just things, the kind of things we used to talk about? I'll tell you all about the garden. . . . It's mine now, and what I'm reading and doing—and—oh, it's so long to summer."

"Please do write to me," Raymond said, bending toward her a little formally. "I mean it. I would love to hear from you."

His eyes were still staring off across the fields. Far up on the slope of the mountain someone had built a house. It looked further away than it was because of the long expanse of snow. The way college had seemed further away to him earlier this morning—and now he was feeling the need to return before there was any chance of again changing his mind. The summer seemed like a definite goal to him now, a finishing of what he had been reluctant to finish.

"But won't you come in? Just a minute?" said Irene. "Please do. Mother will want to see you. And Father will be home in a little while. I know they want to see you. I know." She let her eyes appeal for her. But when she saw they had no effect upon him, that he did not even give them a chance to be seen, she took hold of his wrist in both hands and pulled gently, urgingly. "Oh, I don't want you to go," she cried out.

Then Raymond looked at her. Then perhaps he had to look at her.

Those terribly black eyes were fixed upon him intently, and her face was flushed, proudly, almost defiantly. Her lips were parted a little and he could see the quick, small breath vapors rising toward him. But more than this, more than the unmistakable mute pleading in her eyes, than the tightness with which his wrist was gripped, it had been the momentary huskiness of her voice which had betrayed her. And now, even as he was looking down at her, his own eyes searching, he knew that he was betraying her to herself, and he was furious. He saw her eyes become stricken and the flush on her cheeks change from intense excitement to a deeper hue.

Raymond had to pretend he did not see what he had seen. Even though he knew it was too late.

There was snow in his hair. He stood there, tall, benevolent, almost elderly.

But he had been entirely too late.

For Irene pulled her hands from him, and in her bitterness ran through the gate and into the house.

Raymond Rowiger went down the hill, dragging his umbrella in the snow.

13

As Mrs. Lang was coming downstairs, her mouth flew open and she pressed both hands against her side, then fumbled for the banister and sat heavily on a step. It did not occur to her to cry for assistance, for she was too concerned with the intensity of the pain. When she began to recover a little, she did not feel the need of assistance, though she decided not to delay further in seeing the doctor. She sat there a few minutes catching her breath, composing her nerves so that she would be able to face the remainder of the day, even thinking of the particular things she would have to do, making in the palms of her hands places where she could keep morning, afternoon and evening separated.

The appearance of the hallway had a little of the same depressing grayness and floating sediment it had on mornings when she went downstairs only to discover that she was much too early to be able to do anything. If there was anything unusual in her feelings it was simply that she found herself thinking of even the smallest duties as being attended by vague difficulties which they had never before possessed. And she had been sitting on the stairs much longer than she realized.

She had the curious feeling that the sound of the approach of her husband or daughter would force her to exert herself in order not to be seen sitting there, and that, more than any other reason, urged her to try now, while she could take her time about it. She expected her body to feel unusually heavy and difficult to move, and with a certain reluctance she made an effort, found herself rising with ease, then walking down the stairs with such lightness that it was really a little worrisome. She felt herself and the whole house taller and everything around becoming much brighter and her spirits seemed to be almost radiant. . . .

Then her elbows slipped off her legs and she was dead, there where she had been sitting.

14

Mijack washed immediately and told his wife to fetch his Sunday clothes and the new black shoes which had been worn about twenty times but which were still kept in the white box and the tissue paper. He put on clean underwear, buttoned the front and the flap in the rear, and then put on black stockings and braces and sat down to supper. He ate as he always ate. Then he told his wife to wash herself and dress up as much as she could. He told her to be quick about it.

Susie set part of the dish water aside. While she was upstairs, Mijack fitted the trousers and clean stiff shirt and wrapped the white collar around his thick neck and shoved it down until it met his shirt and squeezed the hat on his brow so that his head was exactly even on all sides and went to the closet and got out the big lantern and shook it to hear how much kerosene was inside. He then reached down a small lard can from the cupboard, took a dollar from it, and put the dollar into the bottom of his pocket.

Mijack walked to town, the lantern sometimes swinging in an arc at his side, sometimes held out before him. He did not look back for his wife. He could tell she was near because their walking was the only real sound in the darkness.

Mijack entered the building, looked around until he was familiar with the contents of the room, blew out the lantern, placed it in front of a row of straight-backed chairs, and motioned for his wife to sit beside it.

He remained standing, hat clenched in both hands. He did not notice the magazines on the table in the center of the room, but did go to the wall, read the diploma, and then returned to the identical place where he had been standing. Ten minutes went by and the hat was not shifted an inch in his hands.

"Make a noise," he said.

His wife did not know how. He rapped on the table. His wife was looking at him with concern.

"Are you sick?" she said, timidly.

She was afraid. She was afraid because she had never known him to be sick. And she knew how he was when he did not feel well.

"Hah!" said Mijack, turning his eyes upon her.

Susie looked at him, then clasped her hands together. Her mouth became a straight, thin line.

Mijack went into the office.

Susie was left sitting alone, her knees making identical bulges in the dress cloth, her legs drawn tight against the rungs. The lantern was no longer warm when she lifted it to the chair beside her. Then she looked about, her eyes behaving as if they were studying a very wide space. The smell in the room nauseated her. When the doorknob moved, she rose and caught the lantern to her and made her coat ready to leave.

Mijack took the lantern from her and grasped her by the arm.

"No," she said furiously. "No."

Mijack led her into the office, Susie holding her coat tight shut with both hands.

"You do as he tells you," said Mijack, "or I'll come in and see to it you do."

Later, Susie emerged, her cheeks aflame, looking straight before her. She sailed out the door without waiting for her husband.

Mijack hurried after her, the lantern jingling. He stumbled down the steps and onto the narrow sidewalk, then turned and looked at the rectangle of white shining through the door, and ran back, fumbling in his pocket for the money he had put there.

At the corner Mijack found his wife, waiting.

"I'll never forgive you for this," she said.

"Faugh!" said Mijack, and turned from her and went toward the mountain.

He did not remember to light the lantern. When he did remember, he did not light it.

Susie had been a sullen girl of continuous, unspoken disagreement with her mother and sisters, but one who had done everything asked of her, and so it had been said of her that she was the quiet one, kind, forgiving. Into this had come a yearning for independence, beginning around her eighteenth year, beginning late, so mild a yearning that she had felt merely tired and uninterested after her sisters married. With a father and mother not so much aging as finding it difficult to take on extra farm work caused by the loss of two daughters, Susie had found these obligations hers and had accepted, changing only by becoming more possessive and authoritative, yet fully within the terms of obedience which had been the core of her education.

So that she had resented the arrival and the offer of Mijack as a further transgression. Then, under pressure of his personality, which made her life seem one of disgrace, she had reversed her allegiance. She had looked at the pale green corn in the fields, at the small, bitter apples in the orchard, and had known, although with a sort of anguish, that she did not want to see them ripen.

What she had desired or expected from marriage never became

clear to her, and, under the pressure of the constant and immediate demands and temper spells of her husband, had become entirely obscured. So she gave him that to which he was entitled, cooked according to his tastes, managed the household with economy far more stringent than Mijack felt to be necessary, sold eggs in the village, and did a vast amount of canning and preserving. She wasted nothing. If this could have brought contentment to Mijack she would never have thought otherwise than that it was contentment for her.

But he had insisted upon revealing himself.

He had gone beyond this, insisting on revealing her to herself, so that something she had scarcely known existed, vanity and pride, had been aroused. That her appearance had been, as she felt, ridiculed, made her cling fast to it and relate it to her moral being; made her feel that he was trying to disgrace her, he, who had disgraced himself; made her look upon Mijack and see the multitude of faults, the oldness of him, the sloppiness and foolishness of his ways, and conclude that she was more than good enough for him. The more he abused her, the weaker her respect for him became, the more nearly she became a match for him.

Yet this night she had been caught on one point where she could not defend, where the entire history of women was against her, where religion was against her. Earlier in the day, as she had bathed and washed her hair, then dried her head over the stove, she had felt an emptiness and loneliness, and had wrapped her hair so tight about that her forehead was flattened and her cheekbones seemed lean. She, who never took down her hair in his sight, had resented him as much as if he had been present, and had done no combing and no brushing.

This night she had been caught. Unnerved, frightened, horridly embarrassed during the period she was undergoing medical examination, even though she emerged furiously angry and indignant, she was not able to throw off the effects of having had her barrenness made apparent to her. It had been cast upon her in the most solitary manner, as clear evidence that her husband now placed the blame entirely upon her.

She could not be sure that the blame was not hers. She took small pleasure from his regular need.

It was she who had wanted to speak with the minister, in the hope that he might be able to advise them.

"The minister is only a man," Mijack had said, "and not the best of men. No, I will not have him speak with my wife on matters of privacy. Faugh, let us look at home, here where the blame lies. Here is our trouble."

This refusal to visit the minister, then his having taken her to a doctor, had appalled her. It made her husband somehow unknown to her, someone whom she could not trust even in the least things.

There had come to her also the realization that her husband was not secure, not the firm, steadfast man she had believed him. Already he had told her something of his past life which had shattered her faith in his moral nature. Now she thought him capable of such foolish action as leaving her and vanishing into another part of the earth. Formerly she had not believed he was strong enough to do this, but now she felt he was weak enough. It was a possibility which she did not fear and yet could not welcome.

Susie hurried upstairs and said prayers for the child which was not yet within her. The thin, straight mouth lost its rigidity. It was a personal terror, something bordering on the mystic, carried through generations of women before her, out of an age when there was neither lamp nor lasting fire in the long nights, when to be barren was a periodic hollowness. It was a personal dread which she related to her religion, to the vapor of her prayers in that cold room, a space wrapped in stone and silence and darkness, a floor that was firm and yet not quite level, so that she always felt lifted above the earth when walking over it.

She spoke her prayer in a whisper, remembering how Mijack had made an explicit request of her father to tell if her sisters had borne children, remembering the deep seriousness with which her father had considered the question and answered, remembering the grave responsibility which it had been for her to watch over children, her sisters and three little girls from a neighboring farm, remembering the gravity and the excitement which the approach of childbirth had always caused in the rambling farmhouse, the silence and the concern, the coming of farm women from all about to help with the cooking and cleaning, and the solemn, spiritual air of necessity which she had seen in the walk and the bearing of her father.

It went beyond failure. Mijack had issued a challenge, had succeeded in making felt the full obligation of womanhood and marriage. She needed to give him children to keep her head high and free of disgrace. She needed to give him a child as a final vindication of her own position, as a post from which she could renounce him, or at least hold enduringly her own moral level. For if she did not fail him in any of the demands or contracts of marriage, then his own failure to find happiness must be his own guilt.

She undressed and got into his bed and waited for him.

In the first years she had been encouraged to make herself attractive. She had hesitated, perhaps had failed, and so had refused. Now Mijack denied her the privilege of wearing the very gifts he had given. His eyes were not interested in her as they had been. He put burdens upon her, exercising his rights as ruler of the house more than formerly.

She drew the covers to her throat and waited. Her obedience was not out of fear. There was too much enmity in her to fear.

Mijack read until he was pleased to go to bed.

"Go on, get out of there," he said. "Go, go to your rug. I don't want you."

Susie looked at him astonished. He handed her the lamp which he had used to light a path up the stairs, and which he usually blew out on entering. It was burning high. And as Susie took the lamp, holding to it awkwardly, clutchingly, as if she did not know what it was, light flew against her face, and for the first time since their marriage he saw her eyes alive. He saw that she was finally deeply offended and shocked.

Mijack was ashamed, but could not retract and so was silent.

He knew too he was going to regret this. Yet somehow he was glad and drew an intense satisfaction from having committed himself, from having asserted a real feeling which had been abiding in him for some months. The time for forbearance was past.

Mijack looked at his wife, took hold of her wrists, and said with great earnestness, "We've got to reach some sort of understanding. I don't know what's come between us, but something has, and whatever it is, it can't be all me."

The walls of the kitchen had darkened, especially in the corner where the coal stove was. But the structure, having its many tiny defects shadowed, had more unity and permanency. It had the originality of having been determined by limitations of equipment and available materials, born out of its own land, and the distinct air of one man's own notions about particular things. There was no hollowness. In the making of the walls each stone seemed to have been selected for strength and for kinship to the stones on which it would rest and those it would adjoin.

"I know I've done wrong. But for God's sake, woman, stop abuilding on my mistakes—or we're both going to regret it all the days of our lives. I don't want that. You don't."

The middle room was better lighted than where they stood. There was no lamp in the middle room. It had the smell of wood burning and a little of the smell of trees and of greenery, and it did not have the crowded atmosphere, the pinched air, that cooking gave to the kitchen during almost all of the year.

"Why can't we get on better?"

Mijack gave his wife more than a fair amount of time; even then he continued calmly, almost beseechingly.

"Haven't I been just to you? On the whole? Don't you feel that's true? Say it. Now's the time."

Outside, the chicken yards were quiet, breathing off in faint driftage odor and warmth that a gentle rain had matted on them in the afternoon. The long, flat garden was bare, winterized, yet very distinct from the land about it, with a softness and an airiness and a yellowish shine in moonlight. Each year the plow had sunk deeper and the clay and stone had been hand-picked. The past summer it had been full and green. It had been dung-fed after harvest, and trapped against the southeast wire was a huge pile of leaves.

"Listen, I'm trying. I'm doing everything I can. But you've got to quit trying to bring out the worst in me. You—you know what my temper is, you know what happens when you keep prodding at me."

Mijack shook his head, despairingly.

"All right, we don't see eye to eye. We don't even begin to. But we can at least be decent, have some decency in the house. Oh damn, woman, you and your confounded silence! What the hell do you expect to gain by it?"

He waited, gathering to him the calm and composure he had so nearly lost. It did not seem to matter what course he took.

"All right," he said easily, "I'm going to keep right on trying. But one day—there comes a time when a man gets a belly full. Mind now."

Susie wanted to visit her folks.

"Go then, go," Mijack said finally. "Damned if I know what good it will do. Be damned if I do."

"None," said Susie, "if you think that way. But if I could feel you meant it, I'd be happier."

"Oh, hell, woman," Mijack said crossly, "I can't think at all any more."

He rose and went to the fireplace and kicked the andirons aside and held his hands over the flame. Yet it was evident the hands had no need of warmth, merely of occupation, expression.

"Go, stay, what difference does it make? With a miserable life like this. I'm not doing my work proper. I'm not taking the care. Not even treating you like I should. I begin to think it's not just you and me. I begin to think it wouldn't make a damn if we had *ten* children. Maybe we've just got a bad God up there. Maybe that's it. If He would—if He would command a pyramid!" Mijack said, his eyes scanning the column of the fireplace. "If he would say to me—but no, that's not his way. He has to deal like a damn robber and thief, in pestilence and boils, in plague and famine. He has to trick a man out of his life. I tell you I'm about through looking in His direction for anything but trouble."

"Shame," said Susie. "For very shame."

Mijack was silent for a time, rubbing his hands together in a manner which indicated they were too strong to ever hurt each other. He darkened the room by standing too close in front of the fireplace.

"Don't say shame to me," he said quietly. "I tell you I'm about fed up. I begin to regret the day I set eyes on this place."

He looked straight at his wife. His real meaning was unmistakable.

"Shame!" Susie screamed at him.

Mijack jerked up proud and erect, then held silence.

Susie picked up a plate and began vigorously drying. She made a distinct cackling sound, a nasty, tart, embittered snicker of laughter.

"All right, all right, you explain it," said Mijack. "Why do I work and save as I do? What damn good is all this plenty? The very food I eat sickens me. The meat is sour with fat. Whose fault is it, if it isn't yours and mine?"

Susie snickered again, and continued with her work.

"I tell you, wife, you don't know me," shouted Mijack. "I'm not the man who brought you here. You failed me. You made your flesh seem unclean to me. I don't know how it came about, but I know it better not continue."

Mijack wheeled and advanced.

"In the name of hell, do you *never* say what you're thinking? Do you find what I say so damn worthless you don't even bother to answer? What in hell *is* the matter with you?"

Susie put down the dish she was drying and then dried her hands also and stood before him exactly as she had the day of meeting, when he had liked how she held her chin high and looked straight before her. It was the same posture, an older face, one more stern and with less color. But there was still an uncompromising courage.

"Samuel Mijack," she said.

And it was two hours before she finished with him.

15

Irene went down to the Bluegill to get a drink of its strong, clean water, minted with cress. Raymond, folding the green and white tablecloth and roofing the jars and other uneaten picnic bits in the basket with it, did so quietly, unwilling to take any risk of breaking the even tenor of her happiness. His face still bore some of the same sterile whiteness that was in the college books he had been bent over all winter and spring, his arms and legs awkward from prolonged inertia on and beneath desks, his fingers twisting and flexing in strange movements they must have learned out of their own impatience while his mind was fixed upon academic matters. He appeared stunned. He had never dreamed that this was to be his golden summer.

The stream came down clean and clear off the cool mountain. Far above, yet less than four miles, the waters of Bluegill ran white with speed and reckless self-agitation over and among rock, not able to bed, not able to settle, plunging with too little weight to groove itself and secure permanent passage. There were yet a hundred turns and broadenings it might choose or at least reconsider, and if the strength of the spring, the cradle of bubbling water which was more important to the existence of the Bluegill than any amount of rain, weakened or shifted its forces, then the creek might lose its straight, eager plunge for the Susquehanna and meander like the weak trail of a urinating steer.

But in the valley before the river, where the land was earth and not stone, where springtime was glutted with brown-red water, where even rain could make etchings on the smooth soil, there the Bluegill lost its haste without halting, settled in pools deep enough to give it new dimension without the least traces of stagnation, and found time to frolic, time to investigate. Still it leaped easily into Irene's hand with the flap and the flap of small pan fish.

Narcissism was one of the possibilities afforded by the creek at this place where it curved like a thigh seen beneath a pale green light, a thigh bangled with small silver ornaments; yet not in truth, for it did not reflect with the accuracy of a mirror, nor even with the pleasing inaccuracy of a mirror in shadow stillness; did not photograph the limbs of trees strung with green, nor the sky across which clouds were dragging like a line of white kites in impudent behavior, nor the face of the girl who was leaning over it, her lips poised to drink, the nearly twin portions of her hair divided around her throat, already wetted at the tips. What she saw looking down was as startling as the minnows which had scudded away a few moments earlier. The water was doing an interpretation, one that made her eyes into long, dark ovals, her lips into red wiggles of laughter, her cheekbones faintly green; only her fingernails at the water's edge were reflected accurately.

It was a reflection in the sense of fantasy, one that avoided the flush along her throat and the alive searching of her eyes, and through elongation and faint green discoloration of her chin, forehead and the shawl effect of thinning her face which her long dark hair gave, sent not only into her eyes but against the whole surface of her face, like a cool, detached reproof, an image more pale and hollow than she had ever seen. It was more poignant to her because she could feel the rosiness and excitement which leaning over the stream forced upon her. It was more poignant because she was the betrayed and the betrayer.

The stones upon which Irene was kneeling were clean and bleached, tan ones with the calcium softness of hen's eggs, others looking as if they had been gently rolled in white flour, all with the rotund warmth and firmness which invites the hand to grasp and the eye to relax and the ear to be keen to the sound of water; one that had been inadvertently overturned was wet with dark slime, and seemed deeply infected. It was Irene who had turned the stone, through a fault of balance, and staring at it had given her a seriousness which she had dismissed with a quick, petulant frown, the way a shadow had earlier forced her to move into a new place, laughing at herself for being disturbed, waving her arms at it as if it could be frightened away as easily as a bird. Now, staring into the pool was giving her a deeper seriousness and a chilling privacy.

The picnic had been an enchantment, the food sweet to her mouth, the green and white tablecloth an adornment to the finer green of her dress where her knees had pressed into the linen. Now her dress was reflected as a faintly blackened silhouette and her enchantment was ended by what should have been a new enchantment. The young lady with hollowed eyes and withered, exhausted expression was giving pain to the deep, probing search of the real eyes above, arousing a fitful anxiety that made the hands clench the round, smooth stones to which they were fixed, and when she saw Raymond's nearness, or the threat of his impending nearness, not as a reflection beside her own, but as a long, thin shadow swinging in an arc across the whole creek, she shrank away from the water's edge and threw her head up, preferring to meet him directly rather than expose what she had seen in the silver-green bottom of the pool. But her eyes were not prepared, her face was not prepared.

So it was that Rowiger saw her more beautiful than she had ever been, far more than when she tried to be attractive, saw her crouched and startled, her lips still fixed to drink from something small, her eyes bright and a little wild. He leaned toward her as if to whisper something, but her face swung to meet his frontally, as if her lips and not her ears were intent upon him. Raymond drew himself stiffly erect. Muttering to himself, he went across the stones to the firm land and toward the oak where his coat was lying, pressed, matted, from where she had been sitting on it.

He shook the coat out and folded it over his arm.

Irene followed, creeping after him, her eyes bewildered, needing explanation for what she had seen in his face, for this renunciation of her. It was something new in their relationship. It was not the hesitation, the kindly awkwardness that made her so often feel a little sorry for him and for herself, but a sudden complete repudiation which struck through all her feelings. Her small shoes trod from stone to stone, making the identical mistakes of his, but with quicker recovery of balance.

"What is it?" she said. "Why did you . . . ?"

Her voice rang clear and imperative, for the previous hour had been passed in silence, in the tinkle of jars and silverware. They were never loud together. Their afternoons were whispers, tense whispers such as the discovery of three pale blue eggs swaddled in twigs in a low branch of the oak toward which Raymond was walking, soft whispers when the squirrel ran down the trunk to see what was going on below, laughing whispers when the sunfish hopped crazily over the pond, trying to capture a big moth. But the heart is a new being, without a past. Especially the heart of a girl.

"What is it?" she cried. "I was only looking in."

"I think we had better be headed back," Raymond said, over his shoulder.

Irene hurried past him and came to stand in front of the picnic basket. When he did not try to walk around her, when he looked at her and smiled, Irene saw that he was more like himself, that whatever had disturbed him for a moment was gone. And her own innocence had a shadow fall over it, and her eyes grew questioning in a way that she could not explain. She laid her hands against his shirt, began picking at one of the buttons.

"Do we *have* to leave?" She mustered a smile.

The sun was in the trees, its light smashing in many directions. The creek acquired its shadows all from their side of the bank, and only the tops of the stones were gleaming.

"Of course not," said Raymond, feeling through his shirt the young awkwardness of her hands, trying not to mind if the button came loose. "Not until—not ever."

"Not ever?" cried Irene, suddenly delighted, thumping her hands lightly against him. "Oh, that's like—isn't that a beautiful thought?" Her eyes swept the sky, seeing not the blueness nor the clouds, but something that was never there, yet always satisfying in its absence. One of the fine qualities of her eyes was their habit of lingering on trees and water and sky, making their worthiness more apparent to those who were with her. "Then I have time to go wading!" she exclaimed.

"Then you have time to go wading," said Raymond, laughing.

She stepped away from him a little, and her hands began to twist water from her hair, first one side, then the other, leaning her head a little so that the drops would fall on the ground. She was unaware of the dark places along and below the shoulders of her high-throated dress.

"And I shall sit here and watch," said Raymond. "There is time for that too."

He spread his coat on the ground beside the oak.

But it was Irene who sat on the coat to remove her shoes. The gallant sweep of his arm which had led her to the coat made her feel a little self-conscious as she drew her stockings from under her dress and bared her slim feet and ankles. Yet she had done this quickly, eagerly, thinking of the water in the exact tenor of feeling in which she had thought of setting her ankles into the blueness of the sky, and it was not until she looked up at Raymond that she felt the nakedness and reality of her feet and laid her hands on them.

"I've never been wading," she said, her voice faltering. "Really, I never have."

Then she laughed about it, seeing it from a new viewpoint. "There's too many never haves," she said, tossing her head.

She waited for Raymond to step backward and give her more space in which to rise, but instead his hand was put down for her to grasp, and when she was standing she found herself airy and splendidly sensitive to balance. After her first step forward there rose a certain careless defiance.

"Why don't you wade too?" she said.

Raymond shook his head and smiled.

"Oh, come on, it'd be good for you."

"No," said Raymond. "Not today. It isn't like the blue eggs," he said. "It's something best when you do it alone."

Somehow his saying this chilled Irene. She had not wanted to think of it in that way. She had, since drawing off her stockings, wanted it to be more like when they passed a ball and got so excited that they sometimes forgot or defied the rules and scrambled for the ball, pushing each other.

"But I'll be watching."

"Yes," she said, joylessly, "you'll watch."

Raymond's eyes studied her.

"Not if you don't want me to," he said. "No, the dickens, I shall watch you all I please." He gave her a little push toward the creek.

Still Irene hung back, looking at the stones over which she must walk.

"I won't go either, then. I wanted you to go."

"Ah-h, very well," he said, and began to roll his trousers. "How obstinate you are sometimes!"

Raymond escorted her across the stones, her small feet perched on the rounded tops while he scuffed and scrunched along. In the little hollow that was almost level with the creek Irene began to feel cool air around her ankles and a vague roominess in her skirt. Raymond reached the edge a moment before she did. He let go of her hand and began to roll his trousers further and untie his shoes. It was in being released that Irene had fear which she had not had earlier, and it came to her as loss of balance, and she caught his elbow and clung to it, even though this made getting his shoes loose difficult. Raymond managed to persuade her to dip her foot ballet-style into the very top edge of the stream, then freed himself from her, laughing, in spite of her protests.

"Go on in. It won't bite."

In sudden anger Irene marched three quick steps into the creek, tossing her head, then moved more hesitantly, and stood still, letting her body grow accustomed to the sensations which each step had altered. The water was deliciously cool. It made her teeth feel splendid. "Stay right behind me," she said, without turning, her eyes fixed upon the deeper place where the next step would take her, looking down through her own shadow, for the rest of the water was too bright. She had no dread of the temperature of the water, but a slight one of the pull of its passage around her legs. She had no real fear because she did not intend to go deeper than her knees. Skirt raised in a manner that allowed her arms to give a little extra balance, she took another step forward, bringing her legs close together. Where her legs touched under the surface, they were faintly new to each other.

"It's co-o-old," she said.

For she had moved forward again, using her toes as unreliable tentacles to keep a grip upon the bottom, until the stream swept past the hollows in back of her knees. Her hands grasped the hem of her skirt more tightly than they need have, and the new coolness of the air made her dress feel very thin and her underclothing tight. The water seemed to rush past swiftly, spangled with jumping light. She thought of the shore as quite distant, and of further movement as hazardous.

"Hurry up," she said, hearing a sound in the stream. "I'm way-y-ting."

In the beginning the sensations had been those of exquisite chilliness which had almost released her into nervous laughter. The current pulling at her had made her feel the slender strength of her legs and a new softness that was in them and a dawning fullness along her thighs. The water had had a clean fragrance that drifted downstream with the current. Everything her eyes had seen had a vividness of color and motion which was more convincing than what her eyes saw.

But that was gone. Her legs were thick with cold and a sort of deadened indifference in which the promise of further movement was only felt in the new part of her leg which would be wetted. She looked over her shoulder and did not see Raymond, and then saw him standing on the shore, his shoes still on. That the shore was much nearer than she had supposed, that she had counted distance in time, made her feel a little ridiculous. But she also felt betrayed and isolated.

"You said you were coming in," she called out.

"How's the water?"

"Terrible," she said, and he laughed. "But it is!"

The water was lonely and meaningless. Her legs felt stuck in it.

"Go on out," Raymond said. "Go all the way across. It doesn't get any deeper."

He laughed at her standing there, her skirt clutched not merely to prevent it from getting wet, but with a tenseness which made Raymond feel a need to force her to laugh, to laugh and forget this fragility which she was always letting dominate her. He wanted her to enjoy life.

"It's not cold," he said, putting his hand in the creek, then holding his pocket open with his dry hand, and with two wet fingers drawing out a handkerchief in a long endless white plume.

"You're mean!" she said. "You promised."

"I'm mean," said Raymond, nodding his head, laughing.

Raymond seemed to stand high above on the shore, near, but a little too distant to see the fineness of his features, so that he seemed to Irene to be merely staring down on her and laughing at her. She felt now the damp blotches on the shoulders of her dress more than the water swirling around her legs. The wet ends of her hair felt heavy. "Don't laugh at me," she said, taking a step toward shore, finding return more difficult than it should have been.

Usually his watching, that warm kindliness in his eyes, was one of the things that made her enjoy being in his presence; sometimes it even made her show off a little, but now it was painful to be exposed to his stare, almost a bit frightening.

"You're going the wrong way," Raymond said, and instead of drying his hand, he used it to splash a little. "Oh, don't!" she said, petulantly, moving another step nearer shore. When a group of almost white drops came high, toward her face, she put her hands up to protect herself, and it was not until the drops had all passed, none touching her, not until she felt the stream pulling at her with new force that she knew her skirt was wet, and in clutching at it stumbled, rushed toward the bank, refused the arm stretched to assist her. She ran across the stones, heedless of the slipperiness of her feet.

She was sitting beneath the oak putting on her stockings when Raymond reached her. She seemed to be trying to get her stockings on hurriedly, but could not because her legs were wet.

"I was only teasing you," Raymond said. "Don't be angry." He knelt beside her. "You'd better wait until you've dried a little."

But Irene put her stockings on and straightened them as best she could.

"Listen, you know I didn't mean to get you wet. You shouldn't always take offense so easily."

"Oh, it's not that," Irene cried out. "It's you—you always treating me like a little girl. . . . Little girl this, little girl that. I can't help it I'm fourteen." Her eyes were angry, resentful, and she was rubbing some of the wetness out of her dress with her palms. "I'd rather not see you any more ever."

"I feel we've been very honest and open with each other," said Raymond, stiffly. "At least until now."

"Maybe you have. I don't know what you—I don't even know why you take me for walks and on picnics. You've never told me why you do anything. And yet you get me to tell you everything about myself, and I never know whether I sound foolish and silly, and if you're not really laughing at me."

"You know better than that."

"No I don't know," Irene said, shaking her head. "I know I haven't been honest. If I were to tell you the truth—oh, you'd just laugh at me."

"Tell me now," said Raymond, firmly.

"All right then. We'll see. I love you. I do. There! Now laugh, go on and laugh."

Irene looked out over the creek.

"Now I'm embarrassed," she said. "But I don't care."

"Of course you love," said Raymond. "And I'm very proud of you for saying it. And were you thinking I didn't? Look at me, Irene. I do. I do very much. You silly, wonderful, beautiful Irene, how could I help but love you?"

Irene had listened to his cool, faintly humorous voice while her eyes still looked out over the creek. She thrust her head backward against the tree and rolled it so that her hair sometimes caught on the bark. There was more wonder than happiness in her expression.

"I didn't think you could love me," she said bitterly. Her eyes fell upon her shoes, which were lying beside him, and they looked small and useless. Even the picnic basket seemed like some plaything which could no longer interest her. "And you don't, do you? Not really? You're only trying not to hurt me, isn't that it?"

When there was no answer, she sighed. "That's what I was so afraid of. That I am . . ." She let her eyes speak the rest, and then she said it. "That I am too young for you. And it's so unfair. I mean it doesn't make sense. It's spoiled everything, and it makes me wish I'd never seen you, never. It's my fault, I guess, but you made me get to feeling this way, you made it hurt." Her dark, grave eyes lanced the air with a swiftness that was quicker than sight could be absorbed. "I didn't want it to happen. Yes, yes I did, back that day when you walked me home through the snow, but that was before I knew you couldn't . . ."

"Irene, listen to me. I must tell you. You *are* too young. Far, far too young. And I'm both too old and too young." There was a bitterness so unaccustomed in his voice that Raymond did not know how to make proper inflection. "But that doesn't matter now. We'll have to take it as it stands."

"But why am I too young?" Irene whimpered. "That's what I couldn't bear. Not knowing why. Because you treat me—well, I'm not as little as you treat me, even if I don't know all the things you know. I remember when I *was* little you always used to be very serious and honest with me, and I was the one who was shy. Now I feel sometimes you don't want me to be honest with you, that you're ashamed of me. I wanted to be able to wait until I was seventeen or eighteen. . . . I thought maybe by then . . . But it's not fair to make me wait. I couldn't. I don't think. So I guess all you can do is just go away from me and not make it worse. I—I don't want you as a friend any more."

"But, Irene, how many times must I say it? I feel almost the same about you as you do about me. I love you."

Irene searched his face with her eyes.

"I'm not sure," she said, biting her lip. "If you really did, maybe this sounds ridiculous, but if you really did, it seems to me you would kiss me. Now there, that's the truth about how I feel." She watched him closely, almost accusing him, and even after she was certain enough to have tilted her head back and pouted her lips, she was not sure and was afraid of being repudiated. But his kiss was long and firm. And when his mouth was gone, his arms were holding her, and there was his chest to lean her head against.

134

"Do you believe me now?" he said, and after a moment felt her head bobble affirmatively. "Did you think I was going to say wait, wait until you get older? Why, that would have been ridiculous. I only wanted to give you time to be sure. I only did not want to rush you and frighten you. And we don't want to rush now either."

But Irene had her face turned for him to kiss.

"Am I too young?" she said, smiling, impishly, yet also with earnestness. "And may I put my arms around your neck? I want to."

"You most certainly are too young," said Raymond. "I don't like being kissed by young ladies who keep one eye open. And I don't like being rushed." But Irene snuggled against him and sighed, and he smiled down at her, and traced with his finger tips the lines of her cheekbones. There was a certain strain in his own features, as he was already considering what was best for her, now that this change in their relationship had been admitted. "Never mind," he said. "We'll do well enough for a couple of greenhorns. We'll learn all about this terrible old thing called love, and have some fun while we're at it. For whatever comes of it, we won't get hurt, I promise that."

Irene rubbed her face against his shirt. "I'm so happy," she said, "I can hardly listen to anything you say."

"You listen for a minute. We mustn't think of love as always kissing. You see, it's mostly the same kind of fun and happiness we've been having. Only we didn't admit to each other how we felt, that's why it hurt." He began to put on her shoes for her and was awkward at it, but she leaned against the oak and offered her feet. "We'll have fun, picnics and walks like today, and we'll go swimming, and to the carnival next Friday, Saturday too if we like. And then we'll have this new feeling for each other, as something special besides." Raymond was the more excited of the two now; it seemed to him possible that this had been the best thing that could have happened. When Irene was prepared to walk, she held forth both hands, a gesture which she had never been free to use with him before. "Now," he said, "let's go back the way we came and take our good old time." They did. But first Irene let him see her reflection in the Bluegill.

Raymond Rowiger liked the young girl enormously. He was doing the best he knew how, bringing her gradually out of the cocoon of seclusion, without exposing her to harshness. It was sometimes a little painful for her—it had to be. His heart never misgave him. Her love was not difficult to manage, there were so many innocent ways of entertaining her.

135

He enjoyed the picnics. The sandwiches tasted as if a young girl had made them. The basket was full of bright colors, of fruits and cold meats and salads which did not always complement each other in taste, but looked wonderful. He would pick pebbles from the stream, wetting his shoes, sometimes demonstrating the difference in water flow, the whole alteration of beauty a single stone, placed exactly, could make.

He coaxed a wren to sit in the palm of his hand. It was the first time in his life that he had been able to do it.

Irene wanted to hear him talk. He told her things out of his own experience and put them into short tales. He sometimes found a sort of glee in talking to her. The tone of his voice would begin to sound pleasant to him, and he discovered that he was interesting, that he actually did have some originality.

When she was full of bits to tell, he would listen attentively, not always with deep interest, for girls are full of trivialities; and when they are in love and loved they are not selective in choosing from among their endless enthusiasms. Irene seemed to wish him to know everything she had ever felt or thought. She did not seem to realize that an experience had to be carefully expressed in order for him to enjoy it as much as she intended him to. Yet she was so astonishingly direct that often he caught something even finer than what she intended him to have. She made herself loved by not knowing how to reach him.

He would have preferred to keep their relationship free of caresses. For that his heart sometimes misgave him. He knew that all he must ever say was, "No, Irene, no," and not even their hands would touch again, unless he initiated the gesture. Yet it was the fragility of her love, one of such intense faith and expectations, which kept him from doing anything which could hurt her.

He knew that she had restored his faith at a time when it had threatened to wane. He knew that she had given him manhood. He decided against politics. He decided to keep his appointment to teach in the fall.

It was his golden summer.

"But what if I'm the one to blame, Father? What if I love him?"
"Then you must wait," said Mr. Lang.
"I am waiting," said Irene. "I'll wait and wait. But what's so wrong with it? What makes you frown? Oh you're both that way, he's as bad as you. I can't see what's so terrible."

"I didn't say it was terrible," said Mr. Lang. "It isn't. I admit I'm surprised to find that you're in love, but I'm not upset or angry about it. I'm interested in seeing that you don't make a mistake. If you were hurt, it would hurt me too. I'm also regretting that I have failed to do for you and with you many many things. Irene, I said I trust you, but what a father really means when he says that, he means also that it is his hope that his daughter trusts him, trusts what he says as coming from the heart and as true—and, Irene, you ought to trust me. I've tried never to give you reason not to."

"I trust you," said Irene, "only—only I trust him too."

"Then I'll say no more. I'm satisfied with that."

Irene went to her father and put her hands on the arm of his chair. She looked at his face and felt returning to her a bond of closeness which she had for a time lost, or not needed. She sensed that here was something stable, something that had no fears and torments. It did not make Raymond seem less tall or less important to her, but it made her realize that her situation with Raymond was not secure.

"Father," she said, "can I tell you about him? Can I tell you why I like him so much?"

Mr. Lang smiled and nodded.

Irene curled herself on the floor at his feet and spoke, at first hesitatingly, sometimes looking out of the window, sometimes drawing invisible designs on the floor. Mr. Lang did not urge her and made as little comment as possible. It was one afternoon when his reserve allowed her to get nearer to him. They arrived at a renewed understanding.

16

Raymond arrived for dinner. He was wearing his best suit, a white tie, and his shoes were polished.

Irene had wanted this opportunity of pleasing him by fixing dinner for him.

When they met at the door she was quite excited and flushed.

There were five roses in a small blue vase on the little table in the vestibule. She took a white bud from where it was hidden in the vase, leaving the five roses appearing as nicely as before, and Raymond put it in his lapel. He had to draw his chin inward and higher to see that he was doing it properly, and he worked at the lapel quite some time before he would accept the pin she was holding toward him.

But this stubbornness only made her somehow glad he was tall.

"Has your father spoken with you?" asked Raymond, in a rather businesslike tone.

"Father will be all right," she said, after the longest time of studying him and deciding. "I'm sure he understands and will be gentle with us." She led him into the parlor and then seated him in a chair, which definitely did not improve his mood. It was one of those soft, cotton-felt chairs which invite relaxation. "He saw me fixing the roses and running around the house. We may have to"—and she hesitated, giving her eyes an opportunity to retreat "—put up with a few smiles and maybe even—but I'm sure nothing very embarrassing."

The tone of her voice indicated that she believed they should have enough strength between them to endure a little embarrassment, and that she was frankly looking forward to enjoying it.

The parlor had not been a good choice. It was a room of many memories for them both. They were accustomed to each other in the fields and hills, under the open sky, so that the walls acted very much as if they were sitting with their hands over their ears and at the same time shouting at each other.

"Mother and I have had a quarrel," said Raymond. "She told me I'm not going to have a future if I'm not careful."

It was seven months since a casket had been in the parlor, and the chairs and furniture had never been replaced exactly as Mrs. Lang had always kept them, and on the carpet there were darknesses which revealed the slight fading which the central portion had. The atmosphere was marked by something else, not dust, not a failure to maintain her standards of cleanliness, but a slight inaccuracy in reproducing the manner in which she had maintained the house.

"I felt so helpless standing before her in this suit and this," he said, flicking the white tie.

The suit had been his graduation present.

But it was his flicking the white tie which struck at Irene more than anything he had said.

"I took a long walk to think over more calmly what she said to me," he said. "And it didn't do a bit of good."

He shrugged, as if to show his present condition.

"And she's talked with your father," said Raymond heavily. "That's the worst of it."

Irene studied a moment.

"I'm sure it will make no difference," she said. "It might make him treat us even more nicely."

"It might," Raymond admitted. "But you can't imagine how my mother talks to people. She puts it on the line."

His hand made a gesture as if to indicate that he was severely understating.

Irene could not understand the grudging respect which was in his voice too. "It will make no difference," she repeated, this time firmly.

She was beginning to feel a little need for concern about Raymond if he met her father as he was now, but not if he was straightforward and loyal to her.

"Maybe not," said Raymond. "But we can't avoid the fact that he knows and that he's been told in the worst way possible. I find it hard to face him."

"You needn't," said Irene softly.

"But you don't understand," said Raymond. "I didn't want you brought into this. I want to do what's best for you."

Irene looked at him, her eyes alert, almost accusing. She sat a little stiff, with her arms drawn tight against her, as if chilled. And then suddenly she relaxed again, and more completely placed herself at his disposal than before.

"Would you like me to talk to him before dinner?" she said quietly. "Or should we have dinner alone? Would that be better?"

"Of course not," said Raymond. "I want to see him. I want us to have dinner exactly as you had planned." He looked rather searchingly at her. "I'm only trying to prepare you for a possibility. I really would like to get everything out in the open now, only I feel so awkward in these."

Again he referred to his clothes, but Irene was not sure he did not also mean the white rose in his lapel.

"Raymond," she said. "I love you."

She said it very carefully, as if explaining something which he might not understand, or had failed to remember.

But when he stood she saw that his confidence had returned and that he was not going to fail her. The dinner began to take on for her an attractiveness which made her own preparations for a nice little occasion in which everything would be handled beautifully and perfectly seem foolish. Presenting Raymond to her father in this situation seemed to her much finer. She saw both Raymond and herself as made of more sensitive and dramatic proportions than the people of the world around them. They would refuse to deal in anything except truths.

Raymond had mustered the courage to go forward and meet the situation, even though he knew it to be much more serious than she supposed. In a very real sense he had never lacked the courage to meet any situation which involved Irene, but he was more skeptical about their having much success. It seemed to him the worst possible time to encounter Mr. Lang. His mood was not the best sort of preparation for what he might have to face. He was acquainted with Mr. Lang and knew him to be liberal and sensible in his thinking, but Mr. Lang was more than thirty years his senior, and acquaintance was often a handicap in a matter of personal importance.

He was relieved when Irene, after stepping into the office-study, departed as soon as Mr. Lang brought a chair into position for him. He felt more capable of dealing with Mr. Lang alone, without consideration for Irene as an added weight. It was his fault that they both seated themselves at the same instant, and it gave him a premonition of having made a very bad beginning.

The two men sat in the leather and wood chairs. The afternoon brightness had died, leaving the calm, clear color of early evening on the windows, so that it was only a little surprising that the room was no better lighted. Mr. Lang expressed the thought that this room was always more comfortable than the parlor, but that he had never been able to decide whether that was true, or only a personal fondness. Raymond found the room had a too businesslike appearance, and was surprised, almost startled, to see that the afernoon had so completely passed in the short time since he had been outside walking along the streets.

Mr. Lang mentioned several new books which he had added to his library, pointing accurately to the position of each in the wall casement, without rising from his chair. The direction of the arm was vague from where Raymond was sitting, even when Mr. Lang made an adjustment in recognition of their differing positions. Raymond scanned the whole shelf, feeling even a little more isolated than before. Mr. Lang chided him gently for having failed to borrow any of his books.

"I ask so few people to take that liberty," he said, "that I feel embarrassed when they fail to do so."

Raymond had by this time begun to suspect that Mr. Lang was not going to say anything. It was of course impossible to be definite about a matter as delicate as this. He had at other moments an almost sickening sensation that it was by silence or by even ignoring the situation that Mr. Lang hoped to deal most effectively with it. Raymond was aware of a sensation of relief and reprieve, a gladness to find that Mr. Lang was at least not going to be clumsy, and yet this made him distrust the strength of his own argument and made him retain a stiffness and formality which he believed might precipitate additional difficulties.

Irene brought in two small glasses of wine. The glasses were chilled. She behaved as unobtrusively as possible until the wine was served, and then, perhaps noticing the strained air which existed in the little room, or perhaps only from the lightheartedness which being alone in the kitchen and preparing dinner for two people she loved had restored in her, she sat on the arm of Raymond's chair and coaxed a taste of his wine. Raymond looked at Mr. Lang before he allowed his hand to be raised. Then, as if to show that she had only been teasing him, she disregarded the glass, kissed him along the side of his forehead, and skipped out of the room, laughing. It was as she was walking along the hall toward the kitchen that she became thoughtful.

Mr. Lang seemed to be put in good humor by it. But as he noticed the young man's continuous seriousness, he put aside his own pleasure to make Raymond feel at ease. The conversation under these circumstances had to be rather intermittent. Raymond, suffering from embarrassment, and, perhaps more correctly, resentment that Irene should have chosen so inappropriate a moment to interfere with the gradual foundation which had been building, was a little angry with himself, because he knew that in another sense Irene had offered to place the truth before her father as simply and honestly as possible, and that it was he himself who had failed.

He found himself saying that he had decided against the offer made by Mr. Tad Stevens. He had decided against politics. No, he was not at liberty to say what he was going to do. He was still uncertain.

Mr. Lang did not inquire further. He said merely that staying out of politics was almost certainly wise, but seldom possible. He went on to illustrate how he had been gradually drawn into the political affairs of the village, until it had actually become an encroachment upon his personal life and his business. "Now," concluded Mr. Lang, "the only thing which encroaches on me, and that very rarely, is time."

Mr. Lang talked very carefully, with the sort of kindness which he had always had when talking with his daughter, trying to show events in a manner which would invite interest for the events themselves, rather than for himself. But Mr. Lang found that his conversation had come to a complete end, that, if there was to be further conversation, he would have to take the full responsibility upon himself. If he showed impatience, it was when in taking his pipe down to refill it, he instead put it aside, on the arm of his chair.

"Raymond," he said. "We are all friends here."

His voice could be taken as nothing less than complete sincerity. Yet nothing else he could have said would have shaken the younger man as deeply. The whole basis for Raymond's formality was swept aside; it also put him in a position which seemed to be untenable. There seemed to be nothing left except to make a full confession of the cause for his behavior, of presenting to Mr. Lang the relationship between Irene and himself and of asking for approval. It went so deeply into Raymond as to touch upon the almost obscured fact that he had not had a father since he was a very little boy. There was also the curious sensation that completely honest explanation of himself and his situation would have in it some of the elements of a betrayal of Irene.

Mr. Lang, seeing that his intention, which had been to put the young man at ease before they did become too much at loose ends, had gone astray, went against himself, and, grabbing up his pipe a second time, tamped tobacco in it with unusual vigor. He instantly regretted a gesture which he knew would have displeased his daughter if she had been present, and letting the room be silent only for as long as it took him to light his pipe, said, "I suppose I am at fault. I suppose I have lost touch with what interests young people these days. If so, I ask you to forgive me."

But then they were summoned to the dining room. Irene had on a different dress and her hair looked freshly brushed.

There were tall red candles on the table. Already a dribble of tallow had made a red mark on the lace tablecloth.

142

Mr. Lang took his usual place, but asked Raymond to say grace, if he would.

Many of the reflectors had been taken out of the room by Irene, so that the candles drew attention to themselves and the table, rather than to twinkles and flickers in mirrors. There was greenery in excellent and simple display, and a faint scent of summer pine, the needles of which glowed darkly in the inconstant light.

The dinner was excellent. Raymond was the only one who did not eat a generous portion.

Raymond knew that he had been treating Irene differently from when they were alone. He knew that he was wrong in doing that.

Irene, in the beginning, had been in sympathy with him. She felt his mood with a tenderness which she did not try to hide from him. And when she saw him trying to meet her fond glances with equally fond ones, his failure to keep brightness in his eyes only roused her hopes. It did not greatly bother her that he had taken little notice of the white scarflet which she had put about her throat, or the care with which she had brushed her hair. It did not matter that her dress had been chosen in the bright late afternoon with her eyes half closed so that she could recall what would be suitable for candlelight. Or that she had hurried into the garden, wanting violets, but having to settle for mignonette, which she had folded in among her clothing. Or that she had tried to make the dining room smell of green wood.

But when she sensed that he wished her not to bring into the situation difficulties which could be avoided, it brought a slight flush to her cheeks. She began to try to tempt a little gaiety at the table, to create an atmosphere in which Raymond could see and feel security, and perhaps be led to join them. She could not help but be proud of her father's behavior toward them, and it was imperative that Raymond be in better spirits when she presented her surprise to him. Her eagerness for every moment of life, with brilliant intuition which allowed her to be intimate and yet preserved her from ever disgracing herself, made her feel angry that he should discourage her from being attentive to him. One of the most important intentions of the dinner had been to show to her father that Raymond loved her. It seemed to her that remained the surest way of attaining real understanding.

Mr. Lang was cordial with Raymond.

Irene began to clear dishes from the table.

Mr. Lang smoked and asked Raymond a number of questions about college.

Raymond gave very civil answers.

Irene was taking the last of the dishes from the table. She decided not to bring in her surprise. She would have to give it to Raymond later, when alone with him.

"It was very good," said Mr. Lang. "Especially so."

Raymond flushed.

"When I see flower petals strewn across the floor," Mr. Lang said, leaning toward his daughter and sniffing. "Yes, as I thought," he said, although he had been unable to smell what he had been seeking, "I can hardly remain in doubt as to what my daughter thinks of you. Even if she had not already told me that she is in love with you." He smiled. "Tall candles and a white rose. Could a father pass those by?"

"I never told him you knew," said Irene, lowering her head. "I told him you might know, but not that I'd talked with you."

"Very sensible," said Mr. Lang. "And I understand better now why Raymond and I had a little difficulty getting our thoughts together earlier this evening."

His pipe, he discovered, had gone out. He held a match in the sidewise fashion of a man who has been accustomed to lighting his pipe by holding a straw into the fireplace and then swinging it very carefully to the level of his eyes.

"My daughter believes you love her, and that you seem to feel there is some complication because of the difference in ages. It sounds a little foolish to say it—we all really know there are certain impediments to marriage now. There are very definite ones against a false friendship. But so far as I can see none whatever against your loving each other."

Mr. Lang made those quick puffs on his pipe which reassure a man that the flame has not been merely a surface one.

"My mother married when she was fifteen, and I in the same breath confess I should not like to see my daughter marry so young as that. I would feel justified in asking her not to. But at the moment we are not faced with anything more difficult than a young woman who loves and does not want to be ashamed of loving. . . . It seems to me, Raymond, that could be your case also."

"Has my mother spoken to you?"

The thought had just come to Raymond that perhaps his mother had not been to see Mr. Lang. It might have been merely a threat.

"Yes . . . And I had to put up with a lot of nonsense," said Mr. Lang. "But that business—that's of course your affair. It could—con-

ceivably—become a problem to Irene. That too is in your hands."
Mr. Lang endangered one of the candles by accidentally blowing
smoke across it. "Basically, it's rather unimportant."

Raymond seemed depressed by this information.

Irene became more and more aware that her father was on their
side, that he, like herself, saw no impossibilities in their circumstance.
She had believed all along that he would not oppose them, but that
he would go so much farther, would try to bring Raymond even
closer to her, was a surprise.

"Those tomatoes," said Mr. Lang softly, "I've had my eye on. Now
they're gone and I have to admit none of us much tasted them. Gone,
along with the trouble and preparations . . . I've never seen Irene
happier than in recent weeks. . . . Her happiness means a great deal
to me." Mr. Lang hesitated, then said, "We *are* all friends here, Raymond."

Irene smiled. She began to suspect that Raymond was pleased,
only, as he so often did, hiding it, holding back until he could share it
with her alone.

"If I considered this an infatuation," said Mr. Lang, "I would
tease you, I would manage to make my daughter blush and tell her
she must not mind a little praise from her father. I would do this because an infatuation should be enjoyed and at the same time ended
as promptly as possible, since it only confuses a girl, or a young man,
about love."

The candles had lost their slender points but were still tall. The
light was a little above their eyes, so that they had to regard each other
from beneath it. The tone of the conversation remained the same
throughout, serious, not formidable, pleasant, not humorous. The air
which prevailed was thoughtful, considered.

"If on the other hand I considered you a friend and nothing more,
I would tell you I'm grateful for your having taken an interest in my
daughter. And then I should have to tell you that your friendship was
threatening to do more harm than good and that it would be better if
you did not return.

"I could have made you more comfortable this evening. I could
have avoided—or you could have avoided it. But, feeling we were
about to create differences which ought not exist between us, and because my daughter is on the verge of being made very unhappy . . .
I hope, Raymond, you will not think ill of me. It's never very good
for a father to risk touching his daughter's heart, and when he feels

loved, as I do . . . More directly between you and myself, Raymond, I like you, and when I see my daughter love someone as she loves you, I find I'm instantly prejudiced in your favor."

Mr. Lang waited, studying the young man with care.

"But I owe it to you as well as to both of you to admit I suspect that you do not love her. I suspect you are not in love, but strongly on the side of love. And since I haven't the slightest notion of how that difference can be determined, and since you have both had more than enough difficulties already—and since perhaps that difference should not be determined," said Mr. Lang, with a reach of thought which surprised himself for a moment, "I'm going to leave you, with your permission, and read a bit. I shouldn't like to get out of the habit at my age." Mr. Lang rose. "I hope, Raymond, you will never feel you are not welcome in this house."

There was silence after Mr. Lang withdrew.

Irene sat looking at Raymond, her eyes gay, almost mischievous.

"Now that's over with," she said. "We don't have to worry about that ever again."

But Raymond just looked at her. "Yes, over with," he said, pushing his chair away from the table. He went to the window and stood looking across the lawn and the garden, though all he saw was vague shadows of the maples and a light down at the stable. He took the white rosebud from his lapel, studied it, sniffed at it, replaced it. He knew Irene was standing behind him for some moments before he turned to her.

Irene could not understand why Raymond still seemed to have missed what her father had been trying to say to him.

"He likes you," said Irene.

"Yes, he likes me," Raymond admitted, slowly, heavily.

Because there was honesty in his voice she was satisfied, and felt that he had been drawn closer to her.

"And I love you, love you," said Irene, rising on tiptoe, placing her hands against his coat, one on each side of the white tie. "More and more. Every day more. That's the way I feel about you." She straightened the rosebud and held a warning finger, that it should behave. "It feels so good to be able to have you in the house. . . . Now I won't have to wait until we're out in the woods to be able to put my arm around you, now we can walk along the street together, we can be in the garden without pretending to be so interested in the flowers. . . . Oh, I don't know, weren't we always sort of pretending before? I mean sort of ashamed to be like we really are?" When he did not

146

answer, she said, "Let's go out in the garden. Or at least on the porch where it's fresh and cool, and we can sort of listen to the sky."

She ran for a sweater and only threw it across her shoulders, then took him by the arm, drawing him toward the door. Suddenly he went quite readily enough, so that it was she who had to hold them up for a minute while she blew out the candles, except two which were near the window and which they might be able to see from outside.

It was darker outside than she had supposed, and since they had been sitting under candlelight, the adjustment of their eyes did not make the night much clearer. But she, confident, needing her eyes only for enjoyment and for Raymond, led him across the lawn and then fixed a place in the grass for him to sit. She too sat very quietly, looking far off above the shadow of the mountain, where the sky was faintly blue.

"Don't be angry with me for telling Father. I didn't intend to, not until the other day when he saw us—when you were trying to peek into the lunch basket and I kept swinging it in circles. . . ."

"I'm not angry with you," said Raymond.

"But don't you think it was best?" she said. "Don't you think we should have . . . ? I mean I liked it being secret, but I really feel so much better now, I feel as if we've found out we are going to have happiness, and . . ."

"It was best," he said softly, but still with heaviness in his voice.

The candles could not be seen, but the window was faintly lighted. Their faces had to hunt each other.

"That was no kiss," she said. "I didn't even feel it."

She was not angry. She was pleased.

She sat there counting her love by memories.

She had learned to dance.

She had learned to swim.

She had learned how to give herself gently into his embrace so that its brevity would not be painful.

The way they spread a tablecloth and sat opposite each other eating identical bites of identical food.

The hundreds of courtesies which, substituted for caresses, had the same joy and excitement as caresses.

The dark hollows in trees which their eyes and perhaps no other eyes had explored.

The summer was ending, the fragrance of things diminishing, part of their love was succumbing too. It was sad and painful to sit and think about something over which she had no more control than the fall of the moon beyond the horizon or the absence of stars. Yet it was not difficult. For she knew it was the beginning or at least near the beginning. It was only a little rest, a little waiting, before the steadier and warmer relationship between them came and pressed down upon them.

"I feel as if I'm falling in love all over again," she said. "Only this time on top of all I already have. It's such a funny feeling, the grass feels taller, and I keep thinking that I can feel drops of rain. . . . I don't know, is it only being happy, is it only because I'm with you?" She hesitated. "When we're out walking, and I come home and bathe and change clothing, I always have to smooth out the dress I was wearing and sniff at it to see if I can catch something which will make me remember better."

As a farewell to the past, an invitation to the new, she coaxed him to comb her hair, which reached now to her waist. She knew it was so wonderfully soft this summer that he could not help but feel a pleasant effect from touching it. Perhaps too he would better understand the faith she had in him. She discovered the mignonette in her pocket and brought it out into her hand and sat trying to restore damage which she had not intended. And she made him know, by the manner in which she kept drawing her shoulders and fixing her eyes upon him, that she was aware of how intimate they were.

Raymond knew it was not good for her. It made her think too highly of herself. But he felt that she needed to be drawn closer to him in order to explain what he knew must be explained. So he did not risk anything which would displease her, except his own seriousness, which he could not overcome. And when she sang to him, in a very quiet voice which let darkness call attention to sound, he had to listen to what was painful to him simply because it was so fine and so delicate. Her voice separated and spread the notes in a manner which made an easy, familiar tune new. It was like the difference between water poured from a cup and sprinkled from dipped finger tips.

Unable to fill the emptiness in his own heart, the longings of her passionate nature, the longings of his own less demonstrative self, he substituted a form of devotion, an attendance upon her. All summer he had brought her gifts of himself and of the world, had bowed before her wishes, urged her to be peremptory in her commands, so that he could better reveal the humility of his attentions. He would still wind garlands for her to choose from, would be servant, tutor, admirer and one who loved her, if by that he could satisfy her longings and intense expectations. But her eyes were on him, and in him were her expectations, and the role of the Magus would not satisfy her eyes.

In love, or on the side of love?

"Irene," he said, "your father did not tell everything."

"Oh?" she said from what seemed like far off, then nestled her head against him.

"I'm going to be disinherited," he said. "I'll probably have to go away from here—here where I want to stay, where I was born." He sighed. "Five years from now, if we still love, marriage could be easily possible, with the sanction of everyone. . . . And now I'm guilty of weaving a fantasy, now, not in five years, and my fantasy is your reality."

"Why do you have to go away?" said Irene, indicating with her arm the enormous freedom of the night about them. She was so accustomed to the warnings and worries which he was always finding, that they had come to seem to be almost a part of her love for him. And so her question had an air of being careless.

"My mother," said Raymond. "Perhaps the whole town. Perhaps even your father, in the end. Why do I have to go away?" he said bitterly, feeling very much older than she was. "Time and place, the very nature of life, myself."

Irene only nestled her head deeper against his chest, but this time with the unintentional intention of making him more aware of her and less of his own thoughts. And it was related to a time long and forever past when she had used to sit with her hands over her ears.

"No matter what I do now," said Raymond, "it can't be for the purpose I had in the beginning. It can't be for you, nor for me; it can only be for or against *them*." He waved his arm at the night. "I have no more freedom."

"I don't understand you," said Irene, sitting erect.

And she did not. She had fixed dinner, had worn her finest clothes and made herself as attractive as she could, and she had brought her father around to a point of view which was certainly favorable. She had kept her head high. She had put a rose in his lapel, herself in his arms. She felt the beginning of an anger with him, a more serious anger than she had imagined herself willing to feel.

"No, this time you don't understand. Can you hide in your eyes all the tendernesses you feel for me? Keep an appearance of casual interest in me?" He shook his head wearily. "Anything I do now is only a form of restitution. And anything you do is a sacrifice."

Irene did not understand. She only, seeing his eyes, sensed that

149

she might lose him. It struck her first as a bewilderment in which everything lost its value, everything except her love, which seemed to sit in her, motionless, isolated. She could not question being in love; at this moment she felt irrevocably committed for her entire life. She could not find the courage to avoid what was the only thing of importance to her, and she said, "Don't you want me? Is it me? Is it my fault?"

Raymond looked down at her.

"I have to know," she said. "You told me you loved me. Is that true?"

Raymond drew her into his arms, although she was unwilling and felt stiff and clumsy against him. "Oh don't!" she said. "Be you!"

"I didn't lie," he said, smoothing her hair and working his fingers until he could feel the small, firm head beneath. "I love you, Irene."

He bound his arms around her and his lips locked upon hers and he possessed her mouth. Irene felt the stiffness of his face pressing down on hers, and the sudden strength in his arms, a strength so wanted by her that his arms were almost weightless against her. She had no way of knowing that he was only making a desperate effort to arouse in himself the kind of love which she had for him, that he was engaged in a renunciation rather than an affirmation. Raymond did not know it either.

And so, later, Irene followed him to the gate. "Good night," her voice rang happily after him as he went down the hill. "Good night."

There was no snow on the earth, and there was no umbrella, but Raymond Rowiger walked down the hill with the same limping drag through the dry weeping of the crickets and the flinty and faint sparks of mid-August fireflies. A young man can feel very old in the summertime. A young man can feel a kind of age which is intolerable because it does not have its foundation in time, but in the secret recesses of his heart, where truth has become utterly confused.

He was walking, with no home to enter, no future to plan for, and no consolation except the love of a beautiful fourteen-year-old girl, a burden and a responsibility. He slept on the porch of his mother's house, and in the morning, when Mrs. Rowiger unlocked the door, after a brief conversation he was allowed to enter. He accepted the conditions which were imposed upon him for the sake of the girl. He accepted his failure.

The blackboard was clean, the floor was shining with wax, and the teacher's desk was empty except for a notebook. It was the opening day of school. The professor, modestly dressed in a gray suit and dark tie, was standing behind his desk, looking down at the students. He was calling seat numbers, and the children were responding with their names, which he was in turn writing in the notebook. He was wearing spectacles, and was either a little nervous or not accustomed to them, for he kept touching and straightening them with his hands.

When all the seat numbers had been called, there was still one girl standing along the side of the classroom, near the door. She was staring over the students and through the big windows.

"What is it, Irene?" said the professor.

"I'm waiting to be assigned a seat."

"You may have any of the vacant ones you wish," he said, waving at the various openings with his hand. "And if any of you," he said, indicating the whole class, "would rather have a different seat, and we can work it out, now is a good time. I notice that seat on the far side is larger than these down front. Perhaps one of the tall boys would find it more comfortable."

"I'd rather be assigned a seat," said Irene.

"Well, then, let's see. What about C-three?"

The professor walked down the aisle, smoothed the top of the desk.

"It has a few bumps, but I guess you can write on it."

Several of the students smoothed their desk tops, looking at ink marks and carved initials.

He began to make a few introductory remarks about the courses he would teach. He wanted to make clear what the purpose of each course was, why it was being taught, and of what use it would be to each of them now and later.

Irene sat erect behind her desk, her knees together, her hands clasped together. She seemed affronted by the teacher's presence. She eyed him coldly, with more poise, with more chilling effect, than a girl ought to have been able to manage. Settling in her seat, she faced the teacher with steady, almost bemused eyes, and was silent for the remainder of the class.

Irene waited for the students to file through the door. She went to the desk. "May I ask you a personal question?" Her voice was soft, almost with the tenderness with which she was so accustomed to speak to him. But she was not at ease.

"Of course, Irene," said Mr. Rowiger, removing his spectacles, smiling down at them, as if in apology for having worn them.

"Is this what you consider so—so beautiful?" Irene said, her eyes flashing. "This? I should have thought you could do better than this!"

Without waiting to hear what he was replying, she rushed out of the room.

The village of Coverly grew until it stretched almost to the mountain. It was becoming fashionable for the original inhabitants to move onto the hill.

Europeans were arriving in droves.

Negroes were finding more and more employment in the open hearths.

Real-estate values were beginning to be affected by new issues and slight pressures.

The Catholic church opened a parochial school.

The steel mill stretched long and dark on the river edge, expanding year by year now that Bethel had bought out Sylvania, and the rail steel from this plant was pouring into the four corners of the nation.

Mijack spent a few anxious days wondering what would happen and whether his job would be endangered. But work went on as before, without stoppage. Mijack's abilities at blacksmithing earned him respect. He was offered assistant foreman and refused.

It was at this time that Mijack discovered he was living on property of the Commonwealth of Pennsylvania. It was brought to his attention when Dauphin County attempted to purchase a strip of land on the opposite side of the mountain.

He was furious. He could not be convinced it was true the land was not his. He held that the state would never budge him from this land so long as he could draw a breath, and he meant it.

But in his heart he was sick. He could stand in the doorway and see houses below, still distant, yet not distant in the calculations his eyes made. The town was creeping nearer every autumn, and winter only brought a silence and a deceiving expansion of the slope below.

He gathered new dark rock from the mountain and mixed with it stones which hand plowing had uncovered in the years since the first garden. He built a stout and high wall. He decided what was not his property by looking over the land with his eyes, considering what portion he actually used, considering also trees and small oddities of the terrain, deciding in fact not only what was his but what he could not endure to see put into the possession of others.

He forged an iron gate, tall and of heavy bars, and when this was erected, his mind was more at ease. But he could not have the same feeling for the land, nor the same respect for the mountain. The wall was not to make good neighbors.

The village grew until its name changed. A referendum was held and Coverly became Nesquehon Foundry, a borough, with four wards. A wooden signpost was erected at each end of the town, and a municipal building was proposed. The main street was paved with brick and a track put in the middle, and soon a streetcar began to go in and out of town every hour on the hour. Harrisburg was made nearer. Workmen from the upper end of town began to catch that first car in the morning, leaving the streets empty until almost nine.

Mijack saw the world around him changing. He bided time, studying over it and his own situation. Then he went into the cellar and took all his money out of it and invested part in Bethel Steel Preferred, part in Power and Light, for he noticed the mill was using more electricity each year. The remainder he put into the bank.

His wife opposed all this. She told him he was throwing their money away.

In the seventh year of marriage Susie Mijack became pregnant, and when he heard this, they were overjoyed. He built a bed for her, larger than his own, with springs of steel coils, and made a crib for the child.

He went to a lawyer and made arrangements to buy the land on which he lived; when he found that it could be done, he cared nothing about the cost, and regained much of his former feeling for the land and the mountain.

His wife made herself a mattress of great softness, using the chicken feathers she had been saving for years.

They came near to that juvenescence of their marriage which they had denied themselves earlier. Mijack realized that his ill-temper, loneliness and despair had been for no more reason than that they had remained two in a house that was built for seven or eight. He told his wife enthusiastically that they must have many children now while it was still possible. He admitted he had never realized how much he needed a son and had never seen the possibilities, the pleasures, that he now anticipated. He saw how unbearable and domineering and even cruel it had sometimes made him.

Yet, even as he spoke these things, there was a hesitation, a wariness. It was as if he was willing to let the past be bygone, willing to form an alliance for the future, an alliance based upon the child and their mutual interest in it, but could not be sure that this would be agreed to. She offered neither consent nor refusal.

In these months, at his wife's urging, Mijack worked harder than was customary, seeking all the overtime he could possibly get, and was for a time in the employ of Mr. Lang, repairing the stable. Yet he would have refused employment from any other private individual in the town, and he even hesitated to work for Mr. Lang, whom he thought of with respect, except that his wife insisted there would be need for more money. She seemed to think of the child more continuously than her husband. They both had waited so long that they were fussy with each other, though unintentionally, and had the sort of haggling quarrels over little household matters which he had scorned to engage in earlier. Mijack worried about her health. He was continually having the doctor come to examine her. He urged his wife to go to the hospital in Harrisburg to have the child delivered.

Susie, on the other hand, fussed at him for spending unnecessary money and would not permit the doctor to give her a complete examination. She was furious with her husband when he made his own breakfast.

Then, later in her pregnancy, she became more irritable generally, and finding her husband willing to give up part of his domination, she took advantage. She let him do far too much around the house. She let him know every bit of discomfort that having a child in her made her feel. If Mijack noticed this, he kept silent.

She was especially worried over the investments.

"You shouldn't have risked our savings at a time like this," she complained. "You had no right. You can't never tell what might happen."

"Faugh!" said Mijack. "Our money's safe enough. It's my son I worry about."

For he never doubted the child would be male.

His wife saw this and had some anxiety, though she was sensible enough not to try to prepare him for possible disappointment.

Mijack took over outdoor chores and made life easier for her, allowing her to do no more than was impossible for him to manage, except for light household work, in which he would not assist.

The child was born. The day was easily remembered, for it was a severe winter, and three days later there was a snow of more than two feet—the biggest of the year 1907. There was a doctor attending. The child was named Isaiah Bartholomew Mijack.

154

Less than a year later there was a second son, Jacob Gilbert, and three years later, a daughter, Naomi Susan.

After the first son was born, the mother returned to her duties, nor was she provided with such comfort or ease for bearing the later children. Again it was as in the early years of their marriage, except that Susie had more to attend to and was more thrifty and that she had the pleasure of knowing that she had borne.

17

Irene graduated from high school at the age of sixteen. She was glad when the end of her formal education came. It had been impossible to pretend to learn what she already knew, and difficult to be interested in such commonplace banalities as history and mathematics. Her expectant soul had shied from the teachers and the plodding shallowness of the students.

After graduation Irene seldom parted company with her garden and her house. The hedge had grown tall. Not even unusual people could see into the garden. From the street beyond—Poplar Avenue of the borough of Nesquehon Foundry—the house had sunk to its windows in green, and there were small lichen smears on the brickwork. The garden was full of new colors, less flags and tulips; wildflowers had been introduced, day lilies, bellflowers, morning glories. There were peonies and the fragile, unpredictable delphiniums.

The poplar tree, which had aged in her childhood, now stood firm, entrenched against a new span of time, with the dignity of bearing of a man with graying hair and a still handsome face. Irene stood tall beside it, still slender, a strikingly beautiful woman, a little sobered in her attitude toward life. There were still moments when the tree summoned an enchantment, though now, with a firmer daily eye, she regarded it as a dear friend and a guardian of many memories.

The quiet of the garden was her favorite spot. She walked endlessly over the lawn and among maples which were beginning to blow out like green frogs. It was a modest little world, but her own. There was freedom to be alone and to converse with herself. She was so articulate with her inner emotions that she had lost the desire to communicate on a casual day-to-day basis.

The house she shared with her father, willingly. Mr. Lang had not changed after the death of his wife. He had worn a black hat ribbon and dark suits whenever he went outside for a year and a month, and in the first months had given his daughter looks of extreme tenderness and kindliness, and smiles that almost hurt. But he had never done anything which could have made Irene feel the difficulty of her situation and thereby made her unequal to it.

He had quietly hired a boy to tend the furnace, and a cleaning woman to lighten the duties of his daughter. The woman came Thursdays and made the house noisy and alien. In the manner that sterilization renders medical equipment unattractively clean, almost untouchable, so the furniture and floors looked after such a thorough application of soap, water and wax. The house smelled odd for hours and the panelwork had a sheen which gave unfamiliar dimensions to the rooms. Irene and her father kept out of the way as much as possible. Mr. Lang found a corner and smoked furiously, as if protecting himself from mosquitoes. Irene would put out of sight all dirty clothing and wash any dishes which were in the sink; she did not wish the details of her life exposed to the eyes of a stranger, a foreign woman, more than was unavoidable. Her own room was locked. She would not have anyone fingering her dresses or pushing or pulling her furniture about.

Except for that one day, Irene was mistress of the house. Mr. Lang was pleased with her, and approved changes in a manner which made them both feel they were sharing the house, that it was as much hers as his. His eyes showed gratitude and pride, and he was at the same time appreciative without being effusive.

Irene shifted dinner from five to six and served her father before setting a place for herself. She was an efficient cook. She knew how much to prepare in order not to have left-overs. The chairs had been moved to positions of more convenience and the lamps changed accordingly. It was not unusual for both Mr. Lang and Irene to have a book open at the far side of their plates and thus to spend several hours over dinner.

Late in the evening she would make sweet fruit tea for him to sip as he read.

Irene was not restless in this atmosphere. There were moments, of course, when she would go to the window and stare into the darkness, or walk on the lawn looking up at the sky, stopping to hear every distant sound. There were nights when she could not sleep and the bed would seem wretched to her legs; she would throw down the covers and push about the pillow. There were times when youth was such an alive sensuousness that she wanted to cry out against the wastage, the arid stillness of the house. But these moments were few, and she began to believe she was detached from the town and the world, that she from birth had been meant to live in tranquillity and isolation. Her beauty seemed to separate her even more from everything, making the sky distant, the lights of the town faint, and the beating of her heart a soft muscular contraction. She felt she had too much pride to seek again for love or step outside the life which she had retained here in this big house.

There was something even more adhesive which held her in suspension, in a state of pause that sometimes made her mouth suck violently at the air in order to feel alive. It was her father's health. It had been a special blessing that he had not changed after the death of his wife, and yet now, three years later, he was changing. He had not merely suffered sorrow, from which he could have sprung back with new vigor, but he had been left shaken and lonely. As is often the case with mild-mannered men who lose a companion who was vigorous and dominant, he had come to find the extent of his loss slowly and with fatal acceptance. He was like a man slowly falling asleep.

His daughter could never fill the emptiness which had been thrown over the house. Irene knew this. It made her more devoted.

Mr. Lang smoked more than he read or thought or attended to the routine of business. He smoked a great deal. The downstairs had a slightly cured odor that was so familiar, Irene could smell it, pleasant, desiccate, only when she came in from the garden. The odor of his office was of autumn grass which had been burning brown for the whole of an afternoon. Yet Mr. Lang never smoked upstairs.

Each of the five pipes on the shelf of his office had a different shape and design, but all were large, heavy and expensive. The rack which held the pipes in dignified, upright positions was hand-carved and had a minor history attached to it. One of Irene's favorite amusements was to guess which one her father would want and carry it to him. The pipes were awkward in her fingers.

She had them identified. There was a thick, squarish pipe that surely made him feel his teeth, a fat one that sat comfortably in the curl of his hand and emitted faint quivers of flame when he sucked on it too rapidly, and one with a long, straight and slender stem and thumb-sized bowl which had a tendency to go out, so that he had to re-tamp the tobacco with pokes of his little finger and pull the match flame deep inside the bowl before smoke would resume puffing cottonishly from his mouth.

But the pipe that could still make Irene giggle had a crook in it, the bowl resting on the edge of Mr. Lang's chin, smoke drifting into his nose, though he never seemed to notice. This pipe he generally chose when he was not doing anything. It had been known to hang from his mouth while he was dozing.

Often enough to make his daughter believe he desired a certain pipe for a certain mood, Mr. Lang told her to take away the pipe he was smoking. But he usually accepted her choices and once said, with a slight smile, "In a few more years you'll know more what goes on inside my head than I will."

But his choice in pipes, his choice in most matters, was guided by something more obscure than moods, by a pattern formation which had been settled during years of careless choice. The feeling in his right hand and a certain heaviness around his lips and the variable dimensions of his mouth often influenced him.

Irene did not quite know what her father thought about. It was for this reason that her respect and admiration could rise to such a height. Yet if Mr. Lang was not what his daughter thought him to be, he was a good man, more than commonly educated, with a fine, even temper and much kindliness and understanding. He would never disillusion her, for he remained shrouded in reserve, never entering into an intimacy which might have placed them both in the crisis of a less favorable light, but devoting himself to his books and his pipes, managing without trying to keep his illusion intact. He had no idea that he was a little mysterious to his daughter. He had no idea that his soft pronouncements had come to be something for his daughter to worship.

When Father was home, the house was full and warm, and when he was away on business, the house was desolate.

A man of thirty-five became a frequent visitor. Owner of the Nesquehon *Daily News* and the Harrisburg *Journal,* a paper of widespread circulation, he also owned stock in Bethel, in the new Gas Central, in Power and Light, and was reported to have holdings in other cities and towns. He was becoming one of the main supporters of the Republican Party of Dauphin County.

Father introduced him as Mr. Pierce, but several times within a single evening Irene heard him referred to as Henry. His father and her father had been friends, and Henry claimed to be able to remember her, holding his hand close to the floor, and wiggling his finger to indicate curls.

Mr. Pierce was broad of chest. His suits struggled with their buttons, cocking them at an angle. But this was true only of his fall and winter suits, and only when he sat in a chair. His summer clothes were admirably tailored, suggesting that they were a more recent addition to his wardrobe. His trousers were a bit suggestive of the contour of his thighs and buttocks, not because they were ill-fitting, but due to his habit of walking about with his hands in his pockets, the hands pulling upward so that the trouser cuffs were drawn far above his shoes, exposing his stockings and even occasionally garters. Although muscular, especially for his age and occupation, he was so genial and relaxed as to give the mistaken impression of stoutness. He had good taste in ties, his hair was neat and recently barbered and his complexion was pink.

Mr. Pierce was quiet, polite and formal. He did not devote much time or attention to Irene. Sometimes he would bring a little basket with cheese and wine, and the two men would sit and drink and smoke and listen to the victrola. Irene was invited, but if she declined she was not pressed. There were moments when she could feel comfortable in Mr. Pierce's presence, and on other occasions the relief of knowing he was not aware of her. The words and sentiments he did exchange with Irene were indicative in content and tone that he considered her an equal. He seemed to respect her and admired the few personal convictions she was willing to venture aloud. He made no attempt to force himself into her confidence.

Once he walked to the bookcase and looked at the rows of books and made comments and gave indications of interest. Irene told him which books were her favorites, and he nodded his head in approval and mentioned a few he considered worth her attention.

His hands seemed to have had special training, for the very manner in which he picked up a book and leafed through it was impressive. He inserted records on the victrola with speed and dexterity. His pipe was manipulated with an ease and grace that made it seem he enjoyed smoking as much as her father. That impressed Irene. His hands were firm and calm, the fingers large and slightly soft; one had a plain silver ring, solid, but not massive. His fingernails were clean and even, without the excessive whiteness of too elaborate care.

Irene was struck by a rather rare honesty. His eyes were never inquisitive. He seemed to admit that there were many things which did not interest him. He never avoided her, nor stared too intently, a fault she had noticed in younger men. It was annoying that people could not or would not refrain from peering into the very centers of her eyes. Irene felt no shyness when stared at, and it was pleasant to be beautiful, but she was irritated by the furtiveness of the glances some young men gave her, as if they were ashamed to look. Only Mr. Raymond Rowiger, besides Mr. Pierce, knew how to be pleasant.

Yet Irene caught herself committing a similar fault in watching and being too curious. For instance, this matter of his hands. Since she thought Mr. Pierce must be aware of and a little embarrassed by her curiosity, she tried to remember not to look, suffering the same sense of imprudent behavior as when she tried not to notice the crippled condition of one of her father's old friends. Whenever her eyes disobeyed and watched longer than was polite, she would blush a little, but look straight at Mr. Pierce to acknowledge her fault. Sometimes he smiled in a manner that made her feel he understood.

Irene resented familiarity and joviality. She demanded sincerity from every human being, and could forgive almost any offense before she could forgive someone for being insincere. It seemed to her that she deserved the same respect her father was given, deserved to be talked to sensibly and intelligently. This Mr. Pierce did.

Irene convinced her father that she enjoyed secretarial work, and she began to expand her activities. Mr. Lang, who preferred to spend more hours in his home and less in the factory, ceased to protest. He was grateful for the assistance. He knew too that the handwritten letters of his daughter were more effective than the bulletins of an office stenographer.

She would sit beneath a floor lamp, her father by the fireside, lifting the pipe from his mouth to say, "I'm going too fast?" or, "We shall respect your wishes in the matter which has been called to our attention," or, "End it with some form of thank you—not too warm," or, "That, I think, is enough for one night, quite enough." Irene would look up at her father and smile, realizing that he was the one who was tired, and sensing that she had for several hours shared his life in a way she had never been able to in the past.

Bit by bit, without ever seeing the persons or places involved, Irene came to know something of the tobacco business and to sense the growing pressure which was being exerted on small independents. Being too young to realize there were tides and trends in business which no individual could alter, she worked and worried more than was advisable. Her father's business was no longer profitable and if it had not been for his other holdings, he would have been in trouble.

Mr. Pierce had a definite position in this business picture. He was giving Mr. Lang a low rate on advertising, in return for which Mr. Lang gave him the support of his stock holdings in Bethel, and in several minor industries. Mr. Lang wished the younger man to buy into his factory, but Mr. Pierce again and again declined, saying frankly that he saw no future in independent tobacco. Loyalty to her father made Irene wish for the factory to continue to operate while he lived, since it represented so much of his life, but she was surprised to find her father bargaining.

Irene did not sketch or paint as well as she had in previous years. She was too busy to allow that to cause her much concern.

One evening, as Irene was writing, she felt a weight descend upon the chair back, and the chair began to feel a little unfamiliar to her. Then the chair was released and that unmistakable right hand was on the desk before her, the silver ring larger than she had ever seen it.

"You do everything beautifully," Mr. Pierce said.

The voice shook her with its nearness. Her head felt the breath that had contained the words, and warm afterbreath made an impression in her hair. The mouth that had spoken was nearer than any mouth had been since the end of her girlhood romance. She had the distinct feeling that if she moved, her head might be touched.

Her eyes were fixed upon the letter she was writing. Her hand had paused in the middle of a line and remained suspended, but now she forced it to go on with its task, forcing her fingers to do with difficulty what years of training had taught them to do automatically.

"My mother wrote a beautiful hand. I always envied her," he said. "But yours is superior."

Irene put the pen carefully into the well when she had completed the sentence. His hand was resting as motionless on the table as the inkwell, firmly supporting part of his weight. Irene blew her breath against the white sheet. Her eyes watched the ink strokes lose their shine. She was afraid to straighten completely because of her head, and of not knowing exactly where he was in relation to her. She tried to think what she would say, and then it seemed to her that she should have already spoken, and instead she put her finger tips on the back of his hand and moved the finger tips until it was clear to her how much difference there was between the texture of his flesh and her own. She sensed that it would be pleasant to touch him, but was not sure she ever wanted his hands to touch her.

Irene was composed and serene again. The brief contact of the small edges of her fingers with the back of his hand soothed her and put her more at ease than any words possibly could have. Taking up the pen, she continued to write, aware of Mr. Pierce's presence only when his breathing touched her hair. She heard him sigh, then walk away, and soon her father and Mr. Pierce were conversing. She finished the letter and began a new one.

It is never known how time passes. It is never known how much time has passed except by some vague feeling, almost a fear, and so it was that Irene knew not too much time had elapsed by looking at how much was written on the page. She paused long enough to listen to the two men talk. They seemed to be far away, and she was aware of and puzzled by the realization that within this house there could be enormous distances separating people. She sensed without looking around that everything behind her was changed. Not since she had been a little girl had the wall seemed so big, the ceiling so far above. She felt that if she were to shout, there would be a faint, faraway voice, a miniature of her own, not even her own.

As she heard the two men speaking, there came to her the impression that Mr. Pierce was a quite different man from the one who had leaned over her shoulder, a man she could not regard in the same manner as she had that unseen presence. She drew her finger tips gently along the surface of the writing table and was thoughtful.

An intimacy began to creep in between Irene and Mr. Pierce, scarcely real, so formed of intangibles, vague intonations and inflections. Quite possibly no more than her own imagination.

But before another month had passed Irene was quite certain that on Friday evenings he came to see her, not Father. It made her a little proud. She did not think it immodest to take extra time at her toilet and select a becoming dress and give her hair sixty brush strokes. She selected from among her shoes a pair with decently high heels, but selected them primarily to make her feet attractive. The best flowers in the garden were marked for cutting in advance, then saved until sundown Friday.

On one occasion Irene realized she had made herself too obviously beautiful. She had dressed in finery a young woman would wear only when going to a party or social event, and she was embarrassed, distressed, though Mr. Pierce said something to put her at ease. From that evening she dressed more casually, more correctly.

In her diary, written while she was in high school, was a brief note. *Love, how often I have thought of love, and of what it is. I think love is the inhaling of morning air above a field of violets. I think love makes my heart like a tall flower.* Now she wrote, *That was all nonsense. I admit I still don't know what love is, but I know what it isn't. Mr. Pierce has made that much clear to me. I suspect he loves me, but I do not hope to love him. I see him as a friend and a confidant. I see him as a sort of interlude.*

How it came about, Irene scarcely knew, perhaps out of the barrenness which was part of the house, but before long most of her best sketches and oil paintings had been shown to Mr. Pierce, and although he spent less time looking at them than she felt they deserved, his opinions were honest and tasteful. He admitted that his respect for art was greater than his knowledge. Irene had to smile. For his forefinger picked out with seeming carelessness all the best original brushwork, while the shadow of his hand hinted at less successful portions. Yet she decided then she liked this man more when he was not quite sure of himself.

One evening Irene gave him her worst paintings to criticize. Weeks of indecision were required before she could bring herself to do this, though she was certain it must be done. It tormented her to be so foolish.

"I have shown him myself at my best. Now I must show him the worst, and he will simply have to think whatever he wants to think."

Irene's worries and sufferings were not justified. Nothing happened to make her regret her decision.

"This painting," Mr. Pierce said, "is not as good as the one you showed me the other evening. The one with so much blue in it. The one where the grass is blue. But I can see how you had to do this before you could do the other."

That same night Irene wrote in her diary, *Question. What made me so concerned about those pictures? Why did I insist that he must see them? Why do I feel so relieved now that he has?* She was sprawled across her bed, biting nervously on the pencil, then looking at the indentations her teeth made in the soft wood. Unable to answer the question, she drew a line underneath, and wrote, *Important question.*

Am I merely flattered by his attention, or is there more to it? This ought to be given deep consideration, because in a way I am flirting with him and I ought not to do that. I must remember this is not: someone who would expect me to. This much I know. I don't want to hurt him and I don't want to get hurt myself.

Note. I've just thought of something. Living here with Father, I don't get to see many young men. I ask myself, if I did, would I still have the same interest in Mr. Pierce? I tell myself I've already had one unpleasant experience with an older man.

18

The model T made its entrance. For the next twenty years it would dominate the land, gradually flattening and paving it.

The New York-to-San Francisco telephone was not a dream. It would soon be a reality.

Immigration was at its highest. Foreigners were finding the hollow wax combs of honey which had been already eaten or was being guarded.

The Rotarians were about to begin.

McKinley was forgotten, and government of, by, and for the people was symbolized in a big stick.

Meat inspection, the Pure Food and Drug Act were resulting in fine print and the beginnings of modern advertising. Lies on bottles were being made into a mockery of American ignorance through the use of technical language. Doctors' signatures were making harmful and useless ingredients into blessings.

Gary and Frick had gotten immunity to buy the Tennessee Coal and Iron Company. There were great days ahead for U. S. Steel.

Bethlehem Steel had gotten the Greek naval contracts.

Roosevelt said, "The benefits of water power belong to the people." And grain mills and fishermen with nets and ice ponds were slowly choked out of existence. The wooden paddles turning on hard oak axles were about to suffer the fate of becoming picturesque.

The United Mine Workers were fighting for recognition. Court injunctions continued to be unjust to the workers. The fake cry, "Play it square," while the big stick put a few lumps on the heads of monopolists, playing into the hands of the corporations, making it clear to them that they were going to have to be tricky and dirty and fancy technically to retain the power which they had accumulated. The Hepburn Act curbed some railroad abuses on freight, but when a hundred and forty thousand Pennsylvania miners struck, because of wages, hazardous working conditions and abuses in weighing coal, T. Roosevelt threatened to use the Army to run the mines.

Nesquehon Foundry was beginning to feel the weight of power and money and men. Levers were being pulled in other cities and states which, passing through the channels of human rights with an indifference such as the world had never before seen, determined the lives of the workingmen, even to the smallest things, whether they worked Mondays or Sundays, whether they bought bread or beer.

The aggression of Bethel was slow and steady. Mark Stevens bested his father in the town elections, and although Tad retained control of the county, the end of his reign was in sight. More than half of the councilmen were favorable to Bethel, and Mark Stevens, with a cigar in his mouth and his pocket jingling with change, was often seen sitting across from Mr. Weaver, who always unhooked his pocket watch and put it on the corner of the table before he began speaking. There was an alliance forming between them.

Bethel obtained a favorable tax assessment, based on minimum value at the time of their purchase from the heirs of Selvinius, and were now trying to get the council to push through a lower and special rate which would give them freedom to expand. The public school was under a subsidy, theoretically called an endowment. Classical education was about to be brought to an end. The new education would be industrial arts, commercial arts, general and scientific. Women were taking over the elementary grades, and the new school board consisted of such men as Mr. Weaver, Mr. Stevens, Mr. Pierce and Mr. Dressinger, who had recently made a profitable sale of land to the company.

The two Nesquehon banks were fawning upon Bethel for its business and pay-check distribution. Foreigners were distrustful of banks, and to have or to appear to have the support and approval of Bethel was essential. There was a bitter fight going on against the postal savings system.

Speereero was playing his million-dollar game on the fringes of law. Earlier he had provided labor at a low pay rate, bringing the men in box cars, bunking them in the Bessemer, feeding them and collecting their pay checks, from which he deducted their debts and interest. But that had become too dangerous, for the workers were learning from the men who had arrived before them, and Immigration was tightening up against illegal entrances. Now Speereero was running a series of boardinghouses, and the Bessemer had become a red-light hotel where flesh was bought and sold: there were women who knew Pittsburgh, Gary, Chicago. Railroaders also were visitors.

Speereero's biggest game was in money exchange and in sending currency abroad. His notary stamp was active. He spoke eight languages and translated letters and offered his services to men who wished to bring their families or relatives from Europe. Without Bethel he could not have risen to the position of being the most wealthy and despised man in the town. And yet he was, in his way, the only clean man among them, for he ate out of the fat of the land and did not pick at the bones.

In her diary Irene wrote not merely facts, events, truths and honest questions about life, but also a great many falsehoods and snobbish remarks. This was not the real Irene, merely another shadow of her loneliness.

The world is an orphanage. I will keep close to my father.

No bee will sting me. I'm sure of it.

I was peeping in the window of the jewelry store this morning and suddenly I felt how precious I am. All the way home the groceries were too heavy for me to carry.

I have been reading my diary. This is not me. I'm not that snobbish. It must be I have moods which aren't really me. I felt as if I were reading about somebody else, somebody I couldn't even sympathize with. It scared me to know I had thought and written such remarks, and I checked the dates of entries, hoping they were all old, but some were surprisingly recent. I'm going to try to be more honest with myself from now on and put down what I really feel.

Yesterday nothing could give me satisfaction. Even the smell of flowers and the garden was sickening. When I woke this morning, the light in my bedroom was so beautiful and the pillow so wonderfully warm against my face and my toes so wiggly, I can't begin to describe it!

I guess I don't find the admiration of others as pleasing as I try to make myself pretend. People are so awful. But it is more than that. I think I find everything in life slightly disappointing, and I must keep that in mind. I'm determined never to disappoint myself. I like myself. I admire my hands, I like to twist and curl them just to watch them. A full-length mirror will always be one of my favorite possessions. I'm beautiful. That's very important to me, and I hope I shall always find it important, and if that's snobbishness, I am a snob, gladly. I realize my beauty is more important to me than to others. But do I include Mr. Pierce? I suppose I do.

I bought a new dress. It brings out the best of my figure, and I can wear it in the house evenings. That's almost too much to ask of a dress. Yet I can't make up my mind to wear it. And I can't go to the door when I think Mr. Pierce might be calling. I feel guilty about creating so many fine distinctions and feel more entangled by them than if I acted with more candor.

I shall never accept less than my expectations. I must not. I sense what would happen if I did.

This is a very important day in my life. I am engaged. It was Father's doing, and he told me he had counted on it for a long time. That surprised me, because he never said a word, not even when I asked some very personal questions, trying to find out more about Mr. Pierce. Father didn't force me to accept. He merely said he thought it would be nice. I'm not very surprised. I think I wanted it. I've wanted something to happen in my life so badly, I don't think I realized how much until tonight, now that it has happened.

The engagement was fun. Mr. Pierce was so capable, yet shy for my sake, as if I were going to be distressed by his proposal. I couldn't help but smile at him. I gave him a kiss. I think he blushed. Oh, I'm sure he's a good man, and I think he understands me in certain ways that Father doesn't. The insides of his hands are much warmer than I had imagined, and I had the definite impression—I'm surely not mistaken—they are gentle. There are many things which shall have to be considered in the near future, and I must, must make more effort to understand Mr. Pierce.

There are so many preparations. I wish I could hide and let someone else do them for me. I'm so terribly ignorant about this matter, no one to discuss it with.

I shall be a lovely bride. He will not be ashamed to have me stand beside him at the altar.

*When I peer into my mirror I cannot see myself for my eyes.
There's something in my eyes that seems to question me, even to peer
at me with scorn. They're clear, bright, almost glowing, but different,
strangely different. Mocking. Questioning. I do hope I'm doing the
right thing by marrying Henry. I do hope so.*

*Winter is almost over. The apple tree on the lawn looks content, I
don't think it wants spring. I do. But still, I like that apple tree in
winter, without its limbs leaf- and fruit-bent. Dear apple tree and my
dear dear old poplar, this is just another spring approaching for you.*
*I was lonely tonight. I liked it after so many weeks of excitement.
I folded my arms across my bosom and hugged it to me. I wonder if,
after I'm married, I shall be able to be lonely? I hope so, at least
once in a while. It's an emotion I need.*
*Tonight I walked out on the porch with Henry. Funny what a
difference stepping outside in the air makes. It was not the darkness,
simply being outside. I kissed him the way I have always wanted to
kiss. I didn't care. I thought this once I would let him see what I'm
really like. Then, after he was gone, I wondered if it would be the best
thing for us to live here in this house after all. I wonder if we
shouldn't have a place of our own? That's foolishness, I'm happy we
will live with Father. I don't think I could bear to move into a
strange house, and I certainly couldn't leave Father alone. But I must
think on this more deeply some day.*

*The wedding day is near and I know so little about marriage. So
very little what my husband will expect of me. I've always been thinking of myself, nobody but myself, and now I'm ashamed. I begin to
see how important* he *is. I ought to have a talk with Father, but
somehow I don't want to. Today in town I met a girl who had gone
to high school when I did. We talked a little. She has two children.
I tried to persuade her to have a cup of tea with me, but she had
shopping to do. I don't suppose I would have been able to ask her
some of the questions on my mind anyhow. I remember I didn't care
much for her at school, but it's funny, I think I like her now. I think
I like everybody a little more than I used to.*

Irene could not sleep. Drawn by a faint ache for excitement and
by some vague restlessness, she crept from her bed and went outside
in her nightdress, the expectation of the morrow making her mind
beautifully confused and urging her toward some action. The house

was too quiet. She went from the murky, wall-formed darkness out into the blacker darkness of night, where her eyes were more useful. The door had to be closed twice. The wind was cool and brisk and did frivolous things to her nightdress and made her lips distinctly separate and put a light tender spot in each armpit.

The garden grass was cool, but the earth was warm, and the blades felt like tentacles among her toes. Clover had no feel at all. Spreading her toes apart, she shoved her feet forward in the grass in the way an unskilled skier moves forward through snow. Her toes squeezed in downward curl, clutching at the grass, and her foot tugged at the earth. It pleased her that she could not break the blades or keep them from slipping loose. It pleased her to feel the strong grasp of the earth, hugging secure and tight everything which it fed.

There had been rain, the kind that softens the earth without wetting it, sufficient to take only the edge from the eternal thirst of the soil. The rain had been a filter through the smoke, smoke which in her childhood had been a far-off grayness, and for a few hours the darkness would be delicate and vivid, and it seemed to Irene that purity and immaculateness were more important to night than to day. The softened earth made her feet feel large and padded on their bottoms, and the appearance of the night was that it seemed held in place. It was the time of spring when there was a great hush, when stillness was stretched across the fields and insects had not yet begun to cry, and she felt freedom as something which was spreading and stretching out all around her.

She picked her way through the garden until she was far enough from the house to feel alone, and waited with slight impatience. She was not satisfied until her eyes were alive and almost disobedient. Then she closed them, suspending sight until all her senses reached the level of excitement which her eyes felt. There was forming in her an awe and reverence deep as when the minister had touched her hair and the flesh underneath with holy water and part of his hand, and she had let her head fall against the railing of the altar in such powerful immediate belief in God that she had been forced to consider all later religious emotions with doubt. Tomorrow she would go before that altar again.

Irene knelt in the grass. Though the damp grass was not more than three inches tall and all curls, she could feel the blades creep along her thighs and tentacle her ankles and bind her to the earth, so that her knees were inside the earth. Her legs seemed to lose their slenderness, to become those of a woman, mature, meaningful, and as she thought for a moment of marriage in a purely physical sense, the best air out of the night seemed to enter her throat. She put this thought from her, not in shame or in fear, but because it was not this which distressed her. She felt prepared for marriage physically. She had felt that for a long time. It held for her the promise of excitement and of passion and of pleasure which she had never tasted nor allowed herself, but of which she was utterly unafraid.

Her torment was caused by something more vague, a fear of dedicating herself to a man she did not fully understand, and to marriage, which she did not understand, and to yet something else, to an atmosphere which would be new and distinct from all she had ever known. Everything felt suddenly remote, forever untouchable, and she, lost and almost trembling in that severe innocence which the intricacy of the mind suffers when it touches upon the finalities of life, struggled against the whispers of her imagination and her intuition. The weight of the world seemed to be descending upon her. That which she had so long escaped was at hand, and she still felt unprepared, almost unwilling.

Irene knelt in the grass and looked up, panic and confusion in her eyes, her hands clinging to and pulling on her ear lobes to keep her head familiar, and she sought among the stars one which would suit prayer. There was in her the same sudden shrill need for utterance that sometimes makes a bird cry out at night, waking itself from sleep, waking the sky for all who are alert. There was in her a need for confession, not the soft, shameful confession trusted to a priest in return for rebuke or comfort, rather one that would have made a church ring with its forcefulness. Yet she whispered.

She sought among the stars. There seemed not one willing to hear, but when she began to pray it did not matter, for her vision broke from its normal piercing straight-line fixity into a sidewise, effortless absorption, so that she saw both more and less than eyes can see, so that the darkness was curved and all the stars visible, unequally smeared.

"I want to give him everything," she whispered. "I want to give him everything I've been told I'm supposed to give You. But I'm a little frightened. I feel I won't. I feel something will make me hold back. Oh please, let me be good to my husband and love him as I love this," she said, spreading her arms to indicate the sky. "Let me wish to hold my arms straight up when he finds me beautiful, and straight out when he has need of me. Let my heart be willing to suffer for him. Let my hands lose their shyness and seek the insides of his. Let my flesh be sweet to his touch, and let me feel my flesh is for him. Give him pleasure. Give me pleasure. Give him happiness. I am happy. I would be afraid to be happier than I am, this moment, even though I am awfully worried and upset. I'm such a vain person I may spoil it all. I want to feel as he does, understand his thoughts." She looked down at the grass, running her fingers through it as through mussed hair, searching her thoughts. "But most of all, let me respect him, let me believe in him, because the rest won't hurt me, the rest I can do without if I have to."

She sought for words that would better express the hope and the fear within her, while the grass became wire beneath the ovals of her knees and the earth narrowed. The earth began to feel wet and hard. The stars were too clear and bright, as if they were mocking. The wind seemed to make a faint hooting. Irene bowed her head, feeling a deep sorrow, knowing that it was insincerity within herself which was beginning to make everything about distract her, but not knowing that she had outlasted the passion which had needed to be appeased. The earth must always become hard to kneel upon.

Forced to rise, she lost all humility in the sudden tallness and slenderness of her body, in the long length of her young legs. She shook her nightdress free where it was damply stuck against her knees, feeling toward the parts of herself that she could see the same strangeness as for her shadow when the lamp by her bed threw it the full height of the wall.

Her eyes watched the earth turn through the sky, slowly, relentlessly, and her legs could feel the torque, an adhesion that had nothing to do with wind—the earth being pulled, by short jerks. She could feel forces in the universe which were not in herself. It gave her a feeling of the world faintly shaking with laughter, and she frowned for a moment, pitting against it her own sense of conscience, but with a quickness that was soon spent, leaving her without seriousness in spite of herself. Darkness was liquid for a time, with the imperfect texture of black shining paint which has been applied by a brush, the marks of the strokes still in it. There was no dizziness. It was only the sky being seen by her eyes now that she had ceased to think of tomorrow and the future. It was the sky being seen by eyes which had faith.

It was a sensation of having been released, of having pulled herself loose from the earth and all bondage and having placed her claim upon the sky, a night sky of more promise than fulfillment, a sky not too filled with brightness for the stars to have that individual shine which is their greatest asset. Now she could go beyond the garden, beyond the town, the boundaries of her life opened, allowing her to include everything, countries and peoples she had never seen, in one immense sensation, as if she were daughter of the whole world, as if the promise of the world hung for her like a garland which she could seize. Night, so bare and spare of ornament, reduced to basic black and white, pruned of detail, was the artistic version of life. It was the sky being seen with faith.

Her mind saw the earth protected and soothed with darkness. Her heart would not believe the sun was shining in Asia.

There was a star shower in which all the stars in a group flung out and took new positions in the sky in a pantomime which had the splendor and confusion of being unrehearsed. She laughed, for it had all come about through a sudden, accidental turning of her head, and had finished before her long dark hair was quite settled in the hollow of her spine.

"Prittee . . . Prit-tee," she whispered, returning to childhood pronunciation, as the sight of beauty often compelled her to.

In playful, impish mood, she made her eyes small and slitted until she could see the enlarged edge of her right cheekbone and dark eyelash fringe with the tiniest flashings tangled in it. Her eyes seemed to recede into her head and be caged in black, thin wire through which sparks of silver leaped at her and pierced her eyeballs without pain, and within this same instant she could feel her navel as certainly and heavily as most people feel a half-dollar in the palm of their hand. The nipples on her small breasts were feeling as they had been one cold afternoon when she had gone walking without a coat, as if they were being tenderly pinched. Irene laughed with happiness. She touched her knees together, curtsied, and watched to see if there were starlighty bits in her nightdress, then made butterfly motions with her fingers in the hope that her nails might shine.

Shaking her hair into less formal position, while the grass screeched faintly moist beneath her feet, she made pirouettes, part imitation ballet, part waltz, wheeling the nightdress in a flirtatious manner. Coming upon one of the maple trees, she danced around it, flinging her heels, laughing, wiggling her body in a way that she had never allowed herself to do before. Then she stopped, and stood before the trunk and wagged her finger at it. "Well, Henry," she said, "what do you think of your young lady now? Isn't she *disgraceful?* Isn't she *awful?* I don't think I would marry her if I were you. She's such a wild, silly creature. You still have time, you know. Time to change your mind. You better think it over, better think, because you're going to have to live with her. Ah, I can see what you're thinking, standing there so still. You *do* disapprove, don't you? Well, I can tell you, the young lady doesn't care."

Irene leaped away from the tree, laughing, and whirled her way into an open part of the lawn. As she spun, ignoring the reluctance of her nightdress, watching the night carnival of the sky, her flesh changed texture and revealed new places on it, and her teeth were extremely white, and had, for a moment, the exact sensitivity of fine frost. Though she was certain a weight of light had caught in her hair, could imagine its downward pull in the arch of her throat, the stars would not spotlight her, nor in any way identify her as their chosen admirer.

Peevish and pouty, she sought the responsibility of mirrors on the great curve of darkness. She was an actress, the world her stage, the sky her audience, an actress not in a drama, but in a solo pageant of beauty, a promenade. She was cavorting in the last hours of her freedom, while her body and her beauty were still hers, her secret and her glory, and as she strolled through the garden there was a flirtatious wildness in all her gestures. It was an orgy of self-worship. But behind it all was a kind of hysteria, a kind of panic which was the result of attaching too great importance to marriage, and of finding herself at the last moment hesitant, doubtful. And, too, unknown to herself, a portion of the nervousness which had made her almost completely irrational was simply too long prolonged virginity. It caused her to behave more foolishly than she had at the age of fourteen, when she had been in love with Raymond Rowiger.

Darkness was between her slender legs, and her hair knew a more delicate vanity than any brush or comb could give it. Darkness was a warm, huggy feeling in which her arms were free to move as they chose. She whirled them in the windmill style remembered from childhood, and had a sudden intuition this was the last time, the last time for a lot of things, a last gambol among a girl's toys and a girl's pleasures, that she, eighteen, was about to enter another world, a world of deep seriousness, and was taking a last fond look backward. It did not sadden her, for she wished to leave, honestly yearned to leave, and was merely a little afraid to know the gate would close behind her, that there was no retreat, no return. But suddenly she did not care. She wanted to throw herself blind upon the future.

She felt the iris of her eye make a faint dilation which permitted a sliver of darkness to enter, and the darkness took on meaning, not merely something seen in the effort to look at other things. She saw in the darkness that which was the most abiding quality of night, a vast loneliness, an utter isolation in which the stars and the moon and the clouds and the shadows of trees and of the hedge could abide peacefully, but in which there was never more than a temporary place for herself. It was this which she had always resisted noticing.

Far above was a lone star that appeared to move further into isolation as time passed, a speck of light, intense, almost suffering. Yet it seemed far more awesome to be human, to be young, to be foolish. Her feet tensed those two arches which were the essential reason for standing on tiptoe, and she offered her arms to the sky in a gesture of extreme loneliness and need. There came to her the futility of struggling, when her body and her passionate spirit desired bondage and perhaps even suffering.

Inebriate from the stance required to look at heaven's straight-above stars, she made her mouth oval and sucked in all the air about her in one enormous, searing breath, and at that instant came the beginning of calm and acceptance. For the first time she knew that she would go through with tomorrow, that she would vow to love and to cherish for better or worse, that she would accept the responsibility of marriage. If her husband needed her, if his hands needed fragile hands, if his capability needed something delicate and weak to protect, she would be grateful. But she would take him regardless, without promise or assurance, and she would find what there was within him, be useful to him, take him small bunches of violets and a smile that would gladden his heart, be satisfied to give and to give. She would settle for being his handmaiden.

She began to think of tomorrow with joy, with a certain fierceness in her teeth, a defiance of her outstretched arms.

PART THREE: 1911 - 1921

19

THE WINDOW was sprinkled with silvery lines. "Whee-ee," Gilbert said, and, leaping out of bed, ran downstairs at a hopping, bouncing gait in his pajama bottoms. The way he ran indicated complete disregard for his bare feet. "Snow!" he shouted. "How deep is it?"

Mijack ordered him upstairs to dress. Gilbert was astonished. He had simply forgotten.

Undaunted, undistressed, he put both feet together and began hopping up the stairs.

"I made it," he shouted.

He dressed with the speed of someone who realized clothes were a nuisance. He knew which button buttoned a shirt, slid both legs simultaneously into his trousers, and his shoes were squashed into the convenience of slippers. All the while he kept trying to warm an opening in the frost-crusted window.

"It snowed!" he said. "Did you see?"

Mijack indicated against his leg the depth. "You talked for it until you brought it on," he said. "Brought on a batch."

The boy had to go to the door and see for himself. A little blew in on the floor.

"Get yourself to the table," said Mijack. "The snow's not going anywhere."

Gilbert ate three bowls of oatmeal, a small pile of butter-bread, and drank a little bitter black coffee, which he did not much like. He had a trick of getting his mouth close to the bowl which enabled him, with a smaller spoon, to eat as quickly as his father. When breakfast was finished, he used his napkin as a washcloth, with good reason.

"Now mop the floor, boy, mop the floor," said Mijack, throwing back his head and roaring with laughter. He did not care how his son ate, so long as the quantity was sufficient and nothing on the plate went to waste. He saw nothing remarkable in his son's appetite. He did not often take into account differences between the boys and himself.

Breakfast was over, the house was warmer from it, the rest of the family were sleeping overhead, and the father and son had a feeling of being very much alone together. Both had a tendency to rise early and a vigorous appreciation for those first hours of the morning, a time of sheer physical response to everything. Frost was glowing on the windows and the light in the kitchen had an odd, false tremble. It, and themselves, made them go outside, where they made a good, hard snowball and passed it back and forth. Mijack understood his son's enthusiasm. Even though he would soon have to tramp down the hill, through town, and over to the East End plant, it did not prevent him from finding his stiffnesses now. It did not prevent him from filing a keen edge on the runners of the sled.

The fresh, crisp snow, the surprise of a winter dawn, was the kind of relationship Mijack wanted with his sons, and it came most when they were alone together, sharing the freedom which morning offered. It was the wonderful feeling of being ahead of the rest of the world, of having some advantage, a high place from which to view and enjoy. It was the time when his own youth was nearest both in remembrance and in actuality, when he could afford to waste energy, when there was significance and truth to be gained from the vast separation of age.

But then the whistle blew far down by the river, and it was time for Mijack to be on his way.

He went down the hill with the lunch pail under his arm, taking long, almost youthful strides. He seemed more vigorous and carefree in wintertime, with the white of his breath trailing behind.

Gilbert watched until his father was beyond the gate, then yelled, and when there was no response, no acknowledgment, ran with reckless speed through snow that had weed tips growing out of it. He ran straight at his father.

Mijack put the lunch pail down, crouched slightly, caught and threw him high into the air. He stepped aside to let the boy fall on snow.

Gilbert loved that. He loved to be handled rough.

"Now get back to the house, son."

"Do it again."

"No, enough's enough."

178

"Do it again, once more."

"Faugh, you're too heavy," said Mijack, "and I'm late."

He had never been late but knew what it was to feel behind, to feel time in the resistance of the wind to his stride and in the minute slippage of his shoes in the snow. Even though he was in fine humor, even though the air around him seemed brighter and the snow more elastic, he could not stay. His thoughts were already fixed upon the second portion of his life, in which he was blacksmith. The responsibility of being a father, strong as it was felt, faded before the approach of something older and more deeply part of him, and perhaps more natural to him.

And so Mijack had to raise his arm and point toward the house, had to stand there with his arm raised in continuous command, mouth silent to give the arm effectiveness, until there was enough distance between them so that he could trust turning and walking on down the hill.

Gilbert, for whom nothing happened often enough, nothing had an ending, went back. Before entering, he gathered logs, had trouble opening the door, but refused to put the wood down. Some of the logs were still striped with snow. He tumbled the entire armload into and around the fireplace, revealing to himself the wetness of his clothes, especially the part of his shirt covering his stomach, for he had a tendency to cradle everything. He slapped his shirt and let it go at that. The logs, beginning to thaw, steamed and hissed and threw into his nostrils a wet moss smell. He stripped a piece of bark, pushed it into his mouth and chewed, then spit the pulp juice into the fireplace. He watched to see what the fire was going to do.

It had been windy during the night, and the fire was too low to bear so much weight of wet wood. With a little tenderness and consideration it would have come along, but Gilbert could not wait. He was alone downstairs, free to use huge quantities of paper and kerosene; soon flame was gushing into the throat of the chimney and the room was full of something like thunder. When the fire became scorching hot he twisted his head from side to side and made temporary shields of his hands. He liked fresh, wild flame, logs with water and juice seething on their skins, wood being eaten, and the reckless noise in fire, the struggle and confusion.

The logs, despite their wetness, were forced to burn, and when it was clear that after the kerosene and kindling had been consumed the logs would not be able to prevent the gathering strength of the real fire, which was not yet flaming, he rushed outside into the crisp coldness of the morning, making his own wind with the speed of his running, carrying against the front of him the overheated smell of his clothes, while his feet tried to break the hot, dry hardness of his shoes. For a time his body seemed less fat, and his head, destined to be always too large, nearly gargantuan, was pulled firm and erect with the effort of running. His mouth hissed unreal smoke at the sky.

He grabbed a handful of snow and ran inside and threw the incomplete snowball at the fireplace and then listened to the sounds. He expected pleasure. Instead it made him thoughtful and less happy. He wished someone else would get out of bed and come downstairs. He did not want to be alone. . . .

Mrs. Mijack made breakfast and Gilbert had a slice of toast and a glass of warmed milk.

"Did you hear the whistle?" he said. "No school. It was no school, wasn't it?"

She tied his shoes, letting him put his finger to hold while she was forming the bow.

"But that doesn't say you shouldn't appear decent," she said.

"Man, I'm going to do things today," said Gilbert, rubbing his hands together in anticipation. "I'm really going to *do* things."

"You're going to study."

She did not mean now. She meant this evening and was getting him prepared for it. He had to be let know far in advance what was expected of him.

"Aw, heck," he said.

"No aw hecking," said Mrs. Mijack.

She fixed his collar and wet her hand and smoothed his hair "Now," she said.

She meant he could move. It had been her hands which had followed his movements, which had only been restrained in distance, even though his effort had been to remain in one place.

"Father and me pitched snowballs. I hit the tree three times in a row."

He was slow in learning to take care of himself. It was the result of awkwardness caused by his weight.

"I suppose that's where the dirt and water came from."

"Where?"

She had to point, choosing one puddle nearest them both. Gilbert put his hand down on it. "That's not much," he said.

"Enough it'd be easier for me to fix the fire than have to clean up after you."

For she knew the real cause. She was acquainted with the various kinds of dirt which were brought into the house.

"Where's a rag?" he said. "I'll clean it."

She told him where a rag was.

"How's that?" he said, after a moment of furious scrubbing. "That clean enough?"

"Yes," she said.

Although there was a trail of such marks leading all the way into the other room, she was satisfied with a demonstration of good intentions. She could not find it in her to ask more of him than that.

But Gilbert had stepped backward into another puddle. He sighed, kneeled, rubbing very slowly, the thought of lasting work distressing him. The flesh on his face thickened from bending and rubbing. His head seemed too heavy for him.

"Finish your milk first," said Mrs. Mijack. "It'll get cold."

He did not understand that she was giving him an opportunity to forget about the dirt. He saw it as another thing which would delay him. . . .

In the bedroom there was a chart with columns on which were noted height, weight, chest and waist measurements, arm reach, and size of fist. Beside it was a map of France, marked with lines which represented the western front, at the bottom of which were a number of notations in pencil. Neatly folded on a chair were trousers, shirt, clean underclothing and shoes clean on the bottoms and along the crevice of the heels, smooth black on top. The shirt and trousers had been altered to fit a narrow waist and the original stitching strengthened with thin white twine, so that the seams presented themselves. In the bed was Bart.

When Bart came to breakfast he took a bowl from the cupboard, washed it with cold water from the well, sniffed at the oatmeal and took two large spoonfuls. He measured out a glass of milk. He broke a little hole in the top of an egg and sucked the raw contents through the shell into his mouth.

"Good morning," he said courteously to his mother.

"And knock off throwing snow at the window," he said to his brother. "If I hadn't been awake, you'd hear more about it."

He sat a little apart at the table, and the care with which he ate made apparent the thick shoulders and strong arms. Bart was ten. Except for the ridge of muscle across his shoulders, which threatened to give him a hunched appearance, he was well proportioned, with a young face of serious cast, rather immobile, and large eyes which had something peculiar about them—not the color, an undistinguished hazel with faint specks of pure green, nor the habits of the eyelids, a steady nerveless blink; the single deviation from normal was that the pupils never appeared to change so that it was impossible to tell what distance the eyes were seeing.

"How's Mother this morning? Better?"

"Yes, no thanks to you."

Bart shrugged. There was a coldness, an aloofness which was not a defense, not a shield against weakness, but an instrument for measuring everything around him. In certain respects he was like his father, but there was a quickness, an alertness, which must have had its roots in an older generation, a strain of blood militant and aggressive. Nor had he inherited his father's flesh, but had smooth white skin, partly feminine, which tanned in summertime without burning or freckling. He had a habit of holding his head too erect and motionless.

"You burned last night's paper again."

"I did not."

But Gilbert was not sure.

"Find it, then."

"Find it yourself."

"Yes, find it yourself," said Mrs. Mijack, at the same time placing her hand upon her young son's arm. "You don't do anything else around here."

"What I get paid for," said Bart.

"Not what you get paid to do either."

Bart had been smiling. It was amusing the way his mother and brother always formed an alliance. He was amused by his brother, with whom he got along very well when they were alone. Bart rinsed the bowl, put it with the dishes to be washed, and went into the cellar.

Their marriage had from the first instant been delicate and even precarious. Mr. Pierce suspected his bride of swaggering a little in the earliest weeks of attempting to live in her new position.

Because of her youth and secluded life, Mr. Pierce suspected she would be a little afraid of the sexual duties and would know very little of what was expected of her. Associating her frailty and delicacy with his own concept of womanhood and feminine sensibilities, he was gentle with her, considerate of the problems she encountered. Allowing her as much privacy as possible, he made every effort to give her a sense of security, and thereby wrought in himself a fine tenderness for her.

It was with a rather confused sense of acceptance, and a moment of actual distaste, that he discovered she enjoyed the sexual aspects and even threatened to become active. Her passion surprised him.

But it was not a situation which caused either of them distress or inconvenience. Mr. Pierce treated his wife in private with every bit of the gentleness which was evident in their daily lives.

He had known from the beginning that Irene was exceptional and that she had a remarkably avid taste for life.

When he had begun to consider the possibility of making Irene his wife, he had been certain of the success of the marriage because Irene appeared already to view him with favor, even though he had not yet revealed to her his true depth of feeling. His unrevealed intelligence and sensibilities were his strongest asset in what was already a favorable situation—a young woman of good family background, interesting and in need of a better setting in which to perfect her virtues.

This could have endangered them.

It was not anything which he had plotted, but the result of circumstances. If their ages were in any manner related to the development of their relationship, it had been in the earliest stages, and in his reticence to approach her as an active suitor. Their marriage proved to be substantially sound and resulted in a period of great happiness for them both.

The honeymoon was so pleasant that Mr. Pierce extended it a week, a month, the better part of a year. He engaged in what even he had to refer to as extravagance. Their luggage and equipment alone marked them as exceptional. He insisted that she select everything of her wardrobe, although he was quite expert at deciding whether the accompaniments of a particular dress should match, subdue or add a bit of dash.

For Irene that year was a sort of passage through time and space into a perfect relationship, in which she was treated with more respect than she had ever known, in which her husband made every effort to bring her happiness. Before the end of the first month she had faith in and a sense of protection from him. It was a kind of atmosphere in which she was allowed to expand indefinitely. Happiness, not timidity, caused her to revert to a very soft and light voice, charmingly

183

offset by a tendency to display her beauty and manners. She was the continuous victim of a delicious shortness of breath, which she admitted to be the result of a preconceived notion of what real love would be like.

This turning of her eyes away from the world and upon him, this turning out of herself, resulted in an even more fragile relationship. They arrived at a stage of intimacy in which everything was discussed at considerable length, and yet their hands and eyes were unmistakably more gentle with each other. Behind this mode of conversation and exploration was a gradual, reticent revelation of themselves which brought them ever closer. It was a desire to share each other in more ways; reticence was like a resonance; they met and touched endless ramifications of personality, and at the same time were so pleased with each other that they kept putting certain aspects off—pleasures delayed until more needed.

Happiness had so many aspects that it was no longer a direct, single emotion, rather one which gained magnitude and stability from echoes, from memories so recent that their minds and hearts would not relinquish them into the past. There was no explaining the delight she felt when her husband was repeatedly mistaken for an Englishman, or his insistence that they should remain awake to see dawn once in each new part of America, or his inordinate liking to see her in summer dresses, or his amusement when she chose gay, fragile hats on windy days.

Happiness was a continuous passing through her fingers of something new. They seemed always to encounter lovely rooms with east and south views. Courtesy seemed to follow them, to lead them. They retained a sense of fantasy and accepted their position as that of two people on a journey which had the sole fault of being seen with too much vividness. They could not possibly retain it all. Irene felt as if she were living in a court, surrounded by attendants and admirers, and she responded by being so eloquently grateful with her eyes that her attractiveness would lead them into new encounters. In these moments of happiness she would be so pretty and charming that those around her could not escape a certain warmth, an overflow from her exuberance.

She was a rarity, a woman who could adore. There was love in her which had been waiting for someone to claim it, take it, need it. The only assistance she required to make that surrender so necessary for the outpouring of love and affection was a little understanding. She offered openly, with determination and even eagerness, not only love (which was his due), but an adoration which could not be bargained for.

Mr. Pierce returned to Nesquehon a content, satisfied man. Irene returned a beautiful and nearly mature woman. Her eyes were serene and poised. Her voice was deep and rich, even at moments a little husky.

Mr. Lang was waiting for them at the station, sitting on a waiting-room bench, smoking at his pipe, marked by the complete tranquillity which was his most apparent trait. For a moment Irene did not have any reaction, she saw him with completely neutral eyes, saw him clearly and in detail, but with no more comprehension than if he had been a stranger. Then she ran to him and hugged him as she never had in her life. Mr. Lang seemed quite surprised at this show of affection, but was obviously pleased. "Well . . . Well," he said, shaking his head. "You're looking fine, Irene. Both of you. Yes, indeed, both of you."

Bart was alone in the cellar, sitting on a wood block stained with chicken blood, beating on an anvil his father had forged, beating on it with a hammer, trying to improve the force, speed and accuracy of his blows.

Then he selected a block of chestnut and five long, thin nails and practiced driving the nails straight, without bend, without hesitation. Only after his arm tired did the hammer sometimes miss or glance off the head of a nail. It was his intention to be able to use every tool. Mijack sometimes gave him instruction, but he was also reaching an age when he was beginning to find things out for himself. He sought perfection.

"I wish you'd go outdoors to make that racket," his mother yelled into the cellar from the door above.

Bart did not bother to answer. He had almost no feeling toward her. She could force herself upon his attention for a brief time, producing in him the kind of annoyance interruptions have for businessmen, but even then with a negative kind of acceptance, without hate, pity, or understanding. She simply was of no use to him. He did not need a mother.

Gilbert heard noise in the cellar. Any noise was enough to make him investigate.

"Can I help?" he asked.

185

"You can watch how you make fire in the morning," said Bart.

"It wasn't nothing," said Gilbert. "You oughta seen the one yesterday."

"Fine," said Bart. "But I for one don't intend ending up a cinder just because you get a kick out of playing with matches."

Gilbert sat on the stairs and watched his brother repair a shoeshine box. He was content to watch. He did not overstep the bounds and compete with Bart or attempt to do what he was not able.

"My birthday's Saturday," said Gilbert. "You gonna buy me something?"

"Hell, no," said Bart.

"Allrighty for you," said Gilbert.

"You're damn tooting allrighty for me."

Gilbert grew restless and walked about, making finger streaks through the dust which had gathered on the jars of preserves, hunting in the potato bin for one that would feel the size of a ball, examining a damp place on the wall. He almost found something of interest in the big can of nails, miscellaneous hinges, bolts, hooks and screws. There was a lot of rust in the bottom.

"Play around," said Bart.

"I ain't hurting nothing."

"No," Bart admitted. He was almost invariably just.

Gilbert spun the handle of the vise, counting the number of turns it would make from one push. When he could not improve on four he hunted for the oil can, but when he did not find it in the first minute, tried to see how tight he could make the jaws of the vise.

He was careful not to interfere with what Bart was doing.

Naomi opened the cellar and started down the stairs.

"Do me a favor," Bart said. "Keep her out."

Bart was justified in wanting to keep Naomi out. She was absolute mistress of worthless questions. "What's that?" she would ask. "What's it *for*? What's it *do*? Show me what it *does*. Why you got it upside down, huh? But what in the world *is* it?"

Bart could stand just so much of that.

Gilbert ran up the steps and braced his arms against the wall and the handrail. Naomi almost slipped past underneath.

It was pretty difficult keeping her out. She could be stubborn. Gilbert was forced to promise to take her sledding, and that only satisfied her enough to keep her from pushing. So he told her what Bart was making, in a tone which pretended not merely to know more about what was going on below than he did, but also implied that

186

he had assisted. He began to feel important and responsible. . . .

Bart waited in the cellar until there was an opportunity to be alone with his mother. Then he came into the kitchen and went over to where she was heating flatirons on the stove lids. There was the faint odor of clean wash which had been sprinkled and rolled, and there was a willow basket full of whites.

"I shouldn't have hit you," he said. "I'm sorry I did."

"A fine time to be talking," said Mrs. Mijack. "After a thing's done."

Bart shrugged. "I decided I owe you an apology. So, there it is."

"You're not sorry," she said, looking straight at him. "Not one bit sorry."

"I've decided, Mother," said Bart calmly, "that we're not going to have any more trouble. All you have to do is keep your hands off me, and I let you alone. Fifty-fifty. Because you see I decided that I don't care if it's wrong. I'm going to hit you if you even so much as touch me."

"I see your father didn't lick you enough," said Mrs. Mijack. "Maybe you'd like me to tell him to give you some more."

"Don't gloat," said Bart. "He beats me, not you." Bart smiled. "And I'm not sure he likes you running to him, Bart did this, Bart did that."

"That we'll see!"

Bart walked away. He would never go out of his way to cause trouble. He was too little interested in her to wish to domineer or to flaunt his independence. It was only that he had a feeling his father would have been a great man if it had not been for this woman, that his father was as disgusted and unconcerned about her as he was, and he did not like to see Mijack being considerate and kindly toward her. It struck against his respect for his father.

Mijack walked up from the steel mill late in the afternoon. Bart was waiting in front of the gate, his young, serious face rather immobile, standing calm and erect, cleanly washed, his hair combed in a style highly individual for his age. He was handsome in the lean, quick style which the A. E. F. was making popular throughout the nation. Kicking aside snow so the gate would open more easily, he went to his father with his arm outstretched.

Hands met. It was not a greeting. Mijack understood and approved. He had to put down the bottles of milk, while the boy's fingers reached about for better advantage. The hands clasped, hardening each into full steadiness, bringing out the lines and hidden tendon characteristics. Pressure was applied by Bart until the white began to show in his fingernails. The father's hand was firm and still, the young one quivering a bit, too small to force blunt and darkened fingers into the curl and clench of a solemn and important handshake.

Mijack and Bart peered into each other's eyes, quietly, with respect.

Yet there was a furious pride in Bart's attitude, so that even though he had to look upward, his eyes were equal to those he was watching; his hand was less small and insufficient, and his fingers, at least momentarily, possessed the same untiring strength his thumb had. He knew he had surprised his father. Yet the young eyes were fixed on Mijack, hunting, seeking, somehow ruthlessly intent and critical.

"You're not trying," said Bart. "I don't like it when you don't try."

Mijack, with a great roar of laughter, increased the pressure and crumpled the small hand within his own. He did not hesitate to let his son know what pain was now that he had felt and measured the strength of the boy's hand in his firmly relaxed fingers. He was neither cruel nor unnecessarily merciful.

Bart sucked his lip and put his uninvolved hand, which now had sharp nerves in its finger tips, flat against his thigh. His mouth smiled so there would be no loose flesh in its corners which might quiver. He tried not to look at where his fingers were crushed into a bewildering tangle of joints. It did not occur to him to use both hands to try to equal the larger one. He did not try to pull free.

"Enough, Father, enough," he said.

Released, he turned immediately and pushed open the gate, standing aside so Mijack could pass. He had to lean hard against the gate to get it started. He put his right hand into his pocket.

"Did I do better?" he said.

"Some better," Mijack replied. "But you tried to cheat in position."

The boy frowned, then ran to get the milk. Mijack went on toward the house.

Bart hurried after him, the quart bottles hooked between two fingers, swinging in careless lantern fashion. As he drew near there was a change in his pace, an imitation of his father's stride, though lighter and more springy, and it became even more apparent that in certain ways they were much alike.

In the midst of dinner, Mijack looked up and searched the room with his eyes. There was a curious alertness in his expression, a listening posture, head held very high the way animals do when they want to hear something far off which they know exists yet cannot identify. He did not seem to be aware that his wife and three children were at the table.

It had been a day when the forge had held perfect temperature, when everything he did seemed to have a fine quality of meaning, a significance not attached to the work itself. Walking home he had taken his leisure and looked around more than usual. He was not tired, never tired when work went right. His work clothes stiffened in the winter air so that there was in his movements something reminiscent of an era of armor. But he did not mind cold. Working over intense heat was stealing from him the capacity to feel anything in temperature except extremes.

He saw something fine. It was not the mountain alone, the steep rock peak which was the only thing in nature other than the river which had refused snow, but the visual freshness of the air, sky which was not fading but brightening in the west. The shadows were longer and thinner, a pattern of parallels, giving grandeur to short, fat trees and shrubs. It was that instant in time when there was still no thought of darkness, when there was no sadness evoked by the loss of pigment which precedes the dying of light, when previous contact with nighttime seemed incredibly distant in memory. And when the astounding clarity of the atmosphere gathered everything available to the eyes, sprinkled it with the delicate scent of drying and crisping snow, and gave a different acoustic plan for the sounds of the earth to gain attention by, and above all justified a man in taking a large, easy philosophy of self and world.

Mijack was just the man to give way to such things and be refreshed by them. His inarticulateness about his feelings was his advantage. He was taken with a desire to strike out upon a long walk, to pass through all these areas which he could now see, to let himself simply by nearness absorb some of it, this terrible health and vigor which hung over it all. Instead, he had come on home, had performed chores and the ritual of washing, yet with a sense of having left something undone and unfulfilled. He had sat down to eat, had bade the children be seated, had felt hunger stir in him and his body and his arms prepare themselves for the dishes which were being placed on the table. Now, midway through dinner, it had become clear to him, and he was feeling the excitement of having it within his grasp. Yet he did not think of speaking out, except that he ate more rapidly, with new eagerness for food, with a sense of haste about getting it into him.

Bart was eating what his father ate, and in the same order, but with the difference that he did not let his stomach fill itself. He wanted to be lean and watched his diet, at least in regard to pie, cake, sweets and puddings. But dieting is usually a defense against gluttony, and Bart, though not without appetite, had no strong craving for any food, and was imposing no hardship on himself.

Mrs. Mijack had been watching the oldest one. She thought he knew why she was looking at him. There was a determined air in the way she had put the dishes on the table and had sat down to her own plate. The proper moment was after the prayer, and this time was past, and so the next suitable time was after her husband had finished eating, and she was waiting to see if Bart would take this opportunity, or whether she would have to do it herself.

"See, what did I tell you?" Gilbert whispered, showing beneath the table the piece of cake. It looked very big in his hand.

"Did you really steal it?" Naomi asked.

"Of course. How you think I got it?"

"Some people have all the luck."

He gave her part. Naomi immediately put it inside her dress. But he was not satisfied and began to eat his at the table, sneaking up handfuls and wolfing them down, eating with a much more exciting appetite than the kind children have at the dinner table. They looked at each other with big eyes. Gilbert even took the risk of tossing a tiny piece in the air and catching it with his mouth. That was as daring a stunt as Naomi had ever seen him pull in front of Father, and it made her scared for the piece of cake inside her dress. She signaled him not to.

"Are you going to tell your father, or shall I?" said Mrs. Mijack. "You!" she said, when Bart did not raise his head. "Either tell him or leave this table."

Gilbert put the last of his cake in his mouth and chewed it the way he chewed meat. Then he reached toward his sister, pushing at her dress where she had hers hidden. She was divided between protecting herself and trying to make it appear as if nothing was happening.

Bart looked up. His sense of courtesy to his father bade him keep silent.

"Well," she said. "You heard me. Now which are you going to do?"

190

"Tell him yourself, if you're so anxious," said Bart.

"What is it?" said Mijack, heavily. "What this time?"

Mijack was for the first time today a little tired and disgruntled. He found it difficult to assume responsibility for what went on within the house while he was not there.

"He threatened to strike me again, that's what. He did and let him deny it."

"Now wait a minute," said Bart. "That's going too far."

"Too far?" said Mrs. Mijack. "Yes, young man, you went a great deal too far. You threatened to hit me. Yesterday you did hit me. And now we're going to find out here and now whether you're going to continue." Mrs. Mijack turned to her husband. "You don't know what he's like. You don't know what goes on when you're at work."

Naomi slipped away from the table and into the other room. Now that her brother had eaten all of his and was out of danger of being discovered, and the beginnings of a quarrel had made the faces around the table stern and hardened, the cake had become a serious problem. She intended to go to her bedroom and hide it, but recalled that her bedroom had little privacy, and so she began to cram big chunks into her mouth, not enjoying them as Gilbert had but only getting rid of them.

Bart waited until his mother had said everything she wanted to say. "Father," he said calmly, "I tried to apologize, and she hopped on me again, and I told her that if she didn't let me alone, I'd hit her. That's what I told her." Bart looked at his mother. "She's just always trying to boss everyone, that's what it amounts to."

Mijack looked at his son, studying him.

"You won't strike her," he said quietly, in a firm voice. "You won't do that under any circumstances."

It made Bart lower his head and not look up. He would have preferred a command which could be broken, one with a severe penalty which gave him the choice of his own decision. But there had been no threat and no command in Mijack's voice, only a tone which made Bart know he could not do anything except obey.

"You bet he won't," said Mrs. Mijack. "I won't have him threatening me. I promised him you'd see he was punished good and proper."

"You had no right to do that," said Mijack turning toward her. "If, as I feel confident, he will promise never to strike you, I think we can put an end to this right now."

"I won't," said Bart. "I won't talk back, either."

For there came to him a sudden belief that he could go for the rest

191

of his life without talking to his mother. And he was almost capable of that. His conviction was exaggerated only in carrying it to the ultimate.

Gilbert went after his sister.

"Gimme a little piece," he said. "Mine's all gone."

"So's mine," she said, chewing hard, holding out empty hands.

Gilbert picked a few crumbs from her hands, then let her lick her fingers and wipe them on his handkerchief. Naomi was at the same time licking carefully the inside of her mouth, because Mother had caught her once by making her open it.

"How's it look?" she said. "Can you see anything?"

"Naw, you're okay."

They returned to the table and began playing a game of looking innocent. It soon made them both laugh.

"Do you mean to say that boy isn't going to be punished?" said Mrs. Mijack. "After what he's done this day? Do you mean you're not going to uphold my word?"

"When he deserves to be punished, he will be," said Mijack.

Bart sat in silence. He was disgusted with himself. He was disgusted that he had made the promise.

"Then he's to be allowed to do as he pleases? To treat me like I don't know what? Am I to have no discipline when you aren't here? So that next thing he'll be telling you lies and you believing them. Is that the case?"

"For God's sake, woman, what do you expect of me? I whipped him just yesterday!"

Naomi was imitating her brother, raising her spoon when he did his; when Gilbert whispered, she repeated it. He tricked her into making a mistake, then wagged his finger at her. That neither Bart nor Father realized what was going on made it more enjoyable.

"I'll know better than to expect from you," said Mrs. Mijack to her husband. "I'll know I must rely on myself." Her anger was gone. "But I'm sorry to have heard you say that, Samuel Mijack. I'm sorry for both our sakes."

She looked around the room, as if trying to fix into her mind those things on which she could still depend.

Gilbert and Naomi took hold of the tablecloth and had a gentle tug of war. They did not pull hard because that sometimes resulted in misfortune. "Oh stop it," said Mrs. Mijack, and they both looked up at her, their eyes accusing.

Mijack took his oldest son by the arm and led him outside, where there was so little light that they could barely see the snow. "You won't understand," he said, "when I tell you that I love living here. Or when I tell you it doesn't take much to make a man free." Mijack put his arm around Bart. "It takes just a little." Mijack laughed. "Not so many years ago I couldn't find anything in the whole country. But that was because I counted things in miles and acres, and in the way they looked. Now I know it's all in how a man feels." Bart was listening intently. His father talked about the sort of things no one else did, about the aims and means of life. It made Bart hunger for the years that were ahead of him and feel haste to be prepared for them, thoroughly prepared. "Land doesn't get old and worn out, not unless a man does it to the land. Why, there's only one cemetery here. Only one! And my father turned up bones every spring. You see the only thing that has changed in my time is that it takes a wall. A real wall outside and another one here," he said, thumping his chest. "My father was against walls, rightly, but what was right for him isn't for me. When your turn comes, you'll remember I'm your father and not of your time, and I'll hate you for it, not so much for it as for the attitude it brings. You'll never understand why I stick with this land, a piece so full of stones that I garden it but wouldn't fool with farming it. You'll never understand when I say, I stay here, I go no farther."

Bart admired his father for being proud and independent. It made him feel more justified in the pride he took in himself.

Mijack stood there, minding the cold less than his son did, rubbing the squarish jaw on which dense black whiskers hard as wire grew amazingly in a single day. His flesh seemed to avoid the issue of age, a thick toughness which time was not able to alter. His appearance had changed little between the ages of forty and sixty, and if there was tiredness, heaviness, there was also unrelenting determination.

"What I'm trying to say, Bart, is that I feel toward your mother about like I do toward my land. It's all in how a man feels. She's not often right, she's most always wrong, she's full of stones and contrariness. But when it comes down on the line, I'm for her. I guess you've seen how she and I got a wall between us, how she keeps putting more walls around her all the time. And I can't find it in me to tell you you've got to be good to her or that you've got to love her. I'm not sure I even got the right to remind you she's your mother. But I can tell you she's my wife, and much as I like you, you'd be wiser not to force me." Mijack studied a moment. "You need more freedom to be free than I do. You're like I was and worse. Or better, depending how you see it. I guess it was just that made me go against my wife tonight and take up for you." Mijack turned toward the door, beginning now to feel the cold, and the uselessness of explaining. "I expect," he said, "it'd be better for us all if we don't have to have a showdown, if we kind of put up with what freedom we have, and not go making more walls than there is."

Bart was no longer listening intently. Listening so often set fire to his own ambitions and sometimes gave him new ones. He liked to hear things which made him proud of his father. But he could not conceal his disappointment from himself, could not but feel cheated.

20

Breakfast was served beside the window. Irene dashed past the maid and into the kitchen where she made an exchange of grapefruit, then returned and arranged the dishes in a manner more attractive than the formal left-to-right setting which the maid had employed. The new positions, chosen in regard to the window and the chair, made the food seem brighter and the odors seem to have more space and separation. But the important change was in making the table seem correct in size and purpose.

She smiled and went toward the stairs with her arms reaching as if to catch something. She was there in time to greet him while he was still above. She had for a moment a feeling, peculiar to mornings, that his attention was to something a little behind her. "Come see," she said, and he allowed himself to be led to the place Irene thought best suited for him. "It's sweeter," she said, laughing. "It's the other half."

Mr. Pierce lifted the dish so that he could see the skin of the fruit better. "Yes," he said, smiling, "you've taken away the side toward the tree and given me the side toward the sun."

"Oh no," said Irene, "I also tasted."

Mr. Pierce shook his coat lightly until it settled around him, then began to eat, while his eyes studied the tone and tenor of the sky, reflecting upon his own opinions. From time to time his finger tips pressed themselves upon the surface of the napkin, although they were perfectly clean, and he ate leisurely, leaving the table appearing as if nothing had been disturbed. He seemed unaware of his sense of neatness.

At the end of breakfast, at the time of coffee, Irene brought her husband a white bachelor's button. It was for morning and early afternoon, the time when he would wear a flower. She stooped near him to fit the flower to his lapel, their heads so near that her mouth was aware of his, but she only made her mouth speak with a voice deeper, richer, more sure of itself. Their eyes were so absorbed in each other that they appeared engaged in a faint testing.

Mr. Pierce had the advantage of seeing her from above, of seeing her shoulders where her hair flowed over them. She was approaching the summit of her beauty. Her body had not changed significantly. It was slender and lithe, still girlish in movement, yet with a distinct provocative quality which his eyes could not determine, unless it was a fine equilibrium, a further development of the feeling which she so often aroused in him, that of being supported only by the small ellipses of her shoes. Her dark eyes had lost the slightly pained, bewildered expression which had a tendency to make people careful what they said to her. Her eyes were serene and poised, almost flirtatious, which seemed only to make her attentiveness more perfect. Her lips were full and soft, her nostrils slightly upcurved.

"I see," he said, "you've had at least a two-hour start on me this morning."

With a gesture of excusing themselves from the presence of others, a gesture which was toward the breakfast table, they went into the garden, where they seemed almost shadows of something which walked a little before them. They could not have picked a better place or time to look at the sky than after having walked over the lawn and its even shade of green. The sky was at its softest and laziest and puffiest, so that they stood in a spatial stillness, with nothing in motion to distract them, with nothing requiring immediate attention. They talked up at the sky. Even their voices had balance and rhythm, her lips' small movements making it seem that her mouth was near something which should not be disturbed. His voice was clipped and precise, but with a splendid sense of pacing. They appeared to sense that movement of speech was not in itself desirable, except as an aspect of time, which was itself unmoving.

Mr. Pierce could sense when the roses were prettiest, when the gladiolas would have full spikes. Irene was the one who would pull aside greenery and reveal a flower which they would never have seen otherwise. She would hear rain in the night and know whether it was going to hurt the seedlings.

Theirs was a harmony of taste and appreciation which could not be explained. They seemed to perform all the physical courtesies, from entering and leaving their carriage, to sitting side by side on a divan of fixed leather surface, with a complementary regard for each other. Their movements and grace were those of a tall, slender woman and a heavily built man who had a touch of priestlike femininity and solemnity. The meetings of their eyes, the touch of their hands, the turn of their necks, the smoothness of their stride, all were part of a continuous sharing.

All seemed to revolve around love. The flowers were more beautiful for it. The lawn seemed in perfect trim. Irene had had the courage to cut the roses to knee-height, and in the cold frame was a plant which they had been assured would not bloom for at least ten years and perhaps as long as twenty. Henry could not imagine anything more amusing in the midst of annual abundance, and it seemed to Irene the finest mode of expressing the permanence they shared, and the continuity of their lives.

Their fingers found intimate contact and tenderly preserved the tiniest feelings. They moved through the garden, doing the right thing at the right time, always in the proper tone, always with excellent results. Caught in a form of limitation, not of themselves, but of human capacity, they seemed to keep their love as something stretched out before them, something still to be encountered, while their eyes admitted colors and sights which they had never seen before. The trip across America seemed to have given them a renewed interest in land which was familiar to them, to have given them an enlarged basis of appreciation, and a common sense of definition.

Everything seemed to happen under illusion, in the happiness of knowing that love was something in itself, a faint intensity within their stillness, a faint stillness in their excitement, and a continuous desire to reach toward a further union and deeper communication. It was the feeling of being substantial flesh and blood, of having a passionate need for that flesh and blood, and at the same time suffering. It was the feeling of having an inheritance, a bit of fortune which could not be struggled with.

Her husband was among the most poised of men. To him it was known where to go, which chairs to choose, which beverage would have the best taste, where the sun would not be too bright, which greenery would give off a fine scent without the dampness which so often attends. To him the possibilities were determined by choice.

Irene seemed to exist in a world of increased awareness, in which attention to details was forever bringing echoes of yesterday and promises of tomorrow. Through her husband she came to understand the slow rotation of the world as suggesting the very permanence of time. Through him she learned how little consciousness would admit within the small area of her mind, while rushes of event transpired at each moment. She learned the inner release from action which was required of her as the pattern of life complicated and intensified. She learned not to fight to recover what was lost, but to go forward with new strength and submission into realms where there was no competition, where the inarticulate was so personal that it did not require eyes, hands, lips, nor even thought, but only feeling.

He had taught her the dignity of love as apart from passion. He made the truth within love almost visible, so that their minds and hearts were always stealing toward or away, never quite touching, never at the distance of pain. She knew the distinction between laughter and mirth, laughter, which was of the mouth, mirth, which was of the heart; and the difference between proximity and touching when she fitted her five finger tips to his five in a nearness which could be easily lost.

As she walked along beside him, in a garden which would have been small if it had not been for their interest in a single rose and a leaf, it was evident that she had retained her own manner of appreciation. It was evident that her beauty was guilty of being the substance of their love, that her fresh blood and young life was the attraction about which it all turned, charming his eyes, eyes old enough to beg their moments of reprieve. It was evident that it was her will to love and be loved which carried her husband beyond his own boundaries.

It was hearing the gurgle of the little spring which made her kneel to wet her hand and then splash a leaf to make it shine and then put her hand in her husband's so he could feel its slipperiness and the extra smallness of her fingers. Then came to Irene the best feeling of the morning, the simple knowledge that her heart would not be hurt when the summer was gone. She realized that her feelings no longer rested on slender margins. She was eager to have the child.

Something had kept her feeling too young and too recently married to have a child; but now her hands clutched with eagerness. It was what she had been feeling all morning, what had made everything pass so rapidly and with such intensity. Standing beside her husband, it seemed something further, some feeling of deeper confidence than they had known. Not a matter of love, it was more nearly an attitude, a willingness to forgo a year of her own life in order to give life. It was an emotional appetite for motherhood as distinctly sexual as her love for her husband, and as honestly so; thus she could accept the burden which a child would place on her—sacrificial, without seeming to contain loss—and could approach the end of the long honeymoon with confidence.

The child would be her first going away from him, her first responsibility which he could not share. She understood now why there had to be the desire to have the child, and why she had worried about pregnancy when she first suspected it. There came to her a glimmering insight into the true continuity of life, which was after all not based on time, but on the flexibility of human sensibilities; it permitted a girl to become woman, bride, wife and mother.

Snow was fun. Especially deep snow. It forced Gilbert to laugh wildly and unreasonably. He threw himself from his sled merely to feel the sliding burn and hurt against his body and the inebriate sensation of whiteness seen by improperly focused eyes. He aimed the sled at trees and then swerved at the last instant, which was sometimes too late. There was something unnatural in the excitement which playing in the snow aroused in him. He was too rough, careless, always hurting someone without meaning to. Nobody would ride on his back. He was so heavy he could make his sled go faster, and in race-fighting it was almost impossible to push him from the track. Some of the sledders would wait until after he had gone before starting down the hill, which went almost a mile, across Main Street, across the canal, into steel-company property. There was the streetcar to look out for.

Since no one else was sledding, Gilbert stacked his sled vertically in the snow and began to run around. He could run at moderate speed for long distances but was unable to make sudden stops or turns. He washed his face and hands briskly in snow until they glowed with heat, stuck a handful inside his clothes and pressed it into melting, then thrust his head to the neck in a white bank and sucked his nostrils full. It was a terrible, searing sensation.

Several boys had begun snowballing from behind white fortresses. Some were at work making the fortresses taller and others were doing the throwing. Gilbert waited to see which side was losing, then charged straight into the midst of the battle, hardly throwing snow himself, simply making a target of himself to give the losing side time to rest; then for less reason, simply to feel the joy of snowballs mashing against him, the disappointment of ones too soft, the sharp sting of ones which fingers had warmed into bluish-white ice.

"You can't hurt me," he cried defiantly, standing erect.

"That one didn't hurt. No it didn't. I ought to know."

"Haw-w-w, you missed."

Boys from both embankments began throwing. He was in the middle.

"No fair," he cried. "That's no fair."

Even his face wanted to be struck, if not too often in succession. He ran back and forth, threatening, waving his arms. It was sheer glee for him.

One really did hurt. It seemed to cut his ear and make an opening along the side of his head. He whirled and saw it had been thrown by Spider Fortiano, from very near. He chased Spider, bellowing at him. His greatest awkwardness was in deep snow, and yet it was the one time when he was less awkard than other boys. He went through a deep drift, plunging, driving, with the peculiar stiffness that is seen in mechanical toys. It was a pleasure as wild as fighting his way upstream against the rapids of a creek. It was possible that waist-high snow made him a bit insane, for he became not merely reckless, but dangerous.

And he would have caught Spider if he had not stopped several times to hurl snow, wasting the distance he had gained. Gilbert gave up the chase. He kept Spider running by hollering threats at him . . .

Bart was below the chicken house and along the wall, taking exercise. His legs were slender, rather long, and, walking or running, they slid past each other with graceful ease. He was so poised, so certain of balance, that walking along the top of the wall gave him no pleasure. His toes were firm and useful. The worth of the lower part of his body was measured in terms of the speed and distance and control with which he could run. He also practiced jumping on the flat white track which he had taken care to jog over until it was firm enough for running.

Satisfied with the performance of his legs, he turned his attention to his arms and biceps, worried and impatient at their slow development. Of quickness and timing he was assured, but to have strength and force was more difficult and required special exercises, varied movements holding stones in his hands, yet taking care to choose nothing too heavy. His hands, of average size, had already discovered the separate functions and abilities of each finger. They had none of the incompetence of co-ordination that makes boys anxious and afraid to become men, that makes it difficult to catch without holding the wrists together. With almost as much accuracy as a cheap watch has, Bart could count a minute by tapping his forefinger.

He did not grow an inch without knowing it. It was impossible for him to hide weaknesses from himself, and he never bragged about his abilities, never displayed them intentionally before any eyes except his own and, on occasion, his father's . . .

Gilbert made certain Naomi was dressed warmly, with gloves, ear muffs and a scarf which wound twice and still hung over her shoulder. He was ridiculously careful, making her hold his hand, telling her how and where to step over snow which had been shoveled into and along gutters, warning her and scraping with his foot wherever he suspected ice. Their own land, in smooth, natural, semi-drifted snow, had been easier to cross than the sidewalk past the Pierce mansion and on toward the center of town.

Naomi did not like all this very much, but since she was not allowed out alone, she had to behave. Mrs. Mijack for some reason believed snow was much more treacherous for girls than boys and seemed to believe it was improper for a girl to want to go out in bad weather. It had taken a lot of talking on Gilbert's part to get permission, and he was still feeling some of the responsibility which had been put into his care.

Naomi liked snow. It didn't make her turn handsprings, but it was okay, sort of crazy. She accepted her brother's protectiveness without much dispute, only it was so ridiculous—holding onto his hand made her slip more often than if she had been free to balance herself. Her occasional, "Leggo, hey?" went unheeded and sometimes caused her hand to be squeezed more tightly.

The brother and sister seemed to be walking solemnly, carefully, gravely eyeing their surroundings. Gilbert wore a thin black woolen sweater, the elbows frayed into holes so large that whenever he put it on his hands appeared at the wrong places. Naomi was hardly able to walk for being so swaddled in clothes. Behind them, coming along in jerks, behaving somewhat like a puppy on a leash, came the sled.

When they had passed below the steepest portion of the hill, he tied the rope differently to the sled and pulled his sister, insisting that she sit up and keep her feet on the guider and hold firmly to both sides. Whenever he was not looking, Naomi let go with her hands, but when this was noticed she was admonished sternly.

"And where's your ear muffs?"

"Home."

"But I put them on."

Going downhill, Naomi was not allowed to steer, but could kneel between his legs if she promised not to fall off. "Promise!"

"Sure," she said.

She did not think life required her to keep every promise.

The ear muffs were of course in her pocket.

So they went down, but just when the sled was beginning to go fast, Gilbert dragged his shoes in the snow. Even though Naomi pounded him on the back, she could not get him to lift his feet.

"What you scared of?" she said. "I'll get some other boy to take me if you don't go faster."

"And maybe I'll take you home."

But he went faster the next time, fast enough for Naomi and then some, although she would not admit it. They stayed off the steep part of the hill and did not enter the main sled traffic.

After his sister had been given a number of rides, Gilbert descended alone, standing on top of the sled, guiding with the rope held in rein fashion, making the runners skid from side to side, smacking one arm against his thigh. "Watch out," he said to children who were pulling their sleds uphill as he bore down on them. "Watch out there." And the sled got caught in a slow section, so that he ran right off the front end and down the hill another ten feet before falling.

His sister had been watching.

"Now it's my turn," said Naomi.

"No sir-ee. That's dangerous."

"Oh foo!"

"Your ears are red," said Gilbert, walking around behind her and placing his hands on each side of her head. "You oughta worn those ear muffs." He made her ears hurt rubbing them. "What'll happen if they freeze and fall off?"

"Agg-ggh," said Naomi. Her brother could be so dumb sometimes.

The hill was getting full of sledders. Children from the flat western part of town were arriving, habit making them come at the same hour school would have let out. One of the sleds came too near as it

whizzed past, and Gilbert pulled his sister out of the way. "Show-off,"
he shouted. "Hell, I can go as fast as any of them," he said. "But you
don't see me aiming at little kids."

A few girls who had their own sleds went down the center of the
street, less daring, with the purpose of letting some speeding boy
catch them and have a collision or force them into the thick snow
along the sides. Gilbert did not like the way they dragged their feet
and ruined the track.

"C'mon, it's too crowded here. We'll go somewhere else," he said,
filled with a sudden urge to go where there would be no sled or shoe
marks other than their own, into fields which were smooth and gleaming with unblemished whiteness. He wanted his sister all to himself.

They crossed a field where the wind had blown the snow into
various depths, sometimes ankle shallow, other times very deep.
The sled stuck, pulled forward like three brown sticks sliding on
snow, and then upset. But Gilbert just dragged it along upside down.
His track was a long straight line of holes. Naomi's was more erratic.
The snow at one place had a sifted sheen which was like white curtains when they are hung beautifully.

"Hey," she said. "Lookee how deep."

Gilbert dropped the rope and went over to where she was standing waist deep. It came just above his knees. But Naomi was satisfied; she had made him forget not to let her. It was one of the things
she liked about her brother, he didn't always remember.

A dog with a thick coat of hair which looked more reddish than it
was against such a white background followed them. It trotted with
dignity across the field, as if proud of its height, though actually merely
trying to see over the snow better. It seemed at first to have more
curiosity about the tracks the children had made in the snow than
about the children. But then it came to them without coaxing and
singled out Naomi for attention. Gilbert took hold and petted the
dog until there was enough familiarity to decide it was safe to let
her touch it. She did. She even pulled its ears.

"Big old horse, stand still," she said.

It was not cold enough for human mouths to make steam, but the
dog's mouth did. There was a faint chill coming upon the late afternoon, forecast of a cold, clear night, indication that the sun was not
merely moving toward the west, polishing the snow crust, but falling
through space to a greater distance from the earth. The light around
them was beginning to have motion and trickiness. The harder Na-

omi slapped her hand on the dog, the better the dog seemed to like her. Gilbert watched, very happy to see her laugh a little.

But when the dog climbed on Naomi and wrapped its forepaws around her and the hind end of its body began to jerk spasmodically, Gilbert rushed over and caught hold of the tail and pulled. Naomi sat down in a heap, laughing, protecting her face a little. The dog did not seem to know its tail was being pulled.

Gilbert finally shoved the dog away, striking with his fists, kicking at it, ineffectively, because of the depth of the snow.

"What you hit it for? It was only playing."

Gilbert seemed to be frightened. He helped his sister out of the snow.

"Here, doggy," she said.

"No, don't call it."

"Here, doggy-woggy . . . You scared it," she said.

The dog watched them and approached warily. It wanted to be friendly. Gilbert hit it with some snow. "Don't," said Naomi, trying to hold his arm from getting more snow. Gilbert took a long look at the dog.

"All right," he said, "but don't let it jump up."

Naomi did not need to stoop to pull at its fur. The tail was wagging, snow flying in all directions, and when Naomi leaned forward her face was licked and hot breath with a curious scent touched her. "I said don't let it."

"Bark, doggy," said Naomi. The dog looked at her. "Ruff," said Naomi. "Ruff, ruff."

"Ruff-ff," said the dog, about three times as loud.

"Ruff, that's bark," said Naomi to the dog, with the seriousness and attitude a first-grade teacher has leaning over a pupil. "Now bark."

The dog just looked at her.

Gilbert smiled, kissed his sister, and held her mittened hands. His feelings toward what had occurred were gradually subsiding, and there was willingness on his part to be satisfied with the manner in which things had ended. Only for some reason the dog seemed a nuisance. He did not want it around.

Sensing it would be a mistake to chase the dog away, he stomped around in the snow, trying to show his impatience to move on. Suddenly, scarcely knowing what he was doing, he looped the rope around the dog's neck and made his sister sit on the sled.

"What's this for?" said Naomi.

"You'll see."

He coaxed the dog to pull. Off they went, Gilbert behind, pushing, throwing clods of snow at the dog to make it pull harder, Naomi laughing, the dog barking. It was a lot of fun. Gilbert kept hollering, "Mush, mush," and also, "Giddap."

The sled got stuck once and Naomi had to get off, but soon Gilbert freed the runner, and off they went again, merrily, more anticipating the enjoyment to come than that of the moment. The dog seemed to have learned what they were trying to do and was eagerly pulling, though making the mistake of turning his head to see if they were following.

By jerks and twists, amid laughter, for Gilbert hit his sister on the back of the head with a soft lump of snow intended for the dog, the sled crossed the crest of the field and slipped down a steep incline. The big dog, feeling new freedom, took off in huge bounds. "Whee!" said Naomi, feeling her stomach rise. Gilbert, stooping to scoop snow, let go of the sled for a moment, and then could not catch hold.

"Whoa!" he hollered, "hey whoa!"

Sliding, stumbling, without the support the rear end of the sled had offered, shouting at the top of his voice, he saw the sled getting further away.

Naomi was laughing. She even turned and looked back at her brother, motioning joyously for him to run faster. Then the front end of the sled met a tree and Gilbert saw her slide against the tree without raising her arms.

He ran downhill the way he usually ran uphill, skidded past the tree, crawled back, and took her in his arms, not looking to see if she was hurt, not looking at anything. He bound himself around her, his forehead pressed against her, and when he heard the yelping of the dog, his grasp tightened so that he shivered from it. His gestures were so frantic that he seemed to be trying to hurt her more.

"Leggo, you," said Naomi. "Hey now, leggo."

His face was wet because her clothes were almost snowman-coated. He had shut out the sky from her.

"Big old damn tree got right in the road."

Gilbert continued to hold and to press his forehead into the rough smoothness of her coat, seeking a place which would bring comfort, in the manner people unable to sleep seek upon pillows some new shape of their head. His entire existence seemed reduced to fierce breathing, to clutching, mute agony. Naomi tried to release herself.

"Hey, leggo. Your head's too hard."

Gilbert looked at his sister. It seemed to calm him to look at her.

There were black marks on her face, marks somehow more noticeable because she did not know about them. With small bits of snow he wiped them partly away, then dried her face with the warm interior of his own sweater. He was still shivering, in a more nervous manner than before, as he helped her to her feet.

"Are you all right? You're all right? Damn it, tell me if you're all right."

"Sure," said Naomi.

Taking the lead, Gilbert almost dragged her up the hill, in the attitude of someone engaged in a serious and hazardous climb, as if afraid they were not going to be able to climb the slope, as if her weight were far greater than his own. He was mumbling something unintelligible. He kept looking about in the manner of someone who has suddenly encountered a strange new land. He stumbled.

Naomi laughed.

Gilbert slapped her across the face, then took new hold on her wrist and led her across the field.

"What's wrong with you?" she said, feeling at her face to feel what had happened to it.

He pulled and pulled, not satisfied even when she ran to keep up. He had never seen the world all white before. His eyes had no time to fix upon the imperfections in the snow, imperfections which are all that keep snow sane and reasonable, habits and obediences which keep it sufficiently related to the world around.

"Why you hit me?" she asked. "You're always hitting."

Gilbert made no reply. When Naomi braced her shoes against the snow, he felt annoyance for her arm and pulled at it. She fell. For a time he simply dragged her through the snow, as unconcerned, apparently, as a little girl is when she carries a doll around by one arm. It was at the same time evident to him what he was doing.

He seemed to recover somewhat and paused to give her an opportunity to get to her feet. Brushing the worst of the snow from her coat, he peered at her, his face held so close and his eyes so fixed that she was a little afraid of him. At a more normal pace, but with a resolute air, he moved on toward home.

The first thing he did once they were in the house was make her change clothes, and kept hollering for her to dry herself well. He persisted in staring at her fixedly, as if still trying to convince himself that she was not hurt. He kept touching her face and arms with one finger, gently, cautiously. He had no recollection of having asked earlier, of having insisted on a reply in an almost screaming voice.

But he did remember the sled and went after it, a long, slow trip across fields and through the darkening sky, where snow refractions kept an appearance of daylight longer than daylight had remained. All the time he was walking, he had a feeling he should not be alone just now. It was an unusual atmosphere, a kind in which eyes suffer from a vague prescience of illusion, from shadows and shades ordinarily not encountered. He hurried. He was almost afraid. The trees, an orchard desolate with winter, were dark and bare, more bleak than the softness and imperfect, diffused shadows they made on the snow, shadows not from the sunlight, but the evening light high above. Loneliness and distance separated them, unreasonably distant for an orchard.

He found the sled. The dog was there too, motionless, dead, hanging from the rope snarled around the tree over a small ledge not four feet deep. Most of the snow had been scratched away from the side. Gilbert had a difficult time untying the rope because the dog was heavy. He coiled the rope and carried the sled under his arm.

He entered the bedroom as softly and secretly as his clumsiness would allow. "Time to get up!" he said in a loud voice. Waking her before it was necessary explained the loudness of his voice. Naomi was sometimes pleased to see the window flooded with early light which did not warm or even deeply penetrate the bedroom. Sometimes she was grouchy. "Hey, sis, wake up." The small mound beneath the blanket elongated, unseeing eyes peeped, while underneath the bedcovers was a struggle for rebirth, all twisting and pushing. Toes wiggled in several directions as they experimented with the temperature. Then for a short while there was no movement, and it appeared she had refound her sleep position. Gilbert waited. He knew his sister's habits.

Suddenly Naomi sat up on the bed, cross-legged, and smiled.

"Eee, it's cold."

She drew the blanket around her in crude shawl fashion.

"C'mon down. I got a whale of a fire going. Wait, let me see your mouth. No, don't touch it. Does it hurt? Is it where I hit you?"

"Huh-uh. Where I bumped."

"You sure it isn't where I hit you?"

"Huh-uh. You hit me here, no, I forget where."

She wiggled her jaw like a man trying to shave.

"Here maybe," she said, pointing vaguely because she had only the most flimsy internal evidence to go by.

"That's all right, then," said Gilbert. "Listen, that dog . . . I did something, when I went back after the sled, you remember when I went back? Well, I—I hit it with the sled. Like this," he said, making an axe-swinging motion with his arms. "But you mustn't tell. Because I would get into real trouble . . . Because they put you in jail."

It was too early in the morning for Naomi to feel endangered by the peculiar responsibilities of a secret. "Me tell," she said scornfully. "Huh!" Then she became thoughtful. "What you hit for? Did it bite?"

"Yes, yes, that's it," said Gilbert. "It bit at me, like this, see—and I got mad and . . . Listen, I killed it."

"Did you really kill it? All the way?"

"Dead as anything," said Gilbert proudly. His eyes were watching, as if seeking to see some particular response. He was impatient to continue talking, without knowing quite what to say.

"Are you glad?"

He waited.

"If you hit it, I'm glad it's killed," Naomi said, no longer doubting her brother, but passing what for her was a difficult moral judgment.

"Yes," said Gilbert, "I *murdered* it."

He stood before his sister, clenching his hands together, trying to make his knuckles crack the way some of the boys at school did. He seemed to be trying to make her say something he did not want to hear. His eyes were quick and shrewd.

Naomi did not seem to be concerned. "Did you break the sled?" she said. "Can't we go sledding?"

"No, but it should have, because I hit that dog harder than anything. Harder than Father can hit, I bet." He walked over to the window and looked down across the white-coated hill at the darkness of the steel mill. The roofs of the shops were large and directly heated so that most of the snow had melted or blown free, and he could see the shop in which his father worked. He punched his hand lightly against the glass. "It didn't bite at me," he said. "That was a lie. But I killed it all the same. I did do that and I don't care if I don't have any excuse." As he turned from the window the room seemed to darken before his eyes. He took hold of the end of the bed and gave it a shake.

"I bet that old dog bit at you because you hit it and all," Naomi said. "Why you always hitting? It's so dumb."

"It didn't bite at me. Don't you see? I just simply killed it!" Gilbert drew himself proudly erect, in sudden clarity of feeling. "For no reason at all. No reason. Not even for you. I—just—murdered," he said, giving a shrewd, mysterious glance, "because I wanted to."

Naomi evidently did not understand. She began to remove her nighty, then remembered she was not supposed to while he was in the room. "I got to dress," she said. "You go downstairs and make the fire bigger, huh?"

Within the walls of his house Mr. Pierce heard almost every day discussions on a wide variety of topics, corn prices, livestock, Bethel, state and national government, county and local politics, art and culture. Through it all ran a thread of apprehension, in every case personal, and yet in almost every instance the apprehension seemed to require a complete statement of proof of external circumstances and a need of confirmation or approval from at least one other person. It was without doubt, Mr. Pierce concluded, that the age of individualism was passing and might even become extinct. It was not that people wanted to be like each other, but that they could no longer define themselves or retain a sense of their identity.

Mr. Pierce was seldom in agreement with his guests and rarely committed himself to sponsoring or confirming an idea. But he had a way of indicating respect for even the slightest viewpoint which was agreeable to almost everyone. He convinced his friends through a kind of sympathy that his mind operated in a manner similar to theirs, that his general feelings acquiesced, and that his hesitancy to commit himself was only the necessary consequence of a life of impartial reflection.

He admitted to favoring a limited republic, holding with the conservative views of Jefferson. He felt America had passed by the real opportunity for a political foundation, through the suppression of Hamilton. Lincoln was the most overrated president, and Wilson was a foolish man. To Mr. Pierce, the retention of property rights was of primary importance, and the Senate was the only decent governing body. These were at least the views he professed to believe, always with a smile of patience.

He had an ability to retract any statement he made, or to modify and explain it at length, putting a more pleasant light about it. He could somehow improve his stature even through making a retraction. When caught in a substantial fault, he would actually bluster and would throw a path of words before him. That was because he was so seldom placed in a position where he had to defend himself.

His knowledge of the weaknesses and faults in people made him charitable and well-disposed toward them. He never called attention to his own preferences, except in the cases of music, wine, sculpture, painting and poetry, all subjects on which there was no objection to a man having preferences. His capacity for detachment allowed him to detect the constant ironies and amusement that went on around him.

Mr. Pierce would have compared himself in character, though with tongue in cheek, to Mr. Lang. He explained himself to a degree by stating to John Broghton, "You poets too often account for people through darkness and light, wealth and poverty, heroism and cowardice. Most of us are really another sort of person. We are idle, yet not yawning, we have refined life to tea and coffee, yet without harming ourselves. We, being free of the scramble to get together money to pay the butcher and baker, neither concentrate our abilities toward a specific purpose, nor allow ourselves to neglect any of the pertinent or impertinent aspects of life. I would suggest we ride sidesaddle. We make culture an attitude of mind, and thereby exert a different influence on society. I should surmise that it is difficult to call us either evil or good, and yet that seems to me one of the most explanatory things I could say."

Mr. Pierce was a man who had never undergone anything deeply emotional or shocking. His closest approach to that had been his marriage, and there was now a fine line of caution about his eyes, as if he were passing to a further stage in which he might remain unaffected even if something shocking did occur. He was turning his sensibilities toward a form of non-participation, with a gathering distaste and distrust for enthusiasm.

Looking up at people with her hand held toward them, never speaking a word, there were sometimes enough coins in her palm so that when she went to the lady behind glass, the lady would tear off a rectangle of red paper, sometimes shake her head and push the coins back. Rose would stand and look up at people some more. Three or four little boys, who hollered at misters for pennies, would push her away. She learned to clutch her hand tight around the coins. She never distinguished between people who put coins in her hand and those who pushed her aside.

There were eight light bulbs in front of the building, one above each letter of "Standard," and it was the brightest thing Rose had ever seen. If she did not have enough coins in her hand before a quarter of nine she would have to run down the street and across the canal and the railroad tracks. She always sat in the front row, where the quick jerky motion of black and white had a strange appeal to her. She liked to hear people laughing, and she liked to hear the piano. She liked to march all the way up the aisle, even though she usually had to wait for someone to lift her to be able to get her mouth against the water.

21

Unlike many stout children, Gilbert was not indolent. He was the possessor of almost boundless energy and seemingly indestructible health. Awake, he sat immediately straight up in bed and indulged in one huge yawn containing various separate noises, then swung his legs over the edge of the bed and rose. He was really awake and ready to go too.

"Church," he said, shaking Bart. "Wake up. Church."

Then he went to Naomi's room.

"Get ready, everybody," he hollered in the hall.

"You better hurry," he told Naomi. "I'm all ready."

He showed her the pale insides of his hands as evidence. His hair was more wetted down than combed. But it looked as if he had tried.

Mijack was outside. He was wearing the same black Sunday suit in which he had married, and which through brushing and pressing and careful usage still retained qualities of newness. Or perhaps it was more his attitude toward the suit which made it seem new. Standing now, looking toward the sunrise, hands stuffed awkwardly into the coat pockets, hands a little stiff because they were not being used today, a clean toothpick in the side of his mouth, it was apparent that he had never become accustomed to Sunday.

He was waiting for his family to assemble at the door. He was waiting to lead them.

Gilbert was sitting on the register when Naomi came downstairs.

"Don't come near," he warned. "It's too hot."

Naomi had on a white dress and white stockings that came above her knees.

Mother came into the room. Her walking had a different sound on Sunday, a sort of swishing which followed her about. She smelled of a rather sterile cologne.

"You go right straight upstairs and wash your feet and put clean stockings on."

"Me?" said Gilbert. "I washed."

He used again his hands as evidence. They were not dirty, but the damp, convincing freshness was gone.

"Never mind that," said Mrs. Mijack. "Do as I tell you."

If she had not been late herself, she would have let him go to church as he was. He was really remarkably improved over his usual weekday appearance.

"You'll find your stockings right on the chair where I put them last night," said Mrs. Mijack. "If you'd only half look. Now hurry."

There was a crispness in her voice which was not usually present. For Sunday was the one day when she could allow herself to show a surprisingly generous appreciation for the family which she had mothered.

Gilbert ran upstairs. In a very little he was back.

"Tie my shoes."

When he tied them himself, his shoes were always loose.

Naomi was not to be depended on for favors. Because when she was ready to go somewhere, she wanted to go.

Bart descended and passed through the confusion and broke the crown of a cold egg and sucked on it. That was all the breakfast there was time for. He was wearing a dark suit with long trousers.

"You look nice," Mrs. Mijack said. "Yes . . . I like that suit on you."

She was indicating gratitude. Everyone had found his shoes cleaned and polished.

"Thank you, Mother," he said, dropping the light, empty shell into the garbage.

Mijack stood looking across town and river as far as the York Mountains, aware of how clear and bright the morning was and of the vast silence which had been broken only once by the faint chiming of the bells of the Catholic churches. The enormous area that could be seen from this height made him aware of the feebleness of sound, even bells. The reason for the brightness of the sky, and part of the reason for the silence, was that the steel plant was operating today on a minimum force. Two- and three-shift operations seemed to have had the effect of keeping the sky darkly pigmented and of making the town shadowed and dirty. Yet Mijack was not as antagonistic toward the town as he once had been.

Sunday was still hard for him. Yet he welcomed the rest and quiet, from the standpoint of physical necessity, and also from greater contentment with the way life was going. He could not feel that he had done badly these past eighteen years. He stood and breathed, gathering sustenance in the form of accumulated air energy, pulling in slow and powerfully as only a man who had been free of tobacco all his life could.

Mrs. Mijack was bereft of her usual precision, tangled in details, forced to adopt tactics of hurry. Among these details was managing to have dinner almost immediately after church. Even though she had been busy since dawn, she would have to have the stove working for her while she was nearly a mile away, which she sorely distrusted. It gave Sunday an enlarged atmosphere, one not confined to the two hours of church service.

Bart put on his checkered cap with the button visor, and went out and stood with his father. For a while he even looked in the same direction.

"It's Mother and Gilbert," he said, "having a time of it."

"Yes," said Mijack. "They're going to make us late."

"It don't make any difference to me," said Bart. "I'd as soon not go at all."

"Ah-h-h!" said Mijack, and looked at his son. "Faugh! My boy, give yourself a little time before you take that attitude." He was not angry, but a little grieved. "It isn't always the best to deny yourself things, and then some day have to come back to them when they ought to be past."

The remainder of the family assembled and indicated readiness. Mijack went to them, in the indifferent, unhurried stride a man takes after he has been waiting too long. "Well, so we're ready," said Mijack, without anger, with more a sense of wonder at how it had come about that his family was gathered together, clean and prepared, and he not having had to shout at a single one of them. "Let's make down!"

It was a fine feeling to set out five abreast and march down the hill

212

and into town. Mijack's hat looked old because it had a new black band. The narrow, detachable collar did not quite match his shirt.

Bart, in a new dark suit and long trousers, worn carefully and almost stylishly, was the one who felt most pride in his appearance.

Gilbert, his hair broken loose from its watered position by the first gust of wind, was in knickers of corduroy brown which covered the worst of his legs but emphasized two dumpling buttocks; the worn-out elastic cuffs had a tendency to work up on his knees when he took long strides. The short jacket had been purchased with the knickers, but so seldom used that it had a distinct tone, and he looked so different from the fresh, modern appearance of his brother that it seemed correct for him to choose the place next to his sister. Yet the family was as proud of him as of anyone.

And Naomi, all in white, so tiny and thin among this family of strong-boned, heavy-shouldered people, was like the badge of their pride. And Mrs. Mijack, a plain, tough countrywoman, one of thousands spread across the farming regions of Lancaster, York, Dauphin and Lebanon, was made to seem unusual by this family which was too much for her to cope with.

For all their dissimilarities they had a unity which they might individually have denied. They were of a different breed from the people of the town, of a stock and blood which came out of the frontier era, a race which had sprung from the early needs of America, strong, simple, formidable: a race which, like all things no longer needed, had vanished, leaving remnants and reminders. The Mijacks had an obvious kinship of life and of purpose such as can be seen in old family photographs. As they entered town, using the street because the sidewalks were not meant for five abreast, they seemed something firm and unyielding in a time when war and industry were changing the customs and attitudes of men everywhere. It was evident that they were more strangers than when Mijack had come alone and chosen his site and his way of life.

This family had risen out of a time when men could think in terms of great tracts of land, of conquest by the individual of uninhabited empires, out of a time when men could not escape struggling with their moral consciences, because a man stood as his own law and his own punishment. And Mijack was responsible for passing this on to his sons, of putting into them the pride and the illusions which he himself had compromised into a smaller and more personal sphere.

They came upon other people going to church and passed in their long, striding fashion, more vigorous, alert, healthy, more prepared for

Sunday and for church. Their greetings were bellowed out in the sincere and warm phrases of people who are not accustomed to seeing friends and acquaintances each day, and they perhaps assumed a greater fame and importance than they had. It was not at all the atmosphere of gawking, gangling yokels coming into town to buy seed and a sack of flour, but a people of great and simple dignity and pride coming down from the mountain to worship in town churches, a people of great loneliness who were for a few hours offering their natural affections to all who would partake.

They had the good will of people who have risen on a bright day and have had nothing happen to spoil their journey. They marched up the church steps and through the vestibule, and as they entered into the dome of the church and took their pew, there was a natural timing of sound and movement that hinted at why the floor of the church should remain uncarpeted, and why the pews should remain wooden and straight. Mijack looked straight at the pulpit, which was still empty, though the organ was playing and the choir preparing their music sheets. Susie took a hymnal from the rack and placed it in his hands.

They bent their heads in prayer. Even Bart. They were the only ones to rise when the minister entered. They stood for the last verse of the opening hymn and remained standing for the Doxology and a portion of the order of service. They rose again for the Apostles' Creed, and for the prayer, and for the whole of the closing hymn and the Benediction. Before their kind of God it was wrong to kneel, and it was equally wrong to uplift their hands, or shut their eyes.

It was the Seventh Day, and they were united, and they were alone in a church that had good attendance.

Mr. Pierce clasped the collar firmly against his throat, raising his head to do so, then fitted links in his cuffs with the same precise care. He slipped his coat on, however, without the assistance of the mirror, shaking it slightly until it settled about him. His suit had been brushed in an earlier portion of the morning, and a selection of clothing had awaited his rising.

In the matter of shirts he had prejudice, wearing nothing except soft collars. He was particular. He picked up and set down his watch, took a last glimpse in the mirror, not in vanity, but for the reason that he could better detect any disarrangement of his clothes. Then, gathering the watch in his hand, he went into the hall, leaving the bedroom appearing as if nothing had been disturbed, the brushes and combs straight and side by side. He was unaware of his sense of neatness and had never in his life tidied or cleaned anything.

The stairs he began to descend were broad and so numerous that he did not have so much to descend as to move forward, and he was not tempted to place his hand on the heavy ornamental banister. He looked down at the room and the table, bearing six kinds of flowers, all chosen for smallness and pale color.

Irene's eyes noticed him, her expression still that of delight with her own activity. Mr. Pierce paused, as if by standing still he would remain unrecognized. He had the faintest sense of discomfort.

Irene came to the stairs and made it necessary for him to be accompanied to the table. There was in his manner a reserve which bordered on resistance. As breakfast began, there was in all his wife did and said an air of romance which seemed unreal to him, a feeling which caused him to pass his hand across his forehead in a shading movement. Yet, by the end of breakfast he could accept a flower in his lapel and feel it an honest pleasure to press the napkin against his mouth.

Mr. Pierce and his wife went into the garden. It was the morning walk. Her fingers were laced at his elbow. The morning seemed to have a fine brilliance, so that no caution was required, everything was lovely, and Irene was uncritical of even the most common things. Mr. Pierce was at his best in such an atmosphere, with his dignity, his faint aloofness. Few men knew how to walk; he did. He had retained a trait of walking through the town and his own garden as if he were a stranger seeing the area for the first time.

Three pigeons with gentle brown eyes and quiet, dignified manners were gathered near one of the white benches; they walked stately along the pathways, proclaiming their right to behave as human beings. They were so bold that it was evident they were from the lawn of the state capitol, and so tame that Mr. Pierce felt them a disturbance to his walking. He was not quite able to appreciate birds. Yet he allowed his wife to tease him into going to the house for peanuts, where he felt the discomfiture of requesting from the maid something which was not thoroughly explained through the very act of request. There was in him a need for the appearance of continuity in his actions.

Mr. Pierce watched his wife feed one pigeon until the others became confident enough to walk in circles near the bench. He spread his handkerchief to sit upon. After a while she placed her hand on his, palm toward palm. It seemed to him an imposition. He sat there and solemnly crushed one shell at a time, removing the brown inner cover, and with some awkwardness tossing the nuts toward one of the pigeons, watching until he was sure they were eaten.

For a few minutes his eyes turned on his wife with an anxious, deep gaze such as they seldom allowed themselves. He envisioned her attractive possibilities. It was an extremely sensitive pleasure to consider the result of the devotion he had given her, and to consider the woman she might become if given all that was in his power to give. What he saw in her was the potential of making life an art.

To accept this was to return to a loneliness which he had for a time escaped. It was the one thing which was denied to himself, denied because he was without the passion required, without the ecstasy which was its foremost necessity; denied because he stood in relation to her as the historian and the interpreter. Mr. Pierce recognized that he had become an inadvertent threat to her happiness. It was again and again the thought of being married to her which forced him to descend into himself.

What he recognized—and it was for some reason more emphatically true as he sat crushing peanuts—was his inability to reach far enough, in the years ahead, to capture and retain his wife's imagination. Only that would enrich the promise her eyes and the independence of her lips and especially hands, resting on his arm, held. If she were divorced from him—emotionally—if she were willing to leave him in a position of lower sensibilities and proceed toward perfecting herself, then he would be released, and could take the satisfactory position of being her husband.

But this was not his position, as it had not been at breakfast, as the flower in his lapel reminded him even now. The position which he had so rightfully held during the first years of their marriage was becoming intolerable. Her adoration of him had come to be the cause. Mr. Pierce was forced to recognize his wife in terms of a weight, easily lifted and sustained for a few years, but which required enormous effort to hold aloft continually. Feeling unequal to holding her aloft forever, he shivered at the vanity of making the attempt. He despised knowing that he could retain her belief in him past the time of importance, certainly past the time of importance to himself. He was at the same time too keen to discard himself as being entirely without value.

They were both splendid traps for idealism, and oddly paired. Irene brought danger through her need of passion and expression, while he

216

was the victim of intelligence and taste. He was able to deal effectively with people of a lower order, yet was at the disadvantage of his respect for exceptional people. He had always accepted himself in certain situations as an invalid.

As a man who had created a deception, he felt the need to take certain precautions which were distasteful to him. As an additional confusion, there was his feeling, at moments, of being capable of continuing to be to his wife the sensitive companion which she needed. At times he felt that his natural self would, after all, simply have to suffice. He could only give her all the attention, kindness and understanding of which he was capable. He could only keep watch over the questions and commands of her eyes. This was not as difficult as he felt it to be, sitting on the bench beside her, sitting on his white handkerchief.

Mr. Pierce was the victim of a curious kind of unhappiness in which everything he did was perfect and was happiness, except that he did not accept it as such. The flaw was interpretation, the renunciation was of himself, though he could not renounce himself. Therefore he believed the best procedure was in making his function more regular and less interrupting. It was necessary for them not to share everything if they were to continue to have happiness.

He was not at the same time capable of believing that he was satisfied with this arrangement. He knew this much—Irene must not be allowed to get as close to him as she desired; that, regardless of the choice he might make as to his position. For within the very closeness she sought was something which made him feel suffocated, even vaguely affronted, as if she were about to take hold of and pull the lapels of his coat.

The children had in no manner changed their essential situation, except to retard its development. Mr. Pierce had the feeling that he must move carefully, that he was on the edge of an antagonism, one which he could not yet comprehend, and which he felt only as a distaste to be sitting beside his wife, solemnly breaking shells by pinching them between his fingers, while the incongruous eyes of pigeons watched him.

Gilbert woke on the morning of his birthday with an inner glee which the quiet and uninhabited atmosphere of the house soon made into something disappointing. Father was either still in bed or not in the house. Mother did not come down at the usual hour. Although he was extremely lonesome, he was hesitant about going upstairs and waking anyone. He remembered how he and his sister and even Bart had been sent to bed.

Father and Mother came downstairs together, and a little later Naomi and Bart. Breakfast was orderly and rather subdued, the family so seldom seated together for this meal that they did not seem to know quite how to behave. There was a strange feeling in Gilbert at seeing the hour pass for his father to go to work, and particularly to see his father pay no heed to it. Then Mother went somewhere in another part of the house and returned with a box. Inside was a pair of short boots, clodhoppers.

When the box was opened, and Gilbert was putting the laces in the bottoms of the boots, preparatory to trying them on, Naomi took the card and read it, then gave it to her father. Bart sat watching both of his parents, eyeing one, then the other. When the card was handed to him, he read it carefully, then threw it aside. "Well, shit," he said.

Gilbert was test-bouncing, and hollering, "Look! Look!"

Bart made as if to rise from the table and leave the room. When his brother came and tried to hug him, he shoved himself loose.

"What goes on here?" said Mijack. "What's this to show?"

"I didn't have anything to do with it," Bart cried out. "I didn't even know about it. It's from them, not me." He pointed with accusation at his parents.

"Hush now, boy," said Mijack.

"Of course it's from all of us," said his wife.

"The hell it is," said Bart. "If I want to give something, I'll give it."

"That's enough out of you," said Mijack.

Bart was silent, and waited at the table until the others had risen, then went and put on a light summer jacket and started down the hill.

Gilbert was one of the happiest children in all America.

He had begged for them, pleaded in vain, for almost two years. Now he actually had them. The card attached read, "Your birthday, from Father, Mother, Naomi and Bart."

He put the short boots on, making them firm and snug, then test-bounced a couple of times, ran around downstairs, upstairs, where they made more noise. He tried skidding on the bare floor. He marched the Kaiser goose step, hupping. Naomi followed him about, clapping her hands. But in a little while he had her almost in tears, with pretended threats of stamping on her feet and telling her in a mysterious voice that there wouldn't be anything left of her toes if she got stepped on by *these* boots. Her toes would be *squashed!*

"You better don't," said Naomi, a little afraid.

Her brother was so excited there was no telling what he might do.

He did not even heed his father's threat to put the boots back in the box.

Gilbert rushed outside and found mud to wade in and water too deep. Then, with great heaviness around his feet, he ran and ran, working the stiffness out of the leather. His feet became gradually accustomed to the boots without forgetting them, and he felt less clumsy and fat with the strong, heavy leather girdling his legs. He felt more balanced and secure, the way football players feel more agile confined in heavy uniforms and pads. He could not run faster, but better, with more determination.

Gifts are seldom valued for their magnitude and not always for the circumstances which enfold them, yet nothing could have given him as much happiness and sheer glee as these boots; they were so obviously meant for outdoors, for freedom, adventure, excitement, meant to cuff and scrape on rock, to clack like hoofs, to pound vibrations across dry, hard fields, to stick in and suck at mud, to slice the bark of young trees and crush weeds and briers, and make deep, wide holes in snow.

When he was tired of being by himself, he remembered school. Naomi had already gone, and he rushed after her, caught up with her, and took her books in his arms, and let her wear his red hunting cap. It was a big red helmet on her, but if she pushed all her hair and the tops of her ears under the cap, it would not blow off. She wore the visor turned up and walked like a Texan in a movie.

Gilbert had his pride today. Both heel and toe were cleated, so that walking on brick or concrete produced a sharp, rhythmic clicking, and, on occasion, even sparks flew. His mind was often preoccupied with listening to his own walking.

In the hallway of the school Gilbert surrendered the books, she the cap, and then Gilbert wore it into his classroom; it remained on his head until the teacher told him otherwise. The teacher merely pointed at her own head with one wiggling finger and Gilbert obeyed, but if she had not done this the cap would have been worn all during the day. Carrying his cap to the cloakroom, he listened to the elephantine sounds on the floor beneath him. Especially in the hall.

He was more aggressive and spirited. He put his hand up often and gave long, exuberant answers to questions. He sharpened his pencil

219

seven times. On the playground he showed off in front of all the children. Visibly and audibly he had been given a means of expressing his pride, and he took full advantage.

It was a warm day, the doors of the classrooms were open. Gilbert asked to be excused to go to the basement. On the way he peeped into the room in which Naomi was seated, and got her attention long enough to make her afraid he would be caught. He found it strange to see her seated among little children. He could not quite understand what Naomi was doing among them. He made a snoot at the teacher, who was not aware that he was peeping in.

So the day progressed. There was always a race to see which one could get out of the building earliest. Naomi won, because the third grade was not strict about time.

"I didn't deserve them," he told her. "I'm the luckiest boy in the whole world."

He was in earnest. Of gratitude he had too great a share. He felt hurt by the goodness of his father and mother, for whom he was nothing but trouble and mischief. He forgot all the mean things which he had thought when the boots had been denied to him.

A bunch of boys were going up on the hill to play. He left his sister and went with them. His furious energy, clumsiness and desire for laughter, roughness and mischief were suited to the fields and hills. His flesh craved sunlight and wind, even rain. He ran to get more wind against him, stripped his clothes to find more sun, in a wild, childish search for sensation. Perhaps stoutness was responsible, but when he ran, laughter would be thrown from his mouth, and the more out of breath, the greater the laughter, uncontrollable, like a fit, making his tiny eyes sightless, making it difficult to keep all the saliva inside his mouth.

As the boys crossed a field they began to jostle each other and practice their versions of tackles and blocks, mostly trying to catch each other unprepared. Gilbert sprawled on the ground, avoiding this, using his new boots to ward off those who were tussling too near him. He chewed weeds and grass, choosing indiscriminately whole handfuls and cramming them into his mouth, later spitting out the stringy, juiceless husks. He caught a grasshopper and held it until there was a glob of black juice on its hind end and then tasted the juice.

Out of disorganized individual struggle rose a battle, as the boys moved onto a corn field that had not been plowed this year, a battle in which it became a great joy to swing heavy, old corn stalks in two-handed-sword fashion. Gilbert was soon in the thick of it, taking more punishment than he gave. His arms hurled yellow and browned stalks with big clods of dirt still around their roots, hurling them like German stick bombs. Then he struck someone too hard, and three or four boys began to beat him over the head. He fled, gathering up a huge clod of dirt, and ran to where there was a young locust tree, bent the tree and let it leap at the sky, intending to catapult the clod of earth at his enemies. But the dirt broke and fell on and around him.

He had no sense of the passage of time. Light had to withdraw from the sky for him to know it was already past the supper hour. Then he would go home in dread of punishment, having offended too often to expect his father to accept an excuse. He was always forgetting. He could not understand it.

But he was saved. Naomi came to tell him it was time for supper. He felt relieved when it was made clear that she had not been sent after him. He was grateful; sometimes she hunted without being able to find him. He had really come to accept it as her responsibility to get him home on time and to be unable to understand how it could come about that she was not able to locate him, when he was *right here* all the time.

Even after she came, he found it hard to leave. He could not get his fill of merriment and wanted to keep on going. Darkness was the end. It meant going home, where he was only a boy with homework to do, going home to obedience and discipline. It was difficult for his mind to bridge the long, dark gap between sunset and sunrise; he wondered why there had to be night. There seemed no use for it. Summer he loved, summer, when sunlight stretched long into the evening.

"Heck, what we eat so early for? Nobody else does."

"What you got to complain about?" said Naomi. "Look at me."

He remembered all the good things of the day and was ashamed that he had for a time forgotten his boots and had forgotten that he had no duties around the house as his sister had.

"Everybody loves me," he said. "I sure am lucky."

He waved toward where he had left a few of his companions.

"Do you know," he said, "when I grow up I'm going to make everybody love me."

That night he set his boots side by side and stuffed the socks into their tops. After the light had been turned out he had a desire to inspect them and see if they had been in any way damaged. Instead he felt over them and then stuck his nose in their tops and smelled how good they were inside. He felt as if he could not wait for tomorrow to come.

"Like 'em?" said Bart, lying with his head resting on his arms in the darkness.

"You bet!"

There was silence. Gilbert finally put the boots on the floor.

"I'm glad," said Bart. "I'm sorry I jumped you this morning. It didn't have anything to do with you."

Gilbert did not understand, but he sensed the friendliness. It somehow completed the whole of a wonderful day.

Bart listened to his brother burrowing into the center of the bed, in the peculiar hole-digging method he had of getting comfortable. In the closet, behind a pile of clothing, was another pair of boots. They were a fine pair which had cost more than thirty dollars, and which Bart had ordered specially, paying another ten dollars to have real silver hooks and clasps put on them. These were knee boots, not clodhoppers, and were exactly what he himself would have wanted two years earlier. He was considering whether or not to give them to his brother.

Bart had never before given a gift. It complicated his thinking.

Bart no longer liked Christmas or birthdays. It made him angry to be told to be good. He sensed the obligations of gifts, the ifs and buts attached. Having never had enough money to buy something really valuable, something which a person would prize and retain through the years, he disdained and was ashamed to purchase "hankies" or ties. He preferred to give nothing and get nothing. He earned money, bought what he needed, and then it was his. Not even Mijack had the right to touch it then.

Bart had seen for nearly a year how much his brother wanted boots. Although he had at the beginning disdained buying them, the coincidence of three events had come together to form a different aspect. For some reason he had felt badly last year about not buying his brother anything. Then he had seen with astonishment that boots of handmade quality were expensive. It made a present he could respect.

The boots had been in the closet more than two weeks. It had been his intention to give them to Gilbert privately sometime during the day. His reaction at breakfast had been to run upstairs and bring down these boots and cast them in the face of his parents. He thought his mother had done this deliberately. His anger at having his name put on something which was not his, with the bitterness of having a better pair upstairs, made him furious with her.

Until he saw that it was his father who had made the purchase. The threats to make Gilbert put them in the box made Bart see how really pleased his father was, and Bart had known then and there that he could not give his brother those he had upstairs. His immediate thought was to return them to the store. But the store was not going to take them back, at least not unless Bart got his father to go with him. Mijack could, if he had a mind to, make a store take back anything.

Now, in bed, he considered wearing them himself. The jealousy it would create was not without appeal. Yet it was just this which made him refuse to wear them, at least at present. Before going to sleep, he concluded nothing more satisfactory than to cover them more so there was less chance of their being discovered.

Springs were his specialty. Crouched by the fire, his eyes extraordinarily bright and large, his mouth dark and unmoving, pumping the bellows with his foot, staring into the core of the flame, he heated a coil cherry red. It was his foot which squeezed air from the bellows and fed color into the flame, his hands which made decisions. His eyes, for all their tenseness, seemed only to have a supervisory purpose. They were prepared to see mistakes. They were at the same time respectful of the movements of his hands, of the slowly visible results of flame against steel. The tongs with which he held and manipulated the spring were gripped as easily by his right hand as a schoolteacher might hold a pointer. He wore a glove which was similar to a sandal in that the backs of the fingers had been removed, and the back of the hand had only a leather thong, so that the glove was held on at wrist and finger tip. He could shake the glove from his hand at an instant's notice and work with it dangling from his wrist.

His features were those of an inarticulate man trying to express a deep and powerful emotion. He was a rather striking man in work clothes, his forearms thrust through sleeves which were blackened at the cuffs, his legs flexed with the steady, motionless ease of forgotten endurance, and the unusual breadth of his neck showing that it was the pivotal position of his strength.

When he saw that the steel had taken all the heat it could safely contain, he dipped the spring in tar, held it aloft in torch position while the tar burnt off, then dropped it into the barrel of oil. Steel was more delicate in its requirements than baking, and had less dependable and observable symptoms of preparation. It needed to be cooled quick or slow, or quick and slow, needed to be handled gently while it was taking a set, or needed a quick blow which would shake the magnetism to one end. It had to be clear in his mind just exactly what the piece of steel was expected to do, whether it was going to be squeezed, pulled, twisted, ground, rolled.

A little later, working heavy iron, making punches and sledges and plate hammers, so much heat was needed that he had to use a helper to work the bellows and feed coal. He worked even closer to the fire, so that the presence of another person would not disturb his attention. The helper knew better than to talk, although Mijack himself talked: "That sucker, how's that for contrary, Sam Hill, halfway doings, get my goat once . . . Now I let for you to decide if that isn't . . . There now, it's for the best after all, and it may be for the best to . . . Put a little kink . . . Right about there . . . It's only bein' a little slow to get the hang of things . . ." So much heat was produced that scale formed on the surface and kept his eyes from being able to detect the exact color of the inner iron, so he chilled it, knocked the scale off, scratched a little place clean, and when the color was not quite correct, thrust it back into the fire, guessing at the present temperature by the response it had to touching the flame.

He trusted his eyes. He did not trust formulas. He did not trust time.

He did not quench the entire hammer, only the part which was to be hardened, the part which would strike the blows, so that the main portion of the hammer would remain resilient and soft. It would supply the firmness which would keep the hammer from vibrating in tattoo. Earlier in the morning he had carried his buckets to the canal, selecting quench water from two different places, and he would never have allowed any of the iron he worked to be quenched in river water.

There was a pile of dark earth which he had brought down from the mountain. To it there had been added from time to time earth which had felt right in his hands and under his nostrils. The pile was kept so damp that when it was not used for several days a green scum formed over it, and there was an odd odor, neither pleasant nor sickening. He was convinced this damp, black earth drew the heat out of iron at exactly the rate which made it most firm, made it least brittle. There were stones and shades of soil which he believed to contain powers and qualities that no man could comprehend, and he was not ashamed to feel an abiding awe for the mysteries of the earth.

No matter how thirsty he became, he never drank water while working over the fire. He sweated under his clothes, sweated slowly and continuously through the dead of summer, but his face and his hands were as dry and darkened as the bark of an old tree, and his mouth, set firmly, had to retain the moisture it had until lunch and then until the end of the day. Water not only weakened a man, but it was the weakness of man.

It was not at work, nor in the town, nor in his ideas that Mijack was failing. It was in the home, where he was accustomed to being the law, where the dictum of his voice was the code for the family to live by. There was an atmosphere which appealed to his sons in the way military schools did. Mijack himself could see that a man could be strong and good and in the main uncompromising with life and still have weaknesses. He knew he had weaknesses. But he was at least clean of that weak, ugly mode of life, of living for money and its security, in the sense that people in the town were living. He was more concerned about damage to his tools than about loss of money. He was more concerned about the perfection of his craft than casting a silhouette which would retain the respect of his sons.

It was an afternoon of sunshine. Mr. Rowiger was playing the role of a browsing investigator of the afternoon itself. He had a habit of walking a distance and then pausing, for no apparent reason, looking all about. The sidewalk was a flat, even stripe of concrete, a constant firmness underfoot which suited his mood and gave his eyes more continuous freedom. His feeling was of having a renewed sense of himself and an increased regard for things that were familiar.

Seeing the garden empty and the gate open, he turned in through the gate and walked across the lawn. Mr. Rowiger was without the faintest sense of the rights of property, and so he examined the lawn as freely as if had come upon something of interest on the mountain side. He was so unhampered by the emotions of possession that he could view walls and boundaries only in the sense of landscape, and was so unaware of his physical presence that it was with surprise that he saw his footprints near some flowers which he had been examining.

A little spring bubbled quietly into a concrete container. Red goldfish played in the bubbles. A portion of the lawn was hooped for croquet, colored balls lying about in the grass, mallets leaning against the maples. The apple tree was gone, but the ground remained humped and uneven, and the grass seemed to refuse to heal over the

225

area. The grass was a good, firm green, but not aggressive. The house seemed to have been scraped into a new red brightness and portions of the walls had been altered to accommodate larger windows. The amount of change made it difficult for Mr. Rowiger to recall whether or not there had been a tree in front of the house.

In the distance the stable was being torn down. There was also a tennis court, the white lines standing out against earth much too red not to have been imported. A colored cook and maid seemed to have taken possession of the rear part of the house, where they were washing and shaking out tablecloths. Mr. Rowiger could arrive at no decision, and with a sense of not having the right to reflect upon the tastes of people who were making an effort to keep their surroundings beautiful, he turned and went toward the front lawn.

Irene tapped against the window. Mr. Rowiger, as he waited beside the porch steps, realized he would have preferred not to meet her. His hesitancy referred to himself.

Irene came out and across the porch and down the steps. Mr. Rowiger was greeted eagerly and asked how and what he was doing. It was of course awkward for him to explain with any sense of preparedness. They were shaking hands long past the time for such a courtesy. Mr. Rowiger, knowing his fault, let his eyes dwell upon her.

Irene seemed spontaneous in her enthusiasm, but quite competent and self-possessed, as if she were feeling none of the hesitancies of which he was so aware. Mr. Rowiger was grateful to her for not embarrassing him with a profuse outward display of feeling, and admired her for a command of herself which reminded him of former times. He told her a little of his past, modestly, genially and admitted that he had no purpose for his visit. The garden had attracted him. He mentioned specifically a rose bush which, curiously, he had given little attention to. Irene stepped away from the house to see better, and as she did so, Mr. Rowiger noticed the quickness of movement which had always delighted him. But her eyes seemed to have the hard, straight gaze that attempts to place things exactly.

His principal feeling was of being dissatisfied with himself. Although tanned and satisfactory in appearance—with the exception of receding hairline—he was plagued by a feeling of incompetence. His glasses had a thickness of which his eyes were fully aware. He was unprepared, after such a long time, to renew their friendship. He was not willing to cross or trespass the time and distance which the diverging lives had gathered, and was at the point of beginning to realize how comfortable his life had become. Yet he quite frankly experienced a sense of emotional obscurity, a sense of lost pitch and intensity, which could be defined only in terms of his present nervousness.

Irene insisted that he should come in. Mr. Rowiger resisted, until he saw that her insistence would place them in an awkward position. He then inquired as to the stable and was told that it was to be the site of a swimming pool. He inquired with some reluctance as to whether there had been a tree in front of the house, pointing vaguely to an area near the gate. There was a vacancy in the exchange. Mr. Rowiger nodded, murmured something, and passed on into the parlor.

The maid took an announcement. There followed a brief introduction to Mr. Pierce, after which Irene hurried to her canvas, explaining that she had just begun a drawing. Mr. Lang joined the two men. Irene chatted while she sketched, drew lines while conversing, and made brush strokes even while laughing. She seemed—slightly unconvincingly—to have brought a portion of the freshness of the afternoon into the room with her.

Mr. Pierce offered tobacco and was faintly amused when it was declined, smiling at the way Rowiger's hand was held in a position of utter refusal. It was a beginning which could have been pivotal, but Rowiger was spared the consequences of his unintentional discourtesy. The offered tobacco was turned to Mr. Lang, who accepted the pouch and dipped his pipe into it. He did not fill the bowl or tamp the tobacco firm, and sat with his pipe unlighted.

A mild, early autumn seemed to have descended upon Mr. Lang, softening and mellowing rather than destroying his features, leaving him free of the ugliness of old age. With his hair white and yet retaining its pleasant texture, he appeared to have regained a touch of youth and a stronger complexion. The most pronounced characteristics still seemed to come from an attitude toward life; he possessed the same calmness and serenity that had always been the source of his real strength. He retained a firmness of posture and a clean, clear gaze which were almost disturbing, simply because he had reached an age when debility and inactivity are expected.

Mr. Rowiger and Mr. Lang were glad to see each other. They made no attempt to hide it, although the presence of others in the room had a tendency to restrict conversation. They changed the seating arrangement which they had imposed upon themselves. It was unusual for two men to spend so much time exchanging commonplaces, but then neither was ever likely to worry about wasting time, and their nods and smiles conveyed more than could have been supposed.

Mr. Pierce devoted his attention to his wife. Irene put aside her brush. From a window, they observed a portion of the lawn which was too distant for Mr. Rowiger to speculate upon, so that his attention reverted to their persons, noting how fine they were in such an atmosphere. Mr. Pierce had thrown the window as high as it would go, yet in a manner which expressed aloofness from the physical portion of the act. It was their seeming reluctance to touch anything, but to stand side by side, using the window as their common bond, which brought Rowiger a fine sense of their maturity and their respect for each other. Noticing from the slight blowing of Irene's hair that there was a breeze coming through the window, one which he could not feel, he sat there, chatting with Mr. Lang.

Mr. Pierce rejoined them and led the conversation. It was curious, the entirely different feeling Mr. Pierce aroused the moment he left his wife and came toward them, holding his head in a position of assumed haughtiness, only the eyes turning, while his mouth minimized the movements needed for speech. His voice was a monitored ecclesiastical, his vocabulary that of a believer in abstract entities. His hands were easy of movement, precise in their finger gestures, almost as if they were intended to convey shades of meaning too slight for speech. Yet Rowiger was soon aware of the easiness and naturalness of courtesy which lay beneath this formal external appearance.

Rowiger then formed a premise which had no supporting evidence, except the kind of courtesy which he received, a premise that Mr. Pierce did not take the slightest interest in him. It was the feeling of having been seen and dismissed. Yet Rowiger could not resent this since it seemed a fair statement of his position. In no manner was there any criticism intended. It was at the most as if Mr. Pierce had looked at him after a game of chess had been proposed and said, "Ah, no, I think not." Being already convinced that Mr. Pierce had a remarkable perceptiveness, there came to Rowiger the feeling that he was also the possessor of a remarkable patience, through which he accepted imperfections in others.

Mr. Rowiger could not conclude whether these impressions were honest ones. It was equally difficult to say whether he had felt being "seen and dismissed" personally, or through indirection, since it was his feeling that Irene was the only person present who interested her husband enough to require him to make acknowledgment. It was perhaps only a form of privacy existing between them which could not be intruded upon.

Rowiger had to take upon himself the responsibility of adjusting.

He felt hampered in his observations by a gathering unreliability in his own reactions. Irene was from his present position inaccessible, at least until enough time had passed to permit them to establish permissible avenues of exchange. Rowiger exaggerated this. His bachelor status tended to make him give more privacy to marriage, as a kind of walled estate, than any woman would require. He placed intimacy on too high and unrestricted a level.

Mr. Pierce proved to be at his best in such a situation. He was in good humor. His reserve had been principally the result of meeting Rowiger through his wife, and once this was set aside, he became the very center of the group, and did much to allay everyone's discomfort. He divided his attention so well that all three could direct their conversation at him, causing momentary confusions and interruptions among themselves, but never causing him to lose his grasp of their meanings. He seemed to make the conversation of more value than it was.

One of the recognitions Rowiger made, during that time, was the willingness, even eagerness of Irene for him to take a correct position. He detected a faint desire, though not quite a request, that he should be more friendly with her husband, and he followed upon this as the most sensible means of clearing impediments. Rowiger then began to see that he was mistaken about Mr. Pierce not being interested in him. It was quite the contrary, and the interest was not in dull exposition of details, but in his aspirations, outlook and beliefs. That his encounters with life had been unspectacular, that they had left him devoid of strong opinions, seemed only to increase Mr. Pierce's regard for him.

As the conversation progressed Irene became a more active participant. She was an excellent conversationalist, independently and as an embellishment to her husband. To a keen instinctive sense of clothing and color, she had added practice and mature judgment. She was not fragile. Rowiger was soon led to suspect it was some fault in himself which kept him from seeing her justly.

Her pride in appearance and in internal honesty seemed only to have diminished in the extent of their individuality. She no longer placed herself on display or made her beauty something to be visually admired. She did not appear to overestimate the value of herself.

Mr. Lang was sitting deep in his chair, quietly smoking his unlit pipe and watching his daughter. There seemed pride in his eyes. Yet there was the definite impression that he was at a greater distance from them, almost as if he had moved himself into some far corner of the room. He seemed to have passed the responsibilities of entertainment to another generation, and was reserving for himself only the pleasure of continued enjoyment. He was keeping the last and perhaps most rewarding pleasure.

The maid brought an announcement which compelled Mr. Pierce to rise and excuse himself. As he withdrew, he made a gesture, assigning to his wife the responsibility of entertaining.

Irene, instead of talking, returned to her painting, where she became so unaware of herself that she came alive physically. A silence seemed to move steadily in upon them. Rowiger felt it painfully. Seeing her eyes with the dreaminess which he remembered, seeing her respond to her internal emotions, it was not difficult for him to accept responsibility for their failure to find a means of communicating. He had never before realized that he was so awkward. He felt as if he were disgracing himself, showing the true narrowness of his adaptability.

He accepted overtures from Mr. Lang, and these were soon turned into a reason for conversation. His position in regard to Mr. Lang had altered favorably, allowing them both to enjoy a sense of friendship which former circumstances had prevented. He found himself more closely attached by nature and interests to Mr. Lang than he had ever supposed. Though their positions in no way coincided, there was nevertheless a vague parallel between their activities. Mr. Rowiger had won respect as a teacher, and was seriously devoted to improving the town. It was a parallel which the younger man was quick to sense.

Mr. Lang was giving his visual attention to his daughter. He was not really paying attention to his own conversation. It was the kind of attention which a young boy might give, an admiration which did not have sufficient foundation. Rowiger found himself wavering between a favorable memory and a rather pathetic view of fondness being carried too deeply and late into life.

Rowiger realized that in his attention to the difficulties of establishing an atmosphere of ease, he had not observed relationships which it was natural to take for granted. Mr. Lang made several efforts to engage his daughter in conversation, but she definitely avoided speaking, pretending interest in her painting. The few occasions when she spoke, she explained her meaning in far too much detail. Once, when Mr. Lang mentioned business, she interrupted with a long series of statements, almost with a gesture of hushing her father.

After that, her response became shrugs and belittling movements of her head, a definite coldness bordering on unconcern. Rowiger could not do less than assume some trouble existed between them. It did not improve the constraint under which he felt himself. Simply to sit there gave him a feeling of the responsibilities which human sensibilities must be prepared to encounter, and which apparently he was not. His discomfort was so acute that he surprised himself by forcing on Irene an aggressive conversation. He pressed so hard that Irene was forced to lay aside her brush and assume a defensive attitude.

She led a busy life, she said. Three children, entertaining to do several evenings a week, a great amount of preparations. She did her utmost to make the social engagements a success, realizing, of course, how unimportant any single dinner was.

She made it clear that she would still fight when under attack, and was still not accustomed to assuming other people were right. What dismayed Rowiger was the extent of her anger with him. He tried to insert into his voice all the friendliness he could. He felt he was at the edge of a discovery that he did not wish to make, at least while his and her eyes were encountering. But it was not long before he was aware that she had escaped. It was with a sense of relief that he accepted this, and he was almost glad when her conversation became neither too serious nor sincere. They seemed to avoid the truth of feeling and statement which had once been their strongest bond.

Admittedly, Irene had become a better person. She appeared to have learned that sacrifice was not necessarily a kindness, and that kindness was itself more important. She appeared to have subdued her temperament. Yet it was surprising that she could have so completely lost sight of her former values and even mistake imperfections for virtues. She seemed to have gained stability at the cost of her earlier brilliance and independence. Perhaps she was simply no longer feeling life vividly any more, and had matured to the point where her best attributes were submerged.

As Rowiger continued to talk with her, pressing in new and safer directions, he had a feeling he understood. Irene had heard nothing except praise from the earliest years of her life. In a more refined atmosphere she would have had obvious faults and would have been sensible enough to repair them, but in this setting she had reached her ultimate. Her curiosity had simply fallen into disuse. It was no more than a feeling of disappointment to Rowiger, especially if he made allowance for his eyes having become more critical, and made allowance for the reality of a person whom he had held in too much esteem.

Yet he could not accept this without feeling he had deserted some of his own values and faiths. Irene had been to him, all these years in which they had not met, a mark of his own dedication. He clung even at this moment to the belief that it was some fault of situation which kept him from seeing her justly. It was again the difficulty of his position. He was attempting to identify an appearance which was as yet too thin to be accepted. There was reluctance to press identification on a woman, who, if he were to continue his present course, would only regret having asked him to visit.

Mr. Lang, who either felt the pressure or was attempting to avert the resumption of silence, rose and expressed willingness to show Mr. Rowiger about. Rowiger complied with a haste that was ridiculous. Irene looked at her father, almost as if her permission was involved.

Finally Rowiger and Mr. Lang did leave the room. As they walked about, their sense of courtesy deprived them of making reference to a number of things which they would not have hesitated to speak about in front of Irene. If it was true that a deeper and more honest friendship existed between them, it was also true a deeper restriction came with that friendship. Mr. Lang's position in the house no longer seemed to permit unlimited openness of opinion.

Rowiger did not prevent himself, however, from expressing surprise at the alterations. Recalling his reaction to the garden, he viewed his surroundings with care, trying not to detect individual changes, of which there were an unrememberable amount, but an essential change. The house had lost its former ease. Something was being hidden, something was being omitted.

Yet it was evident Mr. Lang, his eyes humorous and smoke-pained, was enjoying his explanations. Within the modernization and larger utility, the result of crowding some areas and expanding others, Mr. Lang seemed still to see a continuity. The big fireplace he seemed still to feel was the center of activity. "I'm afraid," he said, smiling, "my generation didn't know what hospitality was. We only thought we knew." The remark was made with such sincerity that Rowiger found it necessary to look about again. Viewing the house from the standpoint of a guest, there was admittedly truth in the remark. That was perhaps the essential change. It was an enormous guest house. Rowiger admitted the sarcasm of his viewpoint as being personal, and knew it was only someone like himself, someone who remembered the house in former times, who would feel resistance. Irene and her father were probably contented.

The new library contained pictures by Ryder, Eakins, Inness. Emphasis on panel wood gave the downstairs a different lighting structure and a more pleasant odor. There was abundance of apple wood. Rooms were of equal attractiveness, inviting choice from among moods and purposes. Guests need not feel restrained to the parlor.

Rowiger's reluctance to approve was based on a personal sensation, a feeling that the house no longer reflected the kind of hospitality for which Mr. Lang was remembered. It reflected a different kind of taste and privilege, something more professional. For Rowiger, who was always ill at ease in luxurious surroundings, his main impression of dislike was the "youthfulness" of the style of decoration, which seemed artificially superimposed on an older and more stable form. There was no evidence of its being lived in by a family, no evidence of the three children. There was only a feeling of an impeccable taste having been at work.

Mr. Lang took him into a room on the ground floor, near the servants' quarters. Rowiger saw two chairs which he remembered as having been in the office. The room was provided for reading, writing and leisure needs, as well as serving as a bedroom. If Rowiger had encountered such a room in a hotel, or as part of his own lodgings, he would have been pleased; but in view of the vast facilities of the house there seemed a contradiction. The room even reflected the possibility of confinement, for there was something too crowded about the furniture for a man of Mr. Lang's tastes. He would never have chosen a room where shrubbery hid most of the window, where light came through in thin rays.

Mr. Lang, however, seemed pleased with the arrangement, hinted that it had been done at his request. It removed the problem of "the stairs." Mr. Lang put his hand against his chest and smiled. Rowiger remembered that he had not seen Mr. Lang fill his pipe since shortly after he had arrived, and there came to him the impression that Mr. Lang was much changed, had been smitten very harshly within, where no eyes could see, causing even a change in moral fiber, which, being a reticent man, Mr. Lang was nearly able to keep to himself.

Rowiger also gathered the impression that few people came to visit Mr. Lang any more. Part of the gladness with which he had been welcomed was indicative of that. He regretted that a stronger friendship had never existed between them. He sensed the path was open, Mr. Lang was even anxious, but it all depended on Rowiger's remaining on good terms with Irene and her husband. Rowiger had a sense of being hopelessly committed to failure. He felt inadequate in dealing with these people. He had never been really involved in personal relations, never at least with someone mature who urgently wanted his assistance. The kind of life he had been living made him unavailable to do much more than observe.

233

Mr. Lang hinted that he was no longer capable of making important business transactions. The affairs of the tobacco factory had been entrusted to his son-in-law. "I have my books," said Mr. Lang. "I've never objected to reading them." He smiled, as if possessing an understanding of life which could not be shared, could not even be hinted.

Rowiger could not share that view, so only nodded his head. He was unable to account for this air of resignation. It was only a few years since Mr. Lang had been competent and had not hesitated to influence the nature of the entire town. Or was it only a few years?

There was so much delay that Rowiger detected a reluctance on the part of the older man to return to the parlor. Rowiger did what little he could to make the atmosphere comfortable. He was glad he had come. It had given him the opportunity to detect a change in himself. Yet he wished too that he had never visited this house again. For the change in his attitude was not merely toward himself and these people, but to everything around him, a feeling that everyone was going nowhere and had done nothing. A sensation of extreme loneliness, almost fear, came to him. It did not touch on the worthiness of life itself, but he sensed the rare good fortune it was to have one's life amount to anything.

It broke the optimism he had felt on the previous afternoon, when, picking pieces of broken glass from the playground, and finding quite a handful of pennies in his pocket, he had spread them carelessly over an area where children of the lower grades would have recess. He saw life was not to be regarded as lightly as that.

Irene seemed trying to live in a manner which was not true to herself. It was an atmosphere of dubious sincerity in which everyone was playing a role neither painful nor pleasant. True, a woman with three children could not be expected to retain the devotion for her father which she had once had. True, she could not be expected to keep even the appearance of that feeling. But she could be expected to retain a little sensibility, just a little enthusiasm.

As he mulled over his memory, there came to Rowiger, reluctantly, the idea that the situation might be quite the reverse. Although it seemed hardly possible, Mr. Lang might be the failing element, might have claimed emotional bondage on his daughter too long, and be suffering now from a kind of resentment which his daughter had turned upon him.

That too, as everything else had been, was speculation.

Rowiger prepared to take leave, assuring Mr. Lang it would not be

234

long before he visited again. He decided to make his visits directly and entirely to Mr. Lang. That did not prove to be practicable, for even before he could get out of the house he found himself promising Irene, who suddenly clasped his hands as warmly as when she had first encountered him, that he would come to dinner.

It was an incomprehensible situation. A few days later, he was confronted with a check for two hundred dollars; the check bore Irene's signature and stipulated that the amount was to be used by him in his work for the poor and for children. With the utmost reluctance, he cashed it.

22

It had snowed during the night, and it did not take long to get the house warm.

Outside, as he filled his red hunting cap with snow, Gilbert saw footprints, and knew Father had left for work. So he had risen too early and too late. The hill was peacefully white and, as far as the eye could see, unmarked by any activity or sign of life, yet he had an urge to follow the footprints, to run down the hill after his father and shout something pleasant. He had a sudden desire to shout something beautiful to anyone, anyone at all, even to the sky, since there was no one in sight.

The snow was glittering with a frost crust that one finger could easily puncture. It was so dazzling bright that the clear skies were a trifle darkened. The trees were blackened and as skinny as the drawings of human bones. Little evergreens had become fat with white. The chicken yard had lost its scratched bareness. The pattern and roll of the wall was more visible. He could feel his shoes even when he stood still, feel the soft compression, the more equal division of weight upon all parts of his feet. He heard the faint tuning that breezes and loose snow made drifting in the shadowed places where there was no crust. He saw the crookedness of the telephone poles further down the hill, wires in deep sag with weight of ice. But the pleasure was not in particular things, in bright flashings which pointed his eyes and forced them to be specific. It was in the freshness and cleanness of everything he saw, fresher than springtime.

He filled the red hunting cap with snow, selecting that beneath the crust, bottom-soft and puffy as cotton, so light it did not feel cold. He went into the house. Passing his mother, he paused to kiss the side of her face, partly in affection, partly because she was less likely to notice what was in his cap. Then he hurried to his sister's room, stole in quietly, woke her with his loudest voice, caught the end of the bed and shook it, then filled both hands with snow and chased her out of the bed more with threats than actual touches.

Squealing and laughing, Naomi struck at him with her pillow. She tried to keep the chair between them. Gilbert threw the small remnant of snow into the air and chased her with his cold hands. Both were laughing so much it was some time before they heard Mother calling. Naomi stopped to listen and then found herself caught.

"Aiee no," she said, bending over in helplessness, her head swinging the long hair back and forth to protect her neck.

Gilbert finally went into the hall to see what Mother wanted.

"Are you in your sister's room?" came the voice from downstairs, which always seemed unfamiliar and unauthoritative when it had to rise through the narrow stairway to reach him.

"No, Mother, I'm not."

"Don't lie to me. I know you are. I can hear you carrying on, and I want it stopped."

"Yes, Mother."

"How many times have I told you not to go in your sister's room?"

"But why?" said Gilbert. "Why can't I? You're always picking at me."

"Never mind why. Do as you're told."

"Yes, Mother!"

"Come downstairs right now, do you hear? I have something I want you to do."

"What?" He shuffled uneasily. "Wha-a-at?"

"Come downstairs and you'll find out."

"In a minute. I promise I'll be down in a minute."

Gilbert listened for a moment, then tiptoed into his sister's room. Naomi giggled, in spite of the fact that he was holding one finger to the center of his lips and shaking his head warningly. "You'll get me in more trouble," he whispered. "Now don't . . . Don't . . . You're going to make me laugh . . . Please, now . . . You know I can't stop. . . ."

236

Naomi put forth both of her hands to help him hold his mouth. "You're still cold," she said, as his hands took hers. Gilbert drew her against him and touched her face at different places with his nose, to give her an idea of how cold he was. Her hair smelled good. She smelled especially clean and fresh in the morning, as if sleep had bathed and scented her.

"I can't understand Mother," said Gilbert. "I must have measles or something."

"Oh her, she's crazy," said Naomi, watching the snow melting in his hat, trying to think of some way she could trick him into putting it on.

On the way home, by a not very direct route, Gilbert and Naomi and Ernst passed a wall higher than any of them. The wall was white. Ernst made it more white at one place by scratching on it with a stone.

The boys had divided her books and were each carrying part. Gilbert allowed this because Ernst was so little and polite and because Naomi had made him her boy friend. Ernst was very pleased and proud and serious about the responsibilities put on him. Gilbert was satisfied to have two little children running around him and to see all the fun Naomi was having.

Somewhere behind the wall a dog was barking.

Gilbert, jumping, could see over the wall, except he did not have time enough to see. But he pretended he had. He said the dog was big and fierce.

Ernst jumped four times. He said he had seen too. He said he wasn't afraid.

Gilbert said he couldn't possibly have seen.

Ernst certainly had. Cross his heart and hope to die.

Gilbert offered to lift Ernst so he could see, but he who had already seen had to pretend he did not want to see.

Naomi was not interested until she was convinced Ernst had seen. Then she had to see too. It was not sufficient for Gilbert to tell what the dog was like, or for Ernst to say that was right. She had to *see*.

So, Ernst, still holding books under his arm, grasped her around the waist and lifted. He could not lift her high enough. Gilbert came over to take his sister from Ernst and lift, but the smaller boy, not convinced that she was too heavy for him, tried to shift Naomi so she would be able to sit on his shoulders. As he did so books slipped, and as he tried to hold them, Naomi fell against the wall and then on the ground. His hanging onto her legs made her fall head foremost.

Gilbert threw the little boy aside, and landed squarely on his elbows and knees, so that his sister was caged in between arms and legs, fully shadowed from the sky. She looked up, face wavering in expression, undecided, waiting for more definite knowledge about herself. "I'm not hurt," she said rather solemnly.

"It wasn't my fault. You pushed me," Ernst said, coming a little closer, trying to see under Gilbert.

"I'm not hurt the littlest bit," she said, more convincingly.

"If you hadn't pushed," Ernst said.

Gilbert rose, face contorted, and glared at the small boy. He had the bewildered, frightened look of someone who did not quite know what to make of that by which he was confronted. His eyes would not seem to turn. Gilbert caught hold of Ernst and hissed into his face, "You don't come near my sister. You stay away."

"It wasn't my fault," said Ernst. "You made me."

Gilbert shook the little boy, and when the talking did not cease, slammed his hand into the boy's face. It was simply an openhand push which probably was intended to cover Ernst's mouth, and a moment later the little boy managed to get free and run along the street, bawling. Gilbert stood watching, then turned, and spying the mark which had been made on the wall with the stone, the same spot which had been vivid white and enlarged, he struck at it again and again, until the flesh was torn and hanging from his knuckles, until he had to lean his head against the wall to bear the pain, and even then could beat only impotently with the base of his hand.

He whirled and looked at his sister with such fierceness that she did not dare to get up from the sidewalk. She crawled some distance from him.

"Go home. Keep away from me," said Gilbert.

"What you hit him for?"

She really wanted to know. She felt something had happened which she had not seen.

"I said get the hell home before I bat you one."

"Why you hit him? You hit everybody."

The hand was too injured to hurt. Gilbert was more concerned with a brush burn on his elbow. He kept rubbing his elbow and glaring at his sister, motioning her away, though she remained there with her head cocked to one side. Gilbert turned away from her.

"Let me alone," he said. "I'm no good. I'm just no good."

Suddenly he began to cry. He screamed with terrible, almost insane loudness, his eyes pinched tight shut, and this continued until his voice was thick with hoarseness. In the last stage the sound of his crying was like strangulation, and his chest and stomach were going in and out too fast.

He became quiet and allowed his hand to be taken and then to be led. He did not open his eyes. He continued to rub his elbow against his shirt.

"That sure was dumb," said Naomi, "hitting so." But the tone of her voice was that of passive pronouncement, without accusation, with complete acceptance of the fact that her brother was to be expected to do things which she could not comprehend.

People seemed to be angered by her outstretched hand. They put coins in the hands of small children, but they ignored her. There was a new theater across the street. Only three of the bulbs above the sign were lighted, giving the name the appearance of "Tan ar." Since Negroes were being admitted the admission price had declined, and people often spoke about the "scratch house."

After the last show had started, the boy who collected tickets motioned for her to pass by. He would do this for her every evening, and she liked him. When he came and sat beside her, Rose was always glad to see him. If she had not been so fascinated by the screen she would have continued to look at him and smile.

There was no longer piano music, and the chattering sound of the projector was in rhythm with the faint jerkiness of the film against the screen. Sitting so far back in the theater, she found it necessary to lean forward, arms resting on the chair in front of her. After the movie she went with him down under the canal bridge.

Gilbert still enjoyed watching his brother at work, and was astounded at how Bart could do and learn things, the way the saw zinged through a piece of wood in seven or eight strokes and nails were little shining dots after a series of springy, resilient vibrations. There was never the loud, flat sound when Bart was nailing, nor did the saw squeak or flex or brown the edge of the wood. Bart made a series of calculations with his hands, placing them one way and another on a board, wrote a couple of figures in pencil, and an hour later there was a storage chest with sliding drawers.

He helped Bart carry it to their bedroom.

"I don't think it'll go," Gilbert said, at the hall door.

"It's forty-one inches," said Bart. "And the chest is thirty-eight."

"It's really swell," said Gilbert, when they had maneuvered the chest into the bedroom. "Can I put some of my stuff in?"

"You can have the bottom drawer," said Bart. "If you sand it."

Gilbert rubbed over it with his hand. He did not see that it needed sanding. But what retained his enthusiasm to use one of the drawers was how firm and strong the chest was, how new it made the room seem. How Bart had made one side exactly like the other was miraculous to Gilbert, who could never make two things more than vaguely similar.

When Bart said he was going to make a lock for it, out of old parts, Gilbert was even more enthusiastic. He was content to sit on the steps and watch. Of course when Mijack came into the cellar, then Gilbert felt he should be doing something, should be given a fair share, a little responsibility of his own. After all, he was not little any more, little, to be sent after tools, or told how to hold a board, or to get out of the way and quit blocking light. Sometimes Gilbert hated the shadow his head made. No matter where he stood, as soon as he moved, darkness would seem to stretch across the whole cellar.

After Mijack began to work, Gilbert made continuous trips for tools and materials. He hurried around because he did not want to miss anything. Then he was sent after a scrap of metal which no one but Mijack could possibly have recognized, and a wedge that had been made five years earlier, which Father described as if he should have perfect memory of it. In the tool drawers were more thingamajigs than namable tools. It might be in the kitchen, attic or outhouse, which now served for storage. Naomi might have put her hands on it—or, and, this was a vague distress which kept him from looking properly, Gilbert might himself have . . .

Mijack was an inventor. He had made a set of chisels, a soldering iron with interchangeable tips, a mold for soft rivets, a set of three-direction pressure jacks, clamps with wide arches, and numerous less common and explainable objects, such as a steel pinch claw which would fit on the toe of his shoe and thus allow him to pluck weeds and dandelion without stooping, a freewheel disconnective unit and spring compressor which allowed the washer, a converted washtub, to be pumped very hard and then continue to wash for two full minutes while Mrs. Mijack rested a little, without the wooden long handle wagging back and forth.

He was now, after several weeks of thinking, experimenting with the idea of a three-roller wringer using a common center roll, in the bottom of which could pass thin clothing, and through the top work

240

clothes and blankets, thus eliminating tightening and loosening of the screw and the overcompression of the coil springs.

"Where you say it was? Where?" Gilbert called down through the register.

"Did you look in the bottom drawer?"

"Yes," said Gilbert, and hurried off to make "yes" true.

Mijack was concentrating on a single aspect of the problem, studying, experimenting, with that extreme patience which is given to few men. He was a slow worker who had to be satisfied one part was fully correct and in alignment before he would move forward. He had studied the place of wear on a single bearing for nearly an hour, until he had been satisfied what kind of wear and where the stress that had caused it really was. He despised "shims" and washers and bushings.

"Don't always look next door for the trouble," he said. "A sore back can come from bedroom slippers, and a snow can come down from Alas-kee."

He viewed friction and "play" as the most lasting and puzzling enemies of good workmanship. He believed firmly in the principle of the fewest moving parts, the least pressure without slippage and in the very best bearings.

"Need me?" asked Bart.

"No, I think the boy and I can make out."

Bart shrugged. He was taking apart four old locks in the hope of finding enough pieces to make one good one.

"Will this do?" said Gilbert, returning, standing midway on the cellar steps.

"What is it?" said Mijack. "I can't see from here. . . . Lord no, boy, why that I made special to go on that filler thing to hold it up straight when the hoo-ger comes on it. Get that piece I told you. That's what we want."

"But I can't find it."

"It's there somewhere."

Gilbert returned slowly to the kitchen. He opened the drawer and ran his fingers across the tools which were piled so thick they sometimes trapped the drawer and made it necessary to run a wire through the crack.

"I can't find it," he shouted.

"Well, look for it and maybe you will!" came back at him.

He wished he were working with Bart instead of Father. Bart would come help look.

241

Mijack was not angry. In this slow-moving process it was natural he would discover the need of a tool as or after it was needed, and there would be a wait while the boy went in search. He understood that the boy needed to be given time and patience, and realized that because he was accustomed to having a helper in the shop he had been too hard on both of the boys, expecting more from them than was reasonable. So he used this time to review what had already been done, to be sure it was right. Then he simply rested and took a look in the potato bin, the coal bin, at the places he was planning to string water pipe and at that part of the wall which was always damp and yet did not seem to be deteriorating. He slapped his hand against some of the stones.

"Pretty solid old house," he said. "I had the right idea when I brought that wall in further than had to be."

Mijack had finally learned how to rest.

Yet Bart was making a timely surmise when he hurried up into the kitchen. He did it because he wanted to be left in peace to finish making the lock.

Bart came up from the cellar, located the scrap of metal in the very drawer Gilbert had searched. He handed it to Gilbert without comment.

It was just that sort of thing which made Gilbert want to hit his brother.

With all the caution, experience, and studying, it did not go right the first try.

"Well, pshaw, now don't that beat daylight?" said Mijack, with respect for the part that had not reacted as it should have. "It goes to show how you never can tell." He immediately, with a pleased happiness hidden beneath the severity of his features and seemingly disgusted head-shaking, began to examine what was to be done now.

"You hold onto these."

Gilbert took the spring and the two small parts in his hand. After waiting about ten minutes in which Father did nothing but look at the wringer, he went over to where Bart was at the bench to see how the lock was coming along.

"You knew where it was. Why didn't you tell me?"

"I didn't know any more than you," said Bart.

"The hell you didn't," said Gilbert. "You just wanted to show off."

"Now who you helping, him or me?" said Mijack. "I wish you'd decide."

Gilbert returned and kneeled beside his father, holding his hand open and outstretched, so the parts would be immediately available.

Mijack was nearing a solution, and with the instinct of a man of long experience, he had reserved his concentration for this time. He had a tremendous power of concentration. His attention would focus upon a minor problem of mechanics with the steady and gradually perfect clarity of a microscope, so intent in eyeing the gauge of a screw that the world could tremble without his noticing. His face seemed to narrow in over the bones, making the forehead and nose line more pronounced.

When Gilbert put his hand on his father's shoulder there was no way of knowing if his hand was being felt, for Mijack continued to mumble and shake his head.

"Faugh! Look at that thing now, will you? That little bugger! Look how it's acting!"

But there was no friendliness in the voice. It was the private, serious talk of a man who was exacting and uncommunicative in moments of importance. He gave a sudden jerk which he had been planning for a long time, and the bearing slipped into place.

"Hammer!" Mijack said, holding his arm overhead.

The hammer was right there beside his knee!

Gilbert picked it up and tried to give it to his father. But Mijack then motioned for the hammer to be withheld, so that he could take another look, so that his hand could reach for the handle and grasp it the way his hand chose to. Once he had decided how the force should be applied, his hand did not change the position of grip or the direction of the blows. He possessed untiring strength and energy for repetitious muscle actions.

When the job was completed, for it took little time after the decisions were made, Mijack smacked his hands together, not so much dusting them, but rather with satisfaction. Completion of a task always put him in good humor.

"Well, boy, what do you think?" he said. "That ought to last a while. That ought to hold up a few years."

He patted the wringer frame, cleaned it with a rag, shook it a little, and then assisted Gilbert in gathering the tools and carrying them to the kitchen. The cellar was so damp that in a few days rust would set in.

"We didn't do so bad for a couple of newcomers, do you think?"

Gilbert's personal gladness was that Father had not needed to call Bart to assist. He went into the cellar to see how the lock was coming along. He felt a faint obligation to have some part in making the lock, since he was going to use the chest, but Bart made it obvious he did not want or need assistance.

"Is there anything I can do?" Gilbert said. "Here, let me hold that for you."

There was no reply. There was never any reply.

After a while the two were leaning over the work table. Gilbert's head kept bumping against his brother, but that was because Bart was keeping him from seeing what was going on. "Do you have a key for it?" There was no reply. "Am I going to have a key?" Bart pulled the piece of pipe from his hands and put it on the opposite side of the table. All that Gilbert had wanted to do, since he couldn't see what was happening to the lock, was to make a spyglass out of the pipe, just for a moment, and surely that was not going to hurt anything!

Bart had collected the tools he would need before beginning, then worked swiftly and silently, and was certain to be annoyed by any unreasonable delay, especially now that he was almost finished. It was very tedious trying to fit the small parts together, so that to be touched made him fear for the result and he shook off the contact with a curious formal movement of his shoulders, with a sort of contemptuous gracefulness. Even words would hurt his ears, so that conversation must not exist.

"Listen," he said, "in the bottom drawer in the kitchen you'll find a flint sparker for lighting gas stoves. I may be able to use the spring in it. Would you get it for me?"

It was only when something unexpected was encountered that Gilbert was sent on an errand. So Gilbert hurried. He found it, about where Bart had said, though moved a bit by his earlier rummaging in the drawer. It was because Gilbert remembered having seen it only a little while ago that he had confidence.

But when he returned to the cellar, the spring in the gas lighter was not needed. Bart had found some other way of fixing the lock. "It works," said Bart. "Now for the keys."

Gilbert took no pleasure in being given the lock to inspect. He was furious. It seemed as if his brother had merely wanted to get rid of him. Father never did that! Father waited for the *right* thing. Bart must think he liked to run his legs off.

Bart worked rapidly, with a trifle less care than Mijack, and when he had finished, there was no show of emotion. Only a sort of relief to have it done. He gave Gilbert a key, and the comment to try to hold onto it for a few days at least. Then he left, with the instructions, "Clean up this mess."

244

Gilbert was alone, with the scraps on the floor to sweep, the work bench to put in order, and the now unimportant tools to gather in his arms. He wondered if he could get Naomi to come down and help him. He went upstairs to see if she was around, but met Bart instead.

"I won't do it," he said. "You can't make me."

He stood there measuring himself physically with his brother, resenting more than ever the year difference in age, resenting at a deeper level.

Bart said nothing.

After that Gilbert was so nervous that he jerked things around and failed to look where he was walking. Mijack's very simple reminder at supper that he had not cleaned the cellar put him in confusion, until finally he rose from the table and went down into the cellar, throwing a glance of furious accusation at his brother, ignoring his mother's command to finish supper first. Down there, alone, secured on four sides by walls of stone, he gradually regained his composure. With something of a martyr's attitude, he gathered the tools, cleaned the floor and refused to eat the remainder of his supper.

It did not put Rowiger at ease to know that there were going to be other guests. Although he would have had to wear the same suit anyway, it seemed somehow less presentable for having been put on without the care which he would have taken for a formal occasion. Mr. Pierce was engaged in a conference. In the brief greeting, he had explained that he was expecting members of the board of a Philadelphia paper in which he was considering making an investment. He admitted jovially that it was really necessary to attend to the matter, since he was in slight danger of entangling his investments at counterpurposes. Rowiger had felt awkward in reference to his own unimportance, and had hastily insisted that Mr. Pierce should continue.

Irene, whose preparations had consisted of bathing and putting on a dress which made her seem slender, surprised Rowiger by coming up and leaning over him and pinning a white flower in his lapel. "There," she said gaily, "now there's no reason to look so glum." Before she had completed arranging him, Mr. Pierce came out of his office and made a telephone call. "Come see," said Irene.

"Why yes, yes-ss," Mr. Pierce said, not moving from where he was standing. He phoned instructions which required him to look at his watch.

Rowiger seemed to lose his discomfiture. But it was more nearly the case that Mr. Pierce's eyes did not take much heed of him. The situation became amusing when Mr. Lang entered wearing a white flower which could have been identical with Rowiger's. It made Rowiger quite embarrassed, however, realizing that in his own expression an improper intonation had existed. He was rather ashamed to look at Irene, feeling that he had been the cause of offense to her. It seemed to him, for some time afterward, that she, even in her lightest and most flippant moments, was on the edge of anger.

Mr. Lang came forward and offered his hand. He had the appearance of having been dressed, or at least having dressed under instructions. He did not seem to reflect his own nature, but the taste of someone else. It was a scrubbed kind of cleanliness not at all suited to him, and which tended to make him appear rather pathetic.

Guests appeared: Mr. Weaver of Bethel, McGroth of the Quarry Subsidiary, Mark Stevens and Mr. Dressinger. Mr. Pierce broke his conference. The members of his staff were in such haste that they did not have time for introductions. The youth of Mr. Pierce's organization, particularly in contrast with the incoming guests, was impressive. Before the guests could be seated, representatives of the Philadelphia paper arrived, and there threatened to be interminable confusion.

Mr. Pierce, however, proved to be at his best in such a situation. Moving about easily, he gradually imposed a sense of form and decorum. Everyone was in good humor as the hour of dinner approached. Only Mark Stevens spoke to Mr. Lang; he gave the older man a harmless pat on the shoulder. Rowiger then went and sat with Mr. Lang. It made Mr. Lang aware that his isolation had been noticed, and Rowiger felt uneasy. But this neglect by men who had known him for so many years was something which Rowiger could not forgive.

Watching and listening to Irene, he realized how difficult it must be for a woman to improve her character when she heard nothing except praise. He realized how necessary it was for a woman to hear her faults spoken on occasion.

Dinner brought the scattered groups together. After an iced soup speckled with new greens, the smoked trout was extremely tasty. The Philadelphians seemed enthusiastic and directed their conversation to the hostess. Irene replied eagerly, too much so. She seemed to find conversation with two young men more entertaining than with the older guests. On one occasion, when Mr. Lang dissented from a line of politics which Mr. Pierce proposed, she said, "Father, you don't give Henry a chance. Let him talk. *I* see what he means."

Weaver and McGroth were discussing the merits of company housing and company stores.

Mr. Dressinger, who owned a waterfront area extending southward from Harrisburg, admitted interest in the location of the tobacco factory, but would certainly not wish to be burdened with equipment.

Rowiger tried to prevent the appearance that he was taking dinner apart from the others.

Irene only sampled various dishes.

One of the newspapermen had taken a paper from his vest and was scribbling brief notes.

Mr. Lang made a remark, distracting his daughter's attention. It appeared that he had had the simple, heartfelt need of conversing with her, and had only mistaken what seemed an opportunity. Irene literally hushed him.

Mr. Pierce rebuked his wife—at least admonishing her with his eyes.

Cruel words slipped from Irene's lips, in a burst of passion. Even though she had been deserving of such treatment, it was unpleasant. Though she was greatly mistaken, she showed that she was willing to fight. She quite suddenly lashed into the men seated around the table, calling upon them at least to relinquish their attention to business until after the dinner was completed. She seemed nervous and impatient.

Mr. Pierce, who did not seem to care to defend himself, but who felt called upon to retain the dignity of his guests, explained that his wife was not wholly in sympathy with his ideas. She was perhaps right for criticizing him for talking politics at a time when his attention should be to lighter matters. "I suppose," he said, "continuous business mouthing is a great deal more offensive than eating with one's fingers."

Irene stiffened. Then she seemed to turn away from the remark.

The Philadelphians consulted among themselves and made remarks on the excellence of the dinner.

Rowiger was angry with all of them. He was convinced there was no excuse for such behavior among sensible people, behavior in which every frown, smile and gesture complicated an atmosphere in which it was impossible to tell the way people were drifting. He felt a need for them to discover their true selves and to cease living in a manner that was shallow and founded on a parsimonious kind of intelligence.

Mr. Lang pushed his chair a little away from the table and took out his pipe, a gesture of placing in his hand a reason for continued existence. There was the air of believing he had earned the right to spend his last years in tranquillity, and was not going to be denied that right simply because there had been a little unpleasantness. In spite of his remarkable calmness, it was impossible not to see that his position in the house had slipped by perceptible stages downward until he was regarded in much the same light as an old servant who had outlived his usefulness.

Dinner was concluded. Mr. Lang excused himself and went to his bedroom. In the early evening, Rowiger, under the guise of looking at the furniture and paintings, but actually motivated by a restlessness, walked about the house. He was trying to arrive at an explanation which would release him from the feeling that he must take leave of Irene for the last time. He could not condone his own position. He was trying to decide how far an immunity to criticism Irene had obtained through her marriage, and whether the types of criticism that he could offer would have any value. He decided the only fair position he could take was not to visit.

As he was preparing to leave, and was in fact hunting for someone from whom he could take leave, he saw Irene pass through the hall into the back of the house carrying a tray with a pitcher and a cup on it. It was the same pitcher which had always been used for sweet fruit tea. He saw too the gentle and devoted manner in which she was carrying the tray. But it only added to his confusion, only made him feel more certainly that he must keep himself away from a house which had become so painfully altered and unrewarding to him.

As he stepped onto the porch there came the feeling that he was avoiding something more unbearable than either of these possibilities. He was avoiding seeing her pretend that her life was satisfactory. He was avoiding being asked to return on the same impossible grounds, a friendship which no longer existed. It had been a very disappointing experience. He had never before realized how deep and lasting an affection he had for her. He went down the hill, the white flower making a dim oval in the darkness, bound never to return and to move onward in a way of life in which his confidence was no longer perfect.

Inside the house, Mr. Pierce was selling the tobacco factory to Mr. Dressinger. They were drawing up the necessary papers. Irene and her father were sitting together, drinking tea.

23

Often Gilbert took his sister swimming and fishing and on hikes. The gang did not mind having her along unless there was going to be a secret meeting or a raid on the Adamson street niggers. She was lots of fun and not afraid of anything. A squirrel could scarcely do better in the trees. Vines that no one else could trust would hold her. She could spit as far, if not as straight, as the best. And boys weren't always being reminded they were with a girl and all that kind of nonsense. There was never any reason for Gilbert to be ashamed to have brought her with him.

But more frequently Gilbert and Naomi went into the mountains alone. If they went alone, there was more freedom, they could both do whatever they wanted. He encouraged her to fill a market basket with good things to eat, and together they would have a picnic. Mijack approved this and allowed them to take as much as they would promise to eat. He even sometimes suggested places for them to go.

Sometimes—although Saturday was a bad day for borrowing— Gilbert was able to get a bicycle, and with Naomi on the crossbar holding the basket, he would pedal seven miles around the mountain to the gap and then on to the Swatara Creek, near the covered bridge. Naomi considered the bridge "spooky" because it was pretty dark inside and gave her a different voice to talk with, and there were places along the side where it was possible to fall through into the creek. Naomi was pretty brave about "spooky" places, for she always had to go inside the bridge; or else she must have liked the feeling of being afraid that came when she was near the middle and the only light was faint splinters from below and two far-off enormously bright circles. Once, when Gilbert did not go with her, since to get the fun of being really afraid she had to go alone, he stood on the bank of the stream and collected a pile of stones, and then when he decided she was pretty far inside, threw so that the stones landed on top of the roof of the bridge and rolled down. She came out running straight ahead for all she was worth.

"Heck, yes, I was scared," she said.

They were both wild about bicycles, and Gilbert could make one go fast. Fishhooks trimmed his old red hunting cap, now relegated to that sport and to Saturdays, and small enough to be always blowing off his head, which was a nuisance, because the hard part was not pedaling, but getting the bicycle started with such balance problems as himself, his sister and the basket.

There was the fishing to do. Gilbert knew where to locate pools of sunfish, rockies and little catfish, and he had about twenty minutes of patience before he would admit they weren't biting. But when they were, he could catch about half a dozen, missing others because Naomi yelled for him to jerk too soon, and so hard that sometimes a little fish would go flying overhead and land in the bushes behind them.

After he had caught a few, whenever a fish nibbled, Gilbert let his sister try to catch it. He would give her the instructions which he himself failed to obey.

But Naomi knew her stuff. She knew bass strike twice on minnows. She knew how a sucker pulls slow and steady and how an old turtle bites by pulling straight down. She had once been thrown right into the stream by an eel that got hooked and tried to lash itself free.

"These old rockies just catch themselves," she said, after cleaning out a pool of nine. "I ain't even changed the worm." And when she caught still another and then took a look at the condition of the bait, "I bet you don't need nothing at all. They just like to bite."

Fishing ended in swimming. Naomi did not have a swimming suit, but that did not bother them. They did not shut their eyes or hide behind bushes or anything silly like that. After all, Naomi was almost nine, and she knew Gilbert was a boy, and there was no sense in getting her underwear wet and then having to ride home on the bicycle, with either her rump sticking to the metal bar and drops of cold water running down her legs, or else ride holding her underthings in the wind to get them dry and Gilbert hollering for her to sit still.

Gilbert swam clear out into the middle and down under the shadow of the bridge where the water was cold. He was graceful in water, and had a porpoise style of rising and dipping which Naomi could not seem to learn. It was only when he tried to go fast that he splashed a lot of water around and did not seem to use his energy correctly.

He swam to where Naomi was coming to meet him, using her "doggy" style, and then when he was in front of her gave the old steamboat treatment, kicking water into her face until she could hardly breathe. When she was a little tired, he let her hang onto his shoulders and took her shoreward. When she was safely within her own depth, she threw off his assistance and, using both hands as alternating pistons, shoved sheets of water in retaliation for when she had been so busy keeping afloat that she had not been able to defend herself.

Gilbert chased her up the bank, caught hold of an ankle, and then, holding her squealing and protesting beneath him, began to slap mud on her back and smear it over her, though careful not to get any in her hair. When he finally released her, she was completely docile, and merely sat up and rather ruefully looked over the extent of the mud damage, and lifted her arms and tried to twist so she could see her back. She did not go back into the water. After sitting and looking at the creek a long time, she decided it was too cold, the flow seemed swifter.

For a while they lay in the sun, tanning, waiting for one another to close their eyes, so that a fly or little bug could be imitated walking. A grass blade made the most effective kind of insect. Once Gilbert got sleepy he was really easy to deceive and would rub and swat at least five or six times before he caught on; even then it was usually giggling that gave her away. Once they heard from the bridge above the big squishy noise of a car as it slapped its way forward on the wagon plates.

Gilbert put his kiss on her mouth. It was the first such kiss, impulsive, loving, without reservation, ever given and received among Mijacks. Gilbert and Naomi realized there was love between them, and Naomi knew that once she was thirteen or fourteen, this, like swimming naked, would have to be altered. But she could see no reason not to accept it now. And Gilbert saw no reason why she should not accept his love now and forever.

He was the fire-maker, she the wood-gatherer. In the red ashes of the fire potatoes shrank into little charcoal balls with white fluff inside. The sunfish and rock bass were wrapped in wet grass and mud and baked. They baked apples and pears. They baked stuff that cannot be baked, and ate it too. They chewed charcoal to make their teeth white. After eating, their hands and faces were black where Negroes are lightest.

Glorious was that Saturday afternoon. The mud dried a white tan which made them feel cleaner than before. Arrowheads could still be found along the Swatara and stones in pointed shapes were taken up and studied as still better forms of spears. Frogs hopped inland and were not always plopping into the creek in terror of sound. There was a brook which joined the Swatara, a brook of knee depth that made their legs blue and gave their child loins the first tingling intimations of future sexual pleasure and made water battles a thing of serious terror. The sky was enormously high because it was above tall trees. Birds seemed to have as much curiosity about what the children were doing as the children had for the birds; it seemed as if it was only the fire that kept them from coming near.

Gilbert and Naomi were in love with life and with each other, were joyous, irresponsible. The same sun tanned both their bodies, the same wind burned their cheeks hard as berries, the same creek took away old dirt and odor. They accepted realities of the simplest and perhaps only authentic form the world would ever contain: thorns bite, legs get broken, water gives colds and sometimes disease, feet accept the same shoes toes won't, feet suffer for their freedom, long-stemmed briers tattoo itchy red welts; but they could also wonder and wander, find small handfuls of mint greens and licorice weed, fight with sticks and stones and fists and words, love out love, and blow their souls high with new innocence and direct complete action, form pacts and promises based firmly on their unreasonable desires.

Saturday, when she was nine, and he was twelve.

Rowiger was at heart a reformer. But he suffered none of the indignation and outrage so common among men who wish to alter the way of the world. It was sufficient to move along placidly, without stubbornness, bending with the wind of opinion, in a slow advance toward goodness. He gathered his impressions almost at random, piece by piece adding small traits of character to himself. Although he understood more than was common, he knew that he could never fully understand anyone, and thus he retained flexibility in his feelings for people.

He was too much divorced from people to understand them fully. Passing a jewelry shop, glancing at the glittering luxuries that were sold under the pretext of utility, the vanity of gold and silver and diamonds spread across dark velvet in the form of watches, rings, table utensils, brooches and pins, cigarette cases and lighters, he would smile at the people who spent or wanted to spend their earnings on these things in the same manner as he smiled at the fondness of children for tops and bubble gum. He meant no harm to them by being amused, and he was the first to admit that luxuries, put into the hands of a sensitive person, had a value which could scarcely be overestimated.

Rowiger did not realize that he was a sentimentalist. He did not realize that his love for children was prompted and strengthened by his inability to comprehend the desperate measures that men and women would take to obtain their ends. He did not realize that he was retreating from encounter with those men and women. All that he asked from people was that they allow him to continue unmolested.

He was unpredictable. One afternoon he went outside and washed a neighbor's car and waxed it. When Mr. Haas came out and asked what he was doing, Rowiger, seeing the inexplicability of his situation, said that in turning the hose on his own car he had accidentally splashed the other and had thought it only fair to repair the damage. That same afternoon, a rather windy one, his hat blew off at least five or six times, and yet it never occurred to Rowiger to pull it more firmly on his head or else to leave it off. He would spread pennies on the playground, would organize picnics, would put himself in debt at Christmas and Easter to get gifts for all the children, would buy fifteen pounds of candy corn and pink pumpkins for Halloween, would stay at home during the four evenings before Halloween so that early visitors would not miss their chance to come in and be guessed at or to rattle the window with corn. Yet he would never give money to the outstretched hands of children and had never given a child a kiss. Shoeshine boys he patronized when he really needed a shine. In the case of ill-treated children, he did what he could for them without allowing them to see that he was particularly interested in them. Yet he took two cases to court, and assisted one woman to obtain separate maintenance from her husband, which was risky in view of his position in the school.

Rowiger, mild, bearing almost too many signs of middle age, nevertheless retained much of his eagerness and freshness of spirit. He was in many ways a young man. His perception was young. It was a gathering nervousness and social timidity which made him seem to have lost his original principles and effectiveness. He had reached an age where he made few new friends. He had lost his naturalness. When guests came to his apartment, he seemed embarrassed at the furnishings, which were clean and comfortable. It was difficult for him when guests needed to stay overnight, even though there was a spare bedroom. He would apologize for the condition of curtains, towels and rugs. His speech had the air of a man ashamed of himself and his mode of life. All men and some women could understand why he was a bachelor. Yet, in the homes of others, he could sit in the worst kind of squalor and never notice it.

He rubbed out obscene words which he found on walls and on the black-asphalt portion of the playground. He did not feel offended, but felt it was an offense against children who were innocent or only vaguely aware of their meanings. Yet, in the basement of the school, where there were pencil drawings, comments on sex and on how to urinate, and the revised history of Paul Revere, Rowiger not only never removed them, he was guilty of reading some of them.

He was full of contradictions. He honored and looked up to people who were of less stature than himself. This same modesty prevented him from undertaking enterprises which he could have easily fulfilled. He did not feel capable of great efforts. He would have been appalled to find himself the leader of a "movement." He even felt unequal to handling the P.T.A.

When Mr. Lang called on him and asked that he be the executor of his will, he accepted. He did not ask about the circumstances which had led Mr. Lang to make such a will. He knew he was giving his consent to a chain of circumstances which could bring him nothing except difficulties, which could even be disastrous.

Rowiger, gentle, generous, was not imposing enough in will or in intelligence to be a great or successful man. He never said anything profound. He would begin talking with all the earnestness of purpose that he could summon, and in a short time would be slapping his hand against his forehead and saying, "Now how did I get off on that?" The few occasions on which life demanded a harsh, forthright voice, he ventured it, but he spoke as if he would rather have jotted his opinion on paper and slipped it unnoticed into the person's coat pocket.

Yet he would risk being involved in a scandal. Despite the most careful kind of life, despite avoiding involvement in political or social issues, he suffered the embarrassment of knowing things about people which he had no right to know. That did not include gossip. It did not include his sense of divining people, of seeing into the secret faults of their natures. He was suffering from outright confessions. Being unwilling to command people toward justice, being unable to entice them toward forgiveness and humility, Rowiger found his own position more uncomfortable each year. He was being made an outcast. Many eyes and mouths which trusted him now with indictments of others and themselves would eventually turn in anger and disdain from a man who knew too much about them.

In spite of these handicaps, he continued to influence the town. In his Junior Garden Club each child was given a small piece of land

and was taught to plant, thin out and weed. A prize was given for the best yield in each class of vegetable. The children were allowed to take their produce home. He was careful not to push children who took no interest. In the case of several boys who were passing papers, he worked out, through talking with them, a system of co-operation.

Yet Rowiger was handicapped. He did not know enough. He spoke with Mijack and with farmers who huckstered in the town.

He tried to get people interested in a Y.M.C.A. He was raising money for a playground. He was organizing a boys' club in the school.

When working with children he instinctively moved toward their happiness, their improvement and toward developing their eagernesses into something permanent. But as soon as he was presented with a similar problem among adults, he shrank from it and felt incapable of assisting. He was a victim of confused thinking. He was running away from kinds of responsibility which were becoming increasingly important.

Rowiger saw better than he admitted seeing. The town was in wretched condition. Honor had become an appearance; law had become sheets of paper. Human endeavor had become a series of specialties. The ruling class of Nesquehon had less individuality than the workers in the mill. Rowiger was haunted by a sense of waste in an era in which machinery made the brevity of life more pronounced. He was scared that people should so easily surrender themselves. The steel mill did not require men to lose the values of life, but it required men to make a more direct effort to retain them, and the men would in the end surely lose them.

As Rowiger was losing his.

Mijack was flattening a sheet of roofing which had been torn from the chicken house by a summer storm. From the mountain in July and August came charred thunderheads that skidded across the town and then over the river. In the late afternoon there would be a firm, strenuous silence in which the sky seemed to pull at the land, and all the heat-bruised greenery would have an inexplicable stickiness. The storm would be vanguarded by puffs of cool air which rooted in the undergrowth and made a thin vapor of the dust. The rain drops smacked hard. The storms were brief, but were bad for roofs and chimneys and windows. Yesterday the chicken house had been damaged. Today it must be repaired.

Bart, seeing that his father intended to straighten the sheet, walked

255

off. Bart never risked being useless. He had things of his own to do. Moreover, of late the elder son and the father had been unable to get along when working with each other, quarreling, glaring at each other, Mijack even shaking his fist.

Gilbert sided with his father, and was making a definite effort to learn to be able to do more, to be of actual assistance. He could not refuse to take advantage of this situation which made Bart and Father distant and critical of each other. He believed he was now actually preferred as a helper. Mijack had taken time to teach him important things and had let him repair household articles without supervision. He was careful to do things as he thought his father would have done them.

Gilbert, sensing that Mijack had a warmer regard for him than he had believed and sensing Mijack had begun to have faith in him and to treat him more as a young man, could not do enough in return. He was surprising himself with what he could actually do. For the first time in several years there had been a contest of speed at the breakfast table, and a real one, because Gilbert could put away the food. There had been laughter. The son had walked with his father to the East End plant, a distance of several miles, and, on parting, Mijack had promised one day soon to take Gilbert through the plant and show him how steel was made and what it was being used for.

Gilbert had walked back toward town and school, feeling his height, sensing manhood was not as far off as he had supposed. He had a feeling it was going to come quick. And he saw now that this was no sudden change, no sudden interest which his father was taking in him, but that it had been there all the while and that it was his own fault which had withheld Father from doing more for him. The time would soon be past when everything was Bart, and what Bart was doing, and what Bart was going to do next. He felt responsibility stirring within and wondered if maybe he should not see about getting a job and making a little money. Now seemed a good time to ask his father about long trousers and better school clothes. . . .

Mijack was pounding at dents with the peen of a massive hammer, while Gilbert held a chunk of wood against the opposite side. He was striking pretty hard for a boy to hold against. That Mijack could concentrate so steadily on a piece of work sometimes caused him to forget that he was not using his regular helper. He had a tendency to consider the mere holding of something so routine that anyone could do it. His wife had often suffered from this during the early years of marriage, from his complete inability to understand that he had given her something she was not strong enough to manage.

While Mijack had been studying over the galvanized sheet to see what sort of kinks had to be removed, Bart had lugged over two of the jacks. This implication that it was simply a matter of applying pressure and squeezing the bends flat had fired Mijack up, and this, as much as any single thing, had decided Bart to clear out. Bart was really weary of the constant quarrels over nothing that he always seemed to get involved in. But Mijack had resented very much that his son should leave without even asking if his assistance was wanted. It was perhaps this that had hurried Mijack into straightening the roof before he was quite ready.

When the wood block was at the right place it was difficult for Gilbert to keep it from jumping. The hammer seemed to strike the palm of his hand and he could feel the bones in his arm as far as his elbow. At moments he could not locate the exact place where Father was pounding, so that the metal sheet made a loud, ringing noise. Mijack would frown and then point at the spot where he wished the block to be held.

Once, although Gilbert was certain he was holding the block exactly where his father had directed, the loud, hollow noise continued.

"Damn, you didn't hold where I told you to," said Mijack crossly. "There. Right there. And don't move until I say otherwise. . . . Keep to your own side," Mijack snapped. "You almost made me make a new dent. You got enough to do without sticking your nose over here."

When the worst bends were removed or lessened, Mijack sent him after a hammer with a small peen, for a big hammer takes dents out by putting little ones in. Gilbert rushed off. He hunted in all the kitchen drawers, searching with one hand, because the other was still a bit crippled and awkward from the constant jarring. The little peen did not seem to be anywhere, and the sound of heavy pounding in the cellar made him nervous. He put both hands behind his back and stared straight into the drawer, making his eyes search thoroughly. This failed. He lifted tools out singly, saying, "Now this is a wrench, this is a file, this is another file."

Finally, in rage, he dumped the contents of the three drawers on the floor and crawled among them on hands and knees. At last he found the hammer and hurried down the cellar steps and knelt beside his father, with the hammer held out where it could be seen.

Mijack continued to pound with the larger one. He was not using the wood brace, but was simply striking the roofing as sharply as he could, raising his arm far overhead. The noise was enormous, making Gilbert want to step away. But he stayed close, and in his anxiety to show that the small hammer was here, that he had found it, he thrust it toward his father.

With a cry, Mijack clasped the right side of his face in both hands, and stood up, the roofing sheet and tools spilling around him. It was a terrible, agonized cry.

"What's wrong?" asked Gilbert, frightened.

Mijack cursed his son and drove him from the cellar.

The table was set for supper. From the stove came faint sputtering sounds of sausage already fried. It was twilight, the windows were lighter than the room, and the family was gathered about the table. But there was no conversation, there was no prayer. A scrambled pile of tools was still lying on the floor. The cellar door was open.

Bart came in and sat down, removed the shoulder belt he used to carry newspapers, and tossed it in the corner. Naomi picked it up and put it around her neck, where it hung like an enormous necklace. It seemed the family had merely been waiting for Bart. It was soon apparent that something else was wrong.

Bart noticed the silence before he noticed that his father's eye was swollen and dark. Bart did not conceal his surprise. He looked at each member of the family, at his father and at Naomi a bit longer than the others. Having so recently entered, his movements had a little of the extravagance of the outdoors, and the room seemed darker to him.

He asked what had happened.

Mijack told, staring at his youngest son severely to prevent interruption or contradiction. It did not take Mijack long to say what he had to say, but there was an intonation in his voice which was rarely heard.

Gilbert glared at his father and his breath whistled a little at places where he would have liked to speak. He saw his father pick up a fork in one hand and knife in the other and then plant one fist on each side of the plate. It was not a gesture preparatory to eating. Gilbert became uneasy and looked out of the window.

"I didn't mean to," he said. "I told you I'm sorry."

Susie Mijack nodded her head that this was true. She did not say anything.

"He might have put out my eye!" said Mijack. "Through careless-ness. Carelessness!"

"What the hell," said Bart. "He didn't mean to do it."

"I only tried to hand you the hammer."

"Either a man's dependable or he's not," said Mijack. "There's no two ways about it. If I can't trust a man I'm not going to have him about me. I'm not going to take a chance. Do you hear me, Gib? You've shown me your stripe, and from now on I want you to keep out of the way when I'm working. I don't want you around."

"I didn't do anything," said Gilbert. "You just like to pick on me."

"Supper will be cold," Susie Mijack said.

"Didn't do anything? What do you call this?" asked Mijack, put-ting a finger near his eye, but not touching it.

"You wanted me to help," said Gilbert. "I was only trying to."

"You have to take his age into consideration, Father," said Mrs. Mijack. "He's a child yet."

"Keep quiet, woman!"

Naomi slipped the shoulder belt off and put it on the floor. She reached across the table toward the potato dish, but Mrs. Mijack shook her head in warning. Naomi was the only one smart enough to know that the way to get supper started was to get food on all the plates. But no one would co-operate.

"No harm's been done," said Bart. "What's a little black and blue?"

"No harm been done! A lot you know," said Mijack.

"Oh, shit," said Bart. "Why don't you be a man about the thing? You act like a baby. No wonder you can't get along with anyone down at the plant."

"What? What did you say?" Mijack banged the table. "Say that again."

"I said, oh shit."

Bart gave his father a look of open disgust.

"Go upstairs!"

"Go upstairs, go upstairs," Bart mocked. "That's all you can say. Why don't you quit being such a jackass?"

Mijack rose and started around the table. Bart waited a moment, then stood up and began to retreat slowly, keeping his eyes on his fa-ther, with body crouched a bit in defense. He seemed to be trying to get into an open part of the room.

"Not here," said Bart, shaking his head at the women.

Susie Mijack closed her eyes and bowed her head.

Naomi leaned forward and pushed the vacant chair so that it partially blocked Mijack's path.

Bart pushed the chair to where it had been. He stood up straight.

"Not here," he said, and made it clearly known that if struck here, in the kitchen, he would strike back. Both Father and son knew a whipping was never to be public, that only upstairs, in private, would the son accept or the father be justified. For this reason Mijack did not strike. For this reason Bart moved slowly toward the stairs.

Naomi shoved at Gilbert, motioning for him to do something. Gilbert did not move.

Susie Mijack, who had been praying, went to the stove and put lids on the pans and touched the sides of the pans to see if everything was still warm. She had appeared to be upset, but was now outwardly calm, trying to make it appear as if the trouble had passed, and as a sign for the other children to keep their places at the table.

But everyone knew it was different. Bart and Father were threatening each other with violence.

Bart had not yet reached the age when he would walk out, when he would deny his father the privileges of parenthood. He was nearing it. He was feeling the need of it. Mijack knew. Mijack understood the real issue he was facing.

Naomi suddenly clambered up from the table and ran to Bart and caught hold of him and smiled at him. She was cuffed sharply. Bart gave her warning to move away or he would cuff her again. Naomi stepped back, but continued to smile in a peculiar manner.

"You'll get yours for that," Mijack warned.

Naomi still smiled. Probably she had not heard.

"Little idiot," said Bart, raising his hand as if to cuff her again. Then he drew back into the stairway.

Mijack followed.

The footsteps indicated that father and son were climbing the stairs at an even pace, that the tension between them was over, that the ritual of discipline was once more accepted. On the stove there was no sound. The pile of tools could scarcely be seen on the floor. The three downstairs almost simultaneously became aware of the gathering darkness. Mrs. Mijack turned on the light, which swung back and forth, lighting one wall and then the other, until finally the shadows of the cups were like the cups.

"I hope he hits back," said Naomi, giving her brother a resentful glance.

260

"Sit down in your chair, young lady," said Mrs. Mijack. "The idea! Taking up for that—that undutiful son—against his own father. The very idea! Who do you think you are? I hope your father gives it to you good and proper, young lady. I hope he gives you every bit you deserve. You'll get no sympathy from me, I can tell you. I've warned you time and again the path you were following, playing into the devil's hands."

"Let her alone," screamed Gilbert, long after he should have, when the mother's words had lost importance to herself and to her daughter. "You're always picking on her."

To Gilbert the entire scene was still vivid, still occurring, as if one end of time had halted and all of the present and the near past were piled against a barricade in his own head, so that his mind was flooded and suffused with too much at once.

"Hush, now," said Mrs. Mijack. "Don't start anything again. We'll have something to eat as soon as your father comes downstairs."

"No, no, no," shouted Gilbert.

He had been surprised and then proud to see his brother speak in his defense. He had wanted to tell Bart how he had not been responsible, how Father had done it himself, and how Father was just making it seem as if he had done something wrong. He had wanted to tell Bart how the hammer had scarcely touched, and how Father had thrown everything around and bent up the roofing worse than it had been. But when Mijack rose from the chair, he had wanted to run, then cover his head with his hands. For a moment he had been terribly alone, and as the exchange of words between his father and Bart moved toward something else, the loneliness grew deeper and more dominating, until he could not center his feelings or interest on either of them.

When Naomi had run to the older brother, Gilbert had tried to catch hold of her dress.

"A fine way to talk to your mother," said Mrs. Mijack. "A fine way, I must say, after all I've done for you. Yes, all I've done."

"I hate you," said Gilbert. He looked around, not at his mother and sister, but at the whole room. "I hate you all."

When his mother had spoken sharply to Naomi, he had not been able to get his breath. He wanted to scream. Tormented by the knowledge that it was too late to speak out against his father, that it was he who should be upstairs, not Bart, he could feel his ears attempt to hear sounds from overhead. But it was impossible to hear. Trembling, furious, he spoke out himself, not in defense of Naomi, but because he could not endure more words inside his head, especially such shrill ones. He wanted suddenly to hurt someone, anyone.

"Yes, yes, I swear I hate you. Do you hear me, Mother? I say to hell with all you've done for me. Now go ahead and call Father. Go ahead. I dare you!"

There was silence. Mrs. Mijack sat there and looked at her son.

There was silence. Gilbert looked at his sister to see if she were proud of him. Then he banged the table with his fist.

"I meant it. I don't take it back. I never will."

It was impossible for him to tell whether Naomi approved or not. He searched her face with terrible concern, to learn what he should do next.

"You can't make me take it back," he said with finality. "So there."

Mrs. Mijack simply sat there and looked at her son. Gilbert watched his sister. Holding out his hand timidly, he touched her elbow. It was cold. He shook her elbow a little, and made his eyelids quiver and his mouth droop in the manner he did when he wanted her attention, but knew he was failing. It became obvious that Naomi was still thinking about Bart.

Suddenly Gilbert's head fell forward against the table, undefended and uncomforted by his arms. He began to make strange noises. Soon there was blood on the tablecloth from his nose. His head rolled from side to side, crudely, without regard for any part of the face.

Naomi watched her brother a little absently. Then, with a change in her entire appearance, she went to him and began to stroke his hair and to pull at it, trying to make him hold his head erect. But this made him cry out more desperately.

"Big silly," said Naomi, "what are you crying about? You don't hear *him* crying, do you?"

Mrs. Mijack still sat there looking at her son, disbelief and a certain blankness in her face.

"Hey, you boob," said Naomi. "Stop hurting your face that way. What for?"

With one wild swing of his arm, Gilbert freed himself of chair, table and sister. He looked about frantically. Then he ran to the stairs and on upward and into the bedroom and then ran against his father. Mijack was standing there with a razor strop hanging by his side, and he did not appear in the least surprised. Gilbert tried to take the strop, but the hand that held it loosely was too strong.

"So you want some too," said Mijack. "Well, we might as well get this settled once and for all."

"Yes, yes, I want some too, you old sonofabitch. Go on." Gilbert pulled at the strop as if to encourage it to strike him. "You won't even hit me as hard as you do Bart. You won't even do that! But Goddamn you, I'll make you, I'll make you."

Gilbert shoved at his father with the childish arm motions which are more nearly defense than attack. He appeared to be trying to hit or scratch his father in the face.

Mijack twisted his son sideways and then began to use full overhand strokes of the leather strop. For a time Gilbert stood under the blows, almost smiling, his eyes keen and unblinking.

"Hate, hate, hate," he said, still smiling, the same word repeated after each blow, but rather softly, and surprisingly controlled.

Then he knelt on the floor, exposing the full length of his back and haunches, his arms hanging unresistant and limp. His breathing was not regular, but his face was more softened than it had been in all the past hour.

Bart stood near his father, viewing coldly and objectively the helpless, humiliating posture of his young brother. It would have been impossible to suppose that Bart had been recently whipped. The slow, deliberate strokes of the leather continued.

Finally Gilbert reached out and took hold of the end of the bed. Then he began to screech. He tried to deflect the strop with one of his arms.

"Bah," said Mijack, and he rolled the strop into a snake about his wrist. "Go wash your face."

When Mijack went downstairs there was pride and bitterness in his heart. He knew he was losing Bart to manhood, and was proud, but at the same time refused to surrender his son before manhood, refused to allow the rope of bondage to fray. The ties must remain firm, the obedience total, until the last instant. He did not intend to let a son of his gradually get out of hand.

Mijack was not very fond of a son who bawled and shrieked. He was a man of pride and was capable of strong admiration, but of little pity.

Mr. Lang smoked a pipeful during his last hour, though he had given up reading quite a few days earlier, because, he said, smiling, "I'd rather not begin a good book than not finish it."

Smollett and Sterne and Fielding had become his companions in the last years of life.

Mr. Lang and Mr. Pierce had a lengthy conversation in which matters must have been settled amicably, for both seemed happier when the talk was concluded. Irene several times motioned to her husband to come away from the bed, seeing her father tire from so long a conversation, and she could scarcely refrain from open speech when she saw her husband light Mr. Lang's pipe on three occasions during the course of the evening.

As is often the case with people who have been really close, Irene and her father did not talk much during the last period of his illness. Their essential feelings were mute and even solitary in the hours of danger. Irene showed her devotion through untiring efforts to make him comfortable, and Mr. Lang revealed his by accepting with grace comforts he did not need or want. Perhaps the real depth of their affection, their mutual sorrow and fear, was most noticeable through the unwillingness of either to depart from the usual routine.

Irene made sweet fruit tea at nine.

Mr. Lang drank the tea without passing any comment upon it. "The children will be a comfort to you," he said, later.

Irene looked at him sharply, and saw from his expression that he was not referring to himself.

"Forgive me," he said. "I never meant for you to be unhappy."

"I have never blamed you for anything," said Irene.

"I have," he said, sighing.

At ten o'clock he died.

24

Rose Lee was a big girl, tall and heavy, but quiet and pliant and very much satisfied with having the friendship of Gilbert and Naomi. She never wanted her own way and was willing to follow them anywhere. They were always playing pranks on her, such as running off and hiding. Rose did not have a very good sense of direction, and so they could giggle and have all the little side tricks which are the real fun of hiding. They would put bugs down her back and she would squirm for a long time before understanding what was the matter. They would let her fish and tell her one was biting when it wasn't. Or get her to swing on a vine that wouldn't hold. It was for her innocence and funny ridiculous little suspicions that they loved her, and if they were cruel at moments, they were nevertheless her protectors and would not have wanted to see anything serious happen to her.

One afternoon the three of them went as far as the middle of the mountain. Gilbert had a whole pocketful of bullets (six) and his fingers were greasy from endless and unsatisfactory pocket mathematics of confirmation. He was boldly leading his small expedition, and was at the same time anxious to get farther into the mountains. Finally he took the pistol from his shirt, where he had been keeping it hidden with one hand acting as cradle, giving him the appearance of Napoleon in a popular painting. He took long strides and looked straight to the front, while the girls joined hands to encourage each other in not letting him get too far ahead.

Naomi carried the pistol a while. She wanted to snap the trigger, but Gilbert said authoritatively that was bad for the firing pin, and so she had to be satisfied with clicking her tongue as she swaggeringly shot up the countryside, killing just everything she saw.

Gilbert told her a lot of things that showed his knowledge. He peered into the barrel and spun the chamber, professionally. "It's too bad the war's over," he said. "I'd liked to be a soldier. I'd liked to kill." He enlarged on that when he saw Rose show interest, and then impressed on them the seriousness of having an illegal weapon. They could all be put in jail. "Because this's a thirty-two," he said, "and it's against the law to shoot anything bigger than a twenty-two."

They walked two miles. Naomi sat on a rock and said, "This's sure an old cannon all right. It oughta have wheels. My old arm's about to fall off."

That meant she was not willing to wait longer or walk farther.

"But listen," he said, "This's dangerous. If you don't hold it right it might knock out your eye. I don't want to scare you, but I've shot it lots of times and I know. So if you don't want to or you'd rather see how I do it first . . ."

"Shucks," said Naomi. "I'll try anything." She stuck a weed in her mouth and chewed it.

"Okay," said Gilbert. "I greased it, so it probably won't kick as hard as it did for me. Rose, see if you can find something to shoot at."

He was pleased at the respectable distance Rose was giving them. He was talking pretty much for her benefit. His sister was so cynical, hardly anything impressed her any more. "Rose, you find anything yet? See how big the bullet is," he said, holding one between his thumb and forefinger. "It has to be something big or it'll blow it all to pieces."

"Heck, I just wanna shoot," said Naomi. "I don't care if I don't hit nothing."

"All right," he said, "better let me load it. Rose, get over here behind me. You stay behind me. All right," he said, putting one bullet in the pistol, "all right, everybody, careful, it's loaded." He let Rose see how a pistol looked loaded, then carefully put it in his sister's hands. "Point it *that* way," he said, giving her the whole upper ridge of the mountain with a sweep of his arm.

Naomi grasped the handle firmly, then put her other hand where the trigger guard was. She closed one eye and moved the pistol around until in approximation her eye saw where it was pointed. She wrapped two fingers around the trigger and pulled. Her arm flew straight up in the air as if she were waving to somebody. Rose shrieked and put her hands to her ears. It was the first time Gilbert had ever seen her afraid. In one moment he became much more her protector than ever before.

"Where'd it go?" Naomi said, looking around, not referring to the bullet. Then she ran a few steps and picked up the pistol. "Heck," she said, "it didn't give me a chance, it jumped like an old frog."

"Are you hurt?" said Gilbert.

"My hand don't feel so hot."

He took her hand, keeping her from rubbing it. He felt the bones and squeezed. "We better not try it any more," he said.

"You bet," said Naomi. "That's too crazy for me."

He felt rather good when she admitted that. "Now you see why I said it was dangerous." He blew into the barrel to cool it off and see if there was smoke inside. But even though she had admitted that she did not want to shoot again, Naomi had not shown the proper fear and respect. So Gilbert told them how if you shot at a rock the bullet might come back and kill you. He took a bullet from his pocket and went to Rose and held it against her chest and pushed a little, so she could feel how big and hard it was. "Imagine that going through you," he said. "Imagine how it would tear you to pieces." Rose was properly awed.

"Now," he said, "*I'm* going to do something. I'm going to shoot straight up in the air, and the bullet will go way, way up, and then it will come down. It may hit one of us. It may hit us right on top of the head. So Rose, you stand here. And Naomi, you too."

Rose did not want to. She preferred to get under a tree. Naomi was skeptical. Gilbert stood and aimed straight at the sky, and as soon as the pistol went off Rose covered the top of her head with her hands. They stood waiting. Gilbert said that when he counted to a hundred they should get ready and listen for it to hit somewhere, and not to look up or it might hit them in the face.

Finally he guessed it was safe, but they stood looking at the sky, three little wind-blown figures caught in the mysteries of life. It did not seem possible that the enormous world could ever be touched by them. It did not seem possible that they could become part of an enormous destruction.

"Do you know," Gilbert told Rose, as they were returning home, "I killed a dog once. Didn't I, Naomi?" He nodded his head gravely. Then suddenly he aimed the pistol straight at Rose and looked at her across the top of it. She seemed further off, and he leveled the sight on the middle of her body. "Like I could kill you now. I wouldn't be afraid to. I might do it."

"You oughtn't point," said Naomi.

But Gilbert, his eyes raising and fixing on the face of the girl at whom the pistol was aimed, saw in her face something that commanded his attention so completely that he did not even realize the gun was pointed or that he was still holding it. He could not have said what it was, something about the way her mouth was, or the way she was looking at him, but he suddenly felt powerful and masterful. He felt the bigness of himself, the strength in his hands, the realization that life was no longer something too large for him to use. Trees were at their right, final size, the mountain no more than a mountain, the brooks never again seen as rivers. What he felt was manhood. He looked at Rose and saw she was not like his sister, that she was old like himself, that she had feelings of his kind, and that, although she behaved like a child, their eyes had exchanged an emotion which was quite distinct from any he and Naomi had ever had.

Irene was in the habit of taking an afternoon nap. It made the children willing. With the house drowsy and feeling somehow untouched by earth, sky or wind, and the summer sunshine reluctant to make changes in shadows which had no movement of their own, and the windows along the lawn open, there would creep through the stillness the laziest sounds from the garden, and odors which excited only the bees.

It made her nights longer and more lonesome. Yet this did not interfere with the pleasure which was hers, lying on the bed, while the curtains moved only enough to make her realize their slight influence on the light. It was the only time she could hear the outside and feel the largeness of space. It was the only time when she could let her ears seek among a multitude of small sounds from which she had become remote.

She heard the long series of little noises which always seemed to come in advance, then the obstacles of the door, and then the slight, shifting pressures on the mattress. The ruthless manner in which children use their feet was one thing she had never become quite accustomed to, and with her eyes still watching the curtains and the garden, she knew Rodger was finding his usual delight in walking on the bed. His hair would be damp as always, his eyes a little too bright, almost feverish. She would never be really able to tell if his hair was black, or if his eyes were blue.

"My sisters won't be ki-et," said Rodger. "Make 'em."

Irene closed one eye and stared at him with the other. He put his hand over the open eye.

"Troot," he said. "An 'at Kat make me get out of bed and pray. Don't I only pray at night?"

Irene stroked his hair, letting him pour his tale of grievances and inventions. Once he had done that, he would be much more reasonable. "You go back and try some more," she said. "Try holding one eye open." It was something he was determined to learn. He was at the stage where he was beginning to find it quite mystifying that his sisters could do it, his father could do it, and his mother could do it. He had the same awe as in watching a light blinking.

"My bed's all terrible," he said.

That had always been his way of expressing an unpleasant event. But he could see he was not believed.

Rodger got down from the bed. He did it by putting his hands on the floor and then finding out what more was required. "Tuck me in, Mommy," he said, trying to open the door the same direction he had opened it on entering. He pushed against everything he should pull.

But he had had the moment of companionship he needed, and so went without too much regret.

Irene lay there, wondering if the mood of peacefulness would return to her. She decided it had not been really peaceful, that this which she was feeling now was much more peaceful. She understood why she did not regret having lost a portion of her romantic dreaminess. It had been replaced by something warmer, and there came to her an intuition of the value which humans have to other humans, a value unlike anything else in the world, and at times worth everything else in the world. Flowers were momentary and their appeal was a touch of fragrance and an instant of delicacy. Wind was refreshing or cruel. The sky was a sentinel's glance at the origin of all color and the searing freshness of light. But children . . .

But children. The very quietness of the house made her sure something was afoot. Irene slipped out of bed. She did not hesitate to go to them in her nightgown, with her hair fallen across her back at full length, and her feet bare. It was indeed the way she was most liked. She scratched on the door and said softly, "Meow," which gave her the privilege of entering.

The children were lying on the floor, talking and dreaming and playing in an atmosphere which they had invented. Kathleen had her tea-party dishes arranged on the carpet. Dorothy was sitting cross-legged. She was holding a cup at the level of her eyes, with her little finger pointed straight. They accepted Irene, made room for her to join them.

"As I was saying," said Dorothy, "I find life quite boring. Quite. Is that the best wine you have?"

Kathleen poured a little water into the cup. Dorothy closed her eyes and sniffed, then held her nose shut and drank. Rodger ran to his mother and she was about to take him in her arms when Dorothy shouted, "He can't eat with the adults."

"I suppose we can make an exception this once," said Irene. "If he promises to behave."

"He won't sleep," said Kathleen, shaking her head sadly.

"Of course not, when there's a party going on."

"If we let him sit at the table, he puts his feet in his saucer."

Rodger sensed a need to defend himself. "She kissed me here," he said, pushing a finger into his cheek. "I don't like. 'At Mommy's place."

"Did it hurt?" said Irene, moving his finger before he remembered to put it in his mouth.

"Sure it hurt," he said, and strutted around the table.

Dorothy was pretending hiccups. That meant she would pretend to be drunk, would go whirling and stumbling around the room, using all the dramatic ballet gestures her father had taught her. Irene saw how near this portion of life was to being ended. Ten, and already the pretense was in its last stages. And Kathleen watching with her one-year-younger eyes, and her dark secrets, which made her whisper everything which she really felt. Kathleen, with her dark hair and impenetrable dark eyes, so like her mother that Irene was a little afraid for her.

Dorothy, whose beauty couldn't wait to find expression, who was destined by her bone structure to be a tall and imposing woman. Her temper was enough for the entire family. As a little girl she had always slept with her hands knotted together and thrust between her drawn up legs, and now she had her own room, decorated as she wanted it, and she gave orders to the servants and only "visited" her sister from time to time.

Rodger, who bristled with energy, who sang aloud to himself and could explain fairy tales by pointing at the pictures. There was always so much to do, so many wonderful things. He had already ruined a floor painting it with olive oil. His flights of fantasy were so purely imaginative that a crooked stick served as his rifle and sword, and even as someone he talked to. . . .

Night had its beginning after the guests were gone and the lights were toned to soft glow. Night began with the last voices calling from the gate, the servants tinkling glasses as they carried them into the kitchen, leaving the house perfect and untouched, not even an ash tray to remind Irene that people had made the smoke which still slightly fogged the rooms, nor a dented cushion to show where someone had sat. It was always a splendid relief to be able to feel the returning presence of the quiet atmosphere in which she and her father had lived, the quiet, late evenings and the silence in which she could hear insects on the lawn. It would bring her out of the nervousness which the constant demands of company put on her.

She would listen beside the stairway for a moment, as she had listened several times during the course of the evening, only now able to feel the satisfaction of believing the children were asleep. There was something so wonderful in being able to feel that they were asleep, and yet it was always the beginning of loneliness. She would hear the tread of her husband's footsteps, and knew that she had no influence upon their direction or intention. She would hear the sounds of doors being locked and window catches fastened.

Her bed had been drawn near the window, and from there she

could see the twinklings on the wire of the screen and sometimes even the stars themselves. There was something shrewd and malicious about them, and it was hard to be amused.

Rose no longer expected the usher to sit beside her every evening. Other boys came and sat beside her, sometimes one on each side. She could watch the movie without feeling where their hands were touching or noticing that her panties were loose. The boys always slouched down in their seats and, when she looked at them, made their eyes avoid her. She had never been kissed. Older people sometimes turned to stare at her and then changed their seats to another part of the theater. It made her feel faintly distressed.

Then one night an older man, without uniform, took her by the arm and led her outside and gave her a push. After that she was never allowed in the movie, even when she had coins in her hand, and the boy who always motioned for her to pass was not taking tickets.

25

In the bitter-cold blowing that had smoothed the snow into flattened broadness and had caused the kind of driftage that puttied shut little holes and ditches, thereby making walking not difficult but tricky, Mijack had gone down to fix the iron gate. The top hinge was broken, and against his principles he had been waiting for better weather to mend it. But the wind made him fear for the lower hinge, which was not made to take all that weight. He could not bear to see something he had made with his own hands ruined while he stood by doing nothing. As he came up the hill from work, the snow, with its nearly straight white lines, made the gate appear more crooked than he had formerly noticed.

So he went down to fix it. He took his lunch pail to the house first. It did not occur to him that he had a grown son.

Nor, when he found the gate stiff with frost and almost immovable, did he think of calling for assistance, though he was tramping through the tracks of his children's comings and goings.

"That sucker!" he said.

The cold was sinking through his clothes, hardening them even as he stood looking down. He had chosen not to wear an overcoat because it made stooping and bending difficult, a restriction he minded more than mere cold. He stood off a moment, hands in his pockets, not to warm them, but to keep them from getting harder to use, and he studied how he could lift and prop the gate until he had an opportunity to see whether the hinge would still hold, or whether he would have to go into the cellar and make a new one. The rapid fall of snow around him, the quick, light movements and the swirling, made such a contrast with his own problem that it was like a faint distraction. He kept wiping the snow from the hinge to see it better.

Mijack thought he saw a way. He knew how to get the most from his shoulders and arms without straining. But the gate proved too much for him; perhaps it would not have if he had not become aware of Bart standing near him. Still Mijack kept silent, thrusting at the gate, no longer so much lifting as waiting, holding onto what little he had accomplished.

"Having trouble?"

Mijack turned his head slowly, out of the fixity to which exertion held it.

"No, I'm kneeling here for my health."

Bart had paid Tim Callaghan to deliver his papers, so he could be early for the basketball game. Coming upon his father at the gate, knowing his assistance was needed, he had felt like slipping past. Yet he could never bring himself to slip past anything. Bart felt he should have gone out on the newspaper route, rather than be caught with something he did not give a damn about. The gate could at least wait until warmer weather. For that matter it was a useless old thing, more nuisance than good, and yet he could not pass by and let his father alone with it.

"Let it be for now," said Bart. "Hell, it'll be dark before long." He said it knowing his father would not quit. He said it knowing his father had lit a lantern more than one night and gone out to fix something or other. His father was right. His father almost always had justice on his side. Yet this only made the bitterness seethe and made Bart want to find some means to end once and forever the unreasonable claims Mijack had over him. To feel the obligations of a son when he no longer believed in his father, no longer believed in the way of life his father had chosen and stuck to, was hard to take.

"Look, I'll fix it tomorrow."

Mijack was still looking up. His face had a little of the helplessness which even the strongest of men cannot prevent when they have been holding something too long and without relief. It was not an appeal, but simply a flattening of the wrinkles in his face, a widening of the eyes. Mijack was trying not to show his disappointment. But it was difficult to feel this way toward his son.

"Give me a hand."

Mijack did not speak for himself, but for the good of the gate.

"I have a basketball game, Father," said Bart. "Tomorrow I'll do it."

"Give me a hand."

"Sure," said Bart, "sure, sure." He stepped in and lifted the gate and did what was harder, fitted it to the hinge. But in doing this he grasped the gate in a manner that did not give Mijack a place to lift. Mijack looked at the marks which the metal had pushed into his hands and said nothing.

"Now what?" said Bart. "Should I hold it until you run get the tools to fix it?"

"You just hold it until I get something to prop with."

"You might at least have waited until it wasn't frozen," said Bart.

"You just hold that gate, and we'll get along better."

"Sure," said Bart. "Take your time, no hurry, I got all night." He was keeping both hands well drawn, dividing the weight. "You know," he said, "this town must have been really rugged in the old days. I bet everybody had stone walls and big gates."

Mijack did not reply. He went to the wall and knocked snow from it and took down one of the stones. He carried it against him, cradled between his arms. Looking down to watch so that he would not slip on the snow made him walk awkwardly.

"The trouble as I see it," said Bart, impatient with his father's slowness because the gate was getting heavier, "is that you made this damn thing twenty years ago. And you made it to last."

"Move your foot!"

"It's going to slip off that," said Bart, as the stone was being shoved under.

"Not if you'll be patient enough to wait until I get another."

"Well, listen," said Bart. "Why don't you let me?"

"Because," said Mijack, looking straight at his son, "I can't hold the gate. It's too heavy for me."

Bart tried to smile. His eyes avoided the directness with which his father was looking at him. He had been trying to force admission only because he was sure his father would never make it. He had a sudden insight into the deep honesty which, for all his faults, Mijack had. He wanted to be able to feel disgusted and could not.

When the stone had been placed so that the two formed both a brace against weight and a lock against movement, Bart made an effort to resume his former nonchalance.

"Now?" he said. "Can I let go now?"

But it did not come off. His father's silence made him know and regret it.

When they were almost at the house, Mijack, walking in front where he had always walked in former years, said, "A strong arm can do more than a weak, you saw that. A hand that contains sureness of what it can do and what it is is a damn sight more useful than a weak one." He talked straight ahead into the open sky, head turned upward, watching the spumes of his own breathing, the vapor forms of his own speech. "I've tried to teach you to respect strength—not idolize it."

If they had not been so near the house and warmth, Bart might have listened better. But Mijack, who never found motion compatible with thought, who was reluctant to carry into the house a conversation which had begun outside, slowed, then halted. He seemed unaware of the snowflakes which were striking and bouncing from him.

"My hands are at the place where I begin to remember what they've done," said Mijack. "Or they soon will be. You put 'em there just a while ago. Just when you're beginning to feel your strength, I'm losing mine, but must that make us like this? Must you make fun of me in the one thing I don't deserve to be made fun of?" Mijack made no appeal. He had not given an inch. He only took it as his duty to admit changes which had taken place in himself, not merely age, but a different attitude. "I can't say I like seeing my hands flub up what they once did so damn easy. And I can't be your judge and say you should respect it. But I can tell you the way you acted over that gate wasn't right by a long shot."

"The gate's done with," said Bart, "so let's go inside and get warm."

"We're going to get something clear first," said Mijack. "I want you to know I'm not the man I used to be. I'm not. My helper's getting the same wage I am, so you know about where I stand." He looked hard at Bart. "I'm still a lot stronger than you'd think, but I can't lift—and I can't see so well. I always hoped you'd be off and gone before this happened. I admit I didn't want you to see it. Not in me. Mind, not because I'm ashamed. But because I knew you wouldn't see it in the right light. And that's going to hurt you, not me."

"Let's let it go."

Mijack was looking down across his land. The snow was still falling, with that deceptive slowness of twilight which made every-thing seem to be under a slight pressure, as if weight were descending from directly above. For all the snow, the stoniness of the land had not been entirely disguised. The wall seemed purposeless now that the gate was erect. He viewed the land as something which did not have much future or promise. Yet even in this he took satisfaction, for the land was at least his to retain to the end of his days, and he knew he would keep it going, not to hang on, but because land carried with it the responsibility of care and cultivation. Land was the only thing with which he had ever been able to develop a permanent relationship, it was the only thing that had never disap-pointed him. The land had kept him alert, had given him poor corn and no peas or melons, knobbed potatoes, but it had never done anything which could convince him that he should relinquish re-sponsibility. For even if it too was marked by time, it was time in such large terms that a man could not do right except by treating it as eternal.

Mijack knew his son would never feel any of this, and it was a disappointment to him. It would have been easier to part with his son if he had been able to feel that Bart had grasped the meaning of caring for something. "I see now. I see I never was a thinker. I only thought what I had to do anyway, I only made up a reason for it." Mijack spit and made a black hole in the snow. He tasted his mouth to see if he had gotten rid of the worst of it. "Your strength's come sooner'n mine did. I wasn't a bit strong until I turned thirty. And you're smarter than I was, Bart, but don't let smartness get hold on you. Don't misuse your strength. If you do, you're not being fair to yourself."

He opened the door. Bart entered first. It was a tribute he was reluctant to accept, but as his father continued to stand to one side, there seemed no other way to prevent further difficulties but to enter. And in passing through the door, the privacy was at an end, and so Bart knew he had been forced to relinquish his right to make a reply. He felt suddenly that he was never going to bother to explain himself again, that his father and he lived in separate worlds, and that there was both hopelessness and hope in that. They would get on better, but they would have less to share.

"Mr. Rowiger," said Mr. Pierce, "you place me in a category little above that of a beast. Yes, my father-in-law held me in low esteem. He had reason to. I was a traitor to every expectation he had of me. I married. I was disappointed in the size of my father-in-law's estate and shocked at his management of it. Let us say I saw his easiness of manner and mistook it for easiness of financial position. It was a practical fool like myself who would overestimate in such matters. This disregards those feelings I had for Irene, which, I assure you, were substantial."

Mr. Pierce was speaking as if he meant to get at the truth. He seemed tired of camouflage.

"I let my affairs go pretty much to the devil while we were traveling. Naturally, when we returned, I was anxious to set things in order. I found out my father-in-law was in poor financial circumstances. He had quietly disposed of a great deal of stock in companies where I was anxious to get a foothold and in companies where I wanted the support of his stock. He had disposed of that stock for no more reason than tradition, an unwillingness to close down a family enterprise, that damn tobacco factory. He came to me, asking me to invest. Not that way, you knew his manner, admirable, I admit, worthy, I admit. But!"

Mr. Pierce looked at the younger man, the man who was not on his side, the man who would try not to understand his side.

"You must understand that my wife didn't care a bit about the factory. She will admit that even now. Her concern was for her father's happiness. Mine wasn't. Mr. Lang believed he had been given the opportunity, through my marriage, through the security I represented, to continue his little fantasy of retaining an old family possession. He was never deliberately after my money, not even when he asked me to invest. But he did think he had, by unloading his daughter on me, freed those funds which he had retained for her— if she had not married. I made what I thought was a clear definition between sentiment and sentimentality. I found myself entitled as guardian of my wife's inheritance to point out to him specific flaws in his intention."

Mr. Pierce seemed angry.

"He was clever. If he had fought me—but instead he bowed out of the picture, suffered in silence, and killed my wife's love for me. Oh, not all in a day. We had been too happy to have anything broken in a day. And I don't say there were no other causes. I was too old for Irene, too weak. . . . Perfect in the beginning, that's the sad part, so perfect in the beginning, breathing life into her, feeding her mind . . . I swear no man has had such a first year of marriage as I had. Nor second probably. And then . . . You know that when a man plays god to a woman, you know he is doomed. The rest, how did the rest come about? At what point does a man say to himself, this woman is too much for me?

"Now, all that I got involved in amounts to less than a twentieth of my holdings, less than a hundredth part of my happiness. Do I want my daughters to find out there is a fund waiting to protect them from me? Do I like my wife knowing that her security is entrusted to you? I'm not blind. I can see that the *protection* was intended to go further than money. It was a temptation. The temptation was for both you and my wife."

"Mr. Lang had no such intention," snapped Rowiger. "He simply saw that you were making his daughter unhappy and felt that he was to blame. He told me that himself. And the only thing he knew to do was to make me the executor of a trust fund."

"Oh come now," said Mr. Pierce, "you know that part of your resentment is simply that it had to involve you. You're only too willing to wash your hands."

Rowiger flushed. "I have not washed my hands. I signed over the trust to you because Irene asked me to do it."

Mr. Pierce smiled.

"Don't you think," Mr. Rowiger said, "you should give your wife her freedom?"

There was silence.

"In fair consideration of the situation," Mr. Rowiger pursued, "even though you've been wronged, as you see it, don't you consider her freedom the only solution? Not even solution. The only chance for her to find some happiness."

"Good God, man," said Mr. Pierce, "there is the exact impossibility. . . . She doesn't want her freedom. She still, in spite of everything, believes in me. She asked you to turn that money back to me not because of a scandal, not because of the children, but because it was her way of giving me still another chance. She still considers me capable of overthrowing all that has gone before. . . . I, who won her admiration ten years ago because I knew a pocketful of magic tricks—I, who never was worth the tip of her little finger."

Mr. Pierce halted, and looked closely at Rowiger.

"If I really thought, sir, that she could have the least bit more happiness, the least bit more, I would be so vulgar as to point my arm at the door of the house and watch her walk out of my life forever. And now, sir, I believe you and I have nothing further to say to each other."

"If I ever again catch you deliberately, deliberately mind you, tearing your pants," said Mijack, "I'll give you a thing to remember."

The idea behind willful destruction of clothing was one Mijack could not regard lightly. It was destruction of property. It was a kind of viciousness, unreasonable and humiliating to Mijack, as if he were being despised for the very duty of providing for his family.

"I didn't try to," said Gilbert. "It was an accident."

"Don't lie to me."

"Well I didn't and I don't care. Oh, hell, it doesn't do any good to talk to you. You never listen."

"You watch what you say to me," said Mijack. "You're getting pretty smart."

Mijack sat down on a chair. He was beginning to feel tired. He was beginning to be tired of everything connected with his family, of his wife and his children. It did not seem to be going anywhere. It did not seem as if he was going to be able to get any principles across to his sons.

"I don't mistreat you. I try to do what's right. Where do you get this idea I'm against you? Where do you get it?" He studied his son. "Listen, when you don't have clothes, come to me, you'll get them. If you don't have shoes, we'll go downstreet this minute. If you don't get enough to eat, speak up. I'm not going to have my family wanting." Mijack spit blackness from his mouth into a big red handkerchief. It would only come loose in his throat from time to time. It would be bedtime before his nose was feeling clean. "You haven't listened. I see right now you don't intend to listen. You like to be pigheaded. Some day I'm going to plug your ears and make you keep 'em that way and see if you don't like listening better then." Mijack looked at Gilbert. "Let me tell you, I want sons I can be proud of. I mean you. You! I'll do everything in my power to have such sons." Mijack studied the palms of his hands. "Worthlessness, that's your danger, that's what's got into you. You've got to stop wanting everything given to you. You've got to realize that in a few years—a few, mind you—you'll be a man, and what sort of a man can you hope to be if you don't start now? Eh?"

Mijack gave his son plenty of time to speak. Gilbert sulked.

"The law says I can guide you until you're twenty-one. The law says that. I say nonsense. If you're not a man soon, you never will be, and the older you get the worse. I do now what I can; you do what you can. It's time you wake up, time you start thinking about something besides what's for supper and what you can wheedle out of your mother. Because this house isn't your life. It's only a cover for your head until you get something into that head. Because you fail me, I renounce you. You're flesh of my flesh, yes, I still renounce you. I have no place in my heart for flesh alone."

Mijack slapped his son across the head, not hard, simply to get his attention.

"You listen to me. I don't often talk."

His anger had become something deeper than when they had begun, turning about what was more important to himself, turning about what he felt should be important to his son.

"I live for myself, my honor, my pride. I lie if I say otherwise. But I live too for you and your brother. I watch my blood flow onward and see how my blood must flow onward, not because of me, but because it must. Bart sees that. He's caught the scent. And you must see it too, because I will not have my life wasted, I refuse to allow you, I will not accept less than what I see in you. So I say and I do and I punish, even if you hate me. I care nothing for what you think of me."

Mijack clenched his hands together. The lines of concentration in his forehead and beside his eyes relaxed into their permanent forms, leaving him looking a little uninteresting. Leaving him definitely past his prime. He saw his thoughts clearly and did not have to struggle to reveal them, and his voice became more powerful.

"I could be proud of a good son who hated me. But never of a bad son who loved me. I mean Bart. I mean you. I mean I know you want to love me and you want to be good, and that is the most tremendous thing a man can want. But my boy, my son, just being good, just loving, without doing those things which are good and are love, without the effort and the accomplishment—no, absolutely no. You have to do and do and do again. Maybe you understand. But not enough. I see not enough. And if your mother thinks it's enough, she's doing you a great harm.

"Listen, I warn myself against false pride, and before the great things of this earth I'm respectful, but for all this, I see that what people need is pride, the pride to stand before God Himself and say, I'm shaped in Your image, I'm worthy of Thee. Will you be able to do that, my boy? Will simply loving people give you that?

"My son, I'm getting old, I get cross, I push at you, I don't mean to. You can't expect perfect understanding from a man my age. Hell, get on your two feet and you won't have these lectures thrown at you. That's all I ask, get on your two feet, give sign that you're going to be a man, that you're going to do something. Because I weaken, I tire, I may not be with you much longer. If I'd died when you were eight or nine, you'd have felt cheated. How'm I going to feel to have to die when you're twenty-five and no further along than you are now, just bigger?" said Mijack. "It's hard for me to accept old age, don't make it harder. I still have pride, I'll never surrender it, I'll never let my sons destroy it. If you make me ashamed, look out, because I won't quit until the shame is where it belongs."

His voice was soft, relaxed, as if he had said what was most important. He was feeling the sadness of never being able to make any change in this son, and the desperation of wanting to give shape and substance. He could not seem, by any means, threat, entreaty, explanation, to call forth his son's real nature. His hands could not relax from their bitter yearning.

"My son, I ache to take of my pride and put it in you. I cannot. I would not. No, it's for you to put it there yourself. If I can have it by no other means than this, this constant miserable talking, I don't much want it. From now on, if I have anything you want, you'll have to come to me." Mijack scanned his son again, this time with sorrow. "I've talked where there's no ear. Go to your toys."

He was not angry. He did not care for himself. He cared only for the boy's sake. The web was already formed, and he could only go on providing. It would come what would come, and what would be Mijack's was a share of the responsibility, but the pride would not be his. He saw that this younger son had, in his own way, become as independent as Bart.

As Mijack looked at his house and thought of himself, he felt it was as well his sons were free. It was well that they had both escaped his teachings and beliefs, because they did not seem to be suitable for anyone except himself. It seemed now only the faith that Mijack had had, a faith he had partially betrayed, which kept something coherent and acceptable running through his life. All there was to show, a stone house, a few acres on which trees had been encouraged to grow, a plot of stony soil, a wall, seemed hardly enough to encourage a man to demand greatness of his sons. Yet it was right, and he had done right, and he could not escape the perplexity of knowing it.

"It's not up to me. If your father doesn't want you to have long trousers, I can't go against him."

"Oh, hell, you always act sick when I want something."

Gilbert left the room without letting her finish. He was disgusted.

Although his mind was centered around this need, this sudden concern about his appearance, it did not exclude an even more general feeling, one of having been abandoned, one of something alien and terrible going on within the house which he could not understand, but which was expressed in a beginning desire to get a job and stay with it this time and earn money of his own. He did not feel secure any more.

As he went through the hall and made the sharp swing into the stairway, he heard the noise of someone moving about in his room, but this merely made him impatient to get downstairs. He heard his father call, "Gib, come in here," but continued to go down the steps, his mind set upon getting out of the house, away from it for a while. It had become habit of late to pretend he had not heard, to go on without glancing back.

But before he reached the bottom of the stairs his name was called so loudly that he could not ignore it. "What? What is it now?" he cried with exasperation, pausing only to hear, then taking a few steps forward, still not turning to look. "What do you want?"

"Come up here."

"Why? I ain't done nothing wrong. I got to meet somebody."

"I said come up here."

"Oh, all right. I don't see why I have to be picked on all the time."

"I've been looking through your clothes," said Mijack. "You really need pants. Why didn't you tell me you needed them?"

"I did. You said I didn't."

"I was going by what your mother told me. I forgot she couldn't get around of late," said Mijack. "Why do we wait? Let's go after them." Mijack put his hand on his son's shoulder. "Listen, there was one thing I didn't tell you. It was part of the reason I talked kind of rough a while ago. It's that your mother's worried about you, and she isn't well, and it isn't good for her to have to worry so. She's worried what will happen to you. And that's why if you could show some signs of finding your way, of wanting to do something, you'd take a lot off her mind." Mijack sighed. "And mine, my boy. You two have been so close that if something did happen, I don't know whether, I don't know that I can make her the promise that I'll be able to do for you."

Gilbert came home from downstreet wearing long trousers. He walked stiffly and erect, closer to his father than usual, taking short strides, part in pride, part in fear he might step on the cuffs. He went immediately to Naomi to show the trousers to her. He strutted back and forth, even sticking his hands in the pockets, assuming poses of nonchalance. Naomi sat and looked at him and clapped her hands in delight. She must have had confused emotions. She must have been getting tired of having material added to her own dresses.

"See how well the waist fits. It don't even need a belt—I'm not sticking my stomach out either—see? You see? I look taller, don't I? Not so fat. Eh? Not so fat? I'm not so fat any more. Do you notice? Maybe I'll get a pair of suspenders one of these days. Suspenders look better than belts, don't you think? Aren't these pants something, though? Do they fit all right in back? Do they really fit? How about when I bend over, like this—like this? Okay? Say, I mean they *do* make a difference. Boy, oh boy, oh boy. And did you see this pocket? It's for a watch. It's what you call a watch pocket, see."

He opened the pocket wide as if she was supposed to look inside.

"Say, are they long enough? I wasn't sure where they're supposed to come, at the top of the shoe or where, so I let the clerk do it, and then made him move the mark just a hair."

Gilbert fingered the still perfect straight crease, pinching, as if to insure its remaining firm.

"Guess how much they cost? No, I'm not going to tell unless you guess. Oh, you'd never guess. Father really put his hand steep in his pocket. He said make sure you get the pair you want, don't worry about the price. I didn't, believe me. Father's okay sometimes."

Gilbert went to his mother. He showed all sides of the trousers to her, although he did not strut and perform as he had before his sister. He insisted that his mother feel the material and tell him if it was good cloth. Susie Mijack nodded her head and pursed her lips.

"I'm going to need a hanger, Mom, can I take one of yours?"

There was no spite, no apparent remembrance of their quarrel. He left the room feeling Mother liked him in long trousers but did not exactly approve of the ones he had chosen. . . .

Gilbert dressed for school and used a mirror for one of the rare times in his life. He took the trousers off the hanger and tried to keep his shoes from getting the insides dirty as he drew them up his legs. He combed his hair with a comb, not the butt ends of his fingers. He brushed his teeth with a washrag and white soap.

Mother ordered him to go straight to his room and take the trousers off. He was not going to wear out a pair of new trousers just to go to school. They were to be kept for Sunday.

There was a terrible argument.

Susie Mijack had her way.

Within two weeks he had prevailed, and he was wearing his trousers when and where he pleased. But he did not forgive her for having stolen from him the glory of that one morning, and he was a little careful of having too much faith in her. She loved him, he knew, but her love did not do for him enough to command his unreserved obedience and belief. Father was right, it was time for him to start earning money of his own and begin doing as he pleased.

Rose Lee was transferred, after failing third grade at the age of eleven, to the class for "special" students, where crafts, hand arts, sewing, weaving and elementary woodcraft were stressed. She had a mother, no father, lived in an apartment and could not have other children in. Since the Mijack children were not permitted to have visitors, there was an established relationship. Children are so unconcerned with past history that, unless parents—as they are apt to do—interfere, they will form friendships on a most unprejudiced basis.

For a long time Gilbert never thought of Rose in relation to himself. He never seemed to realize that she was nearly his own size and age. Most of their time together was spent in the mountains and foothills, alongside brooks and creeks. Rose was always attracted by bright-colored stones and made herself bracelets of moss and wreaths of vines. Her hands were quick and pretty when she was making something. She could toy with a flower for hours without tearing a single petal, simply bending and flexing and peering into all the crevices. She had a way of using the tip of her tongue to taste—or, more accurately, to feel—the flower. All things that tickled made her happy.

Rose liked things which Naomi had outgrown. Naomi's way of discarding whatever she had outgrown forced Gilbert to keep pace; when Naomi laughed at Rose, he laughed too, and made fun of her. "Here," he would say, "there's gold in this stone. Don't say I never gave you nothing." Or he would pick a weed and tell her sarcastically to take it home and put it in a vase of water.

Then he was not laughing at her. He was often looking over her shoulder when she was examining a leaf or a bug or worm or frog or crayfish. Through sitting beside her he learned how much fun it was to watch water skippers and spiders and wind in the trees. He first really listened to a brook and found that, although it lasted only a moment, there was a very pure and pretty music. His loyalty in any important matter was still with Naomi, but he began to prevent Rose from being treated too hard. That she never complained and was always good-natured, and that it took almost nothing to please her, were among the reliefs he found from the demands his sister was always putting on him.

It was healthy and reasonable that Gilbert should turn from his sister and hunt other companionship. It was even better that he did not realize he was turning away, to have it merely happen, to see green leaves and need someone to give affection to, someone who would respond. The fact that Rose was not complicated and did not change from minute to minute was what made him like her. She was direct and fresh in her seeking of sunshine and happiness. She reminded him of the wonderful little world which he and his sister had shared and somehow lost.

There was the time Rose climbed a tree to throw down cherries. Naomi could have done it three times as easy and quick, but she liked using Rose as a kind of servant. Rose got halfway up and then wanted to come down. "Scairdee," said Naomi. Rose started to try to lower herself; she suddenly wrapped her arms and legs around the trunk, hugging it. "Come on down," said Gilbert. "I'm not afraid," she said, "I'm—I'm . . ." Gilbert had to climb to where she was and practically pull her loose. She lay on the ground, panting. Gilbert felt uncomfortable himself.

There was the time Naomi wanted to go swimming. Rose was willing. Gilbert would not.

Looking across the top of the pistol, limiting his attention to the circle of focus, he came to realize part of his feeling. For what Rose and Gilbert shared was a moment of fixation, a kind of passionate exchange between eyes. The firing of the pistol had aroused her, destroyed the calm and serenity in which she usually existed, and she became the receptacle of his emotion.

Afterward, it was never the same. Rose became his admirer, both secret and open. His voice she made her command, his footprint she watched on the ground. She threw off her servant garment. She became more active, and showed more intelligence and interest.

For Gilbert it was a revival of feelings which he had had for his sister before she became too knowing and independent. It was a revival of his sense of daring, which, before the uncritical eyes of Rose, became even more unchecked. Nor was it beyond him to play one girl against the other, to watch their loyalties at work.

Soon it was noticeable that he was giving his attention to Rose. He did not want to go anywhere without having Rose along. Naomi saw and did not mind. She was glad for the freedom it gave her. It was a splendid thing for all three, each finding new pleasures; but it probably had the greatest effect on Rose, who was sometimes simply breathless to see Gilbert. Her eyes were brighter and gayer than ever in her life.

Rose's arms and legs grew away from the small dresses, even from the little edges tacked onto the skirt bottoms. She seemed to be always touching Gilbert. She seemed to be always running her fingers over the material of his shirt or making curls in his long, unruly hair.

Gilbert began to feel uncomfortable when he saw her sitting and looking at something for a long time with that constant calm gaze in which her eyes seemed to absorb rather than see. He got so it was a slight fear that—when they planned a picnic—Naomi might not be able to go with them. On picnics, he was ashamed of the way Rose ate, the way she chewed so vigorously and with such glee; yet he might do the same or worse himself, with all the ferocity he had when hungry. He might carry on and have a heck of a good time— let Rose feed him sandwiches and catch the tips of her fingers between his teeth and make a growling sound.

His sister was frailer and thinner than Rose, delicate in spite of her quick, monkeylike antics. Rose was large and strong, and it was natural there would be more physical contest between them. He was teaching her things, how to spit far and straight, how to smoke cigarettes, how to burn the hair on her arm with a magnifying glass. He put tattoo stickers on her. He taught her how to Indian wrestle.

One day they got into each other's arms and kissed a few times. It threw straight at Gilbert a problem which he had been refusing to consider. He had to decide whether Rose was a child or a girl. The fact that his body had made its decision did not change the importance of the problem, and indeed complicated it. Rose was very mature physically, with a share of the cloying, sweet listlessness and constant, vague physical suffering that is so often the lot of big, heavy girls. He liked to put his arms around her and crush her against him until she got a pained, mute expression in her eyes, a breathlessness, a perspiration. Yet he would be held away from her by the feeling that she did not know what they were doing, that she was innocent of the very desire she was showing. Although he was stirred, and her innocence made him bold, he felt deceived and cheated every time he took advantage of it. He was fighting against a lack of respect for her, a lack of respect which he had never before allowed to come into his consciousness, a truth that he and his sister had always considered her of a lower order than themselves.

Now his feelings demanded that he give her full stature. He hungered to be alone with her, yet did not want to be alone with her. He was, on one side, glad when they could get away from Naomi, and yet did not want his sister to know. Rose stirred in him an emotion that was at times so fierce that he wanted to strike her, hurt her. Her strength infuriated him. And she stirred in him a different emotion, one that was a little sly, a little shameful, a curiosity that he could not bring himself to attempt. The knowledge that she would probably not prevent him, that she would submit in this as she did in everything else, aroused in him scruples and reasons for reluctance.

He came to take a low view of her mentality. He took precautions to make Rose assume that the increasing contact of body and hands was only the result of games. When he brought his face close to hers, it was usually under the pretext of tickling her with his nose or making the sound of a bee in her ear. He would nip her with his teeth and pull her hair until it made her eyes show pain. He would dig his chin into her shoulders, making her roll and toss, laughing, trying to protect herself.

Rose could not seem to understand that they must not do this sort of thing in front of Naomi. He would tell her again and again.

He would have to treat her harshly when Naomi was with them. She wanted to smoke, wanted to take off his shoes, wanted to wrestle. Sometimes he got angry with her. Sometimes he felt sick of the way she had to be always hanging on him, touching him, not giving him a moment to himself.

Gilbert found a pose that was partly successful, that of being an older fellow with two little girls. He would act aloof and unconcerned, very abstracted. He would deliberately not pay much attention to either of them. It was a comfortable feeling to put them both in their places, to let Naomi know that she was after all only a child, and to let Rose know he was not going to stand for her nonsense.

26

Bart became resolute in purpose. The desire to get ahead was becoming strengthened by the moral aspects of his nature, which were highly developed for his age, so that, although he would never be honest in the rather sentimental sense in which honesty is appreciated in America, his values had the foundation of a self-honesty as flexible and inflexible as his own mind. He felt compelled to rule himself, to develop a personal creed, and this was more important than outward power and success, which he also intended to get. He pressed life a little but did not rush it. He could be patient and could measure time with accuracy, and nothing he saw made his eyes blink. Neither good nor evil, in their most shocking forms, seemed to take him by surprise. This was not because he was blind or unmoved, but because he was able to absorb them and remain firm.

It was not long before he reached the decision never to ask a favor of anyone, no matter what situation he might find himself in. He saw that his father had been right in this matter but suspected that Mijack had done it merely out of pride. Bart had other reasons —pride too, but also a conviction that a favor cannot be deserved, and that he wanted nothing he could not demand. He wanted to pay the full price for every inch of life. Yet he did not jump to the usual hard-bitten conclusion, "Ask no favor and give none." He saw that favors were one of the easiest means of gaining power over men, and he would use them as such. Nor, if it did not endanger his own position, would he refuse to be of assistance to others, without having a motive of gain. But he would do it rationally. He would not let himself be compelled by sentiment or personality or promise.

Bart had more freedom than his brother or sister and knew it was only in part due to being the eldest. He had made his own freedom. His aloofness, his unwillingness to share pleasure or pain—his or theirs—with the family, had been deliberate. He had built a fence about himself. This barrier, which was really only an emptiness, had given him time to be alone, and he had found it sweet-tasting. To be alone, to have the continuous sensation of being alone, was one of the most powerful and splendid of emotions. It had an almost spiritual quality, and certainly a great amount of dignity. He found himself free of the conflicting emotions and strains and tensions that arise from the relationships of young boys to their parents, their friends. He had simplified his life as well as shaped it by accepting a method, by choosing isolation as the means of finding not escape from the world, but a place of high importance in it. He almost never said, "I wish," but often said, "I will," and still more often, "I will not." Having seen the advantages of coldness and surliness, having seen that he could keep people away from him, he became more gruff in his manner and speech than his nature required. Yet he was seldom nasty, and found no pleasure in it. And when he saw a person who was deserving of respect, he was respectful and courteous, and was glad in his heart to meet someone who was deserving.

Having once sworn that he would never tell the truth to his father, Bart soon discovered that he did not want to lie to Mijack. He respected his father enough not to lie. But it was equally difficult to respect his father enough to tell the truth, even though Mijack simply was not the kind of man who should have to deal with lies. Bart saw that he had made the vow rashly, under the stress of the moment, and he was disgusted with himself for having done so. It was hard for him to break a vow. It was harder to abide by a foolish one. He went to his father.

"I told you I would never tell you the truth. I was wrong in that. I will not lie to you. I never have, and I never will."

He spoke this with the directness and pride which was always most noticeable when he was in Mijack's presence, and yet was

288

angered when he saw that Mijack was pleased with him, for he suspected that Mijack misunderstood why he was renouncing the vow. In fact, he very nearly added, "You needn't look so happy. It wasn't you who caused me to change my mind." His attitude toward his father was shifting, and he was slowly and methodically forcing Mijack to accept this change. "That's none of your business," Bart said frequently to his father.

Bart was willing to fight any boy he was not quite sure he could beat, but refused to fight boys too old and too mature for him to be able to do more than make a good showing. There was nothing to be gained by losing, by simply proving he was not afraid of being beaten. On the other hand, he avoided conflict with smaller and weaker children, and unless they became loud and overbearing with him, he would never lay a hand on them, nor even be unkind. But he would not allow a child to give him a hard time. He would give warning. Once.

Bart hunted fights. He provoked them. Yet he did not enjoy fighting. It was another stage in the methodical development of his body, as well as a compulsion to be able to defend himself. He could not endure feeling helpless, and thus often fought boys against whom he had nothing, not anger or grudge. Fighting was also another means of isolating himself, of forcing people to stay at a proper distance. He was at his best when his emotions were not involved, when he could calmly face his opponent without having any real desire to hurt. He was patient, waited for an opening, conserved his strength, and was adept at feinting. His tactics were designed to baffle and annoy. Even his face was controlled, assuming a mocking expression against a boy who was angry, and a stern, impassive appearance against anyone who showed fear. His eyes could mislead. His voice was cold. "Watch out for my left," he would say. "You're dropping your guard. What'd you duck for? Huh? What's the matter? Beginning to get tired? A bit scared? What's the matter, huh?"

Bart saw that skill was an asset, but that it was not as important as strength. He had made the mistake of picking on Mike Murray, a big, strong fellow, almost a man in size. He had seen that Mike was slow and clumsy. But he had not counted on continuous bull-like rushes. In the end Bart had taken quite a beating. It did not make Bart feel bad, and he had, in fact, admired the strength and unrelenting stubbornness of Mike, who became one of his few fast friends. After that, Bart forced himself to quit having a tendency to

289

set his legs firmly for one big punch, forced himself to keep on the move, darting in and out. He saw that his real strength was in timing, speed and endurance, not in sheer power. Pounding on the anvil had led him to put too much faith in the strength of his right arm, and now he ceased to depend upon it. Not that it wasn't strong. He had jolted Mike with it several times.

It was not long until Bart was picking fights with boys considerably older than himself. He was getting a bad reputation at school, but that did not matter, and it had advantages.

As often happens, he became an idol of the very boys he had fought and beaten earlier. He became their champion against the older boys. If there was a complaint or a suggestion to be made to the teacher, boys and girls would come to Bart and ask him to do it for them. If he was not too well liked, it was nevertheless known everywhere that he was not afraid to speak out. Bart was the sort of person who would have had many friends, if he had wanted them, if he had been willing to make just a few concessions. But he did not make any. And in certain respects he did not deserve to be liked as much as he was. He had seen the advantages of making children think he was their protector, and he undertook fights, supposedly in their defense, which he desired for a personal reason and which might have been otherwise difficult to provoke.

"Let the kid alone, do you hear? I'll teach you to pick on someone your size."

"He won't bother you any more. If he does, you let me know."

"I said, pick up that hat. You have five seconds before I make you pick it up."

"What was that? Say it out loud once and see what happens."

Such were the disguises that Bart used to start a fight. It would be wrong to say that he was completely indifferent when he saw a small child being picked on, for he was not, and he could not have prevented himself from offering the small child his protection. He had no contempt for the sick, the weak, the stupid, or the helpless, and in certain ways could have more real love for people in this condition than for the rest of mankind. It was people who were capable of defending themselves, but who were afraid, people who failed when they should not have failed, and, above all, people who pitied themselves, who whined, who crawled, that he could not endure. This was not something he had thought out. It was instinctive.

Yet Bart was not really a protector of the children. In the first place, he did not really care enough about them to do anything in

290

their defense which would have cost him any strong effort or endanger him. He would not have allowed himself to do it even if he had felt that he should, for such action would have endangered his plans, his isolation, his whole pattern of belief.

He became even more methodical. He would select the boy he wanted to fight several weeks in advance, watch him on the playground, and at baseball, football and volleyball. His eyes with their unmoving pupils would be measuring, guessing weight, watching for habits and odd, involuntary traits. His ability to measure the physical nature of a person was almost uncanny. It was not sufficient to note weakness. He watched strength and then planned to make it serve him as the greatest weakness. For he saw that where there was exceptional ability, it was almost certain to be too much relied upon. He waited until he was certain he had a good chance of winning, not merely in those moments of furious confidence, but when he was steadily sure. Then he struck.

Bart carried along his physical development with a skill that few boxing managers are able to show in their selection of opponents for a young club fighter. Bart never fought anyone who was easily beaten, unless it was unavoidably forced upon him—it was disgusting not to have to use the utmost of his strength and ability. If he avoided defeat and sought success, then each success must mark an advance, an improvement. He preferred defeat, such as that suffered at the hands of Mike Murray, to a win that had been effortless. The remarkable knowledge of his own ability could scarcely have been as rational a self-judgment as he thought. Despite the charts on which he kept a record of his growth, his body was something he fathomed instinctively, something he knew by a peculiar and temporary odor in his nostrils, by a tenseness of the flesh in the corners of his eyes and by a certain heaviness of his jaw bone.

Bart was not cruel, and would not add additional punishment when the boy he was fighting showed willingness to quit. He never had to be held off by outsiders. At the same time, he was not profuse or apologetic to the person he had beaten, and if he did not offer to shake hands, he also did not refuse. "You were pretty good," he might say, but never did he say it to make the person feel better or to make his victory loom more impressive. Bart when fighting against someone who had taunted him earlier was especially determined to win, so that in his eargerness he was not as merciful, but he still did not lose control of himself. He was capable of desiring revenge, of wanting revenge so badly that he had an almost terrible strength, but once he had emerged victorious, his pride would not allow him to humiliate his enemy. "I waited a long time for this, a long time," he said once, but it was in an almost weary tone of voice. Usually he did not say anything. He did not feel the need to say anything.

Bart seldom realized that he had a brother and sister. He had so freed himself from the family relationships that he did not need to put on the big-brother act of being tolerant and superior. But he was not inhuman either, and was perhaps more kind to them than is usually customary for the eldest to be. He liked Naomi as much as he could like anyone. If he had bothered to think about it, he would have admitted that he preferred her to all the rest, even his father, because she could make him smile. Not many people were able to make Bart smile. She was a pretty little thing. What he liked best about her was that she was the only child he had ever known who was not sometimes afraid of him. He could never really like anyone who had even once shown him the least bit of fear. He called her "little nut" quite often, and pet names were not one of his habits.

Naomi had sense enough not to pester him. There were entire days when his eyes did not have to give her attention or even focus upon her. If she happened to block Bart's path he could gently and firmly set her aside without having to encounter her personality. There was no deliberate cruelty in this. He was grateful to his sister for being able to keep out of his way. He was particularly grateful that she accepted him exactly as he was, without complaint, without too much show of admiration. He liked the way she sometimes dismissed him as belonging to a different world from her own.

Bart never played with his sister or his brother and shared none of his childhood with them. When Naomi had been little, he had occasionally, if his mind was functioning in a manner that did not require a motionless thought-participating body, allowed his hands to roll a ball across the floor and watch Naomi stop it—sometimes —with her hands and knees and dress bottom. He had seemed amused. But if Naomi returned the ball inaccurately, so that Bart was unable to reach it without much effort, she either had to go after the ball and roll it to him again, or the game was over. If it could be called a game.

Mijack had a long conversation with his oldest son, in which many things were settled. When it was over Bart knew that he had underestimated his father. It was firmly understood that their relationship should be established on a more businesslike basis, now that Bart was nearing manhood. At the age of sixteen he was entitled, if he wished, to set out on his own, but once he had left home, he could not expect further assistance; nor was he welcome or entitled, in later years, to assist his father.

"Once you walk out of this house," said Mijack, "I regard us as both free, without obligation. Old age will come upon me before long. I wish it to myself. I don't want to be bothered—and I don't want my son wasting his time with an old man. Do we agree upon this?" Mijack studied his son. "If not, I wish you'd speak now."

"We agree," said Bart.

"Good. Now I have more to say to you. If before you're sixteen you decide you're a man, and you wish to go, tell me, and I will let you go—if I think you're ready. But if I should decide against your going, then I expect you to wait. As long as you remain in this house, I demand obedience. Nothing more. Nothing less. If you believe I'm unreasonable, that's just too bad. You're welcome to tell me—but I'm not likely to change my ways. I've tried to be fair. I've followed my conscience. I don't expect my conscience to be yours. That's why I demand obedience."

Mijack looked at his son to see how much impression his words were making. He did not trust words, and was looking for the mistakes his mouth made. "You're not compelled to leave. I expect you realize that. I don't force you. If you want to remain, you may. And I wouldn't take a penny from you—and I'd despise you. Yet the only price—again—would be obedience. Or if you go away, you run into hard luck, sickness, there'll be food and shelter waiting here. Rely on that much." Mijack paused. "I hope that won't happen. It's not good for a son to return to his father. It's bad for them both. I don't want to be bothered in my old age about keeping peace between us, or what you're going to do next. I'll have enough of the past without being reminded about it. But there is food and shelter here, while I live. I said *here*. Never write asking help, not even for money to come home. Because you'd waste the paper it was written on. No, I won't cheat my sons by making life secure for them. Have I made myself clear on that point?"

"You have. And you needn't worry, I won't come back."

"Good. I knew it. Then I might as well tell you I hope you won't remain here a single day more'n's necessary. I didn't raise my sons to have them hanging about the house. My sons have lives of their own. This is a big country. All things are possible. I speak not with hope, but certainty. You can get any damn thing you want. Big or little. It's even too easy, my son, a little too easy, and that may become your problem. It wasn't easy for me, because I had principles that hindered me. I don't think you have them." Mijack laughed at a thought which came to him. "Why," he said, "why—my trouble was I never found out what I did want. I only found things I had to believe in." He stopped speaking, with an abruptness which was a little too noticeable. He seemed to be considering what he had said, his face strained with the tension of inexplicable things that he understood, but could not share. It was the face of a man to whom nothing came easily, and even when attained it would lie immovable in the concealed, the frozen turbulence of his soul. "My father was a foreigner," said Mijack. "I never mentioned him to you before. Nor would I now, except to make a point. He believed it was my duty to carry on in his footsteps. That's how I came to go down in the mines. These black scars on my hands, they're from coal, not steel." He rubbed over them, feeling at them, as if after all these years he still might be able to remove them. "My father believed in the home, his home, my home, your home, all one. His beliefs, my beliefs, your beliefs, all one. That was good in the old country. It was their hope. It was necessary. There was not much room for walking there. But this is America, and it's big, and we must never behave like foreigners in it. We must not. I've worked all my life among Germans and hunkies and wops and niggers, and I curse them all in my heart. I curse them. They are crucifying my land. *Your land*, my son. Oh, yes, they came here with hope, to build a new life, and then, then like the cowards and weaklings they are, they settled down and lived the same damn way they did in the old country.

"My own father did that, went back to the same rotten life he had fled. Oh, he lived a little better, a little better. . . . That satisfied him." Mijack's voice was angry. "I too, my son. You're right to despise me for some things. I tried to shake my ways, tried to clean my mind and my heart, tried to really see what we had here in this country and what was right to do. I tried! But I too, though I was born here, am still a foreigner. I've seen mountains the sun couldn't get over until ten o'clock. I've lived on the Mississippi, watched the hangings in Memphis, strung trolley wire in Chicago. And always I was the foreigner." Mijack ground his hands together in the fury and bafflement of a man who could not understand himself even after the most active part of his life had passed. "So I came and built my house, and I told myself that my sons would be Americans, and they would be big enough to see and to live and to do. That's why I've never spoken a word of German to you. That's why I built that wall you make fun of. And that's about all I did, about all I amounted to," he said in self-contempt.

Bart looked up. He had been told more than he had ever suspected to exist in his father. And he felt the vague sadness of knowing that the initial splendid belief and respect could never return, that the deepest call and comparison between them had been made, and he turned his eyes away again with a certain bitterness for what he had made of himself. He had taken himself beyond the point of return. For he felt he too stood alone, facing the same prospect, and only a little better armed than Mijack had been.

"I never told you to believe this or that. I told you to obey. For if I was wrong, then obedience would make you hate wrong. And where I was right, you would balk a little, but come back to it. You're still liable to come back to a couple of things. Yes, I often hoped you'd hate me, because I didn't know what you should believe. What I believe was right for me, but it wasn't right for this land. I can smell that every time I bend down over my fire, every time I heat a piece of steel. And it sure as hell hasn't been right for you.

"One night before you were born, by that window over there, I stood and watched lightning. It used to dig into the mountain more than it does now. My house was built, my wife was beside me, the cellar was full, and I was waiting for a son. But that night, as I watched the lightning, I knew I'd taken the wrong road. I knew it. Don't get me wrong, I'm not defeated, I never felt sorry for myself. But I knew that night I'd taken the wrong road, that I'd bound myself and kept the best of myself from living. God in hell, how it makes a man feel to know he has stuff in him and know he isn't using it! You have to be able to work a piece of steel to see what I mean. You have to be able to breathe fire with your mouth and eyes. You have to be able to lift two stones and decide which is a true cornerstone. Even then you only learn what's here, waiting, waiting for someone to know what to do with it." Mijack shook his head. "That was my problem. I could see, but didn't know what to do. Here was America, all of it, and nothing but blind men and men half-blind, like myself.

"Perhaps it wasn't that night, not the lightning. Perhaps I have thought all this since. I lose track of my thinking. I lose track of where and when I began. I think so slow, my son, so terribly slow. A man shouldn't have to think as slow as I do. It's a punishment. It's worse than that. But no one will ever know how close I came that night to walking out of here and beginning the search again. But no —no, I remembered my age, remembered all the futile years, and told myself it was too late. I told myself I couldn't bear to look on the Mississippi again and not know why I wanted to look at it. I couldn't bear to look again at a straight, tall tree and not know why I liked it better than a man, better than you, my son. And now, now it's too late. Much too late. Not because of my age, my wife, my family. No, even today, if that was all that stopped me, I'd walk off, I'd go in the early morning. The truth is it's too late for me to see. I can't seem to recognize what I see. . . . I only remember. My eyes have seen too much flame in the oven, too much smoke in the sky. My ears carry noise in them. My heart's clogged. That's what's too late.

"It isn't good for a man to wait until my age to begin having such thoughts. I'm sixty-nine.

"I'm a strange man, but you're a stranger son. I've watched you. You're hunting. You're strong. You're intelligent. That's about all I know about you, about my own son. I understand you so little that I have great hope for you." Mijack gave his son a firm look. "Don't misunderstand, I know you'll get whatever you think you want. I know it. I could never approve of the methods you'll use. I knew that the day I found out you were shining shoes in barrooms. I was very disappointed in you that day; I thought you had no pride. I know now you have.

"You'll get what you think you want. But one day, after you have it, or maybe even when it's only at your finger tips, you may find it isn't what you want, and you'll feel, as I did, that it's too late to start again. It is not too late. That's the right time. I ask you to take that on trust." Mijack seemed on the verge of saying something further, and Bart sensed that it had to do with himself, something his father had observed. He knew it from the way the eyes were fixed on him, hunting, measuring. Mijack evidently decided to stand upon what he had said. His face relaxed, as it always did when there was nothing further required of him. "Now," he said, "I've made it clear you have no obligations when you leave this house. I've made it clear I don't want to become one of these old men who keep hearing about and talking about their sons. . . . One last thing. I say it now and I'll never say it again. And you will do me the favor of making no reply. None whatever. I chose the right woman for my wife, but I apologize to you for giving you a poor mother."

27

Gilbert thrust his mouth into a pout and smoke went up at the undersides of the trees. The foliage was so dense that there were only momentary shifting peepholes through which sky could be seen, so dense that, although the leaves were brilliant green, they appeared dark and indistinct. His attention was divided between the clean blue which only a small portion of sky, framed and shuttered by trees, can continue to have for examining eyes and the smoke which his mouth was sending experimentally forth in various gusts and quantities. Yet, despite all the shadow overhead, the smoke as it began to rise high overhead at its own lazy pace, having lost the momentum his mouth had given it, had a faintly green cast.

Rose was sitting close to him. She watched his mouth send smoke out. She did not watch what the smoke did afterward.

Naomi was dividing her attention between a mud spot on her dress and a stone which she was trying to break with her hands; it was not a very determined effort, but the stone was filled with air bubbles and grain weaknesses, so that anyone might have supposed it would break easily.

"What's it like to smoke?" she asked. "What does it do for you? Anything much?"

Rose put her fingers on his wrist and then made them run along his arm and burrow beneath his sleeve, striving toward his armpit; Gilbert shook his head, frowning, and his eyes were a little worried.

"Oh, it's . . . It's good," he said. "I mean the smoke goes down and crawls around—makes my chest feel big," he said, taking a deep breath.

He had been smoking in a personal, comfortable manner, but now that attention was called to the cigarette, he assumed the air of an inveterate smoker, and therefore looked a bit awkward.

Rose was able to catch a little of the next plume of smoke with her own mouth. Gilbert gave her a rather stern look. Though he really did enjoy being here. He was having the finest time of his life. Rose made a face, and he assumed a pose of the utmost nonchalance and unconcern, of calm superiority to everything around him.

"Heck, you never explain nothing," said Naomi.

"That's because," said Gilbert, leaning backward against the tree and drawing his knees up, as if planning to take a nap, "you ask hard questions."

"What I meant was," said Naomi, then, "uuh!" as her hands made a last effort to break the stone, then dropped it between her legs where her dress caught it in net fashion, "I want to try."

Gilbert studied the trees overhead, attracted by the idea, musing over it. "No you don't," he said. "It's all right for me, my lungs are already brown with nicotine, so I got nothing to lose."

Rose caught hold of his arm and pulled until her mouth was almost able to get to the cigarette. There was more chance of Naomi hearing them struggle than of looking on her own; she was studying something in her lap. He let his arm relax and be guided, while he kept looking straight ahead, thereby satisfying his conscience.

"Besides," he said, "smoking isn't as hard on a man as on a girl."

Rose blew the smoke to a place where it would appear he had been responsible for it. But not until after he had kept her from blowing it inside his shirt by laying his hand flat and vertical on his chest.

"How come?" Naomi looked up. She was interested in knowing why men could do things she couldn't.

Gilbert was not sure. He offered a couple of vague reasons. He said men were stronger, so they had stronger lungs made of harder skin.

Naomi scoffed. She wet her finger and rubbed at the mud spot and made it both larger and cleaner.

Gilbert offered another reason. Men, he said, live harder. It was one of the most profound offerings he had made, and he felt smugly safe, leaning his weight against the tree. He made his mouth do nonchalant curls to the smoke.

Naomi scoffed. She remembered how he had told her salamanders turn into fish.

It seemed to Gilbert his sister ought to take his word. She ought to know better than to want all her questions answered. He was rather amused.

"I only heard it," he admitted, "but it was a doctor said so, and a doctor ought to know. Doctors study all about smoking."

Rose had pulled his laces. He was holding his foot stiff to keep her from pulling off his shoe.

"They don't know everything," said Naomi, making another effort to break the stone now that her arms were rested. She had to throw it away. She couldn't just keep trying to break one stone all her life. As the stone sailed through the air she wished she had aimed it at something instead of just giving it a fling. "Besides, I just want to try one of the darn things. I ain't going to turn into no fiend or nothing."

"Some other time."

That seemed beautiful to Gilbert, pleasant and sociable; even the words themselves breathed separately and softly, "Some—other—time," seemed to carry with them a vague promise.

"Aw nuts, you wanna be begged, that's all. I ain't gonna beg."

Rose had gotten his shoe off, and was after his stocking. Gilbert simply leaned against the tree and closed his eyes and made his legs comfortable. Yet his poise as a cool young man and inveterate smoker was disturbed by a faint worry of the possibility that his foot was dirty. He never worried about that sort of thing when he and Rose were alone.

"You're some brother!" said Naomi.

Gilbert heard the emotional tone in his sister's voice, the same tone which had always been a command to him. He felt suddenly that he had always been much too lenient with her, giving her her own way in everything.

"Look, I'll tell you what," said Naomi, "you hold it and I'll smoke it. How's that?"

Naomi knew there was no sense in what she said, but it was the sort of thing which would appeal to her brother. He was never logical about anything. He would probably do it just to be able to hold the cigarette and tell her what to do and all that nonsense. She was pretty sure he would.

Gilbert looked around him. There was no purpose in this except to delay answering. He looked at his sister rather kindly, knowing he was being too superior about this matter, and yet he could not prevent himself from being pleased. He felt in such an expansive mood that it seemed he would never again deal with anything seriously, he would only let things come to him, let them happen.

Rose had succeeded in getting his stocking off. His foot was thrust hard against the ground to prevent her fingers from touching the bottom of it. There was in him such a strange mixture of pleasure and annoyance.

"No," he said. "No smoking for you. I won't allow it."

Naomi looked at him in surprise. "Okay," she said, shrugging.

Gilbert felt he had done something good.

The earth was clean in the way of late spring, when there was neither mud nor dust and everything looked as if bright polish had been used on it. They were willing to sit anywhere in their best clothes, with perhaps unwarranted confidence.

Gilbert realized he had not always been teaching his sister the best of habits. He had been careless in what he allowed Naomi to do. Now he felt a more direct responsibility, one which called for a more mature role on his part, more authoritative. He wanted his sister to be more ladylike, better mannered, more particular in her dress and in her activities.

Rose had captured his foot and was holding it in her lap.

"Keetchy-keetchy-keetchy-coo."

"Heck," said Naomi, "aren't we going to do anything?"

"Sure," said Gilbert.

He had just grabbed Rose by the ankle and begun to retaliate. He had just accepted the fact that it did not matter that his sister was present.

Rocks were distinct from the soil in which they were embedded. Shrubs were gorged with brilliant leaves and a thousand spindly winter twigs had puffed with green glory, speaking of the hidden fertility of the barren-seeming soil. It was shade from the trees overhead which kept the brush down enough to give the atmosphere of a slightly crowded but not impassable garden.

"I'm going home," said Naomi. "I got work to do."

"Don't go," said Gilbert, without conviction.

Rose was slapping at his hand with her sandal. He caught hold of her hair and pulled. She dropped the sandal and leaned against him, cuddling close, opening a button on his shirt and making him feel the breath from her mouth, though it was really her nose she was rubbing against him.

"Heck," said Naomi. "I ain't gonna be no chaperone."

She gave her brother a quick, angry glance. She stood up and brushed her dress.

"Wait, we'll be going in a minute," said Gilbert. "Honest."

She gave no indication of being willing to wait.

"Listen, if you really want to try smoking," he said, "why, I'll let you."

"Heck on it," she said.

Rose was nuzzling at his chest. He felt it as a disturbance as he tried to turn to see his sister walking down the path away from them. The bushes hid her almost at once. Rose opened another button and rubbed her whole face against him.

"Let her go," he said, waving his hand summarily.

Footsteps cannot be heard for much distance in springtime. They are too soft and there are too many sounds like them. Gilbert took a pebble and threw it high among the trees in the direction in which his sister had gone, and then he listened.

New mosses were forming about the roots of the trees, with the slime of birth still marking them. Little breezes seemed to creep out of the ground and the small things of nature made way for what must move, bending gracefully. But the tall trees were silent and the distance was silence. One such breeze brought a scent from violets that perhaps no one had ever seen or ever would see, and this was hurried off by a rush of soft wind that had more force but had not found much scent. It coiled in Gilbert's nostrils and gave him his own smell, his own flesh's odor, which had been lost for hours. It made him feel uncomfortable to have Rose's face against him.

Behind the wind, in the hollow the wind had made, came an unintentional bit of gaiety that the creek above them had found against some rock. If the creek had not been so near it could well have been the laughter of a girl who had run far off to be alone, with one hand suppressing a mouth that was twitching with laughter already in her throat and around her teeth. It would have had to have been the laughter of a girl who had just seen something funny and very ridiculous.

"Keetchy-keetchy-keetchy-coo," said Rose.

PART FOUR: 1922 - 1928

28

IN THE JUNIOR-MISS DEPARTMENT of a Harrisburg store there was a bright green dress. It was the gayest and prettiest dress that had ever touched the hands of a Mijack. Gilbert spent an hour walking around the store and four minutes purchasing it. The skirt had the sole fault of a pleat trick which made it appear more ample and blowsy than it was. But to a boy's eyes—perfect. It cost nine dollars. That made it perfect.

Gilbert intended to give it on her birthday, but could not wait.

Never having seen Naomi cry, Gilbert was frantic. But he teased her until she was laughing at herself, and then insisted that she go upstairs and put it on.

He tried to prepare what he would say; maybe whistle and make a big fuss. The important thing was to make her satisfied. He was worried that the dress would not fit or that she would not like it once she had it on. He wished now he had waited until he had enough money to buy a little silk purse to match.

Naomi came downstairs, and he forgot the things he planned to say. The only thing he had sense enough to do was turn on the ceiling light. Naomi smiled at him and did a pirouette so quickly that the skirt had to unwind.

"I'm so proud of you," said Gilbert. "I feel so happy to have a beautiful sister."

Naomi curtsied. It was not her usual imitation of a proper young lady, but authentic, with a charm of its own. It had the grace of happiness and love. The only thing that prevented her gesture from being remarkably accomplished was that her shoes squeaked.

"You're so different, so much taller and all."

The stone walls, heavy and ponderous, which had for so many years made the simple furniture and the family seem hardened and drab, now emphasized the fragility of the silk and the dawning of adolescence in Naomi. The dress brought out the new delicacy at the base of her throat and the slope of her shoulders.

"Sure," said Naomi, "I just looked in the mirror every night and said, 'Grow, you.' And then I slept on the floor. I ate a lot. I waited three years. And I grew. It's easy." There was bitterness in her voice, and their eyes met in that confusion of young people who have allowed themselves to pass too far into the future.

"I shall be pretty when I'm grown, shan't I?" said Naomi. "I thought that just a bit ago when I was looking in the mirror."

"Shall be? You are!" said Gilbert. "It's the truth. I scarcely recognize you."

"I wonder if I shall like it to be pretty?" said Naomi. "I never thought about it before . . . Oh nuts, I *know* I'll like it." Yet she sighed with the weight of things unknown and undiscovered, as if sensing the pressures and the demands involved.

"If you don't I will," said Gilbert, breaking the slight uneasiness by reasserting himself. "I shall say, 'There goes my sister. My beautiful sister.' And I'll follow you everywhere and see to it you have fun, movies, dances and parties, and we'll buy an automobile and—say, you've got to promise me right now, promise Sunday you'll wear this dress and go walking with me. We'll walk all over town—and then we'll go to Harrisburg, to Harrisburg on the streetcar, and walk all over everywhere, around the capitol where the pigeons are, everywhere. We'll go to the museum. We'll go through the park where everybody sits, and along the river where the statues are. We'll have hot dogs and sodas and—and just everything."

"It's a deal," said Naomi, laughing. "Gee, I didn't know a dress could do this. I never knew I wanted one so bad."

"Don't I know!" said Gilbert. "Didn't I want long pants! Say, you look better every minute. I mean it."

Naomi smoothed her hands over the skirt and moved about to get a better look at herself. Her eyes were bright, her face flushed. "When I grow up," she said, "I shall have everything beautiful. I shall have beautiful, beautiful things." Her face became determined. "I will! And I'll do as I damn please."

"Yes, yes, and so will I," said Gilbert.

"It isn't so far off until I'm grown, is it?" Naomi said, wistfully. "It can't be." She looked around the room, at the familiar furniture, and seemed to lose part of her joy. "I can wait, no matter how darn long. And when it comes, boy, look out, I'm going to have fun."

"Listen," said Gilbert. "I bought this for your birthday. But I'll get you another, somehow. A still better one."

"No," said Naomi. "Nuts on that. This one's plenty. It's a little too much. I don't want beautiful things now. Later on, when I'm older, then I'll want 'em. You bet I will."

Gilbert averted his eyes; again the future, this time as a threat; and now a little fear of what the dress had created, someone he still need not protect himself against, but nearing the age when she would be more difficult to understand. "But keep this one," he said. "I don't mean just now. I mean when you have beautiful dresses. Huh?"

"It'll be too little then," said Naomi, "because I'm going to grow tall. But I'll keep it anyhow."

"And say," said Gilbert, "don't let me catch you switching around. You don't need to do that to look pretty. No, I'm serious now, I don't want you . . ."

Naomi pursed her mouth, fluttered her eyelashes, and did an exaggerated flounce with her hips. "Glide but don't slide, hip but don't rip, shake it but don't break it," she said, and they both laughed. It was the popular Nesquehon High saying. It was Naomi who ceased laughing and became serious.

"I like you very much," she said. "Forgive me for—you know, for being such a stinker."

She held out her hands. It was hard for her to do it. Life, day by day, was putting barriers between them, making them more sensitive, more emotional and a bit less trusting.

Gilbert cradled his sister in his arms, a little shy himself, more of the dress than of her, holding in a soft, gentle and awkward manner, losing part of what always filled him with warmth. Yet the important feeling that she was clean and fresh and in need of his protection returned stronger than ever. He was aware of her flesh, visually, its odor, its feeling against him, and he knew it was one of the happiest moments in his life. He adored his sister.

The door was shut. Gilbert shoved until he was convinced it was not merely stuck. He called out. After having shouted and shaken the knob numerous times, he paused and put his head against the door. "Ooo-hoo," he said softly, because he was listening. The silence of the wood panel was something that stretched and pulled. Then he shouted and pounded on the door and the wall beside the door, until he heard, from what seemed far off, his mother.

"Naomi must be sick, Mother," he said. "I can't get her to answer."

Again he heard his mother, enough to realize that she must not have heard what he said, and so he began to hit the door again, trying not merely to beat hard but locate a place on the door that would make more noise. He put his mouth near the keyhole and yelled.

"All right, I'm awake. All right!"

Her voice did not sound sleepy.

"What's the matter?" said Gilbert. "Are you sick? Are you all right?"

"Yes . . . Yes . . . Yes . . ."

"Well what's—what's wrong then?" He rattled the knob to show what he meant. "Didn't you hear me calling? I must have called fifty times."

"Yes, I heard you. Who could help but hear you?"

"Oh-h," said Gilbert, and studied over that a little. "But then," he said, "why didn't you answer?"

"Because I didn't feel like it."

"Well, is there anything I can do? Want me to make breakfast? Want me to bring it up to you? Listen, if you want to sleep more, you've still an hour. . . . I'm sorry I woke you if you don't feel good. . . . But whatcha got the door locked for, anyhow?" There was silence. "Hey, I've got something to show you. It's something you'll like." Still silence. "But don't you want breakfast? Don't you want anything to eat?"

"Oh, go 'way and let me alone," said Naomi.

Gilbert knew that tone of voice. There seemed nothing to do. He went downstairs and tended the fire. There was rain falling, he watched through the narrow window, which always made drops look big and heavier. It was cold for May, the house drawn with gray light that had to spread itself thin across the whole room, finding no reflection on the stone walls, nor on furniture stained grainless and polish dulled to a stickiness.

Naomi came down. He tried to speak to her as he ordinarily would. Talk, which was all that could be risked with her in this mood, was painful, and silence worse. He could not endure to be around someone who would not talk.

Mrs. Mijack made breakfast. The effects of her exertion were heard over the table all during breakfast; she had a rasped breathing which made them all look at her from time to time. Even Bart. It made eating a kind of painful responsibility. Helping her into the stairway, following her with his hands prepared in case she should tire, watching her pull herself along the banister, Gilbert was scared. He was so accustomed to her health and irritableness, and now there was something wrong with her that confined her to her bedroom. Bart had risen and taken the chair out of her way. She had not spoken except once: "It tasted good, I just wasn't hungry." Gilbert felt everything was going to pieces all at once.

He helped with the dishes, but when he threatened his sister with wet soapy hands, there was no response. He kissed her, but it was not spontaneous; instead he had been almost sullen, and when he kissed was quite nervous about it. Her lips were so placid that he drew back. His eyes tried to search hers. But he said nothing and took his place along the sink and made pretense of drying the bowls. It was raining hard, thumping, and there were long, clinging sounds of drippage.

It was so unlike her. That was what he could not get over.

"You're mean," he said.

"Sure, I'm mean," said Naomi. "You don't know how mean I can get."

But she let him carry her books. The rain made them hurry and they concentrated on such things as jumping over puddles and using the doubtful protection of trees. Nothing happened, nothing that he could put his finger on, and yet it was not right. It was as if their former happiness was a dream which had been carefully walled off from them, as if their lives had fallen inexplicably apart, as if she had become without warning tough and hard. It was not a thing of the moment. They were old enough so that quarrels had seriousness and permanent effects. It was a fragile atmosphere in which everything had to be handled like bits of glass, in which the least expressiveness of feature and posture was significant. Naomi was walking along with a mincing stride, with a shy pride that made her carry her shoulders and head differently, and with a movement that made her seem constantly annoyed with her hair. While he, head leaned forward as if walking into a stiff wind, hands deep in the pockets of his trousers, hulked along beside her, bumping trees and walls with his shoulder. They were both too young for a situation which was not a simple quarrel, too young to carry the light touch that was needed, and this made them feel more bitter toward each other. They were both accustomed to dramatic arguments such as their father, mother and Bart got involved in, accustomed to bitterness and punishment and outspokenness at any price. This was something new and something not very nice.

309

"Now what?" said Gilbert, as she reached for her books before they were at the usual place of parting. "What have I done this time? What can I possibly have done wrong?"

"Now what what?" said Naomi. "I just want my books, that's all."

After that they were both afraid to speak. Reaching school, they seemed glad to part. All through the day Gilbert blundered and stumbled, made frantic by the atmosphere of restlessness which rain brought into the classroom. His mind was caught in a confusion of impulses, many without any apparent meaning. It made him uneasy to be confined beneath and behind, his knees forced into the limitations of the desk that caged them. He was unable to hear well, unable to forget that his flesh was against wood, flattened on it. His clothes at the points of contact were moist enough to make a fusion, so that when he found an excuse to stand up, to move about, his trousers stuck to the seat and came free with a tearing sound. He stuck his finger to the second joint in the inkwell and spent the better part of an hour cleaning it with tablet paper. He never did get the rim of blue out from under his fingernail.

He was afraid she would go home without him. He was afraid he would go home without her . . .

Gilbert met his sister after school and asked her to walk with him through the fields above their house. He said quite frankly that there was something he must ask her.

Naomi did not want to go. She had to get supper started. There was ironing to do. There were a million things to do. Gilbert hung his head and followed. Suddenly Naomi turned and her eyes were peering straight into his. "All right," she said.

The earth and the air were warm from several hours of sustained, cloudless shine. The sun had appeared before the rain had ceased, so that puddles sinking into the ground had carried the warmth deep. There was the quick thirst of May that made the earth resilient to walk on and the bushes and weeds stand straight. Crickets, very black, showing off their complex mechanism of threaded and oddly bowed legs, were hopping about to find out what had been done to their surroundings. A hawk that must have flapped its wings sometime in the past sailed over them, a shadow to make them look up; its head was craned forward as it continued its endless search for mice. There was no way for Gilbert and Naomi to know that even as they became more sensitive and complex they were shutting out the natural interest of their eyes by binding sight to their own needs.

Nothing was spoken between them until they had walked a long distance into the mountain. Gilbert's strides grew large; he became more erect. His nostrils opened to the air, pinching it. There was the medicinal smell of warm, wet grass. He kept moving further and further into isolation, leaving the main paths. The farther away from town they walked, the better he felt. He tore loose some wild grass and made his hands sticky with it. His clothing, particularly his shirt, felt lighter and more carefree.

"Let's run away from home," he said. "Just you and me."

"You're nuts."

"No, I mean it. I can get a job. I can take care of you."

Naomi did not bother to reply.

"I could get a newspaper route somewhere, and you could go to school, and even help me pass papers, or do anything you wanted to." He frowned. "I don't want to go back home. Do you?"

"Sure, I have to get supper."

"No, I'm serious. I mean *never*."

Gilbert looked at his sister. He was realizing how intensely personal his relations with her were. He thought how he would like to devote himself to her forever. He thought how fine would be the responsibility of seeing that she got food, clothing, movies and all that she should have.

"I don't want to go home," he said. "It's bad there. They try to make you hate me."

Naomi was picking burrs from her black cotton stockings.

"They do try to make you hate me. You know it's true."

"I still have to get supper," said Naomi.

"But why can't we go off? I know we'd be happier. What's to stop us? I mean, it's not as if we were little and couldn't take care of ourselves. Oh, I know I couldn't get a good job, and I know it would be hard, but I want it. Don't you? Aren't you just sick and fed up with everything down there?" he said, waving toward where he supposed the town was. "I could do things, a lot more than you'd believe, if I wanted to. It's just I don't want to do anything, I mean I'm so disgusted."

It was he who lead the way, walking so rapidly that he had to pause. Naomi seemed in no hurry. The grass was sparser and had a color formed by slanting shadows. But the sunlight would remain on this side of the mountain much longer than in the valley or the town below. Rocks high on the mountain were beginning to have points of glow and a dark purple sheen.

Gilbert's shoes were too old to encourage him to take difficult

paths or test the strength and hardness of things. He was too preoccupied, anyway. He had formed the first clear idea of what he did
want, the first positive solution to his unhappiness. He did not see it
as running away, but as something clean and fine and courageous. As
his spirits improved he became impatient with his sister. He became
more forceful, pounding his hand into his fist as he tried to persuade
her. "But what are you afraid of?" he said. "You aren't scared of going? Hell, what's there to be scared of?"

Once he turned to see Naomi standing at the edge of a wooded
area into which he had already entered; she did not move and seemed
on the point of turning back. In that instant his happiness vanished.
He was suddenly angry. He felt only a little better when he saw her
begin to walk toward him.

She came to where he stood, and said, scornfully, "Do we have to
go further?"

"What's wrong?" he said. "Don't you even like to go walking any
more?"

"Not much."

"What's wrong?" he said, stamping.

"Oh, all you do is talk. I have supper to get. Can't you understand?"

"Jesus Christ!" he said. "What'd you come for, then? All right,
sure, sure, we'll be home in time," he said, calming. "You tired? Want
to rest? Want to go back? We'll go back if you want to. It don't matter what *I* want to do."

"Oh, go on, go on," Naomi said impatiently.

Gilbert walked even faster than he had before. Naomi started to
follow. "Wait up," she said. "Hey, listen—do I look different to you?"
She caught him by the sleeve and turned him toward her. There was
a serious, almost unhappy expression on her face. There was nothing
immature in her at this moment. Only the long black stockings, the
shapeless cotton dress, and the age and tallness of trees near them kept
her small. "Do I? Do I look as if I'm bad? Really *bad*?"

"Then do me a favor," she said. "Don't talk to Mother. No matter
what she says, don't talk to her."

"But why?" said Gilbert.

"Just do it," said Naomi. "Do it." A bit later she said, "No don't.
It doesn't make a damn, anyhow." She looked at her brother, measur-
ing him. "You couldn't do it. You couldn't even run away from home.
And that's easy. It's so easy it's silly." She began to try to break pieces

of bark from a tree. "Have you ever wanted to hurt anyone? I mean really *hurt*?"

Gilbert frowned. "No," he said.

"I don't believe you. Yes, I do. All you ever want to do is forgive. Or run away. Or kiss. Or carry my books." She tossed her head and stuck her chest forward, forcing the dress to show the beginnings of the physical changes she was undergoing. "I don't forgive and I'm not going to run away. I don't forgive even you. I wish I could hate you. You're nothing but trouble—you keep away from me when we're in the house."

"But Naomi, what . . . ?"

"Never mind what. From now on I take care of myself."

"But what're you mad at me about? What the heck have I done?"

"Ask Mother."

"Heck with her. I don't pay any attention to her."

"You don't have to," said Naomi, "but I do."

Gilbert turned and walked on. It was the only thing he knew to do. The vehemence with which she had spoken had somehow loosened the asmosphere. But he did not like the way her eyes had searched his. At last a place was reached where he felt more at peace, with no desire to surge onward. He waited for his sister to sit so that he could choose a place. He did not wish to face her directly, and was not sure he wished to be too near her.

"I'll catch it for not having supper on time," said Naomi, who, knowing it was already late, no longer really cared. They had walked a long distance from the town.

"Did you mean what you said? Did you really mean it, that you don't want me around?"

"Yes."

His mouth made an odd, nervous motion, as if he were testing the jaw before trusting it with speech.

"But why?" he said. "What's wrong? I want you to like me. You must like me. You just have to." He was looking straight at her. "You're not being fair, you know you're not. What'm I going to do?" he said passionately. "Sometimes I think nobody likes me. Not really. Not Father or Mother or the kids at school—and I don't care. Not any more. But you, I never done anything to you, never, and I'd do anything for you, *anything*, and you know I would."

"You talk too much," said Naomi.

"Well, what'm I going to do? Look at it my way. . . . And why don't you like me, anyhow? You still haven't told me why. You don't even give me a chance."

"Oh I like you, then!" said Naomi. "Does that make you feel better?"

"Give me your hand. Give it!" Gilbert said.

"Oh nuts," she said, pulling free, "wadda I want with your old hand? I don't like you any more, and I don't want to, so there! Be mad about it. I gave you your chance, I told you that if you want to do something for me . . ."

"Oh, I hate you," said Gilbert. "I hate everybody."

It was dark when they reached home. Nothing had been settled. Mijack was waiting for his supper. He had been out looking for them. Mrs. Mijack was worse. Naomi fried the potatoes hard as little rocks. Bart jumped on Gilbert for not having delivered his paper route. Gilbert shouted back, "Go get somebody else for your goddamn papers, if you don't like the way I do it."

"Maybe I will," Bart replied.

"It was my fault she was late," Gilbert told his father.

"Oh, but I'm old enough to know better," said Naomi.

Mrs. Mijack:

How was school going? Did he like delivering papers? Sit near her. On the edge of the bed. It wouldn't bother her. Did it take too much time from his studies? He must bear in mind, they were far more important.

What did he do with the money he earned?

. . . . spent it.

It must seem like a great deal of money.

. . . . not so much, Bart made ten times as much.

What did he spend his money on?

. . . . things, lots of things.

Of course, of course, but was he saving too?

. . . . no, not very much

How much? Exactly?

. . . . nothing.

Ahh? Why didn't he?

. . . . he intended to, in the future, honest!

Did he spend on candy?

. . . . yes, a lot on candy.

It was bad for his teeth.

314

. . . . yes.

Did he spend on his sister?

. . . . some, a little.

Only a little?

. . . . only a little, he said a little, didn't he?

Why? *Why* did he spend on Naomi?

Because he wanted to, that's why, it was his money, he could do what he pleased with it.

Mrs. Mijack seemed to take little interest in his replies; she kept smoothing the bedspread with a flat ironing movement of her hand, and looking, not through the window, but at the electric light splayed on the glass. Now that the strong bone features and the thick muscular frame was sheeted with a looser and more gelatinous flesh it was apparent how nervous and high-strung a woman she was.

And didn't he want to go to college? And be a Lutheran minister? And didn't he know that would take money?

And didn't he want a topcoat? Hadn't he said so last week?

And did he think that Naomi wasn't being fed and clothed properly that he took it upon himself to—to buy things for her?

He hadn't said anything of the sort.

No. But did he really think he ought to? Did he think Naomi appreciated it? Did he think his father would appreciate it if he knew about it?

"What are you after? What are you picking at me for?" cried Gilbert. "Everybody's picking at me!"

"What'm I after?" said Mrs. Mijack. "I want to know what you spent on this," she said, pulling from under her pillow a clump of shining green cloth. "I want to know who put it into your head to buy such a thing as this." She thrust it into his hands. "I want to hear how you explain that."

Gilbert stared at it a moment, then began to unfold it.

"But this is her dress," he said. "And it's torn."

"And so it should be. It should be burned!"

"But who . . . ? Did you . . . ?" And the question did not need to be completed, for he saw his mother's face. "But you had no right to. It was mine. I bought it for her." He hugged the material against him, as if to keep her from regaining it. "You had no right!"

"It's devil's cloth," said Mrs. Mijack. "Devil's cloth."

Gilbert stood up and held the dress at arm's length from himself at about his sister's height. He tried to hold it as if it were being worn.

315

"Oh, Mother," he said. He was trembling a little. "Did you see her in it?" he said, in a strangely quiet voice. "She was so pretty in it. You'd be proud of her."

He was still looking at the dress, as if trying to see if it could be worn.

Mrs. Mijack gave her son a terrible look.

"From this moment," said Mrs. Mijack, "you are forbidden to deliver papers, and you are forbidden to have any money, until I give you permission. Until you learn how to use money. Do you hear me?"

Gilbert looked at her.

"Do you hear me! And you will let your sister alone, you will not talk to her unless I'm present."

She saw the strange look on her son's face. It led her beyond what she had intended to say, out of a kind of desperation, out of a last attempt to make the misery of her life and the misery of being sick have some meaning and purpose.

"Answer me. Or shall I call your father? Then we'll see if I've been talking for nothing. We'll see if I'm to be treated so in my own house."

"Call him!" said Gilbert. "I'll call him myself."

He started to leave the room, then halted.

"I'll be glad to call him. And I'll tell him what I think of you."

"Oh but you're ungrateful," said Mrs. Mijack, with real feeling.

"Me? Ungrateful? I sure am!" he said, and there was a bitterness which surpassed anything which his brother had ever felt toward her. "No, I'm not going to tell him," he said, coming back to the bed. "I want nine dollars from you."

He put out his hand. "I want it now. Give me it." He put his hand right against her face. "You owe me it, goddamn you."

"Samuel!" Mrs. Mijack cried out. "Samuel, come upstairs."

She had a slight heart attack that night. The doctor had to be called in twice. But she made no mention to her husband, except to say that she thought she had felt it coming on earlier in the day. And to give a sign of the indestructible hope and spirit and will to live, which suffering and disappointment only seemed to make more vital to her, "Oh, Samuel, I saw colors, and I saw an angel singing, and I was so terribly afraid I was going to die."

Gilbert apologized to his sister, and promised never to buy anything without her consent. He swore too not to trouble her so much

316

and not to get her into trouble. She could count on him to do whatever she thought was best. It was different the way he made this vow, not rashly enthusiastic, but with a solemn, determined air. "I'll never forgive her, never," he said, pronouncing each word carefully and separately, in the most deliberate, calm, unemotional voice. He seemed to have saddened, seemed to have taken a long stride toward maturity.

Naomi was reconciled with him only in part. She told him frankly that she loved him as much as ever, that she thought him the best and kindest person in the world, but that it simply would not do for her to depend upon him and to let him make her life difficult when it could be avoided. She pitied him without being sorry that he was more hurt than herself. And she could not really believe that he would keep any promise.

They never kissed after that. On formal occasions such as birthdays, they relied on pulling ears the necessary number of times—with one for good measure. They never walked with their hands squeezed tight together, or entered each other's bedrooms, or fussed over who was to have the first kettle of hot water or who spent too long in the bathroom.

Yet they remained loyal at heart. And in the early morning—when their fresh youth had not yet had an opportunity to harden into the posed attitudes and nervous worries of the previous day, when entering the world partly new again, when entering the partly new world of skies high and wide and magnificent, streets where the melting tar sticking to shoes would make boys and girls part company or begin the puzzling advance toward love and desire, where girls would no longer climb trees for one reason and boys for another, when night would become a time of restlessness—in those early hours they would remain affectionate toward each other. But it was always Naomi who brought this to an end; she who spoke sharply or criticized. It was she who grew older, while he retained his innocence; more and more he had to follow her around to be near her. She was slipping away from him.

Gilbert began to spend more time with boys.

He acted wild. There was nothing he would not do to win admiration.

Halloween he upset a bird bath and rolled ash cans down the street.

He let the air out of all four tires on Mr. Pierce's new car.

The gang knew Mrs. Wagenbacher lived alone. He climbed the roof and beat on the tin with a club.

317

He walked into a movie, walking backwards, as the nine o'clock show was leaving out.

He put a firecracker in his mouth and lit it.

He and four other boys tried to roll the cannon away from the municipal building. When two policemen came out, he ran straight at them and then swerved and jumped the fifteen-foot wall. One of the policemen chased him, and he ran toward the mountain. The thrill of being chased was so exciting that he ran much further than was necessary, then hooted at the top of his voice. His left knee hurt for almost two weeks. At school he bragged he had been shot at.

For a dime he ate a sandwich of poison ivy, thick as with lettuce. This was especially daring because all the boys knew it was a fact that eating poison ivy could make a person go blind.

He picked a spider from a tree and held it captive in the palm of his hand. His hand was bitten in three places before he finally crushed the spider between his fingers. His hand puffed and got sore, but he was never very concerned about it. Naomi really gave him hell when she heard about it. "Mind your own business," he said.

29

Early in the morning Gilbert went into the fields and woodlands and picked every flower he saw, without regard for size, color, odor, or condition. Wild daisies, purple clover, gentians and buttercups, also a few sprigs of fern, one big wild sunflower and even some red berries. His intention was to gather a great armload, and he was impatient, storming through areas where there were few or none, pulling green stems loose with jerks, root and all if the stems acted like wire.

Though he had roamed these hills for many purposes, it was difficult to remember where he had seen flowers, and he wandered about, scanning the earth. The soil was fertile, there had been fine spring rains, and yet there was not a wealth of flowers. Even violets, which were plentiful, seemed to hide and turn their blue beneath the protection of the grass. Gilbert in his haste passed many singles and many little colonies of color, indeed, even stepping on them.

The sun rose and made bare spots in the trees and gave the fields their customary early summer green. The world was already a little faded with heat and the bleaching tendencies of sunlight. Sometimes Gilbert looked far into the distance, ridiculously far, seeking flowers at a distance where trees were no taller than fingers. He sought whole kingdoms of flowers! It was getting late . . . He started to run at a speed that ignored briers and the binding of grass, ignored curbs and differences of pavement and the slippery polish the soles of his shoes had gathered in the fields. He ran very close to the hedge in front of Mr. Pierce's house and tore loose three or four of the professional-looking early roses and then, sucking his fingers, went on, the town filled with that silence which occurred when school had rung its final summons.

Arriving late in the building made the interior seem darker and enlarged. He ran tiptoe through corridors as if he were a stranger come to peep into doorways, as if he were about to witness faces and events never seen before. He felt surrounded by administration and discipline, as if the very walls and floors along which he was hurrying were part of that influence. Even the bell ringing in the hallway to signal change of classes or fire drill had a new tone.

He rushed into the classroom, past the teacher, to his desk and sat down. He was sitting there listening to and trying to quiet his breathing, when he realized his arms were full of flowers. Or rather realized it was not correct to be sitting there with them. He jumped up, looked about wildly, started toward the cloakroom, sat down again, and began to stuff flowers into his desk. He had to pile some of his books on the floor to manage this. He seemed to think he would find space for the books afterward.

This state of preoccupation, of being semi-aware of his surroundings, continued until the bell rang for recess. Children hurried to the playground.

Gilbert remained seated until the room was empty. It was the same room in which he had had the same subjects and teacher last year. He opened his desk and began to take out flowers in small bunches, handling them with care, trying to impose order and color scheme upon them. This attempt he soon abandoned, and, gathering them in his arms, holding them extra tight after several had fallen on the floor, he walked into the hall.

On the playground he was given a fair share of curious glances. Many of the children thought he was obeying the instructions of Mrs. Garterland and were wondering how they themselves would be affected and what they were going to have to do.

He was beginning to realize the magnitude of what he was going to undertake. In the early morning he had thought of it as a fine gesture, one that would release him from the tangled position into which he had gotten himself. Now he felt he had to go through with it. He saw that he was facing the possibility of separating himself from his friends and from everything which he had been part of. He had the hint of entering another life, darker, more lonely, one which was in part discredited in his own mind, and yet this made his mouth set firmly and his eyes look straight ahead.

He passed his own group and went to where smaller children were playing tag of a sort which allowed the confusion of two or three being "it" at the same time. They were children from the basement of the school. They were children whose eyes dulled and whose faces went into a kind of expressionless comfort as soon as the ball rolled beyond them, children who counted red pegs and green pegs and yellow pegs, who had been in drawing class four and five years and were still delighted to see that blue put onto red made a violet color.

Even as he walked toward them his dream of what they were like began to break, leaving him with the knowledge that they were not the wonderful world of joy and happiness which he had imagined. He had mistaken the games for the children, the toys for the hands which guided them. His sin seemed more terrible now. He had the horrid feeling that he was walking away from all he really wanted and was going toward something which he would never be able to endure. All that he had to keep him walking was a slender idea of remorse and an odd sort of pride which made him confess to himself that he had been very bad and cruel to the girl.

Some of the retarded children had stopped their play. Some went toward Gilbert, some withdrew, and others stood, arms hanging at their sides. It was unusual for them to encounter anyone from eighth grade, and they had the same courtesy and reluctance as before all adults. Rose Lee was in the center of all this, her face flushed, her eyes bright. She was out of breath.

Gilbert walked straight to her, indeed, almost against her, and forced the flowers into her arms.

"These are for my girl," he said in a determined voice.

He glared at every pair of eyes he could see, with quick, birdlike twistings of his head.

He stooped to pick up several flowers that had fallen and were still falling because Rose was not able to get a firm hold on them. He simply piled these on top of the others, with no regard for appearance.

It was evident he was feeling the same sensation of relief as a man who has carried something heavy and has finally been permitted to put it down.

Rose smiled. Her eyes had instantly fixed on his, but now they looked down across the heads of too many flowers to gain appreciation from their individual features, too many even to have the pleasure of recognition and identification. Instead she put her face into their midst and so became conscious of them all, rubbing her face on them in a way that was a tenderness to her and almost a brutality to the flowers.

Looking up, she saw Gilbert was embarrassed. For a moment she looked at him with a faint trace of sadness, the sadness of someone who had never had enough encounter with other humans to bring herself to express her feelings or understand the feelings of others, but this was immediately replaced by a wonderful childish smile. She jiggled the flowers a little in her arms and smelled them, and then, raising on her feet so that she was identically his height, gave him a look of unmistakable adoration.

"Oh I knew you liked me," she said earnestly. "I *knew*."

"Wait!" said Gilbert, perceptibly drawing away. "Wait now! You understand what this means? You understand this makes you my girl?" Her look seemed to have alarmed him. "You must realize this is very serious. You must realize that—that you're mine, mine, and that we're going to tell everybody, and from now on we have to go everywhere together, and we mustn't pay attention to what anybody says." His eyes fixed on her intently. "You have to be mine now." His eyes hunted her face to see if he had made his meaning clear. "We have no choice, understand?"

Rose nodded. Her eyes were bright.

"You mustn't fail me," he said. "You've got to be good and stick by me and help me show them."

Rose did not get an opportunity to answer. All the children had rushed about her, completely surrounding her. They wanted her flowers. There was something too spontaneous in their movements, so individually excited that all courtesy and regard for one another was not merely gone but appeared never to have existed. There were high shrill voices, squealings like animals feeding, pushing and shoving. Gilbert moved away a little. In spite of the most furious individualism, it was essentially a herd movement, as if all of the children had a central mind and desire. Gilbert had a feeling of wanting to sweep his arm and give himself more space in which to stand.

The crush of arms and bodies was around Rose. She seemed to sway easily, unmindful of being touched and pushed, unaware that the behavior about her was in the least rude. She was giving smiles to some of the children. She was a favorite among them. She seemed to command their admiration, because she was affectionate, because she was pretty and healthy, and undoubtedly because she was older and bigger. She was the kind of girl happiness makes radiant, and was accustomed to showing her happiness. She simply whirled about, laughing, protecting the flowers as best she could. The children crowded tighter around her, jumping around with high, stiff knees, moving so swiftly that Gilbert felt them as being without individual shape. He had a sudden feeling that her eyes were beginning to look like their eyes, her movements to resemble their movements, wild and uncoordinated.

"You mustn't fail me," he shouted across the swirl of heads. "Get away from there, damn it," he said, pushing at some of the children, but they just seemed to roll off his arms, and to move about more peculiarly, as if he had been waving his arms in the midst of bees. His height and strength only made him feel helpless, bringing that uneasiness of not knowing how hard to strike without hurting them, and the futility of trying to silence them.

"May I give a few?" Rose asked, smacking one boy on the head, for he had tried to grab the whole bouquet, then offering groups of two or three flowers, trying not to give the left hands of those who had some in their right hands.

"Sure, sure, do whatever you like," said Gilbert. "I got them for you—but if you want to give them away . . . You do as you please." He seemed to be trying to keep his eyes from seeing the swarm of children, fixing them intently on her to be more sure of her attention. "There's a sunflower, you see the sunflower? You keep the sunflower." Now all the children were pressed around Rose and he had less trouble keeping them off himself, he began to resent their familiarity with her, and the way she was being pushed and pulled around. One boy, nearly his own size, had hold of her elbow, and every time she gave him a flower he stuck it in his pants pocket the way a dirty handkerchief might be hastily put away at the approach of someone. "Well listen," said Gilbert, "I have to get back to my class. I have to get back because . . ." and he began to withdraw, walking backwards. "You understand don't you, it isn't—I mean I'd like to stay. I don't want you to think . . ." He turned and walked rapidly, then checked himself, and almost shouted, "But I'll see you after school, you wait for me after school!"

All this had taken place within sight of his classmates, and as he returned to them his eyes were lowered. Some were still basically enough children to be playing and completely absorbed in the game, but most were standing in little groups, looking toward him as if he were a camera about to take their picture. He walked awkwardly and kept biting his lip, then stood at the edge of the group, hesitating to enter, not being able to decide where there was an entrance. For the general expression was neither antagonistic nor with any sign of friendship. He would have felt surer of himself if they had turned their backs on him. He gave his attention to those with whom he was on good terms, trying to discern their attitude, but they appeared to have the exact same expression as all the rest. It made his nostrils quiver and a coldness creep into him; he already sensed that he was going to encounter something which he could not hope to evade or overcome.

He wanted a showdown and there was not going to be one. There was not going to be anything. He was strong and big, with a reputation for fighting, and was not going to be able to use his strength. His eyes were prepared for encounter, and there was nothing. Something in what he saw around him made him begin to feel wary and cautious. There was no place on which to focus an action; he seemed to be on a slow-turning pedestal, going round and round, for all to see and gaze on. He knew that he was in a state in which he could not defend himself. He began to feel as if he were standing behind a window of thick glass, looking through at children who were keeping at a distance from him.

So he hurried on past and into the building. No redemption, no relief and no love. The best he could manage was a feeble sarcasm, scrawling on the blackboard in big white letters, "Gilbert Mijack loves Rose Lee." He did not have the courage to stay, but took the rest of the flowers out of his desk, stuffed them inside his shirt, and went home. He had only a determination that he would see this through. He had only the knowledge that he had done a very wrong thing to Rose, out of spite, desire and opportunity, and he was going to face the consequences. He was going to be good to her and earn her forgiveness. Side by side with this, in the perplexities of his thinking, was the fear that other boys had lain on top of Rose, boys who had been on the playground even as he carried the flowers to her. He was confused and did not know what to do, for what he had believed in the morning would be a moral act had become merely a feeling that he was on the edge of further degradation.

He walked along beside Rose in the late afternoon, but appeared depressed. It was the windows of houses that he watched. Before, whenever he had passed along these streets, there had been pride in knowing people must recognize him, and also a wonderful freedom from their eyes in knowing he lived on the mountain. Now he slunk along.

Rose said, "I'll go on home by myself. You don't have to come with me."

Gilbert did not reply. Whenever he passed a porch on which someone was sitting or standing, his eyes looked straight ahead and he hurried a little. He would not look at her and repulsed the offer of her hand, thrusting his own into his trousers.

After a time, however, he seemed to calm himself, and when they reached the desolate stretch where they would skirt past a part of the town by crossing steel-company property, he told her of gathering the flowers and being late for school. He told her he wished he had brought more. This set him to laughing. Then he broke off suddenly, with, "I used to like everybody. You'd hardly believe that, but it's true. I wanted to be good." His mouth opened and let out false laughter. He turned and caught her by the arms. "But listen, that's not what I want to say. It's you. You're the first person I ever met who's really good. I mean *good*. I can see it in your eyes." He glared at her from the intensity of his emotion. "You've got to help make me like I used to be."

They were nearing the town, and he found himself unwilling to enter. Alone with her, he had so fine a feeling and conviction that he was afraid of going where he might lose it. He asked her to walk across the fields with him. Rose consented. She was serene and happy, and she found his excitement more attractive than his words, his eyes more important than his thoughts.

"Forgive me for being ashamed of you," he said. "Forgive me that."

He walked along beside her, changing his pace in a futile attempt to equal hers. It was his own forgetfulness which constantly changed their strides. He began to tell her things about himself, though he seldom finished one incident, but leaped from thought to thought. His voice was loud, his laughter frequent. If something made her smile, he told it over again, exaggerating. He walked backward, facing her, so that she would have to look at him, so that she would see and enjoy his gestures. They could not walk rapidly in that manner. Rose had to keep looking beyond him, so that he would not bump into anything.

Then he changed again, into a friendly and more quiet attitude, and they walked hand in hand, Gilbert swinging his arm in a manner which made it difficult to walk near him, yet making her wish to be very close. It was still quite light, but birds were making hurried preparations for nesting, suggesting that they too were absent-minded or put things off until the last moment. Gilbert pointed at birds, giving them names, sometimes correct, sometimes thinking he was correct, other times telling fibs. "That's a bob-finch," he said once. He pointed to trees and shrubs and to places where he had been hunting flowers for her. That in particular interested her. He did not seem to realize that he was explaining in too minute detail, phrasing the same thoughts in a number of different ways. Instead he began to feel a genuine desire to protect her. As they passed places familiar to him, he recounted portions of his life connected with these fields.

"Do you know," he said, "I wouldn't trade my life for anybody's, not anybody in the whole world." He stooped and rubbed his hand through the hair of the grass. "Some day I shall be a great man," he said, "and then I'll make everybody see what a wonderful person you are. I promise it."

The sky was in its last full brightness, the brightness of silverish tones which would change into twilight so easily and promptly. The heat began to disappear from the air, leaving the air more lively and more easy to move through.

"Listen, wait here," he said. "I'm going to prove I mean it. Now don't move, I'll be back."

Gilbert ran and went out of sight. Rose waited. She chose a tree stump and sat there until she did not want to wait longer. Then she remained because he had asked her to. When even this was not a reason for her to sit on the stump longer, he came, as a sound through the grass. He dropped beside her, breathing heavily, put his elbows on her knees, and held his hands in identical positions near her eyes. Each hand contained a green earring.

"Put 'em on," he said. "Here, let me. Turn your head and hold still. Hold still! I got 'em for my sister but I want you to have 'em . . . But you have to hold still. Oh you better, I'm afraid I'm hurting you. See how they fasten, like this, now hurry, I wanna see how you look."

"I can't take them," said Rose, though her eyes were so interested that she seemed to prefer looking at them to fitting them to her ears.

"Don't be silly, they're *yours*. Now go ahead."

The earrings made her face small and round. They made her hold her face a little to one side.

Gilbert and Rose sat there a long while, he speaking to her very rapidly. He grew more and more convinced that he had at last found someone who would not change toward him. He felt he was on the edge of love.

"I've had one fight because of you already," he said. "If necessary I'll fight them all. Because I believe you're better than any of them."

Rose talked little, instead looked into his face and stroked his arm, sometimes pinching gently at the fine hair which her fingers encountered. She studied his hand, turning it this way and that, even giving attention to individual fingernails.

Darkness was closing in on them. It was the same hour at which he had thrown her on the ground and pushed himself between her legs the previous evening. He seemed to have no recollection of it, seemed to consider their present relationship as wholly apart from that. Rose remembered it as the proof of his liking her. She did not understand him, she had never had anyone treat her with respect and admiration, but she found pleasure in listening to him. She liked his eyes, liked his teeth, liked how strong and wild he was.

She removed the earrings and put both in one hand and kept the hand tight against herself to remember they were inside.

"Why don't you wear them?" said Gilbert. "That's what they're for."

"They make my ears big."

"You'll have to get used to that," he said gravely.

Rose listened to him and made herself soft and warm against him.

"Everything is going to be fine," he said. "Do you know where we're going? To my house. We're going to study, and we're going to get you out of that class. Because I don't believe you belong there."

She was afraid to go with him to the house. She had never been in anyone's house.

Gilbert was too caught in his own thoughts to give his attention to her. He was walking with a long, firm stride, so that she had difficulty keeping abreast of him, keeping in a position where she could look up at his face. "I'll get Naomi. She's better at teaching then I'd be," he said. "You know I've got to start studying some, too. I didn't take a book home all year." He shook his head disgustedly. "You know I think I could make A's if I wanted to." He could feel a new energy, a kind he had seldom felt before, quick and light, as when he was listening to music.

He led through fields, holding her hand because he knew the paths better than she, talking to her in a tense voice. He explained to her the importance of building a firm relationship between them, the importance of treating each other with respect and being able to look into the faces of other people without having anything to be ashamed of. He explained to her the care they must take not to rush into love.

He felt a need to protect her, a need to build a pedestal for her, a need to redeem himself for having abused her. He wanted her to depend upon his moral strength and to keep their relationship as friends for the present. It was a time for formality, simply to prove to each other that they did love. So that when she put her head against his shoulder, when she assumed the initiative, he felt strongly his responsibility, and was oppressed by a feeling that it was only his moral strength which kept them from doing the same thing again, oppressed by a feeling that she would accept him, without defense, without accusation. He could not avoid seeing that she wanted him to kiss her. He was beset by the feeling that there was no one other than himself to protect her. He looked around, aware of the blackness of the sky, as before he had only been aware of the darkness.

Nothing happened at the house to disturb them. Mijack had already gone to bed. Gilbert found his history book. Rose was afraid he would be impatient and angry with her, as teachers had been. There were so many things she could not remember, things in books.

Naomi discovered she had become much older in relation to Rose, and indeed behaved like a mother whose son was having his girl friend in.

When the dishes were stacked in the cupboard, she came to the table where they were studying, and after she had taken hold of a book and asked questions from it, she became more like herself. She asked the questions in a manner in which Gilbert and Rose could talk between themselves and decide upon an answer, while she, with the information before her, gave little hints and first letters of words and sometimes syllables.

Gilbert looked up from the table, and there was a stillness, but Bart only leaned toward his sister to see the book she had in her hands, and then went upstairs.

Everything went nicely. But Gilbert was worried about taking Rose home at such a late hour, and Naomi would not let her leave before she had a sandwich and a glass of milk. Finally they were outside and walking very slowly until their eyes became accustomed to the dark. "Say, where's your earrings?" he said. "How come you don't have them on?"

"I'm afraid I'll lose them."

They paused while she untied a handkerchief which she took from inside her dress, to prove to him that she still had them. He put them on for her. He felt more pleased that she had accepted his gift than when he had given them to her. He smiled at her until there was nothing to do except smile back, though her face had been prepared to feel pain while he fumbled with her ears. He noticed she liked being touched by him and he was pleased. He liked being attractive.

They walked down the long hill. After stumbling several times, Rose lost caution and quite deliberately bumped against him. He retaliated so forcefully that she put both hands against her ears. Now that darkness was all around her and she could not tell how well he had fastened them, she was afraid the earrings, hanging so loosely, were going to fall. Their least independent movement seemed enormous to her, and she walked with her hands on her ears to keep them from swinging. The palms of her hands were the only safe places she knew.

On the street where she lived, they paused, standing below the street light.

"You don't have to pay attention to me at school," she said. "Maybe it'll be better if you don't. I'll just be your secret girl—like now," she said, looking along the empty and silent street.

"No," said Gilbert. "We're doing fine."

For a while he had forgotten it would ever be necessary for them to do anything. But now, thinking of tomorrow and how he must continue to be firm, he came to himself and hurried her along. "I want to meet your mother some time," he said. "I know I'll like her."

Rose only looked down at the sidewalk.

She tried to lead to the side porch, but he would not hear of it. He went straight to the front and managed the door in doorman fashion, ushered her inside, blew a kiss with his hand, and then went off. He had not walked far when he snapped his fingers, returned to the house and tapped against the large window and tried to peer inside. It did not occur to him that anyone other than Rose might hear or see him. His surprise was that she opened the door when he was looking for her through the window, and opened it so softly that he did not hear. She seemed nervous and kept looking behind her, into some part of the house.

"I forgot to tell you," he said. "I'm sure now I love you."

Then he went home. He whistled along the streets and sang when he came to the open fields.

That night, as he was getting ready for bed, Bart was fixing clothing, folding neat squares.

"Think you can fit that broad ass of yours in these?"

Bart tossed a pair of tan trousers. Gilbert caught them and looked them over, inspecting them not for fitting himself but for being worn out. Bart came out of the closet with another pair. "Try these. If they fit, keep 'em."

He watched his brother slide first one leg, then the other.

"Just so-so, huh? Well, they ought to do for catting around."

Gilbert looked up quick and hard. "Watcha mean by that?"

"What I said. I can't help it," Bart replied, "the teachers come to me with your problems." He pointed toward the floor, meaning downstairs. "I haven't told the old man. Or your mother. But if you don't quit making everything you do so public, somebody else will."

"Tell what?" said Gilbert, throwing the trousers on the bed and standing, hands on hips.

"Tell him about your being fifteen years old and printing your name on blackboards. It's a good way to get yourself named poppa when she turns up with a kid."

"You lie," said Gilbert.

Bart studied his brother a moment, then continued to undress.

"Stay loose," he said. "I'm only trying to tell you something that'll save you trouble later."

"It's none of your business what I do."

"It *is* my business. I happen to be your brother, we happen to be Mijacks."

Bart turned down the cover in a neat halving movement and then sat on the bed to remove his shoes.

"Listen, Gib, don't you know Rose doesn't have all her marbles? Don't you realize she's just a kid whose tits are beginning to itch and doesn't have enough sense not to rub them up against everybody?"

"You lie, Bart. She's not that way."

But he was calm, and his eyes were attentive.

"All right, the facts of life," said Bart, looking his brother straight

329

in the face. "She used to deliver papers for me, remember? All right. At least three guys in this town have had her, one of them older than me. You know who—Spider. There isn't a single guy in the poolroom who'd give ten cents to get in her drawers. There isn't a single one who wouldn't tell you what I'm telling you, and probably more."

"I don't believe you," said Gilbert. His face was white. He knew his brother did not tell lies. "And I don't care," he said.

"Look, all I say is knock off the publicity," said Bart. "You're old enough to take your chances. I've told you, that's the end of it. Except we don't want publicity, not me, not Father and not Naomi. I don't think you want it, either." Gilbert sat down on the bed, right on top of the trousers. "Kids playing in the woods, it happens all the time. Every kid has had the same thing happen," said Bart. "Only we don't make an issue out of it. We forget about it."

"I never touched her," said Gilbert sullenly. He hit his hand into his pillow. "If you want to know," he said heavily, "I love her."

Bart slipped between the covers and turned his head away from his brother. He did not sleep. He lay there with the knowledge that he had never used his own loins, had refused the opportunities which had come to him. It was a bitterness to him that his brother should have experienced, or probably have experienced, that which he considered of extreme importance. For all his cynicism. And that his brother should have chosen Rose seemed to him such a degradation that he could feel it against his own flesh. It revived the feeling his mother had always awakened in him when he thought of her in connection with his own birth. Yet it was only a little later, when, hearing his brother weeping bitterly and softly, he raised his head high enough from the pillow to make his voice free and said, "Maybe I made it sound worse than it is, Gib. You do what you think is right and don't listen to me."

Bart sensed more closely than ever before the relationship between him and his brother. He sensed that they were both seeking to make something good out of life, and that for his brother to choose some poor girl was only what was to be expected and was only his way of trying to do good. Bart remembered that it had been his own sense of pity for her, the pity he had for all people who did not seem to have a fair opportunity at life, that made him give her the job of delivering papers. She had been his best carrier.

But as he lay there thinking, he realized that he was taking a comfortable view of his brother only because he did not have any hope for Gilbert amounting to anything. Gilbert was going to waste his life. It made Bart regard his own policy of strict self-control as wisdom on his part, as a prevention of the possibility of making similar mistakes on a different level.

The sky was deep gray; there was something disturbing about the distance through which eyes could peer without feeling confined. There were shimmers of light which did not have explicable origins. The earth felt a little soft and moist as Mijack, in his black Sunday suit, with his black hat pulled evenly down so that it covered too much of his head, making him appear helmeted and deficient in forehead, pushed open the gate. He glanced toward the mountain, then bent his head as if about to walk into wind and rain. He walked with care, with a certain distrust of shoes which he had never become accustomed to, and which new soles, still bearing traces of gloss, had made still more unreliable.

The street became a path, and the path a vague shadow through the grass, sometimes merely a few green stems standing awry. Despite his powerful build, despite his preoccupation, the black suit continued its domination over him, rendering his movements awkward and mechanical; it seemed particularly to clutch his neck and make his hands useless. He noticed the coming of dawn only when the heads of weeds began to shine. Everything seemed to be exceptionally quiet.

Following the trail across rock was even more difficult; sometimes it was marked by white dust which the sharp, steel-tipped heels had cut free, and sometimes a reddishness had to be scuffed at to prove it was dust. Sometimes he was led forward only by a kind of guess, one which did not grasp at any facts, but which was always correct. Only when a thin whistling began to make his one ear seem large did his eyes look around, still not upward or forward. The trees seemed to have lost the best of their foliage to storm or frost, and the branches were swaying enough to make birds hunch their wings from time to time, partly for balance.

Mijack seemed to be following someone. His whole method of procedure was that of an animal. Yet he was really following himself, following the path which he had taken almost every Sunday afternoon. And when he reached the end of it, he stood motionless, looking upward toward the peak of the mountain. He had never since his marriage been higher than this flat place where he now stood. His age was making itself felt, and as his bones seemed reluctant to obey him without at least forcing him to give some consideration to them, the peak of the mountain seemed inaccessible.

Toward noon he returned to the house and Naomi served him soup and coffee. Naomi had her hair wrapped about her head in tight braids; it made her look thin. Mijack had a cut on one of his hands, and the cuffs of his black suit were ragged and dirty; he asked that his work shoes be brought to him, but then, after looking at them a while, he merely took off the shoes he had on, shook a few grains of sand and stone from them, peered into them as if expecting to find something larger, put the same shoes on, and went out.

Mijack and his two sons ate supper at the table. Naomi served; she had eaten earlier. It was the first time in memory that Mijack sat down at the table without having washed. But the silence was exactly the same as it had always been; there was only the added and deeper stillness of four people who did not seem to be aware of each other's existence. Even Gilbert, who always seemed to be made nervous by the continuous presence of silence, stared straight ahead with unseeing eyes. It was nearly dark, but they did not seem to think of light, not even when the stone walls flickered with passive illuminations of the stove.

Mijack and his two sons went out of the house, past the warm odor of the chicken house, and through the gate. Mijack signaled it should not be closed. Gilbert walked with his hands shoved deep in his pockets. Bart carried under one arm a bunch of cat-o'-nine-tails, and in the other a little bucket. After a while Mijack had to walk in front. It began to rain and Bart walked holding one hand over the top of the bucket. Gilbert turned his face up into the rain and held it there until he could feel the wetness. The brim of Mijack's hat began slowly to bend downward, so that he seemed to have even less face, with only his thick nose jutting out beyond it; his shoulders seemed to creep through the starch of the coat and give him command over his movements.

When they stopped, Bart knelt and dipped two of the cat-o'-nine-tails into the bucket. He let the furry brown ends soak, then handed one to Gilbert, laid the other across his knees. A little later both of the sons stood erect, holding a reed in their right hands, and above them the flame of two torches and the curling black smoke. Mijack was bent over a plain dark rock, which he began to roll. He did not seem to object to the torches being held high. For a time the rock moved in quarter and half turns, but as they came to a steeper part of the hill, there was almost the same steady movement, only slower, of a boy rolling a hoop. Mijack seemed to know exactly when pressure was needed. Bart sometimes lowered his torch to assist his father to see some obstacle ahead on the path, but Gilbert held his high and straight, with his eyes looking up at the flame; only once, perhaps forgetting himself, perhaps for a moment forgetting his sorrow, he began to wave the torch in a circle to see the flame spread into a long and brighter light.

They rested only when there was a need for new torches. The sons, who had nothing to do except walk, seemed more tired than their father. Once, Mijack, in pushing against the stone, slipped to his knees, and for a moment seemed a very old man who had fallen under the burden of life. His tiredness seemed more that of a man who had been carrying something heavy on his back, than of a man who had been pushing. He never once looked at his sons and his sons never bent to assist him, and after the time he slipped, Bart no longer lowered his torch along the path. Inside the flame of the torch stood clear and erect the fuzzy brown core, burnt around but untouched. The rain drops looked white, and the torches seemed to give less light as the grass and bushes became drenched.

At the gate Mijack stepped away from the rock, took the torches from the hands of his sons, and said, "Carry it in." He had never given a stronger command in his life. Bart and Gilbert crouched on each side of the rock, eyeing each other; as they went to lift their heads bumped, but their eyes never changed; as they hoisted the rock their hands and arms became intermixed. Never had they so united their strength; never had they so completely lost their responses to each other. They walked in an odd fashion, as if trying to get into each other's embrace, pushing against the stone and toward each of them, so that their forward motion was almost accidental.

Mijack did not wait to see them carry the stone. He stuck the two torches on the gate, where they would give some light, and went on to the house. As he entered into the real light he seemed to stagger. His face was extremely white. It was as if all the years bent over the fire, all the hardened skin had been peeled away, leaving a flesh so pale and delicate that he dared not show it to anyone. He went straight upstairs, found that the wetness of his clothes had tightened the buttonholes so that his fingers could not manage them, and laid himself face down on the bed.

The next morning Mijack was sitting cross-legged in front of the dark stone which in daylight showed streaks of purple, with hammers and chisels spread about his knees, when the Lutheran minister came. Mijack was wearing the same black suit, and as he rose, did not bother to brush at the dirtiness. For a time the two men talked in low tones; then their voices began to raise, and when the minister made a move as if he was about to go on toward the house, Mijack stepped directly in front of him. "Then you're not a Christian!" said the minister, his voice trembling; but Mijack simply took him by the arm, swung him about so that they were both facing toward town and the river, and forcibly walked him to and through the gate.

Mijack returned to the house and gave some instruction to Bart; then he went back to the stone and sat among his tools. Bart went down toward the gate and sat on top of the wall; bit by bit he shifted stones until he was comfortable. He did not glance downward when Gilbert came through the gate carrying a great armload of flowers; Gilbert had been to the market in Harrisburg and had bought the most that could be gotten for the ten dollars which Mijack had given him.

After a while Naomi came out of the house carrying a bowl. She set it on the ground near Mijack, and he leaned over, caught it between his two hands and lifted it to his mouth. As he drank his soup, he kept looking at the stone, studying it. He was not accustomed to working with a coat on, and it had given him the habit of shrugging, and of raising his hands overhead from time to time.

Bart was munching a sandwich, still sitting on top of the wall, when a group of ladies came up the hill. They were carrying flowers, the two foremost ones, and the rest seemed occupied with the steepness of the hill. Bart slipped easily from the wall and took station in front of the gate.

In a little while the ladies were going down the hill, still bearing their flowers, except for the one which Bart had in his hand, and was blowing into to see the petals spread. Mijack had not once turned his head away from the stone, not even when one of the ladies had called to him in a voice both indignant and distressed.

There was a rather strange silence which surrounded the Mijack house, and it made the chickens seem louder and more quarrelsome. Gilbert walked about with a sullen, slow gait, never seeming to know quite what his own intentions were; for the first time since childhood his head again seemed too large and heavy, and he carried it slumped forward and to one side. Naomi walked on the very points of her feet, and much too quickly; she looked thin and very young and a little frightened. Bart walked and moved too lazily, without his usual precision, as if he were tired and bored. Even Mijack, who was physically remarkable only because he persisted in wearing the black suit and low shoes, worked with a kind of haste, and did not study the rock as carefully as he might have. He made several slight miscuts.

Then, toward one o'clock, the family suddenly burst into co-ordinated activity. A wagon was brought into the yard, and the stone was loaded into it; Naomi brought the flowers and laid them in the wagon behind the stone; it was only the wagon Gilbert used to deliver papers, and with the stone overloading it, she had to tie the flowers with string to keep them from falling off. Bart brought two white poles and a loop of yellow rope. Mijack and Gilbert, bumping their way through the door, brought a large box of new, unpainted wood. Bart and Mijack strapped the poles on each side of the box, and then Mijack and the younger son held one end of the box off the ground while Bart wrapped the rope round and round, until the box was almost girdled in yellow rope. When they lifted on the poles there was the squeaky sound of hemp stretching. Naomi, with her hair darkened with water, and a clean dress, came out and went to the chicken yard, where she threw and scattered hurriedly handfuls of corn. The chickens were aroused to exceptional greed.

Mijack, having lashed the two front poles together and then wrapped the line with rags, gave a signal to his sons. They lifted the box, Bart on one rear pole, Gilbert on the other, and Mijack bearing in coolie fashion, across his neck and shoulders, the front end. They went through the gate and down the hill. Naomi caught hold of the tongue of the wagon; she had a difficult time making the wheels move, and every little stone made the handle of the wagon jerk her arms; but once she arrived at the paved part of the street her difficulty was in keeping the wagon from going too fast. Once she had to run around in back and grasp the wagon with both hands and let her shoes skid over the asphalt until her feet were hot.

Their destination was not far, half a mile, but Mijack held up his hand several times, and they set the box in the street and rested. Gilbert did not seem to like to put the box down; he kept looking up and down the street to see if there was any traffic. Mijack did not seem as strong as he usually was and did not try to hide his fatigue; once, when he put his handkerchief to his face, it looked as if he were crying; but then he spat on the street shortly afterward.

Once, as they were resting, Mijack seemed to take notice of the condition of his clothes. He brushed at them, and then Bart slapped at his back. Mijack tried to clean his hat with the sleeve of his coat, but after examining the hat more carefully, he gave it to Naomi, and walked bareheaded the rest of the distance. They seemed to be unaware of the children who ran along the sidewalk, watching them, and of the curious looks which they received from people standing on their porches. Once a group of women seemed to cluster into a tighter unit as they passed, and to speak incredulously and indignantly of the manner in which Mijack and his sons were acting.

Mijack had always been hostile toward people. Yet he had earned from them a kind of respect, that of being a man of principles, so that he had always been greeted formally. Those who did not know him, but knew of him, respected him through the instinctive form of not attempting to make his acquaintance. He was a man best left to his silence.

But all his stiff dignity of the past seemed as nothing beside the dignity which he had, bareheaded, bowed with the weight of the box, and bowed with the weight of tiredness and the onslaught of age, and bowed yet with something deeper and less explicable. He seemed nearer to humility than to pride. He seemed to be suffering, so that all his former habits, instead of hiding that suffering, made it more visible in him.

They had nearly reached the gate, a great broad gate opening upon a green field littered with white stones and a few small tombs and temples, when the gas sputtering of a motorcycle forced them from the road, where they waited while the long, shiny, black hearse and the stream of cars went past. Mijack did not seem to mind waiting. He did not seem to feel that he was being in any way obstructed.

When the coffin of unpainted boards had been brought beside the grave, he asked the caretaker to inform his sons how to use the roller which lowered the coffin into the grave. Then he went to assist Naomi in pulling the wagon across the soft earth. Bart talked with the young man who had been assigned to this grave, and the two of them walked in a circle around the hole, peering down into it; Gilbert seemed to be about to follow them, when suddenly he sat down on the ground and began to cry.

Naomi had had a problem ever since her father had taken off his hat; it would not stay on the wagon and she needed both arms to pull, and she had not liked to put it on her own head. She had held the brim between her teeth most of the time. In spite of the assistance Mijack gave her with the wagon, he did not really seem aware that she existed.

When the coffin had been hoisted into place above the grave, Mijack opened the top and threw it back. "Take your look," he said. Bart walked forward. He had been walking along with the caretaker, who had been showing him the markers and cornerstones of the lot;

his eyes had a fixity, as if he were attempting to remember everything he saw. But when his father had spoken, he turned so smoothly, so prepared, that he seemed for a moment to keep his own counsel too well.

He stood above the coffin, manly and a little too handsome in dark blue, clean and unmussed. He reached into the coffin and touched his mother, with what appeared to be a gentle gesture, but at the last instant there was a ruder gesture, perhaps only the result of hasty withdrawal of his hand. Then he reached inside his shirt, found it necessary to open two buttons, and took from it a copy of the New Testament, the one she had forced him to sign his name in when he was little, and placed it beside her.

Mijack did not watch. This moment he gave to each was private, as he expected his own moment to be private. "You're next." Gilbert started to step forward, but Bart, who had accidentally kicked some gravel into the grave, stopped and pushed with his foot a little more dirt, watching it fall in the space between the coffin and the edge of the grave. Then, with a gesture of sweeping his arm, as if clearing a large space through which Gilbert could walk, Bart stepped aside and went again to the little rise from which he could watch the other funeral.

The body had been prepared by an undertaker; it had been washed and drained and plugged and clothed in black; it had been scented in a way that did not combine well with the odor of the wood. Gilbert, on first seeing her, almost drew back; then he stood for a time studying the features, seemed about to turn away, when, with a movement which made the whole coffin shift on its rollers, he suddenly reached in and almost drew her out of it, trying to press her against himself. He pressed one side of his face, then the other, against her; then gradually relaxed his hold and let her fall back into the coffin.

"Naomi," said Mijack.

But Naomi shook her head. She did not want to see.

Mijack walked slowly to the coffin. He looked down upon his wife with the same deep affection and the same stern control of emotion which can be seen in a good soldier standing above a fallen comrade. He did not seem disturbed by the fact that the woman below did not look like his wife. It was only as he was about to close and seal the coffin, when Gilbert rushed forward with the flowers in his arms, that for a moment he stiffened, his eyes became confused. Then he nodded, watched while his son placed the flowers in the coffin, seemed to become impatient, and at last closed the lid.

337

Mijack read what he wanted read over her grave. And then he said simply, "She has bowed her head before the inevitable and almighty. May she find peace. We are consigned now to memories, where we shall find for a time her life written more boldly than we dare admit to ourselves. It must lay heavily upon my heart the years of toil and building which this woman shared with me, the sons she bore me and the hypocrisy which we lived. We have done what little justice there is to be done for the dead, and now leave her, as we have no other choice and perhaps no other right, to the mercy of God, until such time as we too shall bow our heads, or perhaps for all eternity. Amen."

30

It was the first he had seen her in more than a month. "Hey Jod, Jim," he said, waving his hand for them to follow. He went across the grass, perhaps because it was more than an hour since school had been dismissed, probably because he did not care. Jod Cauley and Jim Averag, seeing whom he was going toward, followed at a distance, with some reluctance.

Rose was trying to open the door. Mr. Rowiger had been talking with her, and she had walked out of school without her books. She was going from door to door, trying to find one unlocked. She looked at Gilbert with a calm, wistful gaze, and when she realized he was coming to her, smiled. It was a tentative smile, one that wanted to have gladness, but was not sure what response it would bring.

"C'mon, Jod," said Gilbert, "I want you to meet somebody." He offered Rose both of his hands and smiled. "Hello, Rose, good to see you." He waited until his companions were near enough to have halted, with twin reluctance. "Jod, you know the strippers we find on the playground. Meet the girl who puts them there. Am I right, Rose?"

She did not understand. She was still smiling at him and holding his hands.

"I guess I'm not telling you guys anything new. I guess you had your share before I got mine." He laughed. "You know, girls don't go for me. It's my face," he said, distorting his features to make his ugliness more evident. "I had to put on a big act. Flowers and all that crap. Just so I could get some nookie." He was watching the two boys intently. "Of course, after she found out what I had in my pants, I didn't need flowers, did I, Rose?"

Her face was calm, but her eyes were troubled. She understood that he was bragging about his relationship with her, but she did not mind. She had a feeling he was coming back to her. Even hearing his voice was a joy.

"Know what she tried to tell me? I was the only one. I guess she thought I'd pity her or some such thing. Hey, what you guys scared of? C'mere, she won't bite."

Jod and Jim held their ground. Seeing that they were not coming, he took Rose by the wrist and pulled her toward them. He pulled with his back toward her, as if he were pulling a wagon or a weight that did not require consideration, that only required that he lean forward and pull.

She began to resist. He had to twist her arm to get her in front of him.

"Grab a handful," he said. "Go ahead, she likes it."

The two boys backed away. Rose had her eyes closed. Her attitude was more that of being punished than abused.

"C'mon, Gib, let 'er go. We got things to do."

Gilbert's eyes took on a slightly dangerous shade. "Mean you're too good for her," he said. "What's the matter, I admitted mine, I guess you guys are too good to admit yours. That it?"

"I wouldn't touch her with a ten-foot pole," said Jod.

"Yeah? Well what's this Spider tells me about you guys taking her into the hut and making her undress?"

"I never took her in no hut," said Jod.

"C'mon, let's go," said Jim.

"Don't tell me, I know," said Gilbert. "I'm tired of you guys sneering at me."

"Oh, that was years ago," said Jim.

Jim and Jod were out for football and basketball and track, and had real girl friends. Their kid days were over. They did not want to have to remember the foolish things they had done in the past, as they now, with a safe margin of time behind them, despised Rose for not having told on them. They had every reason to want to stay away from her. It was rumored that she was pregnant.

Gilbert advanced toward Jod and Jim, moving toward a place central between them.

"Maybe we've got something to settle, huh?"

Rose went home without her books. She had left as the boys were about to fight, or perhaps only to continue arguing. "Beat it," Gilbert had told her. She felt that she had seen the last of him, that he was never going to speak to her or come near her any more. She could not forget how his eyes had fixed on her, seeming for a moment to be perfectly round.

Perhaps she had not remained awake to hear them return. But she was awake. So familiar were the sounds that she could guess where they had been and with whom and in what mood returned. Dorothy was with a fellow older than herself; she was using her dictaphone tone of voice and excellent grammar. Kathleen was still finding love as fresh and exhilarating as ever, with the boy she had pledged herself to marry at the age of ten.

It was always a pleasure to Irene to hear their gaiety undiminished in the late quiet of the night, to hear a portion of life which she had missed or at least had never really entered. From this distance, with only sound to guide her thoughts, she could get a clearer and more objective view of her children, studying the maturity and immaturity of their voices. They were moving the rugs to dance, and a moment later they were in the kitchen, the girls making sandwiches and coffee for their escorts. One of the boys must have been impatient, for she heard the refrigerator open, and then a squeal of protest from Dorothy. Perhaps it had not been that. It did not matter whether her imagination formed the correct picture.

Irene, lying in bed, felt a faint anguish and wonder for what life was, for what it really was. Without envy or disturbance, she wondered if perhaps her children would not make the same mistakes she had, or if not the same mistakes, ones which would lead to identical results. She heard hooting across time the same questions which her own life had always sought and never found. It was no longer a desire to feel all, have all, be all, but the agony of what was forever gone, the agony of never having consolidated reality with her heart. She felt as if she had filled her heart with good things, and then they had not lasted.

She had not had enough reality, and then too much, and she did not know now whether there had been any reality. There seemed a confusion which was not definable. Hearing the laughter below, she knew that she did not need to decide, that it was perhaps better not to. Life did not present itself, and the most anyone could do was choose the way in which he presented himself to life. She only hoped her children were closer to reality than she had been. But, listening, she wondered if they were.

It was Thanksgiving. Early in the morning four children were moving along the main street. Douglas Getweiler was carrying a ladder with "N.H.S." painted in crude letters on the sides and black rings on the rungs. He was changing the ladder from side to side, pretending his hands were cold. It was a heavy ladder. Kathleen Pierce had an armful of blue and white streamers, and she had to keep bending her head to see where she was going. Rodger ran along behind and picked up any of the streamers that fell or dragged on the sidewalk. He was making himself an endless belt of blue and white. Naomi had her dress hitched at her knees, bagged like knickers, and there were a lot of looped strings hanging from her wrist.

The ladder was put against the lamppost. Naomi climbed to the top and fitted two blue and two white streamers to the lamp. For a while this was the only activity on the street. When they came to the clock in front of the bank there was a discussion. Kathleen did not think they should hang streamers there. Douglas thought it was the best place of all. Naomi wanted to climb and this allied the boy with her. Rodger was no help whatever; he even wanted to hang them from awnings and fireplugs. He kept trying to jump and touch the bottom fringes of the awnings, though most were rolled and cranked fast against the buildings.

It turned out the ladder was too short to reach above the clock, so a sort of blue and white necktie was hung to the central post. Before she would come down Naomi had to put her ear against the metal and listen to the mechanism of the clock working. Rodger began to shout. But Kathleen said, "Hush," and Rodger knew he didn't have a chance in the world of getting to hear the clock. Mr. Pore came out of his drug store, and they gave him six streamers. He was of course not opening his store on Thanksgiving, but was taking this opportunity to give the floor and walls a cleaning. He let Rodger have a lollipop.

The man at the firehouse let them go to the second floor and hang streamers from the windows. He got the American flag and two other decorations and hung them also. The fire house looked like the Fourth of July. Later, a bunch of children, mostly little, began running after them and begging for bits of the blue and white paper. Some were actually pulled out of the armful Kathleen was trying to protect. She was so arm-tired she could just barely carry them. Rodger gave away most of his endless belt.

One boy really wanted a streamer, because he said over and over, "I'm going to the game." So he got one before they gave in and gave the others too. This came about not so much from goodness of heart as the realization that there were an awful lot of streamers and lampposts. Right after that Naomi started hanging six apiece from lamps.

Rose Lee had a piece of chalk and was writing on the walls and sidewalk, "Beat Williamsport," and "Yea Varsity." In the window of the confectionery was a picture of a professional-looking football player, streaming blue ink from his heels. Below the picture was the Nesquehon High football schedule.

Around ten o'clock the band assembled in front of the gymnasium and paraded the six most important streets in the town. Navy blue uniforms, all trousered, with officer's caps, made it difficult to separate boys from girls. Behind them came the cheering squad, twenty-eight girls in blue wool sweaters and skirts, white tams and white boots. Each wore a little gold football over her heart. Behind them came a boy with four blue megaphones, which he carried in dunce-cap position on his head. He was in the middle of four girls with bare legs already reddened by the wind; the girls were wearing thick turtle-neck sweaters and white panties with a very short skirt of feathers, and they were not the prettiest girls, but they had beefy legs and mature behinds.

People were getting their automobiles prepared, piling blankets in the back, some taking lunches with them. There were bells to rattle as the band went past and a couple of Halloween whirrers and a few tooting horns. The band was saving its wind and relying on the drummers.

All in all, around a hundred cars started for Williamsport; most of them had chains in the trunk, for it was rumored there had been heavy snow to the north. Twenty went in one line, tooting their horns all through town.

The band marched down the hill and across the railroad. There was a special train, and many people, some already at the coach windows, others boarding, and a great many men standing around in overcoats, talking. Former students wore dark blue sweaters with a white ring for each year in which they had played sixteen quarters.

There were boys in scrub sweaters, and girls in heavy wool sweaters which made the "N" seem flat against their chests.

Thanksgiving dinner had been a complicated arrangement. Some had it in baskets. Some had eaten early. Many were going to buy theirs in Williamsport restaurants. Young people were impatient for the train to get under way. A few men had a load on already, others holding out against temptation until they were aboard the train and could use paper cups for chasers.

Mijack was there, sitting on the train, the first he had ever ridden on a paid fare. He looked out of place in his black Sunday suit. But he wanted to see his son play. Mijack sat looking out over the river, slightly disapproving of himself.

There were people who were not going to the game, but had come to see the train leave. Especially children. They used their spirit in giving yells. Some attended home games, with athletic cards and fifteen cents. Some were so interested in football that they got on the field at half time and played and tackled and ran. Some climbed the fence, even over the new triangle of barbed wire. Some, with less courage, waited until the third quarter, when the ticket booth closed, and the police were watching the game.

It was a great occasion for the recent graduates, those who had begun the fame of the school. These graduates talked football with enthusiasm, traded shifts at the mill so that they would be free Saturday afternoons; they could never forget that Nesquehon defeated Chambersburg 102 to 0, defeated Dickinson College; a band of ex-footballers had gotten together and formed a semi-pro club which lost to the Carlisle Indians and Jim Thorpe 26-21, and beat the Pittsburgh Steelers 5-0.

That history was only beginning. Six All-Americans were to come from this school. In a few years the greatest player in the history of Nesquehon would break his spine at Annapolis. A senior was going to go straight into pro ball, where he would be the lightest and quickest guard the Eagles ever had. As late as 1952 Penn State was going to have its finest passer and a fine end, Kansas was going to have an All-American who played quarterback, halfback, fullback, end, linebacker and safety man in the same game, and Pittsburgh was going to have a great guard.

The football coach was paid more than the superintendent of the school. The high school guaranteed every varsity player a scholarship. The team was supported by the Lions, Rotary, Elks, Moose and particularly Kiwanis. There was a Bethel trust fund of $130,000 to support the school's football activities. In Bethlehem the team played before 17,600 people, paid attendance. In 1946 the entire backfield was sent to Hollywood, all expenses paid.

There was the pressure on the players of knowing that their fathers and brothers and friends were betting on every game. There were the football pools in every bar and poolroom, pools on picking the score, on total points, on the subtracted score, pools in every way that men could devise to gamble. There was the "Player of the Week" award, and the sports banquets at which boys learned to taste fairly good liquor and lots of beer. And there were men under twenty-five years of age, slumped over bars with defeated eyes, talking of their gridiron victories.

There was another side. The business football brought to the town; it was part of the growing political situation. It was advertising for Bethel. It filled pages of Mr. Pierce's newspapers. It made human ambition center around becoming a football player and then a coach, or making a lucky business contact. It made children despise intelligence, made adults despise children who were trying to become intelligent. There was the money football brought into the school, and there was the promise of glory toward which every boy was striving.

For it had not begun that morning with children hanging streamers. It had already been bet and re-bet and cross-bet in the bars. Williamsport had been scouted in five separate games. Special plays had been practiced at secret sessions. There had been a big bonfire and cheer rally. There had been a special assembly in the school, a talk by the coach and the director of athletics. There had been a high-pressure ticket sale.

It had begun way back in August, when one hundred and four out of a possible two hundred boys, counting freshmen, had trotted out onto the football field. It had begun before August, when the coach arranged for two families from a nearby village to move into town and send two husky boys to Nesquehon High. There had been a weak spot in the line. And there was the business of the concessions for coffee, sandwiches, cigarettes and candy. There was the business of arrangements with bus and train companies. There was the restaurant at which the visiting team would eat, and the restaurant at which the home team would eat. There was the restaurant at which the banquets, at five dollars a plate, were to be held. There were the dances held after the game.

And there was the game itself. The entrance of the field was like a carnival. One stand was selling pennants and souvenirs. Another was selling programs. The reserved-seat ticket booth was already closed, but there were men with hands in their pockets, who would sell one-dollar tickets for two dollars. There was a portable peanut and pop-corn stand.

Parking-lot attendants seemed to ignore cars tooting their horns. Negroes were walking along the stands, shouting taunts at Williams-port, "Five'll get you ten," "Even money and six points," and "Put up or shut up." There was something grim about these people, in spite of their laughter. The Negroes were wearing new gray suits and round-top hats, and there was more warmth and laughter among them than among the professional bettors, but there was something dangerous too.

People were sitting their behinds exactly on top of little white numerals, and already all the high seats were taken from goal to goal. The photographers were walking around, looking at the gray sky, squinting through their cameras. The side-line markers were in-specting their equipment, and stretching the chains. One of the refer-ees was examining the condition of the field.

Nesquehon had never been noted for a good band. They left the matter of musical talent to the other schools. The band could only play three numbers of anything like recognizable music, but they ran onto the field and marched to get their legs warm. Their hats were terrible.

In the locker room Bart was keeping to himself. He would not wear equipment that did not fit perfectly and would not put on a jersey that smelled of sweat. He dressed slowly and methodically.

The other players seemed to give most of their attention to shoul-der pads and the cleats of their shoes. The trainer was taping an ankle. Gilbert was horsing around with a couple of boys who did not expect to get in the game. Nesquehon always took three full squads away to games and dressed them. The coach believed in a full bench.

All of the high-school students stood and applauded when the team trotted onto the field and divided in squads. Most graduates stood too. The band played half a number, and then the cheer leaders waved for them to be silent, and began the long yell, "Ne Ne es es sq sq qu qu ueue hoho hon yea Nesquehon." There followed the national anthem. All the players stood with their helmets in their hands, while the flag was being raised.

Then the captains of each team met in the center of the field. Bart represented his team.

Mrs. Malancic, fifty-three, whose six sons had all played football, and whose last son was now a senior and the center, drew a big round of applause as she went to the edge of the field and waved her umbrella. Her son pretended not to see her, then looked at the bench, and finally trotted over, removing his headgear. He was a big, husky boy, and he stood looking down as she talked up into his face. The Williamsport band struck up "The Old Gray Mare" out of respect for her. But she shook her umbrella threateningly at them.

Then she turned to her son and said, "You play hard. You don't, I get your brothers beat hell out of you. You hear you lazy sonofabitch, you hear your mother?"

The first quarter was scoreless. People were stamping their feet to keep warm. There had been a fist fight at the south end of the field, and the police had rushed there, and so were failing to keep people from walking in front of the stands. That meant the bottom rows were standing up and the middle rows were shouting for people to sit down.

Mijack sat looking straight ahead. For him there was only one person, his son.

Dorothy Pierce was also watching Bart. She had told her girl friends that she was going to be escorted to the dance by him.

Mr. Pierce and Mr. Weaver and other businessmen were sitting in the reserved-seat section. They had a pair of binoculars which they passed back and forth. They laughed from time to time.

At half time Nesquehon led 14-0. Bart scored one touchdown and set up another. Adept at following his blockers, running mostly to the outside, where his speed and sense of timing were at their best, he forced the opposition to spread its defense; then twice he knifed through the guard slot on quick openers.

The crowd remained quiet and sullen. It was not enough that Nesquehon was leading. The talk was of the two opportunities Nesquehon had missed. As the players trotted to the locker room, Mrs. Malancic struck at her son with her umbrella so hard and often that he had to break into a run, covering his head with his hands. "Oh, but you're smart, think I didn't see."

The Williamsport band performed. There was feeble applause. People carrying too many things in their hands were trying to work their way through the stands. People were shoved against each other to keep warm. Men were passing bottles back and forth; the bottles were wrapped in newspaper.

In the third quarter, with the score 28-0, Nesquehon began to

346

substitute. Next year's varsity had their preview. Great rounds of applause went up as one after another of the varsity trotted to the sidelines. Bart, who never made the mistake of running too hard in practice, was exhausted. He went straight to the locker room.

It would have seemed natural for the crowd to relax. But it did not. Their shouting was hoarse and vindictive. They were no longer shouting for victory, but for the utter humiliation of their foe. It was a loud, angry cry which had in it elements of an almost fascist sense of conquest. If it had been only drunks—the police had already broken up three fights, in one of which knives had flashed—but it was the workingmen, young, fanatic women; it was barbers, bartenders, store owners.

There was a prophecy of violence in the attitude of these people. They made victory too important and too ruthlessly sought. They could not accept victory, let alone defeat. They could not find sufficient expression for the dissatisfaction in their lives, and their eyes watched the field with the squint of hatred.

In the fourth quarter Gilbert Mijack went into the game. He was third-string quarterback. His eyebrows were beginning to grow together, giving him a fierceness. The skin hung to the bones of his face. His shoulders were bulky.

Slow starting, he sometimes got caught behind the line, but once under way, was difficult to bring down. His legs were powerful. He bullied his way. His greatest drawback was poor ball handling, and, defensively, a tendency to tackle high, grabbing around the shoulders.

As the game ended, the crowd divided into a riot of joyous and triumphant youth and the grim, raucous criticism of middle age. Youth did not see the end, and the older people were not satisfied with the victory. They turned their backs on the parade, and hurried into the train or went roaring off in their cars, horns tooting, but with haste.

When the train arrived in Nesquehon it was strewn with litter. One seat had been broken. There was a charred spot on the floor where someone had set fire to paper, and there was liquor and urine seeping from the men's room. Two windows were broken out. Restaurants in Williamsport complained of silverware that had been souvenir-stolen.

The next year York fought Nesquehon to a scoreless tie. There was a riot. People lined the streets and hurled rocks and bricks at the automobiles as they passed.

And it was extending beyond football. It was the wrath of men

347

who were being choked by their own narrowness of mind, who were being imprisoned by the nature of their work in the steel mill, who needed to make a declaration of their existence before it was too late. They were dangerous because they did not understand themselves, nor their growing animosity toward life.

Mijack saw his son standing by the wall, motionless as the rocks which held their own steadfast, shineless color, as if the sunlight passed through them without the slightest reflection; aware of the need a man has for solitude, Mijack waited, allowing his son a few more moments in which to enjoy the peace that comes from repose; labor had its solitude, and Mijack remembered a time when a long day of work would have filled his heart to brimming, when the end of a day and the fall of the shadows was a whispering, an indescribable joy of accomplishment; labor had its fruit, perhaps the only worthy fruit on which life could feed, and Mijack had often thought that if only it were given to a man to make fine, pure water in the bowl of his own hands, to leaven and bake bread with the heat of his own fingers, and to churn pebbles from the grinding of his own jaws, then would a man know All; but if labor was all this and more, yet it lacked that fine peace which he saw now within his son.

For Bart was standing there, it seemed to Mijack, as clean and firm as the rocks of the wall, and though the older man could imagine the ambitions of youth swirling inside, the calm, confident posture of this son, taller and more slender than Mijack had been, bore them with the dignity that the sea has, though boiling in its lower depths with multitudes of creatures. There came to Mijack on that instant a conviction that this son would not fail the blood within him. So great a pride welled in Mijack that he wished to bend to the earth, and give it his kiss; he so loved the world at this moment, so rejoiced in the discovery that pride in son could outstrip pride in self, that he could, even though it had to be in secret, tremble with humility at the sight of his own child in man's guise.

Youth came to the aging man, as new as his own youth had once been, and more precious since it was to last so brief a time, if such moments are not timeless, immeasurable. But to feel youth and nothing more would not have influenced Mijack, for that was a common thing, which happened each day, since it could be said in truth that the old feel youth more often than the young; he felt the gratitude a man can have for once having been young, without sentimentality,

348

without yearning. For a moment he lost his son in self-contemplation, but this only brought a more clear understanding of why this hour was given to him, and why this hour was not given to him earlier, and might never return.

He looked where he thought Bart might be looking, and in doing so imitated his son's stance and posture; at first he thought it must be the far-off mountain which was indistinct with haze, but then he became convinced that it was the river, and his heart instantly approved; although the distance was too great to see the flow of the current, and the color too blue for his mind to imagine the river rushing, rolling toward the Chesapeake and the sea, he knew what his son was thinking, and it had to be, ought to be, would be. The grass about them was pale, bright green, for it was May, and already the blades were losing their sharp tips and whetted edges and translucence. The rains were no longer drenching, and the sun would get hot in the middle of the day, and school had ended yesterday. It was time for this son to fix his eyes upon the river.

With the awkwardness which a man not accustomed to standing close or in fellowship with other men always betrays in his step and his manner of approach, Mijack went to his son and placed a hand on each shoulder. There was no timidity in this gesture, but a rough gentleness, and Mijack's fingers were surprised at the heat that rose from his son's flesh, the way they were surprised to find a stone hot from no more cause than sunlight. The two men were of one size, but a few years would separate them forever. Bart showed manhood, but there was in the color of his flesh and the slender frame indication of more growth.

Bart also showed surprise. He had been too absorbed in his musing to flinch, and his body had immediately shown resignation for the hands upon his shoulders, their firm weight; he recognized their symbolic intent, the way a newly commissioned officer recognizes epaulets, and returned the steady gaze of his father; it was a new sensation, one that had come a little too late in Bart's life for him to be able to relax into it.

"When do you go?"

"Tomorrow," said Bart.

"I knew you left tomorrow. What hour?"

"You knew? Yes, I suppose you did," Bart admitted.

"I should, don't you think? I've been watching you prepare to leave me all these years."

Mijack gave that rare, unbelievably warm smile. But Bart turned his eyes from it, finding its meaning too strong, feeling that men who never smile should never smile.

"You're ready to go, son. You're ready to strike out on your own," said Mijack. "And you have my blessing."

Bart looked at his father and realized that they both had passed by an opportunity for real comradeship; he saw that his father was of greater depth than he had been willing to believe, and that the man had failed in his family duties because he could not understand children. He wondered how much Mijack knew of his weaknesses, and whether this conversation was leading to the kind of silent apology that a proud man can barely manage. Bart found himself wishing that Mijack would say aloud, "I failed you," and yet this put a bitterness on it too.

"Ready to strike out," said Mijack. "Life has to be struck at, formed, shaped."

"Yes," said Bart. "Ready or not, here I come." This was bitterly spoken.

"What's that?"

"Oh, nothing much. Just something kids holler when they play hide and seek."

Bart punched at the bottom stones of the wall with his shoe, then seemed to shake off the sadness as quickly as it had come. Mijack took down both hands from his son's shoulders at the same time. His hands had conveyed their message, and he was not one to prolong a gesture. He did not permit an action of his body to outlast its intention.

"I'll have to get at the wall," Mijack said. "I wasn't as careful with it as when I built the house." He pushed a few top stones into place. "One time I wouldn't have liked a wall worth a lick. Now I see they have their place, if the stones don't seem to know it." He examined the marks of time, the history of rain and sun on one stone, no more peculiar than the others, and with as much intensity as a man might study a fine painting, if he had come to love paintings. "Leave early," said Mijack, looking up from his deep study, "early's the time to leave. Early is luck." Mijack smiled. "That's old advice. My father was a fisherman." Mijack bit his lip, as when he felt a thought was not complete. "I guess that's old-fashioned," he said. "I guess that was good in the days before electric light and three shifts at the mill."

"I'm going early," said Bart.

It was easy to agree with his father, with the accumulated experience of generations, now that the experience of obedience was over; it was at the same time strange to know that all the responsibility for his actions, which he had sought after and prepared himself for, amounted to no more than this slight shift, this legal grant which Mijack was now formally making to him; it was this last-minute kindliness, more evident in Mijack's tone than in what was being said, which gave the son a kind of suffering for what had never been and would never be.

His father had become a fine, solid man. He seemed to have thrown off the domination which strong moral fiber and physical power had held over him, without weakening that moral fiber. And just at the hour when Bart himself had finally begun to wear this same power easily and confidently.

"You should have taken me fishing," said Bart suddenly. "I think I would have liked fishing."

Mijack smiled. "No, my boy," he said, "you weren't that kind of son. I was always too old-fashioned for you. With another boy that might have been bad, but you had a knack of finding things out for yourself, same as I had. You did the right thing by yourself and I guess if it's really said, I interfered too much as it was." Mijack put his feet in new positions of the earth. "How you going? By the river?"

"No. Railroad."

"Ah, yes," said Mijack. "I had forgot. I guess it's the same, river or rail." It was a concession to his son, to youth that would not understand that old and new are relative to the time in which they exist. Yet Mijack was not quite free of prejudice himself, for his mind was thinking—the river is slower and gives the eyes a chance to see and measure, the river goes where the land is best, the river feeds the valleys, and if a river doesn't cross a mountain, then no mountain can cross a river, and if a river leads by cities, it was the cities that had chosen the river. For a moment he almost drifted into his own youth, almost began to resurrect what was past, but checked himself. "West?"

"No. Only Philadelphia. Until fall. Then college."

"Oh? College? I had forgotten. I thought perhaps . . ."

"You *hoped* I'd changed my mind," said Bart. It was his turn to smile.

"I'm not trying to interfere now," said Mijack hastily, almost timidly. "It's only a thing I forgot to tell you, my son." Bart was pained to see how sensitive this man could be when dealing with something beyond the boundaries of his own realm of absolute control; there was too much justice in this man, so that it had made him stern, so that in another sense it had made him go adrift from the society of the world; it seemed a shame that Mijack's principles had been so limited; that was what had kept him from rising in the world and had made him a bad father. "I'm not against my boys having an education. But dead set against college. By what I've seen, in my experience at the mill, those college boys have their minds all tangled up with words and thoughts and odd bits of learning that don't set well with what's in a man. Knowing nonsense is worse than not knowing anything. That's why I was proud when I saw you working things out for yourself." Mijack paused. "But that's only my opinion, and I admit I don't have the experience to know I'm telling the truth, so it's better I said nothing. I had my say all these years, whether you liked it or not, and it's about time I quit." Mijack smiled. "You got to forgive a man. He can't change all in a day, even if he'd like."

"Go ahead," said Bart, "I'm interested."

That was easy to say now. It was easy because Bart was free. It was easy because Bart had his own firm concept of life, and did not need to worry that the words of an old man would change it. He realized now that it had been a momentary delusion to believe that he and his father could have been companions.

Mijack looked at his son with new respect, surprised to find that his son was actually in want of advice. It was a boon to him who believed so strongly in a creed of life, who had the conflict of wanting his sons to believe its essentials, its vitals, yet knew it was wrong to force upon them more than a simple, strict discipline; believing that he had lived according to his own truth, he could not find in his heart proof that all men should live as he did, and so it was a reward to him to know that his ideas were welcome in his son's ears.

"Thank you, son," said Mijack. "I'm repaid where I didn't know there was debt."

Mijack looked proud in a new way. With his natural pride to fortify this, it was tremendous to see.

"I will say a little more. It can't harm. I been watching that river a little ago, and it took my eye as far as it could go, and my mind went on across the land. It takes time and a lot of men to change the land, but I guess that's come about since my days. I never got far past the Mississippi; that river always made my heart turn eastward; I saw a good share of the men who headed out toward California, talked with them, but it always struck me as running away: hunting a dream is a poor life, a poor, poor way of making a man feel satisfied with himself. But fulfilling a dream is the best there is." Mijack showed in his face, and by pausing a long time, that he considered that important. Bart considered it obvious, and was silent.

"Son, land isn't so plentiful any more that a man can think in terms of miles all his own—that's greed and trouble now. That was the talk in my youth, to be able to walk four days in your own land and still not see the end of it. But by the time I was the age of wandering, it was gone, except for the West. But I found that a man don't need miles on miles to be free and to honor his God; only enough to give him room to walk a few steps when he has to think, enough land to keep his hands honest and interested in keeping it as good as when he got it, and grow a few things he can't live without. No man should be without a garden, a hog and a few chickens, not if he owns millions. And it would be nice if every man could have his own creek. A well just isn't the same." Mijack looked out over the rolling green of Pennsylvania. "That's what the land means now. I never understood this past war in Europe, not the way the newspapers kept saying about Huns and the Kaiser, but I had an idea that the trouble was some men were still thinking in terms of miles—and that's even worse in Europe than it is here." Mijack shook a finger, but he was really only warning himself, as he always did when he began to go beyond the boundaries of his own knowledge. "Son, get yourself a piece of land. Have all the other ambitions you want, but do that—or you'll regret it."

Bart smiled. "I'll have miles of land," he said, "or else none."

Mijack gave his son a straight look, knowing all he had said had been refuted in that one reply.

"Then get miles," said Mijack, "if that's how you see it. But want them. Want the land for what the land is. Don't just greed it. Get the land honest, and do honest by it, or you may find that the land has a way of paying a man off."

"I'm honest enough," said Bart abruptly, yet attempting to maintain his good humor.

"You're honest for what seem to me peculiar reasons," said Mijack. "But it's too late for talk."

"Sure is," Bart agreed.

"Well, I ought to confess I'm proud of you, Bart," said Mijack, "and I wish you the best. Now shake hands. I expect I'll be off to work in the morning before you're ready to leave. I guess early's about eight for you."

They both laughed, shook hands, and went into the house.

Gilbert started marking spots for the foundation holes. He rolled away several boulders. Stones went crashing down the mountainside. Small ones he lifted and hurled.

Rowiger was trying to pitch the tent and was having difficulty finding ground to drive stakes into. He had already used the trunks of two trees to hitch the pole lines fast. He was bobbing about, snapping his hands together, something prim and feminine in his manner. He could never seem to remember what he intended to do next.

"I warned you it wasn't much."

"It's great," said Gilbert, standing erect and looking over the vast space below.

Rowiger too was looking, but his eyes turned slowly and evenly, like the turning of a beacon. He had chosen this land because of the Bluegill, because it was above the smoke, and the shrubs and trees were still native and original. That the land was poor, mostly rock, seemed to him only a confirmation of its peacefulness. It would be a fine place to bring biology classes. It would at the same time help this boy get himself straightened out.

Gilbert saw it as a wilderness. He saw himself standing alone.

"I think you're going to be surprised," said Gilbert, "when I get through with it." He selected two trees and tied the twine to one of them and then walked from tree to tree until the twine was in four lines. He took the twine in his hand, slashed it with a knife. Those were the dimensions of the cabin. "I picked up a lot watching my father," he said. "The thing I don't know is the roof."

"You get the sides up and we'll cover it with something."

Rowiger was trying to drive a stake with his coat and vest on, his garters showing whenever he kneeled. He paused to wipe moisture from his glasses, then fitted them to his face, pushing the lenses as close as possible to his eyes. He grasped the stake in both hands, and Gilbert picked up the sledge. That Rowiger had such thin wrists and fingers made Gilbert unwilling to bring the sledge down as hard as he liked to. Later, removing a slight sag from the center of the tent, Gilbert jerked the line taut and took a bit of skin from the man's hands. Rowiger said nothing. He did not even look at his hands, only clenched them together a moment.

354

"I'll have the foundations dug day after tomorrow. So if you can bring cement and sand."

"Good as done," said Rowiger. He was encouraged by the boy's enthusiasm, and began to be a little more hopeful. The slow trip up the mountain had raised a good many doubts, and the isolation of the past two hours had increased that uneasiness. Yet he was more than ever convinced that the boy was in need of being alone, alone with a responsibility which was not too great, but sufficient to keep him occupied.

"You're out of shape," said Gilbert.

"Don't I know it," Rowiger agreed affably. "I never had much, but I've sure lost it." Taking a watch from his pocket, he opened the case and studied his whole hand. "I suppose I better head home."

They went down the hill, hunting their way since they had not yet worn a path, Rowiger lifting his skinny legs high. Gilbert came to the car and took the tow line and secured it to the bumper and then around a small tree. It was to serve as a drag brake. "Maybe I better ride part way." He was thinking of the difficulties they had had getting up the mountain. Walking around the car, he kicked against the tires.

"No need," said Rowiger. "Say, maybe you'd rather keep it up here?"

"No." Gilbert looked at the car, appraising it. "I want to be as far away from that town as I can get." They shook hands and Rowiger got into the car. Gilbert watched until the dust that the tree was throwing up hid everything. For a while he stood there, listening to the air get quiet. It seemed to him that all his life he had wanted to be alone.

The high parts of the mountain were bare. Trees put most of their growth into roots which hung down over and between rocks, twisted and misshapen by the deceptions they had encountered in the search for moisture. They had pushed things out of the way. There was a hardened looseness in their grip which indicated the beginning of death. Their purpose had been no more than to break loose rock so that the next seed could take a firmer grip.

The horizon of the sky was below him and the curvature of the earth everywhere apparent. He was standing on the mountain his father had chosen many years earlier.

Gilbert set to work. There was more rock than earth to be dug, and his hands were soon sore from picking. Tiny bits of stone stung his face as they flew up. Once he pulled his eyelid down, blew his nose into his fingers three times, then pulled his shirt off, feeling it stick, not knowing where to lay it because it was wet.

By nightfall he had four holes dug. He went to a tree and pressed his back against it to straighten his spine. He spent the night sprawled among the foundation holes, while the empty tent made noises and moonlight changes in appearance as the wind picked up during the middle of the night.

He woke in the twilight of dawn, put on his shirt, got a bucket and stumbled over the rocks in the direction of the Bluegill. In the early morning the water glittered from its own swiftness and turbulence; as he tried to catch some in a pail, it almost tore the handle from his hands, making him feel how his hands were weakened. He pushed his face into the middle of the pail and washed and drank at the same time. The water was so cold he felt a pleasant numbness. He returned to the tent and started a fire.

He worked steadily, pacing himself, and seemed satisfied to take out an inch at a time. By evening he had the holes dug. Taking from the tent the rifle Rowiger had given him, he went into the lower forest, marking trees that would make good logs. He kept balancing the rifle in his hand, feeling a distrust for it. Between the trees the air was faintly greenish in taste, with an occasional humid cobwebby smell. The treetops prevented the pale twilight from reaching down to where he stood, but above the timberline the mountain shone red and purple.

There came over Gilbert a peacefulness. He sat against a tree, the rifle across his knees. The Bluegill was the only thing that made noise other than himself. The portion of the brook by which he was sitting made light sounds, suckings and wigglings, drippings and giggles. Watching it for more than a few minutes disturbed him. He snorted with disgust at himself and went toward the tent, pushing bushes aside with his rifle.

He did not bother to build a fire. He did not want even that much companionship. He sat hunched over his own knees, breaking one stick after another into small pieces. The stars were bright when next he looked up, a startling white brightness that for a moment made him feel too near them.

Time passed. The stars seemed to become scarce in the vastness of the night, so that individual shine was their only asset, austere and lonely, frozen in their habit of roaming. They had a kind of light that made the pupils of his eyes open too wide.

Below was Nesquehon, a blurred smear of light, a grayish mist that damp sinus-laden atmosphere gleaned from the chimneys of the openhearth and the blast-furnaces. He wished the town were farther away, beyond sight.

Wind was blowing in the valley below, rising as far uphill as it could; there were explosions as trees on the lower level of the mountain stiffened and resisted. One strong gust rushed up the mountain, and because he could hear it, he looked for it, and it caught against him, pressing the flesh on his face against the bones, renewing his self-importance. He held one arm straight up into the air, as if to halt the wind and prevent it from passing him, feeling in the cupped palm of his hand the same good confidence as when a baseball hit there and stuck.

Then he went to bed. And he completed the cabin. But if that wind had not come, or if he had not risen to greet it, he would have walked back to Nesquehon that night.

lets do something
   what
      anything lets do something different for a change
        what
           theres a ken maynard movie the last show hasnt started
              it stinks i saw it
                if somebodyll loan me a dime ill go ive got the two cents
lets hitch a ride somewhere
   where
      anywhere we can get a ride
     ill go   if we cant think of anything better to do
       nobody would pick us up this time of night theres too many of us
         we dont all have to go
since that law against hitchhiking you cant even get a ride in the daytime
  its not against the law
    it is so
      the law states you must have one foot on the curb
        the law says the owner of the car is responsible
          the hell with the law too many people beat on the head thats
         whats wrong
          anyhow we cant all of us get a ride
 if we wait much longer itll be too late for the movie
  i told you once it stinks
    would you please not block the door i dont mind you standing here please
    let people in and
      out he said you heard him
       we sorry

old bastard i dont see anybody wantin by
push me once more i dare you
ahhhesallright
whosallright
doesnt anybody have a car
nats got a ford how about it nat well buy gas
i gotta date saturday if i ask the old man now i cant have it saturday o
night a week is all besides he wouldnt give it this late anyhow
you dont need a million excuses ones good enough
lets just take a walk we can go out by the reservoir and see whats going on
yes lets
all we ever do is take walks
im not going for one i think olga will let me walk her home im going
hang around an see
youve been hanging around her for months an i never seen you spe
to her let alone walk her home
thats my business aint it im doing all right i have my own way
doing things
if shes got a cherry left ill eat it
you lay off you hear
kissmine kissmineown kissmineownsweet
anybody care for a coke dont all holler at once cause i aint buying
im sick of cokes
im never sick of cokes
theres no girls inside just geenan and her crowd
does she have a car
no but she told me once she makes boys get on the bottom when it rains
oh her shes got grass stains clear through on her butt
jesus fellows i couldahadda date   with nancy   if id known this aint
gonna do nothing
what times it getting to be
after nine
that late   time sure flies
id play the machine but you got the tilt out of whack i told you not to ke
shoving it i told you now it tilts just pushing the nickel in
ahhh i guess i can shake it if i wanna you dont own the place
but you werent playing it
so what
so keep your hands off when youre not playing
you and whos big enough to make me
me and myself alone
tata time for all little girls to be in bed
smartie
catch the tilt on that
she aint bad who is she
some kid in diapers

358

i heard the curfew is going on again
   it still blows at a quarter of nine
     yeah but it aint enforced
       i didnt hear it tonight did you
i think ill go home you guys are some guys
   hang around thingsll get going after a bit
coke   thirsty   why not   nothing else to do
   after while maybe   not right now

         who is she
       i dont know your guess is as good
       as mine

            another cunt i didnt think shes so hot
             shes got s a
               shes got that time of month you mean
im going down to the poolroom see if anythings doing
   only one table lit when i came past
     what time was that   not exactly what i call great but not bad
             for young stuff
              but who is she
around eight i guess i went to that damn ken maynard picture at six
   too late now is it playing tomorrow i wanted to see it
     listen numskull i said a dozen times it stinks   out loud
       the last ken maynard picture i saw was pretty good i liked it anyhow
anybody going my way   im going home
   walk down to the poolroom   if theres nothing doing ill walk you up the hill
     no im going straight home
           id just like to squeeze it to see if it can make
          juice
          aw how can girls
          pickles mboy big dill pickles
what the hell it aint far out of your way
   i guess ill know better than turn down a date next time nancy practically
begged me too
     why dont you go along to the poolroom you wanna shoot pinball so damn
bad
       i dont like big chief the cushions are dead you cant judge the spring
       i can beat this one when it aint tilting when guys let it alone i had it up
       as high as thirty-four free games the other day and i cashed twenty
       tuesday   ask donny
         honest to god you wouldnt pull my leg
           i dont doubt it i dont doubt it a bit i never will doubt it i never
           shall
what hit him   dont crap me
hes havin his monthly cant you tell
seven chevvies five fords two plymouths
            i wouldnt crap you son not for the
            world you know that
   isnt anybody gonna drink a pause that refreshes i hate to sit by my lonesome
    is olga still in there if she is ill go in

359

she and darlene left long ago   but who in hell is sh
   she couldnt have i saw her
     go look then i oughta know i have eyes dont i
get your car nat   oh for craps sake tell me who she
         what a bunch of guys you guys a
         youve never seen the day
    the hell i havent i slapped one to her on th
    church steps
shit on you get your own car
  hold it hold it everybody hold it somebody tell me who
  naomi mijack and shes jail bait
    well whos naomi mijack   whos naomi mijack
         ill get my flashlight
how could i have missed her i was standing right here
  im still in favor of going out to the reservoir if anybodyll go ill get a flashlig
  aw nobodys out there its too cold
            nobodys out the
i wish to hell id gone to the movies   too cold i tell yc
i think ill go to nancys see if theres light in her house
yah sue mika suna fima oiny deba la hey shes too fat for me
vrock de da pee on you sis bum bah rah rah rah
  come on go with me   its never too cold for fucking
    where   there goes that stuck up dorothy pier
     anywhere   you used to have a crush on her
look hes gonna close the store   the hell i did
  but where
    anywhere poolroom movie harrisburg middletown even out to the reservo
    i dont care just so we go
     you guys are chicken you never want to do anything
      you just wait man waitll you see me saturday
       cant we think of anything to do
         i did not i never did you cant prove
i can go home and go to bed
  hey what say we go to the roller skatin rink
    nats the one holdin up the works   if hed just get his goddam car
     now listen fellows   fell lows   im saying it for the very last time the ve
     very last time   did you see that
         what
         that rat come out of the sew
IS ANYBODY GOING MY WAY OR ARE YOU JUST GOING TO STAND AROUND

    Naomi came to visit him. She was wearing jeans and a shirt. The
first thing he noticed was the firm breasts prodding into the shirt. It

surprised him, but did not keep him from grabbing her by both arms and kissing her.

"You sure made me walk a long way to see you," she said. "What the heck you way up here for?"

Gilbert did not waste a moment. He showed her all four sides of the cabin, showed her the tent, and let her feel how tough his hands were. He was wearing a red hunting shirt, open most of the way down his chest. His face, unshaved for a month, was tough looking. He was wearing good boots and a wide leather belt, strapped hard against his waist.

He asked about school and home and father. "I've had a hunch he'd be up here trying to make me go back." He began to chew on a piece of bark. "Yeah, I'm doing pretty good," he admitted. "No school, nobody to take crap from, money in my pocket." He stretched himself, pushing his boots roughly among the stones. Then he trotted to the Bluegill and came back with six brown bottles under his arms. "Beer," he said. "Got it in Highspire." He opened a bottle, sniffed it, then handed it to his sister. The next bottle he lifted to his mouth without smelling. "Yeah, I don't keep myself cooped up. I been to Harrisburg and down to Highspire." He offered her a cigarette. "I'm pretty satisfied."

Naomi was drinking her beer faster than she should have. "Hey, I forgot to tell you," she said. "I've got a boyfriend."

Gilbert drained the fuzz from the bottle, bumping it against his teeth, then pitched the bottle down the mountainside.

"He ain't much. But he'll do until I get a better one." She laughed. "He promised me his football sweater."

"Well, you watch yourself," said Gilbert. "If I was you, I wouldn't worry much about boys. You win yourself a scholarship or something." He opened another bottle. "Me, I may not amount to much. I'll probably be satisfied living right here the rest of my life. But you get the best . . . I been thinking of setting up a sawmill, maybe I can get you money to go to college."

"Huh!" said Naomi. "I still got high school to get through."

After her second beer, her eyes were a little shiny. Gilbert drank quite a bit himself. It made him feel good to know she had come to see him, and he felt a sense of protectiveness over her such as he had not been able to feel in a long time. They went down to the Bluegill for more beer, and then they sang a couple of drinking songs, smoking the same cigarette, handing it back and forth. He taught her a song that was a little naughty.

361

Later, he had to carry her to the tent, feeling the weight and the softness of a young woman in his arms, and put her in his cot. He sat crouched in the tent, watching for any sign of movement, his eyes blinking more slowly than usual. It was nearly dark when he woke her.

At the bottom of the mountain he smelled her breath for her and gave her money for chewing gum. Naomi was a little afraid of going home so late.

"Just tell him you were with me. Tell him I wouldn't let you leave."

Gilbert went closer to the town than he intended. When his sister saw that he was unwilling to go farther, she said, "Maybe you oughtn't stay up here. Maybe you ought to come home nights."

He shook his head. "No," he said. "I know where I'm better off."

But as he climbed toward the cabin there were times when he was in such a bad mood that his hands would try to destroy any bush that slapped against him.

"I may come to hate the whole world some day," he thought.

31

There was too much wood. Gilbert built an enormous bonfire, long before it was dark enough to be appreciated, before the picnic baskets had even arrived.

The cabin was finished. Rowiger had told him he could live in it. Gilbert had every reason to feel cheerful. He had shown evidence of his determination, proof he was at last getting himself straightened out. He had finally accomplished something.

Bart came with Dorothy Pierce; they were walking with their arms around each other, walking with the perfect rhythm that only young people who have walked together along many streets on many evenings can have.

Naomi had a boy friend. She was barelegged and wearing a short, tight skirt and was walking exactly the way she had once been cautioned against.

A girl in a light tan dress, a girl he did not care to meet, was looking in his direction. It made him furious that Rose should have dared to come.

Rowiger was talking to Mrs. Pierce. Her movements and hair style would have made her appear a tall girl, if it had not been for the boy standing beside her and the possessive manner in which he held to the sleeve of her dress.

Gilbert threw one log after another onto the fire. He saw what kind of picnic it was going to be. It rankled in his heart that his existence had been so little missed.

Rodger took a knife from his pocket. He pulled at the blade but his fingers slipped off. "I can't," he said, and handed it to his mother.

Irene handed it to Rowiger. "It's a lovely place," she said.

Rowiger studied a moment, as if suspecting some trick or complexity involved, and then opened it. The knife simply had a strong spring. "Yes," he said, "only it gets chilly at night." He handed the knife to Irene, and she stood looking at it.

"But such a relief from the heat down there," she said, looking down toward the river. She did seem to be glad to be away from the town, and Rowiger seemed a little embarrassed. Rodger held the knife with his hands out in front of him and went to cut a green stick. He was going to cook hot dogs and have fun.

Gilbert went to the fire with a new armload of wood. Rose, sitting on a rock, was shielding her face from the smoke.

"Hear you're doing pretty well," he said.

"Fine." Her eyes gave themselves to him immediately.

"A new start, a clean slate," he said. "For you and for me." He laughed. "You see my new start. What do you think of my new start?"

He broke a stick across his knee and threw both parts on the fire.

"I think you've done wonderful."

"Oh sure, really great." He threw a chunk of wood so hard that when it struck, sparks came out around it and whirled as high as they could. Bright bits of light warned of the nearness of night. . . .

Darkness was just beyond the tip of his cigarette. Gilbert kept feeding the fire as if he were in need of light. Little wind gusts kept the bright part of the light flickering and deceptive. The roots of trees seemed to crawl forward and recede, the tops of rocks glinted and vanished. But at the base of the light was a steadier glow which kept the eyes of people particularly apparent.

Naomi was angry with him for keeping watch. He sensed from the moment their eyes encountered that she was ashamed, that it was only spite and defiance which made her keep turning up her face and putting it against Jod's mouth. He felt nothing except contempt. His anger with his sister was for showing cheap taste, humiliating herself.

Then he saw he was mistaken. They were embracing and holding each other tight. Jod pulled her against him in the rough manner that made her breasts hurt, and there was, for a moment, that unmistakable look which no girl can hide, of bewilderment and pleasure.

His fury turned upon Jod, who was older, who was male, who was taking advantage.

Yet he could not do or say anything. Rowiger and Mrs. Pierce were the chaperones. And there in a circle about the fire were others, Tim and Kathleen, Bart and Dorothy, Harriet Kuhnna and Billy Sannich, all in each other's arms.

Gilbert was sitting alone with nothing to watch except people sharing themselves, sharing talk, laughter, hands, eyes and lips. Even Mrs. Pierce and her son, if their difference in size had not been so evident, would have appeared in the shimmering fire light as if they too were in love. Rowiger was alone, but did not look alone, was smiling and wagging his finger at something in the sky. The only young person who was alone, watching Gilbert even now, sitting in a tan dress that seemed white in the firelight, he could not go to. He felt it a bitter culmination to all that he had been doing in the past year, hunting for something fresh and new, hunting for peace and a good life.

He was ugly, his personality was against him, he was neither clever nor intelligent, and if he was going to have any sense of accomplishment, it would be to prove that he was loyal to those he loved. The most he could do was keep himself in a position where he could not be further condemned. He could only stay away from Rose. He could only sit and glare at Jod and his sister. He could only sit beside the fire, alone. . . .

"Heck, what a party," said Rodger. "Nobody likes hot dogs. . . ."

Bart spread the blanket at a distance from the bonfire that indicated he was making a compromise between being too near light and too far from warmth. A chilliness was beginning to settle on the bare earth and rock. Dorothy leaned her head on his shoulder and kissed his neck. "It's only three more years," she said. "I'll wait. I can't see what you're so upset about."

"Yes, my three years, your four, my fortune, and at long last, maybe, wedding bells. No thanks." Bart laughed. "You may as well get that dream out of your head. Me, I'm a boy having fun, and if you're wise, you'll be a girl having her fling—before she marries where her father points his finger."

"It isn't like that," said Dorothy. "It just takes time."

"Yeah? When he tells me amscray? I mean in that yippety way of his. Oh, you'll get what you want. But you won't get me. Because he won't let you. And I'm not going to kneel, not for nobody."

"Now we're getting closer," said Dorothy. "What's to stop us from going to Maryland?"

"Specifically," said Bart, "annulment. If that didn't happen, you lose the key to your house and your papa's wallet. With the kind of life I've planned, well, I'm going to have a tough enough time without that."

"What an opinion you have of me," said Dorothy, drawing away.

"That you're spoiled? Yes." Bart put his arm out and pulled her to him. "That you wouldn't be able to stick it out? Emphatically yes."

"I don't see anything to do except refuse to see you. You don't love me."

"Never said I did." Bart waited for her eyes to react. "But I'll say it. I love you—but unless I'm accepted on exactly those terms, not only by you, but your father—no dice." He slapped the blanket. "I don't think it'll happen. Your father and me—nope." He stretched, making himself comfortable. "So why don't we admit this is a summer vacation?" He caught her hair and pulled her face to where he could get at her lips.

Irene was alone. She was sitting on a rock and looking at the fire without seeing it.

Rodger watched her and watched firelight crawl among the rocks and make them red and purple and disclose new rocks where darkness had been. He chucked a stone into the air in a high arc above the bonfire; it missed and struck the edge of the fire and a portion of the flame changed color and sparks flew and acted bewildered, before they found places to hide in the darkness.

Irene's eyes became large and tense. She looked around, as if seeking something she had lost.

Rodger scrambled across the rocks and sat beside her.

"There's a devil in the fire," he said. "Did you hear him cough?"

He grinned, teeth and eyes bright and impish with borrowed light. He was seated in front of Irene, against her legs, using her knees as a place to prop his elbows and have a steady view of her face.

"Do hold your head that way a little," he said. "There's a scrumptious shadow . . . So lovely . . . There, right there," he said, pointing, then pulling his arm away so his own shadow would not interfere. "Don't move, I'm going to kiss it," he said, climbing on his knees and preparing his mouth.

"Oh, Roddy, do act sensible."

"All right, don't put crinkles in your nose, Mother, it's only the shadow I wanted to kiss," he said, sighing. "You'd better let me kiss you, because when I'm fifty you'll be seventy-five, and no pretty shadows will sit on your face, and I shan't want to kiss you."

He felt with his hand until he found a stone that could be pulled loose. "Better duck," he said, covering his head with both hands, "I don't know where it'll land." Before he had finished speaking the stone struck near his shoe and tumbled away. He tried to find it, but although the fire was bright, the earth was dark. "If it was kisses I wanted," he said, "I'd go to that old smooching machine over there." He meant his sister. "You see Bart? He looks like he's got strawberries on his face."

Irene cradled her knees and bent her neck until her forehead rested on the two flat surfaces of her knees. She seemed to try to divide her forehead equally between them, while gravity untangled her hair and spilled it slowly forward from her ears. Her hair was still so beautiful that she had to cut it to keep herself looking young. But at this moment she was heedless of it. "Please, Roddy," came her voice, muffled by the material of her dress, "I'd rather not talk."

"I know," he said. "But do laugh. Just to please me."

He hoped she would raise her head, but she gave no indication of having heard. Rodger rolled on his back, his head against her ankles, grunting at the discomfort of the stones. "I'll ruin my clothes, won't I? I'm so careless," he said. "Do smile. I'll pull down a star and pin it in your hair. I'll bring down that one over there, do you see it? The twinkling one."

Irene looked up for a moment. She saw one cold, white star. . . .

The only thing Rose could see clearly were his boots shining with light. He was placing branches in a way that would encourage the fire to burn straight up at the sky. His hands worked at a steady pace that could only be maintained when flesh does not mind heat. She saw shadows and glitterings and moments of silhouette, hands folding near the flame to reveal thick knuckles, light on the smooth muscles of his neck, his back tense with the curve of crouching and legs braced as if expecting a great weight to come hurtling down upon them.

She wanted to talk with him. Everything which he had done,

every shame which he had inflicted on her, seemed only to strengthen her remembrance of his goodness and kindness. It was a good love she had for Gilbert, a love which admired and respected.

She rose from the cold stone that sitting had not warmed and held her arms over the fire, as if she were passing benediction on it. Her hands were so near the flame that their color was a daytime normal, hanging from slightly reddened arms. She drew her skirt outward and just high enough to bare her knees, holding the skirt in hoop fashion to catch warmth inside. Then she walked, eyes blinded, into the darkness everywhere equal and impenetrable. The radiant heat was lost from the surface of her flesh and she felt chilled. But she continued to walk, slowly, so she would have time to halt, until the bonfire was a redness in the night. She stood with her back pressed against a tree. Now and then she could see silhouettes or hear a cough or a voice. The longer she waited, the more weight she put against the tree.

Her hair stuck to the bark and was disarranged when she pulled her head free. The tree would not permit her to look straight up at the sky, and she had lived in the town too long to be able to feel the importance of stars. But she could feel the division between darkness and light as the cold northern moon, at its best, passed overhead, illuminating and outlining and blowing clouds fat with vaporish silver. Rose had no expectation of making her mind beautifully confused; she simply lit a cigarette to let him know where she was.

The interference of the trees and the smoke combined to make looking at the sky discouraging. She looked toward the fire and could not see his shadow and for a while her ears were sensitive to sound and her eyes alert. Then his shadow reappeared at the bonfire. She decided it was hopeless. His bitterness would never allow him to come to her.

She walked toward the fire, hunting the stone she had left. Her face took on a different appearance when it knew there was light on it. . . .

Bart folded the edge of the blanket over her legs, with that physical intuition for which she liked him. She took off her shoes and they lay side by side, with their faces so close that she had to draw away when she wanted to see him. They dueled with the tips of their noses, touched the extended tips of their tongues and then brought their mouths tight together. She saw Bart's eyes become sensitive, knew her own were, and slid her lips along his jaw and caught the lobe of his ear between her teeth, lightly, yet not too lightly. When she released him, when his hand was feeling his ear, she saw the opportunity to make him confess his love. "I have the car keys," she said. "We can go tonight."

Bart got up and walked off.

Irene saw one cold, white star. Her own husband was like it.

"The left one's too fat," said Rodger. "Did you sprain it?" He was measuring the thickness of her ankles by gripping them between his hands. He started to remove her shoe, but feeling her foot stiffen in resistance, thought better of it. "Why aren't you hairy?" he said, rubbing his fingers over the smoothness of her skin. "Loan me your hankie, Mother, my hands are all black."

It was difficult for him to tell when his hands were clean, and he turned them one way and another to get light on the parts he was trying to see. He tried to remove the smudges on her ankles, but Irene drew her legs under her and sat on them and smoothed her skirt so that her slender knees were hidden. Rodger threw the handkerchief into the fire. For a time the flames did not touch it and then it vanished in a yellow wisp. "I'll buy you a new one," he said, "out of my allowance. Do talk a little. Even if you don't want to. How about a hot dog, could you eat one?"

"Roddy, you're such a pest."

"Oh yes," he agreed. "I am. I am. Pull my ears sixteen times. I have a birthday tomorrow."

"Why must you lie so, Roddy?"

"Because I want my ears pulled. I want you to touch me." He squeezed his face between his hands. "My head hurts. Do rub it for me."

"Does it?" Irene gave him for the first time the full attention of her eyes.

"Cross my heart, it thumps awful." He wriggled about so his head could rest on her lap. "Please believe me. Say you believe me. I want you to."

Irene felt as if there were a large stone resting in her lap. She stroked it with her hands, seeking the temples, keeping her eyes on the darkness to retain the sense of familiarity which her son had given her by lying still and motionless. Her finger tips traced the cheekbones with lightness. From time to time she brushed his hair back and pinched the tip of his nose, the way she had hundreds of times when he was little. He was still so little and young it made her heart ache.

Someone threw wood on the fire; for a moment there was no light. In that darkness she put her mouth on his.

"Your lips are cool," said Rodger. "I like them."

"Shush," Irene said.

"If I were Father, I'd be kissing you all the time."

Her finger rested on his mouth, gently, until she was certain he would not speak. Then her finger drew away gently, slowly, prepared to return, and she sat looking down at him, with tenderness and fear. Her son seemed to her everything that she had never been, fearless, gay, healthy, talkative, and yet she had never encountered anyone with whom she could have such perfect intimacy. There were moments when she felt he was so exactly herself that she could see in him her own life and her own dream.

"I love you so much, Mother."

Her hands smoothed back his hair, giving her a larger view of his face, and she leaned toward him. For a moment she held his head so tight against her stomach that it was hard for him to breathe. He did not resist, for the odor of her and the partial suffocation pleased him.

Then Irene looked down at him with a stern and surprisingly old face. Perhaps it was a trick of firelight, but her face was so rigid and wrinkled that Rodger had an instant of fright.

"You must never say things against your father. Do you hear? He has been good to you."

"I won't say them. I promise."

"I didn't want excitement and thrills," said Irene. "I wanted a good husband and a good family. I have that. I wanted life to be calm and peaceful. I have that. So you must not talk these things of going away and of your father. They are not true.

"You must not talk these things," Irene continued, "because that is how to make difficulties where there are none. I want my life to remain quiet and calm."

The fire, burning evenly, seemed to acknowledge the rightness of her thoughts. She had nearly resolved herself to accept what her mouth had uttered, when sparks swirled out of the fire and doubt and fear leaped in her heart. But that was not for her son to know or be told, that was for herself to endure. . . .

Some of the people were chilled. Gilbert went to the cabin and brought down his blankets and his thickest clothing. He distributed them by the simple method of walking around the fire and dropping a sweater or jacket or blanket beside each person who did not look warm enough. He did not feel such things himself.

Then he sat beside Rowiger. The only thing he mentioned was in regard to his sister, asking in a soft voice if Rowiger would see to it that she got home safely. Then they sat side by side, looking at the sky, seeking nothing except solace for their eyes, seeing the bluish tint which the moon, too bright, had given to nearby areas of the sky. Gilbert kept remembering how Rose had looked as she stood warming her legs before the fire, and he was proud that he had been able to keep himself from going after her, even though he had seen the invitation in her eyes. He felt in control of himself.

Gilbert shifted his position to break the wind when Rowiger lighted the lantern. They parted, Gilbert feeling as if he had had a long conversation in which he had unburdened his soul. Faith in his sister returned, a faith which he had not had earlier; she was only seeking happiness, he must not condemn her; as he sat there a little longer, his own problems seemed to become clearer and less burdensome. He looked at the fire to see how long it had been since he had put wood on it. . . .

Gilbert walked behind her and dropped something that her hand sought and knew to draw beneath her. "Thank you," Rose said. But he continued to walk around the fire, dropping blankets and old clothing beside everyone. He sat beside Rowiger and Rowiger moved and sat beside him. He said something to Rowiger and their eyes gave each other attention, and then a long period of silence in which the blanket beneath her lost its comfort. The fire was burning away from her, the air that fed it passing on each side of her and between her arms. Rowiger made a couple of rusty, screechy sounds with his hands bent over the rocks and a new small fire sprang up from between the rocks. Only as Rowiger stood and lifted the flame and the glass lighted into glow was she able to tell it was a lantern. He started off into the darkness, carrying the lantern above his head so that it would not interfere with his vision.

Naomi and Jod went running after Rowiger. She saw the quickness and eagerness of their running. It made Rose feel more lonely. It made her remember a time when they had been her friends. She sat with her head on her arms, soothing her eyes from the gathering results of smoke, waiting for the time when she would be able to go home, waiting for time to pass, waiting for a sound in the night. She could feel the steady radiance of the fire, a thin heat which did not warm her, and at moments a hush, a turning of directions, a feeling of being pushed. Her posture made her breasts feel weighted, and she was unaware of the moonlight touching at one spot on the back of her neck. Her body seemed to require no response to anything, only to have response without requiring it, wanting nothing it encountered. She had never felt so useless. It was as if her body had suffered all it was ever going to suffer and was now only moving heavily and unwillingly through time.

She could not resent Rowiger for having taken her from a life in which there had been happiness among children. She could not resent the pains he was taking with her, teaching, explaining. But she had nothing to support her except his kindness and that of Mrs. Pierce, and it made her feel more deeply. She had no right or desire to be among these people. Gilbert had unsettled the little will to improve herself which she had for a time felt, had given her the same odd, sickened feeling as when she had seen him hold a flashlight in his mouth and illuminate himself within, the same sense of distortion as a pumpkin grinning in the night.

She had better ask Rowiger to find her a job in Harrisburg. There would not be this strain of encounter, which always left her feeling badly . . .

Gilbert went for more wood. It was his own fault, using so much. He heard something like an animal scurrying through the bushes and took two more steps forward, alert, as the mountain had taught him to be. The scurrying was whispering, and the first thing he detected was its nearness.

Then he could see and not see, see without detail, two people against the shadow of a tree. It was his sister pressed against the tree, and Jod, who seemed to be embracing both her and the tree. Even as he was about to break forward, intrude, he knew the sound was not whispering. It was the excited breathing and the sound of struggle that was not struggle, short shiftings of feet, abrupt movements and pushings, and the interference of clothing. Gilbert stood with more tenseness and command of stillness than he had ever known could exist, held by that which he could not approach and from which there was no retreat, his eyes verifying everything his ears noted. He had a feeling of being in utter stillness. He stared at the shadows against the tree, dispossessed of brotherhood, witness with his eyes and ears and his heart.

As he continued to watch, his emotion seemed to decline into a callous revulsion, so that he found his position the same as the janitor's had been one Sunday morning outside of the church, trying to separate two copulating dogs. Except Gilbert was going to turn his back and walk away from it. . . .

"Is it better? The headache?"

"It still hurts," Rodger replied, grinning.

"And your throat? How does your throat feel?"

"Good." He moved and saw his shadow against his mother, his shadow bigger than himself.

The moon was bright now that it had pulled free from the mountain. Rodger, tan from swimming, was bronzed by the red light of the bonfire, but Irene, with her pale flesh, seemed chosen by the moon.

She looked up at the moon, more dependable for calm reflections than a fire. When first her eyes lifted bright silver fell on them and silver the weight of dew caught among her lashes and made them blink. She gazed at the moon until it whitened, until it became pale and flecked with thin blue and transparent gray. The faint vapor of her own exhalations had twinkles like miniature stars.

She closed her eyes and there were two faint moons painted on the insides of her eyelids, while a moon of darkness floated across. The tips of her teeth felt as if cold water had touched them and there was something inside her feet that made her point them in ballet style, in spite of her shoes. She sat very still, feeling beauty grope about inside her, seeking for a place to which it could cling, seeking, so it seemed, for her soul. Beauty and the soul, both so shy they would touch and not be touched and therefore never touched, but came, only on rare moments, into proximity. She sat very still, until she could no longer recall the splendor of the moon or the reflective texture of her own mind, until it was her own emotion which she tasted of and was held by. She felt at that moment as if beauty were a delicate frost and a suspension of time, a frost of such thin composition that it could nearly kill the heart. It was not then to be welcomed, but to be accepted with fear.

It was the bright season of the stars, the air crisp and dry, and the stars had the sharp contour and ragged splendor which made the night seem an act of wizardry. The sky had the dark, shining quality of the sea as it ebbed and gathered. She chose among the stars a few favorites. Her eyes were wide open, no longer smitten or awed, but appraising the entire sky, the contrast between the fragility of light and the vastness and fury of darkness, as calmly and as justly as she would have the long stems of roses, unaware that her skirt was drenched with silver, that it seemed to splay out among the dark rock and glitter from her slightest move. Moonlight brocaded her slender arms and painted her eyes and teeth.

Rodger could sense the change in his mother. With his head in her lap he had felt the swiftness of her breathing and the tenseness in her limbs. He looked up at her. Her gaze was so rapt, her attention so direct and impenetrable, that Rodger felt ashamed. He knew her eyes were seeing something pretty, and he looked at the sky himself, and could not find where she was looking, even though he tried to hold his head at the same angle and position. Yet he knew she was seeing something, for that was one of his favorite memories, of how she had sat beside his bed at night and looked out through the window, and then, with her eyes as they were now, told him in her soft voice about the pretty thing she had seen. Every evening it had been something different, and he had been impatient for the time when he could see it himself, see it with her. Now it did not seem to him that he was ever going to see.

"You're greedy," he said. "You gobble all the moonlight. See, there's none left for me."

He held a hand toward the moon, twisting it in the manner in which mirrors are turned to catch reflections, until the palm was nearly white. Then he closed his hand swiftly and pretended to eat what was inside. "It tastes like snails," he said.

"Oh shush," said Irene.

For a moment she did not remember that he was her son and that she loved him. She was still looking at the sky. She had a sudden feeling that this was the last and ultimate opportunity, and that it had come when she was least prepared. It had nothing to do with the sky now, nothing to do with a pantomime of stars or the cold vanity of the moon. It was not a young girl bewildered by life and the thought of marriage. It was not a woman with a cold husband bringing something from the sky to sleep with through the night. It was a need to find resistance against everything which she had selected as the best in life, a need to arm herself against her own sensitivities. For everything which was good and fine in her life had become a debility, not because it had fault, because it was without fault. She had engaged in a sacrifice to time and to her children, to gain her children time, and now that time was not gained, and it had only bound her wrists, and she knew that if she did not soon resist her soul would sink to that place inside where souls hide so effectively as frequently to get lost.

Someone seemed to be breaking sticks high above her and two

yellow stars went whirling far into the night, and Irene looked at the earth and saw one of the children putting wood on the fire. She felt suddenly tired, exhausted. Her eyes, which had continued to court the lights in the sky for their own pleasure and occupation, while she had been caught in her own gathering turbulence, were now aching faintly from incorrect focus. The rock had cut a series of grooves into her knees and along the side of her leg, making her feel older. She sat upright and rubbed and kneaded the skin to remove the marks, but they would not disappear. She patted her hair at the various places which would tell her its condition, seemed satisfied, and brought her fingers to touch along her neck. She could feel the wrinkles and the faint but nevertheless definite looseness of the flesh.

She searched about in the darkness for her pocketbook and a moment later had a lipstick tube in one hand and a compact in the other. The firelight was not bright or steady enough for her to see her mouth in the circle of glass, but she applied the strokes with confidence. It was not the reflection she needed, rather the act of holding something firmly in her left hand, of creating a familiar atmosphere in which the habit of many years could perform itself.

"Let me put your lipstick on, Mother. I can. I've watched you. Please?"

Irene reached out and put a dot on the tip of his nose. Rodger rubbed his nose and looked at his hand to see if it was actually red.

"Well, loan it to me then. I want to put it on my lips. I want to see how it feels."

"You talk too much, Roddy."

"You're right," he said. And then he leaned forward and caught her wrists, and she saw the same grave and at moments terribly black eyes which had been her own fifteen years earlier, and she saw the passionate seriousness which came to her son so seldom that it was always a hurt to her. "I don't deserve a mother like you," he said. "Not really. I mean I'm such a nuisance and all. But I need you. Honest."

Nothing he could have told her would have been more obvious. It was exactly that which had held her in bondage for so long, and in reluctant acceptance of the unhappiness of her life with her husband. It was exactly that which had made her accept less than her expectations, and engage in a hopeless struggle with cleverness, a struggle which time and again made her heart limp and wretched. Yet, as always, the thought of being needed filled her with the same delicious weakness and excitement that the smell of violets brought to her. She had been needed so little in life that she could not refuse, would not refuse, and drew her son's head against her breast and felt the large round spot of warmth it made there.

"Of course you do . . . Of course you do. And I need you, you can't imagine how much at times . . . Only, my love, it's something we can't talk about, we must only feel it." He could feel her breath in his hair. "If we need each other then we will not need so many other things, we can get along on less." She looked out across the fire. "You," she said rubbing her cheek against his hair, "you just keep on being a nuisance. . . . It'll help your mother more than you can know."

They sat there in each other's arms, before the bonfire which shone on lovers of another kind . . .

Dorothy Pierce began to believe Bart had gone home. He was capable of walking off and leaving her, just as he was capable of coming to her the next day and talking as if nothing had happened. It was inability to get through to his feelings that made her furious. Even when he admitted love it was in a cold, careless manner. Yet she was convinced he did care for her.

Dorothy was watching Gilbert. She was curious. She had never been introduced to any of the Mijacks, and as she looked at the bearded shape hunched over the fire, eyes glaring, she supposed him older than Bart. When he stood, as the light on his face changed direction and emphasis, she saw the enormous jaw and smallness of eye, particularly the large, full lips. It made her feel she would never want him to come near her. As he walked into the darkness, with a hulking movement, she was glad at not having seen more of him.

In a short while, before her eyes had left that area, as the eyes somehow always remain after, sweeping up, he returned, carrying the limb of a tree under each arm. He propped one on the ground, held it with one hand and pressed his boot into it. Then he hung it between two rocks and jumped up and down, legs folding almost against his stomach. It was primitive and ferocious. He held the branch straight out in front of him and struck seven times on the rocks. Then he seemed to look at it more closely and admire it, and walked to the bonfire and held the branch while the fire gradually made it two pieces.

His eyes swung and made encounter with hers. His eyes had an almost insane intensity. Dorothy looked into the palms of her hands, even closed her lids a moment. Something made her eyes feel compelled to rise, even though they expected a second encounter. Instead they saw the branch divide, saw him lift the two pieces overhead, red eyes high in the night, and whirl the sticks wildly, creating the effect a child does with sparklers, but with the difference of the sound of wind and of furious expenditure of strength. Again his eyes caught hers, holding them this time in apprehension, staring at her with such wild, open hatred that she felt an actual fear of seeing the flaming sticks come hurtling across at her. Without meaning to, she felt herself crouch, and felt a slight panic that her movement might provoke an action that he had not yet found intention for. Her body knew the vulnerability of being feminine. Instead, he brought the sticks down onto the bonfire with such force that his hands did not have time to release them before they bounced, then settled into the fire.

Dorothy could not watch. She felt as if there had been revealed to her something odious about herself. She did not quite understand. She was accustomed to eyes, to all kinds of looks, but had never seen anyone look at her with such directness, a look that ignored all surface personality, and bore toward her a constant, massive declaration of hatred. The worst was that his eyes had not once recognized her as a person; she recalled the manner in which Bart would draw his head too erect, his eyes chilled, denying her for an instant her existence. There was a comparison between the furious impassioned performance she had just witnessed and the cold, superior leadership, the perfect physical ease that Bart had so often shown her. There was a comparison between the frank, naked hatred which she had seen in those eyes above the fire and the cool, dispassionate warnings Bart had given her.

Dorothy remembered her father's antagonism toward Bart. She remembered how Bart had spoken only once of his family, hinting that they were a strange breed of people, either inhuman or too human, and his eyes had twisted and fixed on her, so that she had known he included himself. There was a feeling of having entangled herself with incomprehensible people, of skirting on the edge of danger, so that all the previous objections to marriage, which had seemed so trivial, stood under a new significance. She sensed that she was about to become involved in kinds of passions that she could not understand, passions that would not tolerate interference, that would sacrifice her to prevent interference. She knew she was still on the side of her father, that she was guilty of making for herself a summer vacation.

For a moment it appeared only as if Gilbert were standing in front of the girl, saying something that made her mouth open wide with surprise. Then the girl was only sitting there, rocking back and forth, making no protest. "Beasts!" thought Dorothy. "Swine!" But for the moment she too was afraid of all men, and particularly of the Mijacks. . . .

Gilbert passed directly in front of Rose, a log slung under each arm. His boots made one sound, firm and heavy, and his trousers a quick, scissored whipping, as he managed to step across her legs without stumbling. Rose, not having had enough warning, was afraid to move for fear of entangling.

Whether it was her foot catching against the side of his boot, or the sight of her cringing, or only what was in his eyes, Gilbert put his boot on her foot, holding it for a moment from a position of conquest. Her eyes looked up at him, startled. Then his boot came down with its full weight and that of the logs. He lifted his other leg so all his weight would rest on one place.

Rose sat straight up and opened her mouth wide and her eyelids pinched tight shut. She remained in this rigid position, quivering, making the rigidity more intense, air going out of her mouth in the same endless flow as a long scream, except there was no sound. Then her hands went out and clutched around his leg, where they seemed to attempt to retain the boot, where they squeezed and clutched at the boot, while her body made a rocking motion, back and forth.

Gilbert went to the fire and knelt and fed logs into the flames in oven fashion. His eyes peered into the flames. The fire seemed transparent and the individual flames thin, weak, devoid of color. His nostrils were clean from the sharpness of his breathing. He could smell the wood smoke in his clothes and distinguish it from the smell of the fire.

Rose sat holding her foot between both hands, holding so loosely that it seemed her hands were only protecting it. Her eyes were closed and she was still rocking back and forth, and she did not make a sound. She was not aware it was getting darker around her.

Gilbert was piling wood on the fire, more and more, until he had shut in most of the light, until darkness crawled to where he was kneeling. When he could not see anyone clearly, he sank back on his haunches. . . .

The fire had burned too long. He wanted to stamp on it with his boots. Fire should be brief, fierce and hardy, and not smother endlessly in its own ash, not linger and prolong existence through slow

377

suffocation. It was painful to watch the embers small into twinkles and twitchings of light and smoke hover above, like fog settling on the earth. He found a few small pieces of wood, which gave his hands no pleasure to touch. His eyes were hunting the best place to drop the scraps of wood, his feet had the stiff-boned air of being uncertain where he was walking, and he did not feel anything when his boots trod on the ashes and made fine dust rise around his knees.

For a moment he felt a little tenderness for one flame which was still trying to burn clean and tall. Living alone, he had come to have feeling for fire. Fire deserved attention and the best wood. It seemed that one flame was the only thing clean and friendly which he had salvaged from the night.

The fire was near death. He wished this night was over. He was breathing heavily and wearily. He pushed a bundle of dry weeds over the ashes until flame jumped up inside the weeds and made a lot of trivial noise. The weeds changed shape and began to unravel and seemed full of thin black wire and crooked splinters, and the flame seemed caged within and not burning them. Then the weeds dissolved into a bright red puff and were gone.

Rose dropped the blanket beside him and walked off down the mountain.

He remembered the disgust with which he had returned. Not honor, love, or passion, only pushed up against a tree, pinned and wriggling. He had felt cool and bitter, and yet with a freedom. Performing the function which had been his all evening, he had dragged in a branch, had tried to break it, and in being resisted had flown into a rage, had stamped up and down on it. His eyes had found himself watched, had swung to encounter with a passionate hatred of a world which would not let him have privacy. And when he had passed by Rose he had not seen her, had only stepped over, as he would have over a stone, until her foot caught his boot. There was no particular reason for having done what he did. There had not needed to be a reason. But after he had already stepped on her, when the pain which he saw in her face had taken on meaning, he had twisted his boot with disgust and hatred and contempt.

A tiny cherry-red flame that did not seem to be able to find anything to burn ran frantically back and forth over the ashes, then vanished. It was how his soul felt, like that. Only a flat bed of embers, the size of worms crawling over the ground, remained.

People were moving about, gathering together picnic baskets, organizing for departure. He kept his eyes on the fire. The sky had be-

378

come more clearly defined from the darkness, and there were rocks with tips faintly purple by moonlight.

The picnic was over. People were moving down the mountain toward where the two cars were parked.

Rowiger and Mrs. Pierce were discussing how they would get the cars turned around.

The young people were discussing who would go in which car.

Rodger had taken hold of his sister's hand and was using it to guide himself. He was sleepy. He had two pebbles in his pocket.

Dorothy gave her brother her hand because she did not have a companion.

Kathleen and Tim were still walking with their arms around each other. Time did not seem to be able to affect them.

Jod walked a little awkwardly because his trousers were wet and sticky against his leg.

Naomi was disgusted.

The fire was so low that only by poking into the darkness of the ground with a stick could he uncover bits of light. He did it with the same curious absent-mindedness which can be seen in a boy who has been fishing without luck.

The moon was going down in the second side of the sky and was nearing the time of swift fall.

Gilbert threw aside the stick, despairing of finding more light, and sat with his head between his hands, as if trying to crush some thought or feeling within his skull. He sat there alone with his boots touching the black ashes of his victory.

At that moment there was a small but distinct noise and a pebble rolled past Gilbert and into the ashes of the fire. . . .

As the pebble rolled past and into the ashes, it uncovered a few flecks of light. If it had not been for those tiny bits of light he would have continued to sit still. Instead he had for a moment the attention of a child who had thrown a firecracker and heard no explosion. He listened down the hill and heard nothing. He rose and stood in a straight upright posture, like a sentinel.

Then he took long, powerful strides through the darkness, his legs making the fullest swing allowed, his trousers so tight the friction made his legs smart. He had a feeling of moving toward some powerful purpose. He could hear himself stamping about, the harsh and weighted sound of his boots. He had the strange heartbroken sensation that his actions were of no moral consequence.

He made no effort to hear. He reached a decision of direction, a

379

decision based on no evidence, and moved heavily and quickly across the mountain. There was one fixed idea in his mind, a suspicion that he was not alone. He began to crane his head forward, peering through the underbrush in a bent, shortened-neck manner. . . .

Exactly when Rose began to suspect she was being followed, she did not know. She felt it first as a sense of solitude and isolation. She halted and listened. In addition to hunting for the brook, she was hoping to see the light of the fire. She should never have tried to start home alone.

She halted, the sound seemed to halt, but with the delay of an echo. She walked as far as a tree and stepped in behind it. She waited and was about to risk walking a little further, preferring to hear the sound again to listening to the silence, when she heard it begin without her having moved. Her fingers had an irresistible desire to break off the edge of bark to which they were holding.

"Who is it?" she called.

The tree seemed her best protection. But after she had stood beside it for a time and heard nothing, she risked creeping away, moving as silently as she could, resisting the temptation to run. Hearing a car, she hurried, since it indicated the direction of the road. She had remarkably good fortune, not striking anything. She ran so heavily, her own breathing was the only thing to be heard. The ground was softer and the brush dense. She moved cautiously, depending on her eyes, with a tendency to avoid places that might have afforded safe footing, simply because they were darker.

There was a hissing. It was the Bluegill. There was no danger of stepping in it, for the banks were crowded with bushes. Cold water warmer than the night had thrown up a mist, making the stream partly luminous. It was strange to come upon steady, pale light after having been in darkness. There was a disturbing unreality even in the sound of the water.

Then came a heavy crashing, and she whirled, prepared for encounter. The stream gave her defense against further retreat.

At that moment a glimmer of light broke through the trees, a sharp twisting blade of brilliant light. She heard another car. It was near. She turned and ran. The light twisted and turned so frequently that she could never seem to run in quite the right direction. She put all her effort into running. The light made a beacon raking that seemed to pass right across her; she threw her arms wide, her forehead spangled with light, her face shining with radiant happiness. There was a moment when she feared she was directly in the path of the automobile. Then the light swung away and in its stead was a small red dot that bobbed up and down.

"Help me," she screamed.

The sound of the car lingered, holding in the air like something which she kept encountering. She ran against a tree, not accidentally, caught hold of it and held herself erect, with her face pressed against the bark. She looked back across her shoulder and saw him coming toward her, with a strip of thin light along his arm, which was upraised. Her mouth opened to speak to him and then it opened wider and her hands clutched at her stomach. As his arm rose again she turned and ran. She veered toward the creek. . . .

Gilbert saw her silhouetted against the white vapor and then saw her vanish. He plunged in too, arms up about his forehead, as if expecting a major test of strength, as if expecting to bump something. He stumbled as he encountered only shallow water, had to put his hands down under the water and scramble forward, boots slipping on the mossy bottom and the tilting stones.

Her arms flew up overhead and she pitched forward. There was no need for him to tighten his grip, for she lay without moving. He did nothing except hold, the slippery skin and wetness of his hands making him distrust, the creek pulling at his boots. He did not use strength until he felt her try to rise. Then gradually he pulled himself up over her until she was pinned among countless loose stones, until his boots could not feel the creek.

"Just let me go," she said. "Please, let me go."

She continued to struggle. Gilbert waited. Whenever she made any serious demonstration of strength, he pressed her face into the rocks.

"You're going to live with me," he said.

Rose began to weep. He could feel the shaking of her body.

"We deserve each other," he said.

There was no bitterness in his voice.

"That's not going to do any good," he said, feeling her try to rise.

There was no sound except her weeping and the roar of the water as gravity hurled it down the mountain. One by one he opened the buttons down the back of her dress. He opened the buttons gently. He rubbed his face in the hollow of her spine, softly, to feel through his beard. He knew it hurt her to lie pressed against the stones. He unbuttoned himself.

"Listen," he said. "You must believe. You must believe we have a chance."

381

She could feel his hand thrusting between her legs.

"Listen, we have the cabin. I have a lease from the state to cut timber. So we're going to be free. I swear we have a chance of being happy."

She could feel his hand in her crotch, trying to excite her. He began to roll her over, slowly, with insistent pressure. He let her summon all her resistance. Then he broke her with one sharp twist . . .

Rose watched him, lying there muscularly hollow, strong enough to keep her prisoner because she had no strength herself. Her spirit was broken. Not physically, since physical exhaustion was temporary; nor by captivity, for that would be a matter of time. She realized that she was never going to be free of him, that he had fixed some meaning upon her. He was never going to let her be free until he was tired of her and had no need for her; or perhaps even until he was tired of himself. Rose thought of her life in the town. It seemed better to go and live with him. She did not believe she could love him as she once had, but she could never again be afraid of him.

She let him help her dress. The wetness of her clothes made the buttons difficult.

"I'll go with you," she said.

She felt herself lifted in his arms and carried into the white mist, the water tugging wretchedly at his boots as he sought footing on the slippery stones.

Another Mijack had taken a wife.

PART FIVE: 1930 - 1936

32

Dorothy had been eager for the party to begin. She thought of him as arriving, with his cool composure, striding straight toward her. But apparently Bart had refused her invitation, and for a while it was important that the party should be gay without him. She saw her father looking out across the floor, and realized suddenly that she hated everyone above thirty, hated them passionately. Several times she went to a window and peered out, refusing to accept the function of darkness.

Later she maneuvered Arthur into taking her on the lawn, where the water could be heard trickling among bushes, but almost before they knew it they were on the steps of the front porch. "Darn!" said Dorothy. "I don't want to go in. Let's go for a walk."

"But it's your birthday party," said Arthur Weaver. He knew he would have to account to his own father. He knew his responsibilities.

"Oh, come along," said Dorothy, and turned as if she would go alone.

They went up the hill toward and then past the darkened Mijack house, Dorothy chattering away in the stillness of the night. She led him toward a stretch of pines. Arthur Weaver's discomfort was noticeable only in the way he talked rather rapidly and disconnectedly. Dorothy took his hand and made him help her past places where the weeds were thick. Then as they began to enter among the pines, she began to tiptoe, and to hold her head as if hearing their secrecy reflected among the trees. She led them on and on, pulling at Arthur's arm.

"Listen," she said, almost whispering, "do you know how to find your way back?"

Arthur looked about him, then faced in a downhill direction. "Yes," he said.

385

"Oh damn! You *would*." Then, looking around, she said, "Isn't it a wonderful place? My boy friend and I used to come here."

She heard his feet move among the leaves.

"Did you know my boy friend? Bart Mijack. He played football."

"I guess I saw him around," Arthur grumbled.

Dorothy laughed, and putting her hands behind her, leaned against a tree. "How many times have you kissed me?" she said.

"Huh?"

"How many times have you kissed me? In all."

Arthur was silent.

"I think a boy would remember such things. How many?"

"None," confessed Arthur.

"Never!" said Dorothy, and she pushed herself away from the tree, laughing. "But why, Arthur? Why? Have I ever told you you couldn't?"

She stepped toward him, and when his eyes only stared at her, she put her arms around him. The scent of the pines was sharp in her nostrils. She drew her waist against him, curving her body backward, letting him feel a portion of her weight. It startled him, so that he stumbled, not much, but enough to let her know he could never be attractive to her. By the time his face had decided to come against hers, she was passive to it.

"And some day your father would let you marry me. Wouldn't he?" she said a little later. "And my father would let me marry you. And our fathers would be very happy." Dorothy peeped her whole face close to his eyes and said, "Would *you* be happy? Would you like to marry me?" She ruffled his hair. There was no pleasure in it for her, only amusement at those moments when he tried to forget his embarrassment and show his masculinity. "Be true to me, and love me," she said, laughing, "and maybe some day we will make our fathers happy—just for their sakes."

Yet, how was it that she did not feel that way in the least? All she really felt was hurt that Bart had not come to her birthday party.

Mr. Pierce was increasing his publications. He divided Pittsburgh from Philadelphia and weakened the influence of both, through the introduction of six local newspapers. The Republicanism of central Pennsylvania was the foundation of his editorial policy, yet he was willing to allow two of the smaller papers to represent Democratic tendencies. He recognized central Pennsylvania as the balance between the two great cities, and that in any real crisis the central counties, particularly Dauphin, carried a political weight disproportionate to their population.

Mr. Pierce had of course more reliable contacts with politics than mere guesswork. At no time did he throw himself into the fray, nor did he allow political leanings to overcome what seemed to him equally important—the retention of farm interest. Several of his papers were devoted almost entirely to rural news, bearing only a minimum of national news and a smattering of items from abroad.

The advantages of central ownership were numerous. The morning paper in Nesquehon could carry the same features as the evening paper in another city. The same news item could be handled discreetly and distinctively by the *Interpreter*, and splashed sensationally across the front page of the *Telegram*. Many homes, during times of prosperity, were being served by two or more papers, all of course his own.

Through the use of a complicated central exchange, staffs were able to be reduced to a single sports coverage, fashion and style staff, literature and art. The articles suitable to each particular paper and area were sent out, and all printing materials and needs were ordered through the central agency. It required clever handling and the stimulation of competition among his own newspapers to get the people introduced to the idea of having the news more than once a day, to the green-stripe extras, and the Saturday-evening football special. But if the central Pennsylvanians were a stubborn and cautious people, they were faithful and firm subscribers.

Mr. Pierce of course recognized that advertising was the heart of all successful publications. And the cost of centralized printing urged him to take full advantage of local sources. He won the faith of businessmen by giving them rate advantages over national competition. He engaged the various small cities in a competition of commerce, so that each city was trying to get the stream of rural trade to come in its direction.

Very few possibilities were overlooked. Banks advertised sedately, stating their financial transactions and the year of their establishment. A representative had been sent to Detroit to see if the automobile industry was interested in a more impressive form of advertising, and in giving support to the local dealers. Housing and construction firms were visited, and markets and groceries were encouraged to compete in prices. Tractor and farm-implement and feed companies were also encouraged. It had been Mr. Pierce's personal contact with representatives of Bethel which had convinced them that articles, supported on the same basis as advertisements, dealing with the accomplishments and aims of the steel industry, would be a healthy communication with labor; this had also led to the annual report of Bethel, a substantial and expensive printing job.

His design and engraving departments were kept busy making samples which could be presented to prospective advertisers. He was quick to use and exploit color advertising in the years before it became too expensive. Among the comic strips which he suggested were the "Katzenjammer Kids," "Mutt and Jeff," "Krazy Kat," "Mr. and Mrs.," and "Polly and her Pals." Later he added "Little Orphan Annie," "Joe Palooka," "Tailspin Tommy," "Tarzan" and "Prince Valiant." John Harvard Broughton, a young local poet whom Mr. Pierce often invited to the house, and to whom he gave encouragement, was induced, as a sort of joke, to try his hand at writing a serial western. Mr. Pierce saw fit to pay fifty dollars for it.

He made annual campaigns to reduce costs, reduced advertising rates to develop more intensive local competition, and on this basis undersold other locals with smaller printings. He developed the idea of printing an all-advertising paper, at very low cost, and distributed at no cost to consumers. This was of course temporary, until competitive local publications were strangled by not being able to get advertisers; after they were ruined, or he had been able to purchase them reasonably, he would bring about a gradual increase of rates to cover his own financial losses during the period of competition.

It would be incorrect to credit specific details to Mr. Pierce; for as he himself explained, they were decisions of the advertising staff, just as editorials were the responsibility of the editorial board. He held out the palms of his hands in faint disclaimer of responsibility for particular minute matters, and suggested that his own connection with the newspapers was nothing more than that of a remote owner.

But Mr. Pierce had what he really wanted, political dependence upon his newspapers. For he knew that in Pennsylvania there was only one avenue to real eminence, politics.

A trio of axes, a handful of oak wedges, a cant hook, a crosscut with a bar between the handles. The lumber yard would make no arrangement with him. In desperation he rented a cart and mule and peddled firewood.

Rose, passive, unhappy, seemed only to serve out a sentence which had been imposed on her. Her cooking was sloppy, her appearance slovenly, and all she washed was the palms of her hands and front of her face. She would not go near the creek. It was enough to hear it in the night, after she had lain beneath him. They shared bed, table and, sometimes, washbasin. She knew he felt as if he were punishing her. She did not care.

It was never a case of not loving, but simply unwillingness to give love under circumstances that would make her despised. Then one morning she woke to find rain along the mountain peak and the entire skyline flashing and glittering like a long line of children playing with hand mirrors, and she realized she was no longer captive, and that instead of being unhappy she was contented. Seeing his determination to keep her and provide for her, seeing the desperation and humiliation which forced him to laugh even as he was filling a sack with firewood chips, seeing him throw the sack over his shoulder and trudge into town and return with a couple of nickels in his pocket, she knew she must give him whatever assistance she could.

She planted a garden in miserable ground which would not even weed thickly. She took hold of the other handle of the saw. She began to believe she was pregnant.

Gilbert seemed to eye her slightly askance, with a mixture of contempt and perplexity, while his tongue lay flat and useless in his mouth. He spent as little time as possible in the cabin. He took long walks alone over the mountain. His rifle could be heard sometimes far below and it could be supposed from the tense quick movements of his eyes that he was killing animals. He never brought anything home, and in the evenings his reaction was a guilt for an expense which they could so little afford.

Then he announced they were going to be married.

Rose was afraid of the ceremony, the church, the Mijacks. The only thing that did not bother her was the possibility of her pregnancy being noticed. She remembered white flowers and the nine people and the command to love, honor and obey.

Gilbert wore boots and had his hair combed back only along the sides. His head was raised slightly, the tightness at the corners of his mouth relaxed. The moral uplift was greater for him than for his wife. He had not invited his sister, but she came, and he found that he held no bitterness against her. The wedding presents were refused, including Mijack's offer to buy a steam saw. Gilbert did not make the refusal until after he had talked with his wife. Rose made only the proper agreements, and yet it was a beautiful moment for her.

Gilbert found work at the steel mill. He liked laboring better than he had thought he would, and even set his sights on a promotion.

389

Life was simplified, nine hours' work, a long walk from the mill. He did not abandon the idea of the sawmill and was putting money aside; the next time he made a try at earning an independent living there would be proper equipment and a truck to haul lumber. It meant waiting ten years. Meanwhile, he would put bread in their mouths. He looked ahead, convinced he was steadier and more determined. Youth was for the first time an advantage, giving time without great cost.

He had exaggerated his loneliness. Everyone liked him, the workers, most of the bosses. There was in him a lovable quality of enthusiastic goodness and unselfish strength which put his hands at the disposal of anyone who needed assistance. His lunch bucket was public property. He was a good man when not trying to be extraordinary. He stood to become popular.

When Bart took a summer job with the company, he felt some of the old enthusiasm return. Mijacks had only to see each other to revive the feeling of being selected for high destiny. He was more at ease among these men than with his brother, but the presence of Bart made him work hard. His father deeply and sincerely approved, not only of his working here, but working in order to get equipment, and thought it wise that Gilbert had not taken the job of helping him blacksmith. There was no future in blacksmithing.

Mr. Pierce was sitting in his own parlor, reading his own newspaper, and watching, from time to time, his favorite daughter. He still had soft, firm hands. He still had remarkably white teeth. There was something too white about them, especially for a man who smoked rather steadily.

Dorothy was flushed and gay, and kept rushing up and down the stairs in her slip and bare feet.

"Mother, Cathy won't let me in the bathroom."

"Have a little patience," came a voice from the kitchen.

"I can't wait much longer. I have a date."

"Then you should have gone in sooner."

"Furthermore," said Rodger, from beside the piano, where his fingers were playing a fantasia on wood, "I, Rodger, happen to be next."

"I've been trying to get in for the past hour."

Irene came from the kitchen and went to the foot of the stairs.

"Kathleen, will you be much longer in the bathroom? Your sister would like to use it too. You mustn't take longer than you need."

There was silence.

"She has," said Mr. Pierce quietly, looking at his watch, "kept Dorothy waiting fourteen minutes."

"Kathleen, do you hear your mother?" Irene turned toward her husband. "Is that so terrible?"

"Oh mother, I'm taking a bath," came through a door upstairs which had been opened a bit.

Rodger made the piano stool revolve. "I'm next," he announced. "And I think I shall take a ba-a-ath. I shall shampoo me."

Dorothy waved her hand for him to keep quiet.

"And if you try to keep me out," said Rodger, "I will write it in my book. You owe me six revenges."

Mr. Pierce frowned. His son was becoming filled with nonsense and bad habits.

Dorothy always had a look of indifference about her. It was most noticeable when she could not have her own way and when she was saying something polite. She looked at her brother as if there were not much to be seen.

Irene returned to the kitchen. Dorothy paced the length of the room, looking up the stairway from time to time. Mr. Pierce's eyes noted her quite shrewdly, and he, in his mildly awkward manner, which was really only an enhancement of his surface perfection, asked her questions which brought her to the arm of his chair. She told him enough to allow him to form a framework of the evening ahead, so that he leaned back in his chair comfortably. She was dating a great number of boys, none too steadily. She showed indications of being willing to tell him about the different boys, how foolish they were, the promises she drew from them. Mr. Pierce chuckled, admiring her more than ever.

Mr. Pierce had a considerable respect for his eldest daughter. If it had not been for the undesirability of a young woman going into business, he might well have encouraged her toward his own career, and perhaps in the distant future have entrusted his heritage into her hands. She was capable, clever. Instead, he was planning for her a marriage of importance, all in good time, when she had tired of the parties and gaiety. Meanwhile he showered gifts upon her, allowed her to prey upon him and be quite spoiled.

His only real concern about her activities had been when she was dating Bart Mijack. He had sat up nights to see that she came home safely, and had admitted to her his anxiety to meet the young man and have a look at him. But at the time when he had begun to take certain steps to effect a cure, Dorothy had stopped seeing Bart, and since that time had been content to scatter her attentions. She would often ask him to greet the young men who came to call on her, and Mr. Pierce would chat with them while they were waiting for her to finish dressing. He was quite amused at how she was able to keep them waiting, and, talking to them with some knowledge of her opinion of them, he would kid them along a little.

Ordinarily he would have suggested to his wife that it was scarcely suitable for Dorothy to be kept waiting. But he had sensed an enthusiasm and haste in his eldest daughter which was extraordinary, and had found himself in a momentarily neutral position in which he could call his daughter to his side and talk with her until the bathroom was available. He stilled her impatience and restored a balance and ease to time, making the evening seem longer and less fleeting. Dorothy sat on the arm of his chair, twirling the car keys.

Kathleen came out of the bathroom, leaving wet footprints in the hall. She went into her bedroom and slammed the door.

Dorothy brought her father a glass of wine before going upstairs. As he sat there sipping, it became evident how particular he was about his collars and his razor, his throat moving against the soft unabrasive material, his chin held slightly high. He seemed to breath the air of the surface of the wine before touching his mouth on the glass, and he held his mouth still, with only his tongue active. After a while Kathleen slipped past him, sounding like someone walking on grass. She smiled at Rodger, who was sitting at the piano, with his elbows propped, and then went to the edge of the kitchen.

"Oh, Mother," she said, "must you always make peace?"

Her voice was soft and low, a bit husky. She was so modest and shy that her tendency to rebel seemed almost a distress to herself. Her protests were voiced in the very manner that Irene could have found herself justified to protest. Yet Kathleen only sensed that in some manner her mother had offended her father and that he was engaged in a form of retaliation. Being young, Kathleen preferred showing her courage to acting with discretion, and thus was making it harder for her mother.

Mr. Pierce's surface perfection remained, his delicacy of taste seemed even more sensitive, and his treatment of the family was perfectly and truly courteous. The atmosphere could therefore not be precisely defined. He had the calm repose and serene confidence of a man who has had much experience in adapting himself to the prevailing forms and creeds of life, without losing the flavor of that which he found particularly satisfactory. His sense of anticipation was so refined that he was freed from the anxiety and haste which attends. He was, after all, in control of life and his family.

Mr. Pierce answered the door and invited the young man to be seated. Turning on a light behind the young man, and dimming another that was in a less favorable position, he slipped upstairs and tapped on the door and entered. He stood there silent for a time, watching his daughter fit ornaments to her ears and wrists and about her throat. There came to him a feeling that she was much too aware of her attractiveness at an age when it was more dangerous to herself than to the young men on whom she practiced her flirtations.

"I confess I feel you've played a rather bad trick on me," he said. "This is one person I don't like the looks of."

"Bart?" said Dorothy. "Oh, he's a laugh." She wrinkled her nose. "He likes *movies.*"

She was wearing shoes that revealed her insteps. The shoes were attractive, they brought out the most beautiful portions of her feet, and made her feet graceful rather than merely small. What made Mr. Pierce sniff was the intention of his daughter, not to appear beautiful, almost as if she did not want to appear beautiful, but simply make herself provocative. He had to admit that his wife had better taste than either of his daughters.

"Understand, this is not an interference in your affairs," he said. "It's merely a statement. He's not right for you."

"Why of course not!" said Dorothy. "What ever made you think . . . ? You're worried for me," she said, running to him and giving him a light quick kiss. Her eyes inspected his face. "Listen, you don't have to worry, you know how I am. This one today, that one tomorrow. But I'm really happy to see you so upset and—and you watch me," she said laughing. "Now go on downstairs." Her eyes for a moment had been frightened, elusive. But now they were bright with genuine merriment, even a trace of mischievousness.

Mr. Pierce went, not satisfied with the conversation he had had, feeling that he had done his duty, but knowing he had chosen an inopportune moment. He sat in silence while the young man made some effort to talk to him.

"And what became of your college career?"

"I found something more important," said Bart.

"I suppose you mean this union affair?" said Mr. Pierce. "I'm afraid you're in for quite a disappointment."

"Perhaps."

Mr. Pierce tapped the arm of his chair. "My daughter takes her time," he said. "But that's her way, and I suppose you're willing to put up with it." Irene came in and placed two wineglasses, and took away the one which Mr. Pierce had had. Bart held his hand over his glass as she was about to fill it, and Mr. Pierce's lips made a faint movement. Then he smiled.

When Dorothy finally came downstairs, she went to her father, and made a pirouette. "Am I presentable?" she said, paying no attention to Bart, who had risen to greet her. Mr. Pierce put aside his glass and leaned his head to one side, watching the slow rotation, seeing her shoulders' breadth and whiteness, shoulders just barely capable of keeping in proportion her rather full bosom. He recognized that the principal difference in his daughter was a lack of tenderness for herself which made her seem more commanding and poised.

"Wait a moment," she said, holding an upturned hand toward Bart. "I'll have to see in the mirror, since Father won't say." Off she went, skipping gaily, and when she returned, she was pouting. "Oh Bart, I can't go out in this. I look horrible. I feel so naked," she said, brushing at her shoulder. "I'll be right back."

"You look fine," said Bart.

"Listen," said Mr. Pierce, "it's soon going to be too late for a movie." Dorothy was already mounting the stairs, and so he turned his voice toward the young man. "She told me that's where you were going," he confessed, smiling.

"Oh, it can't be too late. I want so much to see it," came a voice from high on the stairs. "Bart, why don't you call the theater and tell them to hold it off a few minutes?" Laughing, she vanished down the hall. Mr. Pierce was smiling a little himself. He fitted the wineglass to his lower lip and took sips which only wet his mouth. There was silence for quite a while.

"She asks the most impossible things," said Mr. Pierce. "Call the theater and stop the movie." He laughed. "I must confess it seems to me you're being treated a little discourteously."

Bart's eyes came up quickly. "She likes to tease," he said, "and give the runaround. But appearances are sometimes deceiving."

Mr. Pierce smiled indulgently. "Perhaps," he admitted.

Dorothy appeared on the stairway. She came dashing down. "This is more like it, don't you think, father? More like a summer vacation?" She held out her arms so that her dress could be seen in relation to her figure. But there could be seen more than a mere defiance of convention, something which bordered on contempt for the person she was going to accompany, a frivolity, a carelessness of style.

"You're fine. Let's go," said Bart.

"Oh, it's too late for the movie," said Dorothy. She was twirling the car keys.

"I suspect you could catch part of the feature," said Mr. Pierce.

"Who said anything about a movie?" Bart retorted.

"I don't like going in the middle."

"May I make a suggestion?" said Mr. Pierce. "Why don't you young people put off the movie until another night? We could put on a little music and talk, you could dance if you like."

"What a splendid idea!" said Dorothy.

Bart left early that evening. Mr. Pierce and his daughter enjoyed themselves enormously as they were clearing things away. Mr. Pierce had to admit that he was proud of the way his daughter had handled the situation, and when she explained that she was getting even with Bart for his former treatment of her, he could find no harm in her doing so, provided that she was careful. He mixed a couple of drinks, and he and his daughter sat through the remainder of the evening, and he promised to take care of several dress and lingerie bills which he had objected to.

Dorothy confessed that her real problem was that all the men she knew were bores, there was no life in any of them, there was none of the carefree gaiety which she would have loved to encounter. Then she changed the subject, tried to coax her father to take her to Florida this coming winter. She said she felt the best thing for him would be to get away from the town before he became like all the others, to have a good time, get away from his wife for a while. She leaned toward him and told how she liked to picture him in white trousers and a bright shirt and a polo hat, lounging at a beach table.

There was fun in teasing her father, in making him sometimes believe she was on the edge of being wicked and thoughtless. In making him believe she thought he was on the edge of breaking both his marriage and constant attention to business. But she had become cynical about her father; he was really dull and old-fashioned. She knew he did not approve of her coming to breakfast in a dressing gown, or of running between the bathroom and her own room simply in scanties. She remembered how he had stiffened perceptibly the first time she had let a young man kiss her in his presence, and how he had behaved coldly to her, until she had raised her eyebrows in a gesture which revealed the complete unimportance which she attached to the affection of young men. And she sensed that he took a particular pleasure in being paternal with her, in sharing with her the events of her life.

Yet, one night, she went out to her car and put the keys between her fingers, and Bart got in the other side. The car drifted down the hill a full block before she let the clutch out, jerking the engine into motion. Bart reached across and snapped the headlights on. The following morning they were married.

33

It was Sunday. Gilbert propped the crosscut against a tree, but it was too flexible, and fell with a chattering noise. As sunlight shimmered there seemed to be two sets of teeth at slightly different depths. He found the crotch of a tree, hung the saw, stepped back and waited, not sure.

Rose was on the other side of a log which had been sawed into eight pieces, the pieces still close enough together to give an approximation of the lower half of a tree. She was radiantly healthy. Her dress was tight, showing every line of her body, the palid, washed-thin colors of the cloth seeming to emphasize the deep brown of her arms and face. She seemed to have lost the slow heaviness of movement. Her body was almost too flexible under her dress.

"Goddamn," Gilbert said enthusiastically, "one thing that kid's going to have is a bicycle. I don't give a damn what else he doesn't get, but that's one thing he's going to have." He looked at his wife, grinning. He had become enormous across the shoulders. "No, by God, that kid's going to have everything. Everything I wanted and didn't get." As he stood there, stripped to the waist, heaving, sweat making the hair stick against his skin, it was apparent that in accumulating enormous strength he had lost quickness and flexibility. His hands would never rest on a flat surface, his arms would never fully straighten at the elbow, and his shirts, taut across the back, would always hang a little loose in front. "You know, something happens to kids when they don't get what they really want, I mean not stuff that doesn't count, but the kind of thing that after they've got it they keep right on using it." He was remembering the time Mrs. Cauley had let him borrow her son's bicycle, but with the instructions that he was to use it only on the school playground, and he had ridden it round and round in a useless circle, faster and faster, until he struck the wall and bent the pedal, and then had spent the rest of the afternoon trying to straighten it. "I mean we've got to make our kid feel he's got something, make him feel he's got a chance to be happy."

Gilbert stood there, envisioning against the summer trees, while his wife admired him, the pregnancy between her broad hips only vaguely noticeable, carried lightly and easily because she was unaware of the possibility of miscarriage. Since the child was within her there had become something magnificent in the way she carried herself, in the way she picked up an apple, in the way she hung clothes on the line as if waving signals of good will from the mountain to the entire world below, in the way she smoothed the sheets of the bed and slept with both hands tucked in under her face. She had taken to using herbs for cooking, was more experimental, and seemed revolted by the filth in which she had lived. She took astonishing pride in her skin and in the cleanliness of her body, although the neglect of her hair continued as before. And she had a strong desire for white underclothing, white shoes, white curtains.

"It's going to be all right here," Gilbert said, listening to the creek, and seeing the immense freedom which the trees seemed to insure. "It's ideal here. We only have to watch that we don't spoil it for him." He looked forward to the coming of the child. He thought more in terms of having a companion than of having a son.

Working at the mill had made changes in his relations with his wife. He would come home anxious to see her, to talk with her. He was astonished at his sexual need which seemed to grow stronger as her pregnancy neared the time when it would be inconvenient and even dangerous. He felt a kind of roaring health that made him stamp and curse and strut. He had always been afraid he would tire of her. He had believed that his feelings with regard to sex were too promiscuous for a woman who did not have full claim to his heart to retain his interest.

There were still times when he thought it was not and had never been Rose that he wanted. It had been something in the mountains, some feeling of independence. He felt he would never have taken Rose or married her if he had not been living alone in the mountains for so long; and he would not have minded if he could have been convinced that he really wanted her, if he could have been convinced that he was not merely adding one bondage to another.

Rose had instinctively regarded their wedding as a minor affair. But she sensed that their relationship had strengthened from the moment that they had known of the child she was going to bear. She sensed that the act of birth would put her entirely and forever at his disposal. She accepted it.

Gilbert had continually committed the fault of trying to feel what he could not feel, of trying to make momentary pangs of conscience the foundation of his life. Now he began to see that the essence of a sound basis was not merely control over evil, but holding good impulses to a practical level. He was through acting defiant. He was through being a fool. Rose was neither the high illusion he had first believed, nor the ill-famed, unintelligent girl whom he had despised. He doubted that he loved her, and yet she had a stronger claim to his affection than anyone else in the world, not only through marriage and the child, but out of the kind of isolation they had shared.

Yet he was astonished at his need of her. She had become so aggressive in their sexual relations, so strong and fierce, that their love-making resembled a contest of physical strength, a striving for supremacy. She made love in broad daylight, in the cabin or at the lumber mill, and she had lost the clumsy bashfulness she had felt at exposing herself. She aroused in him at times the need to hold his own, to keep his domination over her, and at other times he was bewildered, finding himself telling her that they must be careful or she might lose the child, finding himself at other moments practically engaged in an assault against the child. He was horrified at the conflicting emotions that he felt, and there came to him a new view of himself in which he was being drawn closer toward destruction.

Perhaps this more than anything else made him strive toward a normal life. He clung to his work at the mill with a tenaciousness that he had never before shown, and made every effort to be sociable, and was thinking of moving into town. He was indeed beginning to be afraid of living in the mountains, afraid that solitude was leading him toward an aspect of his nature which was extremely dangerous. That this was only the thinnest part of him, that he was much steadier and much more reliable, that he could not deny he was pleased with Rose, who had so far exceeded his expectations that he was forced into a position of some humility, only made him more aware of the treacherous nature of his emotions.

Yet, on that Sunday, he spoke of the coming of the child with joy, and he believed in his voice. He cried out not only for the child to have those things which he had been denied, but for the child to be assisted in stepping past those places where he had failed. He knew he had no reason to fear the mother of the child, for her love would be more constant and tender than his own. He was at the height of his physical powers and at the high point of his adjustment to society, having for the first time steady employment and a steady income, having the respect of his fellow workers, having been already eyed by his bosses as a prospect for a future gang foreman, having a wife who had suddenly taken interest in their home and in pleasing him. It seemed as if fate, which had always shattered his best intentions, had chosen the one action for which he did not deserve to be forgiven to become his greatest fortune.

"We've got a responsibility now," said Gilbert.

"You've elected me your union representative," said Bart. "I doubt you know what you've done. You had your choice among four. You could've had Tod Snyder. He'd have done a lot for you. He'd take your complaints straight to your boss. He wouldn't be satisfied until you shook hands. I can't do it that way. It's too damn much like begging.

"You could've had Matt Readinger. Matt fights. Why shouldn't he? He lost an arm. He's doing watchman work at a third the pay, and warned, threatened, to keep his opinions to himself, because his job's a gift. Matt'd fight. He'd never give an inch. But I won't do it that way—because you guys ain't willing to take hard times and trouble.

"Tim Callaghan. Maybe you ought to have him. He'll go through proper channels, he'll give you and the company fair play. Don't look for that from me, I'm no idealist.

"I'm the only one who wanted to be your leader because I like power. I tell you about me. I can spot crap anywhere any time. I'll make this factory realize it's a place where men come to earn a decent living. I'll make this factory see who you are. I stand for this. Good working conditions. Good wages. Retirement at half pay. Accident protection. I mean money and I mean protection.

"I don't stand for no forty-hour week. Nor for time and a half. Nor a national union. Nor forced retirement. You guys fight for that later. I took this job because nobody seemed to have as good a chance as me. Because I ain't going to stand by and see the company beat you guys to death. That's just how big a thing we're facing. From right now get it straight I'm your leader. What I say goes. Vote me out, but, buddy, don't back out. Don't ever back out on me.

"I intend to do just one thing. Break up these slave gangs. When I get that, I'm through. Then turn to Tim and let him point toward the ideal. I can't. I won't.

"I want you guys to know I have a plan. A strike wouldn't get us nothing right now, but the right judge and the right jury might. In a couple of months you'll know all about it. So just stay pat. I want to do this quick and then get the hell out of here and leave you in better hands. I'll at least improve things, that much I swear.

"I ain't going to ask for any sacrifice that's not absolutely unavoidable. That's probably the main thing you get by choosing me, because I don't count on you individually for much. For nothing, in fact, except loyalty. I prefer not even having to count on that. And no dues in this outfit, we ain't going to get caught in that rat trap.

"But get it in your heads, this is serious. Unions are still treason, and union leaders are still Benedict Arnolds. So you can be damn sure the company's going to fight. I want no quitters. If you have any doubts, get out now. Get out and come back later, come back when we're strong. You'll do me a damn big favor by showing your stripe now, not when I need you.

"This constitutes my acceptance."

"No," Bart was thinking, "it don't mean anything, the only thing they'll ever understand is a buck shoved down their throats. It don't mean nothing that I promise my life to an unceasing fight against evil. It don't even mean anything to them that that's the exact reason why they shouldn't trust me too far."

But it was the reason why they could be sure of Bart. Because he was, in spite of everything he had done to kill it, still an idealist.

Girls had always found him attractive. In high school they had fixed their eyes upon him out of basic reactions to sex and popularity in sports; in addition to being a four-striper in football, he had earned his letters in basketball, baseball and track; his sarcasm and aloofness had allowed him to select from among the most highly regarded. Yet, in a truer sense, he had far less opportunity than other boys, who, accepting themselves on a lesser scale, had more freedom to pursue. Then too, Bart, so deeply occupied in making himself live at the utmost of his capacity, tended to shy away from contacts which seemed to him vaguely threatening.

He had his opportunities; in eighth grade and as a freshman he had nearly taken advantage of them. It had seemed at that time a necessary stage in his development; it had seemed that he must be able to know in his heart exactly how strong the attractions of sex could be. But as his ambitions began to focus more intently, he became less and less interested; it was only when a girl showed an exceptional streak of independence and challenge that he made any effort to be acquainted with her.

Yet in spite of this he could make himself agreeable in a social atmosphere. He was a good dancer and could keep his partner entertained and had a good eye for attaching himself to the group which seemed to have best caught the spirit of a festivity. He did not dress badly for his age and had a kind of courtesy which made a young woman feel there was something in his tone which was particularly for her and which he would have given to no one else in the world. This developed during his college years.

Bart never considered marrying beneath his own intelligence and his own physical quality. His egotism was not of the sort which wanted to be set off by a background of inferiority. At the same time, he was equally suspicious of risking marriage into a family of wealth and luxury, sensing that the advantages would have too many false positions attached to them. Dorothy Pierce had been the only young woman who attracted him physically, and she had two qualities which he himself lacked, familiarity with wealth and good taste, and a lack of concern with anything except her own passions. She knew how to manipulate a young man in order to make herself seem charming and attractive, not only to him, but to all who were near.

Bart had at first insisted on keeping their relationship in the tone of a summer holiday. He felt his time was being wasted, that he was giving his attention to a spoiled young woman who did not have the strength to overcome her father's objections; even if she did, he knew he could not overcome some objections of his own which the first sign of animosity in Mr. Pierce had stirred in him. At college he dated a number of different girls, testing himself, testing the strength of feeling and remembrance. He found he was more lenient toward faults in women than in men; women were suited for parties and gaiety, for mischief and moonlight.

The first summer he worked in the mill, he retained the same careless attitude. He treated Dorothy with a mixture of tenderness and indifference. For a time he stopped seeing her altogether. It was not until he had rejected the university, had come into the mill and begun organizing a union, not until he had been deeply moved by the nature of what he was trying to bring about, that he found himself entangled in a passion for Dorothy and a desire to make her submissive. He began to believe she had more strength than he had been willing to admit. He began to believe that she had taken hold of his strength and was raising herself, was making an earnest effort to overcome the influence of her father.

Bart was not so foolish as to fail to realize that the Pierce family was to him an aspect and a shadow of the same struggle in which he was involved with the company. He came to understand that Mrs. Pierce was a long-suffering woman, and both pitied and despised her. Her husband was a boor. In the younger daughter, Kathleen, who on the surface seemed a shy, secretive girl, he saw the strongest sparks of rebellion. At most Bart was only tolerant of this family, and he felt in the vastness of the Pierce home the sensation of not liking to sit around and waste time; he was unwelcome here, Mr. Pierce indicated his displeasure, and Bart knew exactly the risk he was taking as he got in the other side of the car. As it drifted down the hill, without headlights, with only the slightly sticky sound of rubber compressing, he reached toward the horn, intending to sound his victory and his contempt of silence. Dorothy prevented his arm, almost struggled with it, and the car was a full block's distance down the hill before she let the clutch out, jerking the engine awake.

Perhaps Bart should have known by that one gesture that she was still not free. Perhaps he did know, but was drawn toward this further challenge, charged with present success. But he never imagined that in so short a time, in the very midst of their first passionate sex encounters—which, during the early weeks, resembled slashing at each other with penknives, conflicts of pride in which both tried to establish themselves—Dorothy would simply walk out on him, not even bothering to take her clothing or suitcase.

Bart returned to Nesquehon and threw all his energies into gathering further evidence against the company. Then one afternoon he went to the Pierce house and returned her suitcase. He went away feeling stronger than he had ever been, feeling that he had at last been able to make the separation between self and truth. He did not notice that it made him a bit hasty in attempting to bring the wrongs of the company to light. He did not notice that he had come to attach extreme importance to success.

Mr. Pierce, who had been bothered with a cold, was hunting for a soft handkerchief. He disliked pulling at bureau drawers. Seeing something to his liking among a group of white linens, weighing with a slight rise and fall of his palm, he went downstairs holding the handkerchief between two soft manicured fingers, gently shaking it from its packaged shape. Lifting his head a little, he merely caressed his nose.

Stretched upon the sofa with an exhaustion which was not quite convincing, he seemed too careful of himself even in repose, too needful of ease and almost luxurious indolence for each portion of his body. He was quite some time in finding a satisfactory position. It was more nearly a need to rest from boredom, to shut his eyes across a mind recently insulted by the presence of foolish people engaged in harmless business over which he had become unaccountably worried.

He felt insulated from everything, the noises of the house held at a distance, the windows making a slight flue sound at the approach of breezes. As his need to breathe slowly subsided into something small and regular, something that could be handled by slight palpitant movements of his stomach, instead of interminable and oppressive chest expansions, the stuffiness of a summer cold ceased to irritate him. He believed that if only he could cease to be aware of the springs in the sofa, of their slight thrusting, he might get past the drifting stage of filmy shadows which tended to make him restless against the approach of sleep.

He heard the voices of his son and older daughter, like a nagging, insistent chant. It was only after his wife spoke from somewhere nearby that he realized they were all equally distant from him, that he himself had provided the distance; and there came a sudden rushing recollection that his daughter was no longer a child, was as tall as his wife, and this seemed to startle some passivity in his mind, some tendency to lose his firm grip on time and exact events. It was the same peculiar reaction which he had to oversleeping.

"You shouldn't tease him." His wife's voice, it seemed, would never cease to make him attentive. She had had a woman's voice and a child's mouth when he met her, and now she had a woman's mouth and—almost—the voice of a young girl.

"Why not? Nobody went out of their way to make it easy for me." The voices were alike, yet could never be mistaken, a sharpness at the edge, a dramatic twisting of the final sound; in that slight difference seemed to be an explanation. How was it, he wondered, a man could always tell when they were talking about love? Dorothy thinking of annulment, resenting, hurt, and his wife engaged in her tireless pleasure of seeking her son's happiness. But after a moment of reflection he decided Dorothy was only reacting to the disgrace of having her own willfulness set aside, was only covering her embarrassment with little bitternesses which were designed to hurt her mother, that she was, underneath, glad to be free of the responsibility of a hasty action.

"Because he's only twelve. He loves the thought of love. That makes it harder."

"Hun-n-h! Little you know."

Woman against woman, denial of motherhood which had been denied earlier, and a longing to return which could not find enough substance to know where or how to begin. Mr. Pierce felt that he had in certain respects little sympathy for his daughter's situation; hers had been the recklessness of a young woman bothered by her virginity, who teased herself against the shirt fronts of a ruthless young man, and would never have had the courage to run away to Maryland except through being sure he, her father, would interfere. All very sensible. Even clever. Instead of risking the shame and embarrassment of furtive, sordid affairs in the weeds and across the seat of the car which he had been foolish enough to give her for graduation, the car which he had come to hate because of the way she was always spinning the key chain in front of his face, she had taken a way which would satisfy her curiosity and at the same time flaunt her daring, flaunt an independence which she did not wish to have, but only wished to appear to have.

She had struck to hurt her father, and he had been hurt, and although she could depend upon him still to come to her assistance, perhaps to protect her through folly after folly, she could never hurt him again in quite the same way, and that much was forever against her. And, worse for her, he found that she did not hurt him, only embarrassed him.

Possibly, quite possibly, Dorothy's intentions had reached still further. He had noticed since her return a definite subservience and eagerness to be commanded. It was not repentance, as she had in fact, laughing, already referred to the incident as her "trial marriage." At the bottom of her willfulness and wildness might be the very simple intention, unknown, of having her life directed for her; it would not be the first time he had seen a young person so bewildered by the major decisions of life that she had chosen a way which would insure guidance.

"Can you really believe a man ought to devote himself to one of us?" A high, embittered laugh. "Oh, Mother, you better grow some skin. You need glasses or something."

Apparently he had missed part of the conversation, and so was able to consider his daughter's remark purely in abstract, on the merit of itself alone; there was in him a feeling Dorothy was coming to have a very healthy outlook; a young woman should have some callus on her heart, it was much more attractive than sentimental wishwash, much more attractive than the nonsense of his wife, who emptied ash trays and washed them, not to make them serviceable, but to make them pretty. He saw that he had a restrained disposition to forgive, that he was not likely to hold himself apart from Dorothy, after all; the real effect of her going to such an extreme was going to be no more than a shift, in himself, toward amusement, toward further detachment, not only from her, but from himself. It seemed to him likely that he would continue to admire her and that, even if they were a little more distant from each other, it would make more pleasant the curious kind of ruthlessness of which he now believed her capable.

While he was still envisioning his wife and daughter standing together, while listening for some further development in their conversation, something cold touched the back of his hand, then tapped insistently. He opened his eyes and allowed them to stare dispassionately, under the guise of not recognizing; it reasserted in him the faintly humorous feeling of being involved in the act of living only in a technical capacity, so that he could, at moments, capture the superb construction that was perhaps the only real dignity a woman could have; it was a fleeting moment when nothing had to remind him of anything. As he swung his legs over the sofa, planting them a little firmly on the floor, and heard the movement of two released springs, a very faint sound of adjustment, there returned the same discontented feeling which had sent him in search of a soft handkerchief. It was a feeling that by moving he was taking the risk of suffering the same physical nuisances which he had just escaped from.

"What's this horror?" he said, holding the glass at arm's length, as if only manners forbade him to sniff at it. "Ahh, well," he said, after a little, "I suppose if I hadn't been lying down . . . I do think a man should be able to rest on his back a few minutes without his mouth getting so dirty." His lips made a slightly moist, flapping movement, as if the real feeling in his mouth was of clumsiness. He drew his shirt slowly loose from where it was sticking against his chest, and eyed the diminished creases in his trousers with distaste. It would be the third bath he had taken since morning.

"To the party!" said Dorothy, lifting her glass so little as to cast discredit on the gesture. "To happiness all evening."

Mr. Pierce looked at her. He was impressed by the stature of the young woman. Then, after a bit, he raised his glass to where she could touch it with hers. "Why not?" he said, smiling. "I suppose you're entitled to throw one." His eyes fixed humorously on her glass, filled to the edge and a little dark.

"Oh no, I daren't," said Dorothy. "Mother doesn't even think I should appear. I'm supposed to go into hiding for a year and then come out wearing black." She said this with a carelessness which intended to convey that her mother had of course not actually said this, but that it could justly be attributed to her.

Mr. Pierce tossed his head, as at something of no importance; he felt unconcerned about his daughter's conduct, and as he continued to look at her, smiling, it seemed slightly amazing to him that she had ever been his favorite, still was and would continue to be, even though she had lost her initial significance. His eyes regarded her as a curiosity, almost the kind which had made him, passing through a store in Harrisburg, pick up an unclothed doll and roll it back and forth gently, as he did with his pocket watch after winding, simply to determine whether it had movable eyes, closing eyelids, or the kitten sound that was supposed to represent crying. Doubtless he had a deeper feeling for her than that, but, at least at moments, he had none whatever. And yet he was at the point of admiring her more than he ever had anyone.

"I might roll my trousers and we could both throw one," he said. "That would no doubt convince everyone you have my approval."

"Oh no, I'm going to behave," said Dorothy. "I'm just going to encourage the first man who even hints eligibility to tie one on."

Mr. Pierce eyed her. "That would be sensible," he said, meaning it.

"No," she said, "not very. I just want to see somebody act disgraceful in this house. Once. I mean somebody we all think is nice." Pouting her lips in disgust, she gave her glass a careless shake, so that for a moment Mr. Pierce looked down at his knees. "These people you invite! It's always as if they'd like to get possession of what *you* have—not what *I* have. Mothers walking along with their sons to make sure they get a bargain."

Mr. Pierce looked at his daughter approvingly. "You're quite right." He took a sip from his glass, used the soft handkerchief to remove the moisture from his mouth, and then as a pad held against the bottom of the glass. "And I'm afraid mothers will walk even closer to their sons—at least for a while."

Dorothy made a hand wave of dismissal. "Phooey. I know what it'll be like. They'll just all come closer to do their sniffing."

Mr. Pierce raised his eyebrows, and faked a whistle. "You *have* grown up."

Dorothy whirled. "Oh it's not all as much fun as that," she said, "to be given the second-hand treatment."

"Now you're being sentimental," said Mr. Pierce, motioning that she should drink with him.

Instead, she set her glass down hard on the little end table. "Well," she said, "make sure you get a good price for me, we have a right to at least that."

Mr. Pierce took hold of her wrist and swung the pretty, bare arm without attaching any importance to the fact that it gave him no assistance. She was in the most favorable frame of mind that could be wished. Yes, she could be underestimated. Even as he was looking up at her, feeling a definite pleasure in seeing her eyes angry, he realized that perhaps events had worked to advantage, that her potential was only about to be set free. "You mustn't mind your mother," he said. "I don't consider you second-hand." He lifted his glass in salute. "To the party," he said, smiling. He finished his drink without looking to see if she accepted his compliment, and then went upstairs, in good humor, to take his third bath since morning. Yes, there was a good new foundation, a certain expediency and directness of utility which they would never need to disguise, and which could be of service to them both.

34

Dorothy came to him and said, "You're wanted at the door," said it so carelessly that if he had not noticed exposed between lipstick a thin edge of strangely whitish flesh he would not have been prepared. The door was standing wide open and Bart was already inside; he had the swagger of a person who feels he has been born with certain advantages, and the ruthless, watchful eyes of a man who does not trust life enough to relax even for a moment.

Mr. Pierce's immediate reaction was to feel at a disadvantage in dressing gown and slippers, particularly because the gown had been slipped over his shirt and trousers. It was an unpleasant sensation of helplessness, felt mostly in the looseness of his slippers. Though lasting only a moment, it cast a slight nervousness into his gathering composure. Perhaps, as much as anything, it was the dislike of being caught sitting in a chair, he who never remained seated at the entrance of a guest, who greeted people coming toward them with his hand extended.

Bart's attention was being given entirely to Dorothy. She seemed either afraid of him or afraid of what her reaction to him would be; at the same time she was furious at the implied insult in the coldness of his eyes. She was also suffering the embarrassment of not being able to speak, since Bart was in a position in which he could disregard anything he wished to. He had a moral right either to turn on his heel or to walk to Dorothy and hold her firmly against himself. The way he stared made Dorothy feel that her attractiveness was against her.

Mr. Pierce set aside his pipe, laying it carefully on the arm of the chair. It was the gesture of a man who was trying not to consider himself involved in his present surroundings, and who was merely condescending to show a slight curiosity. His eyebrows had the correct height, as he waited rather deliberately, allowing the young people to exchange glances and resentments that could only make his own position more secure.

Bart had seen all he wanted to see. The decision of the court had not simply been parental request for annulment, but had had at least the passive acquiescence of Dorothy. It was undoubtedly that which made Bart so pale, made him seem on the verge of losing control of himself.

Mr. Pierce said nothing. He took up his pipe and stared into space, knowing not only nothing could be done or said, nothing of importance, but that it was rather a good thing for young people to get rid of their last romantic notions. All young people had the most exaggerated sense of their importance to each other.

"Get your suitcase and put in it the stuff I bought you," said Bart. "We're going on our second honeymoon."

Mr. Pierce saw his daughter tremble.

That was exactly what Bart saw and scorned. Looking at the woman he had regarded as his wife until this moment, her eyes a bit large and with a faint sheen of hollowness, her mouth slack and pouting, he was ashamed of her. To see a young woman dressed expensively, daringly in regard to shoulder and arm exposure, to see scarlet slashed across her lips and plentiful shine on her fingernails, to see a woman who was attractive enough to make a man almost predatory in his desire to claim her, and then to see her draw away in retreat, without venturing a single encounter, either of eye or of speech, was the most displeasing sight Bart could have encountered. Even more since he had already once chosen her, had already once sacrificed a portion of his ambitions to have her.

Mr. Pierce saw his daughter's weakness. He saw that there was no more to rely on than the pride of an upstart union organizer to make permanent a separation which his daughter was scarcely sensible enough to hold to. Not even the protection of his age, of the substantial years between himself and Bart, preserved him from feeling hurt and angry. The humor with which he ordinarily regarded youth and its unpredictability failed him.

"Oh come now," he said almost angrily, "haven't we had enough of this nonsense?" He motioned with his pipe. "Dorothy, go in the other room."

Dorothy looked instead at Bart, as if expecting him to countermand the order.

Bart merely tossed his head in disdain. It was a gesture that indicated she would have to come to him if she wanted him. It was evident that he had spoken all he intended to. Bart stood very erect.

"Dorothy, go in the other room—and close the door."

Dorothy looked at her father, almost without recognition. Then, frowning, as if she was thinking of something else, something that had happened at another time and place, she withdrew. She passed through the center of the doorway and continued walking at the same slow, even pace. When she came to the kitchen door she halted only because she did not seem to recognize what it represented.

Mr. Pierce resented the manner of her withdrawal. It had been only in the vaguest sense compliance to his demand, and he made so few outright, voiced demands on his children that it was unbearable not to be obeyed promptly.

Bart continued to stare at the door through which she had disappeared, hands clenched and held at his sides.

"Now look here," said Mr. Pierce, "at least you be sensible. There's been enough foolishness."

Bart glanced, as if to question what possible right this man could have to be speaking. He began to pace through the room. The front door was still standing wide open; he took no notice.

"My daughter made a mistake. You made a mistake. The sensible thing to do is go away and not bother us again." Mr. Pierce put his slippered feet side by side and leaned forward. "You were both victims of an experiment. My daughter acted simply out of resentment for me, and, I dare say, sheer boredom with our kind of life. You couldn't expect it to last."

Bart waved his arm carelessly. "Oh she's mine," he said. "But I'm not going to bother to claim her."

Mr. Pierce gripped the arms of his chair. "You're not even at the place where my daughter was born," he said. Their eyes met and held, Bart recognizing for the first time the full depth of the older man's hatred; curiously enough, he had almost no feeling himself, except of slight scorn. "All you did was stir in her an infatuation and use it for your own purposes." Mr. Pierce almost snarled those last words, but Bart continued to regard him without concern, even beginning to smile. "All you've ever learned, the hard way, as you no doubt refer to it, only makes you despised. People like myself will always regard you as something strictly for hire."

Bart laughed. He eyed the man in the armchair, and then, almost imperceptibly, leaned toward him. It seemed for a moment as if he was bowing, except that his head moved closer and closer to the other man's face, and his eyes remained unmovingly fixed on a spot in the middle of Mr. Pierce's forehead. Mr. Pierce seemed at first merely annoyed, then astonished, and sat with his back straight and his head pushed deep into the cushion of the chair. The head continued to move slowly downward, giving no hint that it was going to avoid his nose, and at the last moment it appeared as if Mr. Pierce were going to be kissed on the mouth. That was when Bart splashed his face with a wet, loud, lip fart. Mr. Pierce turned absolutely white.

Laughing, Bart walked out of the house. He left the door wide open.

For quite a while Mr. Pierce sat there. The first thing he managed to do was peep around the side of his chair and see if there was anyone in the other room. Then, after a little, he rose and, after closing his eyes a moment and wiping his hand across his forehead, went to the door. Without venturing his head outside, he shut it, pushing unnecessarily hard.

Then, in what seemed an action of more decision, he went to the telephone, lifted the receiver and dialed. He stood there, holding the ear tube against his cheekbone, staring at the wall. When he heard a strong male voice against his cheekbone, he continued to stare at the wall. Then slowly his mouth fell open, and there came into his eyes a faint realization of horror.

That evening, when his wife said something to him, he struck her.

The isolation of pride is terrible only when pride is not founded on a suitable nature. For Bart there was no loneliness; his ambitions were too intense and continuous to leave space for remorse or unhappiness. He never seemed surprised; every communication was received as if it had been foreseen, as if, almost, he saw and understood the whole shape and grasp of life. Nothing was less true. He was actually desperately confused, an idealist, not an idealist, engaged in purification and perfection of his smallest actions, finding sometimes purification in the unnecessary and the too rigid.

His eyes were never compassionate when he gazed upon human weakness, his head never acknowledged; it was only by a twisted smile that he gave sign of what he was feeling. But it was becoming apparent, as the full extent of his coldness was witnessed day after day, unending and without relief, how deep and serious was his belief in mankind and truth. He had done that which few people are capable of, had formed his own outward character and made it his law, had constructed it surely and deliberately; it made him an inflexible, unsmiling person; it even did something to his eyes and his forehead.

Since he had gained control of the union, there had come into his bearing a tone of overseriousness which made him appear dangerous physically. He had become almost vicious in his insights, lived with his eyes fixed steadfastly on a single purpose; he was so deeply engaged in the fulfillment of a promise that he missed the opportunity of making deeper insights and contact with things of intrinsic worth. He was particularly ruthless and destructive with himself; his health, the little money he could muster, his personal opportunities—all were sacrificed to the purpose which he had undertaken. It was, on the surface, a dangerous fanaticism, one which would break under stress; yet he had not destroyed his inner self, where he remained extremely resourceful. It was for this reason that he was not going to be easily defeated.

There were other aspects; the speeches he made to the workers during this period belied his true nature. He was deeply moved by the nature of what he was trying to bring about. He was no longer merely testing his powers, but was sustained by a passion, and there were moments when his surface appearance of aloofness was strained to its utmost. The more sarcastic and embittered he became in regard to the assistance he received from individuals, and the more contemptuous he became of workers who were afraid to give formal testimony of the abuses they had suffered, the more deeply he was convinced of the necessity and the rightness of what he was doing.

Bart was becoming more of a gentleman, a more polite and courteous person. He was thoroughly honest both of purpose and method, and was unwilling to use dishonest means of obtaining evidence; even though he realized proof of injustice and exposure would not necessarily straighten things up and knew that law would act only on overwhelming proof, his jaw set itself, and his determination carried him through; his energies redoubled themselves and he forced his way into the open, where he could stand erect and take another look at life with his firm, dissatisfied eyes.

It was a difficult period; only with the utmost care was he able to collect a body of evidence against the company, evidence that included not only testimonials of workers of little value even collectively—but also which in some detail exposed an illegal influence of the company on the public school, the town government and the local police. He gathered exact evidence about a false tax assessment which existed on the four rows of company houses and about profiteering in the company store. One of the things which he was striving to obtain was further testimony in regard to the bonus which had been promised to workers at the end of the war, and a practice of forcing workers to buy bonds. On the inadequate safety precautions he had a sound case. Yet all of these things did not amount to much, except as substantiating material, and it was not until Tim Callaghan made the discovery that "kickbacks" were being made to foremen and that false wage statements were being carried by the pay office that the case began to take on strength.

Bart, sensing that he was near success, turned his back on his own ethics and brought all the force of his personality to bear upon a young woman who worked in that office. In two months' time he had transcriptions of all the important data. Then began the search for legal assistance and the preparation of formal charges against the steel company, which was to be followed by a walkout. After several discouraging conferences with Harrisburg and Philadelphia law firms, who seemed to prefer other kinds of litigation and stronger advance fees than could be obtained, Bart began to favor using one of the professional union legal firms, even though he realized this would lead to control by an outside union. Tim Callaghan opposed this vigorously, and suggested that they get in touch with his young friend who had recently completed law school.

But the important stage was already set. Bart, as the evidence had become more and more substantial, felt his supporters grow and saw a tone of resistance and even arrogance begin to take hold among the laborers. Mijack remained firmly with the company, but honored and admired his son. Gilbert began to show signs of coming to life; he spoke of joining in the walkout. Tim went from shop to shop, talking to men quietly, and in the evenings he went from house to house, talking to the workingmen and their wives. Matt Readinger had already been discharged, and was to be found every morning and evening near the main gate, the stump of his arm swinging, speaking so bitterly that most of the workmen seemed embarrassed as they presented their badges to the watchman.

The company was alert. Bart knew that from this point time would be against him. There were still certain things which he would have liked to have been able to accomplish, particularly to get an unprejudiced press and more experienced legal assistance. He found also that he would have liked to have been able to meet with more experienced union organizers. But there was no time.

Rose went into town, not to persuade him to come home, hoping only to be able to get money from him to buy groceries. He spent evenings and nights in Nesquehon, seemed confused, tired, restless, as Bart drew him further into union activities and organization. In addition to the emotional worries, there had arisen a situation of neglect, no kerosene for the lamps, no milk or eggs. Leaving the child with Mrs. Snyder, so as to be less handicapped in her search, Rose learned he was expected later in the evening at a union meeting. She had three hours; she went to a movie. It was the first she had been to since her marriage.

Somewhere in the time between leaving the child with Mrs. Snyder and entering the theater there gathered in her an uneasiness which she assumed to be the result of not being able to locate her husband. It could be described as an acute sensitivity of her skin and a rather acute feeling of being unable to keep the appearance of having a destination. The manner in which she walked indicated that she was a much younger woman than she accepted herself to be, and her uneasiness reached a climax as she stood in front of the ticket window, searching her purse, uncertain whether there were enough small coins.

Rose found it awkward to get seated, then difficult to fix her attention on the picture. There was a stale warmth in the air which was unpleasant, and she felt herself large and heavy, quite at a disadvantage. The screen seemed to continue to be a series of twisting movements of black and white, and if it had not been for her memory of the gathering darkness and emptiness of the streets, the three hours of waiting, she would not have been willing to sit and look across such a long distance. The room was unusually quiet and there was only the clicking of the projector.

A man took the seat beside her and she had a curious feeling, almost of tenseness, which made her fix her eyes upon the screen and lean slightly forward in her seat. She did not have the least idea what caused her to feel uncomfortable about the man choosing to sit beside her, except that there seemed to be very few people in the theater. The space around her gave her a feeling of giddiness, and she found herself responding to a kind of indignation. It was some time before she realized that her true feeling was a resentment against the possibility of being recognized.

As soon as there was a discreet opportunity, she glanced at the man, not knowing whether this would dispel some of the uneasiness she felt. He was fiftyish, mustached, and as his eyes encountered hers, seemed surprised to find someone beside him. He continued to look at her a moment. His eyes did not make the recognition she expected them to make, and after a bit, she was able to feel certain they never would. Yet she was left with a feeling of being faintly disreputable and helpless.

Bit by bit, she gathered together threads of the past which were responsible for her sitting here, unable to give her attention to the screen. It came to her with a kind of dread that she could be pursued by feelings which had had their beginnings in another person and another world. She felt more aware of and hampered by her past than at any previous time.

In the years since she had married, she had never thought of other men. She had recognized the loneliness of her life and its bleak future prospects, yet had never considered the possibility of living in any other manner. The kind of solution to loneliness which her mother had always chosen would never have occurred to her, and yet she could not prevent herself from being involved, simply by recognizing the man who was sitting beside her as one of those who had visited her mother. The fact that she would never have thought of accepting or making overtures to any man except her husband made her present feeling more distressing. That the man beside her had failed to remember her did not bring with it freedom, but only an avoidance of the necessity of defending herself against that recognition. She actually felt more helpless than if it had been one of the men (at that time boys) with whom she sat years ago in the back row.

She continued to feel molested by his proximity, or by her proximity to him. For a few moments she did nothing, then moved to another part of the theater, knowing now that the uneasiness she had felt walking along the street, hunting for her husband, had been a marginal feeling to the one which she now suffered. She chose a seat beside the aisle and, remembering not only the man with the mustache, but the whole of her girlhood experiences, she sat with a stiff determination and a resolute unwillingness to relinquish her privilege of looking at the screen. She was not as helpless or ashamed of her own past as she was of her mother's, and of the privilege men had of recognizing her as the daughter of a woman with whom they had had intimacies. What she really felt was that she could never have asked the assistance of the usher, just as she would be unwilling to ask a policeman to help her. What she felt was that she could never stop a person on the street and ask the direction of a street (or where her husband was) without a sense of embarrassment. Even worse was the feeling that, if she were ever molested, she would not even be able to feel the correct moral indignation. The fact that her name was Mrs. Rose L. S. Mijack failed to offer her any rights or privileges in society.

The importance of these reactions, which were probably able to take possession of Rose because of her uncertainty as to the strength and protective value of her marriage, and because she was sitting alone, without the child in her arms, was that she saw herself as her husband could see her. There came to her a clear view of herself in which her husband was entitled to be ashamed of her, entitled to consider her an impediment. She began to see how she had disgraced him, how she was responsible for having caused him to disgrace himself. Even without considering herself bad or worthless, her value to him would be forever limited. It was wisdom on his part to keep her living on the mountain, away from contact with people; and it was, for all the loneliness, better for her too. She knew she could never live in Nesquehon and assume the position of a wife and a mother.

Rose felt tenderness and understanding for her husband, and renewed willingness to keep in the shadow of his life. It seemed to her the only kind of atonement that she could make for a shame which he did not deserve to have to bear.

Still more deeply behind her thinking was the child. It was as a threat to her child that she condemned herself. It was probable that the uneasiness she had felt walking along the street and sitting in the theater would have been so disguised from Rose if the child had been in her arms that she would only have hugged it against her. The child had become her most significant protection against the past, her most significant assurance for the future. It was therefore not very pleasant to sit and remember past degradations, remember her own abuses of a moral code which had come to be clear to her. For the first time in her life she suffered the unpleasant feelings of being unchaste.

Later, as Rose walked out of the theater, it was with the determination of having found a destination. She knew she was going to continue to live in the mountains and be more understanding of her husband, more tolerant of his faults. But she knew too that the basis of her actions would no longer spring entirely from her love for him, but from love of the child. The margin of reversal was so slender that it did not have to come into conflict with her love for and devotion to him, and yet it was in this decision, brought about through some inborn tendency toward moral behavior, which, having no outlet, had been suppressed, that the opportunity for happiness was forever lost.

Mr. Pierce frowned slightly and, taking his friend by the arm, led him further along the room.

"These young ones think of men like yourself and myself as Victorian hangovers. They treat us rather like cathedrals were treated during the war, putting sandbags around them. I suppose they are somewhat right. We must seem quaint."

A young man with a red rose bowed to a young lady in a white

416

dress, and water streamed from the rose and splashed against her face. Another young man was walking around the dance floor balancing a broom on the palm of his hand.

"I admit I wince. I really do. My own daughters. Oh, I enjoy them immensely, I enjoy all these antics. . . . I swear the world seems to have become an immense flirtation, not the flirtation of a man and a woman that we remember, but simply a general flirtation about everything."

In a darkened corner of the room a beautifully dressed young woman was standing with her bare feet on top of her partner's shoes, while he shuffled slowly along. Along the side two young women had their arms interwoven and were trying to drink from each other's cocktails, while their escorts stood slapping their glasses together and raising their arms high. Near them, a young man who was talking earnestly to his date kept plucking petals from her corsage.

"I find this a very crude age, and have a decided preference for my father's times. When I look at this generation I find it all a comedy to escape the serious. Trying to walk on top of the water instead of learning to swim . . . Perhaps not, perhaps we're the ones walking the waters. It seems to depend on the point of view."

Out on the lawn a young man was running in circles around the shrubbery, keeping himself a few feet ahead of the girl who was chasing him. He was holding overhead a pair of yellow panties, and shouting, "Who said I couldn't?" On the tennis court a foursome was using real tennis rackets and real tennis balls in the dark. On the porch a young man was walking back and forth, each time pointing a finger at the white post, and saying, "I'm a poet and don't know it."

"But what these young people don't see is that we are a hard lot— much better business minds than they, much stronger sense of values. . . . Superficial yes, but values, values. And I suspect that when it comes to real down to earth, hard-hearted, survival of the fittest—isn't that what they think is such an astonishing discovery—something like that? I expect that in the down-to-earth living we run rings around them."

Some young people were standing on the edge of the swimming pool. In the pool was a young man, fully clothed, with a bottle; it was the only thing that he kept consistently above water. When a young lady reached down her braceleted arm, she sprawled gracefully on top of him. In a little while there were twenty or more people in the pool, all very gay and comfortable.

"They're really children. The most naïve, disenchanted fools the world has ever seen and had to put up with. And how they laugh! Did you ever hear so much and such continuous laughter in your life?"

For the first time he was seeing his own brother. Gilbert felt ashamed that it had to be now, when it was too late, when his brother had lost everything; and there was the sickening knowledge in the pit of his bowels that he had, on first hearing news of his brother's defeat, felt glad that it had occurred; but that was before he knew what his brother had been trying to accomplish; and now it was an ending, it was over before the brothers had clasped hands and sealed their fates in a common effort. For Bart had said less than an hour ago that he was beaten, that his evidence was destroyed and scattered to the winds. Bart was beaten; it could be seen in his eyes, in his posture, in the tone of his voice. Only now could Gilbert, looking at the pale, haggard face that had wept less than twenty minutes ago before this crowd of steel workers gathered for the annual picnic, see how much his brother must have wanted to bring justice to them; already he was deserted and forgotten, except by a few who were suffering for having made his convictions their own. As his brother had wept, Gilbert had seen the shameless smiles, the smug satisfaction of men who would never have the courage to fight for a belief, but who could heal their own cheap souls with the pleasure of seeing a man defeated. There had been audible remarks, some bold, some surreptitious. "Got what was coming to him." "Had it coming a long time, in my books." "Who did he think he was, anyway?" "His old man got the axe too." "They oughta lay all those old bastards off. No wonder we never get a chance." "I hear he told Herman Weaver he was going to have him and Mark Wright and the whole kaboodle in prison." "What's he doing here? He got no right at a steel-company picnic." "I worked in his shop. Slave driver. Nigger lover." "He had me throwed off the police force, just because I was giving an old whore a little fun. But I could tell plenty of *his* goings on." Remarks seem to breed remarks, and the only mercy was the accident of too many men talking at once, which sometimes protected the younger brother's ears. Gilbert glared at offenders, but it did no good, and he felt apathetic toward the use of violence or retort, for he saw that Bart, who usually let no insult slip past him, had no ears. This, more than anything else, had shown Gilbert the deepness of the misery in which his brother was lost. He could see now that Bart had been preparing for this ever since he had been a child, that it accounted for the coldness and the rebuffs, and he

418

saw now why his brother had considered him to be worthless, and he felt that his brother might have been right.

Mr. Weaver was the third speaker and of course his was the major address, which in the first part dealt with the history and achievements of the steel company, and how the town had prospered under its wing; then on to the present, with the end of the company houses and stores, and with the increasingly liberal tendencies, the new workers' benefits. Gilbert noticed that his brother was pale, but intensely alert, and he wondered at what point in the speech this had taken place. Mr. Weaver spoke of the first union, and how the leaders had stolen the workers' money, and he went on to say that a new attempt to make dupes of the workers had just this past week been averted by the vigilance of officials. The steel company did not claim to be perfect, but it was bettering conditions as rapidly as possible for the workers. Expansions within the next few years would open a new future with higher wages for many, and their sons would have a place in which they could be proud to serve; but there was no room for disloyalty, no room for private ambitions and personal grudges, no room for insubordination and threats. That was when Bart rose. Gilbert found that he was on his feet too, and working his way toward his brother, apparently to stand beside him for whatever might come.

Bart stood still and pale for a full thirty seconds before he cried out, "You lie!" The shout was directly at Mr. Weaver, and Bart never moved his eyes from that man. "It is easy for you to boast now, isn't it? But a few days ago you weren't very sure you would be reading this speech, were you? I had evidence enough to put you where you belong. Don't signal for your goons. I'm licked. I stand here only to give you a chance to show this fair play, this glorious future company policy." Bart took a few steps forward, nearer to the platform. "My father has been dismissed without cause. My father has served the steel company well and for many years, and there are a hundred men here who can testify to this, if they will. He had no part in my affairs, did not support me, and I might add, opposed me. What did he get for this loyalty to the company? Fired. Fired, when in three more years he would have been eligible for pension—if you saw no impediment. I therefore suggest, sir, I even beg, that you take him back. If my father is the man I am sure he is, he will resign. But at least allow him the honor of resignation."

Mr. Weaver waited until the man in the audience had finished.

"I couldn't catch all the gentleman said, but I recognize him as

419

one of the leaders in the late unpleasantness. I shall not mention personal accusations and threats which this man has leveled against me, for as an employee of the company I must be above that. I will only state that in spite of all the harm this man has tried to do, offenses for which he could be restrained, it was thought to be fair to allow him to attend the picnic since he worked here part of this year. I should also like to mention that when this young man was in college, we gave him summer employment. Now you see his gratitude."

"What about my father?"

"I know nothing of that. I personally neither hire nor dismiss employees. If your father wishes to appeal his case, I am sure he will have a fair hearing, and that if some mistake has been made, he will have full recompense and apology. But I can scarcely take up such a matter at a picnic, nor spoil the pleasure of the employees, when the beer kegs are already tapped. I might say that in any event I could not accept your view of any matter concerning the company without doubt and suspicion." Mr. Weaver smiled. "I suppose you men are willing to have the speeches, which seem to have been dismantled anyhow, set aside—and the picnic begin."

"Hold it," said Bart. "You misunderstand. I gave you the opportunity to justify my father before all these men. Here. Now."

Mr. Weaver ignored this, and waved for the picnic to begin.

"Then I will be my father's justice," cried Bart, and he started toward the platform.

Gilbert was surprised to find that he had his arms wrapped around his brother, holding him bound. At several points he had nearly joined his brother in shouting at the man on the platform, and he could not explain to himself why, at the last instant, he had seized hold of Bart; he had for the moment a feeling that he was protecting Bart from a worse degradation than he had already suffered, a feeling that at this moment, perhaps the first moment in his life, he was the more sane and reasonable of the two. Knowing how angry Bart must be, almost insanely so to have exposed himself in this manner, he was afraid he could not hold him; but it was surprisingly easy, and he sensed a pleasure in knowing that he was now the stronger of the two, and also a deep pity for what his brother must be feeling, his brother who had never before known what it was to be helpless, who had taken all his suffering in another form. But then he realized that Bart was only stunned, that Bart's face was looking at him with disbelief, and that this changed to anger, to a look of contempt; then it was all he could do to hold Bart, and at moments he was sure he could not last another

420

burst of that wiry strength, not even with the advantage of his grip. But he did, and was in the act of dragging his brother away, when Mr. Weaver, flanked by two company police, came down from the platform.

"Get him out of here," said Mr. Weaver, "or I'll have the police do it. We've had all from that young man we intend to take, and we assure you that none of his blood shall ever set foot in the plant. Now get him out."

The words had no effect on Gilbert. It was the face of the man, ugly, leering, which had made him sick to his bones, and when the man raised his arm, as if he were about to strike Bart, he swung Bart around, and he hissed, "Don't be a fool." Gilbert said it in terrible fear, for he knew that if the man struck, he would have to strike the man; it meant a carnage which could bring nothing but evil, and he had felt again that sensation, a horrid one, that he was destined to kill, that somewhere fate was lurking for him. He had thought this was fate, his heart had leaped with the horror of it, but the man had lowered his fist.

"I will not have hoodlums threatening me. Now get him out, get them both out, officers, if you can without trouble. But if this weren't a picnic," he said, his face pasty with hate, "I would show you what happens to your kind."

"Let go of me," said Bart quietly, and Gilbert realized for the first time that his brother was not struggling, but almost limp. "Take your filthy hands off me."

Gilbert looked into his brother's face; they had come so near to forming that bond which would have been the salvation of them both, and now he saw it would never be; he saw loathing, hate, and he was sick and shut his eyes a moment. "Bart . . . Believe me . . . I did this for you . . . You're too good to have it end this way." But there was faithlessness in the very tone of the words, a sense of the futility of any explanation.

Bart did not even look. Bart walked away, and he was not seen in Nesquehon Foundry for many years.

35

Mr. Pierce began to bring businessmen home with him and intro-duce them to his daughter. In some cases he brought men who were entirely unsuitable, much too old and stable, simply to tease her. In-terspersed among these were a few men whom he considered quite worthwhile. If his daughter had shown any tendency to be attracted by any of them, he would have been pleased. He was rather disgusted with her tendency to date no one except college boys from other parts of the country, particularly tennis players, swimmers and ama-teur golfers.

Yet he paid her bills at college, turned a polite and understand-ing ear to the complaints and forebodings of the house mother, and took a substantial pleasure in seeing Dorothy well dressed; if he no-ticed anything lacking, gloves which did not match perfectly, the need of a brooch, he would shortly make a purchase. He was thoughtful enough to include among the many boxes which were posted little items for her roommate and friends. College seemed to have become rather a playhouse since the war, and yet it was not without delightful aspects.

In her junior year he bought her a fur jacket, took care of a dress and lingerie bill which even she seemed ashamed of. His reward was to see on the wall of one of the fraternity houses a large oil painting of his daughter, a little too glamorous, yet a quite sufficient tribute to the "sweetheart" of the fraternity. Her only two difficulties, it seemed, were grades, of which she was simply careless, and young men, who she claimed were all bores. He suspected, however, that she was really having the time of her life.

He knew she did not love him, that she considered him a bit of an old fuddy, that there were times when he bored her with his moraliz-ing; but in comparison with the rest of the family, he knew he was much more to her liking. It was a nuisance to have her play up to him to get the things she wanted, and at the same time he was amused at how easy she seemed to believe he was to get around.

After graduation, after a summer in Nesquehon Foundry, Doro-thy tried again to coax him to take her to Florida. She felt the best thing for him would be to go spend some of his money, have a good time, get away from his wife for a while. She pointed out to him that there wasn't any life in him, none of the carefree gaiety she would have loved to see. She told him what fun they would have! Of course it was only because he would not allow her to go alone, but it was rather enjoyable to have her tease him, to have her see in him a youthfulness which he had never felt, even in his youth.

Despite all this, Mr. Pierce could never forget that she had twice made a fool of him in front of the same young man. The second occasion had been one of cowardice, and cowardice in women was much more inexcusable than in men. He had always been disgusted with feminine reactions to men who flaunted masculinity, and as he aged, the feeling had become one of nausea. It had been particularly unpleasant to have to rely on the pride and arrogance of Bart Mijack to make permanent a separation which his daughter was not sensible enough to hold to. He remembered how for a moment he had even considered reversing all his former plans, of placing his daughter at the disposal of that ruthless, ambitious man. He had felt like casting Dorothy out of the house. But he had been afraid of the eventual results.

No, he was not likely to overestimate his daughter's strength ever again.

Thus it had been a particular pleasure when a young lawyer, Mr. Fred Kostar, who was hunting an older partner or an established firm, had questioned him as to the advisability of accepting counsel for the steel-company union. Mr. Pierce had been surprised to learn that the union was preparing a case. He had urged the young lawyer by all means to examine the strength of the union's argument. Finding that it consisted mostly of testimonials, along with stenographic transcriptions of documents which had been obtained illegally, it had been a simple enough matter to advise the young lawyer not to handle the case, to, instead, offer him a position as legal adviser to the newspaper, and assist him in setting up a practice in Harrisburg. It had also been simple enough to contact Mr. Weaver, to list the employees who had given testimonials, and state those documents which could be damaging, and, particularly, to advise discretion.

Mr. Weaver, however, had been boiling mad about another matter, a scandal in which his wife—his third—had involved herself. The scandal was not that she was running around with another man, since she had been doing that for several years with several men, but that she had been publicly scorned by the latest man who had caught her

423

eye; it had really been her husband's fault, for talking to her so often about the young union organizer, and particularly by conciliating Bart Mijack to the extent of inviting him to the house for conferences. These visits had been of course only preliminaries to the thirty-pieces-of-silver method which Mr. Weaver was so old-fashioned as to consider as still directly applicable. Bart Mijack, apparently stalling for time, had appeared to show reluctance, had pretended to be tempted, until, unfortunately, he had so scorned Mrs. Weaver that she had found it unbearable not to protest to her husband.

The results had been more dramatic than had been planned, and the information which Mr. Pierce had relayed had not been used with as much discretion as it should have been. Mr. Pierce had been brought nearer to unpleasant publicity than he ever cared to be; even to some of his closest friends it seemed that something like ethics could have been involved, and there had flared into prominence a surprising support for labor, not merely within labor, but in outside circles, which warned of future trouble. Further, Mr. Pierce had been unable to exert his usual influence on Mr. Weaver, not merely because Mr. Weaver's wife had been involved, but because of a sore point which had arisen concerning Dorothy, who had been expected (at least by Mr. Weaver) to marry Arthur Weaver, and who, by her conduct, and now her position as a divorcee, though not technically, had made that impossible, at least for the moment. A man who had been married three times was not likely to approve of his son marrying a divorcee, at least until it was made certain that he could not do better. That Bart Mijack had been involved in both ends of the situation made it more touchy.

But at least Bart Mijack was gone, bag and baggage, from Nesquehon. If Mr. Pierce's role in the removal of Bart had been modest, he was nevertheless quite satisfied with it.

The house was full of roaches and bugs that hid on the stone wall and in the corners and the joints of furniture. The electricity had been disconnected, and in the light of oil lamps there could be seen swarms of shadows. The roaches ran only because light always scared them for a moment, and later some of them would even venture to walk around the bases of the lamps.

The curtains, rugs, cushions, needlework, doilies, vases of paper flowers, the sewing basket and rag bag, the aprons and feather dusters, were still there, dirty with time and dampness. In the cabinet were the pie tins and mixing bowls and wooden spoons and beaters, and on the stove the two pans which Mijack used, and clamped to the edge of the cabinet the meat grinder. On the kitchen sink was the bottle of turpentine and the piece of matted cotton with which he applied it to his teeth.

The curtains had not yellowed, but they were dirty, and they had the stiffness and droop of having hung too long without being touched. The rugs felt sticky against the soles of shoes. Yet the only thing that was changed was the kitchen table, now a bare sheet of wood, and the tablecloth still humped in the corner where Mijack had flung it in disgust. Even the things the children had left behind, clothing, old shoes, a few playthings, hung in the closets and lay on the floor.

Mijack had been gone from the house for several months, and had returned sick. He had always been certain that in every case of behavior there was an absolute distinction between right and wrong, an unwavering line of conduct which one must follow: there was no middle ground, no compromise, no shades or overtones, and no special circumstances. So, after his dismissal from the steel mill, he had packed a bundle and had required himself to walk along the river toward the country to the north. He did not stop to visit his wife's family. He went on past Millersburg and Gratz and Lykens and Wiconisco and then swung back, going as far as Shamokin. He visited all the coal mines which he remembered from his youth, hunting for work.

He had returned sick, knowing it had been his last journey. It was not the money he had needed, but the work, and there had been in his heart as he had walked north a feeling that if he found work he might take still another woman as his wife and raise still more sons. But by the time he reached Nesquehon, sick not as with the typhoid which he had had in Memphis, but sick with the feeling of uselessness, he had known that his memories were never to remember more than one woman and two sons. And he knew then that it was not the money, not even the work which he really had needed, but simply the feeling of being the creator of his own destiny. He had looked forward toward retiring from the steel plant, toward setting himself to pasture. His eyes had always been fixed upon a time when he would have freedom. But he could not accept being rejected, discarded. Because of his favorite son at the hour when he had had the most pride in Bart —pride in a son cannot have much savor unless it is founded on pride in oneself—Mijack had been forced to see that his entire life had been only a small self-representation in the midst of huge forces. His life had meant nothing except to himself.

For weeks after his return, he spent most of his time outside sitting on a tree stump, facing the rising or the setting of the sun. He would sit quietly, contemplative, for part of an hour, and then become restless, roaming his land, waving his arms as if there were still chickens to scare, kicking rocks which had fallen from the wall. It was usually dark before he went inside.

The kitchen began to have the stale smell of bread and of thick milk.

Rowiger was the only one to come to see him.

"Do I look like I'm sick?" snapped Mijack.

"Yes," Rowiger confessed.

"Then if I look sick, I am sick," said Mijack. "And if I wanted to talk, I would."

Rowiger suggested that he would come back another time. He was looking for a carpenter.

That same evening, as Mijack looked about the kitchen, he realized he had been persistently stubborn in avoiding his destiny. He knew that if he were not careful his life would lose even its meaning to himself.

In the days that followed the house underwent enormous changes. He burned sulphur in each room and placed the bed legs in pans of kerosene and aired everything. He made a big pile of all the clothes and curtains and everything which had belonged to his wife and burned them. He kept some of his sons' and daughter's things only because they were still alive. He stripped the house until it was almost as bare as when he had built it, keeping only the rugs and the more useful furniture. The floors were sanded. He even cleaned the cellar, ridding it of accumulated nuts and bolts and odd bits which could be used for nothing, which his own fingers had discarded year after year. He oiled the tools.

Everything went well until he decided to repair the chicken house. Then he noticed that he had to have more time and patience with himself than he was accustomed to allowing. It was as he climbed onto the roof that he made his first full physical insight into age, and sensed that too much experience was a handicap, an extra weight to bear, for he was going to have to find new and easier ways of working. He was going to have to compromise between what he could do and what should be done.

When he had missed a nail twice and struck so hard the third time that the nail bent, he said to himself, "It's time to stop and take stock. You've made the work harder for yourself." He laid the hammer down and looked at his hand; it had a faint, brownish-yellow tinge that was neither sunlight nor fire, but slackened circulation. There was a looseness of skin around the knuckles. He remembered how he had always taken care of his hands, rested them when they were tired.

His hands were not to blame. It was his eye, which he had made look into the fire too many years. Now there was something behind his eye which shimmered and would not let him see as he wanted to; now when his hands were not what they were, he made them do more, made them do what they could not do, work and see too. He felt as if his hands were being patient with him, as if they were still willing to learn new tricks if he had the patience to accept their handicap.

His left hand had always been of little value, good for holding, good for immobile grasping, but never trusted, often getting in the way, disturbing the confidence of his real hand. Because of this his left arm had often hung at his side, so limp and useless that it appeared to be suffering from an injury. His right arm had done extra work which other men would not have required from theirs. Now it was time to change this, time to use everything he had, and he came to see that it was his strong arm which was weakening, and that his arms might some day regain balance, though on a level lower than he cared to think about.

But he still had reason to live, still had a destiny, and it was a more difficult task than any in his life. For it was not physical decline which threatened to make his life meaningless, but the failures of his will, a memory which was neither long nor meticulous, brief, feeble sorrows mixed with periods of sleep and forgetfulness. The mind in decay resembled strongly the mind in growth, and the blessings of age he despised, as he lost his ambitions and desires one by one, without losing his need of life.

He had to keep thinking of what he was doing, had to keep his mind on it. If his mind strayed an instant, he had to say, I have sinned, I have sinned against the only real thing I hold. That helped, though nothing much could keep him from straying a second time, and the secret was never to stray, for he could never return to where he had been, only return near it, across the river from it. And there was each day the loss of time, time to get back to where he could not go.

Mijack came to feel that time was the last secret, the one he would

427

never find out, because he kept it from himself. He could not endure any explanation of it. He would never even know that it was not a secret, that it did not exist in his mind, nor his heart, nor his watch; it was only he who had put it there, now that he could no longer measure life in terms of accomplishment. And that was why he had to keep thinking of what he was doing, because what he was doing refused to have enough importance.

The best that he could hope for was to keep the faults of each day countable on his fingers instead of among the stars. Yet that was something.

There were times—or at least moments—when Dorothy reminded Mr. Pierce so much of his wife, in her physical vitality and her need of passion, that he felt a flickering hatred for her; or rather, not her, since he remained fond of her, but a flickering hatred that his wife had not been more like her—that his wife had so escaped him in her youth. It was a constant reminder that his wife would soon be past the stage of life in which a woman can be most deeply hurt, that she had already passed the heights of her physical nature, and that her intelligence, her curiosity, imagination, would soon be either in decline or untouchable. As he had despised her early in their marriage for her continued faith in him, so he detested her now for having seen through him.

Since these difficulties involving his daughter, there had been a change in him, a more direct antagonism that made him nervous and put him at a disadvantage with his wife, who seemed to welcome his outright anger as a relief from his cool and perfect manners. His control of the family was threatened, and it made him realize that no matter what degree of success he might have in his plans for political control of central Pennsylvania, he would never be satisfied until he had settled affairs with his wife.

His chances of finding affection and companionship within his family were nearly gone. It left him with a chilled bitterness. Sixty was a dangerous age in a man who had not yet resolved or stemmed the animosity that he felt toward his wife, nor finished formulating his intentions in the world around him.

There were almost no flowers growing on the mountain. There was laurel in the foothills and skunk cabbage higher up. Rose kept a single vase on the mantel of the fireplace, in which she placed little dark red flowers, scarcely bigger and not as bright as drops of blood.

428

They were so dry and brittle to begin with that they could be kept almost two weeks, and were found blooming, never in groups, along the edge of the timber line, held on thin, juiceless wire stems, easily seen because there was no other color to attract the eye. Yet she was fond of them, as she was fond of the few vegetables which she could get to grow, as she was fond of seeing the few children and people who ventured this far and high.

Her hunger for those few flowers was not so much prompted by the absence of flowers on the mountain as by the absence of trees where the cabin stood and all above it. Below there were an endless number of trees, so crowded together they had no individuality. It made her feel the bareness of the part of the mountain where she lived, and, looking downward, when the feeling for trees was in looking up at them, made her feel the distance she was from civilization. There were a few trees not far below and even a few above, but with a stern, hard, twisted quality, as if the roots drew their only nourishment from rocks around which they were forced to gnarl themselves in the way blacksnakes hang from limbs.

Rock, endless rock, square, round, time-eroded, chiseled, slashed, frost-cracked. Rock crouched upon rock, boulders hanging in mute, fantastic positions, and above all an impression of tremendous weight balanced for an hour, a century, or eternity, by a few absurd geometric principles. The rocks had been darkened by the rain and melting snow of many centuries. Time seemed accounted for among the multiple fractures and designs of broken stone. The ruin of nature was so obviously the final intention of the sky that the stones seemed to understand the futility of their existence, except as a rough loose armor, perhaps a greater burden than protection, for the earth below.

Rose did not know how to walk any more, not with the easy swinging motion which had been one of the pleasures of her girlhood. There was in the manner the rocks lay the quiet dignity of old soldiers who have required of them nothing except to wait, and yet it was to her more solemn and portentous than she could bring herself to admit. There was the silence, not only silence, but the feeling of being too high for sound, of being held from the lower areas of the earth by a thin layer of air which acted like gauze against her ears. It was a too constant motionlessness to be seen by a young woman who feared she was at the edge of unhappiness.

She had not felt this way about the mountain before the child was born. Hard slaps of lightning kept her in fear from the beginning of summer. The chimney was broken and the logs adjoining scarred black. Sweltering in the reflected heat of summer days, she felt the gathering of storm atmospheres, the sky tense and faintly elastic. The mountain seemed fit only for living with dread of monstrous deeds of nature which had not yet occurred. It made her feel as if she and the child were the foolish accidental witnesses of a contest of forces in which they had no right to be involved.

Winter evenings, when she was alone, snowbound, not knowing whether her husband could return even if he attempted to, seeing from her bed through the window the ropes of snow which netted the peak of the mountain, with moonlight shining on it, she could not even be comforted by the presence of the child. There was a certain cold beauty along the ridge which made her life seem almost unbearable. There was the muted sound of wind passing over snow, while the brook seemed to pass right along the wall of the cabin, rolling slowly downward, held to a slow pace by ice which shawled its edges and made bridges across the shallows. Below, from time to time, there came the choked gargle of water being compressed, a sound like the jerky exit of water from a canteen.

There was almost nothing she liked any more. In the late springtime, when there was only enough greenery to make it evident that the first week of hot weather would dry everything, she planted the few things she knew would grow, radishes, onions, stunted carrots and sometimes beets and kale. The rows were not planted straight, nor seeded properly, because there were places where the ground was too shallow, and as a result, everything grew in clusters, giving a barren air to the whole. Yet there was a triumph in seeing anything grow.

The child was to all appearances healthy, but on the slightest pretext she would carry it into town to have the doctor examine it. She took it more out of fear of her own ignorance of sickness, living where no one could advise her, than of positive fear of its health. She talked with the doctor about the dampness and cold nights. Then too, after the first visit, she was drawn to return because of a feeling which living in the mountains had denied her, the pleasure of possession, the sweet feeling that the child was hers, which, sitting in the waiting room, among the patients, among women who looked at the child and smiled and wiggled their fingers at it, she could find. The feeling of carrying the child into the office, the pain of handing it out of her arms into those of the doctor, of hearing his voice discuss it, a grave voice which seemed to confirm the importance which she felt. There was too the pleasure of being in the town, walking along smooth sidewalks, holding the child near the window glass of stores so it could see the many pretty colored things which it would want to play with in a few more years. Already it had something which rattled, something which tinkled, something which was soft and fuzzy.

Without doubt she was responding to a fear that she was going to be left alone with the child. Her husband was moving beyond her, into a world of interests which she could only vaguely comprehend. She accepted the blame for never having understood. She accepted the blame for pretending that she did, for inviting him to tell her the jumbled contradictions which she had never been able to make sense from. If she had not made such considerable progress in making herself acceptable and agreeable, if she had not made strides toward mature thought and speech and understanding, she would have been less lonely, less bewildered, and would have been more satisfied to remain living on the mountain. The child, for all she loved it, could not provide, either with its mouth, eyes, or continuous needs, the sense of companionship which her husband represented.

It was peculiar that she should have this feeling of insecurity at a time when her husband was most stable, with a good job, good income and savings. He was indeed so satisfied with his present prospects that he had not spoken about the sawmill in many months. He had made a number of new friendships in the town, resumed some which had been abandoned. It was a satisfaction to Rose to know that her husband was on good terms with Mr. Rowiger and Mr. Snyder. There were numerous small changes in his appearance; he had abandoned wearing boots and the broad belt, shaved regularly, wore his hair still slightly long but without deep sideburns, had purchased two suits, one multicolored, but the other a deep, straight brown.

Her worries arose from his enthusiasm and some of his talk. Yet even this could hardly explain her feeling. He talked about sending his sister, who had won a talent contest at the Majestic Theater in Harrisburg, to college or to New York. He talked about her enthusiastically, saying she was hard as nails, she had everything it took to be successful, and that the least he could do, now he had a little money, was help her until she got a start. He talked also about his brother, who was a labor-union big shot out in Pittsburgh, and, although he spoke disparagingly, there was something too suppressed about his voice, something quick in the movements of his eyes. It was when he showed signs of ambitiousness that Rose was most worried, and she could feel a strain begin to mount between them, a strain which no amount of agreement and assent to what he was saying

431

could prevent. At such times, too, he did not seem quite as interested in her or in his child as he needed to be.

But mostly it was the mountain. She believed it was the mountain and its shabbiness and loneliness which was driving her husband toward disregard of her and the child. She believed the long walk home from work every evening was having a bad effect upon him. He no longer felt freedom up here. He wanted to move into town. And yet Rose had to wait, knowing that she dare not suggest it herself, knowing it was herself, or some slight shame which he still attached to her, that kept them in isolation.

Her father was not quite satisfied with her approaching marriage. This would have been true of any man she had chosen, and she knew it was only a matter of time before Mr. Pierce gave his full, satisfied consent. She was utterly cynical about her father. Knowing the man she had chosen would give a worthy account of himself, she knew the eventual relationship between him and her father would be one of mutual admiration and assistance. Mr. Pierce was objecting because he wanted to bring further wealth into the family, and she had been clever enough to see that the one sort of person who was not wealthy and yet could not be denied was a young man to whom he had already given assistance and approval.

It was her mother's unexpressed disapproval that angered her; it did not seem to be Irene's business to interfere in this affair, even through the use of silence. "Why don't you say you don't like him— and be done with it! You know it's not going to change *my* mind!" Dorothy cried out one afternoon, several weeks after the announcement of her engagement. Just because her mother had warned her about Bart! Dorothy had not asked advice then, she was certainly not going to ask now.

On more than one occasion she debated telling Fred Kostar how things stood between her mother and herself, to stop him from being so ridiculously civil to Irene. Sometimes they talked half an hour!

It was the night he had driven his car along the wrong side of the street, shouting and pleading with her through the window, that she had found out there was more to him than she had been willing to believe. "Watch out," she had had to say to him, as a car came plunging down the street, and he had merely pounded his hand against the center of the steering wheel, his eyes still fixed upon her. It was then, driving so close to the curb that the tire sometimes scraped, using low gear and the clutch to manage to stay even with her, looping around the few parked cars, that he had spoken seriously and with decision. Fred did not ask her to get back into the car, and did not say anything when she reversed her direction so that she was behind him, then crossed the street. He simply swung the car across and met her there, the other window rolled down, and continued to speak in a low, serious voice. In front of the house, she had approached the car window, and said, "You're a fool, but I rather like you."

There had been another evening when they had driven close to where the moon was lighting the guard rail of the reservoir. "It's your gas," she had said, and had leaned back and let the car take her. In her purse were her own car keys, and she had sat examining her fingernails, while he drove at the smooth, even pace of having a destination. They had arrived there before the moon was too high, so that he parked with the moon in his windshield. "It *is* cleaner out here," she had admitted. "There *is* something about the moon—in spite of all the jokes." Then seeing the way his eyes had turned toward her, she had added, "I don't mean romantic." After a while, she said, "It makes the past seem past and accounted for. . . . It makes the future careless." Stretching, in that luxurious manner which always made her seem slightly feline, she said, "It makes me more beautiful. But it makes me think of money and jewels and pretty things I don't deserve." There had been silence for quite a while, Fred sitting with his arms braced against the steering wheel, looking very much as if he were guiding the car down a steep hill, Dorothy listening to the sound her purse made as she opened and closed it. "I suppose this was all an accident," she had said. "I suppose this just happened to be full moon."

Fred, not looking at her, had said, "It's not full moon. That's tomorrow night."

Dorothy had looked out through the windshield, feeling the interference of glass, and said, "I used to come up here with quite a guy. He had enough confidence to use my car and put my blankets in the back seat. He even borrowed my car to come up here and cut firewood in the daytime. I remember when I used to like to sit in the wet grass beside him. . . . We didn't bother with the moon." And later she had cried out, "And by what standards do you judge me?" and Fred had looked straight at her, saying, "I've been slapped a few times, if that's what you mean," and she had retorted, "Phoo, you wouldn't know when a girl meant it and when she didn't," and he had stepped his foot hard on the brake, driving erratically because there was nowhere to go.

"I wish I *could* treat you with disrespect."

Dorothy had laughed her high, floating laugh, and said, "Tell me, how *do* Nesquehon Foundry girls choose? By thickness of arms? By wrestling ability?" And still later, she had cried, "Oooh! You're such an idiot. If you would only stop listening to what I *say*." And after she had lit a cigarette from his, "Darling darling darling," she had said, "you have the most wonderful nose. Forgive me for making fun of it." With her forehead against the lapel of his coat, "Marry me in a church." Throwing the door open as he walked solemnly around the back of the car, with that usher-type courtesy that she could scarcely endure, she had said, "I warn you, I refuse to be a housewife, and I won't spend my life in this town."

Dorothy did not consider Fred Kostar nearly as provincial as she pretended. He would make a striking figure as a New York or Boston lawyer. He was still rather collegiate, and had a promising future, and so long as she got out of this town she was willing to wait a few years for Florida and Paris. She craved society. In this town there were no young people. There wasn't even a country club.

Fred was by no means the most cultured person she had ever met, but he had possibilities. He would at least not keep her in chains, not try to make a washwoman of her. She had seen men pour homeward from the central entrance to the steel mill; it was a disgusting sight. To be the wife of one of those ignorant hunkies would be unendurable. Stink, babies, pathetic clothes. Fred was at least a salvation from that disgrace, and a beautiful, cultured wife was a splendid asset to such a man. As his wife, she would be granted freedom such as was impossible for a single girl to ask.

She often imagined how Fred would appear as her partner among the smart younger set in one of the larger cities, in summer white with the splendid tennis tan a few outings in the sun gave him, in golf togs with the light jacket which looked better unbuttoned, by the swimming pool in white trunks and the dark green glasses which made his face handsome, so that his legs, rather ugly around the knees and hairy in ringlets, were almost violently attractive. A single week in such an atmosphere would restore the gaiety and charm which she remembered herself as possessing in college.

She kept him in doubt. She did not hold out her hands to him in complete surrender. She carried her persecution of him to such lengths, actually a few times in danger of losing him, that even she realized she was making him pay too hard a price for her. He was not going to be able to say he had not seen her at her worst. She insisted that he should have the exact ambitions she wanted for him. She poisoned his ear at every opportunity about Nesquehon Foundry. She let him know he was not dealing with one of those hunkie girls who often as not had to pretend pregnancy to get their man.

Yet, even as she treated him with curtness and disrespect, she came to depend on him. She knew she had too high an opinion of her worth, knew her intelligence was not much above average, knew there were limits to what beauty could atone for. But she could not make herself humble. A man who chose only beauty should pay too high a price. Dorothy had no intention of being the kind of fool her mother had been, she was going to keep herself in mind, her husband could come second; none of this yes-yessing, that was how a man got to thinking himself lord and master. She knew she could be hard, cold as ice, and was proud of it. She had already looked in the mirror for marks near her eyes and at the ends of her lips—she knew what she was doing.

Her father, he would give a quite handsome wedding present—perhaps even that trip to Europe. Although she could not count on his generosity, she could still use him to advantage, to help Fred along in a financial way during the first years. Her father did not care about her happiness, and probably would not come to her rescue when and if her happiness was threatened, but he could refuse nothing which would reflect upon the financial circumstances of the family.

This time she knew what she was doing.

36

When Rowiger awoke the light in the room was strange. The room refused to confirm his memory of it, and a faint, gnawing chill in his arms and legs made him feel immovable, isolated in an armchair too big and too firm, while time drifted by him and between his knees.

He had a sudden fear. But it was only a dampness that was creeping out of the fireplace.

He patted the sides of his coat, dipped both hands simultaneously into the large pockets, and soon was fitting spectacles to the familiar marks on his nose.

The sky was autumn dark with threat, but only threat, so when he saw roofs and wet trees and wet street, he looked again at the sky, hunting for rain. The window was clean. The house was silent. It was only something sad and desolate in all he saw that made him decide it was still raining.

The bright green umbrella leaning against the fireplace made his hands grip the foremost edges of the chair, made him come up out of it. As he walked about the room, his hands kneaded each other, as if this would solve the stiffness in his legs. It was to the fireplace, where there was the most chill, that he went to stand, and then to take up the umbrella. He had known for some time now that he was going out into the rain, almost without purpose. He knew at this moment, as he stood waiting without hesitation, that if this had been the black umbrella with the steel spire, he would have started a fire in the hearth, and settled down to read.

Rowiger was struck by his loneliness. He was in fact almost horrified. He took up the green umbrella and went out into the rain, without destination. He did take the time to put on his hat. It was an apprehensive feeling that urged him, but not the sort that would make a man hurry, not the sort that a man can hope by motion to leave behind. More nearly, he sensed that he must not be prevented from taking his afternoon walk, and it was with this sort of determination and preoccupation that he moved along the street. He did not look about. He did not have the hope or even the desire to meet anyone. It would probably have seemed to him a definite though mild agony to have to talk with anyone, for what made him clutch his overcoat close about his throat and hold the umbrella high and forward-slanting was something intensely personal. He was not even disturbed by the drop of water which had smeared one lens of his spectacles.

The roofs of the houses were tin and red, and when he came to a place where there were no trees to hide all the other sounds of rain, he had a sudden impression of hearing thousands of tiny nails falling everywhere. He knew he heard this too clearly for it to be real. He paused, holding the umbrella away from himself, so that he could see everything, and yet he was not really looking, but listening; he felt there was some sound missing. It was the most discontented moment

436

of his life. What was still more alarming, at this moment he sensed that he was a man in middle age hovering near the discovery that he regretted his life, a man who had not walked four blocks and was already feeling the dampness in his shoes and the utter futility of an umbrella. Still more deep in his consciousness was a feeling that for many years his moral nature had been in a state of paralysis, and was now threatened with collapse.

Yet he knew even at this moment that he must draw the umbrella over his head, useless as it was, except in the most practical sense. The rain drops on the sidewalk spread round, gleaming like the coins he had once scattered over the schoolyard . . .

"Can I go with?" said Rodger, crowding close to Rowiger to share the umbrella.

Rowiger shifted the spectacles on his nose to obtain better focus. It was only in this looking down that he became aware of the blurred wetness of his lenses. He could not manage both, so he gave the handle of the umbrella to the boy, and, stooping a little, began to dry his glasses.

"Can I?" said Rodger. His arm was held straight up overhead, yet he still could not keep the spokes of the umbrella from touching Rowiger's hat. The face bent down near his own looked strange, especially the flesh around the eyes. The eyes were looking at him with unusually wide fullness, and the boy saw the near-sightedness in them with a kind of distress. He was glad when Rowiger fitted the glasses around his head and took the handle of the umbrella; which instantly rose with the rush of an escaping balloon.

"I suppose so," said Rowiger. "Go get your raincoat or whatever."

"I'm ready now," said Rodger.

"You'll get wet."

It was a statement of fact, not caution.

"I shall get soaked," the boy admitted gleefully. "See how wet I am already. It runs down my neck." He sprinted on ahead, hair glistening, already sleek and curled. He was holding his face upward, trying to get rain drops to strike against his eyes.

Rowiger had been chilled and miserable. The shoulders of his coat were heavy, putting a curious restriction on the movements of his arms. But the sight of the boy, wetter than himself, was like encountering friendliness.

He viewed the boy as a piece of luck, an escape from his thoughts, even though in a deeper sense the last thing he wanted at this moment was to have anyone with him. Rowiger felt beset by middle-

437

aged nervousness, saw it as such, saw it as utterly unreasonable, and yet was helpless.

Rodger had at this moment run to the shelter of a pine. Just as he arrived, a quantity of water released from somewhere high in the tree fell squarely on him. At any other position he would have been safe, but Rodger seemed to have an instinct for being where things happened.

"You better come in under my umbrella," said Rowiger.

Rodger made a face at the tree. Then, laughing, he ran on down the sidewalk, curving from side to side, testing his shoes to see how much traction they had.

"You hold on," said Rowiger. "We haven't even decided where we're going."

The boy halted, turned. "Is that important?" he said, his eyes bright from the exertion of running.

Rowiger did not answer. He merely looked down into the small, uplifted face.

"Let's just go," said Rodger. "Let's walk and walk."

The boy did, running, Rowiger following, his umbrella bobbing overhead inadequately, as drops struck and splintered into tiny fragments which pierced the green cloth. The slow accumulation of mist on his nose and chin was annoying. Yet he did not feel as depressed as he had; there was something to be said for simply plodding along in the erratic wake of a small boy. He began to feel a patience with life, to the extent that he called out more heartily, "Lead on."

But Rodger had heard the kuh-jugging of a rain spout. He had gone to investigate, grasping the spout in both hands, as if he were trying to pull it loose from the porch of the house. "See how it shakes," he said. "I can't hold it still."

Rowiger carefully stepped over the shallow gutter, grunting an acknowledgment. He plodded on. Further ahead the pavement ended, and there would be mud. Still further ahead were the fields, wet and probably overgrown. He was without imagination today, without any sense of adventure. He felt he could not go anywhere unless there was a clear path to follow. Yet he could not find in the rain, in the heavy downpour, reason to turn back.

Rodger's hands were cold from holding the rain spout, and his pockets wet. They stuck to his hands. When he found a reason to need his hands, the pockets came out too, and hung like two grayish ears. He thrust the toe of his shoe into the white but not very clean spume around the metal mouth of the rain spout, watching the spume climb closer and closer to his ankle, and then, in a freakish gurgle, jump up. Only after he jerked his foot away did the water begin to sink into his shoe. "Yi, is my foot ever wet!" he shouted in glee, louder than necessary. His stocking was uncomfortable, then mysteriously dry again.

Rowiger was moving on. Rodger ran after him, and tried to get his arm. Rowiger pulled his arm away.

"I'm Rodger Pierce," said the boy in a changed voice, walking backward, holding his hand forth gravely. "I'm going to be a musician."

Rowiger, finding himself incapable of walking without fear of stepping on or stumbling over the boy, slowed his pace.

"A great, great musician."

"Perhaps."

Rodger continued to walk backward. He apparently had no fear of bumping into anything. It was Rowiger who kept an eye on what was behind the boy.

"No, it's true," said Rodger. "I found it out this morning. You should have heard me at the piano. Mother can tell you."

Rowiger became aware of the handle about which his hand was closed. The stem of the umbrella felt firm and strong.

"And I'm going to be a soldier too," said Rodger. "I'm going to military school."

Rowiger gave the boy a full, direct look.

"I decided to be a soldier and a musician too," said Rodger. He spoke seriously, with pride.

"I don't think you want to be a soldier," said Rowiger.

"But I do. I'm going to military school next year. Cross my heart, it's true."

Rowiger did not reply.

Rodger was marching along like a soldier, lifting his knees high. "See how wet I am," he shouted. He had just made the discovery anew. "There isn't a dry spot on me," he insisted, proudly slapping his clothes to demonstrate their water content. "I have to run a little to keep warm. You mind?"

"No . . . No . . . But wait there, hold on, I think we better turn back."

Rodger was too far from home to be obedient.

"I think we better get you inside a raincoat."

"You and Mother make a pair," said Rodger. "Always worrying."

Rowiger was not worried. He felt a need to see Irene and talk with her.

Rodger made three jumps for the branch. Rowiger waited until the branch had been released and the leaves had ceased quivering before he stooped, holding his umbrella in the position of a warrior's shield, and crept under.

"I like rain, don't you?" Rodger said. "It makes me laugh."

There were no dry areas ahead. It was raining hard. Big drops thumped the umbrella so soundly that it shook in Rowiger's hand.

"I like you. You listen to everything I say," said Rodger, imitating the man's manner of walking. "My father never listens. Why is that? I mean, gee, after all." He saw a puddle and smacked his foot down on it and made water fly in every direction. "Nothing I say. Heck, how'm I supposed to know what he wants me to say? Do you know what to say?"

Rowiger shook his head. "What military school you going to?"

"I don't know," said Rodger. "A big one, I guess."

They passed beyond the last edge of sidewalk. Rowiger drew the brim of his hat so that the wind was less likely to catch under it; it was really the roughness and muddiness which made him apprehensive.

"Why don't rain drops get big?" asked Rodger. "Why don't they get real real big? Big as my hand even."

"There must be a reason," Rowiger admitted. "But I don't know it."

"What I think is God doesn't want to hurt things."

Rowiger was careful of where he stepped, the thick crepe-rubber soles of his shoes hissing. His shoes had begun to squeak, and the leather seemed tight around his toes. But after a time he seemed to gain the carelessness that is so necessary for a man who intends to walk any distance. He gave up the struggle of trying to keep out of the mud.

"We get on so splendid together," said Rodger. "We see things eye to eye. Father and Mother, I can't never find anything to say to them. And I always thought I'd have more and more to say." Rodger frowned. "The trouble is, nobody's interested in me any more."

"That's nonsense," said Rowiger. "But what kind of soldier is it you're going to be?" he almost shouted. He always raised his voice more in the open. They were walking along a wall, and beyond stood a desolate stone house. The gate was locked with a chain. A few stones had slid from their perches, but it was the kind of wall which would deteriorate only slightly, would rid itself of poorly placed stone without losing its main strength. It had the slope of the hill figured perfectly. "Why a soldier? Where did you get this idea?"

"West Point," said Rodger. "That's where I'm going." He climbed onto the wall and ran along the stones, prancing from one to another, spinning his arms for balance. "Oh, I don't want to be a soldier," he said, pausing, standing on one foot. "Father's sending me."

Rowiger wondered whether Irene was aware that her son was so pliable; it seemed to him, as he remembered their conversations, that she had been counting not merely on her own opposition, but on her son's. And here was the boy, obviously not unwilling to go. Once more Irene was going to be left to struggle alone.

Rodger came down from the wall. He went to the man and gave him his hand. "Mr. Rowiger," he said, "what's wrong with my mother and father? Why aren't they like they used to be?"

Rowiger almost said something, then apparently decided against it.

"I do want to be older," said Rodger. "I'm tired of being a child. I *have* to be older soon." He stamped his foot, with no intention of making the splash he made. "Why do I have to wait and wait?"

The boy shut his mouth in a grim, straight line.

They walked quite a distance into the mountains. There was the pleasant rustle of rain on thick, matted grass. Although it was pleasant by contrast with the splattering sound on the paved sidewalks, there was the feeling of the rain softening the earth too much, streaking it in places with a thin mud slime. The boy occasionally kicked stones, but with this exception his behavior was almost the same as that of the man. They seemed to have either found a purpose for walking, or to have so utterly lost that purpose that they were going on anyway.

"Do you know I feel things terribly?" said Rodger.

"I hope you do."

"But I don't like it," said Rodger. "You know, we think too much. That's our trouble."

"I haven't had much chance to think," said Rowiger. But he had had, and saw that he had all his life withdrawn into the shadows, away from the real crisis, and Irene had done the same. "Or I should say I've only thought I was thinking," he commented acidly, swishing his

441

umbrella, realizing that he had been wrong in trying to improve life through children. The future was not to be trusted to do better, but only the present, only the mature, suffering people of his own age.

"I mean I think too much for my age," said Rodger. "Everybody in our family does. That's what's wrong. You know, we used to be happy and play games and everything, and we don't any more. I think we're unhappy." Rodger looked up into the face with seriousness and trust. "Do you think we're unhappy?"

Rowiger could answer only one thing. He at the same time answered himself. "Yes."

"Can you tell me why?"

"No."

"Oh," said the boy, who had believed this man could tell him. He felt disappointed. "I used to think it was Father. I mean Mother says it's him. Is it my father?"

Rowiger did not answer.

"I just can't see why we're unhappy. I mean me. I don't want to be unhappy. I wouldn't be, only everybody else is. Like last night. Father and Mother fought, just because Father wants me to go to military school. I don't mind going. What do they have to fight for?" Rodger shook his head despondently. "There's something wrong with our house. And I can't see how Father's to blame. Heck, you don't have to listen to him. I told Mother this morning, after I played the piano so good, I told her not to be unhappy. She has me. Do you know she *cries?* She never used to cry."

Rowiger walked on.

"But listen, you think my father's to blame?"

"Yes. Yes, for everything." The man who did not pass judgment on people walked on.

"That's what I really thought too," said Rodger. "I told Mother long ago. But she said it wasn't my father, it was something else. Why did she say that?"

"Because she didn't want you to worry. Now it's time you worried."

Rodger seemed impressed.

As they moved upward the soil became dark and gritty; there were violet and red rocks which looked too clean, for rain does not really wash things thoroughly. The rain made a heavy drumming sound, while far up ahead was silence and bright sky; even though they would not and could not go that high, it was somehow comforting to be walking in that direction. The rocks were slippery, and

Rowiger took short, mincing steps. His shoulders were stiff from trying to fit the area of the umbrella, and he was wet around his ankles
and his knees had wet ovals.

Rodger found a hollow oak and stood inside.

"We better turn back," said Rowiger. "You're shivering."

To his surprise, the boy came out. They began to make the long
return.

"If Mother gives me what-for, can I say I was with you?"

"I guess it wouldn't be lying," said Rowiger, looking on the boy as
something small, foolish, and yet precious.

"No," said the boy, resenting that look. "I'm not afraid. I only
don't want to worry her."

Rowiger noticed the glowing brightness of the green umbrella.
The sun had broken apart the overhead sky. It was still raining a
little.

"I'm going to talk with your mother."

The ground changed color. Bushes and weeds that were slicked
down with rain began to snap upright. Everywhere was proof of the
enormous strength and the power of recovery in nature. Only a few
hollows looked spent, beaten and despairing.

"I haven't the least idea what I'm going to say."

But Rowiger knew what he was going to say. He was going to ask
Irene to leave her husband.

One or two rain drops that must have been delayed somewhere in
their fall through the sky plopped on the ground like heavy bugs and
burrowed their way into the earth. Yet there were little puddles that
would simply have to wait until the earth was ready for more water.
Rowiger was so accustomed to the steel spire on his black umbrella
that it was some time before he despaired of trying to puncture leaves
and pick up bits of weed with the blunt glass tip.

He knew what he was going to say. Ask Irene to divorce her husband. Ask her to marry him.

Rowiger paused before the gate of the former Lang house. He had
no indecision. The sun was almost indignantly bright. He was as certain as he had ever been in his life.

Irene said no.

37

The need of security often comes to men before they have ever felt love, and sometimes must come before a man can allow himself to love. Many a woman can thank this for giving her a husband who might otherwise never have smiled on her. It is not to be despised that a man should say to himself, "Now I'm ready to marry." For men, like grain in the field, have a time of ripening; particularly men who have been obsessed with the idea of remaining single.

Dorothy might have despised Fred if she had known that he had thought of marriage, had met her, and thus formed a feeling of inevitability. "No sooner was I thinking of it—and there she was, sitting across the room," he had said to Tim Callaghan. The right coincidence makes a young man a believer in destiny, and makes the young woman a victim of herself, believing that her charms have been fully responsible for the capture.

Fred Kostar was not averse to having wealth as a part of his wife's background, as a kind of security for their social position. It was a future inheritance which he did not resent; he viewed it as a farmer does a shade tree, when the sun is hot on his back and the plow glinting, and although he has no intention of quitting, there is the comforting knowledge that if the sun gets to be too much for him, the tree is there. Fred Kostar intended to refuse politely any offer of financial assistance, except for wedding gifts; but to insist that he would never accept aid, if a time of need came, was as foolish as to insist that he would never give aid. Fred did not crave independence, and saw the values of dependence and obligation.

He did not make the mistake of believing the path ahead would be forever smooth. He knew Dorothy would not settle for a peaceful life, that he would have to provide her with all his emotions. She was going to be expensive and it was going to be as much a struggle for him to be harsh with her as it was going to be for her to give in. He was spending more than he could afford on dates and flowers and gifts —at a time when he should have been saving. He had spent forty dollars in a single evening, with a private violinist at their table, playing songs of her choice. But he was determined never to make the mistake of enslaving her, because she needed pleasure and fun to be the person he loved. He was too proud of having such a beautiful young woman to risk her displeasure.

He only hoped marriage would tone it down a little.

Bart was never popular among women; they found him attractive, but he was too cold and acid of speech, too inattentive. For a time after his defeat as a labor organizer, he seemed to enjoy using his physical attractiveness. He selected young women who seemed satisfied with their lives, or who overvalued themselves, and derived satisfaction from seeing that he could complicate their lives. Seduction itself was only a consequence, and in a few cases he had turned his back upon women after making it nakedly clear to them that they were vulnerable. The two kinds of women with whom he was ruthless were those who founded their privilege and smugness on intelligence, and those who believed they were hardened emotionally and through experience.

Bart did not like to deal with innocence. He abhorred taking advantage of inexperienced women. Young housewives making their first protests against the approach of unhappiness, engaging in martini-sponsored flings, he viewed with the same contempt as young girls who had already lost all tenderness and romance, who had already experienced the farthest boundaries of physical satisfaction.

But on the occasions when he found a woman who not merely resisted, but showed disgust, it restored some of his former faith in humanity. He was pleased to see pride and honor. There was nothing rare about faithful women, but the rarity was women who were faithful for intelligent reasons. He liked to see women who took pride and happiness in their function of bearing children, who viewed men with open healthy appraisal, and yet did not make of themselves transient possibilities and stimulants for the loins of men.

It was a time when Bart was least disciplined, when he sought to inflict injury on anyone who dared to accept the silent challenge of his eyes. It was a time when he fought with himself against being cruel and brutal, when his desire was to revenge himself for having failed to keep enough distance from life. He blamed his preoccupation and lack of devotion to the union for having been prime factors in his defeat; treachery would never have been able to take place if he had kept his eyes alert. So that now he was trying to destroy once and for all those sentiments and appetites which could cause failure.

Dorothy Pierce was sitting with her back against the tree. She drew deeply on the cigarette so that he would be able to see her face and particularly her eyes. She liked her eyes to be seen when she was angry. Then she threw the cigarette at him. Fred caught and juggled it between his hands.

"Already you've changed," she said. "That's what I don't like about people, they change."

She was remembering the first time his eyes had fixed attentively on her. But the humility of men was brief. Gradually Fred was learning his masculine trade, he was learning to rise and strut in front of her. Next he would throw off romance, and if his reality and hers did not happen to be equal, they would find no happiness.

"Forget we're going to be married tomorrow. Just forget it for a while," she said, impatiently.

She remembered him as he had been, always looking as if he were going to hold out his arms to her, always looking as if he were going to kneel before her. The humility of a man was very brief.

"I wish to hell I understood you," he said. "I wish I knew just once what you're thinking."

"I'm thinking how I got you," said Dorothy. "How did I get you? It's a mystery to me." She laughed. "Was it my soft white flesh?"

God, she was thinking, he hasn't even seen my nipples yet; nor my navel; nor even stuck his tongue in my mouth. What a playground I'll have to make of myself for the next month or two! Well, maybe that's all that can be expected of a second marriage.

Fred was pleading with his eyes. He could see she wanted to quarrel.

"Oh cut it out!" she said. "It's no more surprising that you should make me promises with your eyes than it's going to be when you don't keep them." She rubbed her head against the tree, feeling her hair catch on the bark. "I'm glad I never feel anything any more." But Dorothy did not look glad. "Love is so foolish," she said bitterly. "It's as needless as thirst. It's like having to ask somebody to please give you a glass of water."

"Love," said Fred, "is feeling your heart."

"No thank you," said Dorothy. "I shouldn't like my heart to twitter. I shouldn't like my heart to feel bumpty-bump."

It was always easier for Fred to explain to himself why he was in love when she looked beautiful; her present restlessness gave her an almost feline appearance which the darkness heightened.

"You," said Dorothy, "you're thinking tomorrow I'm yours. You're

446

thinking how hard I was on you and you'll put it among the sweetest memories—until something happens. You don't even realize that tomorrow begins your revenge, but when you find it out—and you'll find it out . . . What a shame I've been through this before, and what a pity you haven't." She caught her fingernails in the bark and pulled loose a few shreds. "What a fool I am!" she cried out.

"I don't know what the hell you're talking about," grumbled Fred.

"What did I say, take me, marry me in a church?" said Dorothy. "Oh brother, I must have had my yellow panties on that night." Her fingers clawed at the grass, trying to find resistance. "At least, for God's sake, stop treating me like something you won in a lottery. At least stop being such a peaceful damn person. . . . All right, tomorrow I stand beside you, I say yes. . . . But if you really want me you better get started and quick."

She rose, swung away from him. But he caught her arm.

"I hate gentlemen," she said, jerking her arm loose. "I detest a man who—who sits calmly on his haunches smoking cigarettes." She watched his anger rise and mocked it with her own face. "I was married before, remember, and I wasn't treated like the Virgin Mary, and I don't want to be."

"You shut up," said Fred. "You get it out and then you shut up."

But Dorothy only tapped his chest with her forefinger. "Fred," she said quietly. "Let's call it off."

The routine was terrible. Naomi had to know whom to let pat her on the buttocks, whom to throw the corny gags to, whom to brush with her knees, whom to let peep in the blouse of her dress. She had to throw out remarks, "Hey man, what you got in your pocket that's so interesting?" then wait for the response, "Money, baby," then flounce her rump at him and reply, "Balls." That was what the owner of the bar called a floor show; that was what the people at the tables expected. It was the giggles of the women which were humiliating, the giggles of women with only a faint remembrance of a time when they had been able to feel obscenity.

When the floor show was over, if it was an evening when there were not many women, she had to dance with the customers. She had to be full of tough lines, "Hey now look, if you want to dance, dance, but stop trying to use me for a you know what," or, "Go sit down and give yourself a chance to cool off." She had to tell the man who was jealous of the man who had danced earlier with her, "What a dope he was. He thought I was going to swoon over him or something, just because I mentioned he had a jazzy haircut. Christ, his hair was the only thing I could stand to look at." She had to tell the young cynics, the ones who were always wanting to know what she was doing in a place so low and vile, the ones who spoke of her talent, her real talent, "I need the dough," or "I only got to sing here one more week, and am I glad, I never saw so many jugheads in one place in my life." There were the men who were proud of their dancing, and the movie-actor types who kept pushing their faces into hers. "You dance like a grown person. You make a girl feel her oats," she would have to say. There were bathroom cowboys, young men who were shy until they got a few drinks, and then tried to play the role of a knight with his fair lady. There were the kind that grabbed her arm when she rose from their table, and if she had said that she was going to the bathroom or even to powder her nose they would have yanked her back into her chair, but because she said, "I'm going to wipe the cream out of my pants," they would grin and wave her on.

Naomi was much sought after, by the married and by those who had no intention of marrying. She was not considered a whore, nor even easy pickings, but most men figured they could get her if they really wanted to. That was exactly what she had to make them feel. In that was her security and the little future which her occupation claimed. She had to be considered slightly disreputable.

Naomi did not care enough for appearances to even try to define to herself where she stood. She would probably marry Dip some day, but she was not sure she loved him. Her bitterness toward life was spent, and in its place was a feeling of the uselessness of everything.

"Isn't it a goddamn shame how the world can get about sixty trillion years old and people still can't figure out how to make marriage a go?" she said to Dip. "Ain't it disgusting to have to think about? It makes me want to puke."

"You just need a vacation," said Dip. "You're just being undressed by too many men's eyes. Or," he said, blowing smoke at her with the slight contempt he sometimes could not disguise, "you just haven't been undressed for the right reasons."

"That's what I mean," said Naomi, her eyes flashing. "You men have to make everything filthy."

"What do you expect us to do," said Dip, shrugging, "when women make us wear little rubber caps to keep us from getting them wet inside, when even the Catholics use a rhythm cycle and avoid crucial days? You expect us to love, honor and cherish?" Dip smiled. "It's no wonder the boys down at the poolroom call it jazzing—you know that definition—a slightly rhythmical kink put into utterly common progressions." Dip seemed to think for a moment. "Men are tired of women who sit in the middle of the sofa and spread their skirts to insure privacy. They're tired of women who wear transparent pajamas and roll on the bed and bite their fingers. They just want something healthy and clean for a change."

"Nuts," said Naomi. "And you know it."

She knew Dip was constantly trying to measure how much she knew about life and how much was simply a front. She was convinced he did know a lot about life and that that was the exact reason he was never really concerned.

"I'm serious," said Dip. "I don't mind women doing wild things. I don't mind them being wicked. But when it gets to the point that all they're good for is a single week-end, then a week-end is all they deserve."

Mr. Pierce was surrounded by comfortable financial investments. His newspaper chain had actually become one of the least of these, which included extensive holdings in Power and Light, Bethel, Limestone and Cement, Lumber Inc., two shoe factories, and a factory-to-you clothier. Also experimental investments in aviation, automobile, real estate and chemicals. Although he had been too late to prevent his father-in-law from selling steel holdings which would have brought him into a bargaining position, manipulation of the Selvinius trust had in part restored his strength.

More important to the future were political gains which had begun quite modestly with the election of a county judge and then a county district attorney. State Republican officials, who were beginning to find resistance in Philadelphia, were glad to trade off county nominations to gain support for their choices to the national government and key administrative posts. In a span of twelve years Nesquehon rose from political obscurity to the position of having itself represented in the county by seven men, and in the state by one. Moreover, more than a hundred people were working in the state capitol on political appointments, with particular strength in the highway department and the revenue department. Mark Stevens' political control continued spreading through the county.

Mr. Pierce was in a peculiar position. He had come to represent in Nesquehon the same advisory position which Mr. Lang had once held, and was possessed of as much outright power, though more diversified, as Selvinius had had. His web spread in all directions and, like a pyramid started from the top, seemed to grow more complex by itself, simply by its necessity for an ever-widening base. The men who entangled themselves in it only made it more firm by their own efforts to gain power and prestige. Judge Hargrove knew where his appointment came from. The district attorney owed his allegiance both to the judge and to Mr. Pierce, which was to owe it twice to the same man. When Mr. Weaver encountered legal complications in regard to a portion of the Pennsylvania Canal which Bethel wished to purchase, a tax indemnity which the county held against it, it was natural that he should visit Mr. Pierce. Later, when charges of river contamination were brought to the State Assembly, it was again through Mr. Pierce (who in turn had to make concessions to high officials regarding November) that Bethel was allowed to continue in its present practice. It was quite easy for Mr. Pierce to have his young son-in-law appointed as a lawyer for the Nesquehon plant.

Mr. Pierce was a manipulator. His position was so complex that often he had to solve both the advantages and disadvantages of particular moves. It was really continuity which he was seeking, a constant advance on all fronts which would retain balance. For continuity and balance were the things most in his favor, and the means through which wealth did beget wealth and power more power. His personal security was assured. He had passed the stage of danger of involvement. For the danger of involvement, under a system of democratic laws, ceases to exist once a man has passed the stage of direct communication with a particular interest.

He was after all only an investor. Even a political upheaval would leave him personally untouched. He was a manipulator, but his manipulations could not be traced, because law is not able to trace the weight of human conscience, nor the power of social loyalty, nor the force of human endeavor, which were the instruments Mr. Pierce relied upon. And if these instruments should fail him there was no need for a hurried burning of files and documents, because there were none, and the nebulous web would leave itself forever invisible. He was a dealer in the ideals and ambitions of mankind, and as long as he did not himself become caught in those ideals and ambitions nothing could harm him.

His newspapers had become so indoctrinated that they really needed very little personal attention. He allowed them from time to time to print editorials of which he disapproved. He realized that some dissent and radical material was needed to give pertinence to the basic philosophy of his papers. He did not even oppose an occasional intellectualization of the news, and removed men for being heavy-handed as frequently as they were removed for wrong thinking. Instead of sending memoranda to his editors, he simply kept files, and when a particular man began to show symptoms of breaking with the basic policy, that file was marked for special attention. If the tendency continued, the man was replaced.

So that his comments, "I wonder what I'm supposed to have an editor for, I shouldn't have allowed this to escape my attention," were intended for the consumption of his family and whatever guests were present. It had become a characteristic trait for him to smile a little whenever he said anything. Life had reached the point where he could afford to play with it.

Bart remained in Pittsburgh several years. He became a student of labor tactics under some of the most efficient and ruthless leaders. Then he moved to Gary and became interested in labor, politics and the underworld. He saw the massive revolution that was taking place beneath a constant diversion of surface activities and counterpurposes. Greed, crime, bribery, extortion and violence were becoming mixed in with idealism and material philosophies. It was a century in which the common man was seeking vengeance for all past history, in which the depression was sinking a fear of life so deep within the hearts of men that they seemed no longer afraid of anything. Even the labor unions were frantically establishing hierarchies to prevent too much of the identical liberty for which they had originally been established.

The tides of power were in flux. The most noticeable strength of the unions was that which they gained through defeat; instead of collapsing as in the previous century, their membership enlarged. The war veterans were becoming a dangerous group. And for the first time men of specialized knowledge, particularly engineers, white-collar workers and the technicians of industry, were beginning to link their cause with that of the laborer. The middle class was breaking apart.

Yet there was very little to be learned from Pittsburgh or Gary that could be applied to central Pennsylvania. Pittsburgh had a great mass of labor with which to bargain and Gary was the keyhole through which the iron ore flowed. Both were vulnerable. Violence would succeed in these areas; pressures would arouse the entire nation. But these tactics could not be relied on to succeed in a subsidiary plant. Bart was going to have to face the particular problems of Nesquehon Foundry and use his own methods.

One thing he knew. It was not through the law courts that the plight of the workingman was going to be solved.

Bart seemed depressed during these years. He seemed to be under a constant strain. After the period of wildness in which he seemed bent on destroying everything, he became morose, silent and rather pale and tense. He did not seem to have the perfect co-ordination or the physical energy that he had always had. He developed a habit of clutching his head between his hands and staring into space.

In Gary he was jailed because of participation in an attempt to intimidate workers.

In Pittsburgh he got beat up by two cops.

He ate in restaurants. His room had only a desk, a bed and a chair.

It was a mistake to offer him assistance, particularly when he was in trouble. He preferred to lick his own wounds.

He lost interest in his attractiveness, preferred promiscuous women with no more than professional loyalty; as far as he was concerned they could leave their brassieres on. He knew them all, women who shaded their eyes, women who smoked immediately afterward, the douche routine, coming back into bed with cold wet skin; the actual encounter a kind of explosion, like throwing water on top of a hot stove. And it meant to him absolutely nothing—it was a form of exercise, about the equivalent of doing push-ups.

He wrote letters and later sent train tickets to Mike Murray and Spider Fortiano. Mike soon became known in parts of Gary as "The Bull."

He received a letter from Gilbert saying he was out of work and wanted to come out to Gary. He wanted to bring Naomi too; she was working in a place that was no good for her. Bart did not answer the letter.

Gilbert was sprawled across the bed. Only his lower legs were naked, one boot lying in the kitchen, where he had flung it at his wife, the other near the doorway, with a few pieces of chinking scattered around it. She was not able to do much with his clothes in that position. His shirt was unbuttoned and she was rubbing against his chest with a warm washcloth.

He lay there watching her, feeling the touch of the washcloth as something very distant from himself. When she went to open his shirt wider, he pushed her away from him. "Let me stink if I wanna, huh?" As she sat there holding the washcloth between her hands, looking down into it, he regretted having shoved her, as he resented that she should try to make him clean. Mostly, he was ashamed he could not remember, ashamed of what he must have looked like to her during the days when he had been recovering from drunkenness.

"Bring me some coffee," he said. "Go on, you don't have to fix every button for that."

He was referring to her latest conciliation, as she began to close his shirt. Then he watched her perform another act of obedience, and wondered if she did not want his abuse, if it was not easier for her to endure than it was for him. He heard her cry out in the kitchen, and in a flash of insight knew she had burned her hand by grabbing the coffeepot without a rag, knew she must have done it because of preoccupation with what had occurred here. It somehow moved him with compassion such as he had not felt for her in many months, for he saw he must be hurting her more deeply than she let on.

"Bring butter," he said.

There was no reply. He lay there thinking how a few years earlier he would have jumped up and run into the kitchen if he had heard Rose cry out; he was saying to himself that he would go now too, when she returned with the coffee. The moment he saw her, he knew he did not care and probably never had cared.

Gilbert took three cups of coffee in silence, while Rose smoothed the bed sheet as best she could without disturbing him. His eyes warned her whenever he felt his coffee was being disturbed. There had been a noticeable improvement in her ability to keep the cabin in order, although she was still basically careless, and much that she undertook had the single purpose of keeping her husband content. Her deference to him was so obvious. Her eyes seemed to be always sleeping. He wished often that she had remained ignorant and savagely afraid in her love-making, instead of being more intelligent and feeling than he could allow himself to give her credit for.

Gilbert raised his hand to his jaw, feeling the hard, sullen lump of flesh his face had become. Once he had been unable to hide his feelings; now his face was a mask, he could walk the streets, torn with emotion, and at the same time confident people saw only a big, hulking man.

It was not until the coffeepot was light in his hand that he grew annoyed, in a petty way which he could have stilled if he had chosen to.

"Where'd the ham come from?" he said. "Where'd you get money?"

"I sold some lumber."

"How much? What did it fetch? Never mind, gimme."

He pointed to the palm of his hand. Rose went into the kitchen, took money out of a glass, and returned.

"I think I better search," said Gilbert, although he was in terror of having this much money in his possession, more than twenty dollars, for he knew that within two hours he would be on his way into town. He would rather have had five dollars. Five was safe. Yet he rose from the bed and searched in a casual fashion, without expectation of finding more, for he had lived with this woman long enough to know she did not hold out on him. His search, in addition to being intended as an insult, was connected with some latent desire to find money hidden, some indication that she found it necessary to deceive him. It would have made him respect her more. It bothered him that she never begged him not to go, not to take all the money.

"I guess you hid it pretty good," he said, abandoning the search, "and I guess the old drunkard is off again, if he can walk to town without falling on his face." He began separating the bills, putting a few in one pocket, a few in another. "I can even afford a pretty woman this time, a little rabbit's foot." He laughed. "Would you make breakfast for her if we came here? Would you mind sleeping in the kitchen?" He reached down and dipped the washcloth into the basin and began to scrub his face, wetting the edges of his hair. "What's going to happen when I can't make it back any more, when you have to come in and fetch me? You will, won't you? You wouldn't let me lie in the gutter?" He smiled a little painfully. "You know, it's too bad no other man would keep you, or you could go away and start a fresh life. You could teach little Julius to say 'Daddy' to some other man, and everything would be fine." He sniffed at the washrag, then rubbed with it under his armpits, so that the shirt sleeve flapped. "But you're not so dumb you don't know this place is better than no place. You never were very dumb. You just said to yourself, 'If I can't find a man like me, I'll take one and make him like me.'" He threw the washrag across the room, and stooping, dipped his hands in the basin and rubbed water through his hair. "Well, if you're not going to say anything, the least you can do is help your old daddy put his boots on."

"No," said Rose. "I'll take care of you when you come back, but I won't help you go."

"Aha!" said Gilbert, not looking at her. "She's got pep and sparkle. She'll wash my ass but not kiss it. . . . Well, for this much booze I guess I can put my own boots on this once." He swung his legs out of the bed and sat up. "I guess one of these days you may up and leave me at that."

"No!"

Rose said this with such unaccustomed vehemence that Gilbert swung sharply and looked at her. But he was reassured when he saw that she was trembling, and he almost smirked, and then he was lanced with a deeper sorrow than her belief in what she had said would have caused him. He had wanted to hurt her, make it easier for himself to go into town, re-establish the old reasons for drinking, which were not quite in control of him yet. But he had not wanted to hear that she was so near the limits of her endurance. He had not wanted to hear that he was coming so near to the end of the line.

"Look," he said, "I'd lie if I said I need to get drunk. But I intend to all the same. Even though I'd rather stay right here in bed. Just the same as I'll buy every sonofabitch I hate a drink. You wouldn't understand what makes a man do that; you wouldn't understand why a man has to be a jackass every day of his life." He stamped his foot down into the boot and then hobbled into the kitchen after the other. "Do you know I took all the money because I knew if I only took part, after I got drunk I'd come for the rest and cause some trouble besides?" He knocked the boot against the wall, shaking fine stones from it. "I once believed I would love you. I once believed . . . That's the whole trouble, I believed. You wouldn't understand how I felt in those days. A man can get castrated up here," he said, pointing to his forehead. "Now you're nothing to me. Nothing but a drag. But do you realize how I must feel, knowing it's my fault things are this way? Your fault too, but mostly mine. It's sort of a laugh; I mean, I went after you in such a big way because I had the idea I would make everyone respect you—when all the time it was me who didn't respect you, me who just had the hots. Some fun. You just went along for the ride, and I never even got the car started, and out there on a goddamn leash, on a goddamn clothesline, is a kid, the only thing we have to show for it all." Gilbert, who apparently had decided to change clothes, put the money he had in various pockets in a pile on the bed, to make it easier to rid himself of his pants and shirt. He stooped and took a little more than half of it. "Take this," he said. "Go straight into town and buy some food. I'll wait'll you get back. Maybe I can even get myself to go give the brat a go-see while you're not around. Maybe I'll explain to him I'm his father and not the boogie man." He drew the belt from the trousers in a way that

455

made him seem about to strike with a whip. "Who knows?" he said bitterly. "This whole thing may work out yet. Who knows? But be sure you spend every cent. Because I got to know there isn't any money in the house. That way I won't come back until I'm ready to flop. That way I won't cause trouble." He saw how long and dirty his toenails were and scratched them on the wood of the floor. "You know," he said cheerfully, "I'm getting to know myself pretty damn well. I'm getting to be quite a master mind. Maybe I'll straighten myself out by the time I'm fifty or so." He frowned, and looked at his wife, hunting her eyes for the first time. "I never used to be sarcastic with myself, and I don't think I like it now, it leaves a filthy taste in my mouth. . . . Am I really washed up, Rose, am I about to go? Or am I going to have to drag through this year after year, until I don't remember where I came from or where I wanted to go?"

38

It was a perfect evening. Dorothy phoned for a taxi while he was still bathing. There was a frenzied rush of dressing, of assistance and hindrance, before they rushed out, banging the doors behind them, Fred with his collar still sprawled about his throat and his tie waving. It did not matter that they were only going to dinner. It did not matter that Harrisburg had only a faintly glittering social world; they were still strangers to it as to each other, were still children bewildered at their own gaiety and extravagance, even though their pictures appeared more and more frequently on the society page. It did not matter that the wedding gifts, except for those foolish items which had evidently been intended to inspire housekeeping, were all spent. Dorothy was so aware of proper sound and soft light, of suitable chairs and clean tablecloth, of agreeable dinner music and attractive glassware, that Fred himself walked briskly and jauntily, snapped his fingers at the waiters, and indulged in an excellent cigar. He did not regret having her choose dinner for them, and there were little things, having flowers sent to the table, more courteous and timely service, a violinist who tried to please them—endless little things which she managed gracefully.

The apartment key felt small and inadequate.

Dorothy had brought a rose with her. She stood beside him, tickling her throat and the underside of her chin with the tips of the petals, then entered the doorway with a provocative movement which made her back look guilty, as if she could never quite suppress that moment in which she was most aware of masculinity and its rigid claim. Fred stepped inside and flooded the room with light and for a moment her jewelry seemed especially bright. Her eyes, peering over the rose which she was sniffing, watched him close and lock the door, with that idle curiosity which always put him at a disadvantage.

She stood waiting for him to come to her, and as he turned and met her eyes, eyes which were always prepared for him, the need which had caused him to fumble with the apartment key was turned into obligation. He knew the boldness which she had in lighted rooms, the savage glint in her eyes, the way she had of suddenly making the material of her dress hint at the softness of her skin. She was one of those rare women who had command of velvet, one of those rarer still who chose her lingerie before she even gave thought to a dress. He stepped toward her with the hesitation of a man who had not yet learned how to cope with his own passion.

Dorothy swung away from him, and went to the bedroom, switching the rose against her leg. He followed abjectly, with the discouraged mind of a man who has not lost anything except the correct moment. In his haste to undress, to get out of clothing which made him helpless, he felt the change in his pocket, a thin sidewise lump against his leg, and was ashamed of it. His pants seemed to cling to his legs wretchedly, while behind him the red tip of a cigarette was from time to time making a thin light on the covers of the bed.

Then, as he stood erect beside the bed, fastening his pajamas, he heard a movement on the bed and the red tip came spinning at him, across and beyond his shoulder, showering sparks where it struck against the wall. He heard her laugh, and caught the covers in both hands and threw them toward the foot of the bed. It was with surprising boldness that she met him in the dark and felt strong as a man against him. He knew then what it was to feel a woman's ruthlessness, to feel her press through her own femininity, to seek and demand as he had thought only a man could. The bitterness with which she demanded pleasure from her own body, the cruelty which she showed for her own loins and breasts, she, who ordinarily had the

457

habit of drawing in her elbows to protect them when he embraced her, and the desperation with which she tried to force him to bring her pleasure, brought on him the panic of a man who feared he would fail himself. He struggled to exceed himself in masculinity, gloried in those moments when he did exceed himself.

And when he seemed on the edge of a night of sensual ecstasy, when he seemed about to conquer, Dorothy lay still, turned her head sidewise on the pillow and blew vulgarly through her mouth the stale air of breathlessness. He knelt over her, undecided. Then her hips resumed their mechanical rhythm as she continued to try to give herself, to give that which could not be given.

Later, Fred, having lain with his eyes open, his eyes hunting, crawled out of the bed. He scrubbed his hands along the floor, encountering his own clothing, shoving it aside. The room seemed bare and enlarged, and the thin film of light that was caught in the curtains of the window made the silhouettes of the posts of the bed seem enormous. Near the wall he found it, and after scraping his hand over the wood, he crept back to bed and under the covers, hoping that now he might be able to sleep.

"Every marriage contains deception," Mr. Pierce said, touching the sleeve with such lightness that only by seeing the hand did Rowiger know he was being detained. "Because marriage is fundamentally a deception. That itself frequently admits a basis for the continuation of an oath—of, shall I say, permanent love. Yes, sensible enough, that. Except—romance, romance, the little pinch of salt which makes the bride feel life has been planned for her, planned to the least detail. Love fairy tales and wander into the furthest corners of daydreams." The hand was soft and white, the bare silver band seeming to choke the finger, revealing not only the plumpness, but a faintly bloated texture. It was skin which, squeezed or struck, took on a pallor of unhealthiness. Yet, to Rowiger, the disturbing feeling was that the skin should show no sign of age, no deepened color, no tendency toward thickness; the softness was a symptom of something further advanced than the normal processes of aging. "Love is a burden to the one who loves. Fine. We accept our responsibilities—or if not, at least remain in the vicinity, watching them parade, scuffing our shoes on curbstones of indecision. But romance, romance is a burden to everyone. It is a temptation to lean back and close your eyes and catch that little bit you think you hear—that little bit you think you always missed the chance to hear—lean back and feast upon the possibility of arriving. Yes, romance is feeling the air passing through the thin spaces between our teeth." The full lips drew a little thin, exposing teeth too white for a man of Mr. Pierce's age. "Romance asks to be placed in the best light, asks the proper color to be seen by—and again you would lean back, you see how it goes? You see the masculine requirements? If it were a poem—it's not. No, romance is no more than a man standing in darkness, with the palms of his hands pressed against his thighs, reading into the white of the moon fancy phrases, while the woman—what is it my daughter always says?—creams her jeans." A nervous spasm seemed to cross his face, making the lips seem carelessly loose, and for a moment his eyes, which had been so steady and yet detached, so innocently amused, dodged, not from the face which they had been fixed upon, but from some internal cause, some unfavorable self-discovery. It was a definite pressure of the hand which this time prevented Rowiger from turning aside, a pressure not of force, but of confidence in its right to detain. And for a moment Rowiger saw the eyes peering into him so deeply that it was as if he had heard spoken into his ear, "We are the same man, you and I, we are the completion of one."

"I chose a woman, wanted her, got her, hardly won her, but got her. I offered her appreciation, offered her the best light and proper color. You see, don't you? You see the catch? The little slip. Oh no, not that I didn't offer love. I did. I profess I did. The slip was romance, you see, her romance. And the romance of a young woman—you have seen my wife, you have seen . . . The romance of a young woman is infinitely more permeating. . . . Have you ever seen two children pitching two balls simultaneously, so that the throw and catch are a primitive form of juggling? Too much, too little, too late, too early, too fast, too slow? I confuse? Or is it clear? Is it clear I am now not speaking lightly? Is it clear that if my wife had been my daughter or my sister—that feeling, the end before the beginning . . . Yet that is not so, not so, for I have seen her stoop and touch her fingers against the edge of water and I would have called out, I would have called out, except I saw it was a woman's gesture and she a woman. She after all a woman. Now do you see? She a woman, that was the line I could not pass. . . . The line you could not pass and I trespassed . . . Tore the woman out of the child, tore the woman and, clutching, ran, chased by the child—or tore the child and was chased by the woman? Eh? Or was that you, for I found my wife in two pieces." The voice had risen, still controlled, still suppressed, but the eyes had for one moment opened wide and looked with as-

459

tonishing hatred. "You see I do not know the signs of suffering or of —why do these women, in their greatest extremities, speak only of their flowers and their fathers and scuff marks on linoleum? Why do they speak at all if not to speak what they ought—what would command a man, give him passion and rage—not this unspeakable, this they call love. Love? Love, that a man should feel the hook draw through his mouth all his innards and stand looking down at a little red pulsing fob, which was all that he had for a heart? I swear no man loves, nor knows what love is. I swear, let a woman, no matter how beautiful, how passionate, how alive to a man's mouth, stand but one extra moment beyond that man's outstretched arms, and he shall never again be able to love or endure to be loved." And it seemed to come to Mr. Pierce, before it came to his listener, that he was speaking not of his wife, but of himself, that he was at the edge of an admission which would make his own face pale and his hands tremble. He turned aside, with a coldly abrupt movement and said, "There's my wife and daughter, there by the wall, looking as if they were alive. Not paintings, not poems, and yet I swear not women, not women as a man seeks, needs, or would have. Women as a man must take, take as a thief to prevent worse than thievery. You see I joke, I make light of the matter, I have my theme, the variants are endless, the ballad goes on, the hundredth line telling no more than the first. Better to be vulgar. Better to be brute, the brute of silence, who stands with eyes fixed upon his wife, daring her to speak to any man.

"Yes, I do not believe that. And yes, I do. For it would be better than to stand here telling a man's small version of what cannot be told, since the one thing which is forever denied to a man is sympathy. Since it should be. Do you begin to know now why I have encouraged you to, shall we say, rescue my wife? Why I have thrown my arm around your shoulders? That in the guise itself was one feeble hundredth part of truth? And yet I have done it really because I am the simplest man alive, a man whose only complication is the method, have put my arm across your shoulder simply because I know my approval will always prevent you from liking your task. I have placed the implication of infidelity in my wife's behavior because it would give my wife the freedom not to care, me the freedom to see her not caring, to see her and myself at least that far released. I have tried to place dishonor on you so that you would be honorable enough to hide within the small pride of being wrongly accused. Don't you see, my poor man, that from the moment you began really to dislike me, from that moment my wife was safe from you?"

460

They were freed now, there need be no detaining hand. It was the freedom of two men who were conversing together for the last time, who would never again even have the courtesy to speak to each other. In that was Mr. Pierce's whole advantage, since he knew the man would one day still have to appear before him.

"My poor good man," said Mr. Pierce, "your position is awful. So awful that I do not even have to threaten you. And yet so is my position awful, since I am forced into an act of perversion. . . . Did you really think I see myself in you . . . ? No, I see my wife in you, and that is why my position is awful. I can no longer stand before you and say that my wife will give me still another chance. She is capable of overthrowing all that went before. You see her there by the wall, that is all I have left of her, a pitiful morsel, and yet—yet perhaps just enough. Enough to find involvement . . ."

He seemed content to say nothing further. Indeed, it became apparent, from the shrewd, detached look which he gave Rowiger, that for all he had said, it was all really pointed toward some response which he was seeking for. And when Rowiger only looked at him, neither with hate nor with astonishment, he seemed to leap forward with one last thrust. "I stand to lose nothing except what was lost, and you to gain nothing except what was lost. Tomorrow I will enjoy life. Very probably a bit later this evening. But if I were to describe life, I would think of a crude lippy cut which is the cause of all this miserable romance."

It was obvious then. It was obvious in the loathing which his face showed, in the hands which shoved deep in his pockets. He was humiliated that his wife had chosen this man, this harmless schoolteacher, as the person in whom she had faith. He was furious that life could have played such a trick upon him. The advantages of noninvolvement, which had placed him upon a pedestal from which he could direct, were ebbing. He was threatened with destruction through the same detached, remorseless energy of mind. He was determined at least to defeat those who had escaped him, to force humiliation on them.

The radiators made the classroom smell overheated. They thumped and pools of water formed on the floor beneath their valves. By afternoon it would be too hot, and the hook on the pole which was used to open the top windows would seldom catch. Mr. Rowiger would have to use a chair or climb on the window sill. All because the janitor had taken the knobs off the radiators.

461

Boys were fighting for choice seats in the back of the room. Rowiger wondered at the value of his policy of not assigning seats. He would have to go to the back of the room and talk from there.

It had to be Monday morning. The blackboard was too black, the erasers were not dusted white, and there were fresh whole pieces of chalk spaced along the wooden tray. Even the wastebaskets had been emptied. Unless he was mistaken, the desk tops had been hastily rubbed with furniture polish; they had an occasional glint.

He had come too late this morning to have time to talk with anyone, too late to hear excuses for homework not done, or explain problems which he had explained Friday and Thursday. Now that he had been teaching twenty years, he knew there had been too many children alike, much too many alike. It was hard to keep seeing them in a new light.

Shoes were hunting positions in which they would be satisfied. Bodies were making the effort of aligning themselves correctly with the front of the room. Rowiger knew then the second and not the first bell had rung. There was the hurried breathing and the forced nonchalance of students late for various reasons, and then, as the room finally settled, two tiptoers, walking with a bobbing motion. Rowiger could not decide if they were trying to pretend they were not late or were trying not to disturb him.

He picked up a piece of chalk. Instantly he heard notebooks clicking. He heard shoes shifting, this time hunting a position suitable to writing. Most children had to lean forward to write; they had to make a tense physical action of it. Note 1, 2, 120, 500. Partial, complete, abbreviated, scribbled, complete but incoherent, coherent but incomplete, coherent but worthless, valuable but not understood. Rowiger felt the despair of dealing with children too well disciplined and too little educated. Whether this was a history class or geography he was not sure, he would have to look some day on his schedule card.

He wrote in large clear letters on the blackboard. "No school today. Class dismissed." Then he turned to face them, listened to the gathering uproar and the astonishment and the joy, and then he raised his arm. He knew why they all got quiet so suddenly.

"You've just been told a lie," said Rowiger. "You've never really been told why it's bad to lie. You've only been told not to. And now you're feeling it. Because there is school, and class is not dismissed. And what you're feeling in your hearts is the exact reason why lies should never be told."

462

Rowiger had been alert for a time. But now, as often when he was hardest at work, when he could not spare a moment, something out of the past stayed his elbow and his mouth and turned his eyes toward the windows. He struggled with it. He knew he would succumb.

When the students were more settled, although still looking at each other, he said, "My lie was worse because you're not accustomed to hearing me lie. Now you're scared to believe anything I say. That too is why we shouldn't lie." Rowiger broke the piece of chalk accidentally, and it made him realize there was tension in his hands, and he put the two pieces down and looked at his whitened fingers.

"Now start writing. I want you to write ten things you are sure are true, and ten things you are sure are lies. I'll tell you right now that it's easier for you than it would be for me, but it's not as easy as you think. Go ahead, start."

He sat at his desk, listening to the silence and then the sudden hissing of pencils. He saw two boys staring at him in utter bewilderment. He knew most of them wouldn't even be able to think of a truth or a lie until after they had looked on someone else's desk, and he pretended to be busy to make it easier for them. Rowiger was not very much against cheating, and he noticed that some boys learned a little that way. A very little. But it was better than the horror of emptiness and a blank sheet of paper with the name written thick and precise.

"As you finish bring them up to the desk."

There were holes in the window shades that allowed bits of light to move slowly and in regular patterns across the desk. He did not mind them. Sometimes he would absently put his finger on a piece of light and try to hold it still. Sometimes he ducked his head when a gleam of light got tangled in the hair at the corner of his eye or made the lens of his glasses wink.

Today he knew he did mind after all. He minded everything.

"When you put the papers on my desk you can go home. Please go quietly."

Pencils that had been poised began to rush, and pencils that had been rushing, paused, then rushed even faster. Rowiger saw how difficult it was to kill belief in the young. He only hoped he could count on the same from their fathers and older brothers.

"I'm saying good-bye now," said Rowiger. "Last night I was asked to represent the men who are out on strike. I accepted. I feel I must give them all my time." Rowiger stood up and took off his glasses. "My eyes are going to be glad to get away from here. My head too. But I think I can say that it has always been a pleasure to me, and I know I can say I'll miss you."

Fred came to see that it did not assist him to allude to any unpleasantness his wife had caused in the past; she had a way of not recognizing any incident to which he might refer, or of waving it away with a light sweep of her arm; she could be so completely without memory that he discovered his own memories were a burden to him. "We're not talking about last week," she would remind him, "we're concerned with right now."

"But you promised specifically . . ."

"I'm sure I made no such promise. If I did, it was foolish."

It was so futile, so impossible. He would feel like grabbing her by the hair and throwing her on the floor. Yet he had enough sense to realize that some way, somehow, she would make him regret any physical violence. In public he would pass it off with a look which was intended to convey the amusement with which he endured the caprices of a charming, if somewhat flighty wife.

Her hat bills were, in honesty, not too large, and her hats were never ridiculous when perched on her head. Fred kept silent, for it was a tribute which he felt was her due, it was expenditures such as these which kept her fresh and lovely. Her lingerie bills embarrassed rather than worried him. He was less reasonable about shoes, in part because she had twenty or more pairs, in part because she treated them carelessly, and also because he did not attach as much importance to the small differences in shoes as in other feminine items.

There had to be extravagance. Fred had come to believe that, yet found himself trying to draw the purse strings; there was no other means of resolving a situation in which he was becoming more and more dependent on his father-in-law and a number of businessmen. On his shoulders rested the responsibility for their living above their means, and it was with himself that he could not come to terms.

Fred sensed that he was more than an indulgent husband, a man who had become indulgent with himself. He sensed the danger.

Yet it was not without appeal, this swift, gay, reckless life they were living. He found himself thinking and feeling that he was satisfied as long as they managed to get by, as long as the bills somehow got paid. He had to admit he found an evening in the Legion more pleasant than an evening at home, with his wife sulking, he unable to concentrate. There were those wonderful nights when they both came home a little tipsy, singing softly a duet, whispering to find out who had the key or where it might be, and he would carry her upstairs in his arms, neither of them thinking it foolish; and those moments when they looked at each other and knew they were young and irresponsible, and how good it was to be young and full of problems and confusions.

Life was not without its appeal. He began to suspect he was willing to settle for this, for slow but sure advancement as a lawyer. He was not going to worry about extravagance in the future unless it threatened to ruin them.

Darkness spread further and further around her as her eyes gained sight. She felt herself in the exact middle of night.

She woke with a strong sense of having wronged Fred, of having been curt and unjust. She felt a need to tell him that she had been at fault.

Fresh awake, alert, she pinched him impatiently and without thought of cruelty, anxious to have his ears attend before her mouth sent out streams of words, a little afraid she would not be able to get him to listen soon enough to hear everything.

"Please, darling, do come out of it."

Fred came near enough to the bed and her presence to sense that his body did not wish to awaken, and thinking without thought that he was being drawn into more sexual expenditure, he rolled away from her, with that innocent cowardice and revulsion to the male function of which he would have been ashamed if it had not been for the authority with which sleep controls the human body.

Dorothy pinched him with real cruelty then.

"What do you want?" he heard his voice cry out, and it helped to wake him.

They had a conversation which did not improve their relationship.

The sky was gray and growing darker every hour. But Irene was hopeful. She argued with herself that an overcast morning was likely to clear by noon. The weather simply could not stay this ugly much longer.

By noon snow had made the landscape unfamiliar.

A bed had been brought downstairs, and fresh linen, and hot-water bottles had been folded under the blankets to warm them. In the kitchen tea was steaming, and a Negro woman was preparing a mustard plaster. All the information Irene had, in spite of her incessant vigil at the windows, was a telephone call from a farmer near York saying he had found a boy who said he was their son and that the boy apparently had been out in the snow quite a while and was sick. Irene had stood uncovered, wringing her hands, while her husband put chains on the car, and never had her impatience with his inability to do anything of a mechanical nature been quite as terrifying; and then he had not allowed her to go along with him. She had exhausted part of her nervousness in trying to have the call traced, and in having the servants hunt through the house in the hope her husband had written the address and left it somewhere.

By mid-afternoon the meadows and corn fields were identical, and the pump and the woodpile were huddled in white. Her eyes had to almost guess at where things were. It was a sticky snow that caught fast wherever it touched, and it seemed to be getting heavier, particularly white against the background of sky. Irene telephoned both her daughters. Then, still not satisfied, she phoned Rowiger and asked him to come to the house; she might have said more, but thought she heard a car coming up the hill.

When she stepped outside of the door it was into a strange land. The wind was firm and strong, and yet the flakes were so heavy that they fell in straight, slanted lines, and their touch was big and wet and cold. They melted much too quickly, and gave off the sensation of being touched again and again by big drops of ice water. She had been right in thinking she heard a car, and could hear the wheels spinning and whining. But after a while there was silence, and when she heard the wheels whining again, it was from further down the hill. Again there was silence and she had to stand there and wait until she was certain it could not have been her husband. She did not realize until she stepped onto the porch that one of the servants had come and put a coat over her shoulders, and then it made the wet dress seem to cling to her.

Rowiger was the first to arrive. She heard him stamping his feet on the porch and opened the door and waited for him to finish. His hand touched hers lightly, yet wholly in a masculine way, and there was in the way he entered the hall something protective and resolute. He had forgotten about the snow on his coat and hat, and he stood looking at the clean floor, perplexed, until Irene took them from him. A servant stood at the end of the hallway, unwilling to intrude upon them. The servants were accustomed to a different mode of conduct when their mistress was alone, and yet on this particular afternoon

466

they would probably have preferred to retain their most formal and dignified and discreet manner. It was not until Rowiger had taken a cup of the tea, now a little strong, that they entered into conversation in subdued voices.

Irene did not belittle her own state of worry. She based it on two facts. Rodger had boarded the train in Harrisburg two days earlier and it was impossible to account for those two days, York being only a little more than an hour and a half's distance. Moreover, the farmer had said he was sick, and Irene knew enough of farm people to know that when they mentioned sickness they meant exactly that. She did not speak, however, about the most definite circumstance of her worry, the atmosphere under which Rodger had left. She said simply that he had been on his way to a southern military school.

Rowiger did not try to comfort her or offer implausible explanations. He did, however, noticing the wetness of her clothes, insist that she change, and proposed that in the meantime he would see whether he could not make telephone communication with the farmer. While Irene was upstairs he found out that the call had been traced, but that the wires were down and service suspended in that area. While he was talking with the operator, a servant went into the hall and ushered in Kathleen and Dorothy.

Irene seemed glad to have something to do, and did not realize that she treated her daughters with the courtesy extended to guests. It was a curious situation in that there was so little of a definite nature to go on that they could be secure only through retaining silence and waiting. Kathleen would have liked to have flung herself in her mother's arms. Dorothy showed her nervousness in the number of cigarettes she smoked. Rowiger had nothing more promising to offer than the opinion that perhaps Mr. Pierce had been unable to get through. He was thinking of calling the highway department to learn if the snowplows were out in that area. But he was really much more worried about the state of the women than the situation, and was astonished that they could all be so gravely certain that they had approached a time of crisis. He had never seen this feeling of fate in the family before, and there came to him the first real inkling of a family unity behind all their apparent disunity.

Finally another car came up the hill, motor and wheels at high speed, while the car itself crept forward. Once there was a shower of sparks. Rowiger and Kathleen went out onto the porch. Dorothy had found a pack of cards somewhere. She was using the arm of her chair for solitaire. Irene went to the window, then hurriedly prepared the bed which had already been prepared, and went into the kitchen to see that everything was ready. The car was so thickly covered with snow that for a time Rowiger stood leaning forward, trying to see through the fog on his glasses. Kathleen seemed to recognize the car at once and ran out into the snow. They both arrived and stood peering into the window, where Mr. Pierce was sitting, looking straight ahead. Beside him was a bundle of blankets, wrapped about something that made them look like a sack. Rowiger opened the door and was met by eyes that stared at him almost without recognition. "I nearly went off the bridge," said Mr. Pierce, and shuddered. Rowiger went around to the other side of the car and lifted out the bundle, while Kathleen helped her father. Mr. Pierce did not seem to know how to get out of the car by himself.

Mr. Pierce did not stumble until he reached the smooth floor of the hall. They all were leaving white clods on the floor. Dorothy opened the door for them and then walked in front, almost as if she were guiding them. Mr. Pierce went and threw himself in a chair, overcoat and all.

Rowiger went straight to the bed, where the mother was waiting. The two of them began the unwrapping, Rowiger lifting the weight, while Irene manipulated the sheets and blankets. Even before they had the boy properly covered, she felt that all her precautions were to no avail. She told Rowiger to phone the doctor and get him to come immediately.

Dorothy, seeing her father's immobility, went over to his chair and thrust a cigarette between his lips and lighted it. For a while he did not help her to make the cigarette burn. "I nearly went off the bridge," he said.

"The doctor will be here shortly," said Rowiger.

Somehow that made them all feel helpless.

Rowiger went outside and brought in an armload of wood which he tried to put down quietly beside the hearth. He stood there, brushing at the wet places on his coat.

Irene had her head pressed against the chest of the boy.

Mr. Pierce began smoking furiously on the cigarette, as if trying to taste and feel it. "God, the roads were bad. I didn't know where I was going most of the time."

Kathleen came down from upstairs with slippers and socks and a towel. She dried her father's feet and rolled the cuffs of his trousers above where they were wet. Mr. Pierce reached his hand forward and touched her hair.

Dorothy was absently scratching the polish off her nails.

Irene was holding her head against the chest of the boy. She also was feeling at his wrist. "Shush," she said, in such a low voice it seemed she was talking to the boy.

Dorothy went to the wall and switched on the light. Everyone seemed startled by it. In a little while the lights in the other rooms went on, reminding them that there were servants in the house.

Rowiger was at the telephone again. "Well, come on foot," he was saying.

Kathleen whispered something to her sister. Dorothy looked down at her cigarette, smoked on it hurriedly to finish it, but seeing that she could not, went into the hall.

Mr. Pierce was still sitting sprawled in the chair. For some reason the towel was clutched in his hand.

Irene stood up. "He's dead," she said.

39

Gilbert returned to the mountain. He was sick, not the retching headache sickness usually associated with drunkenness, but simply unwillingness to get out of bed, exhaustion and inability to keep awake for more than an hour; yet his sleep was shabby, distorted, a sluggish, sullen rest in which his body could find no peace. He scarcely realized he was being fed and cared for.

Rose was away from the cabin much of the day. She kept a pitcher of water on the table beside the bed.

Then for two days he was hungry, eating all the time, yawning, lazy, in good humor but not talkative, sometimes catching his wife by the arm and pulling her onto the bed, making careless love. He did not seem to remember that he had been on a week-long debauch. He simply rested hour after hour, feeling his weight press into the mattress, so much at ease that his buttocks knew more annoyance than his head did. He was still lazy, but in that stage where he was beginning to think of rising and perhaps even going outside into the sunlight and fresh air. There were moments of annoyance when Rose was gone from the cabin, a sort of petulance at being left alone.

Finally he did rise and went into the kitchen, feeling steady enough on his legs, but with a faint distrust of the furniture. Surprised to find two-thirds of a ham strung from the ceiling, after smelling and picking a few choice bits with his fingers, he took the biggest knife he could find and cut big, ragged slabs, not bothering to unstring the ham. Piling sandwiches on a plate, he sprawled on his back across the bed, feeling the plate move on his stomach as he breathed. He never had difficulty eating in this position. He never choked on food.

He was turning the pillow, wet from feeding water too fast into his mouth, when his wife entered. He watched her go into the kitchen, heard stove noises and a few others which did not identify themselves, but continued to gulp down big portions of sandwich by using his hands to crush the bread and meat against his mouth, his hands also forming a cage to prevent chunks of meat from escaping.

Rose stood in the doorway. Her huge, soft plumpness mocked the utility and form of corsets. Her dress was of blowsy Dutch fullness and simplicity, and there was something matronly in the way she carried herself. There seemed even a complacency in the manner in which she watched him.

"I lost track of time," she said. "Coffee will be ready in a jiffy."

He beckoned with a curl of his hand. "C'mere," he said. "Long time no see." He held forth the plate, on which a single sandwich remained. "Feed your old pappy," he said. "He's tired."

There was the briefest moment of indecision, then Rose came and sat on the bed. "I shouldn't, my hands are dirty," she said, while her hands rearranged the slices of bread to make the appearance more nearly that of a sandwich.

Gilbert could smell that she had been sweating and sensed fatigue from her posture. Her arms as far as the elbows had patches of dirt and embedded marks, almost scratches, the kind bark of trees makes. His mouth took small bites to prolong the useless pleasure of being fed, and when the sandwich grew small and triangular, he took the precaution of wrapping his legs around her. The upper portion of his body was relaxed, both hands hammocking the back of his head, finger tips occasionally stirring in his long hair.

Rose made no attempt to free herself, continued to feed him until there was nothing. She pushed at his leg to make her stomach more comfortable, and had the appearance of being resigned to sit this way as long as he wished. She was looking toward the kitchen.

Gilbert continued to study her, his eyes approving of the fact that they did not need to encounter hers. She was not the young girl he had taken by force, nor the young woman whom he had stood beside in boots, his eyes fixed upon the highest of three bronze crucifixes. Her service to him was that of a woman unashamed to bathe, feed and nurse a man who was not deserving of kindness. She had followed him through the worst of his degradations. She had neither judged nor condemned him.

From the moment his legs had circled her they had both known what was to follow. He was merely prolonging the time, while there was still a laziness and an easiness of spirit governing him. But his emotion went deeper, the pain of a man who knows his wife is living a sacrifice and a penance, the pain of a man who no longer cares to be respected. He knew he was trying to disgust her and make her resent the only strong passion which they retained for each other, the only mastery which he still held over her. He was trying to make her ashamed of the one means of pleasing him which had never failed her, offering herself as something to comfort him. Her large, full-blown body had become his best defense against himself.

It was not until the legs began to tighten, making her breathing conscious though not painful, that Rose tried to free herself. She made an ordinary effort to rise, then settled back into imprisonment, giving him a look which might or might not cause her to be released, but indicated she was not going to struggle.

"Hell with the coffee," said Gilbert, catching her nearest arm and dragging part of her weight on top of him. "It'll be good and strong by the time we want it." His hand caught in her hair and jerked rather roughly, in mockery of the half-fond intent which usually accompanied the gesture. He knew her well enough to be sure that this was not one of her more passionate moments, and could sense that her body was tired and preferred rest, but for some reason this was attractive to him. He felt his desire quicken, without confusing or weakening the contempt which he felt, contempt that she should accept him and presume to try to calm and soothe him.

Gilbert was no longer ashamed of his wife. He felt insulted by her. It maddened him at times, the maternal, companionable understanding which she offered, the way she understood how he felt about his sister, the way she understood how he felt about the town. It

471

frightened him that she could remain calm when he was angry and abusive, when drunkenness permitted him to hover along the edge of meanness.

He had the power to rouse her, to make her passionate even in those rare moments when she was unwilling. She had never refused him possession of her body, whether he came to her drunk or with curses or so weak and sick that all he could do was clutch her in an impotent posture of copulation. His wild talk of faithlessness caused her sorrow, but she had never raised her voice in protest nor condemned him. He hated her for these very things.

Rose, trying to look toward the kitchen from a difficult position, made a feeble effort to rise, then gave it up. The legs around her were becoming heavy and tense, shortening her breath, and she twisted a little, not so much because of this, but because it made her feel the soft, loose flesh, normally pleasant, which had been left on her since childbirth. It was when Gilbert pulled the sheet loose from the mattress and began to clean her arms, wetting the more stubborn dirt patches with his tongue, that she grew active. That there were times when he did not wish her near him she had come to accept, but that there were times when he took her with a kind of malicious intent, she would not have believed.

Yet it was their strongest tie. It was the only time he felt a great passion for her.

Outside, their child ran on a leash which slid on the wire clothesline.

"There's hardly any point in sitting by him now," said Irene.

Mr. Pierce was sitting in a chair, facing the coffin, staring at the long panel of wood. He looked up, slowly, as if his head were hard to manage.

For once in his life he missed the intention of her voice. "Please," he said, rising, offering. He simply felt her grief deserved precedence over his own.

Irene went to the window and stared into the darkness. Trees were swaying but she could not hear the wind and it made the house seem enlarged with silence. There was the tiny, flickering sound of sleet so fine it could be seen only at the instant when it bounced away from the window.

Rising, Mr. Pierce had seen his son. He put his hands on the edge of the coffin as he might have on the rail of the porch and leaned forward, astonished at the smallness and thinness of the boy. The four sides of wood seemed high.

In the evening of the second day death had begun to take the form of a faint shade of grayness, and the smell of flowers had settled into something unmoving and stable and without freshness. Neither death nor the undertaker had been able to compose the features into a successful pretense of sleep.

Mr. Pierce was wearing black, the coat and trousers thoroughly brushed to rid them of the shine of pressing, his collar with a minimum of starch, tie a soft knitted black, unadorned, and his complexion bloodless and without moisture. His face seemed particularly fat and large because his hair was trimmed short, without sideburns, and the back of his neck had a band of white flesh.

As he looked into the coffin, his long desire to separate his wife and his son seemed nearest to succeeding, and he could not understand why his head felt so difficult to manage and his hands felt so stiff. It astonished him, the grief that he could feel. And as he turned away from the coffin and saw his wife with her forehead pressed against the window, he found it difficult not to go out of the room.

"He was beautiful," said Mr. Pierce. "Truly beautiful."

Irene's own beauty seemed to give a twist, as her flesh was reminded. Her suffering was intensely physical. She felt as if her breasts were bandaged horribly tight against her, and her mouth felt stretched across her teeth.

As she felt her husband's arms on her shoulders, her head drew back and she turned. "You musn't touch me now," she said, and her eyes were quick, then faded again.

"How I admire you," said Mr. Pierce. "That's all I wanted to say."

"I have no place for that," said Irene, and huddled against the window, so forlorn and without physical resistance that there was nothing his hands could do except release her.

Mr. Pierce slipped his hands slowly into his coat pockets, keeping them straight and flat, and went to the entrance of the hall. He stood there for a time, using distance to feel real distance, seeing the truth, that there was no place in his wife's heart for him, that she found nothing an intrusion upon the stunned condition of her affections. She made only a nominal acceptance of her husband as having more privilege in the house than other people.

He wandered about the house with a keen sense of loss which he

473

could not quite identify, a feeling as if the rooms had been made bare, as if something were missing from every wall. He turned on every lamp he came to, without remembering the previous one, and with a feeling that the electricity was failing. He wandered around the house in vague realization that all these years he had been the outsider, he had been the one who had never had real affection. In one of the upstairs rooms a window had been left open, and although he felt the chilliness, although he brushed at the snow which had blown on the sill and pulled the window down and mopped at wet places on the floor with a handkerchief, there remained a feeling of isolation from everything.

He went back over portions of his life and carefully reconstructed them. He tried to feel that it was his wife who had forced him to involve the children in what had been their own problem. He tried to defend himself. He tried to defend himself from the feeling that he could still respect her, while she could no longer respect him. He tried particularly to think of their sorrow as having arisen out of a former time, out of the first years of marriage, for somehow he could always feel that she was responsible for that early failure. But nothing seemed to have its beginning until after their son had come home, dead.

It seemed to him particularly terrifying that he had never formulated any plans for his son, that there had not really been an excuse for sending him to a military school. What seemed to him horrible was not how he had acted toward his wife, but that he had never once given to his children the affection which he had felt toward them. He knew that he was even now afraid of showing his inadequacy in the presence of death.

He passed through the lower hall, knowing that was as near to his son as he could approach while his wife was still in the room, and he went on toward the front door, heard the wreath flapping against it, and knew that he was forbidden to go outside. At last he went to his room and threw himself across the bed.

He dreamed he was looking at a statue of his son, and even the eyeballs were of white concrete.

Bart was sitting alone at the table. He filled his glass, holding the bottle and the glass at an angle to prevent foam. Beer in a glass always seemed heavy and faintly dirty on top. He seldom finished a bottle.

There was a fat piano player and a young boy with greatly enlarged pupils at the drums. After a great deal of tinkering with the instruments and bending their heads to hear tones amid the usual barroom chatter, after a number of consultations, the fat piano player finally put his beer bottle and an ash tray on top of the piano. Then there was an almost concert-hall exactitude about getting seated comfortably. Taa . . . Taa . . . Dadahdadah . . . Tatatatah . . . Tah . . . Tah . . . Erump-p, and the M.C. came running full tilt across the floor, none of his clothing buttoned, in what was presumably an imitation of a man who is late; followed a comedy of misbuttoning and haste, each time the M.C. looking as if he had been trussed and bound for shipment. Bart noticed it was producing laughter. And the final comedy on clothing, when, in an amazingly short time, the M.C. through a series of swift reversals, stepped to the microphone dressed in cool, suave evening dress.

So this was Dip, thought Bart. Poolroom operator, cemetery caretaker, novelty-shop owner, haberdasher, barber, bingo operator, and now M.C. In one sense it was impossible to put a label on him, in another sense it was the easiest thing in the world.

After a while a young woman came dancing in, tap dancing, but with a split skirt which allowed her to do a few ballet movements intended for sensual eyes. There was a hardness in her face, the impassive appearance many prostitutes have, a third-rate professional smile, fine, narrow legs, and a flexible, athletic body. She went down the aisles and between the tables, making special performances for customers who came regularly. She had obviously been in the business long enough to know which men to flirt with, who would grab, who would pretend to grab, whom it was safe and better for the show to let grab, yet always resuming a cool aloofness which made the men feel a comfortable masculine equality. Bart noticed that there was less attention in some quarters than the M.C. had had. Then she abandoned the skirt and did a straight leg dance and a patter song. She was whistled and applauded back on. She did one more song, one she obviously was overtrained on.

So this was she, thought Bart, little Naomi all grown up and at the height of success. He was left cold by the exhibition, not revolted, but with a completely humorless conviction of its stupidity. He rose from his table and went toward where she would make her final exit. He saw the waitress eyeing him as if he were up to mischief, and it suddenly did make him feel disgusted, for he knew the whole history of this part of the bar and how many drunken and sober assignations had been attempted here. He knew when this hotel had

475

been a straight whorehouse and one of the most notorious in central Pennsylvania.

"Long time no see," said Naomi, as she came off the floor, without surprise, and yet Bart knew simply from the tone of her voice that her spirit was gone, that he was dealing with a woman not unlike some he had had and discarded, a woman who only had the memory of being his sister. And he saw that his affections must have been closer to his family than he had ever realized.

"If you're through," he said, "put some clothes on and come over to my table. I want to talk with you."

Naomi shrugged. "I got another show in an hour."

"Then don't bother to change. Come as you are."

"Okay," she said, and followed him. "What you back for?"

"To finish what I started," said Bart.

"I bet," she said. But she looked at him a little more fully, measuring, and saw the heaviness about him, the different way in which he walked, the solid expensiveness of his clothes. "Married?" she said. "You look married."

"Sit down and tell me what you can do," said Bart. "Because you sure as hell can't go on with this much longer."

"Oh, Christ," said Naomi, "not you too. One brother's enough."

"Gib still at it?" said Bart. "Still polishing your star. Shining, shining star." He gave her a cigarette, and she saw that he was a heavy smoker now, saw it in the way he handled the pack and the lighter and from his first exhalation. "Nothing like show business. I'm not mocking you, sis. I'm just thinking of our whole family. We're great."

Naomi did not say anything.

"But it looks like you're trying to take the cake," said Bart. "You were *really* great just now."

"You're insulting," said Naomi.

"Insulting? How so? The world's full of flesh, some beautiful, some average, some stinking. Tons and tons of flesh. You have to be really great to throw your hundred pounds on that pile."

"All right, watcha want? You're after something. I'm pretty sure you don't care what I'm doing."

"I do care," said Bart. "I care when I see this. I was going to ask you to work for me."

"Work for you?" said Naomi. "Look, Bart, you can't do nothing for me. You've always had to be mister big time. Okay, be it. Me, I know what I got, and it ain't great. But I got three squares and I got friends." Naomi paused. "What's the use? Listen, go see Father before you leave town this time. He's old and he's worried about you."

Mr. Rowiger pushed his glasses tighter against his eyes, and looked at the men seated below him.

"The government," he said softly, "is not with us. By its very nature it never will be. But the government is always forced to make at least some recognition of a majority, and we are becoming a majority. Thus we can by remaining united cause the government to serve our interests."

It seemed unnatural to see such a mild and gentle man standing on a platform, addressing an uneducated audience. Yet he was not nervous.

"That is what the big national unions tell us. This strike has been going on for nearly three months, and it has been hard for all of us, and we would like to get it settled. I have been hearing a lot throughout the town, men like yourselves, some of you no doubt, asking and even demanding why we don't get a big union to back us. I want to tell you why. Because no union of men, unless it is of all mankind, is good, and the larger the more fatal. As we now stand we can keep the right to make our own decisions. We make what we believe are fair demands. We're trying to make the company realize that. We have the privilege of compromise. We can even disband if we vote to do so."

There was something in the audience which was not to be expected from men whose minds and whose bodies were constructed for violence. There was a calm attentiveness. It did not seem that they were men who had only recently passed through a depression and who had not worked regularly during the past four years. It was more the atmosphere of a town hall, of men who were carefully considering justice.

"If we join a national union we gain power. We pay for it. By being committed to policies which are not our own. By having support only when the union believes us deserving, or, more likely, believes it will advance the national strength of that union. I am so opposed to that I can hardly find words to express my feeling. It is like stepping between two big bosses, and being used to push one way and then the other."

Another curious thing about the audience was the number of women present and even a smattering of businessmen who had

477

decided to commit themselves. It was the sort of gathering which could have been expected in church.

"I ask you therefore to stick it out. You have gone through too much to turn back on yourselves now. Your children have seen too much, and they'll never forgive us if we fail. Even the company officials know that they have hung to a wrong belief too long, and they're holding on now only in the hope of breaking us. It's going to be hard. I'm having difficulty raising food, not because our supporters are less generous, but because some of them are now in the same condition we are. We are faced with the need of clothing, and there are whole families without places to live. But I swear to you that everywhere I have been I have seen people making the most honest endeavor of their lives. I for one will not give in."

Mr. Rowiger leaned forward, as if trying to get a closer look at each person in the audience.

"We will vote as to whether to continue the strike through next week."

The Democrats were having a political rally in Depression Park. Three trucks were parked near locust trees which prevented them from entering the park. Men and women were carrying baskets to the pavilion and to the brick fireplace. The lights had already been turned on, bugs had already found the bulbs, and moths had very white wings until they vanished into the darkness above. There was the clang of horseshoes striking the hob and deflecting. One man pitched and others put water on the clay, trying to get it to the right consistency. At the other box a man with a shovel was spading the clay so the water would be absorbed.

The smaller pavilion was already clouded with cigar smoke. Sides were about to be chosen for the dart-ball game. There was joshing about putting all the Republicans on one side, retorts that there wouldn't be enough Democrats to make up a team. Old Mijack, who was in doubt that, with so many men present, he would be chosen for either team, had a handful of darts and was practicing. He had come early, so he would be sure to have time to warm up in case he was needed.

Outside, Sam Benton was putting ice in a burlap bag and crushing it with a hammer, while two younger men took turns cranking the freezer, one stuffing ice and salt in, from time to time poking his little finger in the drain hole to keep it from getting clogged. Two children

478

were standing near, asking questions, offering to help, although their real interest was more foresighted.

Children who had been brought by their parents were surprised at meeting each other. They were a little awkward in getting together, because they were not sure how much freedom their parents would permit, how far they could wander. They were not accustomed to games after dark. But there were a great number of children who had come themselves and were already showing their wildness, running around, paying no more attention to the big people than to the trees, using people as means of getting away from each other, jumping over benches.

Teen-age girls stayed close to their mothers, and there were several groups of young boys, walking about with nonchalance. If it had not been for the neatness with which their hair was combed, they would have succeeded in pretending that they had come for the free food. Their eyes coolly dismissed everyone under eleven and over sixteen, and looked over the heads of girls seated with their parents.

A group of older boys, high-school age, came up the hill. As they came under the light it could be seen that one of them was a girl, with dark, lank hair, which she kept back from her ears by drawing it together and doubling a rubber band around it. She had an abundance of freckles in the center of her face, but her skin was pale. Her legs were thin and muscular, sheathed tight in riding breeches, which made her slim hips and waist seem flexible and easy of movement; but her rather full bosom seemed to weight her posture forward disagreeably. Hanging at her side, almost in the position of a holster, was her motorcycle helmet.

The horseshoes glinted a little as they swung through the air and then settled into the clay box almost soundlessly, except when they struck the hob. Once in a while there was the clear, sharp sound of a ringer, or the high-pitched whine of one which struck too high on the hob and whirled out of the box, making a hollow sound against the wood frame. The men pitching were in their thirties and forties, except for one man, who spat on the second shoe whenever the first failed. He was in his middle fifties. Older men, some of them veterans of these same clay pits, watched and kibitzed about who had his form and who was off. Another man had a wooden board and was manipulating wooden pegs in it, announcing the score only when someone asked, or after one side was above fifteen. He never talked, but sometimes raised a hand and showed a certain number of fingers to one of the men playing, and if his head nodded, the pegs would be moved. The shadows of the insects swarming about the lights had no individuality: the ground seemed less well lighted than the air.

When the hot-dog stand opened, the men pitching horseshoes and those sitting on benches did not move. After a while a middle-aged woman came over and held out a box to each of them. It was only at her insistence that most of them took a hot dog, although one of the men pitching took one in each fist, and put another on top of his hat. He was a plumber with a banquet reputation, and his remarks led a few of the other men to accept a second hot dog. One of the pitchers, who was having a time making his shoes land flat, would accept only a Coca-Cola. He kept shaking his head and saying that someone ought to take his place.

The small pavilion was entirely male, men of late fifty or better, men whose wives did not find it necessary to disturb them every few moments. Sides had been chosen and old Mijack was about to lead off the bottom half of the first inning. He had really had no reason to fear not being selected, at least not on the basis of his hitting, for he was the best singles hitter in the church league. If there had been reason to fear, it was that on an evening such as this someone more sociable might be chosen, since the men were not likely to think seriously about the score.

Mijack walked to the line and placed his left foot almost touching it. He weighed the dart in his hand, smoothed the feathers, then looked at the board, with the long slowness of a man who is studying something on the horizon. His arm moved slowly and smoothly, and the dart moved out of his hand with the same smooth slowness, made an arc, and stuck in the board. "Was that a hit?" he said. "No? A ball?" He took the same care and threw again. It was a hit.

Mijack walked into a corner of the room. He did not like to sit down when he was pitching. He felt his nose and wiggled it to see if there was anything that ought to come out, then gripped firmly with his hand and blew. He looked into the palm of his hand to confirm his judgment of what was there. He took out a handkerchief and dried his hand thoroughly, blew his nose again, this time into the handkerchief, then also wiped across his mouth. "I feel I'm going to have a good night," he said, and then his mouth clamped tight, the jaw pulling upward to eliminate the cavity left by toothlessness.

Outside, Sam Benton had drawn the paddle out of the freezer. While he and the other man were taking the ice cream into the serving stand, the two boys held the paddle between them and licked at the rungs. They were happy that Sam had not cleaned the paddle thoroughly, and their only sorrow was for that which was dripping.

The children had lost their awkwardness, and were engaged in a number of games. Little ones were playing hide and seek, staying in the lighted area, escaping each other by running through groups of people. One boy ran across just as one of the men was about to pitch a shoe, and a bystander grabbed the boy; he was lectured at from many directions before he was released, running just as wildly as before. Another group, in semi-darkness, were playing allee-allee-in-free, and further out on the mountain side there was a game of ring-a-ling, the boundaries of which covered almost a quarter of a mile in each direction.

The opening of the hot-dog stand had for a time brought a halt to the games. There had been so many children struggling to be first at the counter that not many older people would risk going near. But when the hot dogs were really ready, there suddenly came a drove of women and young men. The waitresses handed things over the heads of the children, as women held up fingers indicating how many hot dogs were wanted. One boy, who managed to grab and duck, and another, who shouted his name, which happened to be that of a Democratic councilman, were able to show off their proud possessions. After a while the children began to get their fair share, except for some reason, perhaps because it was feared there was not sufficient refreshment to go around, very few were lucky enough to get soft drinks. Not even orange soda, which few older people were fond of.

Some of the teen-age girls who had been sitting with their mothers were sent after refreshments. They did not seem to like the assignment. Several were embarrassed, after the waitress had handed them a hot dog, to have to explain that they needed four more, and one even pointed to where her parents were sitting, so the waitress would know she was telling the truth. Bill Benton took a whole box of refreshments to the Fischer family, causing some blushing and much happiness to Irene. He was rewarded with a place beside her, and with a discussion by Mr. Fischer of his performance in football. Bill had to admit he was not sure he was going to make the varsity this coming fall.

Bobby Brooks was a more mature boy in his thinking. He went and asked Mrs. Eshelman if she would let Mary sit with him. He pointed to the table which was already prepared, and which he was keeping an eye on, since he knew that at any moment it might be confiscated, or the food stolen. Mrs. Eshelman seemed much more pleased and delighted than her daughter was. It was not until Mrs. Eshelman leaned over and whispered in her daughter's ear that Mary rose and went with her escort.

Six young boys, walking around with hands in pockets and hair neatly combed, were as aloof to the refreshments as they were to everything else. Two deserted, and when one returned with several hot dogs, the leader finally contemptuously accepted a hot dog. Most of the boys were walking in a kind of poised dream, in a pretension they accepted but did not understand. Their leader, who had grabbed, contemptuously took two bites and threw the rest away.

The girl in riding pants was having an argument. As they argued, it became apparent that she and the boy were very fond of each other. She seemed to be giving him the devil. Then she turned away, slapping the helmet against her thigh so that the goggles made the odd, loose sound of celluloid. She walked off, taking long, quick strides. She went to where two girls were sitting, put her foot on the bench and, setting her jaw into her cupped hand, began talking to them.

A group of Italians passed through the park. They halted, all lighting cigarettes from the same flame. There was something careless and tough about them.

Two men confiscated one of the benches and were setting a loudspeaker apparatus on it. Several other men were trying to connect a wire to one of the light poles; they had taken out the bulb, making it apparent that there were only six lights in the park. It seemed for a moment to disturb everyone, but then the people went on talking. There did not seem to be more bugs around the lights than before.

The pitcher who had been shaking his head and saying someone should take his place was disgruntled when Sam Bowers took his place. He had just topped a ringer, and his shoes were sticking better, and he wanted one more try. Several bystanders, tired of sitting, had moved over to the quoit boxes. The ground was in poor condition, had not been covered with rubber pads, and the paint was so knocked off the quoits that they had to study to tell the red from the blue ones. A few old men who could no longer throw shoes joined them.

In the first game Mijack had five hits. It promised to be a great night. "Come on, Pappy, come on automatic," his teammates were yelling. The opposition was yelling at him too. Marvin Herber rubbed his bald head to take away some of his luck, but Mijack just kept saying, "You can't get my goat. You might as well try to throw better." Mijack was not the same man he had once been. His aloofness was gone, and he seemed to enjoy being among men he had found uninteresting in his earlier life. He was weakened physically, seemed not merely stooped, but actually smaller than he had been.

The crowd at the hot-dog stand had begun to slacken. The waitresses were giving sodas to children. Two boys were on their eighth hot dog. There was still a steady business and the ice cream caused a new rush, although there was not nearly enough to go around. Late-comers, who wanted to hear the speeches, gave the stand new trade. The Democrats did not seem to be getting the turnout they expected. The drug-store and poolroom loafers had drifted up, but they remained in the shadows; everything but the drug store and poolroom disappointed them, and they were only killing time, holding on to their beer change a little longer.

The arrival of Rowiger and Mrs. Irene Pierce caused excitement among those who understood the significance of their being here. There was consternation among Republicans who were here to see whether the rally amounted to more than it had in previous years; perhaps Mr. Pierce was switching sides and the papers would run against them. In other quarters a few women talked together on a matter of propriety, but the presence of children caused them to reserve their strongest comments for another time.

The children were becoming rough in their play, a little vindictive. Two boys were throwing rocks at each other. A couple of dogs had found the park, probably by following people, and were hunting for discarded food. Few wore collars, and some were lean and scary. They seemed to be the worst victims of the times. The children were not kind to them, the people seemed to ignore them, but the people seemed to ignore their children too. Perhaps that was what accounted for the roughness.

The girl in riding pants was walking down the path toward the Bluegill with the two girls whom she had been talking with. It could be seen now that they were not girls, that they were only wearing short skirts. One, thin and tall, left a trail of perfume behind her. The other, indolent, plump, innocent-looking, had the look of an easy touch. She had the look of a free throw.

The political speeches had finally gotten under way, with some hurriedness, for now that food was not in demand, there was danger of the people going home. They were people who lived a metronome six-day week, and it was difficult for them to break the habit pattern.

As soon as it began to get late their thoughts turned toward home. The fact that men were out on strike, out of work, or only working two days did not alter their habit patterns. The delay had been in getting the loud-speaker to the park and then in getting it attached.

As the first speaker began to talk, there came a different atmosphere. It was not the liveliness that his voice was trying to convey, but the loudness of the speaker that made people turn their heads and look toward him. Some began to move closer, although they could have heard better at a distance. The same loud-speaker was used by the bingo caller at the endless succession of summer festivals. Penny bingo was the rage, and housewives came faithfully and played to win. The loud-speaker had for them, at least for a time, that same significance. There was more hope in its sound than in the words the man spoke.

A light had been fixed so that it shone on the glossy face of Franklin D. Roosevelt.

The horseshoe players did not interrupt their game, but played faster and seemed to realize it was unfair that the clang of the shoes should make a noise of interruption. Bystanders were faithful, yet it was apparent that when the game ended they would move in a mass to the speakers' table.

In the small pavilion, however, the game went on as before. These were men of an older generation, men who had relied on their savings for old age, and who welcomed the cheaper prices. The banks had failed, but they were not people who lost much through banks or stocks or bonds. Most of them would not have known how to go about purchasing securities. They talked politics plenty, and tomorrow, after they heard different versions of the speeches, they would engage in violent disagreements, which were really an agreement.

Mijack was having a great night. He was up much too late. In the second game, a high-scoring affair, he had a phenomenal eight for eight. Players on both teams were so high in their praise that he became nervous and missed the entire board, and said they should put in a pinch hitter. But his teammates, who seemed amused at his seriousness, urged him to continue. He threw for the two-bagger, and the dart going straight, but without enough force, fell at an angle into the home run, bringing in three runs and tying the score. In the ninth he hit a game-winning double.

The men called him champ. "Pappy," said Mr. Johnson, "you get off that Lutheran team and come down to the United Brethren.

We won't ask you to put anything in the collection as long as you hit like that." Mijack was so excited he ran to the scorekeeper and asked how many hits he had had, and Mr. Harper said sixteen out of eighteen, though it had really been sixteen out of twenty. Mijack asked would he write down on paper the hits for each game, and Mr. Harper borrowed a pencil, and Mijack tucked the paper carefully in his pocket. He did not read it until he was alone, and then, putting his head close to it, he read the numbers over and over, memorizing them. It seemed the triumph of his life.

Children seemed to want to get away from the loud-speaker, away to where they could hear the shouting of their own voices. They went as far into the darkness as they dared. They were aware of the lateness of the night, had lost the joy of freedom, and even their brutality was tempered by a fear that made them avoid trees and hear the weeds and the grass. It was the same fear that keeps children out of trees at night, the advent of loneliness into all things touchable, and even their shrill voices were diminished and shouted from what seemed to them farther distances. Some had gone to sit with their mothers and to be held, peeping out from safe places. A few stared at the loud-speaker, looking between it and the man, hunting in bewilderment for the importance of their own feeling.

The two boys were on their twelfth hot dog. Their rivalry seemed of any time and any age, but in the voracious manner in which they chewed the buns, not in hunger, nor even competition, there could be seen a new trend in life. Despite the difficulty their mouths had to masticate the bread, they were driven by a kind of greediness. It was a possessive greediness so deep within them that they would not have been content to stuff their pockets and carry home a big box of food. Instead they would have gone deep in the mountains, intending to bury it, finding themselves unwilling, as they were unwilling to take it home, and they would have eaten it as they were eating now, eaten until they were sick, and then destroyed what they could not eat, mangled and made useless every bun and bit of meat.

They were boys from average families. They had clothes and did not go hungry. That was where the complication began to form, for they were victims of a feeling, victims of a fear they could not even visualize. The waitresses were laughing at them, were urging them to eat, and kidding them about having bigger eyes than stomachs. Their own parents were amused, and the father spoke about the time he and his cousin had a turkey-eating contest. The two boys identified themselves with that, looked at each other to measure their capacities

485

and seeming conditions. Yet it was not that which drove them; it was the bitterest form of insecurity and the deepest mark of the depression. It was something more destructive than malnutrition.

There was little laughter among the children. They were not lost in their games as in former years, and yet were more deeply lost, hungering for an understanding they could not have, escaping the atmosphere of their lives through one temporary game after another, twisting dizzily as flies in their parodies of escape from being caught, twisting their thin bodies through the shrill shouts.

Three young girls were sitting on a bench. As the loud-speaker focused the attention of the crowd, a group of boys ventured near, freed of a restraint that had never existed except in their own thoughts. The young always feel they are being watched. Laughing, one girl fled in invitation to pursuit, the other two fleeing to the companionship that had vanished from their midst. They fled from a pursuit that had not yet formed.

The leader of the group of boys walked slowly along the path. There was no difficulty finding them, because before the boys had gone as far as they expected to have to go, they could hear giggling. The girls had taken refuge in the outhouse. It confused the boys as nothing else could have confused them, and it made them wait, since none of them was willing to open the door. They were held in the reverse of the same confusion which the girls had brought upon themselves by accepting such an odd sanctuary. Not one of the girls would have, even needing to, used the outhouse for the purpose for which it was intended. They only stood inside, crowded together, forming in their minds a confession of fear and innocent desire. It was a deep indication of the times, of the changed human mind which even in its years of innocence was suffering from a form of perversion.

The girl in riding pants gave a low whistle as she approached the Bluegill, but the whistle was not returned. Only the glowing tips of cigarettes indicated the boys were there. Introductions were made, they divided in two groups, three boys going with the tall, lean girl. There was the sound of brush being trampled as they cleared a space. The boy who had quarreled with the girl in riding pants earlier was speaking to the plump, indolent woman in a low, bitter voice, as she continued to shake her head in refusal. The girl in riding pants began to speak to the plump one, coaxingly.

Finally they persuaded her at least to sit and talk, the two girls doing most of the talking, while the boy from time to time leaned between them and spoke angrily. They were still arguing when the thin, tall woman kicked off her shoes and pulled her skirt above her waist and one of the boys flipped his cigarette into the Bluegill and knelt over her, while the other two chatted.

The political rally was moving along. The speeches were loud and the words were damning, as the national faults and the depression were being attributed to the local burgess. It was the same old dish of tripe, which included legitimate complaints, being voiced by men who could not even read the American Constitution. Yet there was a difference, a certain desperation that caused the voices of the speakers to be hoarse rather than impassioned, furiously angry rather than damnatory. Even the speakers seemed to admit that they were trapped in the confusion of the times and that it was in the very earnestness of their confusion that their right to govern existed.

Women constituted the bulk of attention to the early speeches. It was they who seemed to feel that the depression was the result of politics and government. Yet it was evident that they were not thinking in terms of parties or of voting, were not thinking of their new-found emancipation, but were only hoping to hear something that would explain to them why their husbands were not working and what they were expected to do to keep their families alive.

Foreign women were particularly astonished. They knew it was hard for foreigners to get along, hold their rights, keep from being cheated. They liked America because it was better than Poland and Hungary and Yugoslavia, though not much better. In bad times they knew their husbands would have no work. But it was this thing of nobody having work that astonished them. If there had been a revolution, a war, or a new government—but there had been nothing.

One foreign woman was sitting on a bench, holding a six-year-old child, rocking it like an infant. She had no thought of the child being heavy. She was putting it to sleep, knowing she would have to carry it home in her arms, because it was time for the child to sleep. She was rocking because the child was in strange surroundings and needed something familiar. Her eyes gave undivided attention to the speaker. She seemed to be listening to him, not the loud-speaker, watching his mouth move. Her attention was not broken, her eyes did not stray. It could not have been supposed that she did not understand a word he was saying.

The woman was no fool. She was hunting, as others were hunting. Denied understanding of the words and phrases which were confusing others, words and phrases of hoarse voices which had already caused the nation to select a smooth, confident voice that whispered to the nation that there was nothing to fear but fear itself, perhaps she understood a little of what had happened to the nation.

Men came and stood behind the benches, some dusting their hands from horseshoes, others getting rid of the stiffness which sitting had produced in them. Two political hirelings snapped out the lights over the clay boxes, knowing the light above the speaker would gather people nearer if the other lights were turned off. It was well organized for a town election.

Yet it appeared too that the organization was not sufficient. It appeared as if people would continue to be the victims of their habits, would gather up their children and go home. Some wives were more than ready, were only held back by their husbands, who wanted to hear an earful. Or were held back by the difficulties of finding their children.

Life, even in time of distress, was simple for people who knew only as much as was necessary to live. They had no reason to choke on their laughter, no reason to complain about speeches that promised better times. They had no reason to be influenced by speeches, for their lives depended on the steel mill, not on the burgess or the town council, or county elections, or F.D.R.

The hot dogs and refreshments were a sign of the real fault in the Democratic appeal. They had a loud-speaker to blare, a man to adjust it to different heights for those unaccustomed to this method of public speaking. They had four paid waitresses, who were now closing the refreshment stand. They had a box of fireworks that they intended to shoot off at the high point of the rally. They had four barrels of beer and a pig for the Democratic stag party that was to be held the next afternoon. They had three men with notebooks taking the names and the addresses of voters, promising them transportation on election day. They had placards on wooden sticks which they were waving. And yet they seemed to lack any real vitality or enthusiasm, and did not seem to have any real social leaders.

Then a man who was practically unknown to them, Bart Mijack, stepped onto the platform and said, "I've been accepted as the party's choice for the Democratic nomination. I'll say of myself only that I came back here determined to obtain for you workers the justice and fair play that the steel company has never given you. This is not a good time to do it. So I've decided instead to do what I can to make things easier for you. I should like you to meet some

488

of the people who have decided to support me. I should like them to give their reasons for supporting me."

Then, in turn, came Tim Callaghan, Rowiger, Mrs. Irene Pierce and Mr. Dressinger.

With the turning out of the lights most of the small children ran to their parents. The drug-store and poolroom crowd drifted away, figuring the festival was over, finding it dull and useless. One man was locking up the horseshoes and quoits, eyeing a group of kids he did not trust. Another man was putting out the fire in the fireplace, while the waitresses made bundles of the little food that had not been eaten, intending to take them home to their families. Mountain still-ness was beginning to creep into the edges of the park, bringing with it a slight chilliness.

The three girls who had been in the outhouse ran to the park. A little later the boys came to the park and began to talk to them. They were not bad boys, had no bad intentions; it was only their way of getting to meet girls.

Down at the Bluegill, the thin girl had dispensed with the first boy and the second was with her. She was smoking a cigarette. She felt as if she were being masturbated on. The girl in riding pants and the plump girl were kissing each other, while the angry young man was trying to get the pants off the plump one.

Men were standing shoulder to shoulder, listening to the political speeches, victims of themselves and of a political promiscuity of such a low order that they had to hear spoken and repeated what they believed, or believed they believed, in order to know they had beliefs. By tomorrow they would have forgotten their beliefs and would have to be reminded of them, saying, "That's right, that's what I meant, that's who I'm for, that's exactly what I was trying to say, that's what I've been telling you people all along." One was a merchant, one a steel worker and one a banker. But they could have been anybody with any job. Because that was what America had done to itself, that was what democracy had brought itself to accept as democracy.

The old men in the pavilion, they were the only ones who had beliefs, not mockeries of beliefs, and even then only a few, such as old Mijack, had ever lived by their beliefs. And Mijack in his ex-citement over the game had forgotten that his son was going to speak, and so he missed the only chance to see his son that he had had in many years. Only the old men had beliefs, and they did not need their beliefs any more. They needed only food, medical attention, sleep and dozing and the sight of the sun rising in the early morning.

The world had come to a pretty sad state of affairs. There wasn't much hope anywhere any more.

PART SIX: 1936 - 1941

40

FRED COULD NOT REMEMBER the curtains being such a deep pink.

"Why don't you take a bath?" said Dorothy. "You've been hollering to get in the bathroom for an hour."

Fred put a cigarette to his mouth. "I asked once—once." He blew against the match head, looked at the ashtray full of bent cigarettes, withered tips poking upward, and carefully placed the match on the edge of the dresser.

"Well, I don't like it."

"What do you like?" said Fred. But as she crossed the room, going toward the window with that indifference which made her seem faintly indecent in intimate apparel, with her head and arms bent forward to receive the petticoat, he knew she was not vulnerable to anything. She seemed instead to be aware of the warmth of her own body and of the fresh scent which bathing had given it. She seemed slightly flushed with sensuousness.

Fred stood there, armed with gestures of his cigarette, feeling a coldness toward her. His eyes seemed to blink very slowly, and his nostrils had a hesitancy to breathe. He felt angered that she should be so unmoved by his presence, that she should go about dressing herself, not tantalizingly, which would have given him scorn, but accepting his presence without attaching either value or disvalue to it.

"Fasten me in back," she said, shrugging her shoulders to make herself narrower.

Fred found a piece of paper and held it curled about one finger, then flicked ashes into the hollow. "Yes, your highness," he said, but did not move. He was affronted by the colors of the room, the soft pinks and the shine of mirrors. He wanted a good hard chair in which he could sit and thrust out his legs. Even the smoke of his cigarette seemed faintly offensive, hanging in the air.

Dorothy had one arm looped over her shoulder, and, leaning backward slightly, she managed to hook the buttons. She crossed the room as if she were trying out a pair of new shoes, then gave a few pulls at her dress and watched the results in the mirror. She still had a way of making her dresses sway to accentuate her movements, and more than ever her movements seemed designed to emphasize her breeding. But now she seemed to be trying to make herself untouchable rather than desirable.

Fred walked to the window. He looked outward and upward, seeking that freshness which the sky and the mountains always gave for a moment; but instead the smoke from his mouth spread against the window, making the glass thicker and more impenetrable. Then, as a shadow passed over the window, he caught a reflection of the room behind him, vague and imperfect, yet somehow more lurid and distasteful than the room itself. He whirled around and stared at his wife, seeing her arched back, rather sinuous, looking as if it were going to remain youthful. She was fixing earrings to the lobes of her ears, arranging them to hang properly, then added bits of silver to her fingers. She did not wear jewels any more, nothing except small, heavy bits of silver.

"I ought to make you have a child," he said.

Dorothy did not reply, did not even hunt for him in the mirror; but a movement of touching her fingers against her throat and sitting very still betrayed her. Fred looked at his cigarette, as if to assure himself it was still long enough to be kept safely between his fingers.

"Oh, you needn't worry," he said. "I'm not very likely ever to throw you across the bed. You've spoiled that for me."

Fred had of late taken refuge in a coarseness which seemed particularly effective against her. But he had never spoken in this tone before.

"Oh, I suppose the idea of being thrown across the bed doesn't upset you very much. You'd just smoke a cigarette afterward." And he drew on his own cigarette, mocking the style which she used to keep her eyes unmolested, then blew the smoke at her as if to cloud her from his view. "But I suspect you're rather appalled at the idea of having a baby."

"Yes," said Dorothy, and shivered.

"Yes," he said. "It might spread that pretty ass of yours."

494

She was looking at her own eyes in the mirror. They seemed life-less.

"Or it might look like me, that would be worse yet," he said brutally.

She seemed much more naked than when she had been dressing in front of him. Her preparations for the evening, the make-up around her eyes, the small, square earrings, only served to show more clearly her disorder and her fear. Yet that fear seemed to be directed entirely toward her mirror, toward her own inner being, so that even now she had only a vague relationship to the man who stood behind her, threatening, furious.

"If we didn't take pleasure in each other—but to spite me, to deliberately make our attraction for each other great enough that you know you're even spiting yourself—don't you think it's rather horrible? To say you're tired, when you're really only peeved about something?"

He spoke with the same sarcasm, yet somehow had lost his initial advantage. There had crept into his voice a tone of self-pity. His wife drew her head erect and turned toward him.

"A woman uses what she has. You never gave me any choice except to believe that was the only thing I could use against you."

He stared back, his eyes still angry.

"I haven't denied you anything in a long time," she said.

Fred sat down on the bed and carefully ground out his cigarette. He seemed to have forgotten his repugnance against the bed's soft-ness. "Huh!" he said. Yet he could not reply further because she had spoken the truth; he knew that during the time when she had tried to make their sexual relations something with which to control him, even when she had insisted on separate bedrooms, he had never had such bitter feelings as he was having now.

"Remember when you gave me hell for not taking precautions? That started something. But don't you see—don't you see we're way beyond that now?"

Fred did see and knew he had only been trying not to see, knew he had come up against something that could not be overcome. She had so steeled herself against him that she did not need isolation. She was less his, caught in his arms, far less his, than the night she had locked the door and he had pounded against it with his fists.

They sat in silence. There was no physical reason why they could not even at this late hour find happiness. Fred still loved; even as he

495

sat there, dejected, baffled, he might as well have been holding out his arms toward her. They seemed at least on the point of pitying each other.

Yet something kept Dorothy from allowing them to hang on the edge of reconciliation. Something forced her to keep honesty in their relationship.

"Still got cave-man ideas?" she said.

When his eyes rose, hers were prepared, and stared at him with such insolence that she again felt herself shivering.

"Or are you going to be really honest, go bathe and get dressed, and we shall go out and show our young, gay hearts to the world?"

It was the same evening and there was the same coldness, almost as if she despised that he should notice her. In the taxi as they went toward the club she began to rouse herself and to smile in that way she had of making her teeth look small and sharp.

They chose a table away from the lights and the orchestra. Dorothy smacked down her purse with emphasis and drew off her gloves with sharp, precise tugs at the correct finger tips. Her manicure had too much brightness, her hands too feline with long, scratchy nails. She immediately fitted an expensive imported cigarette to a long tube holder which would eject cigarettes without her having to touch them with her fingers.

Fred was unusually formal in his bearing.

The waiter came and wiped the table with a wet rag, leaving bubbles of water. Dorothy put her pocketbook and gloves in her lap and clutched them firmly against her.

Fred did not even move his elbows. He was watching his wife carefully, preparing himself. He thought for a moment, from the way her eyes were fixed so intently on the waiter, she was going to order something strong to drink. He thought it was going to be that kind of evening.

Instead, she remained quiet, preoccupied rather than aloof. She was careful to make her drink last as long as possible, even though there was an edginess in the manner in which she sipped. She kept looking at the steel workers crowded against the bar and at the kind of women who did not mind being among them. The men were cleaner and drank slower because there was a strike, but the women seemed dirtier and cheaper and more desperate.

Mr. and Mrs. Stevens joined them at the table. Mark Stevens seemed relaxed and unworried, contrary to his usual appearance at election time. His wife had that thin nervousness of a woman who was always much more conscious of her husband's position than he himself was.

Dorothy had apparently decided to make herself uninteresting. She took no part in the conversation. After a while, she hunted in her purse, gathered in her hand all the change she could find, snapped her purse shut, and, without excusing herself, crossed the room, walking briskly.

Fred managed not to turn his head to see where she was going.

"We all seem to have fallen on bad days," Mark Stevens said.

Fred thought for a moment reference to his wife was intended.

"I guess this is a year of the locusts. Thank God it doesn't come every seventh year in my business." Mark dropped his cigarette into the ash tray, then punched at the burning tip with his thumb, with such disregard for the yellowed flesh that he seemed to take pleasure from his own insensibility. "I confess I hate playing the role of a cork bobbing on the tide."

"I don't see it that way," said Fred. "I see it as my biggest opportunity."

"*Was* your big opportunity," said Mark.

"No," said Fred. "Still is."

But he did not believe his own words.

Dorothy returned to the table. She did not sit down. "Nickels," she said.

Fred took out his wallet and placed a dollar and then another dollar on the table. He did not hand them to his wife. He pointed to her drink, jabbing his finger at it emphatically. Dorothy picked up the glass and took it with her. She walked with the flowing stiffness of a woman who was trying to accentuate her height.

Mr. and Mrs. Stevens sat for a short while talking between themselves, giving the young man an opportunity to catch hold of himself.

Through the music and the noise Fred could hear only the initial breaking sound as the arms were pulled down, as coins spilled in the trays. It was not long before he was talking rapidly, telling Mrs. Stevens about the hardwood floors, tile bathroom, electric refrigerator, the chandelier of twelve clustered lights, and the oriental rug in blue and tan. He told her how the sills of the windows had been widened so there would be a place for the flowers to get sunlight. He had bought a set of new cane furniture to alternate with the heavy and deeply upholstered winter furnishings.

"But that's only for now," Fred said. "My wife has in mind a house with lots of glass, lots of porch and garden. Not here, not in town . . . And then having it landscaped and designed . . . And then one day walking up to it, seeing it for the first time . . . Not surprised, delighted, delighted to enter something comfortable and permanent, something which we'll know instantly is going to suit us forever."

It was impossible not to believe his wife had said that. There was too much fervor in his voice. "Only," he said, "it's hard for her to wait."

A little while later, Dorothy returned. "Dimes," she said.

Fred opened his wallet, hesitated, then gave her five dollars. "Should I order you a drink?"

Dorothy did not reply. She crumbled the bill in her hand and turned to leave.

"Your husband's been telling me how nice you've fixed the apartment."

Dorothy stared at the woman. "Yes," she said. "And if we fix the place ever so nice, you've only to go outside to tell what we really have." She went to the bar to get change.

Mrs. Stevens said, "It'll come all right. Women pass through a stage of being ungrateful. I guess it's only because we do pass through such a stage that we always tend to think of you men as being the ungrateful ones."

"Yes," said Fred bitterly. "I seem not to have mentioned that my wife resents my trying to make her happy. . . . . *She* won't go through the cheap business of something a little better and a little better. She resents my using money that was supposed to be reserved for our beautiful home." Fred laughed. "Imagine, she's even afraid that by the time we get a home, she'll have gotten apartment manners."

"She has a point," said Mr. Stevens. "There's not much sense fixing up another man's house."

"I never hoped for much," said Fred. "All I hoped was we'd begin to have friends visit in the evenings instead of always going to restaurants and clubs."

"What a woman doesn't want," said Mr. Stevens, "never give her."

After a while Dorothy returned and sat in her chair. Her presence made conversation difficult. Mrs. Stevens showed the same coldness toward the younger woman which Dorothy had shown earlier. Mark Stevens seemed to be appraising her physically, with a mixture of

498

amusement, attraction and contempt. Dorothy seemed disinterested in her surroundings, yet acutely nervous.

"Any luck?" said Mr. Stevens.

"No," said Dorothy. "I never have luck."

"I expect I've had them tightened up too much," Mark said, smiling.

"I'd rather just think I have no luck."

She sat there making circles with her glass, then wiping her wet fingers. There were instants when her eyes were savage, yet this only made the chilliness of her bearing pronounced. There was in her general attitude, in the way her eyes kept moving, refusing to be held still by conversation, an impatience with herself.

Waiting. It was that which gave the four of them an air of being different from the other people in the club, that more than their clothing or their manners, more than the discreet attention which the waiters gave to them, while in other parts of the room men were banging their glasses on tables or went to the bar where they could shove through an arm; it was an indefinable air of waiting, of having been waiting, of being prepared to sit through a longer time than they expected to have to sit. They were essentially people who had caught themselves on a point of time and hung there, as ill at ease as a group of people waiting to be photographed.

Then Dorothy's eyes fixed on something, singled out something among the crowd gathered along the bar and dance floor, and her whole body seemed to respond, with a stillness, then with a slight uplifted motion as if she were about to rise and walk on tiptoe. Her lips were parted, her teeth bitten together, and when Fred's eyes caught hers, she refrained only through effort from looking hastily away. Her nostrils flared and her eyes peered scornfully and derisively in his.

Fred waited until he could discreetly turn his head, hunting in the direction in which he was sure her eyes had been staring. But it was a wide space and there were many people.

"Quarters," she said. She made an impatient gesture with her hand.

Fred was scared. "No," he said.

She lifted her head, revealing a white neck two strong fingers might pinch. "Very well." She gathered her purse and gloves and took them with her. She went to the bar, opened her purse and took out a blue booklet. In a moment the bartender brought her a pen.

Then the bartender began to place stacks of coins on the bar, and she began sweeping them into her purse.

It cut deep in Fred because he knew she had money in her purse. He watched her cross the room, the swaying of her dress accentuating her movements, bringing out the long lines of her body; again she was making herself unapproachable rather than merely desirable. Only her breasts gave her a tartish air, as if she were unable to suppress them, as if she could not bring herself to restrict or even not accentuate their tips. She walked as if they hurt a little, and yet as if she were delighted. It made Fred recall, in the time when their love had been intense, how she had had a habit of glancing down, sometimes even caressing them with the delicate sides of her wrists as she arranged her collar.

Dorothy passed along the line of slot machines until she found the one she wanted, then emptied the contents of her purse beside it. Watching, his deepest hurt was at seeing her as one of a line of women, all exploring boredom, all preferring the spin of a mechanical dial to the music or the people around them. Beside his wife was a woman hypnotized, her eyes never leaving the small opening in which whirled bars, purple plums, abundance of red cherries, and a yellow gathering of pears and bells. She drew the lever slowly, as if she felt she could control the rate of movement and choose the precise instant of luck. Next to her a woman jerked the handle angrily and did not watch the machine, but seemed to be watching someone on the dance floor.

Next to her was a young woman, almost a girl, who obviously had only a few coins which she had gotten from the man with his back to the bar, his elbows supporting him from behind; in the girl there was a nervousness that caused her to wait long after the machine had stopped spinning, as if hoping for some mechanical accident which would send coins dropping into the tray; the man stood smug and confident, not believing in luck, scarcely believing in the purchase he was making. He was feeling the contempt of throwing away a few nickels. He was building up in himself enough contempt for the girl to feel justified to make his claim later in the night.

Fred saw his wife among these women and felt what she was doing was equally bad. She was not even trying to win. She was only seeing how rapidly she could put money into the machine. It was just another sign of her contempt for his having accepted eight thousand dollars from her father—a "gift" in return for which he was supposed to do his best to prevent the company from negotiating a settlement with the workers. She was scorning him for that weakness, when his real weakness had been accepting the money because he could see no other way of getting out from under the bills she had run up. And he still was not free, the refurnishing of the apartment still was not paid for, and she was at it again, spending, spending. That the amount was small, that the thirty or forty dollars she would put in the machine would not make any real difference in their problem, only made him unreasonably angry.

Fred rose and went across the room. He took hold of his wife's arms, holding them tight against her so that his action would not be as noticeably one of force. "No," he said, "no more tonight."

Dorothy did not resist. "All right," she said, and, released, began to put her personal things into her purse. She picked up one quarter, held it by its very edge. "Yes, go ahead," he said, disgustedly, and watched her drop it into the slot. It was only as her hand paused on the lever, then jerked it down with too much force, that he realized she was looking past him and had been looking past him. He turned in time to see a man pass them.

Bart Mijack nodded politely, so politely that Fred knew the nod was not for himself. Bart nodded again and went on. Dorothy stood watching.

"Let's go," said Fred.

Dorothy smiled, then made a gesture with her entire body, a movement which accentuated spitefully all the allure and restlessness of her physical desires; but worse, the gesture was only seemingly deliberate, only seemingly sarcastic and insulting, and was actually of such hidden violence and emotion that she could not have prevented it.

For a moment Fred wanted to strike her. But he felt weak and helpless.

Dorothy scraped into both hands the silver that was lying beside the machine, looked about, spied Bart standing at the bar. She went to him and gave him the silver, forcing it into hands which simply lay flatly open to hold the weight, while his eyes bored into hers.

"Okay," said Dorothy, taking her husband by the elbow. "Let's go home. I've seen all I wanted to see. Haven't you?"

But neither of them stayed long enough to see Bart's fingers spread, and the silver go splattering across the floor. . . .

There was no strong resistance to Bart in his campaign to become burgess. Mark Stevens, when he first heard of it, laughed; he telephoned Mr. Weaver and said, "Your boy's back again. He's decided to try and creep up my alley."

Bart Mijack was the opportunity Mark Stevens had been waiting for. This promised to be a tough election year. Voters were dangerous when they were fat as pigs or lean as rails. The strikers were in a mood in which they would take out part of their grudge against the company simply by voting contrarily—so that Mark had long ago decided it was foolish to try to re-elect the present burgess. He chose Mr. Kunzmier, a third-ward Lutheran, and, as a precaution, Mr. Crowder as councilman; the young people were getting stronger in that ward, but a combination of the two men should most certainly carry it. The first and fourth wards, predominantly Negro, had been, were, and always would be purchasable.

The second ward Mark almost always lost. It was where he lived. It was solid hunkie.

The fifth ward Mark sometimes lost. It was Catholic.

There had been rumors that Rowiger was going to run for burgess. There had been rumors that Tim Callaghan was going to run for councilman. This had placed the third ward in an undesirable position and could have meant the overthrow of the entire council. Or at least a bad split. It would mean too that Mark Stevens could not depend upon newspaper support and favorable editorials.

So he welcomed Bart Mijack, who would at the most split the opposition. Certainly it made the third ward secure.

But when Mark Stevens attended the political rally at Depression Park, he had said, "There's our next burgess." Mark was a shrewd analyzer of situations, and when he had noticed the methods employed and sensed the money behind the rally, and had particularly noted the people who attended and spoke, including Mrs. Pierce, Rowiger, Tim Callaghan, he had immediately acknowledged defeat. A telephone call from Mr. Pierce the next day, urging him to oppose Bart Mijack with every force available, did not change his mind. And, as he suspected, the newspaper was very late in beginning its editorials, and the editorials were not particularly strong.

Mark Stevens immediately shifted his attention to the councilmen. If he could retain control of the council, the new burgess would be completely ineffective. There were advantages in having an independent burgess during the next four years, because, as Mark saw it, no burgess was going to have blue skies and fair sailing, and it would be just as well for his party to have clean hands; it would be just as well for the voters to get their fill of "independents."

The advantages were with Mark. Nine councilmen were not up for election, and of these seven were his men. Of the ten to be elected and one vacancy to be filled, Mark felt sure of carrying all four in the first and fourth wards, and one in each of the remaining three. Thus fifteen of the twenty would still be solid Republican Party line. Even a surprise loss of two or three seats would not alter the majority.

As the campaign progressed, Mark was surprised at the slight effort Bart made to get anyone elected except himself. Yet, from what he knew of Mijack, it was not, after all, much of a surprise.

Election Day unfolded quite a spectacle. Bart installed a free taxi service, and all day long sedans drove up to the firehouses, letting people out, taking others home. In the morning and early afternoon all of the voters were white. About two o'clock there began to appear, at each firehouse, a number of strange men. Shortly afterward Mark got a report from the first ward that one of his men had been roughed up. The second ward was ninety per cent voted by noon, the third ward was receiving only stragglers after three. A truck with sound equipment kept prowling through the town, urging people to come out and vote.

When the Negroes began to pour in, climbing out of long, black sedans which had been rented from the K-S funeral parlor, Mark knew this was going to be a bad day. He was receiving frantic telephone calls from his ward bosses and precinct helpers. The police seemed a little uneasy.

The election results were even more surprising. Bart was elected burgess by a solid majority. His representatives swept the two Negro wards; but the remainder of the wards elected their usual candidates. It meant that Mark still had firm control, but that his control now depended upon areas in which he had never been very popular.

"Not much trade, huh?" said Dip, peering about the poolroom. "The ladies versus the cue sticks, and the ladies are stealing the day. Well, I guess if a guy meets a dame that fits his tape measure, he's got the right to be gone. I guess when he turns his hot rod into a respectable automobile and makes old Hershey have faith in all kinds of chocolates—just for a girl with eyes the same color and vision the same twenty-thirty as ten million other girls, just for a girl with a mouth about as soft and warm as my thumb, I guess we're all supposed to admire the guy and figure out what we'll buy him for rice day.

"But I wouldn't worry none about the poolroom. Not as long as it's the only place a guy can spit without going to jail. You know, when I owned this joint, guys who wouldn't spit on the street, not even in the gutter, came in here and splattered the joint. No, pool-rooms have too much to offer besides pool tables to ever go out of business." Dip had been peering through the window with "moor-looP s'yekomS" written on it. He rushed to the door and called, "Hi, Betty," to a tall, thin woman across the street. "There's a good kid," he said. "I send her flowers once in a while and write 'Secret Admirer' on the card. No harm, she knows it's me. I got admiration for her; won't wear falsies or pad her hips. A lot of jerks who marry fat little babes would do a lot better with a wife like Betty. Of course it's too late for her in this town. But what I say about flat-chested women, they get the best men or none at all. These fat women may have an easier time getting a ring on their finger, but they always wind up being a pissed-into pillow service.

"Like when I had that clothing store. I turned half the bras back. They'd have sold, but there's some stuff a man's ashamed to sell just to make money. A woman's breast is gentle, not something shocking in appearance—that's not what nature had in mind. Nature thought about men and babies and not cluttering up the body with extra gadgets. That's why men and women can piss and get their vinegar at almost the same time. But when women start wearing pointed bras, then we've had it. Why, a man don't feel like holding them or stroking them—all he wants to do is push on them like a doorbell.

"Men still have sense. They'll still buy a wooden nickel. They'll buy a collar that will collapse, fray and glare. They'll buy preshrunk, Sanforized shirts plastered all over with yellow moons. But a woman, no, she'll tell you the difference between two shades of color that old Michael Angel couldn't have spotted. She's texture-mad.

"I remember this one guy spent the best part of a day in my store. All he wanted to see was every kind of intimate women's apparel I had in stock. I thought he was queer. But he said he'd been married ten years and given up about three years' salary just for his wife's skivvies and still didn't have the least idea about them. You know, one of these women who pays fifty bucks for a negligee and then insists on turning the light out whenever her husband comes into the bedroom. He shook my hand, swore he was forever indebted to me, and went out a thoroughly changed man. Yeah, men still have a little sense.

"I don't see what you keep these jars sealed so tight for. By the time I get the lid off, there's hardly any salt left on the pretzels. Yeah, men sure have a way with women. They really get in love. It's all nice

504

until they have to admit they work in the butcher shop or the open hearth. If women were only pretty or something. Something that would make the nonsense worthwhile. But they ain't pretty. They ain't one per cent pretty. Don't let me forget I'm drinking this. Don't let me forget to leave a nickel. When a man finally does find something he can at least not be too ashamed of, he don't have the nerve to tell her.

"Intellectual women, they're the ones who really give you the creeps. You know, the kind who always think the moonlight makes them beautiful, when actually it makes them look like they've got T.B. And passionate women! They screw their lips in so many positions you'd think you were a bottle they're sucking on. Their mouths need a guy so much he don't get a chance to smoke a weed and winds up wondering if women don't breathe through their ears or something. And when a guy really does get worked up, when he gets in the old prone firing position, they're all fagged out.

"Now we're getting these Christian babes, the kind that sit real stiff and look as if they might spit in your eye. Nice, brainless girls, that's what a man has to let appeal to him. Fill full of whiskey, use a body press, and have a good lawyer or a fast bicycle. If not, they'll wind up stinking up your bed and making you proud you work in the butcher shop. What does the calendar say about the moon? The A's beat the Yanks I see, that's a good love omen. Oh God, give me a woman I can teach to make a side and corner combination shot, instead of this I want her address because I'm a student of nature.

"There goes one. Dot Pierce. Married some lawyer. Got the right measurements, I concede without measuring. I wouldn't be a bit surprised if hers didn't stink. The catch? She's one of those babes who have to make their eyes look like stars—eyewash, I call it. She has to have her wrists jingle-jangle with pure silver, and her neck glitter with upper-middle-class diamonds. If you saw her mother you'd see class, except she looks like a Virgin Mary who's had three immaculate conceptions.

"Oh, I know them, I know them all. The men and the women. I've been a barber and a caretaker at the cemetery. Cornerstones are hell on mower blades. Know what I missed in the cemetery? Not people or spooks, but wind in the trees: there's no trees. I used to let the grass grow high just so I could hear it when there was a breeze. I could tell Negro couples, just listening to their feet move, and don't put on a white sheet, they'll only throw rocks at you. Remember Rudy Surgenic, used to always joke about haunting people? I buried him a foot closer to the surface and never tramped the ground down hard—that's the kind of sense of humor a couple of years of caretaking gives you. I got so I used to change the water in the jars even when they didn't have flowers in them. I remember the little Pierce kid, I guess he was about five years old, pointing at his grandfather's grave, and telling me as serious as can be, 'He's down there in a box.' There was the widow in black, I still have her address. No wonder I have no respect for women—or myself. The best was the day I came across the name Paul Sloniker, and thought, I'll be damned, that's my old man.

"Barber of Civil. What a joke. It's more like giving the Sermon on the Mount over and over fifty times a day. Now freeze, I used to say. You know, some barbers pretend they can cut hair good whether the guy keeps moving his head or not. Others are real patient and keep putting the head back in position. Not me. God, how I got to hate men's faces; that damn look that just because you're knocking their hair off they're being made improved, being made better. And the talk. Of course it's better than bartending, better than that national Protestant confessional. . . . There's something so nasty about men spitting their hearts out through beered-up mouths. I used to be fool enough to think it was educational to know why a guy beat his wife up with a clothesbrush instead of his fist. I used to think it was great to live in Nesquehon, where the only minor is a guy without a dime in his pocket. Yeah, I was smooth with the razor and hell with the scissors. And the lotions men want on their mugs, so strong they can't smell anything for smelling themselves. A man should be clean and a woman should stink a little, that's what nature intended.

"Oh, I was a lot of things. Dance instructor. Salesman. I used to sell those things that set women to wailing in the night, and let me tell you ticklers are as hard to sell as framed Bible verses. I puke every time I see a Christmas card. I was so busy selling one-ninety-eight and two-ninety-eight crap the sweat never got a chance to dry.

"I made a fair living, through one thing and another. I had my bowl of cornflakes mornings. I've lived through prohibition booze and thrown the book at Miss Stone Ache. I've made wild pitches and taken third strikes. It hurts even to remember. I think I might even have had once upon a time something they call innocence. Oh honey, put your anatomy against mine. Put out the fire but keep the home fires burning. Piggly-wiggly is okay in its place. Start making conversation to yourself, because, my friend, that's all there is, that's all we've got left. She's nobody's mother, sister or friend.

"You follow me, you begin to see what I mean about men and women?"

Marriage with this woman had degraded him, and to continue to live with her would be his ruin. He was drinking himself into a whining coward. He was drinking himself below her level. He would not be able to stick it out much longer. Something was going to happen.

Gilbert felt a sense of panic, remembering that several times coming home drunk he had been afraid of himself, particularly the night lightning had struck him. He had felt that nothing he did that night could have moral consequence, and his memory hung upon that feeling as upon a missed opportunity. There had been another evening, when he had stood at the edge of the mountain, a drunken companion leaning on his shoulder, and he had proclaimed, "All this is mine. I rule, I command, I do as I please," and he had gone on home with a dangerous look in his eyes, biting his lip.

Bart had given him the dirtiest kind of work, ward-heeling, making the slot-machine collections, picking up the barroom donations for police protection, carrying booze to the strike breakers. Bart had contemptuously assigned him the role of bodyguard, of spy, of sneak. It was his job to keep stirring trouble among the workers, to get into fights and make trouble. Bart had laughed when he had come to bail Gilbert out of jail, saying, "We finally found something you can do. You're a natural." And as Bart had said another time, "As long as I don't give you anything important to do, you're great." Instead of rising, as he had first hoped, Gilbert knew he was sinking, and his only excuse was that he was paid well.

Naomi was making a cheap spectacle of herself, tapping her way along the aisles of barrooms and singing dirty songs.

To run away, to run once more, without the hope which had always betrayed him, or which he had always betrayed. Simply to prevent worse things from happening. He was not even capable of enduring his constant mistreatment of his wife, for which short periods of kindness could no longer atone. He could never again even try to fulfill his responsibilities as a husband and a father, and his eyes winced at the sight of anything which was hopeful. There was a desire to reach the end, to run beyond the end, where, hanging in space, with his legs flailing wildly, as if thrown from some precipice, there would be the last uncoordinated instant.

He saw himself for what he was, foolish, weak, tormented. Surging through what had once been a generous, romantic nature was the threat of brute force in its most noxious form. He was too enraged to accept the responsibility of defeat, too exaggerating of his own worth to see with clear eyes the world around him. Instead he was becoming hard, unfeeling, even vicious.

The old carpet was tacked at inch intervals. His feet did not lift as high as he wished them to. He could feel walking as a faint furry buzzing against the soles of his feet.

The bathroom had a musty barnyard odor. Mijack spent a considerable portion of his life sitting with patience while the slow drip of urine slowly yellowed the water which he could see between his legs.

The windows were closed summer and winter, and there was an atmosphere of something more lasting than dampness and mold, as if the accumulated darkness of so many years had permanently affected the stones of the walls. There was an air of lifelessness, of the slow drainage of fertility from stone, of the perceptible but incomprehensible mutation which occurs when there is no light, no fresh air, no rain and no activity.

Caught on the bridge of his nose, driving two red scars deeper and deeper, so that the nose was becoming bulbed and loose hanging, were glasses, heavy with lenses, a thin gold wire around each ear. His head never seemed accustomed to the fact that the glasses moved with his head, and seemed to be confronted with the same difficulty his neck had always had with collars.

Mijack seemed timeless, yet with an uncanny sense of time. He slept and ate with a regularity which was annoying to the brief moments of remembered youth within him. Time was only a confirmation of his own inward needs, which had reached a commanding importance, and to which he had become servile. The price of life had become slavery, a slavery so complete that its respite was to be found only in moments when Mijack felt he was tricking himself, an extra spoon of sugar slipped quickly into his mouth, a moment more spent in his bath. He had been unconquerable because he made adjustment to nothing, and now he was unconquerable because he adjusted even before shortness of breath, pain in his bowels, could make their warning. He kept his eyes squinted tight shut when he did not need them.

There was indeed something so measured and calculating in every movement which Mijack made that life as existence, as continued heartbeat, became something contemptible and incredibly ugly, hinting at the deepest reason for the need of death. It took the humor and compassion from Mijack's simple explanation, "I must keep life, life will no longer keep me." It made disgusting his commonplace, "Have a little patience. When you reach my age you don't jump into clothes, you settle down into them slow like you was getting into a bathtub with the water a little hot on your behind."

Freedom from pain had become important; he sometimes mistook it for happiness.

When he laughed, he put his hand against his mouth, by this gesture prepared if his teeth came loose. He had learned to laugh too late in life, so that it was a gargled sound, faintly wheezed, too personal.

He was so accustomed to the aching stiffness in his knees that he emitted a faint ripe groan even when there was no stiffness. He was like an actor deducing emotional reactions, always a moment ahead of himself, living in the shadow of his experience.

The minds of old men are old, and can only unjustifiably be compared with youth and childhood. The narrative items of reminiscence are only an anesthetic, self-applied with brutal mercilessness, to excuse the world and the forgotten god for having discarded old bones and a sack of female flesh. Mijack retained the dignity of knowing he had not found peace, nor truth, and he approved of his youth less than when he had been middle-aged, yearning neither to return toward that youth nor have it pass across the years to him. He stood no more ready now to conquer, even if he had been given brand-new physical equipment, than he had ever been. He knew that he could not see truth, that he had never seen beyond the images which his eyes had given him, and that the utmost he had ever seen of truth was the vague sense of a pattern, like the bending of wheat before an even wind. It was in still being able to stand upright, in being immune to the ignorance which could not be avoided, in keeping alive that which was dying, in keeping honorable terms with defeat, that he continued to have some measure of courage.

No, even greatness. He had submitted to slavery only in the unimportant tediums of life, in the appearances in which his heart had never taken interest, and had thereby retained those things which were of uppermost significance. No roofer had ever been on his roof, and he scoffed at the admonitions of people who saw him that high. The cellar contained four huge jars full of nails, bolts and odd pieces which he had spent weeks hammering straight, so that they would be ready in case of need. He had learned to eat peas in the garden, corn with the ears warmed only by his hands, and saw the dignity which men who had lived without knowledge of fire had had, and the dependency into which mankind had fallen. He cared nothing for his Bible and little for his God and had no fear.

There had come to him sensations and understandings which he had been denied in his youth, secrets which hide at the edges and the end of life, the amusement of living in a world where it never rained while he was inside, the finding of more tribute to life in the squeals of a butchered hog than in the vagueness of flowers. He learned that to see and to hear were the commonest marks of a man's passage through time, and that it was only when a man stood without them, brought to a place where belief and faith can have no outward valuation, that a man could begin to have an inkling of the enormous conquest that is thrown upon and against the human heart every hour of life. Old age was only having swept away that which had never had a chance to succeed from the beginning, but which could not, even as it was being swept along, lost, lost, consign itself to having existed for nothing. Let the reason for living have gone with it, let it have gone, let it never be found, but let it have been. "No man," Mijack said once, in one of his moments of insight, "cares to see God. No man cares if God is alive. But what he must know is that at some point in time, even before time, there was something that might have been or might have been mistaken for God. On that alone mankind can exist mightily and forever."

41

Bart's first move was to test the council. He made a series of proposals, each in line with his campaign promises. A moderate tax re-evaluation of the steel company was rejected fourteen to six. Reorganization of the police force, with the inclusion of Negro policemen, was rejected by the same vote. Purchase of land from Dauphin County, to insure the town of adequate expansion facilities, was rejected. A new municipal building was turned down, eleven, eight, one abstention. Development of the highway and sanitation departments received the same vote. A new water-filtration plant was voted down by a slight margin. Bart then proposed relief and assistance, specifically, flour, corn and potatoes to be purchased in bulk and to be distributed by a welfare society. But this was rejected sixteen to four, although seven insisted on having recorded their specific reasons for voting against the proposal.

The council then proposed to establish their budget for the first half of the year. After the meeting, Bart prepared a report, giving in detail the specific proposals and which of the councilmen had opposed them. A printer rushed out four thousand copies, and these were then distributed to the homes. Bart wanted the eyes of the people to see the exact situation he was facing.

Bart wrote a letter to the state department of health, pointing out the conditions of water and river contamination caused by the steel company's policy of dumping refuse in the Susquehanna. He did not hope for results. He merely wanted to get certain things into the record. Then he decided to call a general meeting with regard to the public schools. He wanted to show people how ineffective they were.

He was in no hurry. He was slowly setting the stage. Yet he presented a surface appearance of agitation and distress, made a point of talking with many people about the difficulties he was encountering, asking advice. He even, about a month after his term of office had begun, went to see Mark Stevens and asked for more co-operation. He wrote a letter to Mr. Pierce, appealing for newspaper assistance. He made contact with various churches, civic organizations. He gave the appearance of a man trying desperately to obtain support. In spite of the fact that he had become heavier and slightly fastidious in his manners, he had at no previous time in his life seemed more earnest. In place of his own indomitable will, his personal vengeance, there seemed to have formed a more peaceful character, that of a man who was no longer seeking justice for himself, but who had not surrendered his interest in humanity.

He began to be more sociable with the councilmen. He began to show signs of understanding their positions. Through the vaguest of hints he began to make them understand that he did not really expect a major reform, but that he wanted to be able to present the public with some token signs, some small concessions, so that he would always be able to say that he had done what he could. Bart was moving carefully and gradually. The first effect of his moderate policy was an uneasiness which the few councilmen who had supported his measures began to show toward him. It was in fact less than five months after he had been elected that a councilman from the first ward accused him privately of selling out to Mark Stevens. Bart insisted that he was only trying to be politic, to gain through compromise at least some of his goals, rather than have the complete failure which direct action had thus far brought.

The biggest surprise came when he not merely approved the budget, but advocated that the allotment to the sanitation, highway, police and water departments be substantially increased. The strongest opposition came from his own councilmen. But the budget was passed and approved.

Bart was, of course, working along different lines. He still had filed away a careful sketch of the malpractices of the steel company. From this he had drawn lines leading to various members and organizations in the town. He was making a specific list of the grafts and crimes of each department—with these divided into two sections, one which was at the present time prosecutible under law, the other substantiating. The police department was vulnerable. There had been for a long time a system of patronage and protection; it had reached its height during the prohibition years, and was now continued in the form of allowing barrooms to stay open after hours, allowing church clubs to use their Sunday privilege far beyond their proper limits. There was also a system of tip-off, particularly when state police were about to conduct a raid. There was the slot-machine protection, with its warning system, and the flimsy plywood panels which could not have hidden candy from a child and yet escaped the hands of police knocking their fists against walls to find hollow places. The Bessemer and the Marigold continued to have their entertainment licenses, under the guise of which were produced crude adaptations of burlesque, including the sensational Negress Maisie, who picked half-dollars from the edges of the tables without use of her hands, feet or mouth; who also smoked cigars, making them puff, by the same means. Although these entertainment houses no longer owned their whores, there was still a system of patronage and credit, including meals. The police had developed a system of seeing that some of the girls were escorted safely home each night. The use of marihuana was growing in some West Side areas.

Behind all of this was a destruction of competition. Tavern owners who were not liked, or failed to meet the obligations of their protection, were being ruthlessly fined and jailed. Old church laws had been resurrected, laws which stated that no alcoholic beverages could be sold or distributed within five hundred feet of the furthest edge of church property.

Bart had gathered a great mass of evidence of corruption. He had also specific charges against individual policemen. Clyde Gold, son of one of the town's doctors, had committed rape in one of the cells. Bart had not only the testimony of the woman, but of his brother, Gilbert, who had been locked up overnight for drunkenness. The woman did not want to bring charges because her husband was a railroader, and she did not want him to know that she occasionally went to the clubs when he was on a western swing. She was also frankly afraid to bring charges against the police. Bart had taken three young Negroes to a Sunbury doctor, where he obtained a written report on the condition of the wounds, and the earliest date at which they could have been inflicted. He had photographs taken of the men's backs. They had been beaten with rubber hose. The record of the jail itself showed that each had been confined ten days, and the testimony of the doctor stated that the injuries could not have been inflicted more than five days previous to his examination. Spider had scared two policemen into chasing him by taking a flash picture of them drinking liquor while in uniform. The picture was taken in the Bald Hill Tavern, and in the upper left-hand corner the clock read forty minutes after closing hour.

Bart did not intend to use this, yet. He had already communicated with several officials of the state police who had for a long time been angered because of the policy which required co-operation between state and local police. He prepared the ground for an enormous raid, and promised to give both a date and detailed information. He had insisted, however, that until that time no one else, either higher or lower in position, should be informed. His position as burgess of the town for the first time did have validity and importance. He was able to take steps which he could not have taken as a private citizen.

The highway department was thoroughly corrupt. Not only its system of employment, in which workers signed slips for one wage, and received a lesser one. The big graft was in equipment and supplies, in the purchase of stone and tar, in sewage pipe. It was a simple case of purchase of first-quality material, delivery of second- and third-grade material, and a splitting of the difference. It was a simple case of false weights of stone. It was an even simpler case of purchasing from certain firms. Councilman Sours owned the stone

513

quarry at the south edge of town. Tar was purchased through the by-products and gas association of the steel mill. Sewage pipe was purchased from Skipney, plumbers and roofers.

The sanitation department seemed free of graft. The men were underpaid. The money allotted to the department was insufficient, causing them to hire only occasionally. It was only as Bart was about to turn away from further investigation of this that he noticed two discrepancies. The cost of a new truck seemed to him particularly exorbitant. He traced down where it had been purchased, a Harrisburg dealer, and found that the standard price for that model truck had been eight hundred less than the sales slip. The dealer spoke of extras. Bart, seeing that the man was suspicious, began to speak of the fact that a new truck might be purchased shortly, but he was not able to get any offer or hint of the possibility of a special transaction. Bart had to leave that for later. That and the enormous amount of money which had been paid for land on which to put the new dump. The land had been owned by Mr. Pierce.

It was a big web, one which reached in every direction; the difficulty was that it seemed almost a communal project among all the monied and business people of the town, and did not seem to have leaders. It was a European kind of greed, small and scattered, and yet so general that it protected itself through involving nearly everyone of importance. Bart had hoped to be able to put the tab of guilt fully upon Mark Stevens and his underlings. But Mark seemed to have been satisfied to take a cut of the profit, to run the slot-machine racket and the two bookie shops, and to gather the rest of his income through legal means. Mark apparently had made a big enough killing during prohibition not to have to take risks.

Even before election, Bart had studied the character and history of each office-seeker and had gathered data on the kind of patronage each was seeking. He had deliberately not opposed those men against whom he had evidence; these he was sure would be susceptible to opportunities to profiteer. He accepted the first budget and enlarged it, giving them rope. But simply to bring before courts of law a multitude of men guilty of petty graft was not his intention. Bart was wise enough not to waste the evidence he had gathered for trivial purposes of personal revenge. He had learned one important thing. What hung over a man's head was far more effective than what was used; men fear the raised stick more than the blow itself.

He turned therefore to the second part of his preparations. He at no time forgot that his real enemy was the steel company. Long before his election, his picked men had begun to circulate among the workers. He himself had gone to see Rowiger. Then in his campaign speeches he made the bold promise to settle the strike on the terms of the union. He had said that he did not simply mean to give them assistance, but to bring the strike to an end. After his first failures at obtaining relief and welfare, people began to believe that he would do nothing. That had been part of his intention. He began to turn a cold ear toward the union, toward the very people who had helped him get elected. First the good impression, then the worst. And then he began to make his real moves.

"All right, you bastards," said Gilbert, "which one first?" His hands were up before him, fisted, poised, in the defenseless style which men accept as challenging and formidable. But the threat was not wholly dispelled by the ridiculousness of the posture, nor by the inept, slow, blinking of the drunken eyes. . . .

"I ain't never left her. And I ain't never messed with other women. You can sneer all you want to. . . . I don't see none of you parading around raving beauties."

Rowiger found him, standing in the middle of the street, caught between traffic, weaving back and forth, too frightened to move even when a motorist stopped and waited for him to get off the highway. Rowiger, who was in about as much terror of traffic as anyone could be, had to go out and lead him to the sidewalk. Gilbert had been kneeling in the middle of the highway, with his upraised hands clenched in supplication, his eyes pinched tight shut. . . .

Sometimes his eyes remained cold and observant, unaffected by drink, and then the eyes would watch the wretched condition of his hands, of his movements. His eyes would fix on something which was nothing except a continuum of color and motionlessness. It was a growing disinterest in everything, so that he did not often know who was seated on either side of him, so that he did not even resent being led outside by the bartender. . . .

"He's all right, he don't hurt anybody, he minds his own business. . . ."

Everything was closed for the night.

Walking, not staggering as in former years, but with a terrible sense of distance, with a heaviness, with an increasing carelessness in where and when he pissed. . . .

Cut enough wood to get beer. . . .

Grasp and bull on her fattened behind. . . .

The physical brawn of which he had once been so proud, that equipment to meet and conquer life, that means of arriving at independence, hung about him in tatters, felt as a heaviness unnecessary for his bones to carry. He could not seem to get rid of either of them, the weight or the strength. The punishment his body could endure made him weary. . . .

Quarrels, impassioned monologues, fits of wild, ridiculous laughter, kerosene dumped on the fire until the explosions sent him reeling away from the fireplace and the chimney rattled with its burden, while his wife gathered the child in her arms and stood near the door. . . .

He boasted that he had been struck by lightning. He proclaimed that first it had stunned him, then made him feel enormously strong.

"I don't mean to be this way," he said savagely. "In the name of God, can't you see I don't mean it . . . ?"

Fred waited until the noise of the night club vanished into the vast, hushed darkness of the parking lot, until the electric organ could be heard only as small, intermittent peals migrating with the wind, before he spoke. He had taken her elbow because he could not see in the darkness, and now his hand began to lift her elbow and guide her because the high heels would not set firmly in the soft, loose gravel, while his own feet were firm, flat pads. They had walked out of the club before the eyes of Fred's wife. Dorothy had been sitting with Mr. and Mrs. Stevens and Mr. and Mrs. Stephonic and their unmarried daughter, Katie; she had looked up when her husband went to the door with this woman, then had continued the conversation. Fred had not looked in her direction, so that he did not know what his wife's reaction had been.

"You understand the reason I brought you out here?" he said, walking with care through an area where gravel had been spread too deep.

"Naturally," said Naomi. "My coat's still inside."

"I want to make her jealous. I want to make her angry. To pay back some things. She's had it coming for a long time." For a moment the gravel felt cruel underfoot, and he tried to scuff himself free. "You can't deal with that woman reasonably."

"Beginning to wish you hadn't come out?"

"Eh? No, not a bit. I don't care how ridiculous it seems, I'm going to show her." Fred smacked his hands together and smiled. "I bet it

516

will work," he said enthusiastically. "I bet this will do more good than anything I could have said."

"You're going to lose her," said Naomi. "You know it, don't you?"

Fred stared at her. He was drawn erect, as if he had been insulted.

"One way or the other," said Naomi, "you lose. Either she walks off, or you crawl back."

"Nonsense," said Fred.

"No, it isn't nonsense," said Naomi.

"All right, she might," Fred admitted. "She might, she's so unreasonable—but I won't crawl back, not after what I've been through." Fred stopped and gathered gravel in his hand and clenched it fast. "I guess this wasn't the best thing to do, but damn it all, what's a man to do?"

"Divorce," said Naomi. "I've heard a lot of these complaints. I'm a regular crying towel for all the married men in these parts." She laughed, probably remembering something. "I used to say, 'Patch it up, give it another try.' Now I just say, 'Divorce.' " Naomi laid her hand on the sleeve of his coat. "I say that because you don't really want to fix things. You want to step out on her and haven't enough nerve. In another year or two you'll be cheating on her, and if she stands for it, you'll keep right on."

Fred stepped back from her and dropped the gravel. He rubbed his hands together, presumably to rub off the stone dust.

"No," he said, "you're wrong in thinking that. Very wrong. I love my wife."

He turned away, and went swiftly toward the building and the music and the noise.

Bart knew small-time corruption was dangerous. It was possible to carry out his complex purpose effectively only by striking at Nesquehon Foundry from many directions. The important thing was to keep people confused. He had promised to end the strike and get higher wages for the workers, but he had not said what price it would cost. If people were foolish enough to believe that Bart had made the promise simply to be elected, they deserved what was coming. The town was riddled with political rat holes, and Bart was forced to pull and to work with meanness and cheapness, but his day was coming. The inch-by-inch method had its purposes, but the time was near to abandon it. He was going to make such great, dark caverns in this town that people would not dare to enter with their tiny torches of light. The essential means of corruption was to stagger man's imagination and leave man dazed and helpless.

Years earlier, a series of robberies had been committed by twins. The aspect of the case that had interested Bart was the panic and fear into which a series of robberies in a short span of time had thrown the whole town. The confusion had been extraordinary. A seed had planted itself in Bart's mind and it had developed, in a more intricate form, into his present plan. Success depended on the corruption already existing in the council, in the local businessmen. It depended, too, on Bart's knowledge of each individual, on his ability to involve men in their own weaknesses, confuse them, and then strike fear into their hearts. After that it would snowball.

The one thing he could not understand was how the town was so corrupt without anyone being behind it, directing it. He had always thought of corruption as having leadership. But in Nesquehon it was almost a way of the world, everyone responsible, and yet nobody responsible. He was striking hard at Mark Stevens, knocking him out of the picture; but he had a feeling it was not necessary to do it. The one real tangible enemy of the town remained the steel mill.

He had a plan for settling the strike. The steel mill was on town property, therefore liable to the normal property tax, but it had always been managed to "allow" the company a special rate, a special assessment at a ridiculously low figure. If this were raised substantially the town income would be trebled and a hardship would be imposed upon Bethel. To prevent this, the company would probably settle the strike, from which it had already suffered a great deal. But if it did not settle, Bart then planned to raise taxes to a fantastic level. With this income he would propose a bill of relief to the unemployed which would continue until the strike was settled.

The problem was accomplishing this with a council almost unanimously opposed to any measure unfavorable to the steel company and in a manner that would carry out certain other purposes Bart had in mind. This was where his plan of corruption entered, and he was so sure of success that a message was dispatched to Rowiger to hold the strikers firm in their original uncompromised intentions for at least three more months. At the end of the message was the following: "I said I'd settle this strike. I meant it. But where I used to have contempt for the workers, I now have loathing. They deserve to starve. I'm doing it only because of my promise to help you and to settle an old score with certain men in the steel company."

The reply from Rowiger: "You owe me nothing and I expect nothing. You're not the man I voted for." It was exactly what Bart wanted, since one of his intentions was for Rowiger to become discouraged and ask the men to go back to work. That was when he intended to step in.

Bart had his general plans settled. He was engaged in setting up particulars. The town was so accustomed to corruption that it did not consider itself corrupt; and although nearly every businessman would engage in individual gain and patronage, each would also hesitate to vote for a measure that would reveal himself or any of his friends as petty crooks. No one had been surprised when Bart began to make a number of deals for "pocket money," although everyone would have been surprised to know that his private funds were being supplied by a national union, on a cash-delivery basis. Bart was buying as well as selling.

But that was not enough. It was his intention to allow enough of his plans to reach the proper ears to create the impression of his being a magnificent swindler. He wanted to create the impression of a man who was some day going to get caught, but who in the meantime was going to live high off of a small hog. This he knew would cover his real intentions better than absolute secrecy, for it would appear as if he were showing his hand.

Bart began to have dealings with a great many men. With some he was blunt, stating that he had information about their various political and financial dealings; with some he pretended to know less than his own files contained; with others he let them believe more information was at his disposal than he actually had. To another kind of man he would say, "I only want one term in office, and I intend to make the most of it. I mean fill my pocket. Now, at the same time, I realize you intend to seek re-election, and I suppose it's not to your advantage to let me go too far. That's quite understandable. But in regard to this contract for six new fire hydrants—badly needed, you know—a fire in that area would be devastating—and they're in your ward. Well, what I'd like to do is award that contract to your brother, if he's interested. It will be of course all legal. I'll tell him what to bid —but what we need is the approval of the council, and it might look good for the record if you got up a petition from some of the people in your ward saying they want fire hydrants."

There was cruel humor in the corrupt means by which Bart could get necessary things done. He was staying clear of the profits himself, but was always creating the impression that it was the profits that most interested him. Instead of taking his cut, he was taking favors from the council, getting a councilman to vote for an improvement. He was trying to get the town conscious of the need for improvements. In his first year of office he accomplished more change in the social and physical structure of Nesquehon than Rowiger had accomplished in his entire life.

But his purposes were not that simple. He was not even going to hesitate to make his thugs earn their pay, if such means showed promise.

"This is the second time, you know," said Naomi.

"I don't care, let's go," said Fred.

"Look, I don't have much of a rep, I admit. And in this town if you're a little bad, you might as well be real bad. But why should I keep doing you favors? What do I get out of it? Not even an admiring glance from you—and don't you dare offer me money!"

Fred blushed, caught at the exact instant of his thought. "I never looked at it from your point of view," he admitted. "Forgive me. . . . I suppose under these circumstances I have no right to ask . . . No, I haven't. . . ."

"I'll go anyhow," said Naomi suddenly, decisively. "Get my coat for me."

Fred did as she bid him, and it was not until they were outside that they spoke to each other. Naomi made herself snug, almost huddled in her coat, before passing through the door, but Fred carried his coat and scarf on his arm. "It's damn cold," he admitted, before they walked far, but made no effort to put his coat on. "We can sit in the car and turn the heater on."

"Take me for a drive," said Naomi. "I need the fresh air. I want to get away from this for a while." Fred did not answer. "What're you afraid of? You want to get your wife angry. Well, then, take me for a drive."

Fred saw her in one side of the car, then walked around to the other and knocked on the glass to be admitted. He threw his coat and scarf into the rear, then had to reach back again and hunt in the coat pockets for the keys. The car idled a moment before he put it into gear, and he did not snap on the headlights until the car smoothed its motion on the highway.

"New?"

"Last year."

"It must be great to be rich."

"Huh! It was a present for being a good boy. The kind of present you never get through paying installments on."

"It still rides pretty nice. Put the radio on." Naomi settled herself more comfortably on the seat, and watched the darkness curl around the headlight beams. "I run away from noise, and ten minutes later I want it again."

"What made you decide to come along?" asked Fred.

"Maybe I'm trying to get my hooks in you."

His eyes turned away from the road a moment. "I don't believe that," he said.

"Maybe that's what I count on," said Naomi, "your not believing me. When a man's unhappy, look out for the woman who gives him sympathy."

"I still don't believe you."

"Maybe I've got an old score to settle," said Naomi, "with your wife. Listen, there's a little bar down this highway about four miles. You drop me off there and go back."

"Changing your mind again?"

"Yes. I don't like this friendly tone you're taking. I like your dancing, you have better manners than most around here, and I'm about half convinced I could get interested in you. I guess I wouldn't mind being the middle woman if there was some real attraction, but being a friend, a pal in skirts, and shaking hands when it all blows over, I can't say that's my idea of a good time. So-oo . . . I got a free taxi, you got what you wanted, we both got some fresh air, and now let's call it quits. Okay?"

"Okay," said Fred, in a disheartened voice.

Bart detested the workers for their belief that fair practices and health benefits and better working conditions would come gradually and automatically. They were only striking for more money. He sensed that the worst of this was that in hard times these same men were falling into despair instead of working up a fighting spirit. He saw they were about ready to give up and go back to work. "You get nothing for nothing, and if you don't go forward you're going backward. Every week your dollar loses a penny, and each year you grow older and more helpless," he would tell them, though he deplored men who had to be worried and frightened into taking up for their rights; it was sickening that when men finally did act, they made of themselves something they were not, made of their necessity a kind of crusade. "What the hell is wrong with you men?" he would shout at them. "Do you think things do things by themselves? Weeds are the only thing that grow for nothing. Can't you see how industry has become? You think that because you can make a joint or a wrinkle that it's going to let you live one bit better than the newest guy here? Marty Grundeiler was one of the strongest and healthiest guys in the whole East End—does that change the fact that he and fourteen other men have been killed by cyanide gas, and about forty other guys have had to quit long before they dreamed of retiring? Spit down on that floor and take a good look at that spit, because that's exactly how much you mean to the company!" Bart would turn his merciless eyes on those of the men nearest him. "For Christ's sake, stick to your guns. Stay out on strike."

"You're afraid of me now my baby's gone," said Irene. "That's all your talk amounts to, simply you don't know what I might take it into my head to do. You're afraid. Yes, you are. You'd settle for my walking off and leaving you. You'd consider you got off lightly." Irene looked at her husband. "You needn't worry, you can breathe easy. I'm not likely to repay you for your kindness. I'm not even likely to feel sorry for you."

Mr. Pierce was as depressed as his formality would permit him to be. He did not seem to listen to what his wife said, and offered her few of those courtesies which, for so many years, he had unsuccessfully given her in place of direct affection. He was dull. That best expressed it. He had always been dull.

"But one thing you will do. One thing I'll make you do. I'm going to see to it that you help Fred and Dorothy. And you're going to help that poor family across the street from us. I'm tired of the miserable role I've had, carrying food to them, odds and ends you wouldn't miss, while you played your grand role of a sanctimonious miser."

Mr. Pierce was depressed. But by no means defeated. The death of his son had been a shock to him, and when he saw its effect upon his wife he knew instantly that she would have to be allowed a larger range of personal freedom. She was showing signs of rebellion. It seemed possible she would leave him. He realized that Irene was not the sort of woman who would wish things "made up" to her. She would despise him for doing so. To a woman who is spirited there comes a time when there cannot be forgiveness. Marriage has a fifth and sixth hour, but not a ninth hour. As Irene herself had said, "To forgive because one ought to forgive is contemptible. Love is the only reason I would ever forgive anyone." Mr. Pierce knew that his security from domestic difficulties rested on the fact that he had become so utterly meaningless to her.

When he saw that Irene was not going to desert him, he did not settle into his usual complacency. He gained for her a respect and admiration. He saw that she had the courage to forget herself and to devote her energies to trying to repair the harm which he had done to his children and to the people of the town. He even tried to facilitate minor matters for her, allowing her to feel that she had a great deal more power over him than she actually had.

It was on the business front that Mr. Pierce foresaw trouble. Less than a week ago, a group of his best friends had with almost hushed secrecy advised him that it would be more secure to make—at least on the surface—an alliance with the burgess. It was hinted that the tide of political power had shifted away from Mark Stevens, and that, whether agreeable or not, it was to their advantage to follow the trend of the times. Mr. Henny, a conservative and respectable tradesman, went so far as to suggest that the burgess was capable of actions of the worst sort. "Henry," he said, "we don't want to see you on the other side of the fence."

"But, gentlemen," said Mr. Pierce, "surely not everyone thinks as you do?"

"There's no way of telling who's changed," said Mr. Koloskovic. "That's the difficulty. But I can assure you some have, and more will. I myself think it advisable to be at least neutral."

"But I have always been neutral," said Mr. Pierce.

It was the intangible nature of this shifting of opinion, an air of fear which had few facts to back it up, which preyed upon Mr. Pierce. If it had been a matter that could be handled through a series of point-blank accusations, he would have acted at once. But there was somehow an insidious threat that these men were hinting at. Mr. Pierce had the courage to demand facts from them. But they did not have the courage to give him facts.

It was a strange feeling for Mr. Pierce to find himself standing alone.

Bart began to make arrangements to sell the town down the river. There were private meetings with all local contractors, offering bids on terms that could not be refused. A new street-lighting system was to be installed—at fabulous cost. Six of the more important streets were to be paved. New steps were to be constructed leading onto the hill at Fourth Street, with the land being purchased from Harv Gill, councilman. The old steps and the strip of land attending were being purchased, very reasonably, by Mr. Dressinger.

Bart arranged for the streetcar and bus franchise ("the railway company") to be renewed at a very small rate, in exchange for which Councilmen Hill and Jess Pulzowski each obtained property in a very lovely district in suburban Harrisburg. The old municipal building was being sold to Speereero, a man who had never cared what the public thought of him as long as the law could not prosecute; a million was not enough for that old man.

Bart's proposed improvements were in each case of advantage to a few men. The high steps would be a broad concrete pathway leading to the two banks, to the mill entrance; the drug store and the diner and the cigar store stood to gain by improved locations. The Bungalow Hill steps would lead to the football field and eliminate an old wooden walkway that was treacherous in winter. School officials and a number of white-collar workers who were trying to increase the real-estate values in that area and the United Brethren church were particularly interested in those steps.

The comfort station and the new municipal building projects were being supported by various women's clubs, by the Elks, Moose, Lions and the Kiwanis, which had become the town's unofficial chamber of commerce. Bart's insistence upon hiring local labor won support among the strikers, who saw through it a means of bringing a little money home to feed their families.

What had begun as private graft was becoming public fever. There was being aroused a community awareness. A twenty-thousand-dollar contract for Christmas displays was changed from a joke into a serious enterprise once Power and Electric and the merchants on the main street were informed where the decorations were going to be placed. The merchants saw their first real chance to stop people from going to Harrisburg to do their shopping. After the firehouses announced that they were going to put on their finest and biggest parade (as a result of the council having appropriated money for new uniforms), and after the bands of seventeen schools accepted offers to parade, offers which had been extended to them by the burgess, and after Mr. Pierce and Mr. Weaver were selected as judges of the parade, there was very little the council could do, without creating a public uproar, except pass the bill.

A project that caught public attention was that of putting walkways underneath the main street. The street was on the main route between Harrisburg and Philadelphia, and since the Army Air Corps had made a huge supply base at Middletown, traffic had become heavy. It was a constant source of irritation to workers and shoppers, and a hazard for the West Side school children. But the big source of conflict was among merchants and property owners; the side of the street toward the steel mill was far less valuable than the side where the banks and the new movie stood. The main street had always had the appearance of having one side semi-wealthy and the other unkempt.

Bart presented the council with a careful comparison of the costs of installing stop lights and stationing police to see that they were enforced and the cost of construction of walkways. He had the support of several councilmen through an agreement as to which contractors should be chosen. He had the solid support of the town's unemployed. Even the steel company favored the plan, since it had offices on both sides of the street, and because a stop-light system would interfere with the truck-dispatch gates. The banks favored it. Only the merchants on the wealthier side of the street, fearing the rise of competition, fought it. Bart conciliated several important merchants by promising that the comfort station would be located close to their stores.

The resistance Bart began to encounter was largely financial. The growing question was where the money was to come from.

The swindles Bart arranged were enormous in magnitude, not so much individually, but in total. He made each plum big and juicy, but was careful not to make it too big. All in all, more than a hundred men in the town, not including council, stood to profit in small and dishonorable ways. Most of the councilmen were committed, in order to get their own favors; often they did not know how far-reaching a bill was, and they knew only that unless their vote was cast, means would be found of withdrawing favor from them.

Bart was relying on more than corruption. He had allowed for the hardness of the times. With business at a standstill because of the strike, many little businessmen who had been too ambitious for their resources were suffering and in danger of collapse. Contractors desperately needed work. The banks were cautious about loans, and at the same time desperately anxious to make them. Bart kept moving fast, before resistance could form.

There were all kinds of reactions. Some men were trying greedily for a bigger share in the profits. Some seemed to feel that Bart was honest and that he was doing locally what Roosevelt was doing on a national scale. Some saw him as a crook who was going to get caught, but did not see themselves as crooks. Some would take no part in it.

Bart was careful not to approach any man he knew to be thoroughly honest. He knew it would not be long before things began to break loose, and when they did suspicion would be cast everywhere; honest councilmen and businessmen were going to be too busy proving their innocence to act effectively against him. The honest councilman was going to be as divided from his townspeople as the dishonest ones.

The net kept reaching ever wider. He was not after the minnows and sunfish, for the webbing of his plan was too loose and the weight would have been too heavy; but the net must scare everyone, so that those who escaped would flee. Bart proposed to the council that the Catholic Church be granted thirty per cent of the school-tax revenue to maintain its parochial schools. Bart knew the town was sixty per cent Catholic, knew the uproar his proposal would arouse, and knew what shadow of doubt certain priests would find themselves walking under.

Garbage disposal was allowed five new employees, water-filtration and purification was allowed three, and the highway department seven. The tax collector was given a secretary. The policemen were informed that they should petition the council for a wage increase and that they would have Bart's support.

The explosion was near. "Crap is crap," said Bart. "I didn't come all this way just to be another crooked politician. I came here to make this town open its goddamn eyes, and I'll do it if I have to blow the place apart."

42

Hunkies built the mill. Hunkies overturned the first ladle and started steel flowing the breadth of a continent. The continent was becoming linked and strangled by that same steel. Men who had fled from Europe had returned there to die, carrying steel in their hands and strapped around them. And now Europe had found a swastika and a sickle, and Asia a rising sun. Nesquehon's cemeteries were full of bones that had once been wrapped with muscle, skulls which had connived and contrived; soon bodies would not rot fast enough, and the people would have to be buried away from the town, and the dead would be buried with the forgotten dead, with those who had paid for perpetual care but had no grandchildren to pay the more modern-type method of "perpetual care." Soon there would not be room enough on the streets, and the sons would have to seek other places.

Yet, for all this, the hunkies were going to overturn the last ladle.

Rain absorbed the sounds of the steel mill and broke the air of its faint vibration. The men trudged home from work, carrying more than their usual gear, carrying extra coats and shoes and odds and ends which had collected in their lockers. At eleven that night there would be silence throughout the town, and the town would have a chance to hear itself. A general strike had been called.

The beginning of the strike made a great impression on the work-ingmen. Tod Snyder went home and propped his wet shoes on the kitchen stove until they steamed. Milt Henny decided this was a good chance to shingle the house. San Benton cleaned out his lunch bucket and used it to keep his radio tools in. Mish Kosevick started on the week-long drunk he had been planning since June.

That fall and winter more men went hunting than ever before. They sat in the barrooms and told tall tales. They planned to go hunt-ing in the mornings and got too drunk to go.

By midwinter it was different. Men were killing game illegally and cutting it up and bringing it home in sacks. They were hunting with a seriousness which Americans seldom display.

By midwinter people were cutting ice from the shores of the river.

Snow was dark against the sky. The flakes looked like the ashes that fall when a large bundle of paper is burned. It was the first snow of the winter and the dirt was too much for it. But there were to be many more snows that winter, clean snows such as the town had not seen in more than a generation. Even the roofs of the steel mill were going to be white all winter.

Santa brought little things for big stockings. People went to the funeral parlor to see pretty decorations. There weren't any in their own homes. The church bells were clear and loud. There had not been a whistle heard in Nesquehon in three months. To hear was so extraordinary that people felt lonely and sad. Trees were selling at fifty cents a foot in Harrisburg.

Rowiger managed a big Christmas dinner for twenty children. I wanna wing! Drumstick! Children don't like white meat. Mashed potatoes cratered with gravy. Battle of the celery—who crunched loudest. Marks of milk of a too big glass against a too little face. It was the child's first olive and went into a mouth too young for complex taste. One little girl kept sticking things inside her dress to take home.

The only trouble, there were more than three thousand children in Nesquehon.

Irene and Rowiger had a lot to share that year. They had moments of happiness.

Spring came. So did mortgages and sheriff's sales.

Women spent more time in their attics. Old furniture and carpets and clothing were the main items, then pictures and books, worn-out hot-water bottles, yellowed ends of wallpaper, old curtains and blinds, useless fuses, clay marbles, blue doughballs, big glass door stops, linen lamp shades, old brass beds, baby clothing, parts of victrolas, stubs of candles, keys, trinkets and old-style buttons, women's hook shoes, discarded army overcoats, iron buttons, centimes with holes. It was a time of revaluation and resurrection. It was the last and greatest era of the ragman.

The snows began to melt and the rains came. The little streams were the first to come rushing at the river. The Susquehanna, broad, placid, accepted these small, raging torrents with patience. Then the Swatara, the Yellow Britches, the Juniata began to flood, and the river began to leap about and show a countering fury of its own. The waters from the north, from New York and the border counties, had not yet begun. They were the most dangerous.

Trestles, foundries, silence. People were frightened. There was no smoke overhead. The mill seemed blacker and harsher in clear morning light from disuse than it had during the fall and winter. The rail switches were green from night rain. The railroad tracks were tawny-colored, and grass was creeping up along the edges of the ties. There was no slag to make the night sky orange.

Prostitutes were not followed into dark doorways. Many of them had bought one-way tickets to Pittsburgh and Gary and Chicago. Bartenders were fortunate to tap one keg of beer. A clerk was absorbed in the effort of picking one white thread from a dark gabardine suit.

Men did not know how to smile. They wrinkled up their mouths in a manner which they believed was acceptable.

The sun seemed to creep down on the mountain, and there was the flashing of ice, not twinkles but explosions of light. There was shattering and breaking, seen through silence, and a huge side of a cliff fell away. It was more water. Williamsport was preparing for flood. Sunbury was next.

528

Pauses in the classroom, children looking toward the windows and the river. Men planting sticks in the banks to check the hourly rate of rise. Several boats had been swept away.

At the north end of the switch center a train was moving heavily and uncertainly, as if it could not find the track it wanted. With a sharp double clicking the cars were dragged over the switch and then moved on. The sound could be heard all over town. It was the high river that made the tracks sound shrill.

There was debris in the river and most of the islands were gone. There was a slow, roaring sound. Harrisburg was alarmed.

People on the West Side began to carry their furniture upstairs. Rowiger had organized a crew of young men to help people move. Bart Mijack had made contact with the Red Cross and had made arrangements for a thousand cots, which were to be placed in the churches on the hill and the fire stations. The steel mill appealed to the workers to return and man the pumps. Bart suggested to the superintendent of the public schools that it would be wise to arrange for a series of typhoid inoculations. He phoned doctors throughout the town.

People were standing along the river banks. All the police were on the alert for looting. Young men with arm bands and nightsticks were patrolling the streets.

The sewers began to gurgle. Little children absorbed in their games of running were the first ones to splash their feet in the water. The filter plant reported that it was unable to continue operations. Bart arranged for Harrisburg radio stations and two sound trucks to broadcast pleas to the people not to use more water than was absolutely necessary. People filled their bathtubs.

The lid of a sewer blew off and there was a geyser. The lights in the stores on the main street were on all night as employees began to move perishable goods from the first floor. People on the West Side were without gas or electricity.

People along the bank of the river were warned to leave before they were trapped. They had to wade through knee-deep water. The sewage stank. A man who had just finished painting his house was cursing everybody in sight. Children were carrying baskets and boxes toward the hill. Young girls were carrying carpets and bedding. The Bessemer had its floor show going, and there was more trade than ever. Two hours later there was water on the floor. That was when the bank went and the only thing above water as far as the main street was the railroad track.

Cellars on the main street began to get puddles in them. Some of the stores had pumping equipment ready.

By morning the main street was under nine feet of water, and the West Side had seventeen feet. Boats were being poled to and from the banks. There were reports of people trapped. The water was almost too swift for rowing and too deep for pole pushing, and yet boats were investigating the second floors, using the lee side of the houses as protection from the muddy current and debris. Furniture floated out of windows, but only two houses collapsed. For once their closeness served a purpose.

Gilbert Mijack felt the river lean heavily against him, felt the twisting water catch his legs and prevent him from using them effectively. A dog passed in front of him, going downstream, chin lifted on the water. It, too, was only trying to stay afloat, and made Gilbert feel as if his strength were deserting him.

Two of the men in the boat were standing. They were arguing whether or not to try to row through a swift area of current which Gilbert had already passed. They had been arguing the same thing when Gilbert had pulled off his boots and plunged into the river, leaving the boat rocking. The only difference was that they were standing and sometimes pointing.

The choppiness of the water prevented Gilbert from seeing his destination. The house was so far under the water that the roof had the broad and wide appearance of an airplane hangar. There was no one on the roof and no sign of life, and he thought of the house only as a place to be safe, a place to be able to rest. The real strength in him was the knowledge that if his strength should fail no one would try to save him. As he came close to safety, his arms beat the water with wasted fury, and then he clung for a time to the roof, unable to pull himself up.

Later, Gilbert swam back. The rowboat met him about a quarter of a mile downstream, and the two men who had been arguing pulled him into the bottom of the boat.

It had only been a rumor. The old woman was visiting relatives in Shamokin.

On the third day the trucks came with water, and people on the hill met it with buckets and old jugs. The schoolhouse had been made a place of refuge. Mr. Pierce opened all the bedrooms of his house to unfortunate friends or unfortunate friends of his friends.

Rowiger addressed a meeting of the strikers. The steel plant had suffered heavy damage, and yet the heaviest damage had been to the

530

workers. Rowiger said that he would understand if the men decided to go back to work after the water subsided. They voted to remain on strike. They seemed to have gathered determination from this new hardship, and some felt they had nothing further to lose.

The worst was after the water subsided. It was going home and seeing sofas and beds and clothing and rugs and smelling the stink. The very wood in the houses was infested. It was not something that could be repaired in a week or a month.

Summer came. Dawn. The milkman with his accidental clinking of bottles, a sound no other glass could imitate, as if milk somehow tuned the bottles to a special pitch. The far-off cry of roosters who seemed to know the vastness of the land. The slamming of screen doors, as men without work still had to rise early.

Most of the people on the West Side were accustomed to going out on the river in summertime to find coolness. The men fished from morning until dark. The women sat with baskets between their knees and sewed bits of clothing. The children played on nearby islands. These were the happier families, ones who had learned to find peace and solidarity in times of unemployment. They were not ashamed to have the smell of cooking carp spread through the neighborhood.

But this summer there were few boats. The flood had taken most of them. Along the shore, sitting on the river bottom, were rotted boats. People only sat on the banks of the river, and it was not the same. The trains from Philadelphia and New York kept passing by, sliding silent on their new electrification. For the first time in many generations one could see log rafts poled.

Along the streets boys were collecting match-box tops for poker and blackjack, and the foil of cigarette packages and chewing gum to make big balls that would sell for a nickel.

Pennies were big and important. Children clutched them in their hands.

The fire hydrants formed fountains from two until three around which children could cool themselves.

The iceman was not worried about ice melting. He parked in the sun. Only when the children became too insistent did he drape a canvas over the ice. His attitude was careless. He sensed no incongruity in delivering a ten-cent piece which had shrunk to five-cent size. And the housewives, at a time when they were bickering over every penny, did not seem to mind. They clung to their usual complaints, tracking the kitchen, being late.

Children followed behind the truck, waiting for an opportunity to grab a few chips of ice to clench in their fists and suck on. The ice-man chased them, but only from the annoyance he felt at being constantly in the presence of children. The wood on the truck bed was rotted, and as they scraped together handfuls of ice, they had to pick out pieces of wood and dirt. Some carried their ice into their houses to wash it.

A group of boys had fixed waxed strings between tin cans and were talking to each other, hollering so loud they could hear two voices, the voice in the can and the voice across the street. There were bicycles and motorcycles, and the whirring of a kind of scooter made of a wooden crate, a long board and roller skates. Another group of boys were walking toward the countryside with potatoes in their pockets; they would pilfer late spring onions and radishes, build a fire and bake the potatoes in the ashes. Some of the boys had ordinary string in their shoes, some had shoes with paper in their bottoms, but none went barefoot.

The main street was crowded. There were more men than could be expected to be seen in the early afternoon. It was hot and there had been no rain. Men were walking about in their shirts, some with rubber bands on their sleeves. Some used their shirt tails to wipe their faces. Others fanned with their hats. There was a whole row of men in front of the firehouse, and men sitting on the steps of the cigar store, and at the entrance to the bank.

Old Italian women were wearing a poor grade of black, without benefit of starch or the enhancement of white breastplates. The Croatians and Serbians seemed to have lost their taste for color and hand-stitched designs; instead of shawls, they wore handkerchiefs around their heads. Two schoolteachers in long dresses were tapping their fingers against the window of a store and consulting with each other. Mothers and grandmothers were out walking with their children. The faces of the mothers were dour and prim, while the grandmothers seemed to have accepted the times.

A flock of small birds skittered over the street, leaving on the people and cars below a hundred daubs of moving shadow. Their reckless flight seemed guided by a single force, and the telephone wires shimmied from the weight which had been removed. The sun had the bright glitter which so often meant there would be no rain, and the heat which had held the air congealed almost since Memorial Day remained unbroken and undisturbed. There was the stink of trees and lawn wilting.

Arm in arm, marching along the sidewalk, forcing everyone who approached them to swerve into the street or step behind Hardinger's Suit Club sign or the penny weighing machine which advertised "Your Fortune," came a group of girls in skirts so tight that the two halves of their behinds were humped into the material, while their knees gleamed. Their sandals flopped and their toenails were red, and their skirts and blouses were of identical colors. Their mouths chewed with the same cudding motion, and they walked with the joyous innocence of girls who are infatuated with life.

Two boys, standing near the bank, with a rope lying across the sidewalk, did not dare raise it when the rush of girls came swinging past.

Rowiger was sitting on a doorstep, breaking into pieces a corner of bread which was apparently too hard for the little child sitting on his knees.

In front of the poolroom. "Man, she's all sex, she don't get past nobody without being mentally laid. . . . You make time with that, go away, sonny." And from the woman their eyes passed to the girls, to thinner legs and tanned skin. Then another car came, and the skinny man with the rotten meat threw a chunk into the street and watched the dogs chase after it. There was a dead dog lying near the curb. "Why don't you cut it out, Spider?" said one of the boys.

In front of the cigar store, men watched women pass by, swinging their possibilities. But their eyes were heavy and tired, and most of them would not have made the effort to follow a pair of thighs a flight of stairs. They had shot their emotional wads. Their conversation was dull and meaningless. "How do you do all you do, now I ask you?" "Harry, get off your lard can." "Well, what do you know?" "I don't know nuttin." "Hey, what goes on here?" "Can you imagine, the nerve of the guy, taking my last cigarette." "Now what in the devil?" "Hey there, Charlie, am doing fine, how about you." "Doing the best I can, all things considered." "Are you doing the best you can, so help you?" "So help me I am, Joe."

In front of the candy shop, five girls, talking. "I take. Do you take?" "Sure, I take. I been taking for two years." "I just love to take." "I took last year." "My mother wouldn't let me take, but I took anyhow. What day do you take yours? I take Tuesday." "I take Monday and Thursday." And on and on, endlessly excited over the "ballet" lessons of the new gym teacher.

Two older and stouter girls wearing peasant-style ballerina skirts, with shiny patent-leather belts, walked past. Their blouses were too small, their breasts flattened against them, the intention of their brassieres destroyed. They walked with the enormous energy and force which made masculine eyes measure them in terms of coital strength and beef. Their abdomens had the little hump which was referred to in the poolroom as fuckbellies, and which in a few years would enlarge and make them uninteresting. As soon as their initial energy was gone, there would be a coarseness of skin and a rounded fullness which, hard or soft, would be unattractive.

They were not prostitutes. They would not become prostitutes. They would marry and provide the steel mill with its future labor. Yet they had nothing left to discover from their bodies except love, and love would come to them with a particularly repugnant morality, and love would flee from them through the long hallway of monotony.

Wild semi-ignorant girls from the West Side, aged twelve to fifteen, were standing in line outside the drug store, waiting for the afternoon to pass. Toward evening they would be standing in line along the "scratch house" waiting for the movie to open, or they would be standing outside the gymnasium toward seven, or they would be in the drug store at eight, making one soft drink last, or they would simply be standing on the street. They were so young they still sweated when boys held them, so young that passion made them nervous. Yet some had steeled their breasts against feeling, some could have their behinds rubbed and their knees hunted among and still clap their hands as a run scored, some could lift their skirts and sit on an exploring hand during a movie. Some knew how to pinch trousers in the right place, some knew where to buy rubbers, some bought them. Some had to be taken to the woods, to the reservoir, to the Bluegill. Some wanted a car ride, some the back of a motorcycle, and some would walk along the streets with their boy friends of one night, one week, and one month, trying the handles of parked cars until they found a place to sit. Some could be lifted against a wall, some could be exhausted of their resistance through wrestling, and a few, a very few, were after money.

They knew it all and yet knew nothing.

The main street was full of boys who had nowhere to go, nothing to do, nothing to do it with. They whistled invitations. But when the eyes of a girl responded, they jeered and forced her away with obscenity. A woman was no longer protection for her daughter; she herself might be insulted. These boys were not afraid of men, and moved along sullenly when the police came.

534

There were discussions of religion. The boys were never able to solve their Catholic and Protestant mixture. Often their parents were unfriendly toward each other. Nothing helped them understand their real differences of belief. They believed and did not know what they believed.

Girls had more sense and kept their mouths shut. But in a few years, as wives and mothers, they would become bigots and send their children forth to commit the same and worse errors.

Religious talk always wound up in a discussion of what a boy would do if he had a million dollars.

There is very little truth in the idea that steel-mill towns are crowded, overpopulated. It is true only by comparison with country-side villages. What gives this impression is the monotony of the streets and of identical houses, and the public apathy toward the ground beneath their feet, and the immeasurable conformity. The Protestant church had become grape juice and a wafer, four times a year. The Catholics were loyal and almost gleefully willing to attend confession, and their faith seemed strong because there was nothing except faithlessness against which to contrast it.

The river was cleaner than it had been in many years. It actually winked in the moonlight. Young men and their girl friends, or often groups of young men, rowed out onto the river and sat and talked and smoked under the light of the stars. It was one place where they did not need money, where they could still feel alive, where they could talk of love and of life without being ashamed. The young ones talked of taking their rowboats to the Chesapeake, to the Atlantic and around the world. But the older ones knew about the dams which had cut the river into little parcels. *Robinson Crusoe* was an impossible fairy tale.

The boys were sitting around the telephone, a handkerchief over the mouthpiece, speaking in low, disguised voices. They were calling girls and pretending to be someone the girl liked. They were calling their own girls and pretending to be other boys. Toward the end they began to say dirty words and make threats. When they could not think of anyone, they began to dial numbers beginning with nine, and if a woman answered, they would say that this was a neighbor who had heard a prowler.

The creaking of porch swings and the small glints of light, and the busy cries of insects, and a boy sitting on the porch steps, in his wallet love letters mended with scotch tape.

Her name was Faye, and she had a good home, but she left. Her sister was sweet, but always seemed to miscarry. Her father was always talking to the nickels in his pocket.

Jake Washington stole copper from the west yard. A week later he tried to sell it to the steel company. "I didn't know nobody else as would want it."

William Kuberlig walked up Nigger Row and shot at everything he saw. He was committed to a home for the insane.

Sam Benton left the front half of his shoe and an equal portion of his foot beside the log he had been cutting. He dragged himself to the edge of town. For some reason he dragged the axe along with him.

Three young girls took Jim Beitener into the woods and killed him. All three had been in love with him. It seemed the only solution.

And the strike was still not settled.

43

"I voted for you," said Mijack. "I'm here as a voter. I had my say as your father."

"What's your beef?"

"My boy, I haven't come to accuse you of anything."

"Only to straighten me out, huh?"

"Call it that," said Mijack. "As long as you know why I'm here."

Bart laughed. "You too, you believe what they're saying, that I'm a crook."

"No," said Mijack. "You're no crook. No more'n I was."

"Then what?" Bart said, sneering.

"Only this," said Mijack. "You always did have to get even. You always could be nasty, if you thought you had a reason. But a job like you have, you have to keep a hold on yourself."

But old Mijack saw it was no use. He left, knowing it was the last time he would ever see his son.

His boots made sharp, cutting sounds, as if they were gnawing at the wood. He crossed to the fireplace and spat into it. His eyes were tiny specks of light as he peered into the swirl of flame which had risen. "I even spit alcohol," he thought, and spat again.

Gilbert crossed to the bar, dug into his pocket, threw down on the shiny brown wood a handful of crumpled money, smacking his hand at the rolling coins.

"Payday," he said, sneering. "Nobody was ever as happy as me."

A few of the men looked at him. Most of them were leaned over the bar, peering into their glasses.

"Hurry up with a drink."

"You look like you've had enough already," said the bartender. But he was carrying a glass of beer.

"Many a time you flagged me," said Gilbert. "Many a night I slunk out of here in shame—but don't give me lip tonight. I'm in a good mood, so good I'll pick you up by the feet and use what's left of your hair to mop this place."

"Big talk," said the bartender, unruffled. He pushed aside the paper money and brushed a dime into his hand.

"I'm somebody tonight," said Gilbert. "Nobody was ever as happy as me."

He roared with laughter. But his eyes were cold and observant, unaffected by drink, and they watched the other men at the bar, and watched the wretched condition of his hands. He would not feel better until he could get his eyes drunk too.

"No rope on my neck, no ring in my nose. A man must celebrate when he feels that way. It doesn't happen often."

"Lost your job again?" said Tod Snyder.

"Lost? Found. Found the job I was born for, and now I'm gonna live," said Gilbert. "You guys know what it is to feel life in every finger on your hand?" He held up a hand and pointed to each finger, as if counting. "Of course not, you've never lived. Nobody in this town ever lived. But I've just found out the secret."

"Does this guy go with the beer?" said one of the younger workers.

Gilbert laughed. "No," he said, "this's the guy who buys your beer. Who'll have?"

The men had been on strike for a long time. It made them sullen to be offered a drink by someone they did not like.

"All the same," said Tod. "You better let me hold a little of your money for tomorrow. Tomorrow has a way of being different."

"Who'll have?" said Gilbert, thumping on the bar.

The bartender stood beside the cash register.

"We don't drink with you," said the same young worker. "You, nor your brother."

Gilbert eyed the worker and took a few steps toward him. Then two more workers turned on their stools, and in a few moments all eyes were looking at the same place, hostile, waiting.

"And you, Tod?" said Gilbert. "Will you have one?"

"Don't drink with him," said the young worker. "His money comes from beating people up and kissing niggers' asses."

"In that case," said Tod, "I guess I'm not thirsty either."

Gilbert went to the bar and picked up his money and left.

He walked in and out of bar after bar, moving toward the clubs in the lower end of town.

The windows of the diner were too steamed for him to see inside, so he pushed open the sliding door. He stood there, glaring. His dirty clothes and unkempt beard were indications of the deeper shabbiness he felt inside.

His eyes picked out the waitress he wanted and he sat where she would have to serve him.

He ordered steak, rare, bloody. He did not use a knife. Taking the meat in both hands, he pulled chunks loose with his teeth. He liked the smell, the hot round spots on his fingers, the animal act of chewing, the strings of meat which caught in his teeth, the thickening of the muscle in his jaw, and the mouth cavity huge and diverse with food pressure. He bit the bone neatly clean, paid the check with money that had the grease marks of his fingers.

"Nobody was ever as happy as me," he said, and roared with laughter.

Last night he had been in the club for a different reason. He and Spider and "the Bull" had come to collect their take of the slot machines. Now the long line of machines made bunchy jingles in their trays with monotonous regularity, and loud, harsh, masculine rumbles from the bar heaved across the room. The people at the tables were crouched low and forward, as if to get under the noise, and exchange words they had exchanged on a thousand nights.

Gilbert pushed in at the bar. He slid his hand deliberately into a pool of wetness and then put his hand against his forehead and cheeks. Finding success in this, he put both hands on the counter, like a man hunting for the place where he had intended to press a blotter, and brought them dripping wet against his face.

A middle-aged woman in young clothes was looking at him.

"Helen!" he said, spreading his arms joyfully.

"Wrong number," she said. "Marge."

"Marge then," he said, taking her by the wrist and pulling her arm aside so that he could get a better view of something that had suddenly captured his attention. He took hold of her other wrist and held her arms eagle spread, and stared at her body. His head began to make a motion like a man slowly and leisurely indicating disbelief. Then he looked into her face.

"Are they real? I mean are they *really* real? They can't be!"

"See for yourself," she said.

He felt with his finger tips and then hunted on her shoulder through the dress material to find the thin brassiere strap and lifted on it, feeling the weight. The woman stood with her arms at her side, watching his face.

"By God! By God, they are! What do you know. Oh—oh this goddamn wonderful earth, this—this—oh, by God!"

"It took me forty-three years to grow them," said the woman. "I'm kind of proud of them myself."

"By God, we must have a drink on this," Gilbert said. "Something like this doesn't happen in a million years."

"They're not only real," said the woman. "They stand up by themselves."

"I believe you, I believe you," said Gilbert, moving so he could see them from the side. He smacked his hand against his forehead. "Do—do you realize—the importance—of this? I mean do you realize?" He went to the bar and pounded. "We've got to have a drink on this."

"I'm forty-three, and I'm going to have bigger ones at fifty."

"What're you drinking?" said Gilbert.

"Nothing," she said. "I have a drink there beside my boy friend." She motioned to a young man who had been watching them.

"Say," said Gilbert to the young man, "ain't they something? I mean, did you ever see anything to beat that!"

"They're the McCoy all right," said the young man sourly.

Gilbert roared with laughter. "Why, why she has something the whole world can appreciate," he shouted. "The whole world! Not many people can say that."

The woman seemed pleased.

"Why, when she dies more guys'll look down in her coffin than ever looked in a coffin before. The undertaker won't charge no fee. I tell you, they'll have to drill holes or they won't be able to close the coffin lid."

The woman laughed.

"No! No! They shouldn't bury them," said Gilbert, one arm held high, finger pointing at the ceiling which he could almost touch. "They ought to be *preserved!*"

"He knows how to flatter a woman," she said to her boy friend.

"Nobody was ever as happy as me," he shouted triumphantly.

An hour later he was shouting, "Beasts, beasts," and shaking his fist vaguely in the direction of the dance floor. And when a woman passed him, he grabbed her by the arm and said, "Say, lady, do you know I never liked being called fat?"

He had been squeezing his legs together to keep urine from squirting out, and in his blundering movements toward the toilet found himself beside the door and then went outside and pissed against the wall. He heard some people pass him and the thin clack of high heels, but he only rested his forehead against the wall and let his guts drain. Then he stepped away, watching the flow of the water, and scraping his shoes. The light at the entrance of the club looked misty and the air felt cool. He went down the steps and looked both directions on the street and set out to walk.

He was at the stage where he would not need a drink for a while, where he did not particularly want to continue degrading himself, was, in fact, merely in the easy stage of continuing habit. The money in his pocket did not make him think of a bus or a taxi. When he crossed the bridge over the canal he leaned over the rail and flung his cigarette down at the black water, and when he crossed the railroad he went, "Whoo-hoo!" without looking in either direction. When he entered the Bessemer, the lights seemed both bright and dim, distant and yet disturbing.

Naomi was singing a patter song in a falsetto Gay Nineties voice. The song concerned itself with a man who was hunting for a cherry in the wintertime, and the hopelessness of the search, and then Naomi sang the chorus line, "Who wants my cherry, who'll take my cherry," holding a cherry by its green stem with her teeth, offering it to a group of middle-aged customers who had bought enough drink to deserve special attention. It was a routine song, brought jeers and cheers.

Gilbert was standing against the wall, looking at the skimpiness of her costume.

Naomi was leaning over, the cherry held tantalizingly above the nose of Fred Kostar, who tried to capture it with his mouth, then finally grabbed it from her with his hand. Mr. Weaver and another man laughed. "Ho!" said Mr. Weaver, "more goes on here than meets the eye." Fred, sodden with drink, patted Naomi on the behind, and grinned at his companions.

Gilbert strode toward the table. Naomi barred his way, putting her hands against his chest. She eased him into a chair. "Don't be silly," she said in an undertone. Gilbert sat there blinking his eyes. When he rose again, Naomi said in a subdued but angry voice, "If you can't do anything but make trouble, stay out of here."

He was quieter after that and sat at the table drinking beer. Naomi sat with him, reminding him of his glass whenever he stared straight ahead too long.

"You're potzed," she said, looking at his glassy eyes.

"I don't want you in here."

"Good," said Naomi. "Give me money and I'll leave now."

"I got money," said Gilbert, crushing down on the table a pile of bills which was thicker than he had begun with, but of lesser denominations.

"That won't take me," she said. "It'd take a lot more than that."

"I didn't mean this," said Gilbert, sprawling it over the table with a sweep of his hand. "If I gave you the money, would you go?"

"Sure," said Naomi. These offers of money which never came about were monotonous. But they were also the most effective way of keeping her brother quiet.

"Okay," said Gilbert. "That's all I wanted to know."

Naomi said she had another number to do, for him just to sit quiet.

"You start packing your bags," said Gilbert. "And keep one empty to put all the money in."

"Sure," said Naomi. "Sure thing."

She gathered the bills together and stuck them in his hand. Gilbert sprawled them across the table again.

After the show was over, Naomi again came and sat at the table, but finding him calm and in an apparently good mood, she left to change her costume.

The three men at the next table rose to leave. Gilbert slowly began collecting the bills together, leaving one on the table, in case he had not paid for his drinks. The three men walked two blocks together, talking a little loudly in the stillness of the night. Then, with waves of their arms and last-moment long-distance conversations, they separated, parting with the regret men have for the end of a stag night.

Although their thoughts already were homeward bent, their thoughts already regrouping around the routines of life which kept them safely intact.

The lone man seemed to hesitate, even to be on the point of turning back. As he neared the railroad tracks, long strides caught up with him and he was grabbed by the arm. Fred Kostar turned his face in time to catch a fist squarely on it. He tried to escape, was caught and spun around, and then hit again and again. . . .

Methodically Gilbert drove the man into the darkness that surrounded the freight building, forced him against the wall. Even after the man went down, Gilbert lifted him, holding with one hand and hitting with the other.

"I guess you won't be petting behinds for a while," he said. "I guess you'll know better than mess with Mijacks."

There seemed no resistance at all from the body as his boot pushed at it. He looked at his hand and wiggled the fingers. "I could kill a man," he thought. "I could kill a man so easy." He stood looking down, watching for a sign of movement which would allow him to use his fist again. There was something in the way the man was crumpled and limp that made Gilbert suspect that he was looking at death.

"What do I care if he is. If he's dead, he's dead. I almost hope he is. The bastard."

He exulted that he had the will power not to kneel and examine the man. He peered up and down the street and saw no one. He put his hands in his pockets and strolled leisurely across the railroad tracks and the canal. He had gone only a short distance before he began to whistle.

Reaching the main street he stopped and called in a loud, clear voice, "Does anyone hear me? I have just killed a man." He looked about, counting houses, counting the possibilities that he had been heard. The stop light changed color, and after a bit a heavy truck came whining by. Gilbert made a thumbing motion, grinned as the truck rolled on past, and then walked on, strolling as leisurely as before.

He went in the diner and had a cup of coffee.

"I haven't been in this place sober in quite a while," he told the waitress. "It looks kinda crummy when you're sober."

"Get yourself a dishrag and start cleaning, if that's how you feel," said the waitress.

"Me, I feel great," said Gilbert. "Nobody was ever as happy as me."

542

A lawyer arrived from Baltimore. He knew nothing of his mission until he arrived. Then Bart opened his safe and unlocked his files and told him to get busy preparing a case for the district attorney's office. But first Bart was concerned about the legality of certain matters. A few of the provisions in a bill he had drawn up might violate his and the council's authority. Moreover, he wanted the proposals in a legal joint form, so that they could be passed by a single roll-call vote.

If the lawyer was surprised at what he saw that day, he was intelligent enough to say little. After studying the town charter, and asking questions on matters that were unclear to him, he stated his objections to certain points in the bill. "Strike them out," said Bart. He would take no chance of having his plans upset. His mind was at ease, and already was beginning to turn over what was to come later. "Do you expect this bill to pass?" asked the lawyer, at the conclusion of their business. Bart smiled. "It already has passed," he said. The lawyer said nothing and began to study the massive pile of data from the files. For almost an hour he thumbed and skimmed his way through material, trying to form a picture of its basic content. Then, with a slow shake of his head, he said, "I guess Baltimore is a pretty decent place after all."

Bart dispatched a message to the steel-company officials, requesting an immediate and final settlement of the strike. The company had until seven that same evening to come to terms, or face a property re-evaluation and a higher tax assessment. The company made no reply.

At seven-thirty Bart read to the council a draft of a speech.

"We're in a mess. A mess is the only way it can be described. We spent too much money on improvements. Far, far too much. I know it and you know it. But what I know that you don't is that we can't get loans to cover those debts. No doubt each one of you can explain to your precinct that this mistake originated out of the most generous motives. Or you can say it was my fault. But I think each one of us has enough to explain—and much too soon. Because the fact remains that this town is contracted for obligations amounting to more than a quarter of a million dollars. A quarter of a million, gentlemen.

"What's to be done? We could save pennies here and there. Mr. Danver, Mr. Hill and Mr. Pulzowski might sell some Harrisburg property and contribute that sum. Tom could lay off those men he hired for garbage disposal. Bowman, I think a law court might decide our highway department is overmanned for a town this size. That law court might ask some questions about kickbacks. I think someone ought to whisper that to the school board. It seems some teachers have

543

given testimony. In short, an investigation isn't what Nesquehon needs at this moment.

"Maybe some of you are thinking, Bart's going to hang, not me. Let me confess that although I have gained nothing in these transactions—which I can prove in a law court—and although I've spent quite an amount of my own money for our noble endeavors—which, too, a law court would reveal, yet I admit I might be suspected of complicity, or at least be regarded an awful fool. . . . I don't want an investigation at present, unless you force me.

"What's to be done? I suppose if you made an appeal, Republicans in other places might signify willingness to help out. They like to keep peace and quiet in the Harrisburg area. And I suppose you're relying on the fact that if a scandal breaks loose, even though it leaves the state machine aghast, they'll do everything in their power to cover up, simply because Nesquehon happens to have too many officials. Particularly since they just got rid of their first Democrat, Earle. But a quarter of a million dollars, gentlemen?

"Again I say, what's to be done? A higher tax rate? Unfortunately, it's not in our power to raise the tax rate without the consent of the people. It seems people do have a voice in government. Not much, but in this case, too much. You know damn well the people won't do it, they won't vote money out of their own pockets, especially at a time when so many are unemployed. Then how do we raise money? We could each one of us chip in ten thousand. That would keep the wolf from the door. How many hands do I see raised?"

"Okay, now listen. You won't like this. It's taking away the candy you've so long enjoyed. I say we reassess the steel-company property. We have the right to do that. The entire steel mill is at present valued, according to our tax collector, at three hundred and thirty thousand dollars. A damn ridiculous figure, and one that means graft where I come from. I've sent a lawyer over there and he assures me that a minimum fair tax assessment on that property would be eleven million dollars.

"With that additional income, we can get loans. We can have a beautiful town instead of a dump. And some of us can stay out of prison. I've got no more to say. I said mine. I call now for a show of hands, first to see whether you want to vote on a tax reassessment tonight, or whether you prefer to wait until tomorrow or the next day."

Three days later the council voted in favor of reassessing the steel company, and also in favor of a general reassessment of town property.

544

It made some men wince, but they did it. In their eyes was hatred for the man who stood on the speakers' rostrum, and they were already having secret meetings, plotting how to get out from under him, and how to get him.

It was the beginning of Bart's revenge. He intended to go much further once he had forced the steel company into submission, to double back and bring his charges against the council, and against many businessmen. He was aiming at a complete purge. It would be at a high cost to himself, but that did not matter. His negativism was at last resulting in positive action. He still kept his mask of contempt, his cold, inhuman look.

But Bethel did not settle the strike. Mr. Weaver, his face white with hate, declared that the company would fight to the bitter end. The company lawyers were already planning an appeal to the courts, an appeal based on the time when the town had been unincorporated. And so Bart had to put back into his files the evidence against the council. He had to take up the fight anew, and he had to find a way to raise money to pay the town's obligations, since until the case was settled in the law courts the banks were unwilling to make loans.

And the worst, and Bart knew it was the worst, was that the resistance movement against him was gathering force. He still saw a way to do it. But it meant the end for himself. It meant an end so disgraceful and humiliating that he began to make preparations to commit suicide once it was over.

His ears had become useless ornaments on either side of his head. The white button in his left ear had a wire hanging from it, a wire that connected to a battery in his coat pocket whenever he wanted to hear. Mijack's one eye was shattered, and over the other a yellow gelatin of cataract squeezed at the light. The eye could look straight at the sun without blinking, and toward evening street lights were its only stars. It led him to walk everywhere as through a dimly glowing long tube, and even the nighttime was never clearly dark, never with the brilliant blackness of background. His belly had broken from its natural girdle and slumped into his trousers, not with the quivering fullness and firmness of corpulence, but hung in the strained weight of guts burst loose through broken muscular walls. He walked like a woman too heavy with pregnancy, while his mouth puffed and sucked from toothlessness. He had to put his finger in first one side of his mouth and then the other to be able to shave.

It seemed all the human indignities had come to this man. Even his right arm, still surprisingly strong, was coated with the soft, white skin of an unhealthy young girl, so that the scars and the blue stains of coal were more nearly defilements than proud marks of accomplishment. The skin of his neck was withered and wrinkled, loose folds hanging over the edge of his collar, and his posture and shuffling walk had the destroyed balance of the syphilitic. He was wearing the black suit in which he had always appeared respectable, but which now hung bagged and filthy.

It was the first time Mijack had been out of the house in two weeks. He had no memory of when he had slept. He had not been able to feel the difference between being awake and being asleep. He had lain on the bed and had felt his eyes open and saw grayness, and the grayness had not come into his eyes, but stood off, so that he had no actual connection with it. The curious thing was that as he had lain there sightless, he had become terribly aware of his eyes.

He had been to the doctor six months earlier and had been told that he must wait until the cataract was ripe, and he had waited, and he was scheduled to go to the hospital next week, and now he was going to die before he had a chance to see again. He was going to die because he had told the doctor about his eye but had been too proud to tell him about his "private." He was not willing to die. His spirit was not broken. He had broken the boundaries of pain, and had passed through suffering for so long that it had become the only security to which he could cling.

He had lain on the bed, which, two months earlier, he had cut a hole through and set a pan beneath, after the mattress had become so sodden with urine that it had made his flesh raw to sleep on it. That had been during the time when he had needed to urinate three times an hour and with intense pain. But the pan under the bed had been dry for three days, evaporation disposing of the little urine which had escaped, and he was suffering from piles, and had not been eating or drinking, in order to stave off as long as possible the accumulation of waste which he believed would cause death.

Friday he had been able to milk a little urine from himself, a pathetic amount, but enough to make him feel that he had gained another opportunity. But by Monday morning he had lost hope of being able to cure himself. It had been with a last sense of duty to life that he had, pushing gradually with his hands, using the pillows and headboard to force his head upward, made himself erect. On going to bed, he had merely unhooked the truss and let it lie on his body, but now, as he tried to adjust and fasten it, he knew he could not endure the pressure which would be needed to keep the protuberance in place. Instead, he pushed and prodded with his hands, gradually easing the rupture behind the muscles.

There had come into his head a buzzing, as of an old fly against a far away window. It was not hunger, and it was not the sound which the steel mill had put into his head, a sound which had remained with him long after he could not hear distinctly. It was the whine of the electric clock, hampered in its mechanical duty by the coldness of the house. He had purchased the clock when he found he could not remember to wind the one which had a cavalryman with a lasso. There had never been a clock in the house until after the children were gone. Having put his hands under his legs, he helped them to swing until his feet rested on the old and very dirty rag rug where his wife had once slept. He rose and with surprising agility began to bend his knees and lift his legs high, testing for cramps in the muscles. The physical pain of movement was almost a relief.

He pulled himself loose from the pale blue pajamas Rowiger had given him for Christmas. He was wearing only the top part of the pajamas, and the muddied bottom was soaking in a bucket of water for the sixth day, the last day on which he had stubbornly refused to give way to weakness and the punctual form of his life. He slipped into slightly yellow cotton underwear and fitted the straps under his heels. It was the same underwear which he had worn to see the doctor the previous time, and which he had set aside for that purpose. The breath from his mouth was faintly visible in the room, but he could not see it. Barefoot he went downstairs, slowly, heavily, his hands moving with fireman caution on the banister.

Downstairs he put on his trousers and shirt and suspenders, once elastic but now as firm as leather. Down narrow homemade cellar steps, aware of their varying widths and depths only since his eyes had failed him, he went, and opened the door of the furnace. He raked it and shoveled out the ashes, shook the ashes through a sieve, saving the small bits of coal. His hands were as knotty and hard as the roots of a tree, but his arms were exceedingly white and flaccid. He made a new fire. He made it even though it would delay him and use the strength which he needed to walk into the town and to the office of the doctor. He made it more because he thought time was running out on him than because of any satisfaction it gave him. He did not need a stable temperature any more, had passed that stage several years before, and now it was enough to heat the house a little each morning, and keep out the worst of the dampness.

His breakfast was oatmeal and cornflakes with a little water sprinkled over them. As he ate he was thinking of how long he would have before the breakfast was added to the waste of which he could not rid himself. He had placed beside him on the table the tin cup in which his teeth were. Although the white ulcers in his mouth and the broken corners of his mouth, raw from where hair had ingrown and festered, kept him from using the teeth, they were there to remind him to try to use them once his mouth got better. And they were a sign of his former dignity, of his former respect for the table and for food. He believed that it was being unable to use the teeth which had caused the waste to block within him.

He spilled part of the breakfast on his clothes. This was not the result of sloppiness. It was the lack of teeth to hold things in his mouth and vision which did not permit him to see anything along the edges of sight. His flesh was no longer sensitive to contact with the silverware, so that to his mouth a fork or a spoon had the same feeling of blunt reception.

On the cupboard shelf stood a succession of abandoned and aged medicines in bottles as dirty on the outside as only partly emptied medicine bottles can get. They were relics of a time when his wife had found hope in them. Although Mijack had no use for them, though he would never have touched them, there was in his attitude, in his refusal to throw them away, a strange faith, as if the presence of the bottles were a force to keep away disease.

Breakfast finished, he washed the dishes in about a quart of water and in an absurdly small pan. He did not break any dishes. He had almost never broken any, and never by dropping them, but by having the handles of cups stick to his fingers when he went to put them down. It made him feel sad to break a dish, not because of the cost or prettiness of the dishes, nor because of any sentiment attached to them, but because his own body and hands were no longer sure. It was the loss of the fine control of his fingers which bothered him more than loss of strength. He washed the dishes with bits of soap that had become too small for his hands.

Then he had put on a detachable collar and a necktie, failing to get the tie under the collar or the collar properly attached to the shirt. He opened a can of dried shoe polish, spit into it several times, and then blackened his shoes. He made no effort to polish them. He closed the door of the house and set out down the hill.

He was exhausted by the time he reached the office of the doctor. He stood outside for a while, afraid to enter while feeling so bad, afraid to be seen feeling so spiritless and hopeless. Yet above all he was repulsed by the idea that he might die in the doctor's office or in a hospital, and he felt, for reasons which he could never have explained, that would be the final indignity which life could offer. Death was much more acceptable to a man when he was alone, when he did not need to fight the surface illness of his body, when he could have his full concentration.

He entered the office and looked around, because he was not able to see clearly. After a while he felt himself taken by the arm, and led, he thought, toward a chair, until his vision had improved enough so that he was able to believe there were more patients waiting than there were. He resisted as the nurse tried to lead him through a door, and said he would wait his turn, if she would be so kind as to find a place for him to sit. He knew that to sit down was going to be the worst pain he had ever felt in his life, knew it might even be impossible, and yet he looked forward to it, not as a delay in seeing the doctor, but as a last test of his will and a last chance to get hold upon himself, before surrendering himself to death. Although he had considerable respect for medicine—much more than his wife had had—he believed that in a moment of crisis he could do more for himself by holding fast.

The doctor had come to the door, and he knew the doctor was looking at him, and that the nurse was beside the doctor. He touched the wire to the battery, heard a whistling, and then through the threaded hum came a mechanical impression of the voices of people whose mouths were moving. He had not attached the wire in order to hear, but because he wanted to speak, and because he had more confidence in his voice when he could hear. "I'll wait here, Doctor, until you come to me."

"Of course," said the doctor, but it was less than five minutes later that he had Mijack in his inner office, having explained that the other people were merely waiting for medicines which his nurse was writing prescriptions for. Mijack stood before him, at first with a kind of dignity, as if he were going to give a cool, detailed account of his illness, and then, suddenly, he leaned forward and said in a very low voice, shaken with emotion, "I can't leak, Doctor."

After the examination, he was rushed to the hospital. The whole urinary area was swollen and bright red, and the buttocks were a pale blue, with the anus area covered with a green fungus. The doctor believed he had about a one in five chance of living, and then only because he knew Mijack, and knew the will to live which Mijack had. He was not disgusted, and he did not admire, and he felt only that it was an enormous shame that human beings should continue to have to exist upon the threads of their youth in the final years of their lives.

When Bart Mijack was told that Mrs. Irene Pierce wanted to see him, he ordered her admitted to his office. He was not the sort of man who needs to study out what is desired of him before granting admittance. Although he scorned the position and the title of burgess, he performed the office with dignity, and was indeed an altogether different man than he had been formerly, more courteous, more formal of speech, and willing to hear the grievances and requests of people he would have refused to speak to in private life. This was no violation of his creed. In his personal relations, he was unchanged, curt, rude, forceful, suggesting that he either had a certain respect for public office, or else was engaged in a mockery of it.

Irene entered in her quiet, modest way. Bart stood and saw her comfortable on a chair before he resumed his position behind the desk. He looked at her a moment in silence, then put his palms flat on the desk.

"Your business?" he said.

"Personal—and I think public," said Irene.

"Difficult to manage, I suspect," said Bart, smiling, yet watching her closely. "I've always considered you forthright."

"There are a number of people who should be here asking what I am about to ask."

"Your husband, perhaps?"

"Yes. But you don't respect him, and that's why I came."

"I hope not to say what he would say."

"No. Not exactly," said Irene. "I came because I feel sure you respect me. I'm right, am I not?"

"I respect you. At least more than most."

"I came to ask you a question. Did you, when you were elected burgess, intend to end the strike? Wait, that's not the question. I know you did. I know because I heard you say it in your speech, and you said it like a threat, and I know you keep threats." Bart smiled on hearing this. "But right after election," Irene continued, "you passed that improvement bill. I know very little about it, but I know that it has ruined your reputation, and after such a bill, after such a mess as you've gotten this town into, neither the strikers nor the company are going to have anything to do with you. So it must not have been part of your plan to settle the strike. I can't imagine why, but it must not have been part of your plan. Am I right?"

"You figure it out," said Bart. "You say I always keep threats. Yet I didn't settle the strike. Up to now, at least. So maybe I don't always keep threats, huh?" Bart smeared the desk surface with his hands, as if trying to erase something. "If all you have is questions, I think we better stop now."

"I'm sorry. You see, I feel it's necessary that you know I understand a little about you, or you won't be able to give a fair answer to something I'm going to ask you to do. In other words, I think you entered office thinking you could solve this strike alone. Now you've found out that you can't. And in your anger, because you failed, you're trying to cover up by being wicked. That is wrong. You know it. I came to ask you to lend your support to Mr. Rowiger, your honest support as burgess of this town, and at the same time to ask you to quit robbing people. We have enough trouble without you."

"You have no right to say any of this to me," said Bart.

"I have every right," said Irene.

"And noble reasons!"

"My reasons are not important. They would not mean much to you. I ask you because people are suffering, and because you are a good man who has done a lot of wrong, and I'm sure you're tempted to do good. I'm sure you want to help us. Do it. Forget yourself for once."

"Is that supposed to be the clincher? Are you ready for my answer?"

Irene Pierce looked at him. "Yes. I'm ready."

"Then you've made a mistake. I'm tempted. Yes. I've often though it would be splendid to change sides, at the very last moment, when success was near. . . . It would be a sort of final touch—you understand?—in my attitude toward life. It would be a denial and a laugh at myself—and at the whole world."

"I don't believe that," said Irene, flushing.

"You better."

"All right, switch anyhow, even for that reason."

"I would if I could. But you see, I never stop until I finish what I begin. I never turn back. That's my weakness. I remember as a boy walking downstreet to buy a pair of shoes. Halfway, not even halfway, it came to me that the money for the shoes was at home. I went on and got those shoes. I had a hard time convincing the man to let me have them, but I got them. Now do you understand?"

551

"But that's absurd!" said Irene.

Bart flushed. His hands drew up into tight curls.

"You better leave," he said.

"All right," said Irene. "If you finish everything you start, how come the strike is still on? Did you finish that?"

"Do you think I like the strike? Do you think I haven't tried?" said Bart.

"Then join us. Together we can do it."

"I said *I* would settle it."

"It can't mean much to you, if you take that attitude," said Irene. "Acting like a little boy, a spoiled little boy, and when people are suffering."

"That's just tough," said Bart. "You go feed 'em, and I'll feed my own mouth." Bart stood and leaned over the desk. "Now get out of here." Irene swung her head as he said this, and she was entirely different in appearance from when she had entered; her face and eyes did nothing to hide her indignation and accusation, which had its effect on Bart, for he beat his knuckles on the desk. "How many times must I say it?" he shouted. "Out, out, out."

"To think I gave you my vote," said Irene. "I can't even pity you, and you're the first human being, and I hope the last, that I can say that of. I almost wonder, are you human?"

For some reason this seemed to restore to Bart more of his composure, and he walked from behind the desk and stood facing her.

"Will you ask your husband to meet me tomorrow at four? And tell him to come prepared to apologize for you."

"I most certainly will not ask him."

"Then I feel justified in this," said Bart. And he slapped Irene Pierce.

44

It was seldom advisable to smile at Bart. He had a talent for remembering every insult. It had always been dangerous to offend him, but now the danger was more immediate, he would lash out like a coiled snake. Of course that meant he was also more vulnerable, that he was near the end of the rope as far as means were concerned, and was behaving more like a trapped animal.

He had changed astonishingly. He looked old and worn, in the same way an athlete often does at about the age of thirty-five, a slightly overprofessional aspect from which all the vigor of youth has been drained. He would have an anxiety for tomorrow to arrive, a necessity for his businesses to be resumed, almost a fear that something would prevent that time from arriving. His nerves were no longer completely under control. There was sleeplessness. He had no fear of things or of people, but there were times when, lying alone, or sitting alone at his desk, he would have a feeling of everything being stripped clean, of the desk being empty and the wastebasket being hollow and the floor a bare single sheet of wood. He would look at the walls and they would seem very high and distant, the pictures like stamps pasted on them.

He was, though he would not admit it, afraid for himself. "Stay loose," he would tell himself, in a fierce whisper, without the calm confidence of his youth. The tolling of the Catholic bells had become something he did not like to listen to, and the whistle from the steel mill was always long and plaintive and at times very thin. It was as if the time schedule of his life, which had never been broken by defeat, was threatening to give way entirely at the very time when he most needed his wits about him. He could not seem to catch up with the thing he had begun. It seemed at times to be getting out of hand, to be going too fast, which was exactly what he wished, but not yet, not until he had insured the direction.

Yet it was the other way too. There was the tension of a formally planned time schedule in the reports which came into his office, and he could see that everything was moving along all right, and that it was he himself who was moving too fast. He had, with every accomplishment in his life, felt a sense of having spent himself, of having used himself hard; and now there was only this increasing nervousness, a need almost to shut his eyes and run blindly and rapidly, as if only in that would there be any relief. He did not think of what he was doing as criminal; the means and even the end were of less importance —no importance, if only he could manage to make his full malignity felt, if only he could destroy and destroy, utterly and finally. Here he was, plunging the town into financial ruin, putting a host of men into a position where public scandal was sure to ruin their lives, and breaking the sovereign power of the steel company; here he was, achieving both his revenge and his long-sought exposure of the corrupt past and present, and out on the street the people were walking about as usual, doing the usual things at the usual hour and for the usual reasons, and this was not going to be changed a bit. He realized that what he had really hated all his life was the imperturbable aspect of the public, and what he had to face now was that it would go on forever imperturbable, that it wore the same manner and the same face year after year, probably century after century; it walked the world and claimed the world, and all the agonies of all the greatest and all the fiercest men, all, all had been for nothing, all would be for nothing. Not a world without end, as Bart saw it now, but a world that was going to end, of which he himself was only a forerunner, a minor figure. For the time was near when the sufferers for the truth would refuse to suffer, would refuse to bleed their hands and hearts to bring forth truths that withered before that imperturbable visage, that mass of humanity which was of greater ignorance than the dust of its composition. And when there were no sufferers for the truth, then there was nothing, then the world had gone back to its beginning.

Mr. Pierce agreed that there was no sense in backing a losing proposition, provided it was possible to make a shift. He was, after all, only the owner of several newspapers, with a number of holdings which had no bearing on political life. He was a businessman, the same as his friends. He certainly did not wish to be left standing alone.

That was the impression he gave the group of men who had come to visit him.

At the same time, he confessed to feeling he was not the sort of man to scrape and bow, and that his alliance with any party or group must be the result of his own decision. To be threatened made his backbone stiffen, and, he said, laughing, caused him to muster some of the authority which he used to consider as his natural due. No, he was not going to be as hasty as his friends. He would take counsel with others before setting a clear path. He had supported the policies of Mark Stevens for many years—many peaceful years—and hesitated to make a move which would set everything adrift. Loyalty was something. If enough men remained loyal, he would too.

That was the impression he gave the group of men who had come to visit him.

Earlier he had visited Mark Stevens, intent upon gaining a statement of facts, and a knowledge of his own actual position; but he had found that to do so he would have to pursue a line of interrogation which would have exposed his own indecision. Mr. Stevens' assurances did not convey to him the strength they once had, and this was perhaps because he needed more assurance.

After his visitors left, he telephoned. "Mark, what in hell's going on?"

"All I know," said Mark, "is that my councilmen don't report to me any more, and the businessmen look the other way when they see me coming. Not that bad, but just about."

"But how? Why?" said Mr. Pierce. "Why men I least suspected of faintness of heart?"

Mr. Pierce compared himself with thousands of businessmen throughout the country and knew that his success had never been through opposition to the political administration, but through utilization of the prevailing opportunities, through affluence and influence. It was therefore wise not to allow his personal hostility to Bart Mijack to alter a procedure which had always been successful. The solution was neutrality, at least until the next election. Yet even this had a danger, threatening to cut him from his outside contacts and leave him without sources of information.

Mr. Pierce was not one to fall on his knees and ask for mercy. Particularly when he was not even sure that he was being attacked. His jaw set itself forcibly and with determination. His assurance, which had been founded on a structure of accomplishment, had lost that firm base simply because it relied upon a widespread division of power. He would simply have to get all the threads in his hands at once and give a pull.

On the other hand, Mr. Pierce could not blame his friends for showing a lack of confidence in him. For they had never known how much influence and power he had over them, and now, at a time when a show of strength and power would have brought them all to him, they could not believe that he was not simply one of them. In fact, as he grimly admitted, his strength was almost obscured from himself. He had contacted high officials, notifying them of the situation in which allegiances were shifting, and they had advised him to wait until nearer election time. He had been so angry with the district attorney that he had reminded the man who was responsible for his election, and had gotten back the frantic reply, "But Mr. Pierce, don't you realize I'm already trying to stall an investigation of most of your friends?"

There had been so many, indeed too many years of peace and comfort, and although Mr. Pierce had been quite busy, it had been routine business, feeding oil to a machine which moved by itself through time, a machine which occasionally needed repairs, replacements, but no significant basic changes. He saw now that his business growth had come about more by the natural process of wealth begetting wealth than by important decisions of his own. He had been a good administrator, had made numerous decisions of importance, small maneuvers and even tricks, from which he had most certainly profited. But he had never faced a determined, ruthless enemy.

Then came a telephone call from the district judge. "I know about the trouble down there," said a curiously impersonal voice. "Hang on. Play along if you must. But don't get involved. We'll soon have enough to get that rascal and get him good." It was the first time Mr. Pierce had ever received instructions which gave him no choice except to comply. He was grateful for them.

Irene was waiting for her husband when he came out of his office. She stopped him as he was about to enter the dining room.

"Have you entered into any business with that man? Mijack? I mean a definite commitment?"

Mr. Pierce looked at his wife rather uneasily.

"Yes and no. Not exactly."

"Explain what you mean."

"My dear, I most certainly shall," said Mr. Pierce, smiling. "I've in fact been desirous of having a talk with you on this—and other matters—for some time. We haven't shared our lives as we should." He threw up his hands mockingly. "No, no, I'm not suggesting that we should."

"I'd rather not go into that," said Irene.

"Yes, yes," agreed Mr. Pierce, "I quite agree. But perhaps once things are more settled, when we see our way clear—this present difficulty, we shouldn't take advantage of each other at such a time—a little matter of divorce, Mr. Rowiger corespondent. But not now." Mr. Pierce looked at his watch. "I should say another week."

"I'm sure Mr. Rowiger will be glad to be of service to me," said Irene. But she was pale.

"Yes, I fancied that. It's such a shame that you two aren't in love. But perhaps being put penniless into the street will engender love in your pale bosom." Mr. Pierce brushed at the sleeves of his coat, holding his arms away from himself so that the lint would not fall against his trousers. "But this other matter. The fact is we're facing a difficult situation. There are a great many things involved. My dear,

I should like to think this out before presenting it. Much better after I've had my bath and dinner. I ask you to be kind enough to wait until after dinner."

Irene knew the impossibility of dealing with her husband when he was in this mood.

After dinner, Mr. Pierce explained the situation as he saw it, admitting a far from adequate knowledge of what had occurred and what might be expected. He stressed the fact that many of his friends had advised co-operation. The friends were named and their separate opinions given, with perhaps more emphasis than they themselves had given them. For this and other reasons he thought it unwise to refuse to see Mijack.

"He behaved politely," Mr. Pierce said with alacrity. "I must say it was not at all unpleasant."

"What I want to know is why he came. I'm sure it wasn't social," said Irene. "What did he want? What did he ask of you?"

"Why, I have agreed to let him run political announcements at a rather low price. That's all."

"That's all! I should think it's enough," said Irene. "Why don't you just go out on the street and begin shouting that you approve of him as burgess?"

"It's not so bad, really. He didn't ask me to cut the price much. I shall still make a profit. After all, I've been doing practically the same thing for years for the Republicans." Mr. Pierce took a handkerchief from his pocket and began to unfold it. "You mustn't believe I approve of him. At the same time, we shouldn't confuse political situations with—with personalities."

"Did you sign a contract?" said Irene.

"I can't afford to take risks until I find out what this man can do to me," shouted Mr. Pierce. Then, seeing the peculiar look his wife was giving him, he patted the handkerchief against his mouth and said, "If I could see my way clear, do you think I would have done it? I honestly don't see what he can do to me, but at the same time . . ."

Irene gave her husband a look of disgust. She sighed. "Then you did sign a contract."

"Of course not," said Mr. Pierce. "I'm making out the bills for the full amount. It was an oral agreement. He'll simply pay me less." Mr. Pierce leaned forward. "Listen, I know what I'm doing. I had a call from the district judge. He told me to do nothing. They have almost enough evidence to get him, and then . . ."

"The honorable judge," said Irene, wearily, "has a brother. His

557

brother is a contractor. He had the contracts for the comfort station and one of the new stairs. Who do you suppose got him that contract for about four times the normal profit?" Irene opened her purse, and began hunting in it. "The judge is trying to keep the bubble from bursting before he can get his own tracks out of the mud, and that's exactly what Bart wants. You happen to be one of the few people Bart does not have anything on. Or does he?"

"I don't know," said Mr. Pierce. "I don't think so."

"Good!" said Irene. "Then charge him the same, word for word, inch for inch, that you would anyone else. And I have some editorials for your paper, beginning tomorrow. We'll see if there is no justice."

"I wish you'd told me this earlier," said Mr. Pierce. "I hardly think I can go back on my word now. It will make him my enemy. You know that."

"He *is* your enemy!" said Irene. "He's out to destroy everything you represent. I'd let him do it if that was all—but that isn't all. I don't know whether we can stop him, but at least don't help him do it."

"I believe you," said Mr. Pierce slowly. "I only want to take the right course."

He was showing every year of his age. He looked closer to seventy than sixty.

"If you don't fight this man . . ." said Irene. "Oh, go play with your sordid divorce case and leave me to handle this. You wouldn't even once in your life be a man. You wouldn't know how to be a man."

Nothing could have been more effective. Mr. Pierce did not think he was a coward. In that moment he pledged to do his utmost to assist his wife.

But later that night Fred Kostar telephoned and said that his wife had left him. She had gone to live with Bart and taken with her material from his files. Even Irene was discouraged, and Mr. Pierce seemed to lose all his resolution.

"But how did it all happen?" he said. "That's what I don't understand."

"So he's totally unconcerned what happens to Dorothy?" said Bart. "He'll hold his head high in the midst of her disgrace." Bart laughed. "I suppose even if I turned her over to your care, he still wouldn't change his tune?"

Spider shook his head. But there was an eagerness in his eyes, and his small, soft lips drew into a tightness, as if he were drinking through a straw. "We could try," he said, sniggering.

"No," said Bart. "This one isn't for you. I'm as well satisfied it turned out we couldn't use her. She's only a dumb kitten," he said. "I'd rather not add her to my list of memories." There was a seriousness in his face, as if thinking of a former time, as if, like a general destined to march across the land of his birth and strew it with ruin, there were still a few things he did not want destroyed. "Now this Pierce, what do we know about him? Clever. We know now who chopped my head off. We know he has influence. Right now, we need him to play ball, and get that wrong slant out of his papers." Bart thought a while. "If he can't be gotten to through his daughter, then he can't be gotten to through his wife."

Bart lit a cigarette. "I made a mistake trying to deal with him as a businessman. A very intangible sort, not the kind who would be a bit upset by his family. Nor probably his business. Yes, as I see him, he's divorced from reality. If we threaten him, he'll probably be very philosophical about it, and have the police breathing on our necks." Bart smiled bitterly. "But if it's true that every man has a weakness . . . Spider, what if instead of a poor, helpless girl, what if you had a nice, plump, middle-aged man, a man who had never had a hand put on him all his life? What if he was taken up on the mountain, say, where my brother has his cabin—yes, there particularly," said Bart, flashing his eyes at Spider. "Maybe some of those games you play with your women. And suppose he was made to realize he had no bargaining power, that nothing he possesses would save him, that you aren't interested in anything he might offer? Not money. Nothing."

Bart blew out a long plume of smoke. "That's the idea of the thing. The details . . ." He shrugged.

He saw the glint in Spider's eyes. He thought at first it was the relish Spider took in his assignments. But then he saw that what the eyes were doing was trying to share with him his own feeling, or what they supposed was his feeling. For a moment he felt repugnance. But then he only felt tired and wanted Spider to get out of his office, wanted to hurry and get this whole rotten, miserable business over with. It had to be over soon. In a little while he was no longer going to have the power of recognition of what he was doing.

Gilbert crossed what she considered her yard because it had a clothesline and the weeds were beaten down, and stopped at the lumber pile, looking at the machinery to see what disuse had done. He tilted one of the barrels to see how much kerosene, lifting at one end and shaking. Rose went away from the window quickly, knowing that if she were seen he would come straight to the house. She went to the bed and sat, hands folded calmly in her lap.

Gilbert came in, finally. He went to the kitchen and poked his head inside. "Put away anything that'll break," he said. He walked around the room, picking up and examining everything that was small and movable. "I said put away anything that'll break." He went to the bed and took hold of Rose's arm and jerked her to her feet. "Put away this, and this," he said. Rose followed him, and he kept pointing at things, but did not touch them himself. When her arms were full, he led her to the closet and pointed inside.

"Now, get Julius," he said. "We're going to take a nice family afternoon walk."

Rose put the things on the floor of the closet. She laid everything out carefully.

"Get the kid," said Gilbert. "We haven't much time."

"You get him," said Rose.

Gilbert wheeled. But something in her face stopped him. He looked around the room. He went to the kitchen and peered in. Then he went to the door and stepped outside, looking at the exact places he had been only a few minutes earlier.

"What the hell's going on?"

"Nothing. Julius just isn't here."

Gilbert turned and marched on his wife. "Cut the funny stuff," he said. "I want to know where he is."

"It isn't funny," said Rose.

Gilbert did not seem to know exactly what to do. He shoved his wife against the wall. Then he went to the window and peered out.

"C'mon, we have to get out of here," he said, and took her by the arm.

He cut through the lumber yard, and Rose could tell from the way he was pulling on her arm that he was taking her away from something. She looked backward and saw three men. Two of them were pushing and shoving the other man. They were going toward the cabin. Gilbert led the way through a group of bushes. "Now sit," he said, "and I mean squat and don't move." Rose sat there chafing her wrist. "I want to know where my son is."

"I'm not telling you anything," said Rose.

Gilbert looked at her and knew she meant it.

"All right," said Gilbert. "I'll go into town after while and check with your friends. You have so few it shouldn't take long."

Once they heard screams from the cabin.

Gilbert kept glancing out through the bushes to see the sky. Several hours passed.

"I guess you know this really washes us up," he said. "I used to think that if you ever left me, you might as well take the kid along. But you've just lost every chance you ever had."

"You'd never have let me take him," said Rose. "I'm not that dumb."

"You're dumb enough that I'm not worried about finding him," said Gilbert. "I have to go into town anyway, so I might as well have somebody to talk to on my way home. I have a couple of nice bedtime stories I want to tell Julius about his mother. He may not understand them, but he'll remember them." Gilbert had taken off his boots to rest his feet, and now he was examining the soles and scratches on the leather. "I've been chatting with Spider about you. It seems he used to be an usher in the movie house. So I guess we can really call them bedtime stories."

Rose knew then who one of the men in the cabin was.

"You can go back now," said Gilbert. "You can start packing. Because as soon as I find Julius, I want that place all to myself."

As Rose went toward the cabin, she saw a man run out of the door and across the side of the mountain, his coat tails flying. He did not look like the kind of man who should be running, and was certainly not familiar with his surroundings, for he kept running into the worst areas. Spider and an enormous man came outside and stood looking; they were laughing about something. It was Spider who wheeled and crouched in the same movement, his hand reaching along his leg. Then he made recognition and cursed. The big man turned slowly and his eyes blinked slowly, his enormous shoulders and hands hanging with a fixity, his neck thick with hair which looked like a black collar ending abruptly against his chin.

"That sonofabitch said he was going to keep her away from here," said Spider.

Rose walked past them and into the cabin. Her eyes gave no indication of recognizing their presence. She went to the wall and took down a rifle and then went to the bureau and tried bullets from the different boxes until she found one that would fit. She did not think of any need for more than one. She went to the door. "Now you get out of here and don't come back."

Rose cooked dinner and before she sat down to eat it was dark. She had cooked only for herself. She lighted the lamps and turned them high. While putting things in the closet in the afternoon, she had noticed a few things she wanted to take with her, and she tried to find space in the two market bags and the knotted shawl. She meant business. She would do what she must do. That was why she felt no need to run away from Gilbert, and why she almost anticipated seeing and talking with him once more. Because she was going, and the definiteness of her conviction was so strong that neither Gilbert nor herself could present any obstruction.

If he did not come before sunrise, she would go without having seen him. She knew that when he came back from Nesquehon without the child he would be like a maddened animal. Yet she sat there, without anything, without need of reading or sewing or any activity. Her loneliness had arrived at a solution which no other mind except her own could have formed, a solution that was perfectly nerveless and without physical symptoms. She did not even feel the breath go in and out of her nostrils.

It was not until she heard sounds of someone approaching that she turned her head toward the window, and sat there with an instinctive knowledge of her big, strong body. She heard her husband's bellow. There was a sharp, thin series of knocks on the door, and she knew her husband was not alone. Opening the door only wide enough to get light on their faces, she saw Gilbert and Spider, who was staggering beneath the weight of the arm thrown across his shoulders. Gilbert's knees were slumped, and he looked almost as if he had been dragged.

Rose let them in.

"He was in a bad way," said Spider. "I thought I better bring him home."

Rose pointed to the bed. Spider freed himself from the arm, ducking his head under it, and as Gilbert fell across the bed, he let out another bellow. He simply lay there. Then, with effort, he rolled his head, loosening it from the covers. "Brought friend," he mumbled. "Time I had friend'n house."

Rose had her arm pointed at the open door.

Spider looked at her. He shrugged.

"Brought Julius," muttered Gilbert. His eyes were closed.

Rose had her arm pointed at the door. She motioned with her head. . . .

Gilbert felt nothing more than surprise. "I finally did it," he thought . . .

He was kneeling in the outhouse, peering into the darkness below the smoothed oval, in the same position in which he had so often vomited. But he was prying loose the boards of the seat. Later he struggled through the narrow door with a body that hung like a slab of steer across his shoulder, folded it at the hips, and shoved it through. It sounded like a big rock landing in mud. Then he went and brought the head, carrying it like a man ready to make a set shot in basketball, dropped it, feeling the hair tangle for an instant in his fingers. He took off his own clothing, except his boots, and threw them in. He nailed the boards in place and put the square wooden rectangle over the round hole.

Gilbert did not bother to clean the floor of the cabin. He only washed himself and his boots and put on a clean shirt and trousers. Then he locked the cabin and left.

Three weeks before the union had been taken over by Bart and two truckloads of men; a mock vote had been held and Bart was made the new leader. "Within one month," Bart had said, "I'll bring the company to terms."

It had made Irene fighting mad. She had rebuked Rowiger for his mild opposition, and urged him to speak to the workers and tell them they were being betrayed. Instead of mere editorials, she ran a full front page. She printed Rowiger's allegations. She wrote her husband's statement, basing it on what little she knew. And in the hotel room, she wrote the story of her husband being beaten up, and had it sent to the office for the morning edition.

People had been coming to her for a week and swarming her under with accusations, mostly gossip and petty jealousies. That seemed to be all she was getting for her pains.

Except the next morning there came a telegram from the secretary of the governor.

The telegram led to a luncheon and the luncheon to an appointment to see the governor.

But by then it did not matter. For it had blown wide open. Everything.

Mr. Pierce passed two people without returning their greeting. He had a feeling of everything being very still and of being more active himself than there was any need to be. He was panting and his forehead was in need of a handkerchief. Yet he was not walking a bit faster than usual. Only the stiffness of his gait was making him tired, an anxiety to be home. The sound of a workingman scraping his shoes on the edge of the porch brought him to pause and stare. The man, rather husky of build, was knocking his work shoes, not in the manner of a man who must have his shoes clean, but with bold arrogance, heralding his entrance. The man made a partial turn, his eyes picking up the heavy and flaccid figure of Mr. Pierce, giving an inscrutable look in which could be discerned a faint hostility.

Mr. Pierce hurried on up the hill, plagued by the feeling that here, within three blocks of his own house, was another person he had never seen. The street which he had traveled for a good many years seemed different. There were trees he had never seen, houses he could not remember.

He felt he had too fine a quality of adjustment to be so completely upset. He could not understand how he could have spent the entire day trying to decide whether to notify the police. He had been brought to the most base and disgusting position, to a state of physical fear such as he could never have believed possible; it had never occurred to him that in a civilized society he could meet with violence.

True, there had been murders and killings in the town, even a gun duel in the Macedonian church. There had been scores of robberies, and a child and two men had been killed in a post-football mob scuffle. It was a town with its share of violence. His own home had been entered, and there had been joking about how neither he nor his wife had awakened, not even when old Joseph, in his nineties, had struck a mattock on the wooden porch flooring, and the prowler had gone straight through the window and down the hill, howling from the cuts of broken glass.

In connection with his position as owner of newspapers, he had never worried; newspapers were no longer important enough to people to cause a publisher unrest in regard to his personal safety. There had not been a political assassination in the state in many years.

Yet this odious thing had happened. His flesh seemed to hang loose from his bones. He was hardly able to endure to think of it. Just when he had begun to despair of his life, when he was so exhausted that terror could no longer keep him from feeling a relief that in a few moments he would be able to close his eyes and slide into darkness, he had been set free.

564

The gun had been shoved into his mouth with the same crude gesture he had once seen an old nurse use putting a hypodermic needle into his son's arm. One of his teeth was chipped and two were broken off, his tongue could feel the sharp edges as it hunted for the pain. His mouth had been dry, terribly dry, although the skinny man had later wiped the barrel with a handkerchief, and he had seen dribbles of saliva on the lapels of his coat. He could still taste the metal and the oil.

He could not explain to himself why this had so completely cowed him, so broken his spirit. He remembered the caterpillars which had been crammed into his mouth, and his stomach was still queasy with the thought that vomiting might not have rid him of them. When they had set him free, he had set out toward the town, running, not sure of his direction; when he had felt distance behind him there had come a revived feeling of all there was to live for, the terrible sweetness of life. When distance had given him a little security, he had paused, crouched behind a bush, and gradually made certain that he was not being followed. He remembered the terrible confidence and cunning that had come to him. He had thought, "Those fools, those fools to set me free." He had intended to go straight to the police. He had had a vision of leading the police there. Although he had been exhausted, he had not found it hard to keep moving. His vision had been fantastically clear. Still with vague fears of being pursued, he had arrived at an open place where he could see the river.

At the edge of town he had walked along deserted streets, sensing the unprotected distances between the houses. It had all seemed strange. He had not even been sure that he would be able to find where he lived. Later, he had passed several Negroes and looked at them warily. The world began to seem bare and unconcerned with any human being, and all of his previous life was something of a myth, remote and useless. He had remembered their words. "We go to his house any time we want, any time we feel like having a little fun." And the lean, nasty-eyed man had stuck his finger out so rapidly that Mr. Pierce's eyelid never had a chance to move and the finger had rubbed over his open eye as if it were testing the firmness of a grape. "He's just a kid. A nice fat little kid. He ain't big enough to play with you and me. We might decide to pull hairs out of his head. It's really hard to pull hair out. Really hard. Four and five at a time."

It had been completely impersonal, as if he had no identity. They

565

had never mentioned his name or given him orders. They had never once said why they had chosen him. They had not accused him of anything. Never since the moment they had encountered him on the street had they shown the least sign of recognizing that they were not engaged in the most normal thing in the world.

It was this that made Mr. Pierce feel so unprotected. He realized that they would not have released him unless they were either insane or extremely confident. He might encounter them on the street and have them nod to him and pass by like the most ordinary of acquaintances.

His mind could not grasp upon any sure bargaining power. All the friendships he had built over the years seemed to count for nothing.

If it were known publicly what had happened, then his course would be clear. He would have to have police protection. He would have to play the role of a girl who has been raped, and sit in court—if the men were caught. He did not trust the local police. And to phone the district attorney would deprive him of the one real protection he had, keeping silent. If that was a protection. What was being asked of him? To follow instructions that had never been given. Not to oppose Bart—if Bart was behind this, if it was not simply two demented men who had chanced upon him as their victim, an impression he had been given in the most lewd manner, poked and pinched. They had squeezed his thighs and patted his behind. It was fantastic to a man of sixty-five. Still more fantastic, he had been sensitive to it, or at least afraid of it. He shuddered at some of the things they had done to him. It had been an attack upon his sanity.

He hoped Bart was behind it. That would give him a certain amount of security. If he did not oppose Bart he would probably not be molested. If he returned to a strict neutrality, or a gradual approval of the administration, he might come through, for his own kind of power was made to absorb that of a man like Bart Mijack. His kind of power was flexible enough to outlast Bart, who would destroy himself.

Mr. Pierce was tired and scared. All his involved plans, all the amusement he had had of seeing puppets act their roles, seeing ambition satisfy itself through becoming parts of the machine, all this had been a fine game which paled before this one experience, the first really shocking one of his life. His own forms of entertainment, which had brought disaster into the lives of so many people, a kind of disaster of which most of them had remained blandly unaware, and

566

which had seemed to him the finest sort of diversion, faded into nothing.

He had never known violence. He had kept his fingers away from it in distaste, just as he had kept his newspapers from printing shocking war pictures. He was the sort of man who has nothing to rely on but the police, and who relies on them only because they do not have anything to do with his own particular life. He could see that skinny man sitting straight up in a courtroom and talking in that chatty, invidious voice. That seemed even worse than his present situation.

Mr. Pierce knew he could safely, bit by bit, convert his holdings into other forms of monies and have them deposited in a large city. He could go off to a different life, perhaps France and Italy. He might even persuade his daughter to go with him and perhaps one or two other young people, to give him a medium through which to enjoy more thoroughly a form of travel that might otherwise lose its interest. Or perhaps, he thought, almost amused, for thoughts of this sort were a relief from the starkness of the situation, perhaps Rowiger and his wife, and he and his daughter, perhaps they might go, and so continue to dally with a situation which he had been breeding. Perhaps it was abroad that his own kinds of pleasures were capable of finding more fertile ground.

Or perhaps it would all break apart. If he could keep up appearances, continue his life as before, and give orders to his editors to stay neutral. He could bide his time and wait for this young man to destroy himself. It was senseless to risk trouble with a man bent upon destruction.

But his impulse remained to pack his bags and leave now, have a taxi come to the house, and then take a plane to New York. Perhaps then, at a safe distance, he would notify the police, and not return or give his whereabouts until after the criminals had been captured.

It was an ugly situation. What he could not forget was how contemptuous the two men had been of him, how they had taken the view that nothing he did could possibly matter, that they were free of the normal laws and forces of the world. If he had escaped from them, he would have gone straight to the police. If they had released him after extracting a promise, he would have acted with contempt for them. But that they had been so sure of themselves implied some hidden reserve. For this had not been their first experience with crime, and they did not intend it to be their last.

Last evening there had been visitors as usual, and he had gone through the experience of trying to retain his composure, at every moment wanting to put his hand on some good fellow's shoulder and whisper in his ear, "I need help." But he had seen the sort of people he was surrounded with, people in whom he had never had the least faith, people he had even less faith in now. Even Judge Wilmot, who would probably preside over the courtroom if the men were captured, who could be counted on to be understanding, who would probably charge the jury harshly with the necessity of maximum sentence, seemed an utterly weak and useless man.

Mr. Pierce really despised himself. It was too humiliating to find himself afraid of violence at a time when he had forgotten that it existed. He knew how afraid he was. He did not hide that from himself—could not. He had not gone to a doctor for fear he would not be able to invent a credible excuse. He was very sore between his legs and his genitals were swollen. It was a severe burn. Much of the hair around his genitals had been torn out when they ripped the tape loose.

Mr. Pierce was a defeated man. His sophistication had deserted him. He had no tongue for light phrases, no thoughts toward books or art, no leanings toward business. He bathed twice, thinking that would relieve him. He found himself remembering the only previous violence in which he had ever been engaged, when, as a boy, his cousin had thrown him on the ground, and had sat on top of him, pounding with his fists; he had been so helpless that he had urinated in his trousers, and his cousin, half-shamefacedly, had let him escape. Afterward his cousin had always seemed ashamed to be near him.

He put salve on his groin. Lying on the bed he found himself reliving the experience. It was the absurdity of having sat there, watching them attach an air pump and rubber tape, and then to sit, unable to prevent the heat and the friction, unable to prevent himself from having an erection, excruciatingly painful, while the man with hollow eyes looked on and made jests. He had nearly fainted. He had writhed. But the full shock seemed not to have reached him until now, and he felt so utterly humiliated.

There was a revolver in his drawer, but since the gun barrel had been thrust into his mouth he did not want to even see it. As the skinny man had wiped the saliva from the barrel, he had laughed and said, "Basically homosexual."

The two men returned. They came to the front door and knocked as anybody else might have.

"How you feeling?" the skinny man asked, grinning.

They came in the doorway, at ease, casual, arrogant.

"We came to take you for another ride."

With utter disregard for Mr. Pierce they began to walk through the downstairs rooms. Spider turned and said, "Show us around. It's always interested me, the stuff a person would be proud to own. I've never had the least idea why people should want to own anything."

Mr. Pierce drew himself up a little.

"Hey, Bull, look how he holds his mouth shut. Didn't I tell you he wouldn't even have sense enough to fix his teeth?"

"Lemme see," said the huge man, moving slowly toward Mr. Pierce. He had big, round, emotionless eyes.

"I've been talking with Bull about your wife," said Spider. "But he's more interested in you. He told me he'd like to take care of you." Spider laughed. "Now me, I'm sensible. I did my thinking about your wife. I think maybe she and I ought to be better friends."

"Lemme see," said Bull, forcing Mr. Pierce to retreat toward a corner.

"Maybe I ought to take her up on the mountain. She ain't bad for as old as she is. We could let her cook and entertain. Of course if you don't want that—we don't care how you arrange it, just so it's done. We'd much rather not have to deal with a woman."

"Lemme see," said Bull, holding Mr. Pierce against the wall and putting one hand against his mouth and rubbing hard against it until it opened.

"We'd probably have to throw her in a ditch somewhere. Permanent. Right beside you." Spider shook his head as if regretting the necessities of life. "It's a shame when a man can't handle his own wife. Especially—oh don't, Jakey, the poor boy won't have any teeth left."

"Please do as I say. Please!"

"What's this?" said Irene. "Whatever's happened to you?"

Mr. Pierce was holding the handkerchief to his mouth. He was extremely nervous. "I tell you, simply listen to me," he said. "I beg you, I implore you—we're going to pack and fly to New York."

Irene looked at him suspiciously. "What is it?" she said. "Tell me."

"This," said Mr. Pierce, taking the handkerchief away from his mouth. "Some men are going to kill us."

Irene looked at her husband, a little incredulously.

"It's true," he said. "Please, I beg you . . ."

"There's the telephone," said Irene. "Pick it up and call the police."

Mr. Pierce threw up his hands. "No," he said.

"Then I shall." Irene picked up the receiver.

"I'll deny it," he screamed. "I'll deny it. I won't get myself into this any further."

He knocked the telephone from her hand. He looked at his hand where it had struck against her.

Irene stared at him a moment, then walked out. At a neighboring house she phoned the police, then waited for them, and returned to the house with them.

Mr. Pierce was gone. Nothing had been touched except his cash box and the revolver in his drawer. Irene gave the police what information she could. Then she packed several valises and went to a Harrisburg hotel. For the first time the house stood empty.

45

Naomi turned to see her brother talking, gesticulating. The door behind him was standing open. She had the distinct impression that he had been talking for some time, even before her ears had heard, although this might have been the assumption of her own broken concentration. She listened intently, at last began to pick up the threat of his intent.

". . . my wife. She wasn't really my wife. That too is why I have this feeling that perhaps I didn't—couldn't have done it. How do I know? I mean it's just as possible I didn't as I did. . . . Isn't it? If I had, don't you think I'd remember, do you think I could ever forget? I'm looking at this from the standpoint of reason. Why should I have . . . ? What reason? I had reason in one sense, but, Jesus, I hated lots of people more than her, and are they dead? I mean—I don't know what I mean exactly, and yet . . ." Gilbert looked into the palms of his hands. "I can't believe I'm evil. I simply can't!" He seemed to put a lot of emphasis into that declaration.

570

Naomi went past her brother and closed the door, pushing it tight.

Gilbert was still facing the desk at which his sister had been sitting, and although his eyes were enormously attentive to each thing seen, there seemed no purpose or continuity in his vision.

"She was taking Julius from me," he said, shaking his head. "I couldn't find him." It did not occur to Gilbert that in the past three days he had made no effort to locate his son. It did not occur to him that he thought of the child in the past tense, as something which had been and no longer existed. "Listen," he said, "a guy made a pass at you. I beat him up. But he didn't die. Do you see what that means? And do you remember when we were kids, when I tied the dog to the sled?"

Naomi had sense enough to tell him to speak slower and less loud.

"Do you *remember?*" shouted Gilbert.

"Perhaps," said Naomi. Her eyes were shrewd and observant, as if attempting to make some discovery. But she was pale.

"But you see, sis, that's what's so important. I didn't kill that dog. I swear. Now, do you begin to see. If I didn't, if I know I didn't, then it's possible I never have killed anything."

This was said almost joyously, so that for a moment it seemed Gilbert had forgotten entirely the physical situation in which he was involved. He was enjoying the abstract possibilities of his own declaration.

"I can't see what difference that makes," said Naomi. Again she seemed to have some purpose behind her statement, seemed to be trying to guide the conversation toward some end of her own. But she did not succeed.

"It makes a great difference," said Gilbert. "It means I did not kill. You see, what's so very important is that I remember how I felt then, I swear I remember—and I feel the same way now. Don't you see what that means? I don't *feel* I killed my wife. There's a fact to go on. At least *sometimes* I don't feel I did it," he added almost wearily, as if something, some new thought, had suddenly blighted the hope which for a moment had made him stand erect. "Damn it, it isn't fair. I'm getting stuck with a lie, my own lie, and the longer this goes on the deeper and deeper it drags me into . . . Sis, do you know the only reason I feel I killed my wife—and damn the evidence, damn the fact I got rid of her body—is simply because I found her dead on the floor."

"Murdered," corrected Naomi.

". . . is not even that, not finding her dead, it's because I told you. I came and told you and stood like a proud jackass, because you gave me hell for beating that guy up, and I wanted you to know what a big brave man I am. I wanted to warn you what might happen . . . That doesn't make sense, but it's true. If I hadn't told you, I would know I didn't, I would know for sure."

His eyes flashed angrily.

"Do you want me to tell you to forget this?" Naomi said sharply. "Is that what you came here for?"

"No."

"That's the first sensible thing you've said. Because if I did tell you it would make no difference." Naomi clenched her hands together. Whatever purpose she had had in the beginning was gone. She too was in genuine moral distress. "And listen, I'd rather you didn't tell me more. Oh, don't worry, I'm going to stick by you. Understand that. Only spare me the details. I'd just rather not know."

"But you're the one who told me . . . I didn't try to kill Fred, I didn't. I only told you that after I beat him up I didn't give a damn if he was dead or not."

"And I told you it was sheer luck you didn't."

"No," said Gilbert. "You told me you knew all along I was going to. You said it didn't surprise you a bit."

"I don't know what I told you." Naomi looked straight at her brother. "I had my heart set on being an actress. That's tough enough, but now you've involved me in fights, brawls, murder and what next? Don't confess to me. Don't explain to me. Please don't." She swung her head, shaking her hair. "I know the fact. Isn't that bad enough? Do you think I have no morals, no feelings, that you can come here and tell me—tell me all the little details? Tell me that you threw her head . . . ? Do you think I enjoy hearing that?"

"You have me all wrong," said Gilbert.

"No I don't have you wrong. All your life, under the pretense of helping me, you've clung and clung. Now grow up. I'm not your big sister, I'm your *little* sister. Remember?" Naomi stamped her foot. "I said I'd stick by you. I will. But remember, sister or not, I'm of no more real help to you now than any stranger on the street."

Gilbert smiled bitterly. "I begin to understand."

"I hope you do," said Naomi. "I just hope to hell you do."

"Showing your colors at last," he said, "calling me guilty. Telling me I've always been selfish. Me, selfish." Gilbert laughed. "That's rich. That's really rich." He took a step toward her. "Is there any possibility I'm innocent? In your heart, I mean?"

"I won't answer," said Naomi.

"All right. Believe then," Gilbert cried out. "Believe every lie I ever told you. Yes, I like to impress you, I like to be important to you, and I guess I even like to scare you. Remember the time I jumped in front of the car? You think I was trying to kill myself. No, I wanted you to feel sorry for me, I wanted you to believe me when I said I was miserable. But don't forget that wasn't a crime. I hurt no one but myself."

Naomi shrugged.

"And I'm glad I beat hell out of that ass-pinching married bastard. He had no right fooling around you."

"That's not your business," said Naomi.

"It *is*. Because I made it my business."

Naomi shrugged.

"What a cold fish you are! You're worse than Bart." He took another step toward his sister and raised his arm threateningly. "You think I could beat you up? Answer me! You think I'm capable?"

"Sure," said Naomi. "Why not?"

"What a fool you are," said Gilbert. "Can't you see that if I committed all the crimes I said I did, I wouldn't be here now? You, who see everything so clear, can't you see this one true thing in me? Can't you see I need help? I need faith?" Gilbert paused, but not long enough to give his sister an opportunity to reply. "If you only knew how I'm suffering. If you knew what it is not to know. Not to *know*. My God, I'd rather I did it, if I knew. Why, it would be a justification, it would almost make my life mean something." He laughed almost insanely, then quieted. "That's not true. I—I loved her. Rose was the only one who knew I meant good—that I . . ." Gilbert looked into space and his forehead gathered wrinkles as if assisting his eyes to focus on something distant and minute. "If I didn't—if—I —didn't, then I know who did." He looked at his sister with cunning. "Yes, yes, *he* could have done it. Why I and not he? But if he, why? Ah, yes, all things are possible in my life." Gilbert seemed agitated, and had a sudden desire to leave, but could not in his confused state find the door, or else could not figure out the purpose of the door. "Thanks so much for talking to me, sis. You're the best. I only wish I could do more for you." This was said genuinely. "Listen, I have a way to get money. . . . You can go, get away from here. Oh, you don't have to worry, I won't steal it. I've never stolen."

"I can't take money from you."

"But why? Oh yes, yes, sure, you're right—always right . . . Well, bless you." Gilbert fumbled with the doorknob. "It just dawned on me. A riddle. You always liked riddles. This one's a scream. There was a man who didn't know. He doesn't think so because—because he thinks he's a coward. That's his evidence. But listen to what follows. He has a hunch. He can know, but in order to know what he wants to know, he has to do what he wants to know if he did. That might put him two deep. If not, it will put him one deep, where he thinks he started. Only this time he will *know*. And if his hunch, his silly fantastic hunch, with no evidence . . ."

"Wait!" said Naomi. "I don't know what you're talking about, but I can see you're getting . . . This is the way you get started." Naomi touched his sleeve. It was the closest she could let herself come to him. "Cut it out, stop thinking whatever you're thinking."

"Sure, I know," said Gilbert, almost cheerfully. "Another thing. Do you know Father is dead? He actually died. Isn't that a scream? And do you know what, the doctor said that if I had brought my father to him a month sooner . . . Like it was my fault—my fault, always my fault. Why, by God, do you know, soon there won't be anything on earth I haven't done. I shall have all the earth's sins, all, and then everybody can be happy and gay and just point at me. Why, why, I'm liable to wind up doing a better job than Christ!" Out he went into the night, leaving wild laughter behind him, and Naomi in terror.

An hour later she phoned the police. Her eyes were closed as she talked through the phone, as if disconnecting herself from her voice.

"What'm I going to do?"

"Marry me," said Dip.

"But that isn't going to stop him, it isn't going to keep him from . . . God knows what he'll do next."

"The hell with your brother."

"But you don't understand . . . I've done something awful, and he knows it. And he still gave me . . . I'm the one who told the police. Nobody else knew. I did it, oh I don't know why, for me, I guess, I was just tired and tired."

"Drink your beer," said Dip.

"And then to have him turn around and give me money—to do it to help me. He said it was time to do something that *would* help me. If you could have seen . . ."

"Where's the money?" said Dip. "Still have it?"

Naomi did not answer.

"Let's go get married on it," said Dip.

"If you only knew my brother. He bought me a green dress once. . . ."

"Swell," said Dip. "We'll use his money for our honeymoon."

"No, I mean it. My brother . . ."

"Look, your brother's a swell guy. I mean it. And my opinion of you and me, not much to brag about. But that's not the point. You and I are people. We belong. We're part of the everyday grind. We can take the bumps. We're two little cogs in the big wheel, and the wheel says thumbs down on your brother, and you said thumbs down on him too." Dip squeezed her hands so hard she bared her teeth. "Stay on the wheel, stay with me. I've been close enough to the edge to know."

There was a stillness between them. Though it had not been mentioned, though neither of them had meant to imply it, there was the feeling that this was the last opportunity.

Dip stood up and walked to her side of the table and put his hands on the back of her chair.

"I planned to go to Maryland. I know a lot of people there, including an old boy who marries people drunk or sober. Coming?"

Naomi picked up her purse and threw it to him. "The money's in there," she said.

Outside, as they approached the car, Dip spun her around and pulled her hard against him.

"Let's live while it lasts," he said.

"My pieces of silver," said Naomi.

"Right, kid, and your punishment—nine kids and a house so little you'll hear all nine at the same time, Miss Career Girl."

They were laughing as they drove off.

Mr. Weaver rose to the platform. He was careful not to make his usual introductory jokes. He strode straight into the body of his speech, into his appeal to the workers. He read directly from his notes, read in a strained, cautious voice, and did not embroider, and mentioned the company as little as possible. He spoke rather as one suffering human being to another.

"It is time to bring this strife to an end. It is time for a compromise. I've been wrong in holding out against your reasonable demands, as you've been wrong in insisting that I comply with unreasonable demands. I feel sure that we can come to agreement. We must not allow the bitterness which has arisen between us to completely distort our sense of justice. We must not allow that." Mr. Weaver's voice began to rise to its old eloquence; he had to pause, allow it to subside. "It's more difficult for you than for me. You're faced with the most primitive of situations, hunger, poverty. It's hard for me to ask you to be reasonable, when I know you're looking at me, now, and saying to yourselves, he's not starving, he's not hungry, he didn't even live beside the river." There was no water pitcher and no glass; he had avoided even this, and it made his pauses seem more nervous. Other company officials were standing near him, but not with that pride of a united group which had always made them stand as if they were preparing to salute the flag or unveil a memorial of national significance. "I have not suffered that. I have suffered instead an incredible loss. A loss of millions. I have seen contract after contract sent to other companies—at a time when every single contract is vital to our existence. I have seen the river destroy some of our most valuable machinery, simply because we could not muster fifty men to work the pumps. One of the open hearths has been practically destroyed." For a moment his eyes looked sternly upon the faces below. For a moment he did not try to be other than as he felt, bitter, angry. "There was a time when I asked you men for faith. Now I don't ask that. It's not yours to give. We must look at each other nakedly, must see each other as we are, enemies, men at cross-purposes. I'm not here to sing. I'm here to tell you the boldest of facts." Mr. Weaver reached in his pocket and took from it a piece of yellow paper. "On this is written our fate. I have been informed that unless this strike is settled by the last day of this month the plant will be formally shut down and the equipment moved to another of Bethel's subsidiaries. This is not a threat, but a fact." Several of the company officials paled. Others looked at each other. Mr. Weaver had deliberately not informed them. "This means, in its simplest form, the heads of all these men standing near me. I don't ask you to have pity. I tell you only this, it means your heads too. It means that it will not matter if we come to terms. It will not matter that you win. Because you lose. You're hungry now. What'll you be when there is no mill? How long will this town last without an industry?" Mr. Weaver banged his hand on the desk. "You're not dealing with me now. You're dealing with fate. You're dealing with your lives."

Mr. Weaver paused, turned to look at his company officials. One or two his eyes seemed to avoid, but the rest he looked at with compassion. He managed a weak smile. "I'm no longer a man," he said, softly, "I'm now only an instrument of Bethel. I am allowed to repeat to you only their instructions. I have here a copy of Bethel's final terms, final offer at compromise. If it is not accepted, before the last day of this month, we must all start searching for new livelihoods. And I can assure you," he said, wheeling toward the audience below, "that no man whose name is listed as an employee of this plant will have a ghost of a chance in any Bethel enterprise in any part of this country."

It was the high point of his speech. It was the last emotional appeal which the company could make. Mr. Weaver was a man standing on the edge of disaster, and he did not realize until this moment his exact position. He saw now the risk he had taken. Several days earlier, when Mr. Pierce had quietly advised that he should take the burden from himself, should submit his authority to that of the central directors, it had seemed an excellent idea. He had felt for a long time that what was most necessary to end the strike was a force which carried with it the conviction of finality. It must be a force which would carry past the inflexible leader, a force which would carry directly to the workers and break the hold which the union had on them.

The response of the central directors had been more direct and commanding than his fondest hopes. It named boldly the final condition. It dealt not in appeal or arbitration, but stated, not threatened, that the Nesquehon plant was not sufficiently important to be maintained in the face of constant loss. Mr. Weaver had been pleased; for a time he had even forgotten his own personality, his own situation, and like so many men who have been for years, for the greater portions of their lives, engaged in a false relationship and a false creed, like any man who has found himself made helpless by a policy which once was successful, he was glad to be able to speak the truth; he was glad to find that the truth was his best weapon.

But now, as he looked down at the terms of compromise, he saw that they were very little improved; they contained nothing of importance which he had not already offered. He began to suspect that his head had been placed on the line. If the workers returned, the success would no longer be his, but that of the central directors; if they did not, he had prepared for his own dismissal. It was easy enough for the central directors to state that a plant was going to be shut down permanently, particularly when it was already shut down.

Mr. Weaver sensed too that he had played into the hands of Mr.

Pierce. A prominent stockholder would hardly place a company official before his own interests. And although Mr. Pierce had been quite silent, there had been without doubt a change in his attitude when the strikebreakers and the national guard had both failed in their intention. Mr. Weaver felt now that he should have conferred with Irene, who had not vacillated, who seemed responsible for the resistance which her husband had lately shown to Bart Mijack. Mr. Weaver sensed that this was a desperate move on the part of Mr. Pierce, a move to end the strike at the cost of the present officials. It was with a sense of alarm that Mr. Weaver realized he did not know the extent of the power or influence of Mr. Pierce. It was becoming impossible to know who were one's friends.

Yet all this could be surmounted by victory. If it was too late to gain in stature, if his first plan of winning a crushing victory over the workers had failed, he could, by settling the strike before the end of the month, probably at least retain his present position. He would at the worst be retired honorably. He would have preserved some measure of security and honor.

And so he hastened to speak, hastened to add to the already grim picture which he had placed before his audience. He stressed even more the fact that they were all caught in the web of a common fate. He stated bluntly that it was impossible to deal with the union leaders, and that the only escape was if the workers themselves would accept this compromise and return.

Mr. Weaver found himself seeking among the faces below one with a certain look. He sought for some indication that he had made an impression on them. But the faces stared back impassively, and made him realize that from the beginning every word he had spoken had been received in silence. He saw that it was an organized audience, that there was a more solid and unbreakable resistance in these men than at any time previous. The faces were those of men determined to have justice, men who had passed the crisis of indecision and compromise.

Mr. Weaver did not realize that he was crying out in his old voice of paternalism, a voice now stricken with terror. The other company officials had begun to look at him uneasily. The police in the corridors stared at the platform with cold eyes and hearts. There was more the atmosphere of a courtroom, of a jury, of men embodied with law listening to the defense of a man who had committed a crime against each one of them. Suddenly Mr. Weaver had a feeling that the whole thing had been staged, that his audience had known what he was going to say, that he and the other officials were the only ones who had not been prepared in advance. His face was pallid and pasty, but there was no hate in his eyes, only a gathering fear. Even the telegram and the threat of a company purge seemed to lose importance before this greater threat.

"I ask you for my sake and your own, this is the time to be reasonable, this is our last chance. If we're not careful we shall destroy everything. I shall read to you now the terms Bethel offers. I shall read you, reminding you that this is no longer myself speaking, but a far larger voice, one before which I am insignificant, one which at the end of this month will make all of you insignificant."

Mr. Weaver scarcely knew what he was reading, scarcely knew where to pause, where to stress his voice. He once even turned his head, as if hunting among his officials one who could be called to finish reading the terms, page after page of them; but as his own strength had begun to fail, theirs had begun to take hold, and they clung to the safety of not involving themselves. They too realized now that he was the scapegoat, and they instantly disassociated themselves.

Before Mr. Weaver had finished a third of the conditions, the doorways of the hall were flung open, and striding down the hall, looking heavier and tired, came Bart Mijack, flanked on each side by a pair of bodyguards. Behind them came a thin, tall man, his coat slung over his shoulder in the toreador fashion which most accented his appearance; he was younger than Bart and seemed much more arrogant and ruthless. Bart rose to the platform, pushed Mr. Weaver aside, and said, "I came here to tell you that we don't have to accept terms. We'll dictate our terms. I have the honor to announce that tomorrow morning no man shall set foot in any Bethel plant. The C.I.O. has decided to begin a sympathy strike; it is also going to give financial assistance to each one of you until the company has agreed to our terms." Bart raised his arms. "I assure you that we are victorious."

There was a deafening applause; and yet the applause was not that of men who have been surprised, but who are only giving tribute to the formal acknowledgment of that in which they have already been instructed. Only a few men here and there seemed not to have known what was going on.

Bart did not prolong his statement. He simply introduced the tall, thin man and then descended from the platform. He glanced once into the face of Mr. Weaver, shook his head in disgust, and, surrounded again by his bodyguards, strode down the aisle toward the open doors. It was Rowiger who caught his elbow and said in a furious, low voice, "And so after all that you have done, after all your destruction, you still had to sell the men down the river."

For a moment Bart's eyes became hard and pained; then he smiled, shrugged, and said, "They're better off with the C.I.O. than with me."

Behind the speakers' platform Mr. Weaver found himself alone with Mr. Dressinger. "But what should I do?" he kept repeating. Mr. Dressinger gave him a very sympathetic look, then said, "Of course you must resign. That's beyond question. But I believe that I would first sign the terms. I believe I would do that." Mr. Weaver looked at him in horror. "I couldn't do that." Mr. Dressinger patted him on the shoulder. "You're still entrusted with the power? Then I believe you should. As a matter of personal safety." Mr. Weaver seemed both horrified and astonished. "But the company would . . . I should have to consult." Again Mr. Dressinger smiled. "The company is going to do the same thing. And there *is* this matter of your personal safety. You see, Mr. Pierce has just been found murdered in his home."

On the speakers' platform, the tall, thin young man stood, eyeing the people below. "I am a representative of the C.I.O. I have been instructed to assist you. I have been instructed also to inform you that the C.I.O. much admires the resistance which you have made. You have made it possible for us to take action earlier than we had hoped. You may rest assured, therefore, that whether or not you men decide to join with us, we shall for the present make your interests our own."

And later, the tall, thin young man stepped down from the platform and walked toward Mr. Dressinger. "At last," he said. They shook hands. Mr. Dressinger looked at the young man and said, smiling, "I believe I was working here even before you were born." The young man also smiled, "I know. That is why I said, at last." The young man showed so much knowledge of the old man that Mr. Dressinger seemed for a moment ill at ease. "And where do you go from here?" Mr. Dressinger shrugged, and then, seeing in the young man's eyes that his future was already known, he said, "Washington."

It was the cash box which stopped him. Mr. Pierce stood there shaking it, trying to feel its weight. Then he slipped into a little hollow between locust trees, knelt, and fumbled in his pocket for the keys.

It was a strange sensation to be without money. He was afraid to risk going to a store to cash a check. He was afraid to do anything. He sat there and whimpered.

When it was nearly dark he crept along the side of the house and let himself in through the back door. He moved straight toward the stairway, not noticing the two men who were sitting on the sofa.

"What's he sneaking around his own house for?" said one.

Mr. Pierce was so frightened that he did not remember he had a revolver in his coat pocket until one of the men took it and showed it to him.

"That was a real nice paper you printed today," said Spider. "Tomorrow's is going to have an even better headline."

"I had nothing to do with it."

"We know. That's why we're waiting for your wife to come home."

"Listen," said Mr. Pierce. "Upstairs I have some money. I thought it was in this cash box, but it's upstairs in my safe. You can have it all—if you'll let me go."

"How much?" said the skinny man.

"I don't remember how much I drew. But quite a bit."

"Lead us to temptation," said Spider.

"Now it's going to be a real pleasure to kill you," said Spider, as they came down the stairs.

"But I tell you I had it."

For nearly thirty years Mr. Pierce had done nothing more strenuous than tennis, and that in such a desultory fashion, against such modest competition, that it had hardly been of advantage to him. He had never felt the need of physical expression, except through fine points, such as his manners, his mode of walking, his way of standing. But now he was acutely aware of himself physically. He perspired an enormous amount and continuously.

"Please," he said. "My wife's the one who printed that. I've done everything you've told me." And later, "I'll get the money for you tomorrow, and I'll go away and never say anything, and you can do whatever you want to with my wife."

But the two men had not spoken to him since coming down the stairs.

"It's late," the burly one said. "She must be getting some nookie on the side."

When the telephone rang, Spider carelessly motioned for Mr. Pierce to answer it.

"Hello, hello, who is it? Who is it?"

"If it's your wife, tell her to come home. Tell her it's time for all good girls to be in bed."

Finally Mr. Pierce put down the receiver. He stared down at the telephone as if he could not understand what function it had.

Then it rang again, and he grabbed at the whole telephone and finally managed to find his ear with the receiver. " '. . . Father, come home to me now, the cow's in the clover . . .' " and then he heard only a few disconnected words, "Papers . . . Safe . . . So much money lying around." And his eyes went shut and then squeezed shut, and his head hunched down between his shoulders, and he heard his voice begin saying, "Help me," and he did not want it to say that. He did not want to start screaming it.

When the knife went into his stomach, Mr. Pierce stood perfectly still. He seemed politely to hand the receiver of the telephone to Spider. Then he was just holding his empty hand out like a man bumming a dime.

Gilbert threw open the door, marched past the desk where Bart was sitting, looking into every corner of the room. "Where's Spider?" he said.

Bart did not look up from the papers he was studying. There was something tired and weary and hopeless in the way he sat slumped over the desk.

"I asked where he is," said Gilbert, coming to the desk.

"I haven't the least idea," said Bart, still not raising his eyes.

Gilbert put his hands on the papers and began to push them aside.

"Go ahead," said Bart. "Tear them and I won't have to sign them. I'll only have to sign another copy that says exactly the same thing in the same disgusting words."

"Listen," said Gilbert, "the cops are after me."

"Then we'll probably meet again," said Bart. "You'll probably find me in jail when they bring you."

"Bart, I didn't kill my wife. I swear I didn't. And I'm pretty sure I know who did. Spider."

"I wouldn't doubt it," said Bart. "I can believe you did it and I can believe he did it, and now please run along. I have work to do."

"I don't go until you tell me where he is."

Bart patted against his chest with both hands. He was hunting for his fountain pen.

"I'll beat it out of you."

Bart took out a sheet of paper and began to test the point of his pen against it.

"Bart, Bart," said Gilbert, "remember me, I'm your brother."

Bart scribbled something on the paper, and then reached his hand to take up the phone.

"No you don't," said Gilbert.

Bart rubbed his hand. "Go away," said Bart. He looked at his watch. "In about twenty minutes I'm going to have visitors. . . . I don't want to have to introduce you."

Gilbert leaned forward over the desk, pushing his face at Bart.

"Not this time. You and I've had something to settle for a long time. A long long time."

"Maybe you've something to settle," said Bart. "I haven't. And even if I had, I don't have time for it now."

"No-o-o, Bart," said Gilbert, making an oval of his lips, and blowing the breath of his voice into his brother's face. "Reach for the telephone once more and you'll make it easy for me. You and I'll settle things right now. The first thing, where's Spider?"

Bart leaned back in the chair and moved his shoulders as if they were tired. He looked at his brother with disgust. "Look, Gib, I don't have time for your games. I've no intention of telling you where Spider is. He's doing something much too important to be bothered. Just as I am doing something much much too important to be bothered." The desk moved as Gilbert leaned forward, but Bart did not; his posture was still relaxed and tired. "For Christ's sake, sit down," said Bart. "You're getting to be as stupid sober as you are drunk."

"I ought to beat your head in," said Gilbert. "I ought to beat you until . . ."

"Start beating," said Bart. "I'm sure as hell not going to bother to stop you, not when the police station is right across the street."

Gilbert turned toward the window and saw that the blind was raised. It reminded him, and increased his need to know whether his life was over or whether he still had a chance.

"But God damn you," he said, "can't you see my position?"

"I can," said Bart. "I told you long ago never to play with matches. But you insisted, and now . . ."

"Now my life's in danger, my *life*, Bart. And I didn't do it, I swear I didn't."

"You didn't," said Bart.

Their eyes met.

"Spider. And he plans to involve me unless—unless you should happen to—understand?"

Bart smiled. "That's the nice thing about having men working for you, they do things on their own. Every fucking man I ever laid eyes on has to do what he hasn't been told to do. That's been my curse. And then one always has a brother to get drunk and set the stage." Bart looked at his brother with contempt. "The hell of it is, you ought to take the blame."

"I *knew* I didn't do it," said Gilbert. He wiped his face with his hands and sat down. He looked even more tired and weary than his brother.

"Until tomorrow you did do it," said Bart sharply.

Gilbert did not understand. He was still sitting there feeling relief from the measureless strain which he had been under. For a moment he closed his eyes.

"And you only have ten minutes to take to the hills. Or you can cross the street and turn yourself in."

Gilbert looked at his brother. Then he smiled. "We can both cross the street."

"No," said Bart. "Tomorrow. Because tonight I have work to do, and tomorrow morning I'm going to the D.A.'s office, and then starting tomorrow afternoon a lot of people can begin visiting the jailhouse."

"Where's Spider? I'll take him in," Gilbert said. "I'll take him in right after he and I have a little talk."

"I have no intention of telling you," said Bart. "Tomorrow afternoon the police'll get a signed statement, telling everything I know about the affair. Spider's already involved in a number of other little matters, so I think you can feel pretty sure your neck'll escape. I also don't intend to report the money you stole from me."

"You knew this all the time," said Gilbert. "All the time I've been running and hiding, all the time I've been suffering, not even sure I hadn't done it. You could have saved me all this."

"I could have let you hang," said Bart coldly. "Now get out of here."

"All the things I've done for you," said Gilbert. "The way I believed in you . . ."

Bart propped his feet on the desk.

"Where oh where have I heard that tune?" he said. "Look, you always told me that if there was anything you could do—well, you've done it. I'm only happy I didn't have to ask you to do it. You'd never have had the guts." Bart scrawled his signature on the first paper. "Tomorrow you'll be free. No wife. No brother. And your sister, I understand, has taken off for other parts. It ought to make you feel good to

584

know she used your money which was my money to get that second-rate gigolo to marry her."

Bart reached for the telephone.

"So—the Mijack name is in your hands. Go join the army or something and restore it."

Dorothy opened her eyes, surprised that she had been asleep, feeling the faint awe that results from not being able to place oneself at an exact point in time. That it must be late in the night plagued her for a moment in the manner of a worry. She wished she had undressed before falling asleep, for her body felt the wrinkled discomfort tight clothes impress on the flesh during sleep, an unevaporated stale moisture, the outline of her brassiere, particularly where it was a narrow thong and metal clasp against her back. There was an itchiness where her legs were confined in the wool skirt, the hairs of which seemed to have worked even through her petticoat.

She remembered that she had been angry with her husband before falling asleep, but now it had become a dull, depressing memory of itself. She felt passionless. She could not remember having ever seen herself so little included in life. At least she had remembered to push off her shoes, so that her feet were not thickened; but they were so cool and free compared with the rest of her body that the contrast was not heartening.

She would take a bath. But first she reached out for the telephone and put it on her stomach and dialed a number. The weight of the telephone made her remember the child that might or might not be forming within her, and she had a vision of some mysterious internal working, a vision not at all frightening or naïve. She thought of it like a groaning of the bowels, only more delicate and silent. Her finger stuck spinning the dial, the telephone slipped off, so that she had to perch it on top of herself and begin again. This time she dialed the operator and inquired the time. She wanted an exact figure.

A bit later she heard her husband's voice. She had a conversation with it. She smoked a cigarette while the conversation with that voice went on, and once blew the smoke into the telephone. She very casually mentioned to him that she had cashed a check. When she hung up and put the phone back on the stand, she lay there on the bed, knowing it would be a little while before she would have to move again and then decide to do something physical, realizing with a sort of amusement that she had not said a single harsh word to Fred. It was rather a good feeling to have let him slip away this once. It was almost a good feeling to have him away from her, to be lying on the bed, doing nothing, going nowhere.

Her arm encountered the ash tray without the aid of her eyes, and she dropped the still burning cigarette inside. Then her hands began to do what little they could to undress her without causing her to move, without committing her to action immediately. She felt what she had done to her hair while sleeping, and had a curiosity to see. Instead, she stretched an arm, caught hold of the wire, and dragged the phone until it fell on the edge of the bed. As her finger toyed with the holes, then made the series of pulling motions which would give her a voice to speak to, even this late at night, she felt that after all this was the best means of communication. And when she heard a voice, she drew her ear away from the phone, listening to the different and feeble sound which carried through and created the feeling of someone trying to be in the room with her. It was odd to have the feeling of someone trying to reach her, to have him shouting with the slight fear of silence, and she held her head cocked sidewise. She waited until she heard the click and the buzzing silence, then dialed again, and as soon as the contact was restored, said, " 'Father, dear father, come home to me now. The cow's in the clover . . .' " She bit her lip thoughtfully. "No, that won't do, but I've thought of one for Fred. It's the one I've wanted all these years. 'Little boy blue, go blow your horn . . .' Don't you think that suits him?" She listened for a moment, then again held the receiver away from her, not so much listening to the thin voice as looking into the mouthpiece. "Oh Father," she said, "I thought I ought to tell you . . . I gave Bart all the papers I found in your safe. He says the ones concerning Selvinius' daughter and her inheritance are interesting. And Father, dearest, you shouldn't leave so much money lying around where it's no use to anybody." And again she listened, then put her finger firmly on the little button, almost surprised at the quick efficiency with which the room became silent. " 'Help me,' " she said. "What a curious thing for my father to be saying." She twisted her head so that she could rub her cheek against the bare portion of her shoulder, feeling a softness in the flesh of her shoulder that she could not find anywhere in her face. "Where have I ever heard that before, 'help me'?"

Then she dialed again, this time holding a little pad open to see the numbers, and sat up in bed, pushing back her hair. She sat with one finger thrust down inside her dress, feeling the very beginning of the rise of each of her breasts. Then, as there was no immediate response, she put the phone close enough beside her that she could still hear the intermittent buzzing, and began to loosen her clothes with a youthful desire for freedom which was only slightly immodest. She sat, bare to the waist, moving her shoulders like a football player who has removed his equipment.

"What do I want?" she said. "I hardly know. I do remember I was just thinking how curious it is to have to look for the phone number of a man who I think has given me a baby. As a matter of fact I was also thinking this might be a good time for you to suggest a name, in case it's a boy. . . . What do I want? Is it important?" Dorothy laughed, then shut her eyes, and put her fingers on the nipple of her breast, feeling where his rejection had hurt her most. "As a matter of fact, I've been lying here wondering what I would like most. Wondering what last remembrance I should like to take with me. Something new? Something old? I was thinking you might want to come stud for old times' sake . . . What? I'm not making sense? Oh, Bart!" She listened for a time, nodding her head. It all seemed so remote and meaningless, and it came to her that the real secret of her life was involved in exactly that feeling. She listened to a voice which she had so betrayed and which had so betrayed her that it could no longer bring any response except a neutrality of conflicting emotions. " 'Little bo' blue,' " she thought, " 'go blo' youah 'orn,' " and hung up, and then disconnected the receiver.

She rose and started toward the bathroom, her dress slipping and then catching along the broad portion of her hips. It made walking feel awkward. She opened the closet to get a dressing gown, and felt utterly frigid and slightly alarmed to find that it was empty. It seemed much larger and darker without the long row of dresses; the hangers made a thin, jingling noise when she thrust her arm inside. And there came to her the utter barrenness of the apartment and particularly of the bedroom, the bureau drawers empty, nothing on top of the vanity except her purse and a comb.

It did not make her feel better to know that a long line of suitcases were at the airport, that the barrenness was of her own making. She could not bring herself to bathe, and even drew her dress so that it hung from one shoulder. Returning to the bed, she found the warmth which she had left, and tried to fit her body exactly to it. Then she drew the telephone to her, handling it with the same absent-minded fondness which she had always shown for the dog. Her intention was to call the airport and have verified an hour and minute which she already knew. Instead there replied the overalert voice of a woman.

"Laura," she said, "could you come over? I know it's late and I know it's ridiculous . . ." As she was talking, her eyes were looking down over her body, faintly distressed that her beauty should still have meaning to herself. She was brushing one foot softly with the other. "There's nothing reasonable to it, nothing in the least reasonable—and yet that's why I called you, I just felt I wanted you near me." She lay there listening to the voice, holding her ear tight against the disk. She heard the protest and the excitement and the confusion in the voice, but what she was really listening to was the feminine quality. "Then you will come . . . Good . . . Wait, don't hang up. I want to ask you . . . Where are you now, in bed? Were you sleeping? How do you look?" She paused, listening. "Laura, would you do something very intimate for me? Would you completely undress yourself, and then just say, I'm undressed? Don't say anything more than that, just those words, I'm undressed." She listened to the other voice, to the nervousness, the anger. She listened until there was silence, and then she lay there, wetting her finger and touching her own navel. She was having the same unpleasant sensation as when she had been a child and the colored woman had washed her in those parts where she did not like to be touched.

After a while, she simply broke the connection, and pushed the telephone away from her. She knew that she had only wanted to find out how the other woman felt toward her. She knew that she would be even more unhappy living with a woman than a man. She knew that she had made the phone calls only to force herself to go to the airport, to force herself to flee what she did not feel like fleeing. She had at least forced herself to do something. Because she felt quite certain that it would not be long before her father and Bart and probably Laura arrived, each for a different reason; and then she would not have such a perfect mode of communication.

Yet these pressures failed to rouse her, and she did not feel the need to explain her actions to anyone. It was not merely the emptiness of the room, but an emptiness in herself, a recognition that she was alone, had been alone, and always would be. She saw that she was doomed to slip further and further into isolation, the one thing she was not equipped to deal with, the one thing her mind and body refused to deal with. She fervently believed that she had been created to behave like a leaf in the wind, to have one mad flight; and now it was over, and it had never been very exciting, and it would certainly not be exciting to force herself to make another attempt.

The airport promised nothing except a passage to another place, to the last place, where, with the money she had taken from her father's safe, the piece of luck that had placed unknowingly in her hands his own desire to escape, and with the check she had cashed against her husband, overdrawing his account to such an extent that he would not be able to repair it—with that money she could have a last fling at unhappiness. For she wanted neither men nor women, nor the child which would have to be aborted. She wanted least of all any of the people she had telephoned.

And yet, if she had only one suitcase here, one tangible thing with which to form a plan of motion, she believed that she would still flee. It was, after all, the sensible continuation of her life. But she could not bring herself to walk out of the apartment with nothing more than her purse under her arm. And when there came a knock on the door, she knew she would not have the courage to open it.

Dorothy went to the bathroom and opened the little white cabinet. It contained nothing except innocent items, pastes and creams, and a little bottle of iodine which she could not even bring herself to touch. "I suppose after all," she thought, "I shall have to go to the airport."

As he stood with his legs bowed, facing the wall of the church, Gilbert realized he was being followed. His first reaction was simply being come upon while he was urinating, and, hurriedly buttoning his fly, he walked on. The footsteps seemed to keep about the same distance behind him. He had the feeling of being followed by someone who did not care whether he knew he was being followed. He passed a street light, waited until he had guessed the distance, turned, and saw them clearly.

He was going to have his chance at revenge after all. His only problem was where to meet them. He felt sure they were not going to try to overtake him before they came to a less populated area. He walked, looking back over his shoulder, wanting them to know he had seen them. In the next block the bigger of the two disappeared, and Gilbert thought for a moment it was an attempt to cut him off. But a porch light went on, and he saw Bull standing on the porch, Spider coming on up the hill.

Gilbert went as far as the next corner and ducked around it. That would make Spider cautious in approaching. He ran to the end of the house, opened the gate, crossed lawn and a low hedge, then came out toward the same street, and the same place which he had passed. He could not be sure whether Spider had yet passed, but knew he didn't have much time before Bull would be along, and so stepped out onto the sidewalk.

Spider knelt and threw one arm against his leg. That was a knife and Gilbert held out one hand toward it, palm open, and then brought his whole right arm downward in an axe motion, striking along the shoulder and neck. Managing to get hold of the blade of the knife, he clutched it in his hand, and kept pounding with his free arm and fist. Spider was kneeling on the sidewalk, trying to dodge the rain of blows, but not really moving, because he was trying to get his knife free.

Then Spider began to scream. Gilbert did not listen to the screams. They were not important; it was what he felt inside himself that was important. He felt exactly as he had one time beating his wife, only this was more final and satisfying. Spider let go of the knife and tried to get away, but a blow knocked him flat on the concrete. He tried to cover his head with his hands. Gilbert was still clutching the blade of the knife, not realizing he was cutting himself deeper. He saw the exposed length of neck, brought his fist down on it and heard bone crack. When the body sprawled limp, he took a moment to look down the street, measuring distance, then stamped down on the neck with his boot. The big man was coming at a run.

Gilbert walked on, and when he was almost a block away, waited to see whether the big man would come after him. Bull was kneeling beside his comrade. Gilbert, as he stood watching, realized he was still clutching the knife blade, and he freed his hand from it. He threw the knife into the street, took a handkerchief and began binding his hand. The handkerchief made something to clench. It gave his hand form. He smacked it against his other hand to see if it was usable. The knuckles were still firm and the fingers had grip. That was all he needed.

At the edge of town he heard the sound of police sirens. The sound seemed to make his body enlarge and he felt at a distance from his feet. He understood then the lighted porch. He had a vision of many porches lighted in the northern part of the town. Gilbert ran. He took the main path. The path had been there for years, but still weeds kept growing; he could hear them snapping against his boots. One by one, the sirens ceased to wail, and the silence gave him a feeling of everything being directionless. He passed fields and began to climb. The wind blew and trees sounded stiff. His hand was beginning to ache and the handkerchief was squishy. After he sensed the distance he was leaving behind, he was calmer. He knew his pursuers would be proceeding cautiously. It had been right to take the main path to make time.

He splashed across the Bluegill, veered upward. By the time he reached the cabin, he was entirely calm. He lit the lamp and the kerosene stove and put coffee on. The water in the wooden bucket was stale. He took the handkerchief off, soaped his hands and washed them at the same time. Not once did he look at the window. He used strips of a sheet to bind his hand, and as he tried clenching it a small reddish patch began to form.

"If I have to use it, I will," he thought. He grinned, actually happy. This was the excitement he had always craved and it was going to take place in an area he was familiar with. He took down the lever-action rifle; it would be accurate for any distance he could see at night; it was also the easiest to carry. From the dresser he took a full box of shells, and emptied a partly used box into his hand. He slipped on a leather jacket, knowing it would be cold high on the mountain, put the box of shells in one pocket, and the loose ones in the other. He still had not looked toward the window, but now he went to it and ripped away the curtain and turned the oil lamp high, watching the light increase on the ground outside.

He went outside and away from the cabin, but keeping himself aligned with the window. He found a rock and sat on it and drank from the spout of the coffeepot, his eyes keeping watch above the rim. The sounds came before the shadows. He heard movements. He had set the coffeepot aside and was afraid of kicking his boot against it, so he did not move. The shadows appeared and hid the whole window. The rifle bounced a little and the shadows remained exactly the same, then one made the quick movement of a soldier coming to attention. The rifle only shivered a little this time, and then Gilbert could see the window clearly. He fired the rest of the clip into the area close about and low, with the wonderful feeling of knowing exactly where men would try to hide, knowing and almost seeing every tree and stone in front of his house.

Then he walked swiftly and silently toward higher areas of the mountain. He was passing into a place where few men had ever been, and knew he was going to give a good account of himself. He had a feeling there were not as many pursuers as he had imagined. He found himself trying to count the police Nesquehon had. He decided he was far enough ahead to smoke; there was no telling when he would get another chance. As he struck a match and saw the first huge flare and brought it to his mouth he had a feeling of being exposed,

591

and he hurriedly shook the flame out. But the glow of the cigarette did not bother him. He carried it cupped in his hand only to keep from bumping it against bushes. He did not look back. He was worried at the stiffness he had felt in his injured hand while trying to strike the match.

He reached the rocky area where trees were little taller than himself. He wanted to get high above before the police came past these trees. He felt like beating his hand against one of them to stop it from hurting. There returned an exuberance; he climbed for the sake of climbing. In the high parts of the mountain he was most sure of himself. He was not bitter, not angry, nor afraid. It seemed fine to be able to discard the past, discard all he had failed to accomplish. He did not think of himself as fleeing. He felt clean of heart.

The rocks were wet. It was odd to come upon the results of rain without having seen or felt it. The surfaces and edges gleamed black in the moonlight. He chose a place and knelt. While waiting, he deliberately tied knots in the laces of his boots.

The moon was momentarily bright. He had good shots at two men and was sure he had hit one.

Gilbert scrambled further up the mountain, deliberately casting aside a chance of slipping through to the other side. He was moving toward the cliffs, where he could not be surrounded, but, too, where he could no longer flee. He would have to make his stand. He could hear guns, mostly pistols, sounding below, and the bullets made whining sounds among the rocks. It was impossible for him to know how near or far they were, but he felt no fear.

He climbed steep and then paused, looking down. It was surprising how little talking he could hear, only a continuous treading, like the hoofs of mules. The moon had vanished and he stood in the blackness, at his full height. He preferred to stand straight, preferred to present a large target. It was like issuing a challenge. There was a long, skinny flash of heat lightning low in the sky. His eyes used it to the full, but when the shot rang out, he was staring into darkness. He would never know. The highest part of the mountain was so near that before the moon had vanished he had been able to see the individual rocks like a line of broken teeth.

He reached the place where he intended to make his stand. He exchanged shots with the darkness, then noticed that the police did not seem to be trying to come nearer. They were not even shooting often. He was lying there, prepared to be crept upon, confident his vision was better than theirs. He knew the places where they would not have cover. But his own rifle was firing as often as theirs, and he had not heard a single sound to indicate that they were approaching.

At a considerable distance below, there was a glow of light, several men smoking. Because he saw only indications of the light and not the light itself, he did not shoot. They were safe behind rocks and could risk smoking. Yet he did not dare to strike a match himself. He reached in his jacket pocket, then lay there trying to think where he could have lost the box of shells. He searched the ground about him, and even crept forward a little, feeling in the crevices of rocks. He did not consider taking desperate measures. He did not retreat nearer the cliff. His body was no longer a wearisome possession to be fed, clothed and sheltered. It was all he had.

"They know no more about me than I about them," he thought. Then he realized they had known something that he had not known. The hour. His eyes began to watch night creeping away from the earth. He could imagine a slight mist along the horizon to the east. He could not believe that it was so near to dawn.

It was much later and still dark when he heard the first sounds of movement. There had been no shots fired in a long while. It was going to be one of those misty mornings when tree scent is strong. Dampness made the rocks stink.

He had been listening too intently to the sounds below. He felt a blow, as if someone had struck him with all his might. It actually pushed him a short distance. He never heard the shot and never heard the sound of his own rifle as he swung it and fired. His feeling was that the man had been standing almost over him, and it was not until after the man toppled and he took more careful aim and shot into the fallen body that he realized there was a distance between them.

He heard the sounds of men running toward him, and he leaped up, clutching the rifle by the barrel. He was filled with the same joyous abandonment as when he had swung corn stalks against smaller foes. He rushed headlong at them, flinging the strength of his arms and his body, the rifle held like a stick. Then something burned in his belly and he bellowed. He did not know he could not see. He felt two thumps against his chest and the bullets push their way inside him, but they did not seem to have any effect, except to make it difficult to move, as if he was wrapped in a tight overcoat. He felt a sense of falling. The last thing he knew was that he had found something to clench in his hands. . . .

Two policemen dragged the dead man by his boots and then knelt over the other man. He was choking.

Bart rolled over and began to vomit. But it was mostly blood that came from his mouth.

"There wasn't no need of anybody getting hurt," said the one policeman, looking down on Bart. "But he couldn't wait until it was light. He had to go sneaking up." But Bart only continued to bleed from his mouth. And Gilbert would never know that he had been shot by his own brother and had killed his own brother. And neither of them knew that they would have to be buried in their father's plot, side by side.

The fabrication building was long and lighted by enormous glass skylights and lighted too by fluorescent tubes mounted along the walls. The floor of the building was white concrete and in a few places cobblestone and brick. Huge ventilators breathed hot air with such violence that men avoided walking directly under them.

The building was divided into halves lengthwise, with a series of arches in the middle, so that there were four sets of cranes, high-speed hydraulic-electric, a set along each wall and a set on each side of the middle. There were twelve of these larger cranes, arranged so that at least two could work in unison in any position.

There was no sign of the furnaces in which the blacksmiths had forged; the tools were cut and molded in other shops, in precision casts and dies. In one portion of the building structural steel was being cut and shaped to size, plates up to four inches thick being cut by a press shears which worked in absolute silence. The cutting of a piece of paper would make more sound than the steel being divided by two edges of harder steel under thousands of tons of pressure. A crane lifted the plate, swung it to the shears, and placed it within three inches of the cutting line; then the shears' operator made finger signals to the man overhead, and the plate moved to within a quarter of an inch. Then the operator stepped on a foot lever which resisted against his foot in the manner of an air brake. The only noise was as the piece which had been cut fell and then slid down its incline.

Beside this was a series of rollers, across which angle iron was rolled toward shears which had two sets of blades and could make cuts of any degree, and even double inversions when fed into from the opposite side. It cut sidewise and downward at the same time, and made a snapping sound when the blades were a little dull. No crane was needed except to haul in the forty-foot lengths and to haul off the stacks of cut material. These shears could mass produce or could do detail work.

594

Beside this, were band shears which cut lengths of straight thin steel at a rate of about forty-five a minute.

On the other side of the arch was a plate bender, which made either barrel shapes or ellipses or odd, rounded curl shapes of large, flat steel plates. It handled the steel slowly, bending at almost infinitesimally small degrees, and yet with the ease with which tin foil can be twisted around one's finger. Hot oil was sometimes applied to inflexible steel, in the way that a steam press mashes down on clothing.

There were few sounds of hammering. Welding was replacing rivets, and almost no hand riveting was done. There was the flash of acetylene torches, but even these were being replaced by chambers in which whole seams could be done in a moment. Holes were press drilled, and unless the steel was very thick, it took very little longer than for a newspaper boy to punch his collection cards.

The loading and unloading areas were marked off by white stripes and the machines had guards and nets surrounding their dangerous areas. The men had lockers in which to hang their clothing and keep their lunch pails. The only things that were missing were chairs and places to sit. There was still noise, plenty of noise, but it was the hum and throb of machinery, machines so large that they required fifteen and twenty minutes to get started, required a motor to start a motor. The sound of steel itself had become a thin tinkle and an occasional shrill screech.

It had become a drama of motion, in which the crane operators hovered above everyone, running their cranes along enormous tracks like spiders running along a wall. The hooks would drop so fast that they would look as if they were going to strike the concrete, and then halt within a few inches of a man's hand, so that he could slip a ring over the hook. It was not the crude movement of the bulldozer or the steam shovel, but a movement of enormous precision, a movement of men who had studied the same area year after year, and could knock a man's hat off without touching his head, could put their hook through any ring which was not flat on the ground. On big loads two cranes would work together, moving like one engine, at the exact same speed, halting at the same instant, lowering evenly.

The pride and the contempt of these crane men could be seen in their moments when they were not busy. They would sit with their feet stuck out through the doors, munching on an apple or a sandwich, eyeing the activity below with careless superiority. They wore clean work clothes and engineer-type hats, and they were the only men who could talk to each other over a long distance. They did their work by signs and signals and by what they saw, and it was rarely that they talked to the men below.

Perhaps the position of these crane men was expressed even better in the attitude of the hookers. There was an enormous trust and faith, which in part the hookers had in themselves, in the correctness of balance with which they had chained the load; but if the crane operator signaled that the load was not balanced or that a chain was twisted, or if he lifted and then set the load down again, the hookers without quarrel would change the positions of the claws. The hookers lived by the unwritten rule that a swinging load was a bad load, and they were the ones to get hurt.

The shears operators paid little attention to what was going on overhead, and yet they too were part of the drama of motion.

And yet there was something wrong, something much more wrong than in the days of the black gang. With all the safety devices, all the machinery, the complicated maneuvering of steel, there was an atmosphere of boredom and of spiritless men. A dollar and a half an hour, two dollars an hour, three, did not change it. Social security and health insurance did not change it. There was being bred a tenacious and fantastically sick and secure tribe of men, and they smelled death where there was death, and yet they stayed where they were.

The work was sometimes still hard, but the better part of the day their gloves were in their jacket pockets. And the threat that they were facing was a kind of universal janitorship. Their eyes still had to see true along a line and their hands had to know when to pull a lever and they had to know how to mark a piece of steel from a temple. But they were janitors. Their jobs were oiling the machines, clearing away the scrap, listening for the right moment to begin putting pressure on the clutch. Their jobs were putting in new parts to replace old ones, putting in shims to make old parts semi-new. Their job was to make the work last, because the machines were too quick. Their jobs were sweeping and spreading sawdust, and using wrenches to flip pieces of steel, and hooking crane tongs and guiding steel along power rollers. In six weeks a man could learn all there was to know, and then he spent the next twenty years learning that he did not have to know anything.

The offices were set off along the walls of the building, soundproof rooms in which the bosses sat at desks and occasionally looked out through small windows. They strolled through the building once

596

an hour just to be reminded of their own existence, and it was no longer in their power to do more than criticize lightly. It was even dangerous for them to give a man a pat on the back. For spread throughout each shop were petty fanatics, ignorant union officials, with their fascist ideas of liberty and the welfare of mankind. And the slavery of the workingman had become twofold, and if he was not union he was still a slave to the same system.

The building itself was a parody of the original intention of steel. The ease with which steel was being cut and twisted and punched, steel which was to be the foundation and the strength of bridges and buildings and machines of war, pointed to the end of a time when armor would be thought of as security, pointed to a time when ships of steel would pass into the same obsolete comedy as wooden ships. The age was not at its end, was not even near its end, but with a long telescope there could be perceived a mist rising on the horizon.

Nothing had ben solved, nothing was being solved. Only human spirit and human dignity, caught in little corners of little hearts, promised a future, after the last banners had fallen in the dust. And perhaps it was even less than this which mankind had to look forward to, not a future, only a continued existence.

ABOUT THE AUTHOR

WARREN EYSTER was born in Steelton, Pennsylvania in 1925. Except for brief periods, he lived with his grandfather until he was seventeen. He delivered newspapers, sold subscriptions, and at the age of fourteen was a collector for overdue accounts.

He graduated from high school in Steelton at seventeen and took a job with the Army Air Corps as a hydraulic repairman. In 1942 he met two friends on their way to the Navy recruiting office. He planned on just walking along with them, but he enlisted and they did not. He found war exciting and the sea both beautiful and free.

He lost a finger in combat and spent some time in a naval hospital and then worked in a mental hospital. After that he became a pest-control sailor on a naval base in swamp land, and spent most of his time hunting down coyotes, rats, mice, mosquitoes and gophers.

After the war he worked at many different jobs, primarily in factories, but he also took a job logging and built a cabin in the mountains. About this time he decided to go to college, and after some preparatory work at Harrisburg Academy, he entered Gettysburg College. Two years later he graduated from Gettysburg. Then he attended graduate school at the University of Virginia.

It was during this time that he started writing. Two of his professors were interested in his work, and he decided that he had had enough education. In 1953 his first novel, *Far from the Customary Skies*, was published, and he moved to Millboro, Virginia, already at work on *No Country for Old Men*.

He married in 1954, has a daughter, Hope, and is at present in Mexico on a literary fellowship at the Centro Mexicano de Escritores.